HE'D LIVE UP TO HIS PROMISE

Esteban forcefully took the black-haired tease by the elbow and swung her around to face him. "Surely you can understand how impossible it would be to convince me that you're innocent, especially when at our first encounter you begged my coin for your favors!"

"Just shut up, San Martín!" Krissoula hissed. "You believed what I wanted you to believe. Why, I'd have slit your cursed throat before you—or any other man—touched me!"

Suddenly Esteban locked his arms about her, slipping one hand about her waist and boldly caressing the curve of her hip before gliding downward. He tangled his other hand in her masses of silken hair, and tipped her head back to gaze deep into her furious eyes.

"Take your filthy hands off me, you blue-eyed *diablo!*" the indignant miss screeched, squirming her hand free to slap his face. "Whatever you think, you don't own me!"

Esteban easily caught her wrist, and with a low, wicked laugh pulled her even closer. "Own you? No, perhaps not. But possess you—take you—make love to you—*sí*, that I will do, señorita. Body and soul!" he threatened huskily, lowering his sensual lips to hers . . .

PENELOPE NERI

MIDNIGHT CAPTIVE

ZEBRA BOOKS
KENSINGTON PUBLISHING CORP.

ZEBRA BOOKS

are published by

Kensington Publishing Corp.
475 Park Avenue South
New York, NY 10016

First printing: March, 1989

Printed in the United States of America

For Karen J. Bento, with love.
You always hear me out, bless you, Karen,
however long and involved the current "plot" might be.
Thanks!

She'd betray her love
To the Devil himself,
Would sell her soul
For a life of wealth,
Relinquish honor,
Heart and health,
For the glitter
Of Gypsy gold—!

Or—was her greed
But a fragile shell
To armor a heart
That had loved *too* well?
Had she loved and lost
And known the hell
Of a gentle heart
Betrayed . . . ?

A Gypsy Legend

"Gold!" cried the Gypsy. "There is nothing on this earth that I love more than gold!"

Hearing his gloating cry, the devil—never one to miss a chance!—popped up from the bowels of the earth. He perched atop a rock, settling down to watch while the Gypsy counted his hoard of golden coins within a desolate hollow upon the heath, far from the covetous eyes of his Romany band.

Nearby stood his Gypsy caravan, his *vardo* made gay with painted designs, and lavishly gilded. A fine, sturdy horse, dappled with black upon its white coat and boasting a full silvery mane and tail, cropped the rough turf and the sweet purple heather. In and out of the golden gorse and the pungent yellow broom, a little girl played tag with a long-eared brown rabbit, her black Gypsy curls flying, her cheeks flushed red with the wind's caress and with the sheer pleasure of life and living. Her name was Belinda, which in the Spanish tongue means "pretty one," and she was the Gypsy's only daughter.

"Ah, my little treasures!" the Gypsy crowed, kissing each golden coin as if it were his grandchild. "Was ever a man so richly blessed?"

"Blessed?" interrupted the devil slyly, inspecting a cloven hoof to hide his eager expression, much in the manner of a dandy inspecting his polished fingernails. "Blessed, you say, Gypsy?" he repeated, though the word "blessed" singed his wicked tongue. "But I've heard it muttered here and there that in money lies the root of all evil! Is that not so, my fine Gypsy friend?" And the devil's eyes glowed craftily, red with anticipation as he caught the tantalizing, exquisite scent of a soul in peril on the breeze.

"Never!" the Gypsy denied, and his fierce black eyes glittered with avarice. "Gold is all that is good, all that is fine in life. If a man has gold to his name, why then he has everything he could ever ask for!"

9

"Everything?" the devil echoed, hardly able to conceal his excitement, for the soul-scent grew stronger by the minute.

"Everything!" the Gypsy declared. "Why, I would sell my soul for the world's wealth in gold, and that's the truth!"

"You'd sell your soul, you say?" the devil whispered, and his pointed tail twitched with eagerness. "Well, then, this is truly your lucky day, Gypsy! You see, it so happens that I might be able to help you there, my fine fellow! What do you say to a bargain between us—your gray and somewhat tarnished soul, in return for the power to turn all you touch into gold?"

"The power to turn all into gold—? Why, 'tis a bargain well met!" the Gypsy replied eagerly. "And here's my hand on it, friend!"

The devil extended a cloven forehoof, and the Gypsy clasped it. There was a flash of reddish light, a sulfurous stink that reamed the Gypsy's nostrils and made his eyes water, and the devil vanished.

"Pah! Too much wine of a night makes a man fanciful the next morning!" the Gypsy grumbled, shaking his head to clear it. "The hair of the dog that bit me will do the trick! Belinda, *mi corazón,* bring your papa the wineskin," he roared, and Belinda, ever the faithful daughter, tripped merrily to do her father's bidding.

But the moment the Gypsy's hand clasped the wineskin, it turned to gold, and there was no liquor left in it to ease his raging thirst.

"No matter," the Gypsy declared, carefully caching the golden wineskin beneath the fire's ashes in the Gypsy fashion, along with his hoard of coins. "A man may quench his thirst in the brook more easily."

The Gypsy knelt over the chuckling brook and cupped his hands to drink from its cold, sparkling flow. But no sooner had he dipped his hands to water than the brook stilled. The icy water became a stream of frozen gold on his lips, and the Gypsy scowled.

"Pah! Neither wine or water have I, but—" and he brightened "—what a wonder of wonders is this! A brook of purest gold will bring men from far and wide, eager and ready to pay a coin to see this marvel, and I shall grow rich beyond belief!"

"But, Papa, I'm hungry!" whimpered his daughter, pouting her cherry-red lips. "Oh, Papa, won't you find us something to eat?"

"For you, my darling daughter, anything!" the greedy Gypsy—in good spirits on account of his newfound wealth—promised expansively. He clambered up into the *vardo* to fetch the pigeon pie left over from their supper the evening before, but as he did so, both wagon and pigeon pie became solid gold!

"No matter," scoffed the Gypsy. "No matter at all. Pigeon pie is

10

fare fit only for the poor, and I'm a wealthy man. Bring me my horsehair snare, Belinda, and in the twinkling of an eye, we'll have a plump rabbit for a fine stew, eh, *caballo?*" He patted his faithful horse, pretending he didn't notice as the faithful beast froze under his palm and became an equine statue of gold.

Belinda sped away and brought the snare, but in her father's hands it, too, turned to gold, and her tears increased. "Now we'll have nothing to eat!" she wept, and her sobs cut her father's heart to the quick.

"Nonsense, little one, of course we will! Don't cry, *pequeña!* Why, I'm not so old yet that I can't catch a rabbit with my two bare fists," he boasted. "Dry your eyes, and you'll see."

As he promised, the Gypsy was light and swift on his feet. An unwary rabbit bounded from its burrow and found itself at once swooped up into the Gypsy's hands, caught firmly by its long ears. "Your supper, *mi hija!*" the Gypsy declared, but his little daughter's tears increased.

"But its ears are gold. Its whiskers are gold! Its nose is gold! We can't eat a golden rabbit, Papa—and I'm so-o-o hungry!" she wailed.

The Gypsy was at a loss as to what to do now, and beginning to wonder—and fear—where all this might end. He found them mushrooms and wild onions, roots and blackberries from the brambles, but no matter what he touched, it, too, turned to gold in his hands.

Day became night, and his little daughter wept softly with cold and the hunger pangs gnawing at her little belly. The blanket her father wrapped around her became a sheet of purest gold, too, at the mere touch of the Gypsy's hands, and the cold metal could not serve to keep the chill night wind that blew off the heath from her bones.

"Aiee, Belinda, my daughter! What have I done to you!" her father cried in anguish the following morning, for Belinda shivered with ague and burned with fever, and pleaded with him to bring her a warming broth, which he could not provide.

Lost in misery and guilt, the Gypsy gathered his little daughter into his arms and wept and begged her forgiveness. But as his arms enfolded her and his bitter tears fell on her cheeks, the child grew still and silent in his arms. Too late, the father saw his folly. Too late, he saw the rich black curls that had so gaily crowned her little head had now become strands of spun gold; the blooming, rosy cheeks were now pale and smooth as any statue's. The cherished body in his arms was stiff and still and no residue of life breathed within its metal casing.

"What a fool I am!" he raged, beating upon his chest with his fists. "What a blind and careless, greedy fool! I bartered my soul to the devil for the golden touch, and now my daughter, my Belinda—once loved above all I possessed—lies still and cold in my arms! Aiee! Aiee! What price now a Gypsy's lust for gold!"

The devil peeped from his hiding place and snickered . . .

Prologue

A small brown donkey labored up the winding cobbled streets, heading for the Ramblas marketplace. The panniers strapped to its back were heavily laden with red earthenware pots. Its young, barefooted master chivvied the beast along with the aid of a willow switch applied generously and frequently to its bony rump, and the little donkey valiantly struggled to increase its speed.

From the shadows of a murky alley, a short, thickset man and a slender young girl idly watched the donkey's passage down the street. The rough-looking man was scowling, and the girl appeared little less agreeable as he continued to scold her.

"You! Pah, you're like that donkey, Krissoula, stubborn and willful, and lazy, to boot!" Hector ranted. "Now, out on the streets with you, girl, and find us a likely mark before sundown!"

"Lazy? Huh! Who's calling who 'lazy,' eh, Hector?" the girl demanded indignantly with an angry flash of her golden eyes. "I'm not the one who stays safe in the alley while others risk their neck— you are! You're not the one to be pawed by those dirty, sweaty animals—*I* am, so don't come bleating to me about laziness! I'll hop to it when I'm good and ready, so there!"

Hector said nothing. He couldn't, for he knew in his heart that the girl was right, and he was reluctant to anger her. After all, he needed her, her looks, her daring, far more than she needed him! For a moment or two, there was silence between them while Hector sullenly considered how best to regain her good graces, and Krissoula idly scuffed her dirty bare toes in the dust and ignored him.

Brilliant sunlight bathed the winding street beyond the narrow shadowed alley, cruelly revealing the shabbiness of the buildings hereabouts without mercy. Pockmarked taverns with peeling painted doors lined the street, each one boasting a tiny flower-filled courtyard before it, where trestle tables and rustic wooden benches

13

sagged beneath the backsides and elbows of a handful of patrons. Rosebushes, heavy with scented blooms, dreamed in the sun by some of the doors, while orange trees laden with their vivid fruits sprang up between the flagstones of others. Far above, red-tiled rooftops looked down into the quiet street, and black wrought-iron balconies bellied out, almost meeting each other. Between some of the buildings, lines had been strung, on which to dry an assortment of shabby laundry. Arched windows, narrow and latticed, betrayed the influence of the Moors who had once ruled Catalonia, and lingered yet in the architecture of Spain, while on the steps of one of the taverns a dusty black cat stretched and yawned and delicately washed its ears with a rough pink tongue, ignoring the plump fantailed pigeons and the cooing gray doves that pecked at the dust scant feet away. It was time for *siesta* on a sultry August afternoon in sunny Barcelona, and far too hot to bother about unwary pigeons, the cat's indolent manner declared. Better to sleep, and dream of the fresh fish to be had for supper, the aroma of which carried to his velvet nose from the nearby quays and wharves of the city . . .

"Well! I'll be buggered—!" the man Hector exclaimed suddenly, straightening up and whipping his hands from his pockets. His sly brown eyes suddenly kindled with greed and a glittering excitement, and Krissoula fancied that even his jug-handle ears twitched, like a hound on the scent of game. "Get an eyeful of what's coming down the street, girl! This 'pigeon's' a gift from God, if ever I saw one! Look lively now, *muchacha!*"

Krissoula glanced up with little interest, for she was well used to Hector's lavish expectations that rarely, if ever, bore fruit. But this time, despite herself and her stubborn resolve to appear disinterested and unimpressed despite Hector's obvious excitement, her eyes narrowed shrewdly as she saw the man Hector had indicated. Standing close to six feet tall, his long, arrogant stride as he made his way down the street, and the elegant cut of his well-tailored clothes, screamed wealth and breeding to the waiting tricksters. Krissoula barely had time to observe the fact that he was also fairly young and very handsome, when a hefty shove in the small of the back from Hector propelled her forcibly out of the shady alley and into the blinding sunshine of the street, taking from her the luxury of choosing whether to make him her latest mark or nay. Damn that Hector's black heart, she thought mutinously, and drew a deep, steadying breath.

Wearing an inviting, sultry smile that betrayed nothing of her true feelings, she crossed the cobbled Calle de Tabernas towards the man. The huge golden hoops that dangled from her earlobes flashed in the bright Catalonian sunshine that cast sharp black shadows off the buildings and onto the cobbles. Her hips swung seductively as she neared him so that her brilliant flowered skirts swished to and fro, and she knew very well that the way she walked was provocative; knew full well it gave the man a glimpse of her bare, slender golden legs, her prettily formed ankles, and an inch or two of fraying white petticoats. After all, hadn't she practiced this walk a thousand times before . . . ?

"You seem lonely, señor?" she purred as she drew abreast of the man. Moistening her lips with a small, pink tongue tip, she eyed him archly with her head cocked to one side as she continued. "Perhaps a woman, *sí*, señor . . . ?"

She let her smoky voice trail away suggestively, and the thick fringing of her sooty lashes fluttered downward as she awaited his answer, so that her slanted golden eyes were hooded, mysterious with promises of pleasure to come.

The tall hawk-faced man—so elegantly and expensively attired he was obviously not of these seedy back streets running parallel to the wharves—gasped in surprise as he looked up into her lovely, delicately formed features, his sapphire eyes widening with what seemed almost like recognition. The curt rebuff that formed on his lips died as he gaped at her, exactly as if he'd seen a ghost!

Krissoula noted his startled expression but gave a mental shrug of dismissal. She had no idea why this handsome *hombre* seemed so dumbfounded by her appearance. But—since she'd long ago grown accustomed to men finding her beautiful and wanting her body— she readily accepted that he, like all the others before him, had been stunned by her looks, or maybe by the unusual, striking hue of her eyes. Few others of her ancient profession possessed more than a faded claim to prettiness, after all!

"A woman?" The man had recovered his lost composure by now and smiled, his finely sculpted face becoming strikingly handsome, the Gypsy-girl mused, for a man his age. Why, he had to be at least twenty-eight, she guessed, a good ten years older than she! He was positively ancient, but a handsome devil nonetheless . . .

"Why, *sí*, I think you may be right, *chiquita,*" he replied with an amused and interested grin, his gaze speculative as sapphire eyes roamed over her bared shoulders and lingered on the thrust of hard, pointed young breasts pressing against the worn cloth of her *camisa.* "The—company—of a beautiful woman might be just what

15

I need to—er—lift my spirits!"

She sidled closer to him then, tipping her head slightly to her accomplice, Hector, who waited in the shadowed mouth of the alley across the street—to follow them as she did so.

"A wise decision, my handsome *caballero,*" she purred, linking her arm through her mark's elbow. "After a few hours of pleasure, your worries will seem far less important, I promise you! Come along with me, señor. I have a room above the next inn that we can use, eh—?" she tempted.

"An inn—on this street? *Caramba,* no, *chiquita!* If it's all the same to you, I've no stomach for the—er—flea-bitten accommodations to be had in this part of town, *gracias!* It'd be far more to my liking if you were to come to my lodgings—say, tonight, at my hotel?" he suggested coolly, cocking a raven-dark brow in her direction.

Seeing her hesitate, and the doubt that flickered across that little gamin face, he whisked a large golden coin from his inner pocket and brandished it, shiny and new, before her greedy golden eyes, which, he noted, widened appreciably. Her hand at once whipped out to snatch the coin from him, but seconds before her nail-bitten, grubby fingers closed around it, he flicked the golden guinea smoothly out of her reach.

"Tut, tut, not so fast, greedy one! First, we must discuss terms, eh? I'm offering you a guinea, to reserve your lovely company for the entire night. You'll receive another of the same when you leave me in the morning. Agreed?"

The *gitana* was stunned. By Saint Sara, he was offering her a small fortune for her favors! But—his unusual generosity made the streetwise girl wary. She frowned in suspicion, her small, narrow nose wrinkling delightfully.

"A whole *guinea,* señor, for what a handsome devil like you could get anywhere in this district for a tenth of the price?" she asked shrewdly. "Why so much, señor?" she wetted her lips. "Do you, perhaps, have—special—tastes?"

"For a woman like you, *niña*—for that face, those wonderful eyes, that body—you wonder why?" He chuckled, and little crinkly lines formed in his tanned skin, winging away from the outer corners of his eyes. "Come, come, little one, there's no need for false modesty, not with me! You know very well what you're worth, so don't belittle your charms. And besides, there's far more where this came from—a guinea's a trifling amount for a wealthy man such as myself!" He dismissed the matter casually as unimportant, his hand lightly resting on the slim curve of her hip now, which was almost boyishly formed. In fact, she was so painfully thin, he could feel the jut of her hip bone against his palm. When, he wondered, had she last eaten a square meal?

"I could take your gold and run!" she dared him, snatching the shiny coin from his fingers and tucking it down her *camisa* between her hard young breasts in a triumphant, breathless way that made his lips quirk in a smile. "You might never see me again, señor!"

He shrugged. "Perhaps not. But that's a chance I'll have to take, eh? Still, something tells me you're a clever, ambitious young woman, and that you'll keep your part of our bargain and collect the balance. So. Is it agreed?"

She nodded. "Very well, señor."

"Then I'll expect you at, oh, ten o'clock, shall we say, at the Hotel Barcelona on Calle de las Ramblas? You may come straight up to suite seventy, or ask for Don Esteban de San Martín's rooms at the desk, and someone will show you the way. I'll tell them to expect you, little one, so don't disappoint me, hmm?" He smiled down at her.

"I'll be there," she promised, her heart skipping a beat at the way his eyes lit up when he smiled.

"Good! I'll be looking forward to it. Until tonight, then—?"

With that, the handsome bastard strolled away, whistling jauntily, leaving Krissoula frowning again as she stared after him.

At once, her partner Hector appeared from the shadows, scowling like one of the ugly gargoyles on the Barcelona Cathedral as usual, the miserable toad.

"He paid you for nothing, eh? Crazy rich bastard, throwing his money away like that!"

"Not for nothing, Hector," she corrected with a sly grin. "He wanted me to go to his hotel room tonight—said he had no fondness for the 'accommodations' in this part of town!" She laughed in scorn.

"What? He must have been as stupid as he was rich, then, trusting a little whore like you to keep her word after he'd parted with his precious money! You don't intend to go, eh, Krissoula?" Hector demanded suspiciously, casting a bleary, bloodshot eye in her direction.

"Of course not, *tonto!*" she lied with a brilliant smile. "Our dear Señor de San Martín has, as you said, thrown his money away! Come, let's buy ourselves something wonderful to eat over at the Paloma. There's enough here to fill fifty hungry bellies, and mine's

17

growling—as usual."

Hector nodded sourly, and his greedy eyes narrowed. "All right, if that's what you want. But remember my cut, Krissoula, and don't squander every peso of the money on food! I know how you are when you're hungry, greedy bitch!" he grumbled as always.

"There'll be more than enough left for a bottle of *aguardiente*, Hector, never fear," she promised, tight-lipped.

Tonight, she decided as she followed Hector down the street, the partnership of Hector Corrales and Krissoula Ballardo would be temporarily dissolved. She would pluck that plump *gorgio* pigeon, San Martín, for herself, keep every peseta of the money, and El Diablo take Hector and his "cut"!

The streets were already dark when she set out, the cobbles lit with hissing gaslights on the corners in this, the wealthy part of town.

She skirted the crowded *plaza pública* with its bubbling fountains and Moorish arches, where countless sweethearts—all dressed in their best and heavily chaperoned—circled about in the ages-old ritual courtship custom of the *paseo,* and reached the Hotel Barcelona and Don Esteban de San Martín's rooms without incident. Ignoring the smirks and lewd comments of the bellboys, she slipped barefooted down carpeted corridors to suite seventy. She was quite dazzled by the opulence she saw all about her, for never had she been inside such a grand place as this one!

Don Esteban, impeccably dressed in a tailored black frock coat with a vest of silver-shot gray brocade beneath it, invited her in on her first knock.

To Krissoula's surprise, a small table spread with snowy linens had been placed before a bay window overlooking the Ramblas marketplace, which in Spanish fashion was still thronged even at this late hour with noisy street vendors selling flowers, fruit, and little monkeys and birds in wicker cages.

Sparkling silver serving dishes with domed covers, and fine china, silverware, and crystal glasses for two had been placed opposite each other. A bottle of expensive wine was cooling in a bucket of ice, and on a side table a bouquet of deep-red roses gave off their sweet, pungent perfume. Roses, she noted with delight, the Gypsies' favorite flower! That was a good omen, she decided, for a successful conclusion to tonight's work! But then, another unpleasant possibility reared its ugly head.

18

"You're expecting company, señor?" she asked, suddenly frightened. After all, she knew nothing about this man! He could be one of those filthy lechers she'd heard about from other women of the streets; twisted men who had strange ideas about what to do with a woman, and sometimes liked to share her favors with others, or watch while others enjoyed their bedsport.

Her apprehensive eyes were drawn suddenly to his hands, which were large, powerful, and tanned a warm brown, with a light sprinkling of dark hair across the knuckles. *Jesús y María!* Those hands were easily powerful enough to choke the life from her slender throat, should he be so inclined . . . ? Her slim, graceful fingers fluttered to her own throat and her mouth went dry. For once the cocksure, streetwise Krissoula felt completely out of her depth, tempted to run. Even the comforting feel of the folded packet of powder in her skirt pocket did little to calm her pounding heart.

"Company? Why, of course!" he responded to her question, and smiled. "Your own lovely company, señorita—?"

"Krissoula," she answered eagerly, forcing a smile. "Krissoula Ballardo." The rush of relief his easy answer brought made her knees feel rubbery.

"Ah, 'Krissoula,' is it? A lovely name for a lovely young woman! It's a Greek name, I believe?"

She nodded, almost shyly. "*Sí.* My—papa—was Greek. It means 'golden one,' my aunt Isabella once told me."

"And a perfect name for you, too, *querida,* with those wonderful golden eyes. Well, come, then, little Krissoula Ballardo, and don't be afraid of me. I won't bite you! I simply thought—since it's long past suppertime—that we'd have a little something to eat and a glass or two of wine to relax us before we—er—enjoy ourselves!"

His dark eyebrows rose, and he nodded wickedly through an open door to where a vast four-poster bed stood in the adjoining room. The crisp sheets, she saw, had been turned down in readiness. Then the man winked in a lecherous fashion, and her heart skipped a nervous beat. Her belly turned over.

Caramba! The dryness was back in her mouth, curse it! What the devil was wrong with her? Hadn't she done this a hundred times before? Then why that niggling feeling of foreboding in her belly, that sense of a trap about to be sprung . . . ?

"*Sí,* I'd like that very much," she managed to reply at length, and gave him a shy smile in return. Blessed Virgin, two feasts in one day was more than she'd dared to hope for! Her misgivings were foolish

19

ones, better left ignored. After all, he believed her a whore. He could suspect nothing more! What could possibly go wrong?

Later, after they'd dined on a fine shrimp paella served on a bed of fragrant saffron rice, while San Martín's back was turned to pluck her a deep red rose from the vase, she deftly emptied the sleeping powder into his wineglass. Her anxiety lessened enormously as he drained the contents moments later without commenting on its bitterness. In a few minutes, he'd nod off to sleep, and then she could do what she'd come here to do and make good her escape . . .

"Mmm, the wine makes me so sleepy and amorous, señor," she murmured and stretched in the lazy, catlike way she knew made her pointed breasts thrust invitingly forward against the thin cloth of her blouse. "Perhaps, if you're in the mood now . . . ?"

He reached across the table and took her hand in his. Raising it to his lips, he kissed her fingertips. "In the mood? Why, that goes without saying, *minina!* And after such a pretty invitation from you—ah, Krissoula *mía,* how could any normal man refuse?"

Smiling still, he led her into the bedroom, slipped off his coat, and quickly unfastened his cravat and the topmost buttons of his shirt. As the fronts parted, a broad golden-bronze chest furred lightly with curling dark hair was revealed.

"Why don't you undress and slip into bed, *cara mía,* while I pour us both a glass of wine?" he suggested huskily.

She knew he was watching her while he poured the wine, but it didn't disturb her in the least. The undressing part was an inevitable drawback of the daring game she and Hector played, and one she'd grown accustomed to long ago; so accustomed that having strange men ogle her in her natural state no longer bothered her at all! Besides, knowing a glimpse of her nakedness would be all those gullible, foolish old goats received for their hard-earned coin gave her a malicious, pleasurable feeling that made what she did easier to bear!

As she tugged her embroidered *camisa* over her head, she wondered if she'd judged the amount of sedative correctly, for San Martín still seemed wide awake. She bit her lip. Hector usually handled that part of it. He alone knew how much of the drug to use. Perhaps she'd misjudged the amount, and put too little, she thought with a moment of sheer panic. Perhaps she'd have to go through with it, and let him tumble her . . . ?

Quite naked now, but playing for time, she reached up to pluck the combs from her hair. She shook it out and let it tumble free in

20

a wild torrent of ebony ringlets that reached almost to her slim buttocks. She heard San Martin draw a quick, admiring breath as she pirouetted gracefully to face him, her hair spraying around her. A slow, inviting smile curved her full lips now, and her thickly lashed golden eyes were seductive, glittering orbs.

"So? Do you like me a little, señor?" she asked coyly, twining an inky tendril about her finger in a provocative pose. "Do you want Krissoula?"

Pouting, she let the fingertips of her other hand trail down over her impudent, honey-tipped breasts and flat belly, knowing full well his gaze followed the path they took. Standing there, she let him feast his sapphire eyes upon her, hating him as she'd grown to hate all men since the betrayal and death of Miguel . . .

"How could I fail to want you, silly little donkey?" Esteban murmured thickly, moistening his lips and setting the wineglasses aside. "You're lovely—quite the most luscious little piece I've seen in a long, long time . . ." He held out his hand in invitation. "Come, my lovely Krissoula! The night, it is wasting, no?" he commanded, and obediently she slipped her small hand in his larger one, padded barefoot to the bed, and lay down upon it.

For a few moments, stretched out there beside him, she fretted again that the powder she'd slipped into his wine had been too little, for he certainly seemed very wide awake still! He stripped off his shirt and undressed down to his breeches, then sat down beside her on the edge of the bed. His upper torso was magnificent, lean and wiry and rippling with hidden muscle like an outdoorsman, rather than soft and pale like a merchant's should have been. The flutters of foreboding she'd felt earlier returned. Something was wrong here—badly wrong—!

But before she could act on her misgivings or protest in any way, he leaned down over her. Broad shoulders blotting out the lamplight, he cupped her face in his palms. His eyes closed as he dipped his head to hers, and she saw how his impossibly long and curling lashes made sooty smudges against his cheekbones in the moment before his mouth captured hers.

His lips, tasting pleasantly of wine, were firm as he kissed her ardently, teasing the margin of her lips and then the little indentations at the corners with his tongue tip. Deepening the kiss, he gathered her into his arms and drew her against the length of his body, so that she could feel his hard male arousal against her hip as his tongue claimed and explored the soft inner recesses of her mouth. His tongue warred with her own tongue in an intimate way

21

that made her tremble uncontrollably, for she'd never been kissed so thoroughly—so expertly!—before, and the feel of his kisses stirred unexpected and unwanted reactions throughout her body. A damnable weakness spread through her, making her limbs feel heavy and loose. A rosy warmth coursed through her veins, sending a rush of heat and color to her cheeks, and a tingling sensation to the very tips of her breasts that was disgustingly pleasurable.

Fortunately, she succeeded in keeping her true feelings under control, and managed to kiss him back just a little. She even managed to utter a few realistic moans as his wandering hands found and fondled her breasts, and to pretend she enjoyed what he was doing to her as he cupped and played with them, teasing the little dark-gold nipples to stand firm and . . .

Pretend? Huh! Who was she fooling? To be honest with herself, this *diablo's* caresses had stunned her, for despite all intentions to the contrary, his ardent lovemaking had stirred her female passions more than a little, and her sighs and moans were more genuine than she cared to admit! What was it about this handsome *diablo* that set him apart from all the other men she'd worked her wiles on in the past? His dark, chiseled face? His lover's skills? *Caray,* whatever the real reason, his passionate kisses weakened her: his exploring hands excited her, made her tingle and glow and grow peculiarly breathless with the warmth of mounting desire. Her counterfeit moans of delight melted into contented little gasps of genuine pleasure against his lips, and she shivered with longing as his hand enfolded her breast and the ball of his thumb teased the nipple to swelling fullness.

But then, just when she was wondering fuzzily where all this delicious madness might lead, the man groaned, sighed heavily, and slumped dead-weight against her, pinning her beneath his body. Krissoula almost sobbed with relief, and maybe—just maybe— with the tiniest, barest twinges of—disappointment?

By Saint Sara, what was this foolishness she was thinking? Had she gone mad, grown soft, merely on account of his gropings and his hateful kisses? She hadn't come here to be pleasured by this rich pigeon, but to rob the fellow blind! And at last, *gracias a Dios,* he was out cold! she congratulated herself, determined to squelch her other foolish notions. She must get on with what she'd come here to do, make good her escape, and none the wiser!

Hefting him up a little, she squirmed from beneath him and rolled his limp body over, onto his back, to make certain he was asleep. His magnificent sapphire eyes were closed, the lashes like smudges of charcoal against his arrogant cheekbones. Beneath his aquiline nose, his mouth was slack, his lips parted just a little. As she looked down at him, a loud snore buzzed from between them and confirmed that he was indeed out cold.

"Sleep well, San Martín, you randy goat!" she wished him with a scornful smile, and added as she slipped from the bed, "And be warned by tonight that, Gypsy or no, Krissoula Ballardo whores for no man, you gullible fool!" she hissed.

Not bothering to dress herself, she systematically searched every drawer in the suite. There'd be time to dress later she decided, for her snoring mark would sleep for several hours. They always did!

But her dismay mounted by the minute as she pulled out empty drawers and delved into empty pockets. Her careful, systematic search became a frantic, haphazard one that left clothing and ransacked personal belongings strewn over furniture, heaped on the floor, or sent it flying in every direction, for not so much as a single peso did she find anywhere in the suite!

"Is this what you're looking for, thief?" San Martín's clipped, stern voice suddenly demanded, cutting through the silence like a steely blade.

Yelping in shock, Krissoula flung about to see San Martín fully awake and dressed, standing by the bed with a hefty roll of bank notes flourished in his hand! With a thin smile at her horrified, guilty expression, he strolled menacingly across the room towards her, looking, she thought, wetting her lips in fear, like a graceful, deadly jaguar stalking a terrified rabbit it had cornered.

"Surprised, eh, *gitana*? Somehow, I thought you might be! Let this be a little lesson to you, Krissoula. You can't teach an old dog— or even a 'randy goat'!—new tricks. And this 'old dog' knows all the tricks in the book! Yours, I might add, has been played by women like you since the beginning of time—and with far greater flair than you play it, unfortunately for you, my reckless little *puta!*"

Escape was her only thought then! Somehow, she had to dress and get out of here! Frantically, she cast about her for her clothes, but they'd vanished, she realized, and her slanted golden eyes grew stark with panic. A sick dread filled the pit of her belly.

"Don't bother looking for the grubby rags you came in, *niña*. You see, I tossed them into the street below while you were busy— er—rearranging my drawers for me!" With a scornful smile, San Martín strode across to the bell rope, and made as if to pull it.

"What are you doing?" she cried, her eyes wide with terror.

"Summoning the hotel manager, of course. Who will, in turn,

23

summon *los botónes.*"

"The cops? But—why?" she whispered, tasting fear sharp on her tongue. "So you caught me searching your things, San Martín—what of it, eh? Curiosity's no crime, is it? I stole nothing from you!"

"No? Ah, but your clothing—which I tossed down to the alley below—tells a rather different story! I'd wager hard money the cops would find a considerable sum of money hidden in your pockets, and, I do believe, a few expensive personal items of my own. Some gold cuff links, pearl collar studs—that sort of thing."

San Martín shook his curly dark head and clicked his teeth reproachfully. "Ah, Krissoula, poor, poor little Krissoula, what a fix you're in, eh? I'd estimate a Gypsy *puta* and thief like you'd get—oh, at least five years hard labor for your handiwork tonight, no? What a waste!"

The color fled her face, leaving it waxy-pale beneath sun-browned skin. Her Romany people had ever been outcasts, she thought bitterly, victims of the *gorgios',* the non-Gypsies', ignorance and prejudices since the beginning of time. Beggars and thieves, dabblers in witchcraft, liars and charlatans all, they called them, drawing away in contempt when they passed by. A wave of hopelessness swept through her. The *gorgio* brute was right! No one—and especially not the authorities!—would believe the word of a Gypsy girl against the accusations of fine Don Esteban de San Martín, with his Castilian accent, his obvious wealth and his cultured air that bespoke breeding! No, never, not in a million years . . .

"Why are you doing this? What do you want of me?" she demanded shakily, feeling vulnerable and foolish standing there, stark naked, trying to bargain for her freedom with this—this *gorgio* madman!

"I have a score to settle with an old enemy, Krissoula," Esteban de San Martín began in a steely, rough tone quite unlike the smooth, cultured voice she'd heard him use before. "Unfortunately for you, my dear, your looks are exactly the bait I need to pull it off. The resemblance is quite remarkable, you see?"

"I see nothing!" she screeched at him, golden eyes blazing. "You're mad, *loco!* Let me out of here!"

She flung herself at the door, then ran to another and another, battering upon them with clenched fists. But as she'd half expected, every exit to the suite had been locked, and the keys removed. That bastard! That sly, conniving, blackmailing bastard! He'd planned this all along, right down to the last detail, she realized too late, and

24

she'd walked into his trap like a lamb to the slaughter.

"Let me go, please, I beg you!" she sobbed, flinging herself at his feet. "I'll do anything you want me to, if only you'll let me go!"

"Sorry, *gitana*—I'm afraid that's quite out of the question, until you've calmed down and agreed to accept my—proposition."

"Proposition?" She wetted her dry lips. "And if I don't choose to, what then?"

He shrugged casually. "In that event, I'm afraid I'll be forced to do as I threatened, and summon the police. And there'd be no question of convincing them that you're innocent! After all, who'd take the word of a thieving Gypsy *puta* over that of a respectable South American *hacendero* such as myself, eh, Krissoula? Now, be reasonable, little one, and hear me out. After all, what choice do you have?"

What choice, indeed? Dread like a weight in her heart, she dragged a sheet from the bed to cover herself, sat down, and grudgingly listened to his "proposition," as he called it, growing steadily more and more sleepy by the minute as he talked on and on.

As a velvety blackness overwhelmed her, she dimly realized in the seconds before she folded across the bed in a crumpled heap just exactly what had happened to the wine she'd drugged. He'd switched their glasses, curse his soul, she thought foggily! She could no sooner escape him than fly.

Unknown to Krissoula, her grudging acceptance of his blackmailer's terms the following morning—rather than risking the very real possibility of spending several years in a filthy jail—would take her halfway around the world, from fabled Old Spain to the exciting, new world of South America. Her life would never be the same again, after that memorable night.

And nor, for that matter, would his . . .

Chapter One

Estancia Tierra Rosa, the Pampa, Argentina, July 1865

"Run from me, would you, you golden devil! You'll be sorry when I'm done with you, damn your black heart—!"

A horse's shrill scream cut through the cool Argentinian air like a sharp-bladed knife.

Krissoula dropped the silver-backed brush with which she'd been brushing her hair and jumped up. She flew across the room and through the open French doors, out onto the balcony. Craning over it to look below, her black hair spilled loose over her shoulders like a curtain as she precariously balanced her upper body over the wrought-iron railing.

In the far corner of the courtyard, where tall walls formed a right angle, a magnificent palomino stallion reared back on its hindquarters. It was furiously striking out with its hooves at the small, brown-faced *mestizo* hand who was advancing upon it, snarling obscenities and threats. The stallion's blond hindquarters were slick with sweat and bloodied by the marks of vicious blows from a whip. Foam flecked its chest, and its eyes rolled dangerously as the man neared it so that the whites showed.

"Leave him be!" Krissoula commanded in a ringing voice from her lofty vantage point on the balcony. "You fool! Can't you see he'll kill you if you try to catch him now? Let him calm down first!"

The man, Alfredo, was either deaf, stupid, or doggedly determined to ignore her caution. He edged closer, hands outstretched to catch the stallion's dangling halter, muttering foul threats as he did so.

"You devil-beast! *Demonio! Diablo!* I'll flay the hide from your precious back again when I catch you!" he swore, licking his lips.

A sheen of sweat greased the *peón's* brow below his felt hatbrim. Oily beads of it clung to his upper lip and his straggly black moustache. The stallion, smelling his hatred, screamed again and reared up a second time, its flailing hooves narrowly falling short of braining the groom.

Krissoula muttered an obscenity of her own. Quickly, she cocked one leg over the balcony rail, then the other. Poised for a second on her bottom over the very edge of the railing, she sprang down to the courtyard below, landing safely like a little cat with bent knees in the thick, prickly bushes of lavender below her second-story balcony. Without pausing to dust herself off, she scrambled to her feet and sped lightly across the courtyard to the man. Grabbing his elbow in the nick of time, she yanked hard to wrench him safely out of reach of the palomino stallion's pawing hooves.

"*Hijo de puta!*" she hissed, her golden eyes raging. "Have you no sense? No brain? Dorado would kill you before you touched him! Look at him, *tonto!*"

The *mestizo* swung around to face her, his heavy, flattish features ugly with rage. There was something about the angle of his body that warned Krissoula he intended to strike her, and she tensed accordingly. Sure enough, his fist swung up and back in the same moment that she nimbly ducked. Then his eyes met hers, and his ferocious scowl faded; the fury dimmed in his brown eyes and was replaced by dismay—and fear—as his arm dropped lamely to his side.

"Why, Doña Krissoula, forgive me—!" he stammered, whipping off his hat and crushing it to his scrawny chest. "Believe me, doña, I didn't realize it was you—!"

Krissoula smiled pitilessly, her golden eyes withering him with contempt. "And if I were not the doña but some other poor woman, what then, eh? You would have struck me without second thought, isn't that so, Alfredo? Pah! Men—! *Caramba,* you are all the same!" she finished with a jeer and a contemptuous toss of her loose black curls. "You lose your tempers and beat your women as pitilessly as you do your horses . . ."

She broke off, realizing suddenly that Alfredo's eyes were widening with amazement as he gaped at her, and it was only then that she remembered she was half naked! The brief lacy camisole and ruffled pantelets she'd stripped down to for her siesta were her only garments! Grimacing, she cursed her stupidity and promptly crossed her arms over her bosom. Caramba! *What's wrong with you, foolish gitana?* she berated herself. *When will you remember that high-born gorgio ladies do not run about in public so scantily clad, eh?* For a lowly groom like Alfredo to see her half naked—

aiee, *Dios,* it was unthinkable, especially here in Argentina where men were, if anything, even *more* fiercely protective of their women's virtue than in her native Spain! What would straitlaced Don Felipe say if he ever learned of this lapse—? She pursed her lips, determining the old goat would never learn of it—or at least, not from her lips—!

"What's going on here?" demanded an angry voice.

Krissoula saw Alfredo's brown face grow pale. She turned in the direction of that all-too-familiar voice, her heart sinking. *Dios!* Why did *he* have to show up now, of all the times to do so!

Esteban de San Martín stood there, his booted feet planted arrogantly apart—and what a handsome *hombre* he was, too, Krissoula thought appreciatively if dispassionately, her golden eyes narrowed.

Tall for an Argentine, the ranch manager was dressed today in the picturesque clothing of a *gaucho,* or South American cowboy. A round, black felt *chambergo* with a cord dangling beneath his stubbled jaw shaded his upper face and concealed his dark-sapphire eyes—which were angry ones right now, she knew only too well by his tone of voice! He wore a black jacket embroidered with fancy patterns worked in yarn across his wonderfully broad shoulders, topping the red shirt that hugged his whipcord torso. A cotton bandanna with a bright red-and-blue pattern was knotted loosely at his brown throat, the ends left trailing. His wide black gaucho pants were tucked into knee-length horsehide boots, belted with a sash of red-and-blue patterns on a cream-colored background. Three huge silver conchos studded the center of the sash, drawing the eyes to his lean waist and hips, then down the length of his muscular thighs where the fringed ends were left loose and hanging. Over his shoulder was slung a creamy woolen poncho with borders of chocolate and black, and from one of his tanned fists coiled a whip with a long, tapering lash. The ugly whip drew Krissoula's eyes like a magnet and filled her with fresh outrage as the furious man strode slowly towards, then past them, giving the pair only a cursory, disgusted glance as he approached the quivering blond stallion.

"Use your whip on that horse, *mayordomo,* and I'll see you whipped yourself—then thrown off the *estancia* before sunset!" Krissoula threatened through gritted teeth, tossing her head for emphasis. Deal or no, she wouldn't idly stand by and witness his cruelty to the stallion, she determined, and her golden eyes flashed.

"Oh, come, come, Doña Krissoula, surely you have more faith in me than that! The whip was for Alfredo here, not Dorado!" the

29

Argentine growled, and flung the ugly black whip far away from him so that it slammed across the mestizo's shins. Hands hanging loose at his sides, he stepped closer to the snorting animal.

"*Basta, mi amigo, basta!*" he crooned in a deep, husky voice. "Enough of your tantrums! There's no reason to be afraid of Esteban. Why, we're old friends, you and I, no?"

To Krissoula's amazement, the stallion tossed its head in response to his crooning voice. Creamy mane rippling, the animal nickered and pawed the dust of the courtyard, visibly calmer when it again stood still. A shiver of powerful muscle twitched beneath its glossy golden coat and a soft sound of greeting blew from its nostrils as the man stepped up to it. He caressed its velvety nose, and ran a knowledgeable hand down its neck, chest, whithers, and flanks to check for injuries. The stallion affectionately nuzzled at his neck as he took the dangling halter firmly in hand and walked the animal in circles to cool it down.

"Lucky for you he isn't hurt, Flores!" he told Alfredo in grim tones as he walked the beast. "You can pick up your gear from the bunkhouse as you leave, but be quick about it! You see, I want you off my *estancia* before nightfall!"

"Leave Tierra Rosa? But, Señor San Martín—!" Alfredo protested in a whine. "—I have a wife, and little ones to feed—!"

"No 'buts,' 'Fredo!" Esteban cut him off with a murderous scowl. "I warned you the last time what would happen if you mistreated my horses again, no? Go, before I lay that whip across your idle backside!"

Gray beneath his brown complexion, Alfredo seemed about to protest further, thought better of it, and scurried from the courtyard, giving the man a look of pure hatred as he left. Esteban turned then to Krissoula.

"And you, doña—have you no servants to instruct—no fine seams to sew?" he demanded sarcastically.

She felt, rather than saw, his eyes travel over her, and sensed he was more amused than shocked by her scanty attire, despite his stern, biting tone. The mockery in his voice confirmed his thoughts and grated on her temper as he added, "Or perhaps Dorado and I interrupted something between you and Alfredo, eh, *muchacha?*"

Krissoula bristled at the heavy innuendo in his tone. Her golden eyes flashed in anger. So, he thought he could speak to her like a serving wench, did he? Pah! a curse on his arrogance! She'd show him once and for all that she wouldn't stand for such treatment, no matter how much he'd paid her . . .

She drew herself up to her full height of five feet five inches, and shot him a scorching glare that would have withered most men. Not this one, however! Esteban met her glare with total indifference and a derisive half-smile that was somehow more insolent, more insulting, than any words could have been.

"Careful how you speak to me, *campesino!*" she snapped, placing heavy emphasis on her insulting use of the word "peasant." "Were he here, Don Felipe de Aguilar would never tolerate such insolence to his—his beloved intended!"

Esteban de San Martín shoved back his hat and let it dangle from its cord down his back. She saw now that his wicked dark-sapphire eyes were shining with contempt, his chiseled lips curled in amusement. "Ah, but Felipe isn't here, is he, Krissoula? And since he isn't, you can drop your grand-lady-of-the-manor act—at least when we're alone. After all, I know better than anyone exactly what you are, sweetheart—and 'lady' isn't even close!"

She paled, leaving only two spots of high color blooming in her cheeks. How dare he talk to her in that way, say such insulting things? *Dios,* he was insufferable! "*Bastardo!* Despite what you think, you don't own me, *hombre!*" she hissed, furious. "Some fine day, I'll be free of you—and then you'll pay for your insults! On Saint Sara's bones, I swear it!"

Unmoved by her threats, he shrugged. "Never mind your tantrums, *muchacha.* You have a job to do for me—and one for which you'll be paid very well, I do believe. Remember our deal?"

"Do I remember? How could I forget?" she retorted sarcastically.

"Just see that you don't!" He paused, carefully watching her volatile face. "Well? Have you found anything yet?"

"Nothing!" she spat out, ill-disguised relish filling her as she saw his disappointment.

"You're sure? You wouldn't lie to me? Wouldn't be considering a little double-cross of your own, say? Because if you are, Krissoula, I promise you you'll live to regret it," he threatened softly, his sapphire eyes cold blue steel now.

"Double-cross? What do you take me for—a fool? Of course not! Like I said, I've found nothing. But—when and if I do find anything—you'll certainly be the first to know, señor. The sooner I'm finished with our little deal and I'm rid of you, the better, as far as I'm concerned!"

"The feeling's mutual, sweetheart!" He bowed mockingly. "Meanwhile, doña," he added with heavy sarcasm, "I suggest you pay a little more attention to your role of high-born lady, and try very hard to keep all your clothes on—at least in public. If you insist on running around half naked like that, questions are going to be asked about the lovely Doña Krissoula Ballardo's virtue—or lack of it, no? And we wouldn't want anything to damage your spotless reputation, would we . . . ?"

Squelching the urge to slap his grinning face, as the old Krissoula would have done without second thought, she uttered a curse, flung about, and stormed off towards the entrance to the grand house.

"Not that way, you little fool! Use the back stairs!" he called after her.

She suddenly pulled up short, belatedly remembering how she was dressed. Stock still now, she considered her predicament, realizing immediately that that damned San Martín was right. *Dios,* she couldn't possibly walk through the front entrance, not half dressed like this! Those gossipy maids would be agog, and without a doubt her duenna, Sofía, would hear of her escapades and report them to Felipe! There was only one alternative . . .

Scowling, she glanced over her shoulder, and her heart sank as she saw that Esteban was still standing there, watching her. The stallion's dangling halter was looped loosely over his arm. His dark head was cocked mockingly to one side as he drew a *cigarillo* from his pocket and deftly lit it with a match struck on his boot heel. Meanwhile, the powerful stallion, docile as a lamb now, nudged his sash pockets searching for treats.

She glowered at him and, muttering a string of ripe curses under her breath that would have done credit to a trooper, she spun about and retraced her steps. Stalking around the house, she passed the lavender bushes beneath her balcony and headed for the rear servants' entrance that led out to the separate kitchens. From there, she could sneak up the back stairs unseen, with any luck.

The man's mocking laughter and the fragrance of his slim cigar followed her as she fled, ringing in her ears, tickling her nostrils. So did his taunting words ring in her crimson ears, and needled her fierce pride as he called after her:

"It would seem our dear *patrón*'s 'intended' must use the back stairs like the serving girls after all, eh, *muchacha?"*

That *hijo de puta!* she thought, grimacing horribly at him as, shoulders squared, back ramrod straight, she stalked away like a furious kitten with its fur bristling. *I'll show him, sí, I will! That blackmailing brute will be laughing on the other side of his handsome face when Don Felipe gets back from Buenos Aires, or my name is not Krissoula Isabella Ballardo!*

And with that thought, she flung about and stuck out her tongue at him in a horrible farewell grimace, before flouncing through the servants' entrance.

The Argentine—utterly astounded by her impudence for a few seconds—suddenly threw back his dark head and roared with deep laughter, his stormy sapphire eyes crinkling with merriment at the corners and the smile lingering about his lips long after the cause of his amusement had vanished.

"Well, I'll be damned, you brazen little baggage!" he exclaimed softly under his breath, shaking his dark head in bemusement. What a little hellion she was—and, *si,* what a little beauty, too, he was forced to admit reluctantly!

The image of her lovely, delicately boned face screwed up in that murderous, ugly expression made him smile broadly all over again. Her thickly fringed golden eyes, framed by a curtain of glossy black curls that cascaded down from a widow's peak at her brow, had been in such shocking contrast to the rudely extended, vulgar protrusion of her small pink tongue as she made her exit! But, except for that unladylike grimace, she'd stalked off with all the salty hauteur of an enraged queen, exactly as the deportment instructors he'd hired to coach her back in Spain had demonstrated. No mean feat to accomplish while wearing only her camisole and underdrawers, which had left a tantalizing quantity of pretty female flesh exposed!

"*Jesús,* Dorado," he murmured ruefully as he grasped the stallion's mane and vaulted astride its bare back, "what the devil have I gone and done this time, eh, getting myself mixed up with a little hellion like her? She's more likely to wreck my plans than see them bear fruit!" He shook his head. "Still, things have been dull around here lately, haven't they, my friend? Perhaps that golden-eyed spitfire will liven Tierra Rosa up a little, eh? You know, Dorado, I could pity my dear uncle . . . almost. *Caray!* What a temper she has!"

Chapter Two

As Esteban led the stallion Dorado back to the corral from which he'd bolted, Krissoula sprawled on her wide featherbed, her arms crossed beneath her head, the disturbing incident already forgotten and replaced by more pleasurable prospects. She was gazing admiringly at the exquisite dinner gown that hung in readiness in a corner of her room; the last purchase she had made before she left the city of Buenos Aires for the grasslands of the Pampa.

Never had she owned such a garment! Of topaz-colored silk that matched her eyes, she knew it set off her vivid coloring to perfection. The exquisite fit also did justice to her petite yet femininely rounded figure, emphasizing the slenderness of her waist and the curves of her small breasts. A smile of pure sensual pleasure teased her lips as she recalled the luxurious, cool texture of the expensive silk, smooth as amber beneath her fingertips.

Resisting the urge to scramble from the bed and caress the fine cloth once again, she snuggled deeper into the bed with a blissful sigh. The gown would still be there later, to touch and admire. It wouldn't vanish like a pricked bubble—none of it would vanish, she reassured herself firmly. But—it was hard to believe. Two years of making do, of scratching out a threadbare living, had made her wary of taking anything for granted . . . The past year of ease and luxury since Esteban's explosive entry into her life had made her doubly determined never to return to such a meager existence. From now on, it was the good life that would be hers!

A bedspread usually covered her bed from corner to corner with a delicate cobweb crocheted in pale yellow thread, but this afternoon the coverlet had been folded back by Estrella, the chambermaid, for her to take *siesta*. She lay now on crisp white linen sheets, edged with a generous four inches of exquisite Valenciennes lace. The bed linens gave off the scent of sunshine and lavender all about her. A plump, lace-edged pillow, filled with

34

eiderdown, cushioned her dark head.

Lovely rosewood furniture, tastefully arranged, dominated the vast bedchamber in which she lay. A carved wardrobe, its doors almost bursting with her trousseau, stood in one corner. A matching rosewood dressing table with yellow-and-cream-flowered skirts of the same fabric as the floor-to-ceiling draperies, lent feminine grace to the room. A cheval looking glass stood alongside the French doors leading out onto the balcony. It was angled so that a fascinated Krissoula—who'd never owned a full-length mirror in her life till now, nor seen her reflection from head to toe except in the mirror surface of a woodland pool—could admire herself as she lay upon the bed. The final touch of elegance was a magnificent carpet the color of butter, with a border of cream-colored flowers and green leaves. The pile was so soft and deep she could wriggle her toes in it as if it were thick grass.

Caramba! *Such wealth, such luxury everywhere I turn!* she thought, almost purring with pleasure. *And it will all be mine, very soon, she promised herself, as the wife of Don Felipe de Aguilar, and* la patrona *of Tierra Rosa!* Her deal with Señor Esteban de San Martín would be history the very moment the priest pronounced Felipe and her man and wife, and then Krissoula, Gypsy dancer, child of the caves of Sacro Monte, Granada, and the back streets of Barcelona, would vanish forever!

San Martín would be livid at her going back on their deal, of course, but that arrogant fool could do nothing whatsoever about it, once she was Felipe's bride! If he attempted to convince his uncle that he'd proposed marriage to a woman who'd been a *puta* and a thief rather than an innocent, convent-raised señorita of breeding, as she'd shyly led Felipe to believe, she'd deny it to the bitter end. Her besotted Felipe would laugh in Esteban's face and ridicule every word he said against her—as, of course, would she!

"Come, come, señor!" she'd protest softly, and with just the right amount of ladylike hurt and reproach in her tone, "why are you telling my dear husband such cruel lies? I was none of the terrible things you accuse me of, Señor Esteban! A thief, you say? I, Doña Krissoula Ballardo, a woman of the streets who—who sold her favors? *Madre de Dios,* have you no shame! How could you tell such terrible lies about me? Is it jealousy, señor—is that why you're doing this? Ah, *sí,* I fear it is! I've suspected for some time now that you loved me and wanted me for yourself. But you must understand that it is Felipe my heart has chosen, señor! I beg you, try to understand, and do not let your jealousy destroy my happiness, nor

35

your false accusations rob me of my precious reputation!"

She giggled at the prudish image of herself her thoughts conjured up, wondering what that old goat Felipe would do if he ever learned the truth? If he should somehow discover that there had been no convent orphanage for "young ladies of good breeding." No pious "sisters of mercy," who'd raised her to womanhood, nor even a fine old *hidalgo* family unhappily left impoverished and decimated in the aftermath of war? Nor, for that matter, had she been that same family's orphaned little daughter, forced to turn her talents as a dancer to good use in order to support herself when she became too old for the orphanage!

Ah, yes, this was the touching story she'd tearfully "fed" Felipe soon after they'd met at the Ópera Florida, where she'd danced the flamenco and earned herself the adoration of Buenos Aires's aficionados, and the prestigious title of "La Reina," The Queen of flamencas!

Her surprising success as a professional flamenco dancer had all come about as yet another part of Esteban's clever hoax, she recalled, quite by accident. Learning she knew how to dance, San Martín had hit upon the idea of using that talent to supply her with a badly needed excuse for coming to South America. Accordingly Esteban, working behind the scenes and pulling numerous strings, had seen that she was scheduled to perform at several grand theaters, convinced—by reasons known only to himself—that Felipe would see her in Buenos Aires and straightway pay vigorous court to her. To her confusion and amazement, on that score he'd been proven correct, curse him, though the critical acclaim she'd received for her performances—both in Spain and here in Argentina—had amazed them both!

Gazing up at the dark-beamed ceiling, her thoughts drifted back to Barcelona, Spain, and the day Señor Esteban had entered her life a little over a year ago. So much had happened since then! The day following her reluctant acceptance of his proposition, he'd hired tutors to teach her elocution and deportment, insisting she must acquire at least the veneer of a lady of quality in order to serve his purpose and carry off her role. For the next six months or so, she'd worked harder than she'd ever done in her life to please him, curse his soul, though she'd seen him rarely in or about the spacious villa he'd rented. Then, when he'd judged her sufficiently ladylike for his mysterious purposes, he'd put in a final appearance.

Indicating a pair of enormous sea trunks filled to overflowing with exquisite dancing costumes, gowns, and everything else she'd need to play her part, he'd told her he intended to leave for South America immediately, and that she—in company with the duenna he'd hired to attend her—was to follow him to Buenos Aires in ten days. He'd given her strict instructions as to what to do and who to see once she reached there, and sternly warned her of the dire consequences of her going back on her word.

"I know a great many influential people both here in Spain and in South America, Krissoula," he'd told her. "Cross me—lie to me—fail to follow through with my instructions—and you'll be looking out at the world from the inside of a jail cell within the hour. *Comprende?*"

She'd understood, all right! And besides, what had she to lose by going along with his little game? Nothing, that's what! Besides, what he'd asked of her seemed ridiculously easy—far easier than the risky game she and Hector had played! She was to act the part of temperamental dancer and lady to the hilt. If approached by one Don Felipe de Aguilar, she had only to subtly encourage his attentions and lead him on. Esteban had been convinced his uncle would do the rest; that sooner or later he'd propose marriage, and invite her to stay at Tierra Rosa until the ceremony took place. How he'd guessed that would transpire was a mystery to Krissoula, but it had happened nonetheless! Now she had only to search the *hacienda* and find the mysterious papers he'd engineered this elaborate hoax to locate, and her job here would be done, and she'd be rid of him forever! She'd be free to go, and would do so considerably richer for the experience.

In all honesty, she'd planned to do exactly that and no more initially—until she'd realized how much greater it would profit her to *double-cross* Esteban and actually marry the wealthy uncle he so hated! That way, she'd have not a few months or a year or two of undreamed of wealth, but a lifetime—!"

"Doña Krissoula? Are you dressed, *niña?* It's almost time for tea to be served!"

Krissoula came back to the present with a bump, to hear her duenna Sofia's sharp knuckles beating a tattoo upon the door, and her shrill voice calling her.

Like the British they so admired and did so much business with, the wealthy, cultured Argentine families customarily took high tea in the late afternoon, following *siesta*, to tide them over until the formal *cena*, or dinner, at ten o'clock in the evening. It was a custom Krissoula had adopted wholeheartedly! No one who'd ever known the gnawing pain of going hungry, of living in the streets with a

37

growling belly nagging at them day in and day out, could forgo the delicious treats with which the Argentines gorged themselves at every turn. Teatime was no exception! Her mouth watered in anticipation of the delicious *empanadas*—little pastries stuffed with tasty concoctions of seafood, meat, or fruits—the tiny sandwiches and thin slices of bread and butter with which the cook, Mamacita Angelina, would load the serving trolley!

"Coming, Sofía! You go on down, and I'll join you shortly!" she lisped in the aristocratic Castilian Spanish which Esteban had hired tutors to drum into her.

She heard Sofía grumbling as she moved away from the door, the click of her high heels on the polished wooden floors gradually fading as she did as bidden. Good, she'd gone!

Krissoula shook her head. Esteban had hired an actor to engage the woman as her chaperone while they were yet in Spain, knowing full well that in order to completely convince Felipe de Aguilar that she was everything she pretended to be, she had to play the part to the hilt. And, since no well-bred, unmarried young Spanish girl took so much as a single step without a duenna dogging her heels, a duenna she must have! Sofía, absurdly naive and trusting by nature, believed she'd been engaged as her duenna by a distant uncle of Krissoula's, and Krissoula had allowed her to go on believing it. It was imperative to the success of his plans, Esteban had warned sternly, that Felipe de Aguilar should never suspect he'd had any part in his hated uncle's meeting and courtship of the famous *flamenco bailaora,* Krissoula Ballardo . . .

She sighed. Poor, poor dried-up old Sofía, destined to spend all her days as the guardian of young girls' maidenheads, without ever losing her own, or ever knowing the fire in the blood that was passion! Krissoula didn't like the chaperone one little bit, but she felt sorry for the old spinster, knowing full well that she did nothing herself to make the woman's life any easier! She'd deliberately gone out of her way on the long sea voyage from Spain to Buenos Aires to lead her a merry dance, straying away from her chaperone's watchful eyes to flirt with the handsome sailors or the male passengers at every turn, dizzy with the heady knowledge that, in her new wardrobe of stunning gowns, she was the most beautiful, most sought-after woman on board, and drunk with all the newfound power her air of culture and beauty could wield!

Ah, but you're a wicked one, Krissoula, she told herself as she rose from the bed and stretched with the lazy grace of a little cat.

Catching sight of herself in the cheval looking glass, she was once again fascinated by the petite stranger she saw reflected there, drawn to her image like steel to a magnet. Was that really her? She pouted and struck a seductive pose in her pantalets and chemise, slanted golden eyes smoldering at her mirror image in the way she knew somehow always made men hungry to possess her.

What was it they saw in her? What was it about her that made them want her? She'd met many women far more lovely than herself, after all! She pursed her lips thoughtfully and considerd the girl who pursed hers back at her.

A mane of tangled black curls spilled down over her shoulders, rich and inky against the gold and ivory of her skin. Her complexion had faded from its former Gypsy nut-brown since Señor Esteban's strict orders for her to stay out of the sun, and was now aristocratically fair. Thick-lashed golden eyes appraised her reflection critically, and then on impulse she swiveled her hips, threw back her head, arched her back, and slowly raised her graceful arms in the first stance of a passionate flamenco. She liked what she saw now very much. She looked dramatic, different, exciting—about to explode with emotion!

Was this the woman she'd appeared to that—that hateful Esteban? Was this how she'd looked in his stormy, sapphire eyes in the courtyard earlier—different, passionate, and exciting? Ah, *sí*, it must have been! Ever since they'd met, she'd sensed his determination to deny the physical attraction he felt towards her—indeed, he'd even gone out of his way to avoid her over the previous year, she knew—but she was certain he found her beautiful, desirable, no matter what his avoidance was meant to prove. Why, his magnificent eyes had betrayed him time and time again! A slow, tempting smile curved her pouting red lips and laughter sparkled wickedly in her eyes as she struck a new pose.

"Fresh from her triumphant tour of Spain and Buenos Aires, I give you 'La Reina,' Señorita Krissoula Ballardo, Queen of Flamenco!" she declared to her reflection. Snapping her fingers in place of her chattering castanets, she twirled once, twice, about the room in her underwear, dark hair spraying about her.

Ah, truly, Esteban, you're far too handsome a devil to be such a dirty blackmailing cur! she thought as she whirled and stamped her bare feet on the soft rug. *How would you like to dance with Krissoula, eh, hombre? How would you like to share little Krissoula's soft bed, rather than just the "business" partnership we share now?*

She giggled, for the idea of that blue-eyed, black-haired *diablo's* hard body pressed to hers was an exciting one! Ah, *sí*, hate him she might, but she was also painfully aware of him as a man, and there was the problem. She'd not felt even the faintest stirrings of desire for any man since Miguel, and never at all for her stick-in-the-mud fiancé, Felipe, who was easily as old as Sofía—perhaps even older. Yet when Esteban looked at her, somehow she melted inside, and yearned to give herself to him . . . Ah, but she was a very, very wicked woman to think such evil thoughts about another man, with her poor "betrothed" so far from home!

She stamped harder, faster, hearing the throb of the guitars, the clapping of hands, and the whirring clatter of the castanets in her mind; feeling the fire course through her veins; seeing the image of Esteban de San Martín's brooding dark-sapphire eyes in her mind as if painted upon her closed eyelids.

She danced until she could see him no more, was convinced she no longer wanted him; danced until the fiery flamenco had once again burned the passionate hunger from her body and soul, and replaced it with the loneliness and coldness which had encased her wounded heart for so long. She needed no man, she told herself bitterly, would never let herself need any man in that way, ever again! As Miguel had used her, she would use Felipe, Esteban, and any other who stood in the way of her plans. She would use men as they had sought to use her, for her own ends. There was only Krissoula now. Only Krissoula mattered—and the dance that could ease her aching heart, and burn the dangerous softness from her soul.

Chapter Three

"Sofía, stop scolding, for goodness' sake! I'm not a little dog for
you to lead about on a string, after all!" Krissoula flared, scowling
as she speared a piece of spicy sausage with her fork and popped it
into her mouth. She waved the fork about and talked as she
continued her enthusiastic chewing. "There's still a whole week left
until Don Felipe's due back from Buenos Aires. I swear, if I have to
spend every day of that week shut up in this house with nothing to
do like the past three weeks, I'll go *loco!*"

Sofía looked as if she'd swallowed a lemon this morning,
Krissoula thought mutinously. Her narrow, sallow face was
puckered up in disapproval, and she grimaced as she looked across
the wide breakfast table—laden with sugared *beignets,* fresh rolls,
platters of fruits, and cups of milky coffee—at her rebellious
charge. Krissoula suddenly remembered her extensive lessons in
table manners, placed her fork neatly across her plate, and
swallowed the last two inches of delicious sausage in one large,
unladylike gulp that almost choked her.

"But it's simply not proper for a young, unmarried woman to go
riding unescorted, *niña,"* Sofía persisted. "Young ladies are
sheltered as strictly in Argentina as the señoritas of our own
beloved Spain. If Don Felipe hears of it, he'll be outraged—and
with good reason!"

"But that's exactly what I'm saying, Sofía! That I want to go
riding, but that I want *you* to escort me, so it'll be proper! Of course
I've no intention of going riding all alone! *Dios,* Sofía! What sort of
loose woman do you take me for, eh?" she demanded indignantly.

Sofía gave her a look of such disquiet, Krissoula wondered if
she'd gone too far this time, and let her ladylike pose slip to an
irrevocable low.

"But—horseback riding?" Sofía gave a delicate shudder of her
narrow shoulders that stirred her dangling earrings of elongated jet

beads and made them clack like old women gossiping. "If you must know, I've never cared for those enormous, smelly beasts! To be honest, they frighten me! My father was a fine horseman, of course, since he never felt it necessary for his daughter to ride so long as she could run a household and sew, I was spared having to learn, *gracias a Dios.*"

"Then you can follow me in the carriage—you *can* drive a carriage, I hope?" Krissoula suggested in a resigned, exasperated tone. Her long, expressive fingers, drumming a staccato rhythm on the polished tabletop, betrayed her bored, restless mood more eloquently than words.

"I've driven one a few times before, yes, of course. Oh, very well, *niña!* If that is what you wish, I'll do my best. We'll go riding," Sofía capitulated with a defeated sigh and a pious sniff. "When do you intend leaving?"

"Later this morning, I thought, if you've no objections?"

"So soon! Then I suppose I should go and get changed right away," Sofía said with the air of one going to the gallows. "I'll need a hat with a veil to protect my complexion from the sun and wind, of course, as will you," she reminded her charge.

"Sí, sí! Anything you say, dear Sofía!" Krissoula agreed airily with a winning smile now that she'd got her own way, though her fingers were crossed beneath the tablecloth so that the false promise wouldn't count. "And thank you for agreeing to accompany me! To show my gratitude, from here on I'll be as demure and obedient and well mannered as even you could desire in a charge, dear Sofía."

Sofía looked doubtful at such a highly unlikely possibility, but nevertheless pushed back her chair, set her crumpled napkin down, and sailed aloofly from the room, starched petticoats rustling, earrings chattering, as she exited.

Suppressing her glee, Krissoula quickly left her seat. She yanked on the tasseled bell rope to summon a maid. She'd ask the girl to see a groom sent up to the house to her, and instruct him that a horse and horse and carriage were to be made ready for her use—*sí,* perhaps that magnificent palomino stallion Dorado, she thought eagerly?

Upon her arrival at Tierra Rosa, Don Felipe had given her a brief tour of the enormous *hacienda* and surrounding out-buildings. The *casa grande* formed a palatial red-tiled, white-walled oasis amidst the rolling Pampa, with several lovely courtyards, patios, a flourishing orangery, a small jewel of a lake that was kidney-shaped and fringed with irises, and a formal English garden that boasted box hedges and sculptured flowerbeds ablaze with color. The stables had been no less magnificent. She'd recognized immediately the quality of the horseflesh the *estancia*'s stables offered. Some of the animals had been bred, Felipe had boasted then, from the finest dams and stallions Old Spain, England, North America, and Argentina could offer. Over the years, Tierra Rosa had won a deservedly fine reputation for her blooded colts and foals, which commanded top prices wherever they came to auction.

Krissoula thought of the shaggy ponies and half-wild horses she'd ridden in the past—many of them overworked, half-starved beasts—and a delicious shiver of anticipation tingled down her spine. To ride such glorious animals as those she'd seen—why, it would be like a dream come true to one like her, descended from a long line of Ballardo Gypsy horse traders! A naughty smile tugged at her lips and glinted in her golden eyes, turning them to darkest amber. She had a feeling she could convince poor old Sofía of her riding abilities in ways the fussy, nervous little woman had never dreamed of; ways that might very well send her into an attack of the vapors should she witness them!

For a second, Krissoula had a fleeting memory of her uncle Ricardo's deep voice instructing her while a shaggy dappled-gray horse cantered sedately in wide circles about a grassy meadow, in perfect response to the gestures of his long whip and his gentle voice:

"Now, niña, jump, jump up! There, you did it! You feel Chico's rump beneath your feet? It's as broad and safe as the grass below you, eh? Come now, balance, Krissoula. Brace your feet apart, bend your knees just a little, grip with your toes! Now, arms outstretched—wider—good! Let your body flow with the motions of your horse, my pretty one. Perfect! Another week or two, and you'll be drawing crowds, my beauty. What a horsewoman! Truly, you are of the Rom, Krissoula, for all that your foolish mother watered your blood with that Greek she took for a lover . . . !"

The image faded, and was replaced once again by her view of the misty Sierra de Córdoba mountains beyond the *estancia,* spied through the lace-swagged windows. The newly risen sun would soon burn off the morning mists with its fiery rays, she thought, and the day would grow fine and cool, perfect for riding. Time was wasting! Where was that maid?

Having received no answer to her summons after waiting for some time, Krissoula muttered a curse and left the breakfast room, going out along one of the three open *corredors* surrounding the courtyard to the kitchens, which were built apart from the main house as a fire precaution. No doubt she'd find that giggly little Luisa and her quieter sister Estrella there, gossiping with Mama Angelina, their mother, who was also the cook-housekeeper of Tierra Rosa.

Her irritation and impatience dwindled as she went in search of them, for in all honesty, she welcomed any excuse to visit the kitchens. They were the only place in the *casa grande* where she could relax her guard, forget her pose, and feel truly comfortable. The whitewashed adobe walls were hung with pretty strings of red and green peppers and onions, and pungent with garlic and saffron spices. The cleanly swept earthen floor was sprinkled with sand or sawdust. This, combined with sturdy, scrubbed furniture of white pine, made the kitchens the only corner of Tierra Rosa that matched Krissoula's notions of what a real home should be. The kitchens reminded her poignantly of the whitewashed caves of Sacro Monte in Granada, Spain, where she'd lived with her family in the winter months, after traveling throughout the spring and summer seasons from horse fair to horse fair across Europe. The *casa grande*, fine as it was, certainly did not invite one to call it cozy!

"Ah, there you all are!" she declared, stepping from the bright light of outside into the shady kitchen. "I've been ringing you for ages!"

Luisa and Estrella were, as she'd suspected, crowded around Mama Angelina. There was another young woman with them whom Krissoula didn't recognize, and the three of them were all cooing and chattering excitedly over something Angelina held in her plump arms. Their chatter abruptly ceased at the sound of her voice, and the three of them turned to face her in guilty surprise.

"Doña Krissoula! Aiiee, pardon us, signorina, but we did not hear you out here!" Angelina stammered apologetically, springing to her feet.

The three younger women swung about to face *el patrón*'s intended, each one wearing identical expressions of guilt and nervousness.

Krissoula felt a pang that they should treat her with such undeserved respect. She wished for a fleeting moment it needn't be so; that she could be one of them, sharing whatever delicious secret it was that Mama Angelina was divulging. But—the moment's weakness soon passed when she remembered her resolve. A life of wealth had its own price, no, but it was one she was willing to pay, even if it meant having no friends to laugh with or confide in

44

ever again.

"You're forgiven," she assured them indulgently, her golden eyes merry, "but—only if you let me in on your secret! What is it you have there, Angelina? Won't you show me?"

"Allow me to introduce my oldest daughter, Guadalupe, Doña Krissoula. Her husband, José Buenaventura, is one of Don Felipe's *gauchos.*" Angelina smiled, and pulled back the covering that encased the squirming bundle in her plump arms to reveal her secret with an unmistakable air of pride. "And right here is my very first grandson, Paulo!"

Lupe bobbed a dutiful curtsy, murmuring, "I'm very honored to meet you, Doña Krissoula," but it was doubtful whether Krissoula heard either Lupe's shy greeting or Angelina's explanations, for as the Italian-Spanish cook drew back the blanket, she gave a delighted cry and started forward, staring transfixed at the babe revealed. The haughty beauty of her lovely features softened into a wistful smile.

"Oh, what a beautiful *niño!* May I?" she whispered uncertainly, holding out her arms for the infant.

Angelina handed the baby to Krissoula, exhanging raised brows with her daughters at the eager way the señorita took the infant into her arms and cuddled him tenderly against her bosom, supporting the little dark head with an ease that surprised them.

"Ah, but you're a handsome little fellow, hmmm? *Sí, sí,* it's true! *'Tía'* Krissoula would tell you no lies, darling," Krissoula crooned softly as if she and little Paulo were quite alone as she cradled the baby tenderly in her arms. "I think when you're grown, Paulito, all the pretty girls will be after you, but you'll break their poor hearts, one by one!"

Uttering cooing baby sounds, she lifted Paulito to her face and nuzzled a plump little cheek, blissfully inhaling the wonderful baby smell that surrounded him. She traced the dark ringlets that crowned his little head with her fingers. Brown eyes, shiny and bright as buttons, gazed back curiously into hers, and then a tiny "Aaaggha!" of greeting gurgled from the infant's rosebud mouth. He smiled and wriggled, fists waving, chubby little dimpled feet kicking free of the blanket. With his smile, something squeezed at Krissoula's heart, tightening fiercely as long-buried emotions bombarded her. Emotions too raw and painful to bear . . .

"He—he's beautiful," she said huskily, then handed him abruptly back to his startled grandmother as if the baby had suddenly grown red-hot.

45

"*Gracias, signorina,*" Angelina said, smiling proudly as she settled Paulo comfortably back into the crook of her arm. "And if I may say so, you have a way with children, Doña. Perhaps, with the grace and blessings of God, you and Don Felipe will one day fill this house with many children of your own, as Don Alejandro always hoped to do!"

Krissoula's jaw tightened, and a pulse throbbed in her temple. The softness fled her face, leaving it as lovely yet emotionless as before. Children? Huh! Even if her plan to double-cross Esteban and marry Felipe succeeded, she couldn't imagine Felipe wanting children, somehow, not in a million years! He was too cold, too self-centered, too jealous. "Perhaps," she agreed stiffly, for politeness' sake. "Perhaps not. Only time will tell, mmm?"

The four women exchanged meaningful glances again, and Angelina gave her trio of daughters a barely perceptible shrug. "Señorita, was there something you wanted?" she asked gently.

"Wanted?" Krissoula frowned for a moment, then brightened. "Ah, *sí,* I'd almost forgotten! I wish to go riding later this morning, and I need to speak with a groom about having a horse and a horse and carriage readied for Doña Sofía and my use. Would you have someone sent up to the house from the stable to arrange it, please, Angelina?"

"But of course, Doña. Luisa, go find Señor Tomás, and tell him the señorita wants to speak with him right away."

"*Sí,* Mama, at once!" the girl agreed overeagerly.

Krissoula guessed that this Tomás must be good to look at, judging by Luisa's reaction. She also noticed the look of disappointment that crossed shy Estrella's pretty face at not being chosen for the errand, and hid a smile. Spain or South America, there wasn't much difference when it came to affairs of the heart!

"Perhaps you'd care for something to drink while you wait, Doña? Some juice, perhaps, or a gourd of hot *yerba maté? Maté*'s the beverage the people of Argentina enjoy more than anything, and it's very refreshing," Angelina offered.

"*Maté* sounds good to me, Angelina—but only if you've no cold beer!" a deep voice declared.

"Why, Señor Esteban!" Plump Angelina giggled, glancing up at the tall frame of a man in the doorway. His entrance blocked the sunlight from entering the kitchen and also prevented Luisa's exit. "For you, I think we can find a glass of the coldest beer in Argentina! Lupe, take Paulo while I see to it, would you?"

"I'll hold him, *mi bonita* Angelina," Esteban offered roguishly.

"That is, if you'll trust me with the little tyke?"

With a giggle at his compliment and a dismissing wave to Lupe, Angelina handed her precious grandson to the ranch manager, beaming with pride.

Esteban grinned down at the infant, whom he held with surprising ease and no apparent discomfort in the crook of his arm, unlike most men when confronted by a squirming infant.

"Well, well, *niño!* I see you're already keeping the prettiest girls of Tierra Rosa all to yourself, eh, greedy one?" Esteban told the baby in a serious tone that, surprisingly, drew gurgles of appreciation from the babe. "Your mama's already been snapped up, worse luck, and your aunties Luisa and Estrella here will not be long in following her to the altar, I wager. What will poor Esteban do then, *niño,* when he hungers for a glimpse of a pretty woman, but can find none?"

The baby blew rude, noisy bubbles at him in reply. Esteban chuckled and glanced up, noticing Krissoula—who'd been holding her breath where she stood in the shadows of a corner—for the first time.

"Oh, so it's you again, is it?" he declared with a grimace. "Well, Paulo, what do you say? Do you think this one's pretty, too? As pretty as your mama and your aunties? What? What's this you say?" He bent his ear as if listening intently to the baby's reply. "Ah, *sí,* little *amigo,* I agree! Pretty enough—but far too skinny and bad-tempered to warm a man's . . . heart."

Lupe, Luisa, and Estrella—left behind while their mother went in search of the beer she'd promised the ranch manager—giggled nervously or gave shocked gasps.

Lupe, the eldest of the trio and the most serious, tried to smooth over Esteban's apparent blunder and cut in, "Excuse me, Señor Esteban, but perhaps you've not met Don Felipe's—"

"—intended? Oh, but on the contrary, Lupe," Krissoula cut in sweetly in the nick of time, "Señor Esteban and I have already met—just the other afternoon, in fact. *Buenos días, señor mayordomo,"* she said, inclining her head graciously.

Esteban made a mocking bow, hiding an amused smile at the polite little charade they were acting out. "And a good day to you, too, Doña—? Doña—?" He shook his head. "Forgive me, doña, but I seem to have forgotten your name!" His sapphire eyes twinkled wickedly, and a roguish smile tugged at the corners of his chiseled mouth.

"It's Krissoula. Doña Krissoula Ballardo, Señor de San Martín."

As he knew only too well, the rogue!

"Aah, *sí*, Doña Krissoula, that's it! An unusual name, doña, but it suits you, somehow." His expression mocked her.

"So I've been told, señor, more times than I care to count," she said pertly.

He chuckled, his sapphire eyes glinting in the gloom of the kitchen as he regarded her silently and intently for moments that seemed endless to Krissoula.

In the glow of ruddy light shed from the cooking fire, her hair—caught back from her temples with ivory combs this morning—was a lustrous, blue-black riot of curls across her shoulders and down over the topmost, golden curves of her breasts, which were partially exposed by the scooped neckline of the crisp cambric blouse she wore above a full skirt of dark red. Her complexion glowed like beige satin, cheeks warmed by firelight to a lovely rose-blushed gold that radiated health and vitality. Her lips were as moist and glistening as the dewy petals of a wild rose.

As he gazed at her with undisguised pleasure, remembering the petite, exquisite nude body he'd held in his arms all too briefly back in Spain, her thick black lashes fluttered downward to hide her eyes and thence her thoughts. Yet her scent could not be so easily hidden. Deliciously perfumed with some subtle floral fragrance he'd never been aware of before, the delicate musk that surrounded her was all woman. It was an exciting and elusive scent, somehow provocative and tantalizing all at once to his nostrils. It aroused his masculine senses in the close confines of the kitchen's thick adobe walls in ways he'd thought himself too experienced with women to fall victim to. Yet despite his every wish to the contrary, he felt a telltale hardening at his loins. *Dios mío,* pretty Luisa and Estrella might not have existed, so extraordinarily aware was he of the petite beauty before him!

Gazing at her, he wanted suddenly to take her in his arms and arch that soft, female body against the hard angles of his. To press her down beneath him into some cosy bed and discover if the wild, sweet passion and feminine mysteries hinted at by her golden eyes and her tempting lips were truly promises—or only teasing lies. *Dios,* she'd been at his beck and call for months at a time before they left Spain. What a blasted fool he'd been to deny himself the pleasure of that lovely body! After all, hadn't he more than paid her price—? At any moment during those months, he could have liberally sampled her charms and driven the lust from his body and mind! Instead, he'd absented himself for days on end from the rented villa, refusing to combine business with pleasure, or to allow the lovely, thieving urchin the slightest chance of a lover's intimacy with him, or develop the trust that was part and parcel of an affair. After all, he was the master of this game, and he didn't trust the *gitana* an inch! *Strictly business, Esteban,* he'd told himself at the start. *You hired the little gypsy* puta *to play a part, nothing more, so hands off! You've too much invested, too much at stake here, to risk everything for a woman!*

But now, after having been away from her for almost two months since he'd left Spain and returned to Buenos Aires, it was as if he'd never really seen her before . . . When, he wondered, had she ripened, grown so incandescently, vibrantly lovely?

Feeling his insolent gaze on her, as keen and intense as if he'd never seen her before, Krissoula waited with bated breath for him to say or do something more, painfully aware of the quickened tempo of her heart as she did so. *Caray!* The hungry way he was looking at her made her breathless and weak at the knees! She was suddenly more aware of him than she'd ever been before. Why, until recently she'd considered him simply another man to be hated, one who'd blackmailed her into doing his bidding in return for her freedom, and the promise of a hefty sum of money when their charade was done. But now, all that had changed somehow; subtly shifted to another, more exciting and dangerous, tempo . . .

The tension built between them as they gazed at each other, one openly, the other covertly. An invisible yet electrical current of awareness, primitive in its attraction of male to female, sizzled in the air between them like a taut wire humming in the wind.

She fought down the ridiculous urge to escape those searching deep-blue eyes that stirred her so strangely, for her fierce pride refused to let her run like a coward; stubborn pride—coupled with her complete inability to move, even had she wanted to, for it was as if she were rooted to the spot!

And then the baby wailed in Esteban's arms, and the shining, charged moment was shattered, breaking into a million sharp splinters of might-have-beens.

He shifted position, bearing his body weight upon the opposite foot now and lifting the child over his shoulder to pat its little bottom and calm its wails. She turned, and in so doing let the tension drain out of her like steam from a kettle in a single, hissing breath.

Sensitive Lupe, fascinated by the sizzling current that had run between the striking pair, murmured an apology for her little son's sudden fretfulness, and reached to take him from the manager. Her rapt sisters suddenly found tasks to busy them about the kitchen and became all bustle and nervous, noisy chatter to cover those disquieting, electrical moments.

"You seem to be settling in quite comfortably at Tierra Rosa, doña?" Esteban observed softly, and somehow she intuitively knew he was thinking nothing of the sort! That he was remembering his last glimpse of her wearing only her camisole and pantalets. She felt heat rush up her throat and burn in her cheeks.

"Thank you, yes, very comfortably," she said aloofly but with equal softness, surprised at the casual tone she was able to muster despite the erratic thumpings of her heart and her burning face.

Mama Angelina returned then, bringing with her a tall glass of foaming beer, so cold the glass was wet with condensation. With her reentry, the last, lingering shreds of the current were banished as if they'd never been. The tension lifted.

"There, *señor mayordomo,* your beer, straight from the ice house! Is it to your liking?" the cook asked with a grin, and in response Esteban quaffed a mouthful, wiped the foam from his mouth with his knuckles, and winked. "Almost as much to my liking as you, Angelina, *mi corazón!*"

Angelina clucked at his foolishness, but her smile belied her scoldings. "*Bastante!* Enough of your teasing! Finish your beer and get back to work with you, lazy one!"

He grinned and waggled a finger at her. "Only you would dare speak so impudently to Esteban de San Martín. When I am *el patrón* of Tierra Rosa, you will regret your sauciness, Angelina, for I will demand you beg my pardon with kisses!"

"Aiee, be off with you, *bribón!*" Angelina scolded. "Even if you have no work to do, I have more than enough!"

Esteban drained his glass and handed it to Luisa. "Thank you, lovely ladies, and *adíos.* I'll see you all later, eh?"

"What did he mean, when he is 'el patrón' of Tierra Rosa?" Krissoula asked when he'd gone, curious to hear what the servants knew of the *mayordomo*'s ambitions. She herself knew very little, other than the tidbits Esteban had been forced to tell her, and what she'd managed to piece together herself.

"Señor Esteban? Why, he's just a boastful rascal, that's all, one who loves to tease us poor women! He was only joking about becoming master here, of course, señorita!" Angelina declared in a valiant attempt to cover up for Esteban's blunder. "Don Felipe is *el patrón* here, as well you know." She appeared flustered.

"Aiee, *Dios*, I forgot the chickens! Excuse me one moment, Doña Krissoula!"

And with that transparent excuse, she escaped outside.

"Do you know what the *mayordomo* was implying, Luisa?" Krissoula asked casually after Angelina's exit, knowing the girl for a chatterbox who loved to gossip.

"You truly do not know about Señor Esteban, Doña Krissoula?" Luisa asked slyly, then amended, "Ah, but of course, it would hardly be proper for Don Felipe to speak of such things to his intended! What could I be thinking of!"

"What things?" Krissoula persisted. "You can tell me, Luisa!" she coaxed. "I promise I'll say nothing to your mother or Don Felipe, if you will?"

"All right," gossipy Luisa agreed, smiling eagerly across at Krissoula. "I'll tell you, before someone else does! Don Esteban is the son of Don Alejandro. His illegitimate son," she added in a low whisper.

Esteban, a bastard? Krissoula hid a gleeful smile. Well, well, that was a juicy piece of news! For all his arrogance, Esteban was no better born than she!

Luisa continued. "You knew, did you not, that Don Felipe inherited the ranch from his brother, Don Alejandro de Aguilar, upon his death two years ago?"

"*Sí*, I did."

"Well, the way Mama tells it, Don Alejandro was married to the daughter of a fine old family, named Doña Manuela de Córdoba y Castellano. After a year's honeymoon by the sea at Mar de la Plata, the newlyweds returned to Tierra Rosa to begin their married life. Everyone expected that theirs would be a marriage to envy, for although Manuela's parents had arranged the betrothal, there was love on both sides. But things did not seem to be going well between them any longer. The poor doña would spend hours in her room, crying until her eyes were red and swollen. And although Don Alejandro would plead with her, he could not coax her to come out, nor to smile, nor, it was whispered—to share his bed." Luisa blushed and whispered the latter tidbit in hushed tones. "Soon, everyone noticed that Don Alejandro spent less and less time with his wife, and had taken to visiting Córdoba—a little town to the north of here—very frequently and staying away for days at a time. You know how gossip spreads, señorita?" Seeing Krissoula nod, Luisa continued. "Well, the rumor spread like wildfire in these parts that *el patrón* had taken a mistress, and that he'd set her up in

51

a pretty little house there! She was a beautiful widow whose name was Maria de San Martín, and she'd been Doña Manuela's personal maid and companion before her marriage—the same maid who'd traveled with the couple to Mar de la Plata to attend the doña during the first year of the couple's marriage! The gossips whispered that it was there, during those months spent by the sea, that lovely Maria had caught *el patrón*'s eye. Sadly, it seemed the stories must be true, for when she set up house in Córdoba, Maria brought with her her infant son!"

"That would have been Señor Esteban, right?"

"*Sí,* Señor Esteban," Luisa agreed.

"Did he love the child?"

"Very much, Mama said."

"Then since he sired no other sons, why did Don Alejandro not recognize the child as his heir before he died, instead of leaving everything to his brother?"

"Oh, he intended to, señorita. But—before he could do so, he was killed."

"And my Felipe inherited," she said softly, realizing now why it was Esteban hated his uncle so. To lose an inheritance like the vast lands and hacienda of Tierra Rosa, all for the sake of a little scrap of paper—*caray,* what a blow that must have been!

Luisa's little tale had, to Krissoula's secret delight, answered many of the questions she'd had about Esteban's past, and his reasons for blackmailing her. He'd needed someone he could trust—for one reason or another—inside the *hacienda*. Someone with the ability to come and go. Someone who could move about the house and wage a thorough search of its every nook and cranny for proof of his paternity, without arousing Don Felipe's suspicions!

Esteban was no fool. He'd probably realized long ago—as she'd come to realize since her arrival—that if she found the documents he needed, she'd hold his entire future in her hands! Once she'd meekly handed them over to him, he'd have all the evidence he needed to prove his birthright, and to legally oust his hated uncle from Tierra Rosa and take over himself. And then where would she be, mmm? Back where she'd started, give or take a few thousand pesetas, which certainly wouldn't last forever!

But—if she found such documents and destroyed them—or simply denied ever having recovered them—she could marry Don Felipe, become mistress of Tierra Rosa, and Esteban, curse him, would be left out in the cold! A little thrill ran through her. Either

52

way, how could she possibly lose? Her future was as good as assured! The only question Luisa hadn't answered was how Esteban could have been so certain that she and no other woman possessed the means to attract Felipe, which assured her being invited to Tierra Rosa? Something indefinable like the attraction between a man and woman had no guarantees, after all . . . ?

"Señor San Martín must have been very bitter when his uncle took over Tierra Rosa," she observed thoughtfully. "Having been raised here, it must have seemed he lost his home, as well as his father."

"But he wasn't raised here, señorita!" Luisa supplied. "Mama told me that when he was—oh, perhaps three years old—something happened. Nobody knows just what, exactly. Perhaps Doña Manuela had only just learned of her husband taking Maria as his mistress and of the child she'd borne him, or perhaps there was some other reason, who knows? But whatever it was, it is said that Doña Manuela went to visit Maria in Córdoba—it's an old university town about fifty miles to the northeast of here. After the doña left Maria that day, the neighbors say that the woman packed up her belongings, took the child, and went away. When poor Don Alejandro next went to visit them, the woman and child had gone! And although he searched for them from here to Buenos Aires for many long months he could find no trace of either of them."

"*Dios mío!* That cold-hearted bitch!" Krissoula exclaimed, quite forgetting her pose. She reddened and quickly amended, "I mean, how terribly heartless of the doña! The doña must have been jealous because she couldn't—or wouldn't—share her husband's bed, don't you think, and so rather than give him the child he craved, she must have threatened Maria somehow, no, to make her take the baby and run away?"

Luisa shrugged. "No one knows, señorita. Perhaps what you say is true. Many people thought so. Whatever reason lay behind it, poor Don Alejandro saw nothing of his son for many, many years. Indeed, he feared both Maria and the child dead in the summer cholera epidemics that take the lives of so many each year, here in South America, especially in the cities. But then, when Don Alejandro had long given up hope of ever seeing him again, and was already a widower and ailing himself, Señor Esteban arrived at Tierra Rosa a grown man."

"And Alejandro was united at last with the son he'd given up as lost! How romantic, *si?*" Krissoula concluded the tale with a satisfied smile, for she loved a story with a happy ending. Or at least, a *partially* happy ending, she amended with a tiny twinge of conscience. Unless Esteban eventually regained Tierra Rosa, the story could never have a *completely* satisfying conclusion. And, since she couldn't allow that to happen and firmly intended to double-cross him—! She gave a mental shrug.

"*Sí*, that is so! Mama said he was so happy to have Esteban here. He made the young man his *mayordomo,* his manager of the *estancia,* and swore that he would teach him all he knew of the running of a ranch and its herds, so that when he passed away, Tierra Rosa would be in good hands. The next few years passed very quickly, as time has a way of doing when we're happy, and Don Alejandro realized that he was no longer young, and could not postpone such an important matter forever. He made plans for him and Esteban to go to Buenos Aires, and everyone thought he'd have his lawyers there draw up the necessary papers naming Esteban as his legitimate son and therefore his only heir. A big fiesta was planned for when they returned! But, before he could carry out his plans, Don Alejandro died, and it was his brother Felipe who inherited Tierra Rosa, instead of Esteban."

"Then why does San Martín stay on here? It's obvious he has no liking for Don Felipe, and yet he must have agreed to manage the *estancia?*"

"He stays, he says, to protect the dream his father and grandfather worked so hard to build, because he knows his uncle Felipe is a fool where the running of any business is concerned—Oh! *Dios mío,* what have I said!" Luisa's plump hand flew to cover her mouth, and her eyes were round with horror. "Please, you must forgive me, señorita? My tongue runs away with me always!" The girl apologized, horrified by what she'd blurted out to Don Felipe's intended.

"I promised I would say nothing, and a promise is a promise, Luisa," Krissoula reassured her, hiding a smile. After all, her own opinion of Don Felipe to date was far from high, her betrothed or not!

"Luisa! What have I told you about gossiping?" snapped Angelina's stern voice as the woman returned to her kitchen carrying a metal pan, which she slammed down on the table, her annoyance with her daughter obvious.

She snatched a brace of fresh-plucked chickens from the bloody pan with one hand, took up a meat ax with the other, and began deftly chopping the carcasses into neat portions for cooking. Obviously, as far as Mama Angelina was concerned, the subject of

Esteban de San Martín's birth was now closed. *"Pollo* with rice tonight, señorita! Your favorite, yes?"

"Wonderful, Angelina," Krissoula agreed. "And now, I suppose I really should go back to the house, and get ready for my ride. Sofía will be frantic, wondering where I am! Send Tomás up to the house, would you, please?"

She headed for the door, pausing to caress the baby in Lupe's arms one last time before she left.

"Your son is beautiful, Lupe. You should be proud of him," she said huskily as she looked down at the suckling infant, tugging greedily at his mother's swollen brown breast with little smacking noises of pleasure. His cheek was flushed from nursing. Chubby fists thrust energetically at his mother's bosom. "I enjoyed holding him so much. Thank you for letting me."

"If it would please you, José and I would be honored for you to come and play with Paulito any time, doña," Lupe offered shyly. "Our home is not very grand, but you are always welcome there."

Krissoula nodded gravely. "Thank you, Lupe. I'd like that very much. Soon, God willing!" And with that, she was gone back to the main house, leaving Angelina and her daughters exchanging astonished glances.

"Well!" Luisa exclaimed "What do you make of that?"

"Of the way Esteban and the doña looked at each other when Mama was gone—or the way she took to Paulito?" guileless Estrella asked innocently.

"Both!" her sister Luisa retorted, giggling. "Aiee, *Dios,* if looks could burn, Esteban's eyes would have scorched the señorita to a cinder!"

"Nonsense!" their mother denied. "The señorita will marry Don Felipe in three months, and such talk is malicious and can only harm her good reputation, poor *niña!"* She shook her head, frowning. "She might have a wealthy husband and a life of ease coming to her, but somehow, she seems sad and lonely to me, rather than happy. Her smiles are all on the outside, not from within."

"Aiiee, *mamacita,* you read too much into the smallest things!" Luisa scoffed. "Why should she be either sad or lonely, with the easy life she's always known, and the one of luxury that lies ahead for her! Besides, you weren't here when she and Esteban stood there, gobbling each other up with their eyes . . . If Don Felipe doesn't marry the doña—and soon—she'll not stay lonely for long, I shouldn't wonder!" Luisa insisted mischievously.

"Bite that thoughtless tongue of yours at once, Luisa! Mama's right—the señorita did seem sad, somehow, despite her smiles. And as for you, little sister, and that loose tongue—aiee! Mama should cut it out with her axe! You mustn't go around speaking so loosely and rashly about the doña and Señor Esteban, and what happened here in the past, Luisa. You know how swiftly gossip travels at Tierra Rosa, and a wicked tongue like yours could harm them both! Why, what if Don Felipe got word of it?"

"Oh, very well, I'll be quiet about it in the future," Luisa grumbled. "But—I wonder why the doña was so curious about Esteban? Could it be she likes him, too, do you think? Just a little?"

"Enough! There'll be no work done at all today if you stand here gossiping all morning, Luisa!" Angelina scolded her youngest daughter sharply.

With sweat running down her face, she browned the seasoned chicken pieces in sizzling olive oil, using a heavy-bottomed skillet. "There are beds to be made, *hija,* so get on with your work. And as for you, Estrella, to the dusting and sweeping with you! We've wasted far too much time on idle gossiping this morning—so, hurry now, little parrot, to your work!"

And with that, she booted her giggling daughter from the kitchen, and rolled her eyes heavenward in exasperation to quiet Lupe and Estrella.

Chapter Four

Was there any country lovelier than Argentina, Krissoula wondered as they rode across the lands of Tierra Rosa later that morning?

She'd traveled far and wide with her mother's people, the Rom, and had seen almost every country in Europe from the swaying seat of a painted caravan; had slept under the starry skies of Spain and Portugal, of France, Italy, and Greece. She'd wandered the green, rain-washed valleys and winding country lanes of England and the desolate sweep of her heaths and moors, where the yellow broom showered the turf with gold or the purple of wild heather, but never had any land been as beautiful as this, the heartland of Argentina!

The sky was a more vivid blue here, an azure vault that was as endless as time, trimmed with wind-shredded clouds. The pampas, spreading away in every direction beneath her mare's hooves, were more lush, more richly green and fertile than any grasslands she had seen before, and the wildlife they harbored was exotic, fascinating to the eyes of a Gypsy such as she, who loved and respected all wild creatures, and called each one "brother."

She'd seen a long-necked, dun-colored rhea speeding away from their approach at an ungainly lope shortly after they set out, and moments later—much to her delight!—had spied an armadillo trundling down a little hill before it disappeared from view, looking for all the world like Don Quixote, a knight in heavy armor waddling quickly away, to tilt at windmills!

The bare branches of some of the trees they'd passed had sheltered the homes of the common little birds the local people called *los horneros,* the baker-birds, because their dome-shaped nests built of mud looked for all the world like ovens! She'd also glimpsed amongst the leaves and branches the brilliant red caps of scarlet-headed blackbirds, and the startling red breasts of black, crowlike *caciques,* too. Earth mounds lying above patches of

57

stripped grasslands like miniature Inca cities betrayed the burrowing of the *viscachas,* the gopherlike animal of the grasslands.

She looked eagerly about as they rode along in the hopes of spotting one of the pampas foxes that she'd heard about, too, curious to learn if what was said about it was true. The gray foxes, she'd been told, froze in place when startled by something, and would not so much as flinch or bat an eye even when a man struck them . . . ! But alas, she was unlucky this morning, she decided, perhaps next time, and with a disappointed sigh, she shifted her attention to the beautiful vista off in the distance.

Far to the west, the snow-capped Andes sprawled like a hazy giant reclining beneath frosty blankets, while much closer, the Sierra de Córdoba ranges flaunted every shade of green imaginable with the sun spreading its rays in wide arcs over their velvety emerald slopes, like a coquettish señorita opening her painted golden fan over the world below.

The temperature was quite mild today, for all that it was July and winter in this part of the world. The wind's fragrant grass-and-earth-scented caresses were like the kiss of crisp, feathery wings against her cheeks. She felt alive as she'd never felt before; in love with life and the sheer, unmatched beauty of the world around her! What more could she ask for, she wondered, almost bubbling over with happiness, than what she had now? Truly, El Señor moved in ways mysterious for mortals to understand! But when He did something right—as He had when He changed her life for the better—He spared no pains! She had three delicious meals a day now—four, if one counted teatime. Clean, pretty clothes were hers for the choosing, and each night she slept on a soft feather bed between lace-edged sheets, instead of on the hard ground with a ragged blanket teeming with invisible bedmates clutched about her shivering body. She had a beautiful house to live in, servants to please her every whim, and wonderful, blooded horses to ride whenever she wished. Could any woman be so fortunate as she, she wondered, ignoring the nagging voice that asked her what good it all was, if she had no one she cared about to share that life with? That old goat, Felipe de Aguilar, her unwitting "benefactor," didn't even enter her thoughts . . .

The mare she rode that morning was yet another palomino, chosen for her mount, she suspected, because she was a pretty, showy little animal blessed with a placid nature and a gait that was pure silk. Her coat had been curried to a shining pale blond. Her mane and tail had been brushed until they flowed in the brisk breeze like tassels of silver. A few lumps of sugar before they set out, and Krissoula had won her heart, and the mare hers!

In answer to her questions about the fiery stallion, Dorado, which she'd yearned to ride, Tomás, the *domador,* or head groom and horse trainer of Tierra Rosa, had explained that the mare, Girasol, which meant "sunbeam" in Spanish, was Dorado's dam. Her magnificent son could not be ridden this week, Tomás mumbled with a red face, since Señor Esteban was putting him to the mares of Tierra Rosa for breeding.

The scent of the mares in season, corraled somewhere nearby, had probably been the reason Dorado had escaped Alfredo that day and bolted into the courtyard, Krissoula guessed shrewdly, for stallions were driven mad by the scent of mares, and could detect their presence from amazing distances.

She smiled as she cantered Girasol down a shallow grassy incline, one of few that dimpled the flatlands, remembering the tactful way poor Tomás had described Dorado's unavailability for riding as "being used for breeding purposes." What would the shy groom think, she wondered, if he knew that the delicate señorita, the innocent, virginal "intended" of Don Felipe, probably knew as much about the violent mating of stallions with mares as he did— maybe more?

Had she not helped her uncle by holding the bridles of reluctant mares to calm them and keep them still while the stallions mounted them? It was a task that only a woman could do without arousing the jealous fury of the stallions, for the lust-crazed beasts saw all males, horse or human alike, as rivals in their excited state. And had she not seen for herself the savage beauty of their mating; a beauty that, to an innocent girl on the brink of womanhood, had been strangely disturbing, quickening new pulses and awakening dormant senses within her budding body she was too young to fully comprehend?

"So it is with all living things, Krissoula," her uncle Ricardo had said solemnly after one such mating. "For every male, there is a female. The fire in their blood compels them to mate and reproduce their kind. It is a siren's song few are strong enough to deny, be they human or animal. When you are older and a woman, you, too, will hear the call, and feel its power in your blood. But choose your mate well and wisely, little Krissoula, for you will be a woman, not an animal. Answer that call not only with your heart and body, but with your head!"

And had she heeded his wise counsel? *Caray,* no, she had not!

For when Miguel entered her life, all reason had left it . . .

"Mi sobrina, this man is not for you!" Ricardo had reasoned gently when she'd told him her decision. "He's a *gorgio* who knows nothing of the vagabond life we Rom lead! How can he share with you a life he knows nothing of?"

"Do you forget that my father was also a *gorgio,* Tío Ricardo? Besides, it doesn't matter to me that Miguelito is not one of us. You see, he's asked me to stay with him in his village when our band moves on, and so it is *I* who must learn his ways, not he ours! I love him so, Uncle! I'd follow him anywhere—even to the very ends of the earth!" she'd declared with all the passion and conviction of youth. "When you move on to Portugal, I won't be coming with you. I shall stay here in the village with my Miguel, and become his wife."

"Pah! It is your lust for him that rules you now, little one! Share his bed, if you must have this man!" he'd suggested, shocking her speechless, for Gypsy menfolk guarded the virginity of their maidens at all costs, and his suggestion brought home more forcefully than countless arguments the depth of his anxiety for her future as Miguel's bride. "We'll wait here for you," he'd continued, "and in a few weeks, when your blood has cooled, you'll be sensible again and come with us."

"No, Tío Ricardo, it's not just desire I feel for Miguel. I love him! That love won't lessen when I share his bed. Remember, Tío, you taught me that my virginity was a precious gift, to be given to the man I chose to share my life with? Well, I've chosen to give that gift to Miguel—the man I'll take for my husband, as well as my lover. I'll spend the rest of my life with him and the children we make together! Don't wait for me, Uncle, for I shan't be traveling with the Rom again."

"Ah, Krissoula, Krissoula, you have eyes, and yet still you are blind!" her uncle had cried. "You look no deeper than a man's handsome face, but what about his soul, eh? *Sí,* he has a pretty face, your *gorgio,* a pretty body, your Miguel, but trust me, he is not the one for you! You need a strong man, one who can meet you as your equal. You need a man with your fire, your intelligence, your strength of will.

"Would you harness unmatched horses in the shafts of a wagon, one weak, the other strong? Never! A *vardo* team must be well matched, with both horses pulling the weight of the caravan equally. You know very well that a badly matched team would overturn the wagon! So it is with life, *chiquita.* A husband and wife are the team, and the shafts between which they must pull is the marriage they make together. The load they haul is the conflicts we all must face in life and strive together to overcome, like ruts or hills in the wagon's path. Miguel is no worthy match for you! Find another to share life's harness with you, *mi sobrina*. One who is strong enough to accept the burdens as well as the joys, and will pull his weight beside you in the marriage shafts."

"No," she'd refused stubbornly. "I've made my choice, and there is nothing you can say to change my mind."

Tears had filled her uncle's eyes. "Krissoula, listen to me, I beg you, and remember what happened to your mother! If you defy me, if you take this *gorgio* as your man, the council will cast you out! You will be considered 'unclean' henceforth among those who love you, and no longer of the Rom! Don't throw away your life, your people, for this pretty young man. He isn't worth the price!"

But Ricardo's pleas had fallen on deaf ears. She'd run away from the Rom and the life she'd known one night, and married her pretty *gorgio* soon after, finding out too late that her uncle had been right, and that there was no turning back . . .

Heart aching, she wrenched her thoughts back to the present and the horse beneath her, halting the mare to look back over her shoulder for Sofía.

She was jouncing gamely after her, perched on the seat of a little four-wheeled carriage with broad, sturdy wheels well suited to the grassy yet flat terrain of the pampas. The duenna's face was shaded by the fringed sunshade fixed over the carriage, but Krissoula could see her expression was a determined, if grim, one, and her heart softened towards her chaperone. Poor Sofía! She tried so hard to be the perfect duenna! She turned Girasol about and they cantered back towards the bouncing surrey, slowing to a walk alongside it.

"*Dios,* the day grows warm, winter or no, Sofía! Shall we rest for a little while, before turning back?" The offer was made for her duenna's benefit, since she was not in the least bit tired herself.

"*Sí, gracias!*" Sofía agreed gratefully, hauling back on the reins. "Aiee, how my arms ache!"

"Poor Sofía!" Krissoula sympathized. "But I confess, you've surprised me today, *amiga mía,* for I'd not suspected for a minute that you could drive a carriage nearly so well!" she praised craftily.

Sofía's sallow cheeks grew pink with pleasure beneath her severe black mantilla, giving her narrow features a surprisingly attractive, *human* cast. "You know, you're right, Krissoula! I did do rather well, did I not?" Sofía said with a smug air Krissoula had never

61

guessed her capable of before. "Here, take this and help me down, won't you?"

Krissoula swung down from her horse—which she'd ridden astride, despite Sofía's exclamations of horror and her veiled hints of the disastrous effects it might have upon her "virginal" body!—and looped the reins about a low, spreading bush, before reaching up to the carriage to take the basket Sofía held out to her.

"*Caramba!* What's in here?" Krissoula asked, surprised by its weightiness. She guessed teasingly, "Your dowry in gold, Sofía *mía?*"

"On the contrary," Sofía teased back with a rare display of humor, "it is your *almuerzo,* your lunch! Since you always eat like one of Don Felipe's hungriest *peóns,* I asked Mama Angelina to make it a big one!"

Krissoula's eyes widened with delight and surprise. "Why, Sofía, you angel, a picnic? What a wonderful idea!"

"I thought you might approve," Sofía murmured dryly. "I've noticed you're always far sweeter to me when I give in to you, *niña,* and do things your way. But when I do not—" her duenna shrugged—"then, *Dios mío,* you become a *diabla,* a she-devil!"

Krissoula pouted. "Well? Isn't everyone at their sweetest when life goes the way they want it to? But I promise I'll try to be much better in the future, Sofía—if you'll promise to give in to me once in a while. Agreed?"

"Agreed!" an exasperated Sofía promised, and allowed Krissoula to hand her down from the carriage.

Tasty *empanadas,* pasties stuffed with shredded beef, and hard-boiled eggs, black olives, a salad of tiny tomatoes sliced with raw onions and sardines, tangy oranges and wedges of juicy melon, disappeared into Krissoula's hungry mouth soon after. At a slower, more dignified pace, an astonishing amount also disappeared into Sofía, leaving only bones, crumbs, rinds, and orange peels scattered over the linen cloth when they were done. Krissoula took a last swig of watered red wine from her enamel cup, patted her belly in a most unladylike fashion, and groaned in satisfaction.

"That was marvelous!" she declared. "Why does a meal eaten al fresco always taste so much better than when one's inside?"

"I don't know, but all this fresh air and exercise makes me sleepy. I think I'll take a little siesta right here, before we make that long ride back to the *casa grande.* Krissoula, you will wake me in twenty minutes, yes? And *niña*—do not wander away unescorted, *por favor?* There're gauchos scattered everywhere across these grasslands, and to all accounts, they're rough, uncouth fellows, every one of them." She lowered her voice as if they were in danger of being overheard as she added, "Many of them even have a dash of Indian blood, and I'm certain you can imagine—knowing that!—how uncivilized they could be! Those *mestizos* would not recognize you as the intended of Don Felipe, nor care that you're a high-born lady. They'd see only a helpless woman, and try to rob her of her innocence, as such rough fellows will, you understand?"

"*Sí,*" Krissoula promised demurely, hiding a smile. "I understand. I'll sit right here and relax beside you under the trees until you awaken."

She was able to keep her promise for a full ten minutes, but no more, before boredom and restless energy had her fidgeting. After all, she'd not felt in the least bit tired to start with, and had agreed to a halt only for Sofía's benefit. In reality, she itched to be mounted again, and galloping on across the endless grasslands astride Girasol!

With a sigh, she took off the smart, flat-brimmed sombrero she'd donned for riding, and toyed with the silver braiding about the crown and brim, picking at it with her fingernails until it frayed. When that novelty palled, she slipped off the short bolero jacket of chocolate-brown velvet she wore over a crisp white shirtwaist and carefully inspected it for lint, before tossing that, too, aside. Knees bent, chin resting on her fists, she sighed again and wiggled her toes, admiring her calf-length boots of soft suede, which were the same color as her jacket. Ah, what a pretty contrast they made appearing saucily beneath the deep-gold cord of her divided riding skirt! High-heeled and sassy with their elegant pointed toes, they were the very height of fashionable country wear for the discerning horsewoman, the cobbler in Buenos Aires had promised, but—they pinched and made her feet hot! She tugged and hauled until she had them off, and her stockings with them, and could wriggle her bare toes in the thick, cool grass. She sighed contentedly. One of the true blood, one of the Rom, as was she, never felt completely free unless she went barefoot, with Mother Earth beneath her feet.

When that little pleasure palled, she sat and watched pretty Girasol, who was quietly cropping the lush grass. After a few moments, a wicked, speculative gleam came into her golden eyes. She glanced across at Sofía, and grinned in satisfaction. Her duenna was already fast asleep, lounging against a tree trunk with her hands folded across her breasts and her mouth gaping open like a stiffened corpse.

63

Reaching across, Krissoula carefully unpinned the fob watch attached to Sofía's black silk bosom and adjusted the tiny hands, turning the hour hand backward a full revolution before replacing the tiny gold watch. There! Now she had an hour and ten minutes to pursue her own interests, and no one would be the wiser! The duenna was a heavy sleeper. She rarely took *siestas* lasting less than two or three hours. When she'd accomplished what she was tempted to do, she'd wake Sofía like the dutiful charge she'd promised to be, and they could return docilely to Tierra Rosa!

She slipped away from the small grove of *quebracho* trees where Sofía slept, and went to Girasol. Stroking her gently and talking to the mare, she rubbed her body against the horse to let the mare learn her scent and with it, the knowledge that she meant her no harm. Then, when she was certain the animal trusted her, she uncinched the girth strap and hefted off the heavy saddle and sheepskin blanket beneath, discarding them in the long grass before vaulting astride Girasol's bare back.

Jacketless, hatless, bootless, she rode the palomino mare across the pampas for several miles, glorying in the freedom she felt with the wind streaming through her hair and whipping her cheeks to a bright cherry-red, before turning her horse back towards the *quebracho* grove where she'd left Sofía sleeping.

Not once in all that time did Girasol's gait alter and so, when she judged the moment was right, she gripped the mare's silvery mane and leaned forward over her neck. She drew first one leg, then the other, up beneath her, until she was no longer astride, but kneeling precariously on the mare's back.

For a few moments, she let her senses absorb Girasol's rhythmic canter, and then she slowly drew herself up and back, until she was standing with her bare feet braced apart on the widest part of Girasol's broad rump, one hand outstretched for balance, the other holding the reins taut. Girasol, bless her, never faltered nor missed even a single stride, despite the fact that her rider was now standing on her bare back, rather than sitting sedately astride.

"Ah, yes, my beautiful Sunbeam, yes! You and Krissoula were made for each other, no? This little adventure will be our secret!" she cried.

Laughing out loud in delight, she shook her hair free of its remaining pins and let it stream behind her in the wind like an ebony banner. She could still do it! She'd forgotten nothing that Tío Ricardo had taught her all those years ago!

She'd almost reached the spot where she'd left Sofía sleeping when she saw a lone rider, sitting his horse as still as a statue upon the crest of a nearby low-lying hill. The man wore the fringed woven poncho and black *chambergo* of a gaucho, she saw as he suddenly moved, riding nearer. Her golden eyes widened, then she frowned. *Dios,* he was circling down from the foothills and heading straight as an arrow towards her! In fact, so purposeful did his approach seem, she almost lost her balance before righting herself and slipping quickly back astride her mount.

Who was he, she wondered as the rider kicked his horse into a canter to catch up with her? One of the rough-and-ready *gauchos* Sofía had warned her of, or a half-Indian *bandito* with rape and robbery on his mind? She shrugged fatalistically. Whichever, there was no sense in trying to make a run for it. His huge bay horse dwarfed Girasol, and he could easily overtake her. Besides, she was no coward who'd ride off and leave poor Sofía alone and defenseless while she slept! The sensible thing to do was rein Girasol in, let the man approach her, and find out what he wanted.

She quietly sat her horse, her heart thudding as she waited. But as the man rode closer, she recognized him and her apprehension turned swiftly to anger. *Dios, no!* she groaned. *It was that damned blackmailer again!* Her heart gave a peculiar flutter as he rode nearer. Perhaps she should have ridden off at a full gallop, after all, and done so without looking back—? Perhaps—*sí,* perhaps she still would!

Chapter Five

"*Hola* once again, *chiquita!*" the hateful man drawled with a grin when he was still some distance away. He swept off his *chambergo* in a graceful yet mocking flourish, as if she were truly the grand lady she was pretending to be. "I'd no idea the circus was in town! Where the devil did you learn to ride like that? In one of your Gypsy camps?"

"Where's no business of yours, *hombre!*" she retorted rudely, furious to see him again so soon. She gathered the reins about her fists, every muscle in her body tensed for flight. "And what is it with you, anyway, eh? Always you turn up when I least want or expect it, like a bad penny! Are you my shadow, San Martín, that you must go everywhere I go? Do everything I do? I told you the other day, I've been searching for your cursed papers, but—no luck! When— and if!—I find them, señor, you'll be the first to know, I promise you! Meanwhile, just go away, *bribón!* Stop following me!"

With that, she let out a yell and drummed her heels into Girasol's sides. The valiant mare obediently sprang forward, stretching out moments later into a swift, ground-eating gallop that gobbled up the feet, then yards, between them. Krissoula leaned forward like a jockey over the mare's arched neck, her face almost buried in its silvery mane, and gave the palomino her head.

The grasslands streamed beneath Girasol's hooves in an endless, blurred green stripe. The incredible speed at which the swift mare carried her away filled Krissoula with a wild exultation; a fierce, sweet joy. She glanced over her shoulder, and saw San Martín belatedly kick his bay into a gallop to race after her. Giddy, defiant laughter was torn from her, then lost on the breeze. Let San Martín catch them—if he could! She and Girasol were racing the wind!

Esteban recovered swiftly and, with a rogue's grin, kicked the bay after her.

"*Pronto,* Barbaro!" he roared, slashing the reins across the

66

straining stallion's flanks. "Faster, boy!"

Barbaro was eager to gallop, and needed no further urging. Four black stockings pumping like pistons, the stallion streaked after the mare, following its thundering passage in and out of the Sierra de Córdoba foothills that skirted the Pampa in undulating folds.

Esteban saw Krissoula cast a hurried look over her shoulder. Heard her silvery laughter ring out on the crisp air before it was whirled away and lost on the wind. Her scornful laughter needled his pride. That little hellion! That golden-eyed witch! She was laughing at him, challenging him to catch her, he realized. He grinned as the bay thundered up a grassy incline and then skewed sharply down a rock-littered slope, fringed with thorny chapparal. If she wanted to play games, well, *por Dios,* he was more than in the mood—!

One of the *puestos,* or line-camps the *gauchos* used when far from the *hacienda,* mushroomed into view. Esteban spotted it first, and with a broad grin he turned Barbaro's head eastward, circling around the golden horse now in a wide arc that would herd the palomino in the hut's direction.

Too late, Krissoula realized his ploy, and muttered a foul curse under her breath. Damn his black soul! Damn that sly, sneaking weasel of a man! While she'd been intent only on outdistancing the bay, that cur San Martín had outwitted her!

She tried to rein Girasol in, to turn the mare west before he cut off their escape route, but there was nowhere to go but forward! Girasol careened onward, and moments later, San Martín's stallion was racing along beside her, their two mounts neck and neck as their hooves flew over the rough turf. Reaching across, Esteban swept Krissoula from her mount's back with one powerful, crooked arm, tearing her hands from Girasol's reins as he slung her across the saddle before him. Chuckling, he reined the bay into a walk, and then, finally, a halt.

"Bastardo!" she hissed from her ignominious position, slung like a sack of cornmeal across his saddle. Her little face was reddened with fury and exertion, her golden eyes glittering shards of topaz in the sunlight. "Dirty, cheating bastard!" she jeered. "Because you couldn't beat me fairly, you must cheat, eh, dirty cockroach?"

"Damned right," he agreed amicably, unperturbed by her insults as he yanked her from his saddle by the waistband of her skirts to stand before him. "'Victory at any cost,' that's my motto, *bombón!"* And he chucked her beneath the chin.

He grinned as she jerked her head away from his touch, relishing

67

the disheveled picture she presented now. With her composure lost, fury spitting in her golden eyes and blistering curses rolling off her lips, she was magnificent, like a furious kitten with its fur standing on end, bristling with tigerlike rage. Her mane of inky ringlets spilled wantonly about her furious, flushed face. The two topmost buttons of her blouse had become unfastened by the wildness of her ride, and the luscious curves of her heaving bosom swelled into view between the parted cloth, tempting his lips and hands and drawing his gaze like magnets. "Rest assured, *minina,*" he added softly, his hooded sapphire eyes darkening with desire, "I seldom lose . . ."

She read the hungry expression in his eyes for what it was, and panic filled her. "There's always a first time, señor—even for you!" she countered, tossing her head and sounding far braver than she felt. "Now, I must get back to Sofía. She'll be wondering what's happened to me . . ."

Peculiarly breathless, she turned to catch the mare, who was quietly cropping the grass a few yards away. But before she'd taken more than a step or two, he took her by the elbow and swung her around to face him.

"Let go of me!"

"No, fierce little one! Your precious Sofía is fast asleep beneath the trees, snoring like an armadillo! As well you know, it's unlikely we'll be disturbed for quite some time." His dark eyes caressed her, lingering on the seductive fullness of her lower lip, the graceful, elegant arch of her throat where a tiny pulse throbbed madly; on the darkened valley that lay between her breasts.

"What of it?" she demanded, her heart pounding uncontrollably now.

"What of it! Come, come, surely you haven't forgotten so soon, darling? We have unfinished business between us, no? And what better time to see it—satisfactorily—concluded than now, while Don Felipe is away. And rest assured, I won't fall asleep this time!"

The dangerous, silky purr to his voice made the hackles rise on the nape of her neck. Little feathery quivers of fear tickled in the pit of her belly.

"Business?" she echoed, her voice faint, though she knew only too well what he was referring to.

"*Sí!* One golden guinea's worth, as I recall. Now do you remember?"

Oh, she remembered all right! How she remembered! The golden guinea he'd given her lay wrapped in a shawl in the bottom of her lingerie drawer. She'd left it there to remind herself of her gullibility in going to San Martín's rooms alone that fateful night, and of the far-reaching consequences of her stupidity and greed.

"You're *loco,*" she accused instead. "You—hired—me to find the papers for you, San Martín, nothing more. The other," she blushed furiously, "was never part of our deal!"

"No? But I say it was! I paid separately for your favors after all, *minina*—and my guinea was never returned to me, was it . . . ?"

"Think what you will, señor, but I was no whore!" she protested hotly. "A thief, *sí,* but a *puta?* Never! I'll—I'll see your money returned to you, I promise, if you'll just let me go?"

"Never a *puta?*" He chuckled and shook his head. "Forgive me if I call you a liar, but I'm sure you can understand how impossible it would be to convince me—of all people!—that you're innocent, especially under the circumstances of our first encounter?"

He smiled and drew her to him, slipping his arms about her waist like a velvet vise, and holding her so close she could feel the heat that rose from his body. "It certainly wasn't clothes-pegs or lucky white heather you were selling the day we met, was it, now, my little Gypsy? Your—wares—were something rather different, as I recall—and far more to a man's liking!"

"Just shut up, San Martín!" she hissed, cheeks flaming at the innuendo in his tone. "You believed what I wanted you to believe, that's all. Why, I'd have slit your cursed throat before you—or any other man—touched me! Pah! You men, you're all the same—rutting, randy pigs, easily dazzled by the sight of a naked woman. Show them a glimpse of a ripe breast, the curve of a shapely rump, and they forget their purses and think only of the bulge in their breeches!" she jeered. "Why should I have suspected you were any different? It was a role I played to fleece you of your money—just like the one I'm playing for you now—so just—just let go of me!"

"No."

Seeing the lust and steely determination smoldering in his eyes, she quickly looked away, unable to face him down. *Dios,* she seemed to have shrunk as she stood trapped in the cage of his arms, feeling smaller and more uncertain and vulnerable than she'd ever felt before! It was not a situation the tempestuous Krissoula cared for, and she swallowed to cover her anxiety. If she pretended to go along with his game, could she catch him unawares and escape? It was worth a try. For if she allowed him to take her, if she succumbed to the compelling attraction he held for her, how then could she go through with her plan to cheat him? It would be child's play to double-cross a man she hated and resented, but double-cross her lover—? No, not easy at all, for one with even a shred of conscience left her . . .

"Ah, but I fancy you've grown bold of late, Krissoula!" he observed, mistaking her silence and apparent composure for hauteur. Nuzzling the dark cloud of her hair, his arms still locked about her, he continued. "Perhaps you've been playing the grand lady too long, if the simple truth can sting you so, force you to make such flimsy excuses for your past? Why, I think you're starting to live the part I chose for you, aren't you, sweetheart? To believe you're a grand and innocent lady! Maybe you need reminding of exactly what you were when I found you, eh . . . ?"

One hand slipped from about her waist and boldly caressed the curve of her hip before gliding downward. He splayed tanned fingers over her skirted thigh and caressed its slim length, before sliding his hand between her knees possessively as he tipped his head back to gaze deep into her furious eyes.

Dios! His touch burned her flesh like the smarting stripes from a lash, even through her thick skirt, and her heart fluttered with—with *something,* although exactly what, she wasn't sure . . . She drew back her booted foot and kicked his shin, yet his boots were of thick horsehair, and he felt nothing. Worse, her childish display of temper made his smile broaden.

"Take your filthy hands off me, you blue-eyed *diablo!*" she screeched, squirming her hand free to slap his face. "Whatever you think, you don't own me!"

He caught her wrist easily, and wrenched it down to her side before the blow landed. With a low, wicked laugh, he stepped forward and hauled her effortlessly into his arms again, this time sweeping her off the ground and holding her fast, although she struggled wildly to escape him.

With their raised voices, Girasol nickered and tossed her head, scampering a few feet away before lowering her head to graze once more.

"Own you? No, perhaps not. But possess you—take you—make love to you—*sí,* that I will do, *minina.* Body and soul!" he threatened huskily, only too aware of the aching at his loins, the swollen pressure of his desire for her. "*Caray,* I must've been a fool that first night!" he whispered, his hawk's face stark with passion as he searched her face. "I should have taken what you were selling first, little one—and afterward played the mark and let you rob me!"

"I—said—take—your—filthy—hands—off—me, you slippery cockroach!" she panted again, wriggling in his grip and trying to pluck his fingers from beneath her knees one by one, but without success.

"No!" he ground out, his eyes an even darker sapphire now as he added more softly, "No." His large hand cupped her chin, and he tilted her head up to his. "Come, pretty *puta,* why fight me—why fight the inevitable, eh? I paid your price long ago. Now it's time for you to pay mine!"

Their eyes met and locked for agonizing seconds, tawny gold to piercing dark blue. Krissoula's were the first to uneasily look away, for it was as if Esteban could see clear into her soul and unmask the real Krissoula; the Gypsy urchin and thief who was neither cocksure nor streetwise, who still hovered there like a frightened, forgotten woman-child, desperately needing the love and protection of a man. The girl-woman who found *this* man in particular more disturbing, more attractive than she dared to admit, even to herself, and who was trying valiantly to deny that potent attraction even as it stirred and came fully alive. A tricky child who, in her heart of hearts, fully intended to double-cross him, given the slightest chance, no matter what her feelings for him were . . .

Her heart was pounding so fast and so hard, she feared it might escape from her breast as he cradled her fiercely to his chest and strode with her to the ramshackle cabin. That *diablo,* that devil! He was so tall, so broad, so dark and stern—she'd never be able to escape him, not if he was so set on taking her!

He had to duck as he entered the hut, for the mantel beam was set too low for his tall frame. Casting about him a moment or two, he selected a spot against the far wall, and wasted no time in carrying her to it.

"Since I'm forbidden entry to my dear uncle's house, I regret your bed must be humble leaves, mi'lady," he apologized mockingly, and set her down atop a heap of dried grasses and crackling dead leaves that crunched beneath her weight. Gazing down at her for a moment or two, he tossed off his hat, yanked the woolen poncho over his head, then dropped to his knees beside her.

Her frightened golden eyes were drawn as if by magnets to his mouth in the shadows. Her lashes fluttered nervously, and she thought she might faint as she stared at his lips, unable to look away. They were slim lips, yet firm and attractively molded, the sensitive flesh a dark-rose color against his sun-and-wind-browned skin. He could drive a woman to madness with those lips, she sensed, almost feeling the moist warmth of their caress tracing the knobs of her spine . . . A reluctant shiver of excitement moved through her as she imagined him doing just that! Unable to bear such unsettling, unwanted thoughts, she raised her gaze to his magnificent, brooding eyes, surmounted by brows like inky slashes.

71

The irises were so dark blue they rivaled the indigo of a starless night sky, fringed with thick charcoal lashes. Those eyes were gleaming wickedly as she gazed hesitantly up into them, as if he could see through her clothing to her body beneath!

"So," she said slowly, and her voice sounded shaky, she knew. "I suppose you mean to leave me no choice, señor?"

"None at all, *minina,*" he agreed amicably, his lips quirking at the corners as if he wanted to smile. "Surely you can see that it's a matter of principle? I paid your price, and now, sweet little *bombón,* you must deliver the 'goods' I purchased! Such is the way in business matters, no?"

Smiling, he lowered his dark head. His lips grazed hers, their touch so light, so fleeting, she was stunned. His mouth and tongue continued to play about hers with such a delicacy that, despite her intention to remain stiff and unmoved by his kisses, she felt herself beginning to respond, her flesh growing warm under his enflaming caresses, her tension ebbing like an outpouring tide.

"Kiss me, *minina,*" he urged, and his warm, masculine scent filled her nostrils. "Kiss me back as if you mean it!"

Summoning all her nerve, Krissoula gave him a quick, pristine peck upon the lips, at once withdrawing her lips as if scalded.

"*Caray, mujer!* You call that a kiss?" he scoffed softly. "I've kissed nuns with more passion in their lips than you! No, little kitten, this—*this* is a kiss . . . !"

So saying, he gathered her fully into his arms and brought her hard against his chest before she could wriggle free. One hand cupped her buttocks, the other firmly gripped her chin to hold her head upturned to his. His ardent mouth came down over hers, stealing her breath away with the sweetly savage ardor of his kisses. The hand at her chin moved to twine instead through her hair, twisted in it so tightly she could not turn her head aside, while the other hand stroked or firmly squeezed the globes of her bottom as he crushed her hips hard against his.

Pressed so tightly to him, she could feel his manhood like a hot, hard iron against her belly, and her heart turned crazy flip-flops in response! Little tongues of fire flicked through her loins. She struggled furiously at first, but the handsome brute just kept on slanting his mouth back and forth across hers in a hungry, greedy way that demanded some response of her—and which stirred a tiny, treacherous pulse between her trembling thighs.

Feeling her body soften in partial surrender against him, Esteban gave a low growl of triumph deep in his throat. *Caramba!* How soft and ripe she felt in his arms! How deliciously rounded and female!

His pulse quickened. The lust for her that had been building since their meeting in the kitchens earlier that day pounded in his veins, hardened his loins unbearably. Holding her still tighter, he sought entry to her mouth with his tongue as if it were his god-given right, and thoroughly ravished its inner sweetness. To his delight, she uttered a throaty whimper of surrender, and yielded whole-heartedly to his mouth.

Uttering a breathless moan, Krissoula surrendered, quite forgetting her resolve. Parting her lips, she took his tongue deep into her mouth, answering its sensual probings with tiny flickerings from her own tongue, and with gentle sucklings that fanned the buried embers of her passionate nature into blazing fire.

His scent was full in her nostrils, a delicious mixture of soap and clean, manly flesh with the faint undertang of leather and tobacco to it. His arms were like bonds of silk and steel about her, strong yet gentle as they imprisoned her, held her captive against his broad chest. His kisses made her hungry for more. Like a greedy child with a dish of sugar plums set before it, she couldn't stop at one—! Sensations, yearnings, needs she'd thought extinguished for so very, very long were instantly rekindled by his fiery kisses; by the feel of his warm, aroused male body pressed to hers. With a melting sigh, she softened still further and thrust both breasts and hips shamelessly against him of her own accord, ignoring the warning bells in her mind that clamored to be heeded. Common sense demanded she call a halt to this madness, before she was lost. But—she turned a deaf ear to it and let passion rule her.

He moved his body over hers, shifting her beneath him in the crackling leaves so that now he lay half across her. Broad shoulders looming above her, his weight pressed her deeper and deeper into the bed of leaves and grasses. Eyes closed, she felt him shower hot little kisses over her face and throat; heard him whisper scandalous promises in her ears while he reached beneath her skirt to stroke her bare legs. Then his knee moved to press her thighs apart, and to Krissoula's surprise, they moved with a will of their own to loosen and accept his intrusion. A delicious sensation resulted when he firmly pressed his knee to the sensitive mound of her woman-hood, and she moaned with longing against his mouth, his name breaking from her lips like a prayer. *Dios,* how could she think of refusing him now, with her body growing so warm and tingly with passion in his embraces? When she ached to feel him inside her, and give vent to the wildfire raging in her blood?

Her nipples had ruched into swollen buds that were exquisitely sensitive. She knew he must be able to feel them nudging against the broadness of his chest as he kissed her, despite their garments, and the knowledge excited her. His mouth was savage on hers now, devouring her soft, yielding lips hungrily. Her breathing quickened, became a husky rasp deep in her throat; almost a she-cat's purr of pure pleasure as she answered the building hunger of his mouth measure for measure.

"Esteban . . ." she murmured. "Aiee, *querido mío . . . !*"

She tugged his shirt free of his belt and squirmed her hands beneath it to his warm, bare flesh. Her fingers clawed a path across his broad back, over his rippling shoulders, to bury themselves in the crisp, glossy curls at his nape. Even his neck was powerful, her fingertips told her, the muscles standing out as sinewy cords down its length. Her grip tightened as her passion mounted. She knew by the way he strained against her, by the feverish caress of his hands, his demanding lips, that he wanted far more than kisses now. He intended to take her very soon. To possess her, brand her as his woman . . . and, God forgive her, she wanted him, too! She wanted—in that single, wild moment—to belong to this powerful, virile man. Perhaps Esteban could cauterize the wounds love had dealt her in the past, she thought hopefully. Burn away the numbness Miguel's betrayal had left in her heart and soul? Perhaps she'd come truly alive again when he took her body in a blaze of passion, and made it his? Even her beloved dancing had never achieved that wonder—the miracle of draining the hurt and mistrust of her past away, so that she could be whole and able to *feel* again.

Her beloved dancing.

It was her only talent—but it was the one that had brought her to the notice of Don Felipe, and soon after, his proposal of marriage. The art that would, in just a few weeks, all going well, make her *la patrona* of Tierra Rosa, with all the comforts, wealth, and position she'd ever dreamed of . . .

Suddenly, she felt cold instead of hot with passion, as if a bucket of ice had been thrown over her. *Dios,* what was she doing here, writhing beneath this gaucho Romeo, stupidly risking discovery and with it, the loss of all she'd ever wanted? Would she throw everything she'd worked for away, in return for a few moments of passion in the arms of this handsome, blackmailing brute, who, without his lost inheritance, was in truth little more than a penniless nobody? No. *Never!*

"Señor, no, get off me!" she began, struggling to free herself from his arms, tearing her mouth from his. "Someone will find us! Your plans will be ruined! *Bastante,* I say! Enough!"

"Enough? No, not nearly enough!" Esteban whispered ardently, laughter in his voice. "Ah, but you make me reckless, darling. You make me set aside my ambitions, make me forget them completely. Your body does that to me—it drives me wild! Ah, kitten, I must've been blind to wait so long! I want you, Krissoula, and I'll have you, darling—*all* of you—I swear it . . ."

His fingers moved to unbutton her blouse, freeing them one by one. Folding back the cloth fronts like a child unwrapping a longed-for gift, he bared her lovely breasts to his lips. In the meager light that filtered through the cabin's narrow window, they rose proudly before his eyes, golden apples crested with swollen buds that were the color of sweet, wild honey from the comb. He dipped his head to the shadowed cleft between them, and as he tasted her satiny warmth, suckled her treasures, he groaned with pleasure.

"By *Dios,* I've discoverd your hoard of Gypsy gold, *minina,*" he murmured between his ardent assaults on her breasts with mouth and tongue, gentle teeth, and wicked, teasing fingers that tweaked and fondled and licked and nipped her to the brink of passionate madness. "*Sí,* Krissoula, all of your treasures are golden! Your bewitching eyes . . . your silky skin . . . your hard little breasts . . . even your little nipples are nuggets of gold! Ah, *querida,* your body tastes sweeter than golden grapes, taken warm from the vine. Your lips are the amber wines of Andalusia, tasting of sunshine and gold-kissed lemons. Your skin is softer, more fragrant, than the scented breezes that blow from the south. Open to me, my Gypsy witch. I'm under your spell. Let me love you!"

His hand slipped between her thighs, and his intimate caresses as he explored her soft, secret flesh fanned her smoldering passion into blazing fire. She felt herself grow moist and ready with his touch, and wanted more, much more. Gritting her teeth, she fought for control of herself. But oh, her treacherous body! His enflaming caresses made her want to moan with pleasure, instead of pleading for him to stop; to beg him to take her, rather than demanding that he let her go! But she mustn't weaken, she mustn't relent. In a moment or two, she must demand that he stop . . . and she would, oh, *sí,* she would . . . in just a moment or two . . .

But—never had she been so aroused! Never had she been made love to so ardently, so expertly! By contrast, her young and inexperienced husband Miguel's rough lovemaking seemed coarse and shallow now, the eager fumblings of a greedy little boy, seeking only his own relief. They were as different from Esteban's lovemaking as day was to night! Esteban's touch, his caressing voice, his flattering phrases, left her weak and yielding with the urge

75

to give of herself, and go on giving. His lovemaking built a female hunger within her she'd never known before, a knot that tightened and tightened, deep in her belly. She hummed like a strung wire, trembling on the brink of some marvelous revelation she'd never imagined could exist, knowing that sooner or later, the humming wire inside her must snap—but with what result? She had to know!

With a soft, yielding cry, she let him do what he would with her, trembling as he drew the garments from her and she lay bared in the leaves, moaning helplessly as he kissed and caressed her everywhere, sealing his burning lips to her breasts, her aching nipples, her belly, and the silken inner flesh of her thighs.

When he could delay no longer, when she was whimpering and tossing her head from side to side with her need, he knelt between her thighs and raised her up. She opened joyfully for him, and cried aloud as he plunged deep between her thighs and began to ride her, plunging again and again into the sweet, tight warmth that sheathed him until he felt her grow tense beneath him. Wave after wave of tiny contractions caressed the length of his aching shaft, filling him with delight.

Krissoula closed her eyes and her lips parted in a silent cry of wonder and disbelief as the wire inside her finally snapped and hurled her headlong into rapture. Sunbursts exploded in her mind, imprinted in scarlet and gold upon her closed eyelids. Sensations of such intense pleasure and relief sang through her veins, spread like melting honey through her limbs, she couldn't think straight. She could only feel, and go on feeling! She clutched blindly at him in her wonder, panting hoarsely and crying his name again and again as her fingers clamped over his shoulders.

He gathered her up into his arms and let her cry out her rapture against his chest, while his own body succumbed at last to the fierce, sweet pleasure in throbbing waves, the pressure at his loins building and building until it culminated in an explosive release that made him roar her name to the cobwebbed rafters and shudder with the force of his release.

In a tangle of limbs, their bodies slick with a sheen of sweat, they fell back, exhausted, to the leaves, breathing heavily.

Esteban's arms were still wrapped fast about her, his lips lost in her hair. She wondered dreamily if it would always be this way with him, for she enjoyed the way he held her in the aftermath of their passionate coupling. Miguel had never done so! His lovemaking had been begun and ended in only a brief, unfulfilling moment or two, and then he'd rolled from her and ignored her utterly, as if

76

she were a—a thing to be used, a ready vessel into which he emptied his pleasure, giving nothing in return, while Esteban—aiee, *Dios,* what wonders he'd shown her—the meaning and reward for her woman's part in passion!

Heavy-eyed, her body drained and loose with contentment, she sighed and rested her head against the crook of Esteban's arm, staring up at the spider's web in the angle of the rafters above them. Idly watching the spider's laborious spinning and spinning on the fairy threads that glistened in the patches of sunlight fingering through the broken windows, she knew she'd never be able to look at a spider's web again without remembering this moment in time. Never be able to walk through drifts of autumn leaves without remembering the crunches, the crackles and rustles of the leaves beneath them today as they made love. Strangely, she could remember nothing of the nights she and Miguel had coupled, unless it were the after-sensation that lingered like a foul taste on her tongue and left an aching emptiness and heaviness in her heart; the sense of being used, shamed, neither loved nor cherished, and unworthy of anything better. The only good thing that had come out of her disastrous marriage to Miguel had been her little Nicki, and God had taken him from her . . .

"I never dreamed anything could be so wonderful!" she whispered, and she dropped a kiss to Esteban's chest.

He chuckled, tousling her spill of inky curls where they pooled across his chest like the ripples of a dark stream. "Never? Ah, *querida,* I find that hard to believe! But—if it's praise you're fishing for—I'd say my guinea was well spent. And with interest!"

"Your guinea—!" she whispered, chilled to the heart by his callous words.

"*Sí, minina,* keep it!" he urged casually. "After all, you earned it, no?"

And he grinned and tweaked her nose, his words and his actions underlining that, for him, their passionate interlude had held no more significance or meaning than a romp in the hay with a willing servant girl, or a furtive mating with some faceless whore in a darkened alley, while for her—for her it had been—so—so very much more—!

A flood of such hatred rose through her, its bile stung the back of her throat like acid. He'd used her—used her as the whore he believed her to be! She meant nothing to him—no more than she'd meant to Miguel! With a strangled cry, she scrambled to her feet and snatched up her clothing, began hurriedly shrugging into her garments, clumsy with her upset and haste to be gone, to be anywhere but there, with him.

"Was it so distasteful you have to run about like a chicken without its head?" he demanded, looking aggrieved and irritable as he sat up. He ran his fingers through his disheveled hair, extracted a leaf from it, and scowled.

"*Sí!*" she spat at him, her golden eyes blazing like torches in the shadows. "Yes, it was loathsome, every minute of it! Wonderful? Ha, I lied! I've tumbled gouty old men who were better lovers than you! Young, fresh-cheeked boys who had more skill, more passion in their little fingers than you in your entire body!" she jeered, wanting to hurt him with words as he had hurt her.

"Liar!" he rasped. "You wanted me, too, *gitana*. You were as hot for me as I was for you, no matter how you deny it!"

"Wanted *you?*" she scoffed. "Wanted my blackmailer? Pah! Never! Don't make me laugh, San Martín! If you were the last man on this earth, I'd spit on you before I shared your bed again!" she raged "I hated your lovemaking, San Martín, maybe even more than I hate you! Well, you've had your golden guinea's worth of Krissoula Ballardo this afternoon, no? Lay a finger on me again, *hombre,* and I swear before God I'll cut it off—*and* anything else you might be stupid enough to point in my direction!"

She was halfway to the door when she halted and swung about to face him. Before he guessed her intent, she leaned down and dealt him a ringing slap across the face. Simultaneously, her booted foot slammed into his unprotected groin where he sat. The blow left fingerprints emblazoned in crimson tiger-stripes across his tanned flesh, she saw with satisfaction in the moment before he groaned and doubled over in agony.

And with that far from tender farewell, she whirled about and ran from him, from the hut, from her hurt, battling her way through the broken door and out into the sunlight.

"That *canallo!* That swine! That *bastardo!* That filthy, blackmailing whoreson cur!" she hissed as she scrambled onto Girasol's back, her tumbling hair a wild black mane down her back, her golden eyes hurling sparks. Mounted now, she glanced back over her shoulder to see if he'd tried to follow her, and saw him standing in the doorway, watching her with a murderous expression in his eyes. With a tight smile, she made a fist at him in the Italian fashion, and kicked her heels into Girasol's flanks. Without a backward glance, she rode away.

"You vicious little cat!" he gritted, wiping the trickle of blood from his lip on his knuckles as he stood there, guarding his bruised middle with his free hand. "But I'll tame you yet, Gypsy! By God, I swear it!"

Her breasts were still heaving with fury and in reaction when she returned to Sofía's side in the *quebracho* grove. A scarlet-capped blackbird was singing his heart out, and in her black mood, Krissoula could easily have wrung its joyful little neck.

Gracias a Dios, Sofía was still fast asleep, she saw, and a peek at her duenna's fob watch revealed she'd been gone less time than she'd feared. With shaking fingers, she raked her hair through to tidy it, twisted it into a knot, jammed on her hat to keep it in place, then put on her discarded jacket and boots once again.

"Sofía! Sofía!" she called sweetly when she was done, in as even a voice as she could manage, considering the violent, upsetting interlude with Esteban. "I believe it's time for us to start back!" She shook Sofía's shoulder, and the woman stirred and yawned. "Come on, Sofía, sit up with you! You poor dear, you still look half asleep, but we must start back if we're to reach home before nightfall. I'll tie Girasol to the back and drive the carriage for you, how about that?"

"Would you? *Gracias,* Krissoula, my dear. To be honest, my arms are still aching from this morning."

"I'll be happy to." In all honesty, her knees were still so rubbery she doubted she'd be able to ride anyway, thanks to that whoreson San Martín, God rot him!

The sun was just beginning its dive towards the horizon when Krissoula halted the carriage in the flagstoned stableyard of Tierra Rosa. The *casa grande* awaited them, cool and regal with her whitewashed adobe walls and red-tiled roofs rising proudly from amidst pretty gardens of green lawns and manicured shrubs, towering trees, and even a miniature lake fringed with irises nodding purple heads. The sight of the *hacienda* strengthened Krissoula's resolve. Truly, no man, however attractive, however *macho* and exciting he might be as a lover, was worth losing her chance to become mistress of all this—and especially not a man who'd never believe she was anything but a *puta*—! Perhaps she should thank San Martín for the valuable lesson he'd taught her today, she thought bitterly?

Tomás Cabral, the head groom, came out to take their mounts. He handed Krissoula down from the carriage, and lifted Sofía down after her.

"You had a pleasant time, I hope, ladies?" he murmured in his shy, engaging way.

"Very pleasant, *gracias,* Tomás. We must do it again very soon, mustn't we, Sofía?" Krissoula suggested, smiling at her duenna. Thankfully, to all outward appearances, she'd regained her lost composure during the long ride home.

Sofía gave a thin yet genuine smile in return. "Certainly! I would have no objection to doing it again. But, please—might we wait a few days until the stiffness from this time has passed?" Forcing herself to laugh lightly, Krissoula took her chaperone's elbow and steered her towards the main entrance of the house. "Of course, Sofía! But I promise you'll feel much better after a long soak in a hot tub," she promised. "You'll see . . ."

Tomás grinned at their conversation as he unfastened Girasol's reins from the rear of the carriage. Immediately, he examined the mare for injuries, as was his habit after each of the animals under his care had been ridden. Don Felipe was the type of rider he hated most; one who tore his horses' mouths with a brutal hand on the reins, and was overly fond of using his quirt. So fond of inflicting punishment that even Dorado, the biggest and most fearless among the stallions of Tierra Rosa, hated him. The huge beast snorted and kicked and acted up whenever Don Felipe so much as came near him! Doña Krissoula had also seemed a little on the headstrong side to Tomás, and he'd feared she might prove as rough on his precious horses as her betrothed. But to his relief, Girasol seemed not only sound after her experience, but even more affectionate and good-natured than usual. The outing had obviously done her good.

He was unsaddling the mare and had a stableboy, Pepe, waiting to water and curry her down when he was done, when Esteban strode into the stable, his expression like brooding thunderheads. Raised crimson welts showed against the sun-browned skin of his weathered cheek. Fingermarks? Tomás wondered silently, stifling a chuckle. *Dios,* she must be some woman to have refused the handsome Esteban's attentions! He was used to women falling into his hands like ripe plums off a tree!

Tomás opened his mouth to offer a greeting to his friend and inquire after the cause of his livid expression and the welts that accompanied them, but then thought better of it. Esteban had a notoriously foul temper, and an unpleasant habit of venting it upon whoever was handy at the time! Tomás had no ambition to be his unfortunate victim today. Pretty Estrella, the maid, had smiled shyly at him that morning as she swept the hall, and he wanted nothing unpleasant to mar such a golden day . . .

He'd steer clear of his friend until whatever "ill wind" that had caused Esteban's foul expression had blown past!

Chapter Six

There was an hour or two remaining before high tea once she'd finished taking her bath that afternoon, Krissoula realized as she briskly toweled herself dry, and she determined to put it to good use.

The fiery need to repay that damned San Martín for taking advantage of her that afternoon still burned hot and fierce in her breast, and what better way to have a glorious revenge than by finding the papers he so desperately wanted—and destroying them, she thought wickedly! Perhaps she'd even tell him she'd done so, and laugh in scorn when she saw the anguish in his face. Ah, by Saint Sara, she swore, that rutting *gorgio* bull would learn the hard way that it was dangerous to cross a Gypsy!

In light of her ambitions, it seemed foolish to waste even a moment, when Don Felipe could return any day now from his business trip to the city. Her systematic rifling of every nook and cranny the sprawling *casa grande* possessed would have to be far more furtive once he'd returned. Her opportunities to search the place might be few and far between—or even nonexistent. She'd feel far more secure, she decided, if she had her hands on the papers that cursed San Martín had blackmailed her to find *before* Felipe returned. With all proof of her betrothed's illegitimate nephew's claim to Tierra Rosa removed, her future as the wife of the wealthy *hacendero,* Don Felipe de Aguilar, would be secure, while as long as even the slimmest chance that some written proof of Alejandro de Aguilar's acknowledgment of Esteban as his son and heir existed, she'd never be able to breathe easily . . .

When she'd dried off, she threw on a yellow silk robe and tied the sash tightly about her waist before slipping out into the long corridor. She looked up and down it, then breathed a sigh of relief. Good! It was quite empty. She slipped down the corridor, her movements sure and swift, with no hint of uncertainty.

81

The suite she intended to search lay at the very end of the long corridor, the door facing down it. In answer to her casual inquiries several days ago, the maids Luisa and Estrella had referred to it as the entry to "poor Doña Manuela's apartments." The door, she'd discovered days ago, was kept locked—had been since the death of *la patrona* years ago. But that little tidbit of information hadn't fazed Krissoula, *Dios,* no! The long, sturdy hairpin she carried in her palm would make short work of such a simple lock as that one.

Sure enough, after only a few moments the lock clicked open in answer to her pryings, and she was inside. Quietly she closed and bolted the door from within, then let out a relieved sigh as she looked about her.

Tall French windows, draped in swags of lace and blue brocade, afforded glorious views in two directions from the room, one of the distant misty mountains to the west, the other of the courtyard and the formal gardens beyond it. The furniture—a heavy four-poster bed and various chaises and chairs, dressers and bureaus—had been sheeted to keep them free of dirt. The air was heavy with old sunshine, dust, and—*sí,* the faintest traces of a woman's perfume— lily of the valley, perhaps?—that still lingered long after the woman who'd favored it had been dead for many years.

Krissoula frowned and bit her lip. Searching Felipe's study, bedchamber, and the library downstairs had given her not a moment's pause, but, strangely, she felt guilty, an intruder here. It was as if, in some peculiar way, Manuela de Córdoba y Aguilar's spirit still hovered here, and deplored the wicked Krissoula's ruthless search of her mortal possessions.

"*Tonta!* Fool!" she scolded herself for such fanciful thoughts, and superstitiously made the sign to ward off the evil eye, her hackles prickling nonetheless as she crouched before one sturdily fashioned, carved dresser. Flinging up the dust sheet, she yanked out a dresser drawer to begin her search.

You could tell a great deal about someone by what they kept in their personal drawers, Krissoula reflected as she systematically searched the suite of two rooms. The woman Manuela, she decided, had been a totally feminine creature, one who favored underthings edged in yards of exquisite lace, and whose taste in colors was—in Krissoula's personal opinion—deplorably pastel. There were several gowns hanging in an armoire, still in excellent condition. All had been cleaned and pressed and shrouded in black tissue paper to keep their fragile colors unyellowed by time. Rose-pink, dove-gray, gray-blue, off-white—pretty enough colors, to be sure, but Krissoula thought with a grimace that she far preferred her own vital hues of gold and flame and scarlet. Now, there were colors that lived and breathed!

Continuing her search, she found drawers neatly arranged with dozens of pairs of gloves, some kid or silk, others sturdy wool. Other drawers held nothing but shawls and fans, silk stockings and lace collars, and frilly garters. There was precious little paperwork of any kind to be sifted through! What there was fluttered from between the pages of a thick book to the polished floor when she drew it forth from the back of a narrow drawer.

Expensively calf-bound but worn, the book's pages were secured by a little padlock. The small slips of paper had been too narrow to be hampered by the clasp, and had slipped free. Krissoula knelt to pick up the little slips of thick paper and scanned them curiously. There was a receipt or two, much yellowed by time, obviously for some of the feminine folderols she'd already found in the drawers. Also, a beautifully penned list of possible Christmas gifts to be purchased, with the prospective recipient's name neatly written alongside it.

Alejandro—a new saddle of córdoban leather? Inquire of Domingo Cabral.

Maria de San Martín—a silver rosary to replace the one she lost last month?

Mama—a vicuña wrap?

There were more entries, all on the same thoughtful note, but Krissoula found herself unable to read any further. *Madre,* it was so very sad, this little Christmas list for people now long dead, penned by a woman who was likewise gone, she thought, feeling an uncomfortable lump form in her throat. Had Manuela given her loved ones the gifts she'd planned so carefully? Had they liked them? And had the thoughtful gift intended for Maria de San Martín ever been given—or discarded when Manuela learned that the woman she'd considered her friend had been her husband Alejandro's mistress and, furthermore, had borne him a child out of wedlock?

Her curiosity thoroughly piqued now, Krissoula used her hairpin and tried to pry open the padlock that bound the book's yellow-edged pages, but it was rusted and refused to budge. Definitely a job for her nail file! With a shrug, she tucked the book under her arm, intending to take it back to her own room and examine it at leisure. It was probably nothing more exciting than a household accounting ledger, the accounting book in which Manuela, as mistress of Tierra Rosa, had jotted down her expenses for running the *casa grande,* but she was reluctant to leave any possible avenues unexplored.

There was nothing else worth looking at a second time here, she decided—nothing that could either help Esteban, or harm her. With a quick glance about the suite to make sure that everything was exactly as she'd found it, she turned and started towards the door, pulling up short with a startled cry at what she saw directly ahead.

A life-size painting of a woman, framed in ornate gilded wood, reached almost from ceiling to floor. In the dying rays of the afternoon sunshine that fingered through the lace draperies to touch the faded oils, the woman had, at first glance, seemed alive! Indeed, Krissoula's second thought—hot on the heels of her initial shock—had been that she was looking into a mirror, for the woman reclining gracefully on a low chaise, her pastel blue skirts swirled elegantly about her and a long-haired lapdog curled at her feet, was her double!

She stepped towards the painting, unable to believe what her eyes were telling her, but even close up, it was still so. With the exception of one feature, the face she was looking into might well have been her own, painted on a day when she was taken by a rare serene frame of mind!

The hair was the same inky black as her own, a riot of raven curls forced into glossy order by pins and brush and curling tongs. The complexion was the same, a flawless beige and gold, as was hers, the rich curve of the lips no less generous and sensual. Only the eyes differed, in that, unlike her own golden-brown ones, the woman's eyes were deep blue, a lovely contrast against the inky ringlets of her elaborately dressed hair. A small brass plaque had been attached to the bottom of the picture frame which read, *"Doña Manuela Inocencia de Córdoba y Aguilar."*

A piece of the puzzle suddenly dropped into place! Looking at the painting, she knew immediately why Esteban de San Martín had been so astonished the first time he'd seen her. He'd obviously seen this portrait, too, and had recognized immediately her startling resemblance to the long-dead Manuela! She frowned. But, that being the case, what had led Esteban to believe her resemblance to the woman would guarantee Don Felipe's attraction to her? What had Esteban known—or suspected—about his hated uncle's feelings for the woman? Could Felipe have been in love with his sister-in-law—was that the answer? *Sí,* it must be! It was the only answer that made sense! And knowing that much,

Esteban could have been reasonably certain that her appearance would guarantee Felipe's notice, at the very least!

Had Manuela returned Felipe's love, she wondered idly, or remained faithful both in spirit and body to her husband? Krissoula shook her head. The clothes in the armoires and drawers, the feelings and impressions she'd gathered about the woman, suggested not. Manuela, she felt strongly, had not been a woman to cheat on her husband. For her, marriage would have been forever, a holy oath taken before God and a priest that bound her to the grave. But—perhaps she was wrong? Perhaps those blue eyes that had gazed so serenely, so innocently, at the artist, had been as deceptive as they were lovely . . . ? Only Felipe knew the answer to that question, and Krissoula suspected her close-mouthed *novio* would keep it that way!

With the leather-bound book tucked snugly under her arm, she slipped from the room and back out into the empty corridor. A quick glance assured her she was alone. Crouching down, she relocked the door, then sped down the hallway, back to her room.

"Why, Señor San Martín! I'd no idea you'd planned to pay us a call this evening?" Krissoula gritted, livid to see that loathsome man once again the very same evening, this time standing below her in the hallway alongside a giggly, smiling Sofía. "To what do we owe the—honor—of your visit? I do hope there's no trouble with the *estancia*—or the stock, perhaps?" she asked with a calm coolness she was far from feeling.

"Fortunately neither, Doña Krissoula," Esteban replied, playing the perfect *mayordomo* to her perfect *patrona,* curse him. "I'm happy to say this is merely a social call on my part."

"How very nice," Krissoula ground out, thinking something else entirely. Wearing a plastered-on crocodile smile so forced and fixed it made her jaws ache, she moved with a dancer's grace down the last three steps of the staircase as Esteban de San Martín came towards her across the black-and-white tiled hallway.

Knowing Sofía was watching them from the drawing-room door now, the ever-vigilant duenna, she politely accepted his bow and offered her hand to be kissed, wondering if—after what had happened that afternoon, and the manner in which she'd taken her leave of him—he might actually *bite* off a finger, rather than kiss it!

He did nothing untoward, to her relief. He merely kissed her hand, straightened, and offered her his arm with a gallant inclining of his head and a foxy smile. With such a lead, she had no choice but to let him escort her across the hallway and into the *sala,* the very image of the perfect hostess!

"I've an unexpected business problem to take care of at the Aguilar salting plant near Córdoba tomorrow morning," he announced in a carrying voice that Sofía could not help but hear unless she'd suddenly become deaf. "The problem could take several days to resolve. I thought, in Don Felipe's absence, I should let you know where I'll be, and reassure you that in the event of any trouble here, Tomás Cabral will be in charge of the *estancia* during my absence. He's a reliable man, Tomás. You need have no concern on that score, doña."

"Oh, I'm sure he is!" Krissoula murmured, anxious to be rid of him. "And, since you no doubt have many last-minute details to attend to if you're planning on an early departure in the morning, I won't keep you a moment longer, *mayordomo. Vaya con Dios.*"

She extended her hand in farewell, obviously intending that that be an end to their conversation, but San Martín had other ideas. He merely smiled and ignored her hand.

"To be honest I'd not intended to stay, Doña Krissoula, for the very reason you so cleverly guessed—my hope to make an early start tomorrow. However, before you joined us Doña Sofía graciously suggested that I join you both for dinner, and I accepted. I trust you have no objections, doña?"

His black brows raised in cool, mocking inquiry over his piercing sapphire eyes, and Krissoula thought—not for the first time—what a wonderful actor the unprincipled cur would have made, under different circumstances. That *diablo* looked as if warm butter wouldn't melt in his mouth!

"I, object? But of course not, my dear *mayordomo!*" she purred silkily. "Why on earth should I! Felipe's trusted *employees* will always be welcome guests in my—our—home."

He smiled disarmingly despite her deliberate insult, and it was a smile that only Krissoula would have recognized as conspiratorial as well as amused.

"How gracious of you, as always, doña! And may I also say that you're looking lovelier each time I have the good fortune to see you? Gold is obviously your color, señorita," he complimented her with a mocking bow, and it was no lie. The gorgeous little bitch! With her raven hair, her slanted golden eyes, and her petitely rounded body set off by the full tissue skirts of the gown, she was exquisite!

"You're far too kind, señor!" she said coyly, making him a little curtsey. "To be honest, this particular gown holds very special memories for me. You see, I commissioned your famous South American designer, Maximilio, to create this very gown especially for me. I wanted something to commemorate my final triumph at the Ópera Florida, you see. Ah, how wonderful it was!" she declared, her eyes sparkling. "After my last dance, the audience stood and demanded encore after encore, and all those wonderful, silly young men tossed yellow roses onto the stage at my feet and called me their 'Queen of Flamenco'—didn't they, Sofía," she continued airily with a glance at the duenna, who nodded. Fingering the tiny gold-silk rosebuds that trimmed the plunging neckline and skirts of the gown as she did so, she eyed Esteban over her fan and asked flirtatiously, "So! Was Felipe's money well spent, señor?"

"It was, indeed! He's still not back from the city, I take it?"

"No, not yet," she confirmed with a wicked little smile. "That's why I thought I'd wear this gown tonight, since Felipe loathes to see me in bright colors. Aren't I naughty?" She smiled beguilingly. "Alas, we don't expect *el patrón* back until the ninth of the month, next Saturday."

"Independence Day? Then it's unlikely Don Felipe will be back until at least the day after? He's more *porteño,* city man, than *hacendero,* after all, Doña Krissoula, and anyone who's anyone stays on in Buenos Aires for the weekend celebrations. It's as much a chance to make business contacts and cement new deals as a patriotic celebration, you see."

Krissoula shrugged airily. "On the contrary, I'm confident Don Felipe will be home on Saturday, Independence Day or no! You see, before he left, he instructed the servants to prepare a grand *asado* for that very day, and had Sofía send invitations to all the neighboring *estancias* for the occasion—didn't he, Sofía? Oh, dear! I see you didn't know anything about that?" she amended as his eyes snapped like blue steel and his brows lifted in surprise. "But I'm sure you'll find your invitation awaiting you on your return home, no?" She added with a sly smile, "Don Felipe also hinted that he intends to make the official announcement of our betrothal that evening, so you see, I'm certain he'll be back just as planned, because he promised." She smiled and fluttered her lashes. "Certainly my company rivals that of any old business associates, wouldn't you say, Señor de San Martín?" she asked with a charming little pout that made her lips seductively full.

Esteban smiled a thin, mirthless smile. "Oh, I've been hopeful on exactly the same score, my dear—as well you know! However," he added, still using the same lower, threatening voice that only Krissoula could hear, "seeing you here, acting the grand lady of the manor in every respect and obviously enjoying the role to the hilt, I feel I should caution you about becoming overly comfortable here, or too confident of your hold over Aguilar. Need I remind you, *querida*, that—despite what happened this afternoon—*both* situations are merely temporary?" he menaced.

"But of course!" she agreed with a little trill of disclaiming laughter. "Poor, poor Señor de San Martín! Surely you didn't think I could have convinced myself otherwise?"

"In a word, yes! You're a clever, vicious little cat, and you've become adept at playing the grand lady, Krissoula. I wouldn't put it past you to think you could go on playing it indefinitely, just to try and get back at me! Why, I could almost forget you were ever other than what you appear myself—*if* I knew no better."

"Why, thank you, señor! You *did* intend that remark as a compliment, didn't you?" she asked, brows arched innocently.

"Yes, you minx—but don't let it go to your head," Esteban growled, unable to help a smile. Immoral little gold-digger she might be, but she could be a damned engaging one when the fancy took her! Despite the dull ache that still lingered in his vitals from her well-placed foot that afternoon, he realized that, miraculously, he still desired her—perhaps more than ever. He looked up, and caught her wearing a peculiar expression on her face, definitely secretive and maybe even a little smug. What was she up to now, the tricky minx, he wondered? Revenge? "And however appealing it may seem, Krissoula," he warned her, certain he'd not misinterpreted her expression, "don't make the mistake of hitching your wagon to Felipe's star! When I'm done with him, he'll be ruined—finished!" he added, and his sapphire eyes gleamed with anticipation.

"You must hate him very much?" she observed softly.

"Hate? No. The hatred's long since burned itself out. Despise would be a better word," the Argentine corrected curtly. "I despise him!"

"And your uncle's never suspected that you feel this way?"

"Oh, Felipe knows how I feel about him all right!" Esteban said with feeling. "And he doesn't enjoy the situation one little bit! He's forbidden me entry to the house, but although he fears what I might discover—and with good reason, eh?—he needs me here to run things for him, and so his hands are tied in many ways." He grinned.

"One day, some day, he'll slip up, and I'll be here, waiting . . ."

A little shiver ran down Krissoula's back at the cold, calculating way Esteban said this. *Dios,* the violent undertones she sensed in the man before her were frightening! If he should ever seriously suspect she intended to double-cross him, *caray,* her very *life* might well be in danger, she thought, suddenly robbed of breath by the anxiety rising through her!

She was grateful for the sudden entry of the maids and Mama Angelina, bearing the meal. The electric tension in the air dissipated, and with it, her feelings of panic.

"Well, we simply must talk more over supper!" she suggested brightly, in a much louder voice for Sofía's benefit. "Come, *señor mayordomo,* you shall sit here, on the right, next to me," Krissoula gestured with the air of the perfect hostess, taking her own seat at the head of the heavy table as if to the manor born. "And you, Sofía dear, if you would sit opposite Señor San Martín . . . ?"

The supper was, as Angelina had promised earlier that day, Krissoula's favorite, chicken with savory rice, but first they were served a platter of various cheeses, salads of tiny tomatoes and onions, and crisp lettuce leaves with a tangy, vinegar-based dressing, accompanied by bread that was still warm and crusty from the oven. They ate with enjoyment, interspersing their appreciation of the delicious foods with idle conversation.

"I've never been so hungry!" Sofía remarked, finishing her dessert much later with unusual gusto. "Our outing today must have given me an appetite."

"Outing?" Esteban echoed politely, innocently, sipping his cup of thick black coffee.

"*Sí,* Don Esteban. This morning, Señorita Krissoula and I went riding, across the Pampa," Sofía confided.

"Alone?"

"Why, yes!"

"Do you think it was wise, to allow such an excursion? I very much doubt that Don Felipe would have permitted such an outing, were he here!" Esteban exclaimed, scowling. His dark-sapphire eyes snapped angrily, and his sensual lips thinned.

Krissoula saw Sofía's rare smile fade into a worried frown, and leaped to her crestfallen duenna's rescue. She did so as much to anger Esteban and to try to ensure that there'd be similar freedoms permitted her in the future, as to rescue the poor little woman from his wrath.

"Oh, come, come, Señor San Martín, you make far too much of

nothing! Why, there was nothing wrong in what we did—and Sofía never left my side for an instant, did you, dear Sofía, so my reputation was in no way compromised."

"Never, Sofía confirmed, tight-lipped. "The *niña* was at my side constantly."

"There, you see?" she challenged Esteban, daring him to contradict her at his own peril. "If you want to scold someone, then you must scold me, not my Sofía, the poor dear! I badgered her into it!"

Krissoula tilted her lovely head to one side and eyed Esteban challengingly through hooded golden eyes as she ran her fingertip slowly around and around the wet rim of her wineglass. "Besides," she continued throatily, "boredom tends to make me reckless, Señor San Martín. And when I grow reckless, I do wicked things— things I often bitterly regret later. I'm sure you'd agree that Don Felipe would much prefer I found a fitting outlet for my energy, such as horse riding, rather than becoming . . . reckless?"

Their eyes met, and Esteban was forced to back down under the implied challenge in her golden ones, much to his annoyance. He knew quite well what she was threatening: to do something— anything!—that would jeopardize the success of his plans! Perhaps even tell his uncle what had transpired in the line-camp hut that afternoon? And, knowing Krissoula as well as he'd come to know her over the past year, he didn't doubt for an instant that she was capable of carrying through with her threats! She was greedy, he knew, but she was also headstrong and proud. The large sum of money that he'd agreed to settle on her once she'd served his purpose could only go so far to keep her in line. If he pressed her too far—as he had once already today—her volatile temper might well explode. Once it did, she might just as easily toss caution to the winds and tell him in no uncertain terms what he could do with his money than stick to their deal! Frowning, he wondered not for the first time if he'd been a fool to choose Krissoula for what he intended. Better, perhaps, if he'd found someone more biddable, more easily controlled; less like a loaded pistol about to go off at any second . . . But—where else would he have found another whose looks suited his purpose so perfectly, they'd practically guaranteed the success of his plan—? Her resemblance to Manuela was uncanny.

"Oh, very well," he conceded with a furious scowl. "My apologies, ladies! I suppose I overreacted a little, but in Don Felipe's absence . . . well, I feel it's my duty to see you come to no harm. The foothills are crawling with bandits, you know, and the thought of the two of you, out there without an escort, alarmed me more than I can say!" His sapphire eyes bored into Krissoula's. "I'm certain your ride was quite proper, señorita, but you know how dear your safety and reputation are to our beloved *patrón's* heart!" He added silkily, "I'd never be able to forgive myself if anything— terrible—happened to you." He turned to the duenna and inclined his head contritely. "Please, forgive me for snapping at you, Doña Sofía?"

"Your apology is accepted, señor," Sofía readily accepted, and actually blushed as the *mayordomo* flashed her a dazzling, contrite smile, Krissoula noted with disgust. "But now, if you'll excuse me, I have some correspondence I must attend to before retiring, time permitting." She glanced at her fob watch and then at the one on the wall, and frowned. "*Dios,* my watch is over an hour slow! How on earth could that be—? Ah, well, no matter! I'll be just next door if you should need me, *niña,"* she told Krissoula pointedly, indicating she would be within shouting distance. "Good night, my child— and a good night to you, too, Don Esteban."

San Martín moved gallantly to her chair, and pulled it back for her. She thanked him with a shy smile, turning beet-red upon meeting his eyes as she did so.

"Good night, Sofía!" Krissoula called sweetly after her duenna as she left them for the adjoining room.

Alone with Krissoula now, the need for his pose as no more than her betrothed's faithful ranch manager dispensed with somewhat by Sofía's exit, Esteban relaxed his guard. He unbuttoned his formal jacket and poured himself a hefty brandy. Extracting a small pair of special clippers from an inner pocket, he drew a slim cheroot from Don Felipe's own humidor, which had been set on a grotesque, ornately carved side table. He snipped off the end and lit it, exhaling with obvious pleasure. Fragrant blue smoke spiraled up to the high ceiling, wreathing about the dark beams and the ornate chandelier, which was ablaze with stubby candles.

"You should be more careful, San Martín," Krissoula cautioned. "Sofía is very proper, the perfect duenna. Make a habit of scolding her in that way, and she'll start wondering what business it is of yours what Don Felipe's betrothed does! She might even seek another position, and then where would you be?"

"Once you've found the papers I need, the old dragon's usefulness will have come to an end, so why worry? I hired her only for appearance' sake, after all. You couldn't have played the part of the carefully chaperoned young lady of breeding without her, Krissoula, what with dancers and actresses being considered of notoriously loose morals nowadays, eh?" He grinned.

"Don't you think I know that?" she snapped crossly. "That's the whole point I'm trying to make! That if Sofía hadn't acted *precisely* like the fussy old-maid chaperone that she is—hovering over me, demanding my gentlemen admirers never visit with me unless she was present also—Don Felipe would never have given me the time of day, let alone believed me sufficiently virtuous to court and propose to! For that, if nothing else, you should be nice to Sofía, señor! The success of your plan owes just as much to her as it does to me. The poor old thing! She believes she's to stay on here as my companion after the wedding. What'll she do once she learns my betrothal was all a hoax, that her future is far from secure? How will she live when that day comes? We both know that once you've pulled off your little triumph, neither she nor I will be welcolme within a thousand miles of Tierra Rosa! I know I can survive, San Martín, but what about poor Sofía? Did you consider her at all?"

"What concern is it of yours?" he demanded. "You do your job, get your money, and then you'll be free to go where you wish." His ebony brows rose as he regarded Krissoula thoughtfully over the rim of the brandy snifter. "*Qué?* Surely you're not being pricked by a twinge of conscience, my cold-hearted *minina,* not at this late date? Well, well, what a surprise! I didn't think you had a conscience—or a heart, for that matter!"

"I don't," she snapped back, irritated. "But Sofía's no longer a young woman, nor an independent sort. I don't think she can survive on wits alone. Certainly she'll never find another position as chaperone, not after your little scheme comes to its successful conclusion! *Dios,* you're a cold bastard!"

"*Dios,* aren't I!" he rejoined with a sardonic chuckle. "But I don't recollect hearing you complain before—nor offering to share your future wealth with Sofía—despite your concern. Would you rather have stayed where I found you, in the filthy slums of Barcelona, earning your livelihood on your back?"

She winced. "You know better than to ask!"

"Then forget about Sofía. You can make a good life for yourself with the money that will be yours when this is over and done with. And thanks to me, you can use your dancing talents in a way that will make you somebody! Who knows, with your art, combined with the breeding and culture the tutors I hired gave you, you might even land yourself a wealthy husband! Certainly you'll never have to sell yourself again, unless you wish to. Not bad for a thieving little Gypsy whore, eh?"

She felt the blood drain from her face at his easy insult, and anger and denial rose in a scalding flood inside her. She'd told him she was no whore just this afternoon, but obviously she might as well have held her tongue, for all the good it had done her. He'd taken her anyway, and now seemed inclined to act as if it had never happened, God rot him! Well, his day would come, and then—! Why, he'd be laughing on the other side of his face! And so, despite her anger, she said not a single word in self-defense, instead sipping her wine with a sulky, thoughtful expression.

She and Hector had been masters in the risky game they'd played, true; she the pretty, inviting bait in the trap that brought the men running, Hector the muscle to step in if her cheated customers turned nasty or awoke too soon from the drugged wine she'd slipped them. If things had continued the way they were headed, though, she probably would have been forced to sell herself long before this, if not for the man sitting beside her. She sighed. Like it or not, in a perverse way San Martín had proven her salvation with his blackmailer's threats. Without his forceful means of persuasion, she'd have fled that night, gone back to her old life, and might well have resorted to whoring for her daily bread by now. Then so be it, San Martín, she thought bitterly, her golden eyes narrowing. Go ahead. Think what you will! Call me what you wish! I'm done arguing the point. One day, you'll learn that you've overestimated your control over little Krissoula, but by then—ah, yes, it will be far too late! By then, I'll be mistress here . . .

Her lips glistened with moisture when she set the glass aside, and she delicately licked them with the tip of her small pink tongue in a way calculated to bother Esteban. True to her expectations, he noted the provocative gesture and his scowl deepened—in direct proportion to the sudden shock of arousal that stabbed through him.

"What's going on in that devious little mind of yours now, Krissoula?"

"I was wondering just exactly what it is I've gotten myself into," she retorted. "Why don't you level with me, San Martín, and tell me everything? It could benefit us both if I knew *exactly* what it is you hope to accomplish, and why?"

He said nothing for a few moments, but continued smoking with a thoughtful expression for some time before nodding agreement. "Perhaps you're right," he allowed. "There are certain risks in-

93

volved, and I suppose it's only fair you should know exactly what you're up against, since your life might very well be in danger."

"My life!" she exclaimed, sitting bolt upright, all ears and eyes now. "Not at Felipe's hands?"

"Ah, *sí,*" Esteban confirmed, watching her expression. "Especially at your precious Felipe's hands!"

"Oh, come now, señor! Just because you dislike the man doesn't mean he's capable of murder!" Krissoula denied.

"Liking or disliking him has nothing to do with it, little fool," Esteban countered. "You see, I have reason to suspect he's killed once before. What's to stop him doing so again, if his ambitions are thwarted?"

"Ah. Your father, yes?" she guessed at once by the grim expression he wore.

"*Sí,* my father," he agreed in a tone laced heavily with bitterness. "You see, Krissoula, according to our laws here in Argentina, all property is divided equally between a man's male heirs upon his death. Accordingly, my grandfather's will split his properties equally between his two sons, Felipe and Alejandro. Alejandro, my father and the youngest of the brothers, received Tierra Rosa, a summer house at Mar de la Plata, the vineyards, and the *saladero*— the meat-salting plant near Córdoba—upon his death. Felipe, the eldest, received the Aguilars' comfortable city residences in Buenos Aires and down in Rio, and the lucrative Aguilar import and exporting business based in Brazil, which dealt in furs for the European markets, orchids, and in supplying exotic South American animals for the European zoological gardens, and so on.

"But although both benefited equally from my grandfather's death, Felipe was greedy. He'd always been jealous of his younger brother, Alejandro, and he coveted this *estancia.* To my mind, in light of that jealousy and Felipe's sorry financial state at the time, coupled with the circumstances surrounding it, my father's sudden death was more than suspicious."

"But even should you disprove your uncle's claim to Tierra Rosa, what court would recognize the claim of Alejandro de Aguilar's bast—illegitimate son?" Krissoula asked with a shrewd grasp of the situation that took Esteban by surprise.

He looked at her through new eyes as he explained, "Illegitimate children may also inherit here in Argentina, provided they were officially recognized as their father's offspring during his lifetime. But, as you know, I've been unable to find any written proof that Alejandro officially acknowledged me as his son prior to his death.

Nothing would please me more, Krissoula, than to see Tierra Rosa taken from Felipe! The *estancia* belongs to me, not my father's murderer! Living here, within Tierra Rosa's walls, you have both the time and the opportunity to make a thorough search, which I certainly don't. Find me the proof I need to claim what is rightfully mine, and you'll find me a generous man."

The brandy had mellowed him considerably, Krissoula thought, stealing a glance at him from beneath her sooty eyelashes. He seemed amicable now, almost friendly—and, curse him, he looked so devastatingly handsome with the candlelight gleaming in his jet-black hair and softening his tanned, angular face! Remembering that afternoon, her heart beat a little faster as she murmured, "I'll do everything I can, rest assured, señor."

"Despite this afternoon?" he asked, almost holding his breath, and she wondered if he'd read her mind.

"No. Because of it!" she retorted, lying through her teeth. She smiled thinly. "I'm doubly anxious to be gone from here now, you see!"

He ignored her dig and asked, "Where have you gone through so far?"

"Well, let's see. I searched the drawers in Felipe's desk the first day he was away, and then the personal papers he keeps hidden in a small casket in his room the day after." She grinned impishly, and her golden eyes danced with mischief. "The lock was but child's play—I picked it easily with a hairpin, ánd *el patrón* 'll be none the wiser when he gets back! But—I found nothing inside but bills and angry letters from impatient creditors demanding he pay them! You suspect Don Felipe found the document you need and destroyed it soon after he came to Tierra Rosa, don't you?" she guessed from his expression.

Esteban shrugged, his sapphire eyes veiled. "I've always hoped not, but—who knows? If there was some written proof, it's unlikely that Felipe would have kept it, when it could be so dangerous to him to do so, don't you think? On the brighter side, perhaps he found nothing himself, but suspects that such damning documents exist? After all, why else would he have reason to fear me? Why would he forbid me entry to the house? But then, my dear uncle is a law unto himself. Who knows what he'd do!"

"What makes you think your father didn't die a natural death?"

"They said he must have fallen unconscious in the stables after he returned from riding—apoplexy, the doctors suggested—and been trampled to death by his favorite stallion. But it's always felt like

95

too much of a coincidence to me that he should die the very eve of the day he planned to officially recognize me as his sole heir at a grand fiesta—especially when Felipe had arrived that same day in something of an upset, begging my father to make him a hefty loan to get his creditors off his back! But—no one will ever know the truth for certain now, eh? We can only guess! Alejandro's buried here at Tierra Rosa, beside Doña Manuela. Ironic, is it not, that he should share his wife's last resting place throughout eternity, when he never shared her bed when they were wed!"

"Sí. That Manuela was a cold bitch, from what I've heard!" Krissoula commented offhandedly in her gutter Spanish, and yelped in pain as Esteban's fingers suddenly closed about her slender wrist and squeezed so hard, she thought the bone would snap in two!

"Manuela," he rasped harshly, "was by all accounts a lovely woman of virtue, beauty, and sweetness. In essence, she was all that you—despite your similarity in looks—could never hope to be!"

Slowly, he released her wrist and scowled at her across the table as she watched the red marks he'd caused fade slowly away. "My father loved his wife very dearly until her death. He made it plain to me that, despite the distasteful gossip about their unhappy marriage, he had no regrets. He never uttered a word of blame for her inability to be a true wife to him—and nor can I permit anyone else to speak ill of the woman when she can no longer defend herself."

Rubbing her painful wrist, Krissoula nodded contritely. "I'm sorry."

The anger drained out of him in a heavy sigh. He was no longer the angry, threatening figure he'd appeared moments before, but a man who believed he'd been cheated of a father and a future by a man he hated, and now had little more than his thirst for revenge and justice to give his life purpose—with precious little hope of obtaining either. She almost pitied him as he nodded, draining the brandy snifter to the dregs.

"You're forgiven, minina, but I'd prefer that we speak no more of Manuela, nor her unhappy life. In fact, I must insist that we do not! It's a painful subject for me, under the circumstances, knowing my father loved her far more than he ever loved my mother, his mistress Maria de San Martín.

"Now, it's getting late, and a long ride home still lies ahead of me. I must be on my way."

"Can we look forward to seeing you at the asado?"

"With or without an invitation, I wouldn't miss it for the world!" he murmured with a grin. "Thank you for a most delightful dinner, Doña Krissoula, and please offer my deepest regrets to your *novio* that I missed him tonight."

A heavy lacing of sarcasm tainted his louder, formal farewell for Sofía's benefit in the adjoining room as he took her hand and bowed low over it, brushing his lips against her knuckles as he murmured a parting warning. "And remember what I said, *cara mía,* and don't get too fond of your role! It's only temporary, after all, you do understand that . . . ?"

Moments later he had gone, leaving Krissoula frowning after him in deep thought. Well! That was news! Felipe, a possible murderer? To be honest, she wouldn't put it past him! There was a certain look in his cold eyes that hinted at a ruthless streak running through him.

Still pondering what she'd learned, she called Sofía to inform her that the *mayordomo* had left, then summoned Luisa and Estrella to clear the supper table and snuff out the candles. Within minutes following Esteban's departure, she and Sofía had retired to their rooms to prepare for bed.

After she'd undressed and brushed out her hair, she went out onto the balcony to take the air before going to sleep.

Standing there in the silvery-gray moonlight, she inhaled the cool night breeze that ruffled her unbound hair and fanned her bare arms. Along with the rich scents of dew-moistened earth, lavender, and gardenias, she fancied she could also discern the fragrant smoke of Esteban's cigar, rising from the courtyard below.

Idly curious as to why he should have lingered at Tierra Rosa when he'd implied he was headed directly for home, she leaned over the balcony and searched the shadows below her window. Sure enough, there was a man standing down there, as she'd thought. She could see the red tip of his slim cigarillo glowing like a single red satin eye within the velvety darkness. As the man tossed the cigarillo to the ground and stepped forward from the dense shrubbery to stub it out, she saw by the way he moved that it was Esteban, after all.

As if sensing her eyes upon him, he glanced up towards her balcony, and for a second, as the moonlight glinted in his eyes and on the silver buckle at his belt, she was certain his sapphire-dark eyes could penetrate the night, and that he could see her there, looking down at him!

Involuntarily, she gasped and quickly drew back into the

concealing shadows of her room, relieved she'd been too lazy to light the lamp. Had she done so, it would have illuminated her from behind, and Esteban couldn't have failed to see her standing there in only her filmy chemise, silently watching him. She grimaced. *Caramba!* She had no wish to give that arrogant brute the satisfaction of knowing she was spying on him, not after what had happened this afternoon. It might give him lusty ideas again . . .

Her heart pounding, she remained frozen in place by the French windows as the melancholy sound of whistling rose, sweetly haunting, on the cool night air, grew fainter as Esteban strode from the courtyard and away to wherever it was he made his bed. The song he whistled was a popular *Triste,* one of the old and not-quite-decent *gaucho* ballads lamenting a faithless sweetheart. This one had been popular in the cafés and bars of the common people of lively Buenos Aires when she'd danced at the Ópera Florida in the city two months ago:

> *. . . So beware, my young gauchos, of women,*
> *And learn from a fellow like me.*
> *While you remain constant as flowers,*
> *They'll flit bloom to bloom, like the bee . . . !*

As the whistling grew fainter, she leaned back against the wall, trembling all over. Her face grew hot as she closed her eyes and pressed her clenched fists to her racing heart, for she could recall in infinite detail the way Esteban's lips had felt as they savagely devoured her own that afternoon: the feel of his hard, virile body mastering her softer curves as she lay helpless beneath him. The sensations those memories recalled made shivers of excitement lick through her body like tongues of fire. *Dios,* how he had throbbed with power between her thighs, like a virile young fighting bull, and, *caramba,* the unexpected pleasures he'd awakened her to—!

I want him.

That blackmailing bastard! No matter how he's used me, I want him again!

A quiver of yearning uncurled in her belly. It remained there, a tiny, feathery-liquid pulse that tickled maddeningly. Her nipples swelled into aching buds that yearned for the caress of his hands and the sweet torment of his lips, growing so sensitive she crossed her arms over her breasts to ease the bittersweet pain. Once—so long ago it seemed a lifetime past!—she'd been a gentle, giving woman, eager to love and be loved in return. She'd thought that softer, passionate side of her nature forever dead and buried, along with Miguel and her past. But today, Esteban had resurrected that other, fiery Krissoula, brought her back to painful, feeling life again with his ardent lovemaking . . .

Madre, *how she wanted him! How her body hungered for his!*

Somehow, she must stop this craziness she was feeling, before it raged like wildfire out of control and consumed her, left her plans in ashes! She closed her eyes and moved her lips in silent prayer, beseeching El Señor to give her the strength to resist her sinful desires for Esteban. Yet her prayers went unanswered. Even when she fell into a restless sleep after tossing and turning for what seemed like hours, it was Esteban's devil's eyes and mocking smile that followed her down into the velvet depths of sleep; him she dreamed of; his muscular arms that imprisoned her in a fierce embrace, and whose lips she welcomed with eager kisses as he made wild, passionate love to her.

I was right, she thought, fitfully hovering on the brink between growing fully awake and falling asleep, *San Martín's a dangerous man! Far more dangerous and disturbing than I'd ever dreamed. To want a man like him is tantamount to playing with fire—and I have no eagerness to burn!*

From now on, she'd have nothing whatsoever to do with him, she told herself. Deal or no, she'd avoid him like the plague until her revenge was assured!

Chapter Seven

July 9 was a holiday for *hacendero* and peasant alike; one of two national holidays the patriotic Argentines observed to celebrate the independence they'd won from Spain in 1816, after decades of struggle.

That Saturday dawned bright and clear, the perfect day for a traditional *asado,* the outdoor barbecue in *gaucho* tradition enjoyed by the *hacenderos,* or ranchers, of Argentina on festive occasions.

Shortly after sunrise, whole carcasses of beef—the hide left intact—had been spitted on five-foot-long iron skewers known as *asadors.* These spits the *gauchos* planted firmly in the dirt in the center of the courtyard at a semi-upright angle, over a huge rectangle of glowing red coals. When the fat melted as the meat slowly roasted all day, it would run downward through the beef, basting it continually. The end result would be juicy and delicious! Moments before the gathering was ready to sit down to eat, the *gauchos* who manned the spits would add dozens of *chorizos* to the sides of beef. These delicious sausages of minced beef, pork, and spices that traditionally accompanied the other barbecue fare, would quickly be browned for the feast.

As morning wore on, smoke and steam rose into the air from the charcoal fires, and the tantalizing aroma was carried to the room where Krissoula lay with her mouth watering and excitement bubbling through her veins, and tried, as Sofía had ordered, to take a long *siesta* and rest in readiness for the evening's festivities.

Alas, resting was one talent Krissoula did not possess in abundance, any more than the gift of patience, which had also been denied her! She alternated between trying fitfully to sleep, and in selecting and reselecting what gown she would wear that evening, all the while interrupting her selection to run to the window and peer from it to see if Don Felipe had returned. In all honesty, it was in the hope that he would *not* return in time to join the gathering that she repeated her vigil so frequently, though Doña Sofía believed differently! The unsuspecting duenna smiled indulgently at Krissoula's antics, thinking her charge was distracted by eagerness to see her *novio* again after his absence of several weeks!

"Patience, Krissoula *mía,* patience! Don Felipe will be here soon enough!" she cautioned, industriously embroidering the new altar cloth she had elected to make for the tiny chapel of Tierra Rosa.

"That, Sofía *mía,* is exactly what I'm afraid of!" Krissoula muttered, bewildered by her own perverseness. On the one hand, she wanted the old goat to return today as he'd promised, for his doing so would prove beyond doubt the attraction he felt for her, and consequently, her power over him! On the other hand, she disliked the man intensely, and wanted him to stay far, far away from her for as long as possible, so that she could have a little fun!

"I'm sorry, *niña*—what did you say?" Sofía asked absently, rethreading her embroidery needle with sky-blue silk.

Krissoula smiled with every appearance of innocence. "I said that I'm afraid Felipe won't be back in time for the *asado,*" she lied guiltlessly.

"Ah!" Sofía said with an abstracted nod, and continued her intricate stitches in a slow and methodical way that made tempestuous Krissoula ache to scream, or wring her neck, just to get some lively response from her!

In the kitchens, as late morning gave way to afternoon, Mama Angelina and her daughters and the other house servants worked like demons to prepare dish after tasty dish to accompany the succulent barbecued beef.

Great platters of onions and tomatoes were sliced, and tossed with torn lettuce bathed in oil-and-vinegar dressing for salads; various platters of creamy pasta, seasoned with flecks of green herbs, oil, and spices were mounded in wooden bowls, alongside porcelain tureens of ravioli swimming in a savory tomato sauce. Chicken and fruit *empanadas* were brought golden-brown and steaming hot from the ovens. There was a pot of *noquis,* potato dumplings in an herb and tomato gravy, and another of *locra,* a thick soup of corn, pumpkin, white beans, and beef. There were skillets of fried potatoes, steamed squash, and a huge kettle of *pulchero,* the traditional country stew of boiled beef, squash, carrots, onions, and whatever else took the cook's fancy, bubbling or frying or steaming in their turn over the kitchen fire. Chicken, lamb, or fish dishes might be good enough for everyday fare, but certainly not for a festival! Such celebrations demanded staggering quantities of the Argentines' favorite meat, prime beef, cooked and served in every conceivable fashion!

And, in the icehouse, four gallons of Mama Angelina's delicious *almendrado,* ice cream made from her own secret recipe and rolled in crushed almonds, waited packed in ice brought from the Andes to keep it firm and cold; the perfect surprise dessert with which to crown the sumptuous meal!

Meanwhile, the grooms and stableboys erected ladders and festooned streamers of blue and white ribbons, the colors of Argentina, from the eaves of Tierra Rosa. They also unrolled a huge national flag which they spread across the red-tiled rooftops so that its broad blue horizontal bands flanking a central white one emblazoned with a golden sun could be seen for a mile, maybe more.

At long last, it was time for Krissoula to get ready. The maids trundled a heavy slipper-shaped tub into her room, and filled it with kettles of steaming water. They offered her their assistance, but Krissoula laughingly refused, telling them she could manage to bathe quite well for herself.

"You run along now, *muchachas,* and finish your work quickly! Then you'll be able to join in the dancing later, *si?"*

"*Sí,* Doña Krissoula. *Gracias!"* chorused Luisa and Estrella, obviously in high spirits themselves today. Still giggling excitedly, they did as she told them and left her alone.

As soon as they were gone, Krissoula undressed and swept her heavy mane of hair up above her head. She fastened it with a length of ribbon into an untidy pony tail from which inky tendrils escaped to frame her little heart-shaped face with wisps that curled from the steam. Moments later, she was immersed to her shoulders in the hot water made deliciously fragrant with her favorite wild orchid bath oil. The unusual, light perfume—a product of Brazil's finest parfumiers which she had discovered in Buenos Aires—was so subtle it was almost elusive. The light floral yet slightly musky fragrance reminiscent of lush green rain forests filled the room as she took up soap and washcloth and scrubbed herself vigorously. And as she bathed, her thoughts dwelled apprehensively upon the coming evening.

Sofía had implied that everyone of any consequence from the surrounding *estancias* would be at Tierra Rosa in response to the invitations she'd sent out at Don Felipe's request. She'd also hinted that they would be coming more out of sheer curiosity to see

102

Krissoula, Don Felipe's intended bride, than to enjoy their host's hospitality. The idea of dozens of wealthy *criolla* strangers staring down their noses at her, evaluating her, was a terrifying one! She tried to remember all the little points of etiquette the tutors Esteban had hired in Spain had taught her, yet, of a sudden, it was as if her memory had sprouted as many holes as a sieve, and she could remember nothing! Panic filled her, and she lathered herself furiously in an effort to calm herself.

Her efforts, combined with the soothing effects of the warm water, succeeded at length. Before long, she was herself and under control again; the cool and calculating Krissoula Ballardo, urchin of the Barcelona streets who feared nothing. Pah! Tonight was no true challenge, not really! Hadn't she scrambled over city rooftops to evade the irate marks who'd awakened too early to find themselves robbed, and wanted her blood in return? Hadn't she pulled her knife and singlehandedly fought off the foul animals who'd been overeager to bed her, until Hector'd stirred his bones to finally come to her rescue? *Sí,* she'd done all that, and more!

Then how much more dangerous could this evening prove? So what if she made some little mistakes here and there, she told herself? Who were these people to criticize her, anyway? Snobbish *gorgio* nobodies, that was who, with more money and blue blood than common sense! By the standards of her people, the Rom, she was as highborn as the best of them, the niece of the Romany "Count" Ricardo Ballardo, who'd worn the single golden ring of leadership in his ear, she reminded herself proudly.

If she slipped up, she'd just smile and murmur airily, *Dios mío!* You simply must forgive my ignorance, Doña High-and-Mighty, but in Europe, we do things quite differently from South America! Why, yes, Doña Hoity-Toity, in the most prestigious salons of Paris and London—to which I was fortunate enough to have entrée, of course—the current trend in entertaining is a far cry from the rather formal gatherings you enjoy here. Parties have become charmingly casual! Perhaps to you delightfully old-fashioned Argentines, such informality would be considered a trifle gauche, but, alas, since I was raised in Europe, I do as the Europeans do . . . !"

Let them make of that what they would, she thought with a wicked little smile as she squeezed warm water over her small, hard breasts and admired the shapely firmness which nursing a babe had not succeeded in distorting.

"Golden apples" Esteban had described her breasts the other

afternoon, tipped with "little nuggets of gold," and Dios, what pleasure his flowery words had given her. Pah, that whoreson dog! Lies, he'd spoken nothing but flattering lies, would have said anything she wanted to hear in order to make her spread her thighs for him, she thought bitterly, and muttered a curse under her breath. Dismissing the tarnished memory of that afternoon, she returned to her former train of thought.

The society families of Argentina, she'd observed soon after her arrival, slavishly followed the styles and customs of Britain and France, particularly those of Paris. If they believed Krissoula Ballardo a true product of European drawing rooms, by month's end every woman in Argentina would be holding "charmingly casual" gatherings, as opposed to formal dinner parties where rigid rules of etiquette held sway! She grinned broadly, for it was an idea she rather liked; that of the snobbish *porteño gorgios* aping the manners of a little Gypsy nobody! Somehow, she'd get through the evening!

Later, glowing from the hot soaking and a vigorous toweling, she applied wild orchid perfume to her wrists, throat, and cleavage, and dressed in the gown she'd selected; one that was gloriously and boldly modeled after the costumes she wore to dance; the festival dress of the *gitanas,* the Gypsy women.

Of scarlet satin trimmed with narrow bands of black lace, it boasted two-layered bell-shaped sleeves that reached to her elbows. A deeply curving neckline exposed her throat and delicate collarbones to advantage, but modestly bared only a tantalizing glimpse of the topmost curves of her golden breasts and the shadowed valley between them. The skirts were tight across her stomach, but ruffled from the lower hip, each deep ruffle trimmed with narrow black lace that matched the six black lace petticoats she wore beneath it, over her lacy drawers. She decided to dispense completely with stockings, and slipped bare golden feet into pretty, high-heeled scarlet slippers with rounded toes and straps across the instep. The petticoats were new and stiff and she felt confined enough by them without adding stockings and garters to the torture! Besides, the evening promised to be a warm one, from nerves if not from the weather . . .

Seated before her mirror, she dusted the merest hint of powdered rouge over her high cheekbones, and reddened her lips ever so lightly, just enough to emphasize their generous fullness and pretty shape. Satisfied she was ready, except for her hair, she rang for Sofia to help her dress it. She'd have her duenna pull the unruly black mane severely away from her face and twist it into a heavy coil at the nape of her neck, with only a single daring spit curl in the center of her forehead. The dress would declare her intention to play the Gypsy tonight. Let the gathering think she'd dared to dress her hair to match! The graceful, black lace folds of her mantilla, supported by a tall comb of ebony wood, would charmingly soften the severe effect created by her hairstyle.

Ah, Krissoula, you're beautiful tonight! You'll stun them all, leave the men with their greedy criollo *tongues hanging down to the ground, eh, niña—and that San Martín with them!* she approvingly told herself an hour later, turning this way and that before the cheval looking glass to admire the clever way Sofía had dressed her hair. The door opened, and she glanced up as Sofía swept back into her room, her favorite jet earrings clattering as usual.

"I have my shawl and fan now. Are you ready, little one?" Sofía asked.

The duenna was not unattractive herself tonight, in a gown of bronze taffeta that softened her plain, somewhat angular features and warmed her sallow complexion, Krissoula noticed. Her gentle brown eyes held a sparkle of excitement, too, that made her look years younger. Why, Sofía—whom she'd always considered plain—was not really so plain after all, she amended! She had attractive features that had simply never been made the most of.

"As ready as I'll ever be!" Krissoula smiled up at her duenna, then frowned. "You however, Sofía *mía,* are in need of just a little color, I believe!"

Before the duenna could protest, Krissoula had deftly applied her fluffy rouge brush to Sofía's lovely, high cheekbones, adding new definition to her face. "There!" she declared wickedly, golden eyes sparkling with the heady excitement thrumming in her veins. "Now we're both the very picture of innocent, blushing virgins!"

Sofía opened her mouth to scold, caught a glimpse of herself in the mirror, and smiled with pleasure instead as she stared at her reflection, patting her hair almost coquettishly. "So we are!" she murmured in an awed tone, as if unable to believe her eyes. "Why so we are!"

Taking up their fans, they went below.

Esteban de San Martín, with or without an invitation, was the first of her guests to arrive, much to Krissoula's relief. Hate him or not, she badly needed the moral support his presence would give her tonight! Out of earshot of Sofía, he complimented her warmly on her appearance, which he judged a clever balance between being either too immodest or too insignificantly drab. Then he proceeded to stand at her elbow as the first guests, riding in grand carriages, began to arrive, sweeping up to the front entrance of Tierra Rosa, where a splendidly dressed Tomás and his grooms waited to take their horses to the stables or coachhouse.

Now that the moment was here, there were butterflies in Krissoula's stomach despite her brave, boastful promises to herself. And, since there was no indication as yet that Felipe intended to return today as he'd promised her, she welcomed Esteban's whispered suggestion that he act as host for the gathering in *el patrón's* absence. She needed his confidence badly!

Between welcoming guests and seeing them served some refreshment after their ride, Esteban suggested that she fulfill her duties as hostess and inspect the huge, covered patio, which had been arranged with numerous tables and chairs and potted rubber trees, palms, and other greenery, and the array of tempting foods that weighed down the snowy-draped trestle tables. She could find no fault with either, and praised a nervous Mama Angelina so lavishly, the plump woman blushed beneath her olive skin.

"Truly, Angelina you're an angel by name, and an angel by nature!" she teased, and to Angelina's surprise, the señorita hugged her and kissed her on the cheek, before turning to greet yet another guest Esteban was leading across the courtyard for her to meet.

"Doña Krissoula, good evening! Dare I hope you remember me? I was fortunate to meet you in Buenos Aires with Felipe, after your farewell performance at the Ópera," the slim, bearded man declared pompously, bowing low over her hand. His palms were damp with sweat enclosing hers, and Krissoula had to fight down the urge to rid herself of all traces of his touch when he was done.

"But of course I remember you, señor!" she simpered instead. "Don Jaime Ramirez, how could I forget? How lovely of you to come tonight!"

"The pleasure's all mine, my dear doña. And this strapping fellow's Felipe's *mayordomo*. San Martín, allow me to present Doña Krissoula Ballardo, soon to be the wife of my dear friend, Don Felipe, and your mistress here at Tierra Rosa. I'm sure you want to offer the doña your greetings, before you get on with your duties, eh?"

"Señor San Martín, my pleasure," she murmured politely.

With Ramirez's words, Esteban's jaw had tightened, she saw. A

106

nerve danced dangerously at his temple, and a flare of anger sky-rocketed in his eyes. But, to his credit, he covered his blazing anger at Ramirez's insulting introduction very well—at least to all outward appearances and casual eyes. He at once stepped forward to take her hand, so smoothly that Jaime Ramirez, watching the pair, suspected nothing awry that he could later report back to his old friend Felipe.

Krissoula blinked in surprise, for the rough-and-ready *gaucho* she'd once scathingly termed a "peasant" was completely gone tonight, replaced by a handsome, distinguished-looking devil she hardly recognized. Why on earth hadn't she noticed earlier how wonderful he looked, she wondered, wanting to pinch herself? Was she so preoccupied with her role as the "grand lady" it had taken that horrible Ramirez's mealy-mouthed introduction to open her eyes to the dashing figure Esteban cut? Apparently, it had!

For the first time this evening, she noticed that he sported a dashing black sombrero atop his short, wavy, jet-black hair, with a slim rawhide cord fastened beneath his obstinate jaw. A superbly cut, short black jacket made his wide shoulders appear even broader, his waist even narrower. And his breeches—aiee, *Dios!*—they hugged snugly to his flanks and his powerful horseman's thighs, emphasizing his masculinity and the well-muscled leanness of his build.

Beneath the jacket, the snowy contrast of a crisp white shirt, high collared at the neck and ruffled down the front, made his tanned face, curling black hair, and snapping deep-blue eyes doubly striking by contrast. The shirt's snowy whiteness was offset by a gleaming royal-blue satin sash that spanned his narrow waist and by a short V of tanned bare throat where he'd left the top button undone, for, as was traditional, he wore no tie of any kind. Except for the dangerous glitter in his eyes, he would have been perfectly at home in the grandest salons of Spain, or anywhere young men of style and intelligence gathered to discuss the pressing affairs of their country. She must have been blind not to notice the difference in him sooner!

As she echoed his name, he swept off his hat and took the hand she offered, decorously brushing his lips against the back of it—or at least, to all outward appearances that's what he did! In effect, the second before he straightened and released her fingers, she felt him turn her hand over, palm-uppermost. His moist tongue tip darted out to flick the tiny hollow of flesh in a bold, suggestive way that was far from decorous—and which made her knees suddenly weak!

"Ah, but the doña and I have already met several times, Ramirez," Esteban said softly, reminding Krissoula of a tamed jaguar about to erupt into jungle violence. His dislike of Felipe's crony was obvious in his repugnant expression as he stepped forward. "However, Doña Krissoula, it's always a pleasure to meet a lovely woman such as yourself again," he murmured gallantly, smoothly, and his flashing eyes lifted to her face and scorched her with their heat.

She read a threat in their dark depths, too, for he was a proud man, was San Martín—every bit as proud as herself!—and he did not take kindly to being treated as a servant, as Ramirez had so insolently done. His expression said as much, warned her that she would regret her little game if she sought to humble him by being a party to it, but in all honesty, such a thought never crossed her mind. It was one thing for *her* to insult him in private, she thought irrationally, but quite another for someone *else* to do so! She was almost as annoyed by Ramirez's degrading manner as was he, and in a far better position to do a little something about it . . .

"Gracias, Don Esteban," she said levelly, her eyes locked to his. "And may I say in return that your gallantry and impeccable manners—so unusual in this new and somewhat savage land— make every such meeting a pleasure to which I look forward each time?" and she dropped him a deep and exquisitely graceful curtsey. Touché, Ramirez, she thought maliciously as she rose to find that Ramirez's face had paled to a sallow yellowish color, and that his black eyes were ignited with anger. There's one in the eye for you, you sweaty-pawed little weasel!

Stepping back, a startled Esteban gave her a disarming, grateful smile that somehow made her feel as she had in the kitchens earlier that week—stark naked, despite her clothing, and deplorably weak-kneed.

He murmured, "As always, you grace Tierra Rosa with your beauty, charm and elegance, Señorita Ballardo."

And incredibly, he sounded as if he meant every word!

Dios, Krissoula thought, a warm blush of pleasure filling her cheeks, he was pleased at what she'd done—although his pretty words and proper gestures didn't deceive *her* for a moment, that clever devil, that smooth scoundrel! He was still furious at Ramirez—close to throttling him—but handling his anger so beautifully, he made Ramirez appear the ill-mannered, arrogant clod!

She had to fight down the wildest urge to giggle nervously, to

108

smother his handsome face with passionate kisses as she begged him to forgive her for ever thinking of double-crossing him, and implored him to take her away somewhere . . . anywhere . . . and make love to her again, on whatever terms he chose . . . *Caray!* What was wrong with her? Such mad impulses had to be sternly dealt with, before they slipped her control! Instead, she aloofly inclined her head, summoning every ounce of self-control she possessed to quell her naughty thoughts.

"And now, alas, señores, I regret I have other guests to attend to," she apologized huskily. "Drinks are being served on the patio, and the tables are groaning with food. Please, make yourselves at home, and help yourselves to the buffet, gentlemen. After all, my house is your house," she simpered, fluttering her lashes coyly. Esteban de San Martín was not the only one who could act a part when the need took him, and Krissoula could give as good as she got any day of the week!

With that courteous yet transparent excuse to quit their company, she wandered off to where Mama Angelina and her pretty daughters presided over the groaning supper tables. Krissoula's golden eyes narrowed jealously as she followed Esteban's path across the courtyard, noting how the women's eyes lingered longingly after him, and the excited whispers they exchanged among themselves.

It was some time later when Ramirez cornered her again. She'd escaped to a secluded part of the courtyard to catch a breath of air away from the crush of people, and was fanning herself vigorously when he loomed out of the shadows.

"Why, Doña Krissoula!" he exclaimed, and she knew that despite his surprised tone, he'd followed her. "What can you be doing here, all alone in the shadows? A jealous man might wonder if perhaps you'd escaped the crowd to rendezvous with a lover, no?" He smiled.

"A jealous man, uncertain of my affections, might well imagine such a thing, señor," she countered smoothly, bristling at his nerve in suggesting such a thing. "However, a *gentleman*—as my Felipe surely is—would wonder no more than the truth. That I have missed him these past few weeks, and sought only a little solitude to ponder on my loneliness."

"Prettily put, Doña Krissoula. Felipe is a lucky man."

"Thank you, señor. As I am a very lucky woman." She fanned herself vigorously.

"I understand the *mayordomo,* San Martín, was in Spain until

109

quite recently—a business trip to persuade the Spaniards to import Tierra Rosa beef, I believe?"

"I've no idea, I'm afraid, señor. Don Felipe has not seen fit to discuss his business matters with me as yet."

"Then you'd never met San Martín before coming here? You didn't, perhaps, make his acquaintance in Spain?"

"I hardly think the circles in which I moved would have included Don Esteban," Krissoula evaded. "We theater people—dancers, singers, actors—are notoriously close-knit, you know."

"So I understand. I must admit, also, that they are a people I have always found to be singularly vulgar and flamboyant, with little of breeding and manners to commend them."

"Are you implying that I am also vulgar and flamboyant and ill-mannered?" she bristled.

"On the contrary, you are the wonderful exception to the rule, doña! But then—" he continued, "—I was given to understand from Felipe that you are of good family, left unhappily orphaned and impoverished by circumstances, no?"

"You're very well informed, Señor Ramírez. That was my unfortunate lot in life, yes. Happily, through my dancing I was able to better myself."

"From where did your family come?"

"Granada, señor."

"Ah, lovely country, Granada! And the history that surrounds it! Unfortunately, on my one rare visit, I found the beauty a little tarnished by the presence of those damnable rogues living in the caves there."

"The Gypsies, señor?"

"Ah, yes—or should we say, thieves and layabouts?" He smiled superciliously, and she had to squelch the strongest urge to slap the smirk from his face.

"Believe what you will, señor," she said instead. "I personally owe much to that people, and have learned from personal experience that they are badly maligned. You see, Don Jaime, it was on account of a Gypsy woman's generosity of heart that I was taught to dance the flamenco."

"You have no relatives who would have taken you in?"

"A distant bachelor uncle, one with little time or money or inclination to raise a daughter. Except for him, I'm quite alone in the world."

"But for Felipe?"

"Sí, except for him."

"Then your sad little tale has a happy ending, does it not? The destitute Spanish princess of unquestionably noble blood finds herself a wealthy foreigner for husband, and lives happily ever after in the lap of luxury!" he said with ill-concealed distaste.

"*Sí, señor,* happily ever after!" she agreed with an edge of defiance to her tone. "And now, I really should get back to my guests—?"

"I wouldn't dream of keeping you from them a moment longer! By the way, what was this uncle's name again?"

She turned in her retreat to face him, brows arched. "Didn't I mention his name? How remiss of me! His name is Ricardo, señor, Don Ricardo del Campo. *El Conde del Campo,* if you prefer," she said with complete veracity, for, after all, her uncle was truly an "earl of the countryside" in a manner of speaking!

One of Ramirez's eyebrows quirked up in surprise. "A count, you say?"

"*Sí, señor,* a count! And now, by your leave?"

And with that, she sailed aloofly away.

"Ramirez knows!" she whispered hoarsely when Esteban came to take her arm much later, and led her to meet some latecomers. Her golden eyes were wide with the fear of discovery, her composure perilously close to being lost. "He's seen through me, I'm sure of it! He cornered me a while ago and asked me question after question about Spain, my family, how I came to be in South America—everything!"

"Don't panic, *tonta!*" Esteban growled. "He can suspect nothing, as long as you stuck to your story. You did stick to it, didn't you?" he said tightly.

"Like a cockleburr to a fox's brush!" she insisted, indignant that he would think otherwise.

"Then Ramirez was merely fishing. You insulted him by being so gracious to me, and he simply decided to repay you for your slight by questioning your background. I warned you, didn't I, that Felipe de Aguilar is no gentleman? Well, *querida,* neither are his fawning friends! A true gentleman would have ignored your insults, but Ramirez—? Never, *minina!* He's too afraid of what your marriage to Felipe might do to his friendship to welcome you wholeheartedly as Felipe's bride!

"You see, I happen to know he relies heavily on Felipe's good will in the form of large loans. Consequently, as Felipe's luck runs, so does his own! He's afraid your marriage will cut off his source of ready cash, so naturally he'd have little liking for you, my dear. So,

111

after you'd shown your claws and, in effect, defended me before him, he bared his teeth in return, and decided to make you uncomfortable, that's all. Now, calm down and pull yourself together! Everything is going perfectly, and it'll continue to do so, *minina*—as long as you remain in control."

He smiled and elbowed Krissoula into doing the same as an older couple and their middle-aged son approached them.

"Ah, Doña Selina, Don Alfonso! Señor Jorge, my boy, welcome! Señores, may I have the honor of presenting to you Doña Krissoula Ballardo, Don Felipe's betrothed? Doña Selina, Don Alfonso, Doña Krissoula Ballardo." She murmured a polite response, and gave the disheveled-looking couple a warm smile.

"Don Felipe was expected home from the city today, but alas, he appears to have been detained. Luckily, we have our charming hostess to more than adequately take his place until he returns," Esteban explained with that disarming, flashing smile again that he used to such devastating advantage—although this time on the frumpy-looking Doña Selina, who visibly melted under its impact, Krissoula observed with the barest twinge of jealousy. "Doña Krissoula, won't you offer Doña Selina some refreshment after her long ride, while I escort Don Alfonso and his son in search of some stronger, liquid means of fortification?"

Krissoula obediently did as he asked, thinking as she took the large woman by the elbow and steered her away that Esteban was more suited to the position of master of Tierra Rosa than she'd ever have believed until tonight. Seeing him act the perfect, charming host was something of a shock, knowing him before this only as a blackmailing, conniving rogue!

After a while, her fears regarding Ramirez's suspicious questions were forgotten as she was forced to concentrate on her guests and on maintaining her role. Never had she been on display before so many watchful eyes, nor carried off her masquerade as a lady in so distinguished a gathering as this! After an hour or two, the strain of maintaining a welcoming, gracious smile began to tell. *Dios!* how her jaws ached!

Thankfully, each new guest had been properly welcomed and led to the laden tables when the moon rose over the courtyard. She ordered the torches lit and escaped to a quiet corner to relax and enjoy some of the delicious foods for herself, though she'd not risk taking even a single glass of wine with Ramirez sniffing around her like a dog after a bone! It might go straight to her head and ruin everything!

112

After supper, she drew a deep breath and began circulating again, complimenting one guest on the loveliness of her gown, and another on the exquisite old lace of her ivory mantilla, while Angelina and her daughters hurried to clear the supper tables. When everything was set to order, they would escape to their little homes to freshen up, change into their finest, Sunday-best clothes and return to the courtyard for the music and dancing that would follow later, and in which everyone of the *estancia* was expected to participate, from *el patrón* himself to the lowliest *peón*.

While the guests enjoyed their after-dinner brandies and cigars, or tiny cups of thick black coffee, musicians garnered from the ranks of the *gauchos* and house servants took up their instruments and began playing.

Soon the lively strains of guitars and the *bandoneón,* an instrument halfway between an accordion and a concertina, filled the torchlit courtyard with the indolent *habanera,* a Cuban dance, and Krissoula listened avidly. Her attention rapt, her guests forgotten, her red-toed slippers tapped out the stirring beat beneath her skirts, while her fingers itched to snap along with them!

While staying in the city prior to receiving Felipe's proposal and his invitation to spend the months until their wedding at his home, she'd heard rumors of a shocking new dance that was being performed in the back-street areas of the city. In the communities known as the *barrios,* where the poorer people of Buenos Aires lived and worked, a new dance had been born from the strange mating of the Spanish country dance, the *malonga,* and the throbbing, sensual music of the freed *negros* of the Rio de la Plata area. It was said that the tango, as the resulting dance had come to be known, was immoral, and that the couples who danced it—the *compadritos* and their volatile mistresses—appeared to be making passionate love as they danced!

Descriptions of the *compadritos* had also captured Krissoula's curiosity, for it was said they were a colorful type of men, more often than not strutting petty crooks who'd been born in the slums, and reputedly ran the *barrios* as overlords or princes, in their own ruthless fashion. They were of the sort of men she'd come to know only too well from months lived in the back streets of Barcelona, although others were bored young men of good families seeking the thrill to be had from leading a wild, dangerous lifestyle, far removed from their staid upbringings.

Rumor said the *compadritos* enjoyed wearing the flashy, colorful clothing of dandies, and carried pistols or knives in their belts, ready to battle anyone who besmirched their rigid code of honor. It was also said that many of them were brave fellows, even charismatic after their own fashion. A true *compadrito* would never back down in the face of even the most daring challenge or life-threatening situation—and neither would he let an attractive woman pass him by without giving her an insolent if flattering stare, or paying her an outrageous compliment called *un piropo!* To Krissoula, they'd sounded very much like her old partner, Hector, a *gato* who'd possessed all of the *compadritos'* dubious qualities—but had sadly lacked their color, intelligence, and streetwise charm.

Her fascination with the dance itself and the breed of men and women who favored it, combined with the knowledge that it had been banned by *el presidente* Mitre of Argentina, only added to the tango's fascination for Krissoula! Not only did she yearn to see it, but as a professional dancer herself, she longed to dance it—and with a true *compadrito* as her partner throughout every shocking step! What, she wondered, would staid old Felipe think of that, the old goat . . . !

A voice calling her name broke into Krissoula's thoughts, and she turned to see a short, bearded young man whom she recognized as Jorge, the only son of the Marin couple, gesturing to her. He'd been watching her covertly ever since his arrival, and she was just about to turn away and pretend she hadn't seen him signaling when he hurried over and nervously asked, "Please, Doña Krissoula, won't you dance for us? We've all been dying to ask you, but didn't want to impose on our gracious hostess—!"

"*Sí*, Señorita Ballardo, just one dance, we beg you!" one of the other female guests chimed in as they all suddenly clambered about her. "We've heard so much of your talents! Unfortunately, we weren't able to see you perform when you appeared at the Ópera Florida, for, alas, there wasn't a ticket to be had in all of Buenos Aires, was there, Rafael, my son?"

"Not a one," Rafael's bossy wife confirmed for him. "Oh, you simply mustn't disappoint us, Señorita Krissoula! We're old friends of the Aguilars, and Felipe is like a cousin to us!"

"Surely you'll dance just once, to please us?" they wheedled.

"I'd love to," she admitted, fanning herself gracefully, "but I promised Don Felipe, on the night he honored me by asking me to become his wife, never to dance in public again."

She lowered her lashes and laughed self-consciously behind her fan as they groaned their disappointment, well aware that their eyes

114

were upon her, judging her, looking for the slightest crack in her well-bred demeanor, however charmingly they might plead with her to oblige them, those two-faced old foxes! It would never do to appear eager to dance for them, and so she demurely explained, "I'm afraid Felipe does not wholly approve of my former profession, you see? And naturally, I would never willingly do anything to displease or embarrass my future husband."

Again, she lowered her golden eyes in modest fashion, praying silently that they would insist; that, as their hostess, she would have no choice but to graciously bow to their wishes, for then—then Esteban could not help but see her dance! Oh, Krissoula, wicked Krissoula! Like a child with a box of matches, she feared burning— but could not resist the deadly, fascinating prospect of teasing and courting the fire!

"But surely your fiancé couldn't possibly object, not with your wonderful duenna Sofía here to chaperone you, and all of us looking on to see that everything is quite proper?" Doña Selina insisted, gawking down her large hooked nose at Krissoula like a beady-eyed crow eyeing a succulent worm that both fascinated and repelled her at the same time.

Dressed all in somber black like a huge tarantula festooned in webs of lace, the aristocratic woman was of pure *criolla,* or Spanish, blood, and her family one of the legendary Two Hundred, as the elite descendant families of the original Spanish colonists were known. If Selina de Borges y Marin wanted her to dance, the rest would insist upon it, Krissoula realized with a suddenly racing heart!

Sure enough, Selina's remark resulted in a chorus of further pleas for her to perform for them, and in the end Krissoula shrugged helplessly.

"Very well, what can I say, when you've all begged me so charmingly, señores? I will dance for you, but only if my duenna agrees that it would be acceptable. Sofía, darling, what do you say?"

Sofía gave an indulgent smile, her better judgment mellowed by several glasses of wine and the heady atmosphere of the rich and influential all about her. "What else can I say but yes, when you beg me so charmingly, *niña?* Angelina, send one of your daughters to fetch the señorita's castanets, if you would?"

"Ladies and gentlemen, won't you find yourselves comfortable seats?" Jorge Marin suggested with a beaming smile. "You're in for a rare treat this evening!"

Chapter Eight

Krissoula was soon ready, the polished wooden castanets looped in her damp palms.

Although traditionally the flamenco was danced without castanets—accompanied by only the guitars and the dancer's own clapping, called *palmas,* the foot-stamping called *zapateados,* and the fingersnapping known as *pitos*—audiences enjoyed the castanets' dramatic accompaniment, she'd discovered, and she'd decided early in the game that to give her public what they wanted could only increase her popularity and fame, and, consequently, her wealth!

Her knees trembled, and she realized suddenly that she was more nervous about dancing before the snobbish gathering here than she'd ever been about performing for the crowded theaters of Barcelona or Buenos Aires! Or—was it the knowledge that Esteban would be watching that made her so nervous? Was it him she wanted so badly to impress, to dance for and be noticed by—? Guiltily, she knew that despite everything, it was . . .

Seeing her hesitate, the man who tormented her thoughts came across to her and took her by the hand, leading her to stand in the center of the torchlit courtyard.

Looking down at her, he smiled. "It seems you're a success tonight, little one. I must have overheard a hundred compliments to your graciousness, your beauty, your modest behavior! Felipe will be pleased," he murmured in her ear, "as am I, *querida!* I congratulate you on a superb performance!" Then he gallantly kissed her hand and strode away, nodding to the guitarists to get ready as he went.

Krissoula, breathless with excitement, hesitantly murmured the name of the piece she intended to dance, and asked if the musicians were familiar with it. The guitarists grinned and nodded. Did they know it? Why, it was only Doña Krissoula's most celebrated number, the one that had taken her audiences by storm in Buenos

Aires! The piece of music had become popular everywhere since her performances last month, and now floated out from every restaurant, tavern, café, and corner bar. Of course they knew it—and very well, too!

Moments later, the first rich, commanding chords of *La Gitana de Sevilla,* The Gypsy from Seville, thrummed on the smoky air that wreathed like mist about the courtyard, riveting the expectant onlookers in place with their dramatic, stirring rhythm. All heads turned in her direction, and an expectant hush fell amongst the onlookers as she took up her stance. Graceful arms raised in elegant, overlapping curves above her head, the black lace of her mantilla falling from its tall comb and down over her arched back like her own tumbling river of blue-black hair, she waited.

And then, so suddenly some of the watchers actually gasped aloud in surprise, the two guitars burst into full-throated song. The powerful, passionate rhythm of a *farruca* exploded on the sultry hush, just as Krissoula simultaneously exploded into movement!

Her high-heeled scarlet slippers stamped an impassioned tattoo upon the flagstoned patio. Form and color dissolved, became a scarlet blur as her feet drummed faster, faster, each footfall cracking like the lash of a whip as it hammered the ground, stirring the blood in the veins of the onlookers with its frenzied heartbeat. She grasped her skirts in her fists and shook them furiously, like an angry kitten shaking a toy, the ruffles of her petticoats swirling and flirting as she stamped and whirled. And then her arms rose high above her head. Long fingers and slender arms weaving patterns above her in the graceful, sinuous movements known as the *filigrano,* she circled the torchlit courtyard like a scarlet flower whirled by the wind. Castanets throbbing, gazing seductively over her shoulder, she searched the blur of pale, rapt faces for that one, very special, disturbing face.

Her golden eyes were smoldering cinders of passion, her lush red lips curved in a bewitching smile of temptation when at last she found him, standing apart from the rest beneath an archway like a lean, dark shadow.

A crystal wineglass was raised to his lips, and as the glass caught the torchlight in a miniature ruby sunburst of light, Esteban felt her eyes upon him and raised the goblet to her in mocking salute. Over the shining rim of it, their eyes met, and her heart faltered and skipped a beat.

His scorching sapphire eyes were locked endlessly—or was it for but a moment?—to her golden ones! The brooding intensity of his

117

lambent sapphire gaze made her heart pound madly, as if it would burst from her heaving bosom. *Dios,* how his dark eyes pierced her soul, seemed to impale her like a crimson butterfly impaled by a pin! How that look devoured her! And what was it he asked of her with those brooding eyes? What message was he trying to convey? *Caray,* the expression in their depths was masterful, compelling her to look at him, bending her will to his, daring her to betray him . . . to desire him . . . to dare to love him, the man she hated!

As she gazed on, mesmerized, helpless to tear her eyes from his, his firm grip upon the stem of the glass tightened. The delicate wineglass shattered, tinkling shards cascading to the flagstones. The warning sound broke the spell in which Krissoula had fluttered for seconds that had seemed an eternity. Suddenly breathless, unable to bear any longer the disturbing quality of his dark eyes riveted fiercely upon her, she forced herself to look away, to dance on, to flick her head and break the magnetic contact; to seek out other faces, other eyes, before the gathering sensed the electrical current that had leaped like lightning between them, and paused to wonder at its cause.

The courtyard of Tierra Rosa faded. The *casa grande* vanished as if into thin air as she danced. It became instead a horseshoe of painted *vardos* or Romany caravans. She was Krissoula, Queen of Flamenco, no more, but simply La Gitana of the music she danced; a young Gypsy woman, driven mad with grief at surprising the man she loved in the arms of another . . .

So closely did her own sad past reflect the message of the dance that soon it was no longer Esteban de San Martín, but the *gorgio* youth, Miguel whom she danced for on the hillsides overlooking Sacro Monte. The cold flagstones beneath her feet became springy turf, scorched hard and dry from too little rain and too much Andalusian sunshine. The writhing torchlight became the flickering golden flames of Romany campfires under the stars and the spilled gold of a Gypsy moon. Her elaborate costume of red and ebony became a simple *camisa* embroidered with flowers, her skirts swirling red ones with bands of varicolored ribbon at the hems.

Bare-legged, bare-armed, her ebony curls spraying free about her with no combs or pins to tame their wild beauty, in her imagination she spun and whirled to the music of violins, the chinking heartbeat of tambourines, and the wild chords of the guitars, until the sound was in her head and she was in the sound; until she was the music, and the music *was* her. She was La Gitana, the Gypsy! The pulse in her veins, the very breath in her lungs, the soul and spirit and life in her body—they were the instrument and the music, and she and the dance and the music were one! She danced until she knew not where one finished, and the other began . . .

And then, a man's deep voice began to accompany her dance and the softly played guitars, the *duende,* or emotion, of his singing partnering her own. The timbre of the singer's voice was harsh, laden with sorrow, vibrant with feeling as only the *cante jondo* can be. The wrenching grief and the terrible beauty of his singing and the words he sang raised goosebumps on the arms of the watchers. He was the spirit of her lover, the man La Gitana had stabbed in a jealous rage, and he begged her mournfully:

> Forgive me, *querida,*
> For not loving you better—
> As I forgive you for the
> Taking of my life.
> Now a cold grave holds me
> To the bosom of Mother earth,
> Not your loving arms
> To the warmth of your breast.
>
> If only I could return—
> Have a second chance to love you!
> But—like the Gypsy fool of legend—
> I sold what I loved best
> For an illusion.
> I betrayed your trust
> For another's easy smile,
>
> For the false glitter
> Of Gypsy gold . . .

As the voice, ragged with emotion, trembled moodily on the night wind, Krissoula's movements slowed little by little, until she barely seemed to move at all. Haughtily, she flicked her head as if to rid it of some lingering, foolish dream. Her golden eyes closed. Her moist lips parted as if in a wistful sigh. Only her wrists and tapering fingers moved now, painting filigree patterns in the smoky air as the tasseled castanets whirred.

Crr-cla-clacking high above her head, the deeper notes of the male quarreled furiously with the higher voice of the female, until finally the angry sounds grew softer, muted, as she brought the pair together again at last, bringing her hands closer and closer until they met. Above her head, her arms twined in winding, snakelike gestures about each other that were peculiarly erotic. Her long fingers were moving so slowly now, the castanets purred with lazy pleasure and whispered teasingly to each other in the languorous voices of lovers whose quarreling is done.

> You will feel my lips in
> The night winds
> As they kiss your cheeks.
> You will hear my pleas in the
> Rustle of the leaves.
> 'Forgive me . . . Forgive me!
> I am desolate
> Without you.'

The guitars sobbed away into silence. The voice died on a last melancholy note, laden with pathos.

Krissoula grew very, very still, standing motionless there in the courtyard like a lovely statue, the torchlight glistening on the sweat that slicked her brow, her arms, and trickled down the valley between her breasts. Seconds passed, and there was still no movement from her . . .

And then, while all in the courtyard still watched, spellbound, scarce daring even to breathe for fear they would banish the magic she'd woven, Krissoula suddenly yelped, startling them all!

"Aiee-ya!" she cried. "*Infiel!* Faithless one!"

She tossed back her wild mane of loosened hair, kicked out a foot, twisted a hip gracefully, and her skirts swirled up as she burst back to life, like a crimson ember exploding into flame from the ashes of a dead fire!

Another second, and the rippling chords of the guitars were driving her swiftly again, sending her spinning across the courtyard like a top on a soaring crest of music, her slender, catlike body arching and flirting between the shifting light of the torches and the shadows.

A glimpse of flashing golden eyes—
Spin!
moist red lips—
Stamp!
graceful arms weaving patterns in the air—
Spin! Spin! Spin!

Faster, faster, she whirled and stamped her heels, *zapateado*. The frothy ruffles of her black lace petticoats billowed up beneath crimson overskirts trimmed in bands of ebony lace; red and black, the colors of birth and death, of heartbreak and passion, magic and mystery. Krissoula danced them all with a wild Gypsy fervor that throbbed and pulsed with emotion!

Long, sleek golden legs and firm, slender thighs were bared as her skirts flew higher, and the men held their sweethearts and wives just a little bit closer, and thought of the long night yet to come.

A tempting smile from curved reddened lips, a flirtatious sweep of thick, dark lashes, and Tomás felt his collar grow unbearably tight about his throat, and cast longing eyes upon an enraptured Estrella across the courtyard.

A trickle of sweat disappearing beneath the tight bodice of Krissoula's gown or slithering wetly down a sinuous arm, and sweat suddenly streamed from the brows and palms of the watching gauchos, and sent them reaching thirstily for their glasses of potent *caño*. Her impassioned dancing reminded them all that their beds were lonely ones, and the hunger for a hot-blooded woman filled the men and tightened their loins.

Sofia watched, transfixed, from her chair, fingers clamped over the carved arms. She felt an unfamiliar stirring and heat in her own tepid spinster's blood that she must surely confess to the priest before receiving her next Mass! And Mama Angelina and the older folk sighed and remembered the days of their lost youth, and unforgettable nights spent in the passionate arms of lovers or husbands, mistresses or wives.

Yet it was really for Esteban de San Martín that Krissoula danced. For him and no other—though every male watching her was convinced she danced for him alone! *Look at me, want me, take me, querido mío!* her eyes seemed to implore, and all of them burned to answer her plea!

But—not Esteban. No, the young *mayordomo* never answered her plea, and nor did he linger to witness her triumphant finale. The man who'd dominated her every thought of late drained his fresh glass, gave her one last burning, enigmatic glance, and silently slipped away from the courtyard.

When Krissoula was finished, an enthusiastic chorus of "Olés!", "Bravos!", and a flattering burst of applause followed. Breathlessly, she took her bows, laughing in delight and triumph as she graciously accepted the congratulations and flowery praises of the gathering. Yet even as she thanked them, her eyes anxiously strayed

121

beyond them, searching the shadows and the faces for the one face she most wanted to see.

He's gone, she realized, looking about the courtyard, and she felt heartsick, crushed with disappointment. Esteban had gone, and her finest dancing had been for nothing, for he'd not stayed to see it, curse his soul! And suddenly, she wished that they were *all* gone; every last one of her fawning admirers. That she could be alone with her disappointment hugged jealously to her breast, if not the lover she desired . . .

"Excuse me, my friends," said a rasping voice. "But I'd also like to offer my thanks to the señorita whose dancing has delighted us all!"

"Why, bravo, Felipe, you're here at last!" cried Ramirez in welcome, his black eyes glittering.

"About time, too, you old rogue!" offered another, slapping the tall man across the back.

The crowd about her parted to let him through, and Krissoula raised her flushed, glowing face to the tall older man with graying black hair who stepped between them. For a second, the welcoming smile that curved her lips wavered, but then she deepened it and swept him a graceful curtsey.

"Don Felipe! Welcome home, at last! Why, we'd almost given you up for lost, señor!" she chided prettily.

Without smiling, Felipe took her hand possessively and tucked it through his elbow, squeezing her wrist and fingers as he did so with a firmness that bordered on being painful, though only one of the guests observed his cruel gesture. Oh, no, thought Esteban, concealed deep in the shadows of an archway, wearing a contemptuous curl on his lips, Tío Felipe was far too clever to let the gathering see his secret viciousness to the talented, lovely young woman who'd just delighted them with her performance! His guests saw only an older man who was deeply in love, and touchingly anxious to reclaim his young *novia's* company after they'd been parted for several weeks—which, Esteban knew, was exactly what Felipe intended! And if Doña Krissoula had grown suddenly pale, then surely it was exhaustion that made her so, not any cruelty on Don Felipe's part—?

"That you believed I wouldn't return tonight is only too apparent, Krissoula *mía,*" Felipe de Aguilar ground out coldly in a low, rasping whisper intended only for her ears.

Maintaining his tight grip so forcefully she feared her slender fingers would snap in two like chicken bones, he led her back to the patio like a chastened child about to be punished. There, he yanked her sharply down to sit beside him, saying harshly, "Had I thought for a moment that my absence would encourage such vulgar, theatrical displays on your part, my dear, I would have timed my return sooner. It seems you cannot be trusted to behave modestly unless I am here to ensure that you do, is that not so, Manuela? I must see that such opportunities are few and far between henceforth!"

"As you wish, señor," she replied in a husky voice choked with tears—though of rage more than hurt. "But," she added bravely, for all that she'd grown pale about the lips with the pain of his grip, "angry with me or no, I would remind you that my name is *Krissoula*, señor—not Manuela. No woman enjoys being called by another's name, especially not when that other woman is long dead. It is most—unflattering."

"Is that so, *Krissoula?*" Felipe taunted softly, and she itched to slap his cruel, hawklike face. "Then I must be sure to remember that on our wedding night, mustn't I, little one?"

He smiled at her, but it was a chilling smile that never reached his stony sapphire eyes, nor softened the harshly handsome angles of his lined face. It was a smile intended for the guests and friends that surged forward to greet him, not for her, and totally lacking in human warmth.

And she was plotting to marry this cold-blooded animal, this cruel *bastardo* of a man, she thought, incredulous at her own daring? *Dios*, she must be mad, utterly mad . . .

As if someone had walked over her grave, she shivered.

Chapter Nine

It was after three when Krissoula returned to her room, yawning hugely and rubbing gritty eyes.

Felipe had invited the Marins, that nosy, hateful Jaime Ramirez, and another couple to be his overnight guests at Tierra Rosa, their *estancias* being over thirty miles away. And so, when she'd ruefully told those few guests who still lingered over drinks on the patio that she hoped they would forgive her, but she was exhausted and really must retire, Felipe had kissed her hand and bade her run along with an indulgent smile. His rare benevolent mood was more the result of the vast quantity of wine he'd consumed, rather than any gentling on his part, she knew only too well, but it had nevertheless provided the exit she needed! Murmuring that she'd look forward to seeing them all over breakfast in the morning, she'd escaped to the house, barely containing her glee.

Closing her bedroom door behind her, she sighed and held out her left hand. She angled it this way and that, wriggling her slim fingers so that the moonlight caught the trio of enormous diamonds in the heavy golden betrothal band she now wore. Its facets reflected the light in sparkles of silver and purple.

She'd almost forgotten Felipe's earlier cruelty now, for its importance had paled beside what had happened an hour or so later, when he'd gathered his guests about him and made the formal announcement of their betrothal! Afterward, he'd slipped the huge ring upon her finger, and kissed her cheek before everyone. She'd almost collapsed from sheer relief when he did so, for in all honesty, she'd been afraid he might have reconsidered his proposal after returning to find her dancing again in public, in flagrant disregard of his orders!

Once their health and happiness had been toasted with champagne, the guests had surged forward to congratulate them both and demanded to know their wedding plans, and the next hour had been spent fielding their questions and basking in her private glow of triumph.

Beloved Saint Sara, it had worked! Gracias a Dios, *it had worked like a charm!* Now all she had to do was marry the crazy old goat, and her future was secure, his wealth her own. And that blackmailing Esteban, their deal, his threats of imprisonment, could all go hang! A handsome devil San Martín might well be, and desire him as a lover she might, but looks and passion—pah, they dwindled over the years, while wealth, wisely managed, invariably increased tenfold!

"Not bad, eh, *gitana?"* she murmured aloud, a smug little smile curving her lips as she admired the heavy ring once again. "No, not bad at all! *Caramba!* This little trinket is *some* knuckle-duster! Poor old Hector would sell his soul for it!"

She smiled impishly as she tore her eyes from the ring and set about undressing. Wrenching the mantilla from her hair, she carelessly tossed it aside, the combs and pins following and showering to the floor. She shook out her unbound hair, and then, wriggling like a circus contortionist, she managed to unhook the scarlet gown in back unaided and stepped from its ruins, leaving it where it fell in an untidy heap to gather wrinkles. A trail of six black petticoats marked her passage about the room as she lit the bedside lamp, turning the wick down low so that only a gentle amber glow illuminated the newly created havoc of her bedchamber. Sitting on the edge of the bed wearing only her filmy chemise, she sighed, yawned hugely again, and kicked off her scarlet slippers. One after the other, they went flying across the room in the direction of the French windows, which she'd left ajar, and towards the balcony beyond.

"Madre de Dios!" exclaimed a deep, pained voice from behind the draperies. "Must you always be so damned violent, *minina?"*

"What—!"

Krissoula sprang to her feet, too astonished to say more for a second. In the same moment, Esteban stepped from concealment behind her flowered draperies, rubbing his dark head and holding one of her high-heeled slippers in his hand.

"Don't scream, *Cenicienta!"* he warned her quickly as her eyes widened and her jaw dropped, his bruised head forgotten as he raised his finger to silence her scream of shock.

"Don't call me Cinderella! It's not as if we're friends, after all, *hombre!* Now, what the devil are you doing up here?" she gritted, furious that he'd so boldly force his way into her room when Felipe

125

was drinking on the patio below with his guests, mere yards away. Her golden eyes crackled with indignation as she added, "And what's more, how did you get in here?"

Fists planted on his hips, he grinned, his eyes gleaming chips of dark sapphire, his teeth a wicked flash of white in the muted light.

"'How' is easy to answer!" he responded with a casual shrug. "I climbed up from the lavender bushes—the same way you climbed down the day I fired Alfredo Flores, remember?" He winked. "And don't act so outraged, sweetie. It could hardly be the first time a strange man has invaded your boudoir, now could it?"

She ignored his pointed observation and snorted in disgust. "You climbed up from outside? *Madre!* Now I've heard everything! Don't you care what would happen if your uncle found you here, with me? Your little game would be up then, San Martín, and no mistake! Felipe would have you thrown off Tierra Rosa on your backside—or else thrashed within an inch of your peasant's life— maybe even killed! And then where would your precious plan be, eh? Aiee, *hombre loco,* what the devil possessed you to do such a crazy thing?"

"To be honest, I'm not sure why I'm here," he answered with disarming frankness, stretching out upon her bed and leaning back on his clasped arms, his long legs casually crossed as he yawned lazily. "But I suspect my motives are far from gentlemanly, though. They usually are . . . !"

He grinned up at her wickedly, and saw the heat rush up to fill her cheeks and add a dangerous brilliance to her eyes before continuing, "Perhaps the *caño* was at fault, eh? That damned rotgut rum your precious fiancé dishes out to his gauchos has made me reckless, I think! The last thing I remember—or rather, that I remember *clearly!*—was watching you dance, and then seeing my dear uncle take you by the wrist and drag you away. I had the craziest urge to choke his cursed neck and carry you off somewhere we could be alone." His eyes darkened sensually. "Now, I wonder why that should be, unless I'm drunk, eh, little one?"

Her lips tightened in a prim expression that was wildly incongruous, considering the earthy sensuality of her vivid beauty. "If you think you can force your way in here and use me like you did the last time, forget it, *hombre!* Felipe is easily within screaming distance this time, remember?" she hissed, frightened by the lusty gleam in his eyes, and praying her reminder would divert his thoughts to safer ground.

Esteban casually shrugged and uncoiled to standing again with the easy grace of a wildcat.

"Scream your little head off, then, *minina,* if that's what you want—to see Felipe gunning for me?" He strolled a pace or two across the room, towards her. "But somehow, I don't think you're that stupid! We both know Felipe would never believe for a minute that I hadn't bedded you if you sounded an alarm, and that he'd run a mile barefoot over hot coals before marrying a woman whose honor has been compromised in any way, and then where would *you* be, eh, *querida?* No Don Felipe. No Esteban de San Martín— and no lovely money from either one of us for poor, greedy little Krissoula, either! Think it through carefully before you scream for help, won't you? And then, if you decide you don't give a damn what your precious Felipe does, or whether you get to keep that vulgar hunk of jewelry weighing down your pretty little finger, go right ahead. Scream your blasted head off! But remember—you stand to lose just as much as I do!" He smiled insolently, calling her bluff.

He was right, and she knew it. She couldn't scream! However innocent it might be on her part, the last thing she needed was for Felipe to ever suspect she'd been alone in her room with a man— and especially not *this* man! As Esteban had implied, the wedding plans would be canceled in short order—and with them her plans to someday be the widow of the wealthy *hacendero!*

Fighting down the jumpy feelings Esteban's presence bred in her, she steeled herself to move and walked across the room, slipping into the yellow silk wrapper that hung from a peg in the rosewood armoire to cover her state of undress. As she did so, she could feel his sensual hooded eyes devouring her, and grimaced ruefully. It was getting to be something of a habit, she thought, arguing with San Martín in her underwear . . .

"Aaah! Spoilsport!" he commented with a disappointed groan as she knotted the sash of her wrapper tightly about her waist and turned back to face him decently covered.

"Shut your filthy mouth, *gato!*" she hissed back, golden eyes flashing as her short-fused Latin temper exploded. She tossed her head irritably. *"Silencio,* you tomcat! If you have nothing better to do than leer at me, climb back down the way you came—and I'll pray to all the saints you break your cursed neck in the process!"

"Oh, I can think of a dozen better things to do to you than 'leer,'" he threatened wolfishly, "and I guarantee you'd enjoy them all, remember, my luscious little *bombón?"*

She tossed her head, ignoring the little thrills his reminder sent shooting through her loins. "Pah! The devil I would! I told you before, your lovemaking leaves me cold, *gato!* And quit calling me *bombón!* Save your sweet talk for the silly maids who are naive enough to enjoy it," she suggested waspishly, furious that he had her at a stalemate, "and tell me what it is you really want?" She couldn't call for help, as well he knew, not without endangering herself, so how on earth was she to get rid of him this time—?

"All right," he agreed resignedly. "The truth is, I have another little—how shall I put it?—task for you to do for me?"

"Oh?" she observed, suspicion etched in every feature. "What task?"

"My uncle and that Jaime Ramirez—they're up to something. I know it, but I'll be damned if I can figure out exactly what it is! I was wondering if—while you and my precious uncle are billing and cooing like turtledoves!—you could ask a few discreet questions, and try to worm out of him what's going on?"

"If I agree, you'll leave?"

He frowned. "So soon—and after I climbed all the way up here, too? What's your hurry, *querida?* I'd been hoping we could dispense with business in short order, and spend what's left of the night in far more pleasurable ways—hopefully the same way we spent those few stolen moments the other afternoon in the *puesto?* Come on! What do you say, kitten? Will my *minina* sheathe her sharp claws for the night, and let Esteban teach her how to purr?"

He reached out and stroked her cheek with the back of his hand. His smoldering, sensual eyes never left her face as he spoke, and she could feel color and warmth rising to fill her cheeks beneath his knuckles as his gaze devoured her. Oh, God. A single touch, and the urge to melt, to lean against him and surrender to his lovemaking was overpowering! Self-conscious and trying to conceal her weakness, she hurriedly looked down—and immediately regretted doing so, for her treacherous gaze fell upon the straining line of Esteban's tight-fitting breeches. His arousal was quite evident, and remembering how it had been between them upon the rustling, whispering leaves in the shadows of the line-camp hut made desire suddenly quiver through her loins like the silvery shimmer of a heat wave rising from sun-baked ground. Her heart skipped a beat, then two. Her mouth felt suddenly dry, her tongue knotted. So that's why that rogue had really forced his way in here! Not to ferret out Felipe and Ramirez's plans, but to seduce her again. She'd been right about him all along! *Caray,* the blackmailing brute had balls, no, to coolly contemplate bedding her again, and beneath Felipe's very own roof, too, while the man entertained his guests in the patio below! Well, she'd reward his boldness in no uncertain terms!

"Pah! Maybe you are drunk, as well as *loco,* to think I'd willingly let you lay a hand on me, *hombre!*"she flung at him with a nervous, brittle little laugh. It was all she could do to speak, let alone come back at him with the cutting retorts she wanted to make, so powerful was the urge to yield to his blandishments and give herself over to the pleasure she knew she'd find in his arms!

"Am I?" He grinned. "After watching you dance this evening, I don't think you'd put up much of a fight! You were sending out signals that only a fool—or a gelding—could fail to read, darling! And I'm neither, just in case you need reminding—! Ah, *minina,* I'd bet more than one poor bastard on Tierra Rosa's spending a restless night, tossing in his bed and thinking wicked thoughts about you!"

"Then why don't you join them, San Martín? Go toss in your own bed—alone!" she spat, her golden eyes glittering in the lamplight, "And leave me be!"

"Perhaps I'd rather stay here, and enjoy what your dancing dared me to claim? It *was* me you danced for, wasn't it, *querida?*" he demanded softly.

"You?" she sputtered. "The devil it was! You think I'd dance just for the likes of you, you blackmailing snake? Pah! You're an arrogant fool!" she jeered in a scathing tone, lying through her teeth, for her body was already afire for him, aching with a longing so fierce, she trembled inside. "If you were the last man alive, I'd kiss a—a baboon before I gave myself to you!"

But *caray,* how her poor knees shook, how her heart thumped— so loudly, she was certain he must be able to hear it from across the room! Had her innermost secret desires really been so transparent as she danced tonight? Had her hunger for him been so easy to read? *Madre de Dios,* it must have! Then little wonder Felipe had been livid with her . . . !

"Oh, I think you'd do more than just *dance* for me, Krissoula mía, or simply kiss me, given half the chance," he said silkily. "Much more—coin or no coin! You're the fool, if you think a man can't tell when a woman wants him! And I do want you, *minina,* you know that, don't you, so—where's the harm in it, eh, little one? You're a young, passionate woman, and you want to share the pleasure we shared that first time. There's nothing wrong with that. I'll give you a night to remember, *querida,* if you'll forget your role, just for tonight?" he coaxed, stepping closer. "Let's be nothing other than what we are for a few hours. Not blackmailer and spy, not Krissoula and Esteban, but simply a man and a woman who need each other. Come to bed, *querida!* Let me love you . . ."

As he spoke, he reached out to caress her again, and something inside her snapped. Curse his soul! That he should expect her to so eagerly surrender and spread her thighs for him again infuriated her! It meant nothing to him that she was Krissoula Ballardo, niece to the Gypsy "Count" Ricardo Ballardo, whose virginity had once been a priceless jewel to be treasured until the day of her marriage! He treated her as if she were a lusting female animal, not a person whose feelings and wishes were worth considering! He treated her casually, as if she were not La Reina, Queen of Flamenco, whose favors had been sought after by the wealthy *hidalgos* of two continents, but instead propositioned her as if she were no more than a raddled, ten-peso whore selling herself in the cribs of the Madrid wharves! Reaching behind her, she picked up a hairbrush from the dressing table and flung it at him, following it with her porcelain box of hairpins and the hand mirror in swift succession screaming, "Go to bed with *you,* you foul-mouthed whoreson? *Dios,* you really are mad! *Bastardo! Canallo! Hijo de puta!* For the last time, g-e-e-e-t o-u-u-u-t of here!"

He ducked and twisted, and her missiles, fired with deadly accuracy, glanced off him, crashed into the wall at his back and shattered. On the stillness of the night, the impacts sounded deafening. Alarm acted upon his arousal like a bucket of water. His expression darkened swiftly to one of anger, rather than passion.

"Cut it out, *tonta!* You'll have all of Tierra Rosa up here in a minute, you little fool!" he hissed, genuinely shocked by her total disregard for caution. Perhaps it wasn't entirely an act, after all, he wondered uncertainly now? Perhaps—despite all appearances to the contrary that time in Barcelona—he'd been wrong, and she wasn't a *puta?* Was, in fact, far more of an innocent than she seemed? Her outrage certainly seemed genuine enough—or did it stem from something other than innocence? Perhaps he'd misread her completely, and she felt nothing but dislike for him, as she'd insisted all along?

"So what if I do wake everyone? Think what you will, but *I* have nothing to fear!" she retorted, too angry to guard her tongue now. She was bent on brazening it out all the way, of gaining the upper hand over him for this once, curse his arrogance, and with Krissoula, when fury flew in the door, common sense left by the window! "Let Felipe come up here and find you, *gato.* I don't give a damn—though I wouldn't want to be in your boots when he does!

I'll swear that you surprised me while I was undressing. That I was forced to defend my honor! That I threw things at you to protect myself! I'll swear you threatened to stop at nothing to prevent our marriage and take Tierra Rosa from him, and that your—your plan was to seduce me, his innocent *novia,* to do so!" she finished triumphantly, the rash words escaping her in a powerful, heady torrent more potent than an intoxicating wine as she saw the devastating effect her threats had on him.

The grin faded abruptly from Esteban's face, and was replaced by a murderous scowl. "So you'd squeal on me, would you?" he growled, his tone a rough, threatening purr that was laced with menace, and somehow sounded more of the *barrios* than the well-to-do world in which he moved.

"Sí!" she gloated, certain she had him at the disadvantage now. "If you won't leave right this minute, I'll tell Felipe *all* about you, San Martín! And all about how we met in Barcelona, and your clever little plans to cash in on my resemblance to the saintly Manuela to find proof of your birth, and have Tierra Rosa for yourself! Oh, once Felipe heard my story, he'd make certain that you'd never succeed, I know he would! Right now, he has the law on his side, remember? Whether you like it or not, he's the *patrón* of this *estancia.* He's in control—did you forget that, San Martín? Push me too far for your own ends, and I swear that within three months, I'll be his bride and *la patrona* here! If you try to force me to your bed, I'll spill my guts, I swear it! I'll tell Felipe everything— every last juicy little detail of your plans—and you, my fine *mayordomo,* will be left out in the cold on your bastard's backside, looking for a job!" she jeered.

"Over my dead body," Esteban swore, his expression dark and frightening now in its intensity, all traces of banter and wicked humor gone. He looked quite capable of taking her by the throat and squeezing the life out of her, but Krissoula was oblivious to his expression. In her anger, she'd gone beyond fear, for the time being.

"If that's what it takes, then I'm sure Felipe will be only too happy to oblige you, *hombre!*" she hissed. "And I," she added bloodthirstily, "will dance a fandango on your grave!"

A strange expression, frightening in its dark intensity and purpose, filled Esteban's features. His sapphire eyes were shadowed in the muted light, but anger glowed in them like banked coals.

"You've gone too far with your threats this time, Krissoula," he said so softly she almost had to strain to hear his words. "You've obviously forgotten, *chiquita,* that I'm master of this little game,

131

not you! I'm the one calling the shots here, and it strikes me you need another little lesson in obedience. A reminder of just what you were when we met! Take off the robe, little *puta.*"

His harsh command was a low purr, like the deadly, threatening rumble of a dark panther preparing to spring. When she hesitated, torn between defiance and flight, Esteban's powerful hand streaked out and gripped the slippery silk front of her robe in knotted fingers.

"You heard me, Krissoula. Take it off, I said!"

He wrenched the fabric, jerking her roughly, and the loose garment fell away from her shoulder, baring a breast. He jerked the other front, and the garment slithered down her slender body, coming to rest in a yellow puddle about her feet. Before she could react, he gripped the front of her brief, filmy chemise and tore it from her body in a single move. The fragile cloth gave with a little scream of protest, leaving her naked, and Krissoula swallowed a terrified sob. Her graceful hands flew up to shield her bared breasts. God in heaven, he was a madman!

He sprang towards her with all the grace and speed of a leaping jaguar, gripping her by the forearms and holding her roughly for a second before he dragged her against his chest. His mouth came down over hers, hard and brutal in his determination to punish her for her threats of betrayal, to instill such fear in her, she wouldn't dare double-cross him in the future, not if her very life depended upon it!

Hungrily, he ground his cruel mouth over hers, ravaging the sweetness of her inner mouth with his tongue, bruising her lips with the hard, fiery heat of his. His large hand found and roughly fondled her soft breasts, forcing an anguished sob from Krissoula that was half pleasure, half pain. She tried to twist free of him, to escape his grip by pushing at his chest with her palms, yet his lean brown fingers pushed her hands away and swept down over her body insolently stroking across the flat plain of her belly to plunder the soft, dark nest at the juncture of her thighs. Despite her fear, despite her fury, she was shamed beyond words as he slipped his hand between her thighs, knowing that when he touched her there, as he must, as he would, he would find her aroused and ready. Oh, damn him—damn her body's betrayal! Must he win even now, even this battle of wills—? Must he turn her own secret passions against her?

His arm curled about her waist, dragging her fully against him so that her feet left the floor. He raked his mouth over the swollen fullness of her lower lip, reddened by his earlier kisses, and commanded in a thick, strangled tone, "Lie down, Krissoula. I'll have you now."

"Please—"

"Lie down!"

"But I didn't mean it! I'd never double-cross you, I—I swear it!"

"No?" he gritted. "Little liar! Lovely treacherous little liar! You'd double-cross your own grandmother, for a price. Lie down!"

"But I—I won't betray you, I swear it—! Don't do this to me—please don't!"

"Lie down!" he barked.

Trembling, she drew herself from his punishing arms and turned hesitantly towards the bed, turning back to face him with an imploring expression on her face. "Esteban, you must listen—!"

"Oh, but I've already heard everything you have to say, *minina!*" he rasped, tugging his shirt up and over his head. He flung it aside, baring his broad bronze chest, his muscular shoulders. His flesh gleamed like tan satin in the lamplight as he strode slowly towards her. *"Sí,* I've heard more than enough! You can add tonight to the little tale you tell my damned uncle—should you ever grow rash enough to betray me! Now. Enough of this stalling. On your back, *muchacha!*"

As if he were only waiting to see her bowed beneath the force of his will, obedient to his harsh, hateful commands, the minute she lay down he was upon her. He forced his knee between her thighs and loomed over her, his lean, handsome face dark and savage in the muted lamplight as he braced his weight on his hands, planted on either side of her shoulders. Her long-lashed slanted golden eyes were wide with apprehension as she gazed up into his, and her lower lip quivered. For a moment, that tremulous quivering almost undid him, swayed him from his purpose, and the urge to make love to her with tenderness swept over him. But then he recovered, steeled himself to his original purpose and set his jaw hard as he reached between them to unfasten his breeches and bare his rigid shaft.

Without further caresses, without endearments or kisses, he thrust deep into the softness of her woman's body, riding between her thighs and roughly fondling her breasts as if she were truly no more than a *ramera* he'd bought and paid for. She'd find no pleasure whatsoever in their coupling as she had the last time, he swore. Tonight, she'd learn that he was her master, she the hireling, be damned if she wouldn't, he vowed! By his mercilessness, his cruelty, he'd instill such fear in her, she'd never dare to double-

133

cross him—!

But Esteban had reckoned without Krissoula's unexpected response, nor had he paused to consider that at heart he was not a cruel man, nor one given to abusing his women.

As he took her, the sweet, encompassing tightness of her body enfolded him in sensations more pleasurable than those enjoyed in his wildest dreams. Her slender body, so perfectly, petitely rounded, bore his weight, pillowed him in delight. Her pointed breasts were crushed beneath the wiry roughness of his broad chest, but he could feel the hardened tips against his skin, and he shivered with sensual pleasure. Her hips arched eagerly upward to meet the driving, flexing power of his flanks, embedding and drawing him ever deeper into the velvet caress of her sheath. With a groan, he wound his hand through her tumbled raven curls and kissed her deeply, drawing her fevered lips to his, drowning in the honeyed taste of her mouth as it moved tentatively against his. The feel of her arms embracing him, of her graceful hands slipping over his shoulders and down his back, caressing him, made him shudder with the escalating force of his passion.

"Esteban! Oh, God, Esteban—!"

She cried his name, and although her words were muffled by his mouth as he tore his lips from hers to draw breath, the cry brought him to his senses, reminded him of his original purpose. He felt the stillness grow in her, and, looking down, saw her glorious eyes cloud over like veiled jewels, their color darkening to misty gold as her passion peaked. He felt her body arch like a bow beneath his impaling weight, and knew her release was imminent. For the lesson to be learned, he should withdraw from her now, and deny her the pleasure she craved. But—his own need was too pressing, too compelling to deny! He could no sooner end it now than fly!

The pressure at his own loins gathered, built, like stormclouds massing above the mountaintops, swollen with rain. Sweat beaded on his brow and trickled down his back as the sweetfire tension mounted in his aching groin; growing, expanding, and then finally exploding, filling him with a heady rush of relief and pleasure that made him gasp aloud, and reel like a drunkard, intoxicated by the astonishing sweetness of its draught. Still shaken, he drew away from her, from the bed, hearing only dimly her cry of disappointment as he untangled himself from her arms and reached for his breeches.

"How could you—!" she whispered. "How could you! Aiee, *Dios,* how I hate you! Hate you!" She rolled over onto her side, and

134

buried her face in her pillow.

He set his jaw and made his expression hard as he fastened his breeches and drew his shirt over his head. Fully dressed, he strode back to the bed and leaned over her. Taking her chin between his fingers, he forced her to look at him, surprised by the complete lack of tears in her eyes, despite her wounded expression.

"Let tonight be a lesson to you, *minina,*" he gritted mercilessly. "Breathe a word, and you'll regret it! *You'll* be the one out of here on your pretty backside, not me, make no mistake, darling!" he threatened, his sapphire eyes blazing into hers. The icily controlled violence of him now somehow terrified her more than his earlier fury. "Just a single, careless word out of turn, and I'll see you walking the lowest *barrios* of Buenos Aires, spreading your lovely legs for every drunken sailor with a spare peso in his pocket," he rasped. "How would you like that, eh, *ramera?*

"Now, we made a deal, you and I," he menaced, "and I mean to see that you keep your part of it, to the last letter. You'll do as I tell you, no more, no less. And be warned; if you still harbor any ideas of double-crossing me, little one, I'll make sure you live to regret it for the rest of your life! There'll be no city big enough to keep me from you—no hiding place I won't be able to ferret out. I can be a good ally when this is over, *querida*—or an enemy more deadly than any you've ever imagined! *Comprende?*" he growled, jerking her so roughly by the chin her head flopped about like a rag doll's.

For a second, she was too stunned to answer him. She merely gaped up at him, pale-faced, as if she'd never seen him before—and in truth, she hadn't, not this side of him!

"I asked if you understood me, girl?" he ground out again, taking her by the shoulders and dragging her up, off the bed, so fiercely her feet left the floor.

"*Sí!*" she whispered. "*Sí!* But, Esteban, you must believe me, despite what I threatened, I never really intended to tell Felipe anything, I swear I didn't! I was just angry that you . . . that you . . . Oh, damn you, yes, yes, I understand!" she acknowledged as his fingers tightened cruelly around her arms, biting into her tender flesh. "Please, you're hurting me! Let go!"

He gazed deep into her eyes and seemed to believe her, for he nodded, just once, and murmured very softly as he released her, "That's better."

"*Krissoula! Señorita, is something wrong?*"

Her head jerked sharply about as furious knocking sounded at her locked door, breaking the roaring silence between them

135

as they stared into each other's faces. For a fleeting moment, she had a sudden premonition that, despite his fury, despite everything, he meant to kiss her again, but then the moment passed and was gone forever.

"Niña! *Are you all right? Did you fall? Answer me,* niña!" pleaded Sofía's anxious voice.

"Are you leaving—or sh-shall I get rid of her?" Krissoula asked. Her voice sounded far calmer than she felt. The situation had grown so quickly out of control, he'd become so deadly so very, very fast, the shock still lingered, slowing thought and speech and movement.

His moody dark-sapphire eyes were enigmatic as he scowled at her. "*Sí,* I'll be leaving for now, *chiquita*—but remember tonight, and what I've said, and don't do or say anything that you might later regret!"

With that parting threat, he slipped between the opened French doors and out onto the balcony, much to Krissoula's relief.

"Coming, Sofía!" she called shakily, and after checking that his tall frame had disappeared over the balcony, she hurried to answer the door.

Sofía, her hair done up in rags, was standing there, wearing a prim flannel nightgown buttoned to the chin. She held a candlestick in one hand, the slim flame guttering in the draught.

"Are you hurt? Did you fall? What on earth were those crashing sounds I heard?"

"I'm all right, except for a bruise or two on my shins," Krissoula lied, pressing her knees tightly together to still their trembling. "As for the sounds, well, like a fool, I—I turned the lamp wick too low to see by, and stumbled against the dressing table while I was getting ready for bed!" She opened the door a little wider. "Just look at this mess! My porcelain pin box went flying, and that lovely mirror, too! *Aiee, qué tonta!* I'll see the mess cleared up first thing in the morning, Sofía, don't worry about it tonight. You go on back to bed."

With a relieved nod and her wishes for a good night's sleep, Sofía went back to her own room.

Krissoula closed the door in her wake and leaned upon it for a few seconds, eyes closed, while she recovered her composure.

"San Martín? Are you still there?" she whispered softly moments later on the silence, wanting to make sure that he was really gone. To her relief, there was no answer. Hurrying to the French doors, she locked them, making a mental note never to leave them open at night again, air or no air. To do so only invited trouble!

Still too disturbed to sleep, she tossed and turned restlessly for over two hours. By then, the night sky had grown flushed with rosy color beyond her window, but she was still unable to find sleep even with the coming of dawn.

Daybreak found her tired and weepy and still furious with herself. What a stupid, stupid fool she'd been to blurt out her intentions like that, just to be rid of him, to gain the upper hand, foolishly thinking she could later laugh off her words as idle threats! Men like Esteban de San Martín made dangerous toys! What could she have been thinking of, to show her hand so rashly and so soon, and play with him that way? Well, she'd been royally burned for her rashness, and no mistake! He'd shown her who was the master of their little arrangement, using her and tossing her contemptuously aside the way he had, with no thought for her pleasure whatsoever. Dare she still risk double-crossing him after his threats? *Dios!* The very idea terrified her now! When she'd first stupidly threatened him, he'd seemed quite capable of killing her in his fury! Dare she risk her life for the sake of a comfortable future, go ahead with her plans, and pray that Don Felipe would take care of that hateful San Martín when and if the time came? Or should she take the safe way out, do what she'd agreed to do, find his cursed papers if they existed, and meekly vanish from Tierra Rosa when she'd served his purpose?

It was the hardest decision she'd ever had to make in her nineteen years! And, if she decided wrongly, she had an awful feeling that San Martín might see to it that she never saw her twentieth . . .

Chapter Ten

Esteban saddled his horse and mounted up, urging the black-stockinged bay swiftly away from the *casa grande,* where Felipe and his remaining guests still lingered over their drinks, and out onto the moonlit grasslands of the pampas.

He was forced to slow his pace after a while to keep a careful watch on the trail ahead as he rode, for potholes that might trip a horse and leave it with a broken leg were all too many in these parts, thanks to those damned little *cuis,* animals similar to gophers, which made their burrows in the grasslands of the pampas.

A half hour's ride brought him to the little adobe house which his position as *mayordomo,* or ranch manager, of Tierra Rosa earned him, rather than a space on the hard dirt floor of the bunkhouse, where the *gauchos* not needed out on the grasslands to ride herd over *el patrón*'s vast herds made their bed.

Any other night he would have joined them, the hour being late and his gut fiery with good red wine and cheap *caña*—the pale, rotgut rum which Felipe had doled out to the manservants and cowboys for the festive occasion on his return. But, not tonight. Tonight, after that disturbing interlude with Krissoula, he needed to be alone with his thoughts.

After unsaddling and watering his horse, he turned it out into the corral with the rest of his *tropilla,* or string, which numbered six horses in all, each one of them black-stockinged bays and so alike they could have been womb-mates. The bays came to nuzzle his hands for treats, and so he lingered awhile in the bright moonlight, fondling their soft, velvety noses and calling each one affectionately by name.

Building a string of horses that were matched by color and size was an old *gaucho* tradition, but few of the *gauchos* now living practiced it anymore. Nevertheless, Esteban had heard of the custom and liked the idea. Although not a *gaucho* himself, he'd bought and traded horses over the past few years until he'd built up his own *tropilla,* which he enjoyed displaying at fairs and festivals about the countryside, dressed in traditional *gaucho* costume. His father had done similarly in his lifetime, choosing to build up the number of palominos in his tables and corrals until, at the time of his death, he'd owned over twenty of the beautiful blond animals, along with his other fine horses. And not one of those twenty, including his father's favorite stallion at the time, a huge horse named Rayo, had possessed a mean bone in its body, he recalled grimly, although Rayo had been blamed for his father's death nevertheless. Felipe had ordered the stallion shot immediately when he took over the *estancia* soon after, and since Esteban, sick with grief over his father's death, had not been there to countermand the order, magnificent Rayo had been destroyed.

Two years ago, that had been, and Esteban still felt the same frustration and anger he'd felt then, on hearing the father he'd grown to love had been killed. Time had softened his rage, but hadn't succeeded in ridding him of it, nor in lessening his determination to learn the true facts of his father's death and avenge his murder. That, more than anything—his burning desire to ensure that his uncle Felipe should not profit from his crime, that he be called to account—was what drove him mercilessly to prove his claim to the *estancia.* Becoming master of Tierra Rosa was only secondary.

His huge dog, Rojo, bounded forward to greet him as he approached the house, barking joyfully as his master led the way inside. The two-roomed cottage he called home—for the time being, anyway—was no *casa grande.* Measuring only sixteen by twelve feet in all, the stark interior boasted two small rooms of whitewashed adobe, clean but unadorned except for serviceable pegs to hold his belongings, saddles, tack, and so forth. The humble abode was in brutal contrast to the opulence of Tierra Rosa that he'd just left. Tossing Rojo a bone from the screened meat-safe in which he kept his perishables, he lit a lantern and hung it from a beam above his head.

"Soon, Rojo, *mi amigo!"* he promised the dog as he lit another match and squatted on his heels to start the fire in the stone fireplace he'd built himself. "Soon we'll be living in comfort, instead of Señor Felipe de Aguilar, eh?"

Winter nights could be cold and damp on the pampas, though snowfalls were rare. Yet few of the settlers' hovels boasted a real fireplace, as did his. Esteban had seen no need to deny himself this one small comfort, as had those other *perezosos,* lazy ones. Too idle to do more work than was absolutely necessary for their survival, they did little to better their lot or even keep themselves clean, although there was a plentiful water supply from the countless little streambeds that crisscrossed the grasslands; more than enough for drinking, for keeping a man and his clothing washed, for watering his stock and irrigating his few crops. In fact, there was fresh grazing everywhere in abundance to raise enough livestock to feed a large family; fertile land for the growing of vegetables, or a little grain to provide variety and bread for the table—no excuse whatsoever for men to live in filthy hovels, wallowing in their own dirt worse than any animal! That might suit others, but not Esteban de San Martín. Even in his early years, when he and his mother had lived in a single room above a tavern in one of the *barrios* of Buenos Aires, he had never gone dirty. Hungry, yes. Sick with fever in the summers, yes. Shivering with damp and cold in the winters, yes. But dirty—never! His mother, María de San Martín, whose name he'd taken, had seen to that.

"To live a good life, a man needs only God, and pride in himself, my son," she'd always told him. "And how can a man stand before his God with a dirty neck and ears, eh?"

Now the memory made him smile, but at the time he'd always nodded solemnly.

Gazing into the growing flicker of light as the fire caught and grew, he added fresh kindling to the flames and remembered how she'd also told him, time and time again, that he was the only son of a wealthy *hacendero,* a man named Alejandro de Aguilar. His father loved them and wanted them with him, but could not take care of them because someone was looking for them, some mysterious, wicked people who wanted to hurt them or perhaps even take Esteban away from his *mamacita.* They must remain in hiding until the danger was past, and he must promise, she'd told him, he must swear before God, that he would *never* tell anyone his real father's name until she said it was time to do so, and he'd solemnly promised and sworn and kept that vow to the bitter end.

That last year, cholera and yellow fever had taken hundreds of lives in the city, claiming both rich *porteños* and the dwellers of the *barrios* alike. María de San Martín had also fallen ill, and there'd been no money for doctors, nor any cure for what sickened her even could they have afforded one. Whether his childhood sicknesses had protected him from contracting the dreaded cholera from her, he never knew, but in a few short days she'd died, and he'd been left healthy but alone, the promise from which she'd never released him the only thing of worth he had left.

Ten years old he'd been then, with no one to turn to, and not even the shabby little room they'd shared for shelter, with his mother dead.

"To my knowledge, dead women can't dance, *pibe!*" Luigi, the dance-hall owner had told him with macabre humor, speaking in *lunfardo*, the peculiar, Italian-rooted dialect of the slums. "And no dancing means no money to pay for your room. Besides, you're a man now, *pibe*, ten is old enough to make your own way in the world, and so—*chau!* Come back when you're rich, eh, and buy old Luigi a drink!"

With that, Luigi had kicked him downstairs and into the filthy, rutted streets, which were dusty and stinking with refuse in the summer heat.

The people of the *barrios* were close-knit, as a rule, and helped each other out in hard times, but Luigi had been an exception. He'd wanted lovely Maria de San Martín as his woman, but Maria had refused him to her last breath. In his bitterness, he'd not lifted a finger to help her when she fell ill. Nor would he help the little son she'd left behind.

Having nowhere else to go, nor any limits on his time, young Esteban had wandered down to the riverbanks, and watched the Negro and mulatto washerwomen pounding dirty clothes on the rocks there, running away with a reddened face when they teased him and called him a "handsome little rooster," and asked him slyly if he was still a virgin.

"So! Have you had your first wo-mon yet, *gallito?*" they'd asked throatily, he remembered with a grin, and they'd rolled their liquid dark eyes and nudged each other. "If not, little mon, Consuela help you out, eh, Consuela? She like her men young—the younger de bettah! That girl, she drop her drawers for you anytime, handsome—won't you, 'Suela-girl?"

"Better dan that, Rosie-girl!" slender Consuela, a pretty mulatto woman, had teased back in her lilting voice. She'd lifted her arms from the soapy yellow river water to flourish the most enormous pair of frilly woman's drawers he'd ever seen in his direction! "I've already dropped dem, don't you see, mon!"

He'd fled as if the hounds of hell were after him—or at the very least, one of the evil spirits the *curanderos* cautioned everyone against!

It had been a long time before he'd dared return to the riverbanks and face the washerwomen's merciless teasing—almost four years—but when he had, he'd changed. And they hadn't teased him, not anymore. They'd looked him over with expressions he'd learned to recognize by then as ones of female approval, and more than a little interest, and had greeted him in their dark, sensual voices that always made him think of rich chocolate sweetened with brown cane sugar, for by then he'd left childhood far behind. By then, he'd become a man, and was a virgin no more.

Life hadn't been easy. The first few weeks after his mother died had become a blur now, each day having blended endlessly into the fog of the last. He remembered only hurting inside with a grief so deep he wanted to die, too, just so he could be with her again and not have to bear the aching loneliness.

Hunger had been his only companion, fear his only watchdog in those terrible days. He'd slept in filthy, littered alleys, making his bed on heaps of decomposing garbage, for there it was at least a little warmer—and safer—than prowling the dangerous dark streets. Each evening, he'd rummage amongst this rotting "bedding" for scraps of food, daring to slink out and take his turn only after the bigger, stronger, older scavengers who roamed the dark back streets of the *barrios* were done, for even here, amongst the human castoffs and vermin who lived their lives in the streets, there was still a pecking order, and it was the strongest, always the strongest, who survived.

And then one night, the clawing hunger had grown too much to bear; any risk had seemed worth taking if it filled his belly, no matter if he disobeyed his mother's stern warnings never to steal, or even lost his life in the process.

It was the long, gray hour shortly before dawn, and Esteban had found himself loitering outside the house of a baker, Señor Mendez, his mouth watering until it gushed saliva like a mad dog's as fragrant, yeasty aromas escaped from Señor Mendez's ovens out into the streets below.

He'd known from other mornings spent standing there, going through the same self-imposed hell of smelling without ever tasting, that at first light a horse and cart would pull up in front of the baker's house. Soon after, the baker and his sons would carry out baskets of bread loaves and rolls, buns, and empanadas, and stack them in back of the cart. Then the cart would lumber away to deliver the baked goods to the baker's shop in the rich *porteño*

142

districts far from Barrio San Timéo. If he moved fast, perhaps he could snatch a loaf or two and run away quickly enough to escape the baker? And if he didn't—well, what did it matter anymore, he asked himself with a fatalistic shrug of his bony shoulders? Who would care if come tomorrow, there was one less urchin prowling the streets, and one more corpse floating in the yellow waters of Río de la Plata? Not he! He'd gone beyond caring.

He timed himself to the second, erupting around the street corner in the very moment the unattended baskets of bread were most vulnerable, the instant after the baker's son had set them down in the back of the cart, and turned to go back inside for another. A dark-haired whirlwind had whipped past Mendez Junior. A scrawny bare brown arm had flashed out, and a long loaf of warm bread had leaped into a small, dirty hand.

"Why, you little thief!" Mendez Junior had bellowed, but in another second, Esteban had been tearing off down the street for all he was worth, ducking into the first alley he came to, scrambling over piles of rubbish and offal, shinnying up walls and springing down to the other side, before dragging himself upright and stumbling on down alley after alley that formed the rabbit warren of the *barrios,* trying to put distance between himself and the baker.

He ran for an hour without once looking back, before he finally clambered over a crumbling wall and into an area that seemed safe, far from the sound of San Timéo's bells, to catch his wind.

The courtyard he'd stumbled into was empty and unfamiliar, close to the wharves and littered with crumbling fountains and withered orange trees. It was surrounded on all four sides by high walls—not a good place to rest in at all, if he'd thought about it, for escape from such a box would be slow and difficult if he was forced to run for it again. But somehow, the high, blank walls had made him feel safe and hidden instead of wary. And besides, he'd been exhausted and so very hungry, and the bread—! Oh, *Dios mío,* how delicious it smelled! How warm and heavy and crusty it felt in his hands! He'd cradled it lovingly to his bony chest for an instant, trembling all over with such giddy anticipation, it had made him dizzy. In fact, his hands and knees were shaking so badly, he was almost afraid he'd drop his prize, and so he squatted down and opened his mouth to tear into the loaf.

Yet his lips had barely brushed the golden crust, his teeth had yet to sink into its buttery shell, when a shrill voice demanded, "Hey, you slug, gimme that!"

Shocked, he'd glanced up to see a ragged youth about four years older than himself standing arrogantly before him, fists planted on his hips, dirty bare feet braced apart. There'd been a belligerent expression in his hard brown eyes that had boded ill for Esteban. Three other boys of similar age and appearance had stood in back of him, and Esteban's belly had turned over with something more than hunger to see them there.

"No. It's mine," he'd said softly, stubbornly, surprised that he could speak, let alone find words to resist.

"Yours? Dirty liar! You stole it, slug! And if there's any thieving to be done in La Boca, we do it, *comprende?* This is our *barrio*—and you don't belong here, worm! Gimme that!"

With this, the boy had reached out to wrench the loaf from Esteban's arms, and no one was more startled than he to find himself filled with an outrage so great, he snapped his head forward and sank his teeth deep into the youth's wiry, skinny arm, drawing blood.

"Yowch! Why, you dirty cur! Bite me, would you! I'll have your teeth for that—*sí,* and your balls, after!"

The next thing he knew, Esteban found himself flattened under the boy, the bread knocked from his arms to the dirt, forced to defend himself.

Anger still blazing through him, he landed a good sock or two on the boy's face and chest, and tore out a hank of thin, greasy black hair as the two of them rolled over and over in the dust of the abandoned courtyard, furiously scuffling. He even began to think that against all odds, he might be winning the fight when they rolled over again and he somehow managed to end up on top.

A hatred he'd never dreamed existed in him surfaced. Looking down at the youth's now bruised and bleeding face, he experienced a savage, unholy joy at this evidence of the damage he'd inflicted. He'd not seen himself in the urchin at all anymore, nor anything even remotely approaching another human being. He'd seen only hunger and loneliness, grief and despair, the unfairness of life that had taken from him the only person he'd ever loved, and he'd struck out at life's injustices and cruelty in the only way he knew how. He'd rained blow after blow from his furiously clenched little fists, until everything before his eyes became a crimson tide of rage!

Seeing their leader being beaten by this little shrimp, the other youths had leaped to his aid, piling on Esteban and dragging him off. Four against one now, Esteban hadn't had much of a chance, but the anger was still there, and it seemed to give him new strength. They might take his hard-won loaf of bread, but he'd be damned if they'd get off easily, he swore!

Three of them had bloody noses, all had at least one black eye, one had lost a tooth, and bloodstained spit was dribbling from his lip when the first boy pulled a knife.

The air in the courtyard subtly changed; it grew tense and charged, expectant and lethal. Everything stilled. All that happened after that moment seemed slowed, to Esteban's thinking, as if everyone, every action, moved through a syrupy, dragging fog. Before he could recover from his shock at seeing the glittering blade materialize in Antonio's fist, they'd jumped him, pinned him to the ground, and though he struggled and writhed under their weight, he couldn't escape.

"You'll pay now, *perro!*" Antonio had menaced, shifting the long-bladed switch-knife from hand to hand so that it flashed evilly in the first rays of the sun coming up over the city. "I'll cut out your stinking little heart, and eat it along with your bread—! We'll teach you to stay where you belong, *amigo,* but good—!" he'd jeered, and the other urchins had snickered their agreement.

He'd tried to escape their hold, but one of them had kicked him in the ribs several times. Another had lifted his head by the hair and slammed it down against the hard dirt again and again until he saw stars, and a pounding agony in his skull made thought impossible. Another had sat on his legs while the fourth, Antonio, ripped open the front of his dirty, ragged shirt and bared his chest. He'd known then that they'd do as they'd threatened, and cut out his heart and eat it with his bread—and also that he could fight no more. His strength had gone. They'd won!

The narrow square of pale blue sky above his head tilted, and darkness crowded in. He'd felt the sting of the sharp blade as it crisscrossed his chest, a warm, wet splash that was his own blood, and known it was all over for him.

"*Madre!*" he'd whispered through swollen, bloodied lips. "*Mamacita,* will I see you now?"

And then the sky had gone strangely black, as if the sun had been blown out like a snuffed candle, and there'd been nothing but that wonderful, velvet nothingness until he'd opened his eyes again, and seen the *compadrito,* Rolón Severino, standing over him . . .

He blinked to dispel the old memories and straightened. The fire was going well now, and spilled warmth and light over the room, casting his and Rojo's shadows like giants on the whitewashed walls.

Finding a little sack on a shelf, he ground a handful of the rich

145

Colombian coffee beans he loved and tossed them into a pot, which he propped over the fire to boil. Soon, the fragrant, spicy aroma of coffee filled the room. Esteban poured himself a scalding cupful and sipped it black and unsweetened, then lit himself a slim black cigar and smoked, cursing the overabundance of liquor he'd consumed that had made him maudlin and nostalgic.

His days of living hand to mouth in the *barrios* were long past. But—although he'd sworn to Rolón Severino he'd never go back there, to where life was cheap and it was the brute force and fickle whims of the *compadritos* that determined who lived and who died as often as poverty and sickness—go back he had from time to time, to the Ciudad de los Niños, the City of Children that huddled on the banks of the Plata, only to find that nothing had changed for the better. *Nothing, damn it!* Little children were still left homeless and hungry, sick and frightened, as he'd once been, and without vast sums of money, there was little he could do to better their lot. Frustration, impatience filled him. *Dios,* if only Tierra Rosa were already his! If only he could guarantee that one day, some day, she would belong to him, instead of floundering around in this agonizing sea of doubt! *Madre,* the things he could do for the *niños* then, the changes he could make!

His fists clenched around the enamel coffee mug, and his sapphire eyes were fierce with determination as he gazed intently into the flames. Then he sighed, and his shoulders slumped. Hell, what good did brooding about it do? Better he think of the present and the future, and leave the past where it belonged: firmly behind him.

As he exhaled thin plumes of smoke through his nostrils, he gazed again into the fire and saw the golden eyes of Krissoula Ballardo in their depths, blazing with anger, or alternately soft and warm with invitation. Ah, *minina,* my little kitten, what a tempting, infuriating mystery you are, he thought, bewildered by the conflicting emotions he felt for the girl.

Despite the threats she'd made to betray him—and they'd been very real threats, despite her belated protest to the contrary, he knew instinctively—a warm smile softened his lips as he recalled how she'd danced only for him that night, her magnificent golden eyes seeking his above the rim of his wineglass and flaring with desire.

Sí, she'd wanted him, although she'd denied it. Not only her eyes, but the way she moved her body—the things she didn't say as well as the ones she did—all betrayed her feelings. No stranger to women, he knew it as surely as he knew that he wanted her, too—and that he would have her again, sooner or later. Some things defied all logic, and this was one of them. A single, electric glance in the kitchens of Tierra Rosa that day, and he'd known that sooner or later, they would be lovers, and that he would know the mysteries of her woman's body. That the fires of passion that leaped between them might consume and destroy them both in the process was also a possibility he'd reluctantly accepted, for neither of them was capable of lukewarm passions. Hell, no! Love or hate, anger or joy, passion or greed, the emotions they felt were felt intensely, and with an all-consuming fire, flaring up and blazing with the threat of self-destruction implicit in their intensity. Gazing into her catlike golden eyes tonight, he'd felt even more strongly the tug of fate pulling them together against their strongest wills . . .

He shook his head at the irony of it. There'd been many women in his past, women of both breeding and virtue, and delightful scores of others who'd had small claim to either. But never had he felt more for them than a passing desire, an idle curiosity, perhaps, and the thrill of a brief challenge to woo them to his bed that they had conveniently—eagerly!—supplied, before he moved on to the next woman, with no hard feelings on either side. He'd promised them nothing more permanent or meaningful than a brief and exciting affair, and they'd asked for no more.

Krissoula, on the other hand, could be neatly pigeon-holed into none of the categories of women he had known in the past. She was beautiful, there was no denying that, with her wild mane of ebony Gypsy curls, her seductive eyes and delicately boned face, her slender, graceful body, but many of his other women had been more beautiful. No, it was her fire, her sensuality, that set her apart from the others; that aura of intense sexuality, that promise of unbridled female passion in direct apposition to a strangely vulnerable, childlike, and innocent air about her, that attracted men to her like moths to a vibrant flame, eager to learn which of the two was the real Krissoula, bewildered child or fiercely passionate woman, cloistered nun or born courtesan . . .

But—there was more to it than that for him. There were qualities Krissoula possessed that he'd instinctively recognized and responded to from the very first, because they were qualities he possessed himself—the stubborn instinct for survival, the will and the drive to overcome the odds, and the stubbornness and obstinacy to succeed despite them. Being a fighter himself, he admired that trait in others, had no liking for women who wilted

147

and whimpered when adversity crossed their path.

His little kitten had known what it was to go hungry, to be alone, to grieve uncomforted. To have to struggle day in and day out in order to stay alive, just as he once had. He'd watched her most of the evening, even when she'd not been aware of his eyes upon her, and the signs had still been there, for one who recognized them to see. The tutors he'd hired hadn't succeeded in eradicating a lifetime of hard living, nor the wariness that came with it!

He'd seen the way her body tensed fractionally when he'd introduced her to her guests tonight, and then relaxed just as fractionally when they'd moved on, with the barest hint of triumph playing about her sultry little mouth as if to say, "See! I handled them, didn't I, *hombre?*" He'd heard the almost stilted way she offered them her greetings, an accomplished actress prettily reciting her lines, outwardly confident and poised, inwardly terrified. He'd observed how she always positioned herself so as to have an escape of sorts at her elbow, be it open doorway or the moral support of his nearness. He'd also noticed how she'd carried her platter of food to a quiet, inconspicuous corner and had eaten it with a dedicated relish and guarded watchfulness that few who'd lived a life of plenty ever applied to a mere meal, leaving not a morsel even for politeness' sake when she was done.

"Ah, *sí,* what a woman she was! She had courage, intelligence, and an undauntable spirit that any man would envy! That was why, he fancied, he'd steered clear of Krissoula that year in Spain. She was far too dangerous to be around without succumbing to her allure. The attraction he felt towards her was too real, too intense, and so complex it could only stand in the way of his goals, if he were rash enough to let it blossom into a full-blown affair. Accordingly, he'd done the only thing he could, and put distance between them. Let her consider him only a "dirty blackmailer," he'd decided back then. Let her hate him and chafe to be well rid of him, and get the job he'd compelled her to do by his threats of imprisonment over and done with, as soon as possible. There was less chance of her ending up getting hurt that way, he'd decided, for he'd seen the spark of female interest in her eyes when she looked at him, and had determined to do nothing to encourage those feelings. After all, there could be no future in it, for either of them, so why complicate matters?

But now—since that unforgettable afternoon in the *puesto*— everything had changed. Instead of satisfying his lust for her, their lovemaking had only served to whet his appetite for more, to deepen his craving! *Dios,* the memory of her lithe golden body arched beneath his tormented his sleep! The feel of her soft lips moving against his mouth . . . her honey-nippled mound cupped in his hands . . . her silky thighs enfolding him . . . her hips cradling his body . . . her hands guiding him to that secret, honeyed warmth between her thighs—started the fire within him all over again . . .

"So, what do you think, Rojo? Can I trust her, or no?" he murmured to the dog. "And do I really have a choice?" He smiled. "No, I think not! That lovely little hellcat holds all the cards. She's no fool, and she knows it. When she gets over the fear of God I put into her tonight, she'll realize that. And what will she do then, eh, Rojo? I wonder! What would I do?" He paused, then added, "No question about it! I'd put my money on Don Felipe, and San Martín and his 'sometime' promises of payment be damned!"

He threw back his head and laughed. It was a wicked, calculating laugh that made shaggy Rojo whine uneasily.

"No, she can't be trusted, my friend, promises and protests notwithstanding. She's a survivor, and she'll do whatever she thinks she has to to come out on top, and choose the option that'll keep her there. In this case, by marrying my uncle and double-crossing me! I'll have to watch her, Rojo, watch her like a hawk!" he murmured at length, and took a long, thoughtful swig of the scalding coffee.

Somehow, it was a prospect he found not in the least unpleasant . . .

Chapter Eleven

The vast herds of Tierra Rosa spread out across the rolling Pampa in every direction; a great, constantly moving dark blot against the tall yellow-and-green grasses. In summer months, a dust cloud hung like a thick swarm of locusts over the herd. But in winter months—as it was now—the rich black soil was churned to mud under thousands of hooves, the grasses flattened.

Much like their North American counterparts, the cattle barons of the West, Alejandro de Aguilar and Esteban's grandfather, José, had built their herds from the staggering numbers of scrawny, long-horned wild cattle descended from those which escaped the *conquistadores* three centuries before, and multiplied in incredible numbers. They'd also applied for a *vecino's* license to catch and corral the wild horses that roamed free over Argentina in huge herds, and had broken the sturdy broncos to the saddle for their *remudas,* the strings of replacement horses used to ride herd on the cattle.

But the disappointingly small amount of beef which the slaughter of the scrawny half-wild cattle had yielded for salting and export, coupled with the toughness and poor quality of the meat, had compelled Alejandro and his father to find ways to improve their herds. The introduction of Scottish stock noted for its heavy production of prime, marbled beef, had seemed the obvious course by which to do so. Accordingly, they'd had several Aberdeen Angus stud bulls purchased for the Tierra Rosa herds, and by judicious cross-breeding of these enormous beasts with their own hardy yet far smaller semi-domesticated cows, their herds had, in a few years, been vastly improved and beef yield tripled.

Esteban leaned on the pommel of his saddle and looked out over the grazing herds with a shrewd eye. The herds were quiet for now, the *gauchos* who herded them circling from time to time to ensure that they remained so, mounted on their nimble little broncos.

There was a distinct nip in the air this morning, and Esteban observed that, like himself, all of the cowboys had opted to wear warm woolen ponchos against the chill.

Those who were not actively patroling the herds had congregated beneath a few *quebrachos*, "axe-breaker" trees, to enjoy an early-morning cup of fresh-brewed coffee, or perhaps a steaming gourd of *yerba maté*, a favorite with the cowboys. Already a side of fresh-killed beef was angled over the fire, slowly cooking for the cowboy's single meal of the day, to be eaten late afternoon. The steam curling up from the mugs into the crisp air, and the richly fragrant, dark aroma of the coffee did not go unnoticed by Esteban, who enjoyed the brew far more than the traditional *maté*. He rubbed his chilled hands together beneath his poncho to warm them, wondering, as he glanced up at the sky, if they'd be treated to a rare winter snowfall before afternoon. Snowfalls were few here on the pampas, but in the winter months of July and August, not unheard of. He decided it was unlikely. There was no hint of snow in the sky above him, which was pale blue with wisps of fleecy cloud.

Touching his heels to Barbaro's flanks, he urged the bay on, dismounting by the campfire.

"*Hola,* Tadeo!" he greeted the foreman. "Everything quiet out here?"

"*Hola, mayordomo! Sí,* everything is very quiet—now." Tadeo grinned. "But you missed the excitement earlier this morning, señor!"

Esteban gave him a sharp glance, but the foreman's smile reassured him, and he relaxed as he squatted alongside the man. "What happened?"

Tadeo shrugged. "What else? A party of starving Indios showed up just after daybreak—and a dirtier bunch I've yet to see! Their *cacique,* their chief, old Blue Devil, looked a little better than his men, but not by much. They made the usual demands."

"You gave them what they wanted?"

"Of course, señor. Was that not what you told me to do?"

"Just checking," Esteban said with a grin. "How many head?"

"Thirteen, señor. None of them prime stock, you understand? I chose all older, injured beasts cut from the herd. Some of them were so ancient, my *gauchos* hardly needed the *boleadoras* to bring them down—they would have dropped of their own free will, in a day or so. *Por Dios,* I hope those poor *indio* bastards have strong teeth and jaws! They'll need them, that's for sure!"

"Why so many?"

151

"There were several in Blue Devil's band, señor, and the *cacique* made certain that I understood that their wives, children, and old ones were very many. He was such a scrawny old armadillo himself, and his men looked more than half starved—how could I send him off with but one or two head, and still sleep soundly tonight?"

"How, indeed!" Esteban acknowledged, knowing Tadeo for a good man with a conscience. "But I'll have to report that many gone to *el patrón*. One or two, there'd be no need, but thirteen won't go unnoticed—! *Dios,* I wouldn't put it past our beloved Don Felipe to think I've been rustling his herds!"

Tadeo shrugged eloquently. "But of course you must tell Don Felipe, señor. And I'm sure *el patrón* will understand, and would much rather lose a few worthless animals than have his entire herd run off like before, no? It is only a fool who learns nothing from his mistakes, after all!"

"You and I know that, but Don Felipe—? Who knows!" Esteban said grimly. "Give me a cup of that coffee, Tadeo, then I'll ride on up to the hacienda."

Two hours later found Esteban waiting in Don Felipe's study at the *casa grande* of Tierra Rosa, idly moving about the room and examining this and that while he did so.

Memories of hours spent poring over accounting ledgers and production reports, discussing the management of the ranch, or its salting plant, and formulating plans for the future with his father were inescapable in this room.

The cumbersome ox-blood leather chair in which Alejandro had sat to work; the huge, ornate Spanish desk topped with the finest leather and brass studs; the walls of books ranging from the classics to the latest on farm husbandry—all reminded him sharply of his father.

He glanced about, looking for further poignant proof of his lingering presence in the room and noticed suddenly that the portrait of Doña Manuela de Córdoba y Aguilar was once again hanging over the fireplace, as it had during Alejandro's lifetime. He frowned. So. Felipe had seen fit to have the painting brought down from Doña Manuela's old rooms, had he?

Shortly after Esteban's arrival at Tierra Rosa, his father had ordered the portrait taken down and rehung elsewhere, whether out of respect for Esteban's mother Maria de San Martín, or to rid himself of this reminder of his unhappy marriage, Esteban had no idea. Other than remarking once that he had loved the woman until the day she died, and that the unkind gossip which had plagued her during their marriage had offended him, Alejandro had never discussed Manuela with him further, nor commented on the portrait. But now, it was back.

He sat in the chair, hands clasped behind his head, and considered the painting thoughfully. He'd had incredible luck, he decided. That firebrand, Krissoula, was so like Manuela, the resemblance was uncanny, although Manuela's features were more aloof than the girl's, her mouth less lush and warm with the promise of passion. Both women possessed a beauty that was as much their curse as their blessing!

He'd learned of his uncle's love for Manuela quite by accident, soon after his father's death. One morning, he'd gone to the tiny family graveyard on the rise behind the *casa grande* to pay his respects at his father's grave, and had seen Felipe crouched beside Manuela's headstone, his arms filled to overflowing with flowers, his face contorted with grief and wet with tears. Quietly, he'd slipped away before Felipe had noticed him, pondering the implications of what he'd seen.

It had come as no surprise to him, really, that Felipe—perennially jealous of all his younger brother, Alejandro, had possessed—had also coveted his brother's lovely wife. And having learned that was the case, Esteban had known the very minute he set eyes on Krissoula on that last business trip he'd made to Spain (to finalize new contracts to export Tierra Rosa's prime beef to that country) that he could use her uncanny resemblance to Manuela to gain entrance to Tierra Rosa. Accordingly, he'd blackmailed the girl into returning to South America with him, and into finding the proof he needed to rob Felipe of the lands he believed his; lands Esteban believed he'd killed to acquire, as he'd confided to Krissoula.

Esteban sighed heavily. He feared the future boded ill for little Krissoula, should she decide to betray him and cast her lot with Felipe's. To all accounts, the dead Manuela and the petite yet fiery Gypsy girl were as different as chalk is to cheese! Krissoula, he thought with a surprising pang of pity, would never be loved for her volatile, tempestuous self by Felipe, but rather for the sake of the memories her appearance recalled. And if her behavior should differ violently from that of the dead woman Felipe was trying to resurrect, what then . . . ? What lengths would Felipe go to, in order to bend the girl to fit the mold he'd created for her? He frowned, suddenly fearful for her. Unless he'd seriously misjudged his uncle, her very life could well be in danger if she displeased him, or failed to live up to his unrealistic expectations of a second, saintly Manuela . . .

Although he knew the many drawers the desk possessed didn't hold the documents he sought, he pulled them out one by one, and idly sifted through the paperwork there. His troubled expression deepened to a dark scowl as he glanced through an accounting ledger and saw the neatly penned red figures that only confirmed what he already knew; Felipe had no head whatsoever for business. The figures spoke more eloquently than words could, neat little inked columns detailing costly, unnecessary expenditures or luxuries, as well as several hefty payments of cash to one Señor J. Ramirez, all offset against dwindling profits, while badly needed items had been disregarded, or their purchase postponed.

He slammed the ledgers back into the drawer with an irritable curse. Given free rein with the finances of Tierra Rosa for a few more months, on top of the past two disastrous years, Felipe de Aguilar would bring about the *estancia*'s ruin, destroy everything Alejandro and his father José de Aguilar before him had worked so hard to build! He couldn't let that happen . . .

"Looking for something, San Martín?"

Esteban barely glanced up as his uncle stepped quietly through the study door.

"You know better than to ask, Tío Felipe," he said insolently, his sapphire eyes scornful. He didn't bother to do the older man the courtesy of standing, nor did he apologize for rifling through his desk. Why be a hypocrite, and pretend a respect for the man he didn't feel? "I'm always looking for 'something.' And you know very well what—and where—that something is, don't you? One day I'll find it, and then you'll be out on your ear, Uncle."

The threat, so softly spoken, was nonetheless loaded with menace.

Felipe's face darkened with anger beneath his olive complexion. His dark-blue, almost black, eyes crackled, but he chose to ignore Esteban's pointed comments, saying instead, "I've told you before—don't call me 'Uncle,' San Martín. To you, I'm Don Felipe, your master here. And as far as I'm concerned, you were my late brother's *mayordomo*, nothing more. That position can be taken from you just as easily as it was given!"

"You think so, eh? Well, *Uncle*, I took a quick look through your ledgers before you came in, and from what I saw there, you need me far more than I need you! A year—two, at most—and Tierra Rosa will go under, unless you mend your ways and stop making that snake, Ramirez, loans you can ill afford—and which I very much doubt he'll ever repay! Oh, you can hire yourself a new *mayodomo*, true. But you won't find another manager with such a vested interest in the well-being of the *estancia* and its businesses as I have,

154

I promise you."

Felipe could think of no ready comeback, for in his heart he knew that what Esteban had said was true, damn him. A hired manager was only as good as the man instructing him, and there was still so much about running the ranch he did not fully understand . . .

In the years following José de Aguilar's death, Felipe had watched the lucrative importing business and properties he'd inherited from his father go under as a result of his own bad management until, at the time of his brother's fatal "accident," he'd been on the brink of ruin, the wealth and high regard the Aguilar name had guaranteed him all his life perilously close to being lost. Alejandro's timely death had eased matters considerably, but now—with Ramirez sucking him dry like a leech after blood—he was in desperate straits yet again.

His fists clenched at his sides, the knuckles bled white beneath olive skin. After all he'd done, all the risks he'd taken, he couldn't afford to lose Tierra Rosa, too, but—neither was he willing to relinquish the promise of the fat government position which Ramirez dangled before him like a carrot before a donkey! He wetted his lips and bit back his anger towards Esteban. He could get through this, so long as he kept a cool head for a week or two more, he told himself. The arms' shipment from North America which his "loans" to Ramirez had helped to finance should be here any day now. When it was, Zamora and his men were waiting and ready, Ramirez had sworn it. If he could just hang on . . .

"Perhaps the accounts could stand going over," he admitted reluctantly, to Esteban's surprise. "I've been too busy lately to give them the attention they require. You'll take a look at them next week."

"If I have the time."

"Make time," Felipe snapped, angered now beyond caution by the young man's coolly contemptuous manner, which reminded him so much of his brother when angry. Oh, yes, much as he hated to admit it, he had little doubt that Esteban was Alejandro's natural son. There was a strong physical resemblance that marked all the Aguilar males—himself included—which couldn't be hidden, any more than their resemblance in temperament. Alejandro and their father, José, had been intelligent, ambitious men, with the same bold drive and hunger to succeed that Esteban displayed, and with it, the vein of ruthlessness needed to assure that success. And, like his father, Esteban had also inherited the quick Aguilar temper, and had little time to waste on fools, which was exactly how his bastard nephew always made him feel—like an incompetent fool!

155

Well, all that would change when Mitre's government was overthrown, and himself a member of the new Presidente Zamora's hand-picked Cabinet. Ah, *sí*, San Martín would be forced to look at him through new eyes then!

Squelching the urge to toss caution to the winds and flaunt his plans in Esteban's face, Felipe added, "Meanwhile, I'm sure you didn't come here simply to pay a social call?"

"Hardly," Esteban scoffed. "No, Uncle. I came to tell you we handed over thirteen head of cattle to the Auracanians this morning. I thought you'd want to know."

"Thirteen! Why so blasted many?"

"According to Tadeo, the Indians looked hungry enough to turn nasty if they were refused. He decided a show of generosity would keep them sweet and persuade them to think twice about running off the main herd—like the last time, when I was away in Europe, when you refused to give them even a single calf, remember?" Esteban added pointedly.

Felipe remembered, all right. It was one of his most painful memories, and had forever stamped him as a greedy fool in his nephew's eyes, he knew.

Over a year ago, a party of Indians, along with their old chief, the same Blue Devil, had showed up virtually on the doorstep of Tierra Rosa, threatening to attack the house and create havoc if their demands for several head of cows were not met. Such Indian visits and their subsequent attacks on remote *estancias* were relatively common in these times, but nevertheless, against Tadeo's most heated protests, he'd stubbornly insisted that he would not be blackmailed by a bunch of dirty savages. He'd had his *gauchos* run the Auracanians off with their bull whips—with disastrous results.

Several nights later, he'd been awakened by screaming servants to the smell of smoke and the unwelcome news that the outbuildings and storerooms of the hacienda had been fired and that mounted drunken Indians armed with lances were trampling the courtyard to a quagmire, looting and destroying everything they could lay hands on. Simultaneously, it transpired, a second half of Blue Devil's band had stampeded the herds out on the pampas. It had taken weeks for the *gauchos* to round them up again.

"I remember," he acknowledged with palpable reluctance, his lips thinning. "I suppose Tadeo acted for the best. I'll make a note of it."

"Do that," Esteban said brusquely, and rose from his seat behind

156

the desk, striding for the door.

Felipe, reluctant to let him have the last word, called him back. "One thing more, San Martín!"

"What is it?"

"Alfredo Flores came to see me. He said you'd fired him while I was away in Buenos Aires and had him run off the *estancia?*"

"That's right. What of it? As *mayordomo* here, I don't need to ask your permission for firing that lazy drunkard, surely?"

"Permission, no. But—I would have preferred that you'd discussed it with me first. As you know, Alfredo and his family came with me here from Brazil. The man's always been loyal to me, and I feel he deserved a hearing out, at the very least."

"The devil you did!" Esteban snapped. "The man's more trouble than he's worth—and more fond of his bottle than a babe in arms. Loyalty be damned. You mean he was your yes-man, don't you, Uncle—your *compinche,* your crony! No job too small or too dirty for Alfredo, eh?" Esteban jeered. "He was sly and insolent, lazy and light-fingered, and what's more, I didn't like the way he handled my horses! I warned him once, told him what would happen if he ill-treated Dorado again. You know I don't hand out warnings a second time, Uncle."

"You won't take him back?"

"Not even to lick my boots."

"And if I insist? The man has a wife and children, for Christ's sake!"

"How touching your concern is—and how uncharacteristic of you. But Alfredo should have thought of that before he took the whip to Dorado. Insist all you want, *Señor Patrón,*" he mocked, "but if your dear, loyal 'Fredo sets so much as a foot on Tierra Rosa again, I'll horsewhip him within an inch of his life, as I should have done the last time. And when I'm done, I'll run what's left of his scrawny backside clear off this land—again."

Before Felipe could comment further, Esteban gripped the doorknob and flung it open, strode through it, and was gone, leaving his uncle feeling as if a tornado had just swept through the study in his wake.

Felipe went to the open door and stood there, deep in thought for a few moments, before calling softly, " 'Fredo! You can come out now."

The squat, brown-skinned *mestizo* appeared, hat in hand, from a shadowy corner of the hallway. *"Sí,* Don Felipe?" he murmured, shuffling his feet.

In his greasy poncho and baggy *calzones,* or breeches, of grubby white cotton, he appeared even more the coarse peasant than usual, Felipe thought with a flicker of distaste. But unfortunately, he needed the man. There were few things that the faithful dog would not do for his master, he'd discovered, however distasteful those little services might be to other men, and he never knew when he might require Alfredo's dubious "talents" again.

"Señor San Martín has gone."

"Sí, señor."

"I asked him about reinstating you, but he refused."

"Sí. I heard him, señor."

"Then you heard the reasons he gave, too. I'll have to go along with him, 'Fredo. I know very little about ranching, and I need his know-how. If I anger him, he'll quit, and then where will I be?"

"Sí, Don Felipe. It is all right. I understand."

"Good," Felipe acknowledged. "Then you'll stay away from the *hacienda* when San Martín's around?"

"I will."

"Here, take this," Felipe added, fishing deep into his pockets. "It'll tide you over for a while, if you don't fritter it all away at the first *pulpería* you come to."

"I have a wife and little ones, señor. Food for the table will come first, of course," Alfredo whined in the obsequious manner that Felipe alternately loathed and enjoyed. "What father would think of going to a saloon, when his children are hungry?"

"Quite," his master agreed with obvious disbelief. "Be off with you, now. I'll get word to you, if I should need your—services."

With a sullen nod, Alfredo slunk down the hallway and was gone.

Felipe returned to his study, and stood gazing up at the portrait of lovely Manuela above the fireplace, lost in memories.

"Such innocence, Manuela," he murmured. "Such virtue! I would have given all I possessed to make you my own, but that wasn't enough for you, was it? What did Alejandro have that I didn't, eh? What was it about him that made you refuse me, my innocent one . . . ?"

His dark-blue eyes were wet with tears as he stood there.

Esteban made his way to the stables, and sought out Tomás there. They exchanged greetings and then discussed the Indian incident, Esteban warning Tomás to keep a sharp eye out for the next few days.

"According to Tadeo, Chief Blue Devil seemed content with their peace offering, but in case they turn nasty, I'd post someone to keep a lookout here at night, just to be on the safe side."

"It's as good as done, *amigo!*" Tomás readily agreed.

"Bueno. And while you're at it, have someone take some provisions out to the Flores's shack, would you?"

"For 'Fredo's family?"

Esteban nodded. *"Sí.* I won't have his wife and children suffer because their father's a lazy, good-for-nothing bastard."

"Should I include a bottle of horse liniment for 'Fredo?" Tomás suggested with a wicked grin.

"Do, and you'll join him!" Esteban retorted with a grim smile.

"All right. I'll see to it myself, right away. I'm about finished here for the morning, anyway, and I'd welcome a ride before *siesta.* Beans, flour, maybe some dried beef—will that do?"

"Sounds fine. And tell Angelina to throw in a wheel of cheese and a little butter, if she has extra. And a crock of fresh milk and some fudge, too, if she has any made. You know how little ones love sweets?"

"You've a soft heart underneath that foul temper, eh, *amigo?"* Tomás observed, knowing it to be true. Esteban had never forgotten his early years of struggle in the *barrios* of Buenos Aires, and though he'd sworn never to return there to stay, he'd made a difference to the lives of the ragged, orphaned children of the *barrios* in other ways, making several visits a year to bring them much-needed food staples and other items. "The children in the Ciudad de los Niños don't know how lucky they are to have you, San Martín—and nor do those snotty-nosed little brats of 'Fredo's."

"Luck has nothing to do with it. I'm just repaying an old debt, pure and simple, *amigo."* Esteban curtly dismissed the subject, embarrassed by Tomás's reference to his visits to the city. Few people knew of his commitment there, and he preferred to keep it that way.

"Well, forgive me if I cut this short, but I'll be leaving now. If you're still around when I get back, maybe we can enjoy a drink together, eh?"

"Eager to be off, aren't you?" Esteban's dark brows rose suspiciously. "It wouldn't have anything to do with the fact that pretty Estrella should be helping her mother in the kitchen right about now, would it?"

"Nothing at all!" Tomás cheerfully lied. *"Hasta luego, amigo."*

Chapter Twelve

Esteban was still grinning when he ducked into the stables, having decided to take a look at the colt, which had been sickly a few weeks back while he was at Tierra Rosa.

His eyes took a few moments to adjust to the gloom, and he blinked as he made his way along the rows of stalls, each one of which boasted a divided door opening out onto the stableyard, the top halves left open to the light and air. The scent of horses and hay, leather, liniment, and saddle soap tickled his nostrils. He inhaled it with pleasure, for his love of horses was equaled only by his love of Tierra Rosa.

The colt, a pale blond replica of his older half-brother, Dorado, was on his feet, and looking far more spry than he'd been the last time Esteban saw him, he noted, much to his relief. The colt tossed its head playfully as Esteban entered the stall, and came to him as tame as a pet dog, nuzzling at his hands, while his mother, a beautiful red-chestnut mare, turned her head and nickered a welcome.

"*Hola*, Churro, my beauty!" he crooned, reaching up to scratch the mare's pricked ears. "How's Rubio today, eh? How's that baby of yours?"

So involved was he with his beloved horses, it was several moments before he realized someone else had followed him into the stables. The sound of Krissoula's voice—low, honey-sweet, and gentle as she talked to the mare, Girasol, in a stall farther down the row—alerted him. With a grin, he crouched down in the hay and eavesdropped shamelessly.

". . . Oh, how I'd love to go riding with you again, pretty one," she was murmuring, "but that stuffy old Felipe has forbidden it—*sí*, he has! What a grouch he is, no? He has not your joy of life, Girasol, nor mine." She sighed heavily, resting her cheek against the mare's velvety muzzle.

Esteban's grin deepened.

"Dios," Krissoula continued softly, "how could I bear to spend the rest of my life with such a hateful man, I wonder? If he had his way, *mi bonita,* he'd have me on my knees in the chapel every minute of the day, saying my rosary, or making endless confessions of my every little wrongdoing!"

She giggled softly, and Esteban smiled as he imagined her lovely, vibrant face transformed with muffled laughter.

"Perhaps—though it is a very wicked thought, 'Sol—perhaps Felipe would not live for very long if we were wed? Perhaps having a young, hot-blooded wife such as I to share his bed would prove too much for the old devil, and his heart would go 'poof' with excitement! Oh, if I were to become his wife, I would pray each day that it would be so! And then—ah, then I should be a rich young widow, free to take you riding every single day, and to dance away each night! Wouldn't that be wonderful, 'mmm, Girasol?"

Watching her, Esteban fought down the wicked responses to her fanciful comments that he itched to make, and instead gave himself up to the considerable pleasure of looking at her. *Dios,* but she was lovely, he realized—even lovelier, if that was possible, than the night he'd surprised her in her room three weeks ago, with such disastrous and unsettling results.

A wide ray of sunlight falling through the opened upper half of Girasol's stall deepened the green-flecked gold of her eyes, and struck bluish lights in the rich cascade of her hair, tumbling loose, black, and curling to her mid-back. Delicate apricot color warmed her cheeks. The fluid, graceful line of her throat was cast in silhouette, disappearing into the lighter neckline of her simple cream-colored blouse. The color made a rich contrast against the pale gold of her skin. Her long, flaring skirt was of a rich, rusty shade of velvet, belted at the waist with a wide, braided belt. She'd thrown a flowered fringed shawl over her shoulders for the chilly walk from house to stables, but it had been discarded now, and lay in a heap at her feet, forgotten amongst the straw. She made a delectable picture, bathed in that broad ray of sunshine, and Esteban felt the familiar hardening in his loins that betrayed his desire, despite all wishes to the contrary. Hadn't he decided, the morning after the *asado,* that his lust for Krissoula was dangerous, and counted for nothing when compared to his plans for revenge on his uncle? That no woman, however desirable, however beautiful and alluring, was worth jeopardizing the fulfillment of his dreams? Nevertheless, he knew his deepest feelings hadn't really changed.

161

He wanted Krissoula with a hunger that bordered on madness, though after the last time they'd been together he had little hope that she'd welcome his attentions!

Moving stealthily, he crept up behind her and snaked one strong arm about her waist. The other palm he clamped firmly over her mouth to cut off her inevitable cry before she could utter so much as a squeak.

"*Silencio, mujer!*" he growled roughly in her ear. "Not a word, or the evil *bandolero,* Esteban the Wicked, will have his way with you!"

He felt the initial tension of shock gather in her body, then slacken only marginally as she realized his identity. *That blackmailing San Martín again!* he could almost hear her thinking aloud. She again grew rigid in his arms, and he realized ruefully that, in this case, time and absence had solved nothing. She was still furious at him, the little cat! A chuckle of amusement rippled through him as, grinning broadly, he turned her to face him thinking, then so be it! Let her fight him and pretend she loathed his touch, abhorred his kisses, detested his caresses! He liked nothing better than a challenge, a little token resistance to sharpen his lusty male desires and fire her blood, so long as he and the woman both knew what the ultimate result must be, and both craved the same happy conclusion. Ah, *sí,* she wanted him all right, he knew that as surely as he knew his own name! Despite her outraged-innocent act, the protests she'd raised, she'd enjoyed him the last time, thoroughly enjoyed him, as he'd enjoyed her luscious little body. After a few initial protests for the sake of pride, she'd succumb all over again, and what a fine lusty time they'd have of it, here in the hay . . .

As he turned her to face him, he realized with surprise that he'd forgotten how small she really was, a finely boned little slip of a female. Somehow, she always seemed to him a far more imposing creature than she was—but maybe that was a result of her gigantic temper!

"So! Did I scare you?" he demanded roguishly, looking down at her with twinkling dark-sapphire eyes.

"Of course not, *loco!* I was just—startled, that's all!" she rejoined, a little breathless. Despite her denials, she *had* been scared, just a little. He'd been so very angry the last time they'd clashed wills, she'd purposely kept close to the house for the past three weeks since then, in order to avoid him. Now, however, his fury that night seemed a thing of the past, she realized with

162

enormous relief.

"Only surprised, *minina?*" he countered. "In truth, little one, you have nerves of steel to show only surprise when a wicked blackmailer waylays you like a bandit from the shadows!" Grinning still, he boldly ran his hand lightly down her arm, and felt the nerves leap beneath the crisp sleeve of her blouse in response to his touch. "And then again, perhaps you have something softer than steel under here, eh? Shall we find out . . . ?"

His voice was low, a caressing purr as he lifted her little hand to his lips. He dropped a lingering kiss in the tiny well of her palm, then kissed each fingertip in turn. Blood rushed to her cheeks, he noticed, and her eyes glittered, but to his surprise she made no move to pull her hand free. She left it resting in his like a curled flower even when he was done kissing her fingertips, and his heartbeat quickened. Could her resistance have softened? Could she possibly be eager and ready to accept him as her lover? He swallowed, such a possibility shaking him to the core. The thought of her giving herself to him freely, with warmth, passion, and eagerness, was almost too arousing to contemplate!

"You shouldn't be here," she whispered. "The last time we almost . . ."

She tried to sound stern and annoyed but failed utterly as her voice trailed away, and looking into her face, he saw that she was remembering that last time all too clearly. Color flooded her cheeks, but to his delight, he saw the suspicion of a reluctant smile twitch at her lips, then spread to kindle in her golden eyes so that they glowed like twin topazes in the sunbeam that made a halo about her head. He flattered himself that he was right, and that the smile confirmed that she had indeed been thinking about him just a little since he'd seen her last—and clearly with somewhat less than hostile thoughts!

"Ah, *sí,* the last time! To be honest, your threats that night terrified me, Doña Krissoula!" he whispered teasingly, his expression all roguish innocence. "They made me quake in my boots! *Por Dios,* I've not slept a wink since, fretting about them. Tell me, my merciless lady, have you betrayed me yet to the terrible Felipe? Should I expect a challenge for your honor—perhaps pistols at dawn—or, knowing my uncle, more likely a stiletto in my back?"

She giggled, and her entire body suddenly quivered with relieved laughter in his loose embrace. "You're quite mad, *campesino!*"

His eyes darkened suddenly as his gaze came to rest upon the rich

163

curve of her mouth. The urge to kiss her, to drink from the wine of those lips, was suddenly overwhelming. His embrace tightened around her. "I know," he agreed huskily, and gazed deep into her golden eyes. "I must be, mustn't I, *minina,* to risk being here alone with you like this, and not give a damn about what discovery could mean to my plans?"

"And what of mine?" she protested faintly. "I have plans of my own, too, remember—and you play no part in them, you wretch . . . !"

But the moment was irrevocable, the one they'd both been moving towards, craving, from the last unsettling time they'd made love. Her voice trailed away to a silence that was charged with emotion.

Time hung suspended for a moment as he reached out and gently rubbed the ball of his thumb across her full lower lip. Her mouth was like a crushed flower, warm and ripe with color and infinitely tempting.

"*Dios!* To the devil with plans, *querida,* both yours and mine—!" he murmured huskily. "Plans have nothing to do with what we're feeling here, now! We must *both* be mad, Krissoula *mía* . . . because you want me, don't you, little one, just as I've wanted you from the first . . . ?"

He leaned towards her, his curly dark head lowering, his mouth gently claiming her soft lips.

The sweetness and warmth of his kisses stunned her, made her tremble uncontrollably. Any lingering protest she might have raised dissolved under the sweetfire tenderness of his mouth moving on hers, for it was so unexpected that he would be gentle like this after his last ruthless seduction of her.

From the very first night in his hotel suite back in Barcelona, she'd sensed the undercurrent of violence in him, the temper held in check that could nonetheless explode at any moment, and had finally seen her fears become reality the night of the *asado* when he'd warned her against double-crossing him, and taught her the consequences of betraying him by mercilessly using her body to slake his lust, heedless of her protests.

Truly, he could be a *diablo* when angered, forceful and single-minded in the pursuit of his male pleasure! But—his kisses today revealed another side of him entirely; a tender, gentle side. To find him so unexpectedly tender, coupled with the heady physical attraction he already held for her, was more than her dormant senses could withstand! Something tight and controlled, a painful knot of wariness and mistrust for men that she'd buried inside her, uncurled like a flower bud unfurling in the sunshine's warmth, unraveled and floated free.

Heart pounding, she gave a muffled cry, which he shushed with his lips on hers. She responded eagerly to the pressure of his mouth with a sweet, wild warmth that made him shudder. To his delight, she moved closer to him so that their bodies brushed against each other, hers pliant and yielding as a willow against the hard-muscled angles and planes of his. The soft curves of her breasts and the swell of her hips grazed his chest and flanks, and the electric contact of her female roundness made him shudder anew and tighten his embrace about her. Reaching up, she wound her arms about his neck and tousled the crisp-soft waves that lapped and frothed over his nape like a restless black sea. The sensation of his hair was like raw silk beneath her fingertips, curiously vital, crisply voluptuous and alive.

His lips moved from her mouth and traveled downward to the soft line of her throat. He inhaled deeply, and uttered a growl deep in his throat.

"Ah, *querida*, you smell sweet as any wildflower," he murmured, and she felt his ragged breath fanning her skin as he kissed her arched throat, and darted his tongue tip into the shadowed little hollows at its base. His fingers caressed her tumbling black ringlets, grazed lingeringly down over the slender curves of her shoulders, and slipped behind her to her back. He traced each little knob of her spine through her blouse and skirt down to the rounded swell of her buttocks. Once there, he splayed his hands to capture the taut little mounds of her bottom and gathered her gently against the hardness of his flanks so that she could not help but be aware of his arousal.

"Do you feel, little one, how very much I want you?" he whispered, his voice ragged and thick with passion. "Let me show you how wonderful it can be between us . . ."

A moment later, and his hands were caressing silky, bared skin, skimming over her body beneath the cloth of her untucked blouse to find her rib cage, then a pointed breast, and cover it with feathery caresses. The soft little peak rose hard against his palm, courted the touch of his knowing fingers. A delicious thrill ran through her from breast to loins in a lightning silvery ripple as he thrust up her blouse. He pressed his mouth to the tip of her breast and drew the hardened peak between his lips, suckling gently, swirling his tongue

165

about the swollen nubbin. She gasped, her longing for him sweeping through her. Her nails dug into the hard, muscled flesh of his shoulders as he dipped his head and continued to fondle her; the ball of his thumb like the stroke of fire against one nipple while his mouth consumed the other with liquid heat.

"*Sí,*" she moaned softly, clinging to him like ivy to a wall, her hips arching closer to his of her own accord, rubbing against him. "*Sí,* oh, *sí,* I want you, too, San Martín! Take me, *querido mío,* take me—before I come to my senses!"

Her husky, throaty pleading sent his passion sky-rocketing. With a deep-throated growl, he dragged her full against him, his mouth sweetly savage now as he held her fast and kissed her deeply. He devoured her mouth like a man starved of kisses and Krissoula, aflame with longing now, was little less sweetly savage than he. Pressing forward, she eagerly kissed him back, her lips parting beneath the pressure of his mouth, thrilling to his kisses as she thrilled to his hands playing upon her breasts. Her own hands shook with impatience as she tugged his shirt free of his breeches at the waist and ran them up beneath it, over his torso.

Oh, how lean and powerful he felt, she thought giddily! How beautiful he was, this man! The muscles braided to his shoulders and upper arms were like the taut strings of a guitar, and she could feel the play of sinew and cord beneath smooth flesh as he suddenly swept her up into his arms, and held her cradled there as if she weighed no more than thistledown, his lips still drinking thirstily from hers.

Her lashes fluttered as she gazed up at him and saw the hunger in his expression. His desire was raw and naked, blazing in his sapphire eyes. It made her quiver deep inside with an answering hunger. *Now!* she silently implored him, *Now, before I recover the will to resist you, my love!*

"Ah, Krissoula! *Minina,* my little kitten! Krissoula, *mi amor . . . !*" he breathed, and her name dropped like a prayer from his lips as he lowered her gently to the fragrant straw, following her down into their warm, scented love nest.

In a nearby stall, a furtive shadow moved and was as quickly gone, taking with it Krissoula's discarded shawl. But the lovers saw nothing, suspected nothing, heard nothing but each other's low, caressing voices murmuring words of passion and love, so lost were they in their private world of kisses and endearments and swiftly escalating passion.

Her skirts tangled about her waist, Krissoula felt Esteban's hand slip inside the waistband of her undergarments and seek out the warm cleft between her thighs, already honeyed with the passion he'd aroused in her with his kisses and by fondling her breasts. She felt him bare her lower body, heard the hiss of silk as the cloth whispered down her slender legs, and moaned softly as his knowing fingers found and teased the tiny bud of her passion. He explored her hidden petals in ways that made her utter little birdlike cries of delight as her womanhood swelled and flowered, like an orchid blooming under his touch. Eager to delight him in return, she stroked the hard plateau of his belly, then tentatively caressed the hardened ridge of his manhood with her palm. Even through the heavy cloth of his breeches, she could feel the burning male heat of him, the swollen urgency at his groin that demanded release.

"Free me, *querida*," he whispered huskily, nibbling at her lower lip. "Free me to love you . . ."

Her breathing ragged against his hungry mouth, she eagerly complied. Finding the laces that fastened his breeches, she slipped them free.

At once, his manhood sprang from its confinement, erect and ready for its task. The arrogant spearhead slipped hard and hot into her hand, steel sheathed in hot velvet, a sensation so exquisite it made her gasp with excitement and wonder. She took his length in the warmth of her palm, her fingers curling about it, her long nails teasing the engorged shaft, then trailing down to his inner thighs and the soft weightiness just above them, gently rubbing and squeezing and cupping until he could bear her touch no longer.

A shudder moved violently through him, wrenching a groan of unbearable agony from his lips. Taking her upper arms, he kissed her fiercely as he fitted her beneath him. Trembling with longing herself, she lay back upon the scented straw and parted her thighs, offering him the ease he craved, the solace of her woman's body. With a low cry, he bore her beneath him, crushing her down into the straw under his weight. In a single, fluid thrust of his hard-muscled flanks, he filled her utterly, began moving upon her, deeply within her, in the sensuous dance that is older than time itself.

His body was dark, golden brown skin sliding erotically back and forth against the paler gold of her creamy beauty, his muscles flexing as he loved her. Her inky river of hair flowed about them and spilled in raven commas across the pale gold of the straw, silken whips that flayed his flesh and spurred his desire. Apart and together they moved, soft breasts to rough, hairy chest, hard belly to velvet stomach, yet the haste, the urgency of their first joining

167

had lessened now. Haste had been replaced by a slow, easy, spiraling, a steady building toward the ultimate pleasure, the little heaven on earth they knew awaited them. His thrusts were deep and languorous, and wrung little sighs from her lips. His stroke was unhurried, and accompanied by lingering, sweet kisses that melted like winter snow in summer sun against her lips, her throat, her breasts.

"Oh, how you love me, *querido!*" she whispered, the beauty of their mating bringing the sheen of tears to her eyes. "Esteban, oh, Esteban, my love—I cannot bear it! Blessed God, if I must die, then let it be here, now, in your arms as you love me—!"

She arched her body to meet the flexing of his loins, partnering his fluid grace to a rhythm that sang through both their bodies, that filled their hearts and touched their souls. He was the music, she the dance, and the dance and the music were one. She knew not where one ended and the other began! They were united, inseparable, two imperfect parts made perfect by the joining . . .

God, how elusive she is! Esteban thought tenderly, pressing a burning kiss against the corner of her mouth. She writhed beneath him, lovely, all-female, passionately giving him her body, responding to him with a beauty and fiery willingness that defied words! And yet, there remained a part of her that held itself aloof from his passion and mastery, he sensed, a tiny part of her will that refused to yield to his lovemaking, or his dominant part in it. A rebellious part that maddened him, drew him, fired him with the urge to possess her utterly—body, heart, and soul—and left him with the frustrating, bewitching sense that he could and would never possess her utterly. That he might spend a lifetime in quest of that elusive chord, that single, sweet note she denied him in their dance, and never capture it, call it his own! Ah, *Dios,* she was woman and girl-child all at once, surrender and defiance, passion and purity, magic and madness, all woven into one delightful rhapsody of womanhood—!

Faster he moved now, answering the silent music between them, obeying the quickening temper of passion's dance that throbbed like a racing heartbeat in their veins. And she danced with him, beat for beat, measure for measure, step for step, their cries at the last commingling on the straw-scented air in a last crescendo, a triumphant finale that flung them heavenward, and left them spent in the velvet peace that echoed in its wake.

For a few seconds, there was silence, broken only by the shuddering gasps of her breathing, the hoarse panting of his, the low blowing of a horse in a nearby stall.

Then he murmured with feeling, "Aiee, Sweet Madonna Mary—!" and rolled from her, to her side, at once pulling her into his arms, and holding her fiercely to his chest as if he feared she might escape him.

"Hola, amigo? *Esteban! Where the devil are you?*"

Tomás's voice.

Simultaneously, the lovers both froze, startled into statues. Esteban felt Krissoula's heart skip a beat, then suddenly accelerate beneath his palm as she stared wide-eyed at him, horrified that discovery was imminent.

"Todos los santos! Are we cursed, *minina?"* Esteban muttered in exasperation, sitting up and running his fingers through his tousled hair to rid it of wisps of straw. He tucked in his shirt, rapidly tied the laces of his breeches, and stood. "Last time, it was Sofía who interrupted us, and now, Tomás, blast his hide!"

He added an obscenity for good measure, then pressed his finger across his lips to warn her to be silent. "Stay here and don't make a sound, *minina mía!* I'll see what he wants, get rid of him, and come back to you as quickly as I can, *sí?* A few moments, and we can carry on where we left off, *mi corazón.*"

But the moment was gone, shattered like glass; he could see it in her eyes as he left her and hurried towards the sound of Tomás's voice, and the knowledge infuriated him. There'd be no taking up where they'd left off, not this time. Damn! Was he destined to spend only stolen moments with her, and never the endless nights he craved?

"What do you want?" he growled, scowling darkly as he exited the stables and saw his friend there, astride a chestnut gelding. After the gloom of the stables, the bright light of outdoors dazzled his eyes, and made his scowl appear even more ferocious.

"I thought I'd better let you know before I left—your old friend Alfredo's come back for a visit!" Tomás explained. "He was hanging around the kitchens earlier, Angelina said, asking for handouts. She thought he seemed to be nursing quite a grudge against you for firing him, *hombre.* She's afraid he might try doing something to get even!"

"All right. Thanks for letting me know. I'll look around before I leave, make sure he's off the *hacienda,"* Esteban reassured him. "Damn! If that fool of a *patrón* didn't encourage the drunken bastard, it would make our jobs far easier, no?"

"You don't say!" Tomás agreed, and then his eyes shifted to

someone or something beyond Esteban, and he swept off his hat. *"Buenos días,* Doña Krissoula!"

Esteban swung sharply about as Krissoula exited the stables, looking—he suspected—far more calm and composed than she felt.

"And good day to you, Tomás," she responded graciously, giving the head groom a sweet smile. "Señor de San Martín here was kind enough to show me Girasol's stall. I brought her a little treat, you see. You will make sure that she's exercised regularly, won't you, Tomás, since I've been forb—since I'll be unable to ride her for a while?" she amended.

"But of course, señorita!" Tomás agreed with a solemn nod.

"Doña Krissoula, if I might have a further word with you before you go—?" Esteban began, striding quickly towards Krissoula as if Tomás no longer existed. Before she could voice an excuse and escape, he took her elbow and drew her aside, speaking in an urgent whisper.

"You can't go like this, *querida*—I won't allow it! By God, I want more than a few stolen moments in the hay, afraid someone might surprise us! I want to spend the night long making love to you, *minina!* To wake up and find you cradled in my arms, and then make love with you all over again." His dark eyes caressed her, and his fingers tightened painfully on her arm with the urge to drag her against him, and taste again the sweet, crushed flower of her reddened lips. "I'll come to your room tonight, just like the last time! Wait up for me, darling!"

"No!" She gasped, obviously terrified by the thought. "Don't even think of doing such a crazy thing! Forget what happened between us today. It was all a mistake—a very big mistake—to think we could ever mix b-business with—with pleasure. It would never work! Now, please, I really must go inside now. Sofía will—!"

"To hell with Sofía," he growled. "If not tonight, when can we be together again? Name a time, a place?"

She shook her head vehemently. "Never!"

"Then I'll be damned if I'll let you go, Krissoula!" The intensity in his low voice gave it a harsh, rasping quality, so different from before. His grip on her arms tightened almost brutally.

"Can't you see it's impossible?" she beseeched him. "We're from different worlds, you and I, and however wonderful you make me feel, there can never be anything more than passion between us."

"Isn't that enough, to begin with?"

"No, not nearly enough! I've been hurt once before in my life, Esteban—and I—I don't intend to be hurt again. Not by you, not

170

by any man! Now please, let go of me!"

He let go, and she fled him, making no promises, giving him only a last, anguished glance before she slipped from his grasp and was gone, black hair swinging over her shoulders as she ran from the stables to the house as if the devil himself snapped at her heels.

Standing in the bright light that flooded the stableyard, watching her small figure flee quickly from him and vanish through the huge, studded double doors, Esteban could quite readily have murdered Tomás for his untimely interruption.

Drawing a *cigarillo* from his pocket, he viciously struck a match on his heel and lit it. He gazed broodingly up at the towering white house, at the charming patterns the arched, grilled windows made against the whitewashed adobe walls and red-tiled roofs without really seeing them. He scowled moodily, drawing on his smoke, the raven-wings' slashes of his black brows almost meeting across his tanned forehead as he did so.

"My apologies, Esteban," Tomás said softly, regretfully. "It would seem I interrupted something, eh, *amigo?*"

"Go to hell, Tomás!" Esteban suggested, but without rancor.

"If I did, it surely couldn't be any hotter than the one you're creating for yourself right here! Don Felipe's intended, eh? Aiee, *Dios*, you're asking for trouble, *amigo!* If you play with fire, don't be surprised when you get burned, eh?"

"I won't," Esteban agreed tersely. He gave an evil grin. "Besides, Tomás, the risk is half the fun, no?"

"I'm sure it is—to you. For myself—" he shrugged "—well, I could live without such dangerous pleasures!"

"To each his own, my friend," Esteban said curtly.

"*Sí*—it's your choice, I agree. But—what about her? What about the señorita? If you're discovered, my friend, she'll pay the price as well as you, will she not? And our Don Felipe is a cruel *hombre*, no? If I were to care for a woman, I would not expose her to such dangers."

Esteban shot him a glare that would have withered a lesser man, knowing only too well that decent, honorable Tomás was quite right, although his friend had no knowledge of the true relationship between Krissoula and him. Oh, yes, he knew what he was doing was wrong. Hadn't he told himself time and time again he'd steer clear of her in the future, deny his desire for her? He should leave the girl be, let her play the part she'd agreed—albeit under duress— to play, and then pay her off and let her go. But—she'd gotten under his skin. His desire to be with her, make love to her, chafed at him

171

constantly, each day apart pricking like a burr under a horse's saddle, rubbing him raw day in and day out. He could no sooner follow Tomás's advice than he could halt the sun in its path across the heavens—and nor did he want to, in his heart of hearts.

"Thanks for the advice, my friend, but what I do is my business."

"You're right," Tomás agreed ruefully. "But—one more thing before I go?"

"What now?" Esteban snapped.

"You have straw in your hair, *Señor Mayordomo!*" Tomás observed with a grin, clicked to his horse, and rode away.

After Tomás had left, Esteban remained standing there in the stableyard, painfully aware that Krissoula's fragrance still clung to his body and shirt in the winter sunshine. It was the subtle scent of the wild orchid perfume she favored, and another, subtler perfume that was her own musk. Her scent still had the power to move him, to arouse him, even apart from her as he was now, he thought, inhaling deeply. What was it about her that drew him so, like a moth to flame, or steel to a magnet? He'd thought he knew, that he'd analzyed the cause of it, but it still remained elusive, an indefinable *something* that was more powerful than anything tangible could ever have been.

Somehow, he knew he'd find a way to see her again, if only on the pretext that he wanted to tell her he understood her fear of discovery, and of Felipe. Or to promise her that there'd be no more impetuous trysts in the stables. He'd promise to be more careful, completely circumspect from here on, so she need have nothing to fear from his uncle.

And, when he'd set at rest her smallest doubts, and she was nestled in his arms, he'd drive her crazy with longing for him, sweep aside her protests in a blaze of passion that would consume them both all the long night through, and make love to her with an ardor she'd never forget until the stars paled from the sky!

Chapter Thirteen

Krissoula ran through the house like a woman possessed, racing down the *corredor* in the direction of the stairs. She knew only that she had to get to her room, had to be alone to think through the crazy thing she'd done!

Blessed Saint Sara, what madness had possessed her! What insanity had allowed her to give herself so readily to that man— *what?* And now that she'd let him make love to her, it could never be undone, never. He probably thought she was exactly the sort of woman he'd taken her for from the first now, and he had every reason to . . .

"*Niña?* Blessed Mary, what's wrong? Why are you running?"

Krissoula was brought up short on the third tread by Sofía's sharp voice. Her fingertips poised over the wrought-iron balustrade, she stood stock-still and fought to control her breathlessness without turning to face her duenna, afraid of what her expression might betray.

"I'm running because I didn't want to be late for tea, Sofía, and I still have to change! It *is* almost teatime, isn't it?" she explained breathlessly, crossing her fingers so that the enormous lie wouldn't count as a sin. Or if it did, as a smaller transgression.

"*Sí,* almost," Sofía acknowledged, looking pale and tense. "But where were you all this time? I have such an aching head, and was hoping you'd massage my temples."

"I'm sorry, I didn't think to tell you. I—I just went out to the stables to give Girasol a little treat," she supplied casually, "and I lost track of time. When I realized how long I'd taken, I ran all the way back to the house to make up for it! Oh, Sofía, Felipe's always so busy! I hardly get to see him at all, except at teatime and *comida,* and I did so want to talk to him, about our wedding and the future and everything . . ." She made her voice sound wistful to cover her agitation, wondering as she did so if her soul would burn to a cinder

173

in hell for her lies, her wickedness!

"Your eagerness to spend time with your betrothed is commendable, but you simply must not race about the *casa* like a hoyden, *niña*, for whatever reason! Don Felipe would not be pleased by such behavior, as well you know! Remember that you will be mistress here very soon, and that *la patrona* of any great household must always comport herself with grace and with dignity."

"I'm sorry, Sofía," Krissoula apologized dutifully. "It won't happen again, I promise. Now, if you'll excuse me, I really must change! Then I'll massage your temples if you'd like, you poor thing."

She beat a decorous, if somewhat hurried, exit up the winding staircase, but once out of Sofía's sight, she almost flew down the hallway to her room, closing and locking the door behind her.

Only in the privacy of her own four walls could she permit her calm facade to crumble. Swallowing, she crossed quickly to the mirror and stared long and hard at her reflection, anxiously wondering if there were not some outward mark upon her? Some sign of her secret sin that Felipe would recognize? She looked a little flushed, perhaps, a little disheveled, and her eyes were certainly very bright, but other than that, she was outwardly the same Krissoula, she realized with relief. There was nothing to betray that only moments ago, she had lain in the straw of the stables in the arms of Esteban de San Martín, her fiancé's *mayordomo*, and eagerly let him use her as his *puta!*

Her face burned with shame and anger at herself for giving in to him—and to her own desires—so easily. The enormous lump that had choked her when she fled from Esteban was back, yet she knew the choking knot of agony couldn't be dissolved by tears. The normal female release of tears was one long denied her for some reason. A punishment from God, perhaps, for the wicked life she'd led? Whatever the cause, she hadn't cried for over two years, not since she'd held Nicki for the very last time . . .

Nicki! Oh, mi hijo, *Nicki!*

If only she had a friend, someone to talk to, to listen as she poured out her heart. If only she had someone who loved her to offer their advice and their arms to comfort her . . . But in all this wide, wide world, she had no one to turn to, no one who cared for her, just as she'd had no one back then. She swallowed, and the old grief and self-pity welled anew in her throat, constricting it painfully. Unwanted, unbidden in her upset state, the memory of the dreadful, dark day she'd lost Nicki came flooding back in all its

174

brutal clarity, reminding her of her aching loss all over again. When Nicki was born, she'd been so happy, knowing she wouldn't be alone anymore, that she'd have someone who was her very own to shower with love, and to love her in return. But the sole joy of her life had been cruelly taken from her, leaving her with nothing.

She sighed heavily. She'd wept a lifetime of tears in the days, weeks, and months that followed the morning she'd awakened to find her little son dead. She'd believed ever since that she had no more tears left in her to shed, and it seemed she was right. She couldn't cry now, even though she badly wanted to.

Cursing her vivid, hurtful memories, she yanked off her clothes so roughly, the delicate blouse tore at the seams in her haste. She poured cool water into a porcelain basin, and taking up soap and a cloth, she scrubbed herself from head to toe, hoping that in her efforts to rid herself of the lingering reminders of Esteban's touch, his scent—which still clung to her skin—she could rid herself of her guilt, too.

But it was useless! Although her body smarted from the thorough scouring and toweling she punished it with, her lips still tingled as if his kisses had freshly seared them. Her breasts felt swollen and sensitive in the wake of his caresses. And above all, the treacherous, delicious contentment of his lovemaking still sent a warmth surging through her veins, had kindled a lasting glow in the pit of her belly that could not be considered in any way unpleasant, yet was so at odds with her remorse for what she'd foolishly done.

How long had it been since she felt eased by a man's loving, her restless body at peace? Aiee, *Dios,* an eternity, a lifetime, for she'd never known the joy of passion that Esteban had shown her, nor the exquisite relief that was passion's prize. Miguel had been too clumsy, too selfish, too impatient to take the time to slowly bring her to fulfillment, even had he cared to, or—for that matter—known how to do so. Their lovemaking had been pleasant enough, for the most part, but it had always left her feeling tense and angry, aching for something more she couldn't define, something that would equal the enormous pleasure Miguel had obviously derived from their coupling. Ah, yes, too many lonely, empty nights she'd yearned for a lover's touch to awaken her dormant senses as Esteban's had done, and had that yearning denied her! More lonely, empty nights than she cared to remember, for since Miguel, she'd desired no man until now, until San Martín—that handsome devil—had touched some buried spark within her! A blackmailing, dangerous rogue he was, true, and a penniless nobody unless Tierra

Rosa should someday fall into his hands—and yet, *Dios,* how wonderful his loving had proved! So very much more tender and passionate than she'd ever dreamed a man could be, she'd forgotten her resolve until it was too late. Well, it wouldn't happen again, she told herself firmly. Enough was enough. She'd put her mistake—or rather, two mistakes—behind her, and start afresh, and waste no more time on self-reproach. She was only human, after all, and surely El Señor forgave a mistake—or two?

When she'd finished her toilette, she dressed demurely in a warm gown of charcoal velvet that she knew Felipe would approve of, and which suited her penitent mood, then swept her hair up tidily into a knot at the crown and secured it with pins. She allowed no softening wisps to escape and detract from the demure effect she wished to create. If it was another Manuela Felipe he wanted, then by *Dios,* that was what he'd get from now on! She gave herself a last appraising glance in the mirror, and saw a colorless hag staring back at her. *Caray,* she looked as drab as a sparrow, as sexless as a nun. Without a doubt, Don Felipe would approve wholeheartedly! With a bitter smile, she went downstairs to tea.

It was still early when Felipe, in an unusually mellow mood, offered his apologies and left her for his study, with the excuse that he was expecting a visit from Jaime Ramirez within the hour. They had important business to discuss, he explained, and he asked Krissoula to remind the maids that he did not wish to be disturbed.

Perhaps, she decided, with free time on her hands until supper at ten, and no one to share it with—Sofía having withdrawn to her room still complaining of a throbbing headache—she'd force at long last the lock to the leather-bound book she'd filched from Manuela's rooms, and see if the pages contained any deep, dark secrets. Her face screwed up in a frown of disgust, for she doubted they would. After all, what lurid secrets could that saintly woman who'd favored pastels have possibly possessed? Probably nothing more exciting than that she'd cooked the household accounting books in order to buy herself a hair shirt, that pious ninny! Dear sweet Manuela would have made no mistakes the like of the wicked Krissoula's, that much was certain!

But the reluctant urge to delve into Manuela's secrets had lessened somewhat by the time she reached her room. She lay on her bed, dressed only in her wrapper, and stared miserably up at the ceiling, trying to imagine Felipe as her husband, and their wedding night.

The image of that olive-skinned, hawklike face looming over

hers, those cruel fingers plucking first at her garments and then at her naked body, filled her not with anticipation, but revulsion. *Dios,* how could she bear to have that old lecher touch her? Although rather distinguished looking—in all honesty quite handsome for a man of his years—he was already past his prime. His hair was more silver than black, his hands blue-veined, with the beginning of liver spots. His body was tall, but no longer firm with muscle. Rather, he'd grown loosely fleshed, almost gaunt, after a life of ease and self-indulgence. She thought of Esteban's lean, beautiful brown body, and shuddered at the thought of sharing Felipe's bed. And yet somehow, if she intended to go through with her plan to double-cross Esteban, she must not only submit to Felipe's lovemaking, but convince him she was a virgin bride, to boot! That part didn't scare her too much, though. The whores of Barcelona had told her of the tricks they played on men who lusted only for virgins, using chicken bladders filled with blood and a few strident, well-timed screams to convince such men of their innocence. One girl had even sold her "virginity" over a hundred times, Krissoula recalled with a smile, so how difficult could it be? *Sí,* she'd come this far, was so very close to seeing her dreams bear fruit, there was no way on earth she'd be stupid enough to risk losing everything she'd worked for, not for the sake of San Martín's body or his strong, protective arms, she decided. Let him think she'd regretted her rash threat to betray him. By the time he realized she'd been conning him, it would be too late!

Feeling calmer now that she'd finally made up her mind, she discovered her lethargy had vanished. Delving beneath her layers of lace-trimmed underwear, she pulled out the calf-bound book she'd hidden there, and made short work of the rusty lock with her nail file.

The fat little book wasn't a household-accounting ledger at all, she discovered, but Manuela de Córdoba y Aguilar's personal journal. The pages were yellow and spotted with age, and smelled musty as she riffled through them. Five years, she realized, quickly scanning the dates on the first page and then the last. Five years of the saintly Manuela's dreary, perfect existence and saintly thoughts, scribbled down for her to wade through, with little hope of finding anything interesting.

With a sigh, she settled herself comfortably on the bed, propped up on one elbow. She turned back to the very first page, neatly dated February 14, 1834, and began to read the small, feminine handwriting:

"Today, Dear Diary, something wonderful happened!" it began sickeningly, and Krissoula rolled her eyes in disgust. *"At the fiesta my father gave for my fifteenth birthday tonight, I met the man I want to marry. Oh, he's so very handsome, Dear Diary, quite the most handsome man I've ever seen, with glossy dark hair and such melting brown eyes!"*

Melting brown eyes? Krissoula snorted. It was even worse than she'd feared!

"His name is Alejandro de Aguilar, and I do believe, from the looks Mama and Papa exchanged when they introduced him to me, that they would approve if he should ask for my hand. His father was very wealthy, their family one of the Two Hundred, as is ours, and he owns several thousand acres of land to the southeast of Córdoba which Alejandro's grandfather named 'Tierra Rosa.' Don Alejandro smiled when he bade me good night, and said that he hoped to see me again, very soon. Maria, my duenna, had turned her back for a moment, and so I took advantage of her distraction, and was shockingly forward! I told Alejandro that I also hoped to see him again very soon, and he winked and laughed in the most engaging way that made me laugh, too. Dear Diary, am I in love? Sí, I think I am!"

That gushing, dramatic declaration concluded the first day's jottings.

Krissoula sighed and yawned hugely. It promised to be a long, long night . . .

Chapter Fourteen

Felipe's meeting with Jaime Ramirez that afternoon had obviously gone badly. The man acted like a bad-tempered bear towards the two female members of his household when they came downstairs for dinner that night, sharply criticizing Krissoula's choice of gown, which was—for her, at least—a somewhat demure taffy-colored silk, and taking Sofía to task for permitting her charge to dress so "gaudily."

"I do believe Ramirez is right," he'd accused the poor duenna coldly. "You're far too permissive with your charge, Señorita Moreno! Kindly see to it in the future that my betrothed is attired as befits her future position here as my wife—in pastel colors that reflect a modest manner and a more refined taste!"

Felipe's frosty silence punctuated by murderous scowls affected them all throughout supper that night. Sofía seemed about to choke on every morsel of food she put into her mouth, and wouldn't meet Felipe's eyes nor answer his curt questions without stammering and turning an awful shade of salmon pink, while Krissoula seethed with frustration at having to bite her tongue and keep up her demure front when she'd rather have told that old goat where he and that weasel Ramirez could put their sniveling opinions and just exactly what she thought of them, in no uncertain terms!

Fortunately, she managed to curb her impulses long enough to escape to the privacy of her room once again. There, she volunteered an innocent bolster to play the part of Felipe and proceeded to pummel it into feather-shedding oblivion and heap every foul insult and colorful obscenity she'd ever learned on its erstwhile "head." It was less satisfactory than venting her feelings on the man himself but far safer under the circumstances!

When, her rage abated, she resumed her readings of Manuela's journal, it was to learn that Alejandro de Aguilar had indeed asked

179

for the fifteen-year-old maiden's hand, and that his suit had been accepted by her papa. The girl's bemoaning what promised to be a lengthy engagement of two years, and her eagerness to become her Alejandro's bride, interspersed with glowing accounts of her *novio*'s every word and deed, jarred violently with Krissoula's simmering frustration.

"Pah! You're the cause of all this, you, you simpering, scribbling, pastel-favoring *virgin!*" she muttered, and flung the diary from her, across the room, in ill humor with the author who, even long after her death, still managed to affect the lives of others in such adverse ways.

Over breakfast the following morning, Felipe curtly announced that he was forced to leave Tierra Rosa for a day or two, citing yet another mysterious "meeting" with Jaime Ramirez and several other unnamed business associates at the Ramirez *estancia* as the reason. It was obvious that he would rather not have left the *casa grande* again so soon after his last absence, but for some reason felt compelled to do so. As a consequence his temper was foul.

He responded to Krissoula's apparently innocent request to accompany him on the trip with a curt refusal, suggesting instead that she occupy her time more fittingly by embroidering, prayer, and good works, or in pursuing some other suitable female task in his absence. She had no choice but to obediently comply with his wishes—at least on the surface—for she fancied she detected a definite cooling in Felipe's manner towards her this morning, and suspected that Ramirez was in some way responsible. Had the man's dislike and suspicions of her since the night of the *asado* encouraged him to put doubts about marrying her in Felipe's head? She had a sneaking hunch they had, and consequently didn't dare argue or plead to go with him or do anything else to deepen his displeasure.

"Very well, Felipe. I shall stay here and do as you wish," she agreed contritely but with a heavy sigh and a little pout. "But every day will seem a lifetime until you return, *mi novio!*" Beneath the tablecloth, she crossed her fingers so the outrageous lie wouldn't count as a sin, a superstitious quirk that was becoming something of a habit these days since Felipe's return from the city, as lies piled up upon lies!

This wistful observation on her part seemed to soften Felipe's displeasure a little, for he told her good-bye in almost affectionate terms, and even went so far as to press his lips to her brow in platonic farewell, murmuring, "Patience, Krissoula, my dear one, patience! Soon I will be your husband, and when that time comes, every day and night will be ours to share, *sí* . . . ?"

She'd paled, she knew, at the implication of his words, but he'd only chuckled—probably believing her faint with longing for him, the vain old lecher! Moments later, he'd clambered awkwardly astride Dorado and hauled savagely on the stallion's tender mouth in a way that made her wince with sympathy for the poor beast. The palomino had screamed in pain, and they'd ridden off. Luis and Pedro, a pair of *gauchos* he'd chosen to serve as his bodyguard against possible attack from either *banditos* or Indios had followed him hot on his heels, riding their *criollo* ponies.

Dare she hope he'd run afoul of both bandits and Indians, Krissoula wondered, smiling wickedly as she enthusiastically waved her lace-edged handkerchief until he'd vanished from view? Should she pray that he'd meet with some exquisitely agonizing death, perferably one that was drawn out and long in coming? Better not—or at least, not until she could be assured beyond doubt that all the benefits of wealthy widowhood would be hers in such an event!

As always when *el patrón* was absent, the atmosphere in the *hacienda* lightened appreciably with Felipe's departure. Mama Angelina prepared all the foods she knew were Krissoula's favorites—enormous broiled steaks, heapings of pan-fried potatoes, empanadas and a hearty, savory *pulchero* stew for luncheon—and hummed happily in her kitchen while she worked. Estrella and Luisa were all smiles and giggles and noisy, infectious chatter as they cleaned and dusted and polished about the house. Even Tomás, out in the stables, whistled while he oversaw the care of the horses, and the *peóns* in his charge exchanged grins. Was it merely because Don Felipe had left Tierra Rosa that Señor Tomás smiled so broadly this morning, they wondered? Or had he received a smile from pretty, shy Estrella to gladden his heart and give him hope that she would allow him to pay court to her?

Whatever the reasons, Tierra Rosa took on a festive, jubilant air that gradually extended even to Doña Sofía, who'd been even more reserved than usual since her scolding at Don Felipe's hands the day before, and who had at first flatly refused to so much as consider the pleasant, innocent little outing Krissoula suggested.

"Come, come, Sofía *mía*," Krissoula cajoled, smiling her own most melting smile, "enough of your pouting! Since Don Felipe is not here, we can't ask him for permission to visit Lupe and her baby now can we? Therefore, we will do so anyway—and worry about his approval later!"

"But, *niña,* he expressly forbade us to go riding!" Sofía protested with a worried frown. "When he learns we have disobeyed him yet again, he will send me from Tierra Rosa!"

"But we don't intend to go riding for pleasure like before, my silly Sofía," Krissoula rationalized patiently, her golden eyes dancing with mischief. "Visiting the workers of the *hacienda* and the *estancia* and their families to enquire about their well-being is quite a different matter from galloping across the pampas like—like hoydens!" The corners of her generous mouth twitched with ill-concealed merriment. "Why, it is my solemn duty to do so! You told me yourself that it is up to *la patrona* of any household to ensure that her husband's workers and servants are well fed and content with their lot, did you not?"

"*Sí,* that is so, but—"

"'But' nothing!" Krissoula cut in quickly. "If, by some chance, Felipe should learn we left the *hacienda* while he was gone—and I certainly won't tell him!—then we have a perfectly legitimate reason at heart for having done so—the 'good works' he told me to busy myself with. Even stuffy old Don Felipe himself could not help but consider the smooth running and well-being of his *estancia* important! What could he possibly find to disapprove of?"

"From what I've learned of Don Felipe, *niña,* I have no doubt that he will find something!" said Sofía with surprising frankness and a definite bite of anger to her tone.

"True," Krissoula allowed with a giggle, "but he'd be far angrier to learn that I'd gone to visit Lupe and little Paulo unescorted, no . . . ?" She let her words trail away unfinished, and pointedly arched her brows.

"Oh, wicked girl! You wouldn't do such a thing—!" Sofía exclaimed, aghast.

"Oh, but I would, Sofía *mía,* and you know it! Although with the utmost reluctance, of course," she amended contritely, but determined.

"*Sí,* I know it! Ah, Krissoula, someday, you will prove the ruin of me!" Sofía prophesied, throwing up her hands in dismay, but her unhappy expression was now a thing of the past. She was reluctantly smiling, and Krissoula knew she'd won yet again. "Blessed Virgin, what am I to do with such a willful girl!"

"What are you to do with her? Why, simply enjoy her company, for the time being, *amiga,*" Krissoula retorted gaily, "and the adventurous moments she brings to your dishwater-dull life! And if

Felipe finds out, and he's angry, I'll take the blame, I swear it. I'll not let him hold you to account for *my* naughtiness."

With that understanding, the two of them set out, Krissoula riding astride upon a frisky Girasol, and Sofía following sedately in the surrey behind her.

The head groom Tomás had insisted they also take with them one of his stablehands to act as their escort, a good-natured, middle-aged *mestizo* man named Ignacio, since Blue Devil's band had been unusually cantankerous lately. He'd given Krissoula instructions on how to find Lupe's cottage, as well as a conspiratorial wink as he handed her up onto the palomino mare's back, murmuring, "Rest assured that my lips are sealed, Doña Krissoula! Don Felipe will hear nothing of this morning's doings from my mouth."

"Nor from mine, Tomás!" Krissoula had responded impishly, flashing him a teasing smile that had made her eyes sparkle like topazes in the morning sunshine as she looked down at him. *"Gracias, mi amigo,"* she'd finished warmly, and Tomás had been both pleased and embarrassed by her friendliness and lack of formality as he watched the little cavalcade ride away.

Lupe was delighted, although a little flustered, by their surprise visit. She ushered them into her little house, one of a row of such simple adobe dwellings. All belonged to families whose fathers or mothers, or more often both worked for Tierra Rosa as *gauchos,* horse-handlers, or serving women. She hurried to find them seats at the table and to prepare *maté* for her guests, welcoming them with blushes and beaming smiles of pleasure. Despite this, she was obviously a trifle nervous to see them, for she whisked imaginary specks of dust from the simple, rough-hewn furniture of her already immaculate little cottage, and tucked tiny wisps of stray hair into the heavy coil that rested prettily on her shoulders.

"Please, you must forgive my house and my appearance, Doña Krissoula, Doña Sofía. I was not expecting guests, you understand?" she apologized breathlessly, smoothing down her crisp white blouse and black skirt.

"Oh, but you have absolutely nothing to apologize for, señora," Sofía said gently. "Your home is immaculate, and both you and your little one are simply charming!"

To Krissoula's surprise, Sofía had been almost as taken with little Paulo as was she! There had been a brief battle over who was to hold the baby and play with him first, before Krissoula graciously

183

yielded to her duenna and followed Lupe outside to the fire and the dome-shaped adobe oven, housed beneath an open-sided *ramada,* or shed.

"I'm sorry I didn't warn you we were coming today, Lupe," Krissoula apologized softly. "I should have sent word to ask if today was a good time for us to visit, shouldn't I? It was inconsiderate of me to arrive unannounced like this, I know. But to be honest, I didn't even think about that until it was too late, and we were already on our way! You see, Don Felipe left on business only this morning, and since I'd been wanting to come and visit you for weeks now, today seemed the perfect opportunity, and so here I am!"

"Ah, but you must not apologize, señorita," Lupe denied, lifting a huge black kettle from the fire. "Did I not tell you that you are always welcome in our home, at any time? And it is so, truly it is. If I seemed unhappy to see you, forgive me, for it was not intended. It's just that I—I'm not accustomed to having guests such as you and Doña Sofía. I was afraid that perhaps you would find my home—uncomfortable—after what you're used to?"

Krissoula laughed, thinking she was used to far humbler dwellings than Lupe's. "Oh, don't be silly! Your house is charming, Lupe, and so very neat. You should be proud of it, not apologizing! Aiee, *Dios,* I'm not a tidy person at all myself. If it were not for your sisters and the other maids, the clothes I wear would stay where I leave them—tossed on the floor and gathering wrinkles—and there would be enough dust everywhere to plant corn for tortillas!"

Her airy confessions set Lupe immediately at ease. She smiled. "Truly, Doña Krissoula? You are teasing me, yes?"

"No, truly. On all the saints, I swear it!" Krissoula vowed solemnly, her hand pressed to her heart, and the two young women giggled companionably, the barriers of position broken between them.

Sofía was uttering strings of cooing nonsense words to an enraptured little Paulo when they returned to the cottage later with the steaming kettle, but whether it was her words or her dangling jet earrings that jiggled tantalizingly just out of reach of his chubby little fists that delighted him was debatable!

"My turn, Sofía!" Krissoula insisted, and the duenna reluctantly handed the squirming armful to her mistress with a farewell pat to his little bottom.

Paulo's gummy smile and crows of delight when she softly greeted him seemed proof to Krissoula that the baby remembered her. Lifting him up, she kissed his warm cheeks and buried her face in his soft, inky curls. The baby responded by chuckling and gurgling aloud, grabbing fistfuls of Krissoula's hair, and stuffing it into his little mouth as if starving, which he obviously was not!

"Oh, doña, he'll ruin your hair!" Lupe exclaimed, hurrying to take her son, but Krissoula shook her head.

"Who cares about my silly hair, eh, Paulito, eh, my little angel? Tell your *mamacita* not to worry—I love it!" she disclaimed.

Reassured by her shining eyes and the smiling curve of her lush mouth, Lupe returned to preparing refreshments for her guests, pouring boiling water over the dried herbs to brew the *yerba maté* and slicing a golden loaf of crusty, homemade bread, which she spread with butter and honey. Sipping the bracing, somewhat bitter Argentine *maté* from little globe-shaped brown gourds by means of silver straws called *bombillas,* both of which were a traditional part of the ritual, Lupe chatted more and more easily with Sofía as the minutes passed, her earlier nervousness forgotten.

Meanwhile, Krissoula was in a world of her own, cuddling little Paulo on her lap, playing the singsong childhood games she'd once played with Nicki as she counted his little toes and fingers. The lump was back in her throat, but the memories were easier today, somehow. All the love she'd buried inside her since Nicki's death now came pouring out to the infant in her arms, an emotion so surprisingly fierce and full she wished she could keep him always. She even guiltily acknowledged in her heart that she felt envious that he was Lupe's son, and not her own.

Was that how Manuela had felt, she wondered thoughtfully as she bounced Paulo on her knee, on discovering that Maria de San Martín, her duenna and later her companion, was to give Alejandro the child she'd been unable or too fearful to give him? This same, aching envy in her breast that she was feeling now? What could have gone wrong after the joyous day they became betrothed to have changed Manuela so dramatically from joyful bride to the unhappy wife who'd given grist to the mills of gossip?

At first, she'd wondered—sifting the tidbits of gossip she'd gathered here and there through her mind—if Manuela had fallen for the wrong Aguilar brother; not the one her parents had chosen for her husband, but the older brother, Felipe, and if perhaps that had been the cause of her unhappy marriage. But, after reading page after page of Manuela's diary last night, Krissoula knew that was not the case. Manuela had hardly mentioned Felipe in her writings. But her joy over her betrothal to Alejandro of the "melting

185

brown eyes," and her mounting excitement as their two-year engagement passed and their wedding day approached was perfectly genuine, she was certain. She'd have to read on before she discovered if that love had lasted . . .

After they'd enjoyed the refreshments Lupe provided, they went outside with her to meet some of the other workers' families, all of whom greeted the future *patrona* of Tierra Rosa with awe and reserve, except for the children, who welcomed her with shy smiles, giggles—and no reserve whatsoever!

One dark-eyed little angel of a girl even invited her to join in the game of hopscotch which her unexpected arrival had interrupted. To Sofía's amazement, Krissoula agreed, lifting Paulo from her hip and returning him to his mother for the first time since she'd taken him in her arms. Moments later, she was hoisting her riding habit to her knees and showing her petticoats, hopscotching in the dust with the little girls, her black hair bouncing over her shoulders, and laughing and tossing her pebble like a little girl herself.

Lupe, who'd been watching the way the doña walked through the little village carrying Paulito astride her hip in the easy, comfortable manner of a peasant woman, was quietly thoughtful as she watched the señorita win the hearts of everyone in the tiny village in turn. Whether it was by playing games with the children, or complimenting the women on their exquisite embroidery or by admiring the ingenuity with which the ancient *gaucho,* Xavier, turned the hide taken from a dead colt's hind leg into an unseamed boot, or watched another old one, a *viejo* named Roberto, carving a *taba,* or gambling piece, from a cow's knucklebone, they were won over in a matter of moments, their shyness and reserve forgotten. And then, to everyone's amusement, the young woman lingered to try one of Roberto's finished *taba* for herself.

"Heads, Roberto! I win again!" she declared, after tossing the *taba* a few times.

"*Caramba,* Doña Krissoula, with such good fortune, a man would be foolish to bet against you!" Roberto declared, shaking his snowy head. His leathery olive face was wreathed in smiles amidst the deep wrinkles that crisscrossed it, his mouth sunken in around his gummy grin like an overripe squash.

"*Sí!* But lucky with the dice, unlucky in matters of the heart—isn't that what they say, Roberto, *mi viejo?*" she laughingly disclaimed, giving the old one a hearty nudge and a wink. "That being the case, you must have many, many sweethearts, eh, *amigo?*"

Everyone laughed.

Lupe, looking on, wondered if any of the others had noticed that the señorita now spoke with the common accent of the Spanish people, rather than with the lisping Castilian of a highborn *criolla* that she normally affected, or if she was the only one who'd noticed that her manner was far more relaxed and far less reserved than usual?

The time flew past! Before Krissoula had realized how long they'd stayed, Sofía was reminding her charge that it was time to leave. Amidst cries of farewell and invitations from everyone to come again, Ignacio gave Krissoula a leg up onto her mare, handed Sofía into the carriage, and they made ready to leave.

Krissoula led the way, throwing a kiss and a wave to Lupe, who watched them go with Paulo cradled in her arms, before kneeing Girasol into a brief canter.

She was startled to see another rider coming towards the village as they left it by a grove of *quebracho* trees—a rider whose black-stockinged bay horse she recognized long before she recognized him. *Esteban.* Oh, *Dios,* no, not him again!

She tensed as the distance between them closed, knowing she'd have to acknowledge him in some fashion or risk drawing Sofía's attention to the omission. But her stomach bunched up in a knot and her hands trembled on Girasol's reins as he drew nearer. *Madre,* what a handsome figure he cut as he rode towards her, horse and lean, dark rider moving effortlessly as one. This afternoon he wore a crisp white shirt under his customary black jacket with the embroidered shoulders, and the whiteness of it emphasized his tanned throat and hard, angular good looks. She bit her lower lip. Those striking good looks somehow never failed to hit her with the force of a blow to the belly, driving the breath from her in a purely physical, female response—and today was no exception!

Somehow, gathering up her courage, she managed to nod politely as he rode abreast of her without meeting his mocking sapphire eyes and tossed out a curt, *"Buen día,* Señor San Martín," to him as their horses passed on the narrow track.

He politely tipped his *chambergo* as he rode past her, but uttered only a single low word in response to her greeting. Her face flaming, she gritted her teeth and urged Girasol into a canter, for the single word he'd murmured had been a wicked threat, a scoundrel's promise, a roguish invitation, all rolled into one.

"Tonight!" he'd said as he rode past. *"Tonight."*

The rest of the day seemed to fly by, as if somehow time had been accelerated as part of a conspiracy with that *diablo,* San Martín! No sooner did the wintry sun sink beyond the mountains than it seemed the sky had fully darkened, the moon risen, in the blink of an eye! The customary late-evening dinner hour the Argentines preferred, after the Spanish fashion, also seemed to come and go just as quickly, and although Angelina had prepared her favorite foods yet again for *comida,* five minutes later Krissoula could hardly remember what she'd eaten!

She tried to delay the hour of retiring by persuading Sofía to play cards with her, and Sofía good-naturedly obliged for an hour or two until she could no longer hide her yawns.

"Forgive me, but I'm going to bed now, *niña,"* she said at last. "Another moment, and I'll be asleep sitting up!"

Krissoula had no choice but to retire likewise, though she lingered over snuffing the candles and by dousing lamps, and in slowly climbing the long, curving staircase, putting off the inevitable solitude of her room and, with it, all opportunities for succumbing to the temptation that pulsed in her veins!

She'd just lit the lamp to undress for bed when she decided it would be far wiser to leave it unlit. A lighted lamp shining from her window would signal that she had retired, and might be mistaken as an invitation for Esteban to join her! Consequently, she blew out the flame and leaped away from the lamp as if scalded, instead stumbling and groping about in the gloom to undress and ready herself for bed. She'd lock her balcony doors securely, she determined, but since she couldn't be one hundred percent certain that her flimsy French doors would serve to keep that determined rogue out, she was still far from confident that she was safe from him!

After she'd washed, she brushed out her hair and went to the French doors that led out onto the balcony, first risking a glance over the railing to the area below her window, and peering at the darkened shrubbery and the courtyard beyond washed in moonlight. There was nothing there. No suspicious shadows, no darker, man-shaped bulk against the lighter masses of the foliage. No lurking, lovesick Romeo bent on scaling the ivy-draped walls to her balcony. Her heart fluttered, but whether from relief or crushing disappointment, she honestly wasn't sure. Curse the man! she thought, angry at herself for letting his wicked threat bother her. Did he have some power unknown to her, that he could continually invade her every waking thought—and far too many of her dreams?

Resolutely she went inside and locked the doors. Afterward, she drew the flowered draperies behind her, plunging the room into inky blackness. Satisfied she'd forgotten nothing, left nothing to chance, she made her way to the bed. Throwing back the covers, she scrambled naked beneath them, but lay there like a stiffened corpse instead of dropping off to sleep, staring wide-eyed up at the ceiling.

An hour passed, but she was still unable to sleep, although she tried desperately to do so. And, since nothing hinders sleep from taking its natural course so much as *trying* to attain the state, she was still wide awake another hour later, when the yowling started!

The first loud squalls brought her bolt upright in the bed, trembling all over with the suddenness of those blood-curdling, screeching howls that rent the hush. *Indians!* she thought initially, her heart pounding, *The casa was under attack! What else could it be?*

The second, unearthly chorus of yowls sent her flying to the French doors and out onto the balcony to discover their cause. Fortunately, she had the presence of mind to tug on her wrapper as she went, for she saw that on the next balcony, a white-robed figure was also craning her rag-tied head over the railing to look below.

"Did the noise wake you, too, Sofía?" Krissoula whispered, plumbing the darkness below. The scent of lavender and gardenias was overpoweringly sweet on the chill, damp air.

"*Sí,*" Sofía agreed, doleful-eyed, smothering a yawn. She crossed herself piously. "*Dios,* what a racket! At first, I was sure it was all a part of the awful dream I was having. The souls of the wicked, doomed to burn in purgatory, were screeching in agony—!"

"*Dios!* That must have been *some* nightmare!" Krissoula exclaimed admiringly, staring at her duenna with new respect. Perhaps Sofía had hidden depths she'd never suspected, till now? She certainly seemed blessed with a deliciously lurid imagination!

"*Sí,* it was!" Sofía gave a shaky laugh. "And then, I realized it was only *el gato,* and I was embarrassed by my foolishness!"

"*El gato?*" Krissoula echoed, feeling faint, for *gato* was the insulting name she always flung at Esteban. *Dios,* no! Surely it wasn't him howling like that to attract her attention—?

"*Sí,* of course! Don't tell me you haven't heard the howls *el gato* makes when he's prowling about at night before this?"

Krissoula was frankly shocked by now. "When he—he's p-prowling? No, I—I haven't, but then, I sleep like the dead!" she denied in a whisper, wondering just how much more Sofía knew about San Martín's peculiar nocturnal habits that she'd yet to discover for herself.

Another yowl sounded, louder and more ear-splitting than any before, if that were possible.

"There! That settles it! Tomorrow, I shall instruct Tomás to set out a trap for our amorous *Señor Gato* and drown him!" Sofía said firmly. "We can't have his noisy mating calls keeping us awake every night."

Krissoula's jaw dropped and she blinked in wide-eyed astonishment. She'd always considered Sofía a gentle, retiring woman hitherto, but now, hearing her speak so calmly and cold-bloodedly of trapping and drowning a man simply because his "mating calls" disturbed her night's rest revealed a vengeful side to the woman's character she'd never suspected existed!

"I—er, well—do you not think drowning him just a little extreme?" Krissoula suggested, her voice faint with shock.

"Certainly not! Besides, Angelina tells me he's sired quite enough litters of kittens that Tierra Rosa will never be short of mousers, thanks to that great, evil black brute! We'll miss nothing about the beast but his noisy singing each night!"

Litters? Kittens! Krissoula thought, trembling now with outrage at what seemed irrefutable evidence of Esteban's rank promiscuity and astonishing fertility amongst the serving women of the *estancia*. But—*mousers?* What on earth had Sofía meant by that—?

And then the truth suddenly dawned on Krissoula, and she started to laugh, helpless giggles and wild, unladylike snorts of bawdy amusement that shook her body uncontrollably so that she had to hang onto the railing for balance.

"Aiee, *Dios,* Sofía, you mean he's a—a—tomcat?" she managed to gasp out between gales of laughter. "I thought—I thought you meant—aiee, *Dios mío!*—what I thought—!"

But she couldn't tell Sofía exactly what she'd thought, no, not at all! It would have given too much away!

The Spanish word *gato* had several meanings, one the meaning she'd usually attached to Esteban, implying a man who was a rogue, a rascal, a petty crook, but it could also refer to a country dance, known as the *gato.* Still another meaning was, of course—a humble tomcat! She'd called Esteban a tomcat, too, so her initial confusion was understandable on reflection, but an amusing mistake, for all that. *Caray!* The idea of Esteban being trapped and drowned by Tomás—of him siring countless litters of "kittens"—was hysterical! And poor, poor Sofía, looking so terribly confused and comical in her prim flannel robe with its numerous buttons fastened clear to her small, pointed chin, her mousy brown hair all done up in rags for sleeping like some fantastic Mardi Gras wig, was just too much, under the ridiculous circumstances. Krissoula erupted into hysterical laughter again, clutching her sides.

"Humph. I really don't see what you find so amusing," Sofía said, but fortunately Krissoula was saved from having to explain by more strident tomcat yowls below that made them cover their ears.

"It's nothing, really, Sofía," Krissoula gasped when silence prevailed. "Here, I'll fix your amorous *'Señor Gato'* for you! We won't need to drown the poor old thing!" she promised with a wicked smile, and stepped back inside her room. Taking up the porcelain water basin, she returned to the balcony and waited. When the howls sounded again a few seconds later, she hurled her dirty washwater into the shrubbery below in the direction of the sounds with a satisfyingly loud splash.

"Maadre de Diioss!"

Silence. Absolute. Complete.

"Why, that tomcat sounded almost human when the water drenched him, didn't he, *niña?"* Sofía observed curiously moments later.

Golden eyes shining in the moonlight, Krissoula smiled wickedly. "You're right, he did sound human—almost! But then, mating cats always sound like babies crying at night, don't they? You can go back to bed now, I do believe, Sofía. I don't think *'Señor Gato'* will be back to sing us his mournful *Tristes!"*

"I hope you're right!" Sofía said fervently. *"Buenas noches, niña.* Sleep well."

"You, too, Sofía. God bless," Krissoula murmured, instead thinking, That rogue San Martín! The nerve of him, to howl like a tomcat beneath her balcony to get her attention! Well, she'd fixed him, once and for all. He'd go home disappointed and wet tonight, that much was certain—and without the reward he'd been eagerly anticipating, too!

Still smiling to herself, she slipped back inside the room and closed and carefully locked the door behind her, drawing the parted draperies closed in her wake. In inky darkness once more, she replaced the porcelain basin on the washstand and fumbled about her for a heavy upright chair. After wedging it firmly beneath her balcony doorknob as an extra precaution against forced entry, she made her way back to bed. Groping about in the darkness to find her way, she encountered the edge of the feather mattress and stretched out, rolling over to lie on her side.

At once, two powerful arms wrapped around her waist from behind and tightened. A deep, masculine voice shaking with laughter suddenly purred in her ear:

"So! Did you get rid of your pesky *gato, querida mia?"*

Chapter Fifteen

"Why, you conniving rogue—!" she hissed, fighting his hold.

"Can it be you're not pleased to see me, darling?"

"The devil I am, *diablo!* Get out of my bed, you cockroach, and let me go!"

"But why, *querida?*"

"Because—because—I hate you! Aiee, *Madre,* your hair—it's soaking!" she hissed as he reached across the bed and pulled her by the waist towards him. As he did so, droplets of water showered again from his hair to wet her arms and shoulders. But, her silk wrapper slippery against the fine sheeting, she was no sooner able to resist his tuggings than fly. She slithered smoothly across the bed and into his arms as if skating on ice!

"And whose fault is it that I'm wet, eh, you minx?" he countered huskily, turning her smoothly to face him. "No one's but yours!" With her body snuggled firmly against his, imprisoned gently by his arms, he nuzzled his damp head beneath her jaw to rain hot little kisses over her throat.

"Pah! You deserved far more than a good soaking, Señor Gato, howling like you did!" she accused. "I just knew it was you, and not some poor, lovesick tomcat, and I was hoping the cold water would cool your ardor! You woke Sofía, you know—and the rest of the household, too, more likely than not!"

"If you'd been a little nicer, you'd have left your balcony door ajar, and we could have avoided my little 'act,' *minina*—and spared me a dangerous journey up the back stairs, into the bargain!" he pointed out ruefully, but she knew by his tone that he was grinning, and it infuriated her.

"I left the lamp unlit for a reason, *loco*—because I didn't want you here!" she hissed, and added with far less conviction, "And still don't!"

"No, *querida?* Then tell me to leave," he suggested reasonably, tracing the elegant curve of her cheek with his fingertip, and following it down to the corner of her mouth and the adorable little indentation there. His thumb brushed back and forth across her pouting lower lip as he repeated, "The choice is yours, after all. It's not my way to force a woman, however desperately I desire her. Tell me to go, *querida,* and I will, I swear it."

His warm breath fanned her cheek, raising goosebumps on her arms as he ducked his head and pressed his lips ever so gently to the sensitive pulse spot just below her little ear. His warm breath raised gooseflesh on her arms, and she knew she was lost as his maddening tongue delicately circled her shell-like ear. Being here, lying so close to him, his kisses like warm rain dropping everywhere on her skin, and his strong arms holding her close, her desire to surrender was far greater than her will to resist . . .

Oh, Lord, what harm could a last night of passion possibly do, she rationalized? It would give her something to think about, to cherish throughout her dreary years of passionless existence as Felipe's wife, a precious, golden moment to hoard forever in memory's storehouse. Besides, her body acknowledged his mastery, even if she could not. It was coming alive, responding, growing warm and tingly in expectation of the pleasure it had learned to expect at his hands—the traitor!

"Well?" he asked again, cupping a hard, pointed breast and fondling it wickedly until the little crest ruched and swelled between his fingers. "Still want me to leave, *bombón?"*

"Yes, I want you to—*Madre,* how I want you to! But—but somehow, I can't tell you to go!" she whispered helplessly, her voice breaking. "I just can't, you rogue—and you know it . . . !" she wailed.

With a soft chuckle, he planted a brief kiss full upon her lips, then leaned in lower to deepen it with an appreciative groan, his tongue parting her lips and ardently exploring her inner mouth in a way that turned her loins to melted butter.

"Mmm, wonderful!" he murmured, his words muffled by her lips.

He was right. It *was* wonderful! She felt as if her bones were melting as he kissed her, dissolving to leave only a mass of insubstantial, hungry flesh in their wake. Her willpower was even less substantial. With a defeated sigh, she kissed him back with open mouth and darting, eager tongue, her arms winding around his throat, then framing his handsome dark face as she pressed her aching breasts against his chest. Madonna! Being in his arms was like coming home, somehow, she thought, familiar and comforting. And he tasted so wonderful, smelled so wonderful, felt so very wonderful! His lips were warm and salty on hers, his musk a mixture of clean male flesh and soap in her nostrils, with just a hint of *caño,* the fiery local rum, tobacco, and woodsmoke.

But then—to her dismay—just when she was really beginning to enjoy his kisses and kissing him back with a fervor that amazed her, he untangled her arms from about his throat and slipped from the bed.

"Wait! Where are you going?" she cried in dismay, afraid he meant to leave her after all. Now, having decided to succumb to temptation once again, she couldn't bear it if he left her this way!

"Going? Why, to draw those infernal drapes, where else?" His eyes gleamed wickedly in the sudden, silvery light as he did so, then he turned back to face her, fists planted on his hips, and she saw that he was laughing. "What? Surely you weren't afraid I'd had a change of heart? Ah, there's no fear of that, *minina!* It's just that I want to see you—every pretty inch of you!—as I make love to you—and this room is blacker than the pit of hell!"

Relieved, she sank back against the pillow, replaying his words in her mind as he strode back across the room towards her, his tall silhouette framed by the starry heavens wheeling beyond the windows.

". . . as I make love to you!" he'd said, and *Dios,* how his words excited her, sent thrills skittering up and down her spine like leaping cats! His rich, sensual tone made warm, quivery feelings tremble in the pit of her belly, and she clutched the lace-edge corner of the sheet in her two fists to steady herself.

It seemed a lifetime, but only moments later the bed gave to his weight and he stretched out beside her again, at once taking her in his arms and kissing her hungrily. He laced his strong, tanned fingers in the cascading ringlets of her hair to hold her fast for his eager mouth, although she returned his kisses with an eager, greedy hunger that delighted him, teasing his tongue with her own, and making no attempt to pull away.

"Still want me to leave?" he asked roguishly when he broke the lingering kiss again at last and drew back to gaze deep into her golden eyes. Catching the silvery pallor of the moonlight streaming through the window, they shone like twin candle flames beneath a thick fringing of sooty lashes.

"No, *diablo,* no!" she whispered throatily, running her fingertips down his cheek, his throat, to his chest. "You drive me crazy,

194

hombre—you make me forget what is right! You make me think only of what Krissoula wants, and not what Krissoula should do, damn you!" she accused.

"And what is it that Krissoula wants, mmm, little one?" he teased sensually.

Her glowing eyes, her rapid breathing, gave him the answer he craved more eloquently than words. But, lips slightly parted, glistening with a moist sheen that was tempting beyond his wildest dreams, she whispered smokily, "You, *querido!* Krissoula wants you!"

His gut lurched. His pounding heart skipped a beat. The hard weightiness of his groin tightened in response, and his manhood surged. That bewitching little minx—she drove him wild, too!

Restraint and caution vanished as he lowered her gently to the sheets. Felipe, her dreams of a lifetime of wealth and comfort, her promises to herself, no longer mattered. Nothing and no one mattered but him, in that moment. For her there was only Esteban de San Martín, her lover, and the aching emptiness that he alone could fill.

With a muffled cry, she reached out, cradling his head in her palms as she eagerly sought his mouth, pulling his head fiercely down to hers. She was dimly aware as their lips met in a searing kiss that he was loosening the sash of her wrapper, thrusting the silky folds clear up to her hips, then tugging the sleeves down to bare her breasts. As he undressed her, he paused to kiss her again and again, slanting his lips across hers and sliding his tongue between them to explore the inner sweetness of her mouth as he flung the robe aside. She felt him draw a ragged gasp at the feel of her soft, bare curves pressed to his, the exquisite sensation of her body trembling beneath his touch.

"Ah, *querida,* how lovely you are . . . so soft, so silky everywhere I touch. Do you like it when I caress you here? And how about here, between your thighs? Ahh, darling, *sí, sí,* tell me, tell Esteban what it is that pleases you most . . ."

Her fingers tightened their grip in his damp curls as his hands moved lazily over her body, cupping her buttocks, pressing up her breasts to feast upon them with hungry lips, knowing instinctively where and how to caress her and give her the greatest pleasure, until her body hummed with sensation like a taut wire, stretched to its limits.

"Esteban, *mi amor!* Oh, *mi querido,* don't stop, take me!" she pleaded softly, burying her face against his chest in shame that his touch could make her want him so. But in moments, shame was no more. His fingers found the sweet, wet core of her, and he began to play upon her senses like a musician upon a well-tuned instrument, plucking forth the sweetest, purest chords of pleasure until her body sang with joy, vibrating like a harp in the wind. She sighed under his caresses, writhed with a sweet, wild joy as he readied her, and she surrendered to his loving like a leaf whirled in a fierce, hot wind and blissfully let it carry her away.

She felt the current of cool night air from the open French doors fanning her bare skin. Felt the slippery, lace-edged texture of her sheets sliding away beneath her. Felt the hard warmth of Esteban's bare, hairy chest pressed hard against her crushed breasts, the wiry roughness arousing her nipples to tingling life—all three at once—and shivered with the exquisite, wide-open awareness of her senses. It was as if every inch of her skin had been turned inside out, the nerves exposed, ready to absorb the slightest sensation like a thirsty sponge! Sí, *I'm a sponge,* she thought, made drunk and giddy with desire, *I'll absorb every moment, every touch, take every memory and keep it, like a thirsty sea sponge!*

When—how?—had he removed his shirt, his breeches, she wondered dreamily, feeling the roughness of his muscular legs brushing against her own silky limbs as he rolled towards her. But when or how really didn't matter. His naked male body felt alive and vital, virile and beautiful beneath her hands as he knelt beside her, the corded muscles rippling beneath his flesh. That was all that mattered; that, and the wonderful way he was making her feel . . .

She felt the graze of his hand limn the curves of her hips, stroke across the flat expanse of her almost concave belly, and slip downward again to caress her ankles, her instep, each little curling toe, then her slender calves, rising slowly upward to press apart her thighs once more.

Like a flower unfurling, the creamy columns parted at his command. His warm fingers were slightly rough with calluses, yet oh, so very gentle as he caressed the inner silkiness of her thighs, drawing maddening circles there that made her gasp with pleasure. She arched her back, raising her hips to meet the questing fingers that fondled the soft dark curls that crowned her mound. She shivered and tensed with pleasure as they trailed lower again to tease the hidden, velvety little crevice of her womanhood and the tiny, sensitive bud within its petals that ruled her passion.

His touch found a welcome there as dewily moist and warm as her mouth had given him, and he growled deep in his throat as the pressure in his loins mounted. Stroking her delicately, he built the yearning within her, playing fast then slow, gently then more urgently, pressing and penetrating until his caresses grew unbearable, until she could think of nothing but easing her torment. Bones and substance had melted away. She was all aching, wanting flesh, trembling with his touch and the need for more of him, to feel him inside her. She ran her fingers over his lean body, rubbed his tiny brown male nipples until they stood erect, then followed the rough, wiry line of his chest hair down over his rock-hard belly to his straining loins. With trembling fingers, she sheathed his velvet hardness within her palm, giving him pleasure even as he gave pleasure to her. She saw his eyes darken, and the rise and fall of his chest quicken as she stroked his rearing shaft, grazing her nails across its swollen arrowhead.

Her eyes pleaded with his darkly magnificent ones in the shadows.

"I want you so—I want you now, *querido* . . ." she whispered urgently, her voice husky with passion, her touch enflaming him. "I'm ready. So ready! Please, *mi amor,* don't wait any longer . . . ?"

Gazing hungrily down at her, he saw that her lovely face was transported with desire. Her slender body was bathed in moonlight and shadow, her pearlescent skin patterned in silver and gray tiger stripes like a pagan goddess's. Her head was flung back upon the fragrant sheets, framed by an inky river of hair. Her golden, long-lashed eyes were closed in rapture, lips parted and glistening with a dewy sheen.

He shuddered at the glorious picture of wild abandonment she made. Her back was arched, her pointed breasts presented high and taut in offering to his hungry lips, her thighs flung wide to flaunt the crimson flower of her womanhood. Leaning over her, he gathered a mound in the cup of his hand and suckled the pointed crest, drawing each swollen bud deep into his mouth until she uttered frantic little cries and ground her hips wantonly against his fingers as he plundered her treasure. *Dios,* how lovely she was in her passion! How his loins throbbed at the nearness of her! He wondered—for just a fleeting instant—if he could control himself, if he could postpone his own release long enough to give her the ease she craved, so great was his need—so very exciting was she in hers!

Drawing his lips from her breast, he came into her arms as naked as she, fitting her beneath him as he loomed above her.

She ran her fingers down over his hard belly between them, each

197

touch as soft and fleeting as the warm trickle of rain down a windowpane, and then she heard him gasp aloud as she enfolded his hardness again. She felt his shaft stir in pleasure at her touch, and heard him murmur her name again and again as he fondled her breasts, kissed her throat, her hair, her lips. Wild for him, she teased and tempted him, tested his control to the utmost limits by caressing him until he could bear it no longer, until he knew just another, featherlike brush of her palm, another gentle rasp with her teasing fingernails against his sensitive flesh, would undo him.

Drawing her hand away, he guided himself to the portals of the sweet, warm sheath between her thighs, and poised there a moment, both of them savoring a delicious second of anticipation, before he slid his palms beneath her bottom and filled her with a single, plunging thrust.

Her cry of rapture as he entered her trilled high and sweet on the hushed gloom, like the cry of a songbird in the dark of night. Prolonging each powerful thrust, lingering maddeningly over each withdrawal, he moved deeply within her. Sweat beaded his brow with the strain of denial, for the tightness of her woman's body enfolded him like a glove, sheathed him in delight, the tremulous quivers of her womanhood stroking him like tiny caresses, even as her nails had tantalized and tormented him moments before.

"Ah, mi amor, ah, qué magnífico!" she murmured throatily. His thrusts were so slow, so deliciously deliberate and powerful, she wondered if she'd faint with the sheer ecstasy of his loving! And then his mouth sought hers, his tongue delving deep into its sweet, wet recesses to mate with her own, and she responded fiercely to feel them joined so utterly—mouth to mouth, soft breasts to broad chest, hip to hip, and met his driving hips with a joyous arching of her own. She caressed his shoulders, raked his powerful back, moaning uncontrollably against his rough cheeks as he made love to her wonderfully, wonderfully. With whispered endearments, she urged him on, telling him throatily of her need, how virile he was, how his lean hard body pleased her, until speech became impossible. She could only utter little cries of incoherent delight that rose higher and higher, one after the other, note upon fluting note.

As their desire mounted, he tore his mouth from hers and uttered an anguished groan, riding her swiftly, deeply now as their passion soared. His half-closed sapphire eyes were liquid stars as he gazed down at her, and caught the moonlight like shattered gemstones. His hard mouth had grown softer and more sensual in passion.

Gazing up at him, she saw his lips were parted slightly with the ragged quality of his breathing.

"Now!" he commanded hoarsely. "Now, *querida,* soar with me—!"

She moved beneath him, twining her legs about his waist, meeting the driving power of his flanks with a response that was instinctive, eager, unrestrained. She gave herself with a fierce, wild sweetness no woman had gifted him with before . . . if indeed any woman had existed for him before Krissoula. *Dios!* In that heady moment, he no longer knew or cared . . . There was only the lovely tigress in his arms! Only her . . .

The gathering pressure in his loins coalesced, built in bittersweet torment for moments that were endless, before freeing him in an explosion of pleasure that left his senses reeling.

He felt the roar of triumph building in his throat long before it was ever born on his lips, and in the same moment felt Krissoula's nails grind deep into his back. Her body tightened in uncontrollable spasms around his, sheathing him deeper and tighter in the honeyed velvet of her sex as waves of ecstasy crashed over her.

"Never before . . . !" she moaned helplessly. "Never, until you, *querido!* Aiee, *Dios!* I never dreamed . . . that . . . it . . . could . . . be . . . like . . . this!"

Her lips parted to utter sobs of delight, sobs he knew he dare not let her voice—not here, not now. It was too damned dangerous! He stanched both their cries with his mouth, swallowing her sobs of rapture, kissing her savagely as the shattering climax convulsed them both and left them spent and trembling.

Esteban came back to reality first. He rolled from her and lay on his side, facing her. Krissoula's eyes were closed in the moonlight streaming through the window. Her lashes rested like sooty moths against her flushed cheeks. Her face was lovely and serene, blurred with spent passion, totally at peace. In that moment, she appeared softer, more feminine, more exquisitely beautiful than he'd ever seen her before—*si,* irresistibly so! He leaned over her and kissed her closed eyelids and her soft mouth, drawing her close against his chest so that she nestled in the crook of his arm like a sleepy kitten in a warm basket.

She stirred and opened dreamy golden eyes to gaze at him searchingly for a few seconds, before her eyes suddenly darkened as if in remembered pain. She brushed the back of her hand down his cheek, and he caught that hand and kissed the palm.

"We are well matched in some things, you and I, no?" he murmured with a teasing smile, adding, "if not in others!" He kissed her cheek and pulled her closer, resting his chin upon the soft curls that crowned her head. Funny, that, no? he thought. She curved so perfectly against him, it was as if she'd been created with no other purpose in mind . . .

"Esteban?"

"Mmm, *minina?*"

"What now? What happens next?"

"You have to ask?" He laughed deeply and turned her a little to kiss the tip of her nose. "Why, we make love again of course, *querida,* the very minute I've recovered my strength! And we do so as many times and in as many glorious, different ways as it pleases us to do before sunrise—when, alas, I must leave you to see to the *estancia.*"

His hand drifted down from her upper arm, and grazed teasingly across one pert nipple, tweaking it gently to stand erect yet again, then cupping the fascinating soft-firmness of one perfect breast in his palm. "Be patient, my lovely, golden-eyed kitten, for just a moment or two longer. With a lovely woman like you to fire my blood, my recovery won't take long, I promise. Ah, look, darling! See what you've done to me? Already the bull wears horns again!" he laughed, grinning wickedly as his manhood stirred against her thigh.

"I didn't mean tonight!" she murmured, a catch to her voice. "I meant what will happen about us later—tomorrow, and the next day and the next? What about when Felipe comes back? What then? Will we still be lovers, or must it end? Oh, Esteban, I thought I could go through with our deal. I truly believed I could carry it off and find the information you need. Oh, I swore I would, I know that. But now, since you and I have been lovers . . . !" She bit her lip and shuddered, shaking her head. "I don't think I can keep up the pretense any longer, I loathe Felipe so! And he—he scares me, Esteban! I think he'd kill me, if he ever learned we were lovers—"

"I know, darling, I know. But I'm never far way, *minina,*" he tried to reassure her. "If there's trouble, you have only to cry out, and Tomás or I will be there in the blink of an eye, I swear it, never fear."

"And after this is over?" she persisted, propping herself up on one elbow to look into his face. "If I find the papers that will make you master of Tierra Rosa, what then? What about me—about us?"

He couldn't answer her the way she wanted him to, he realized.

200

He couldn't commit himself or make golden promises for the future that he might later regret. It was not his nature to lie to a woman, any woman. If he told her the truth—that he didn't know about the future, and that he hadn't thought the consequences through any further than satisfying his dominant goal of making love to her—she'd be hurt and furious. While a woman loved with her heart, a man made love first and foremost with his body. If he confessed as much, she'd accuse him of using her—and not without reason.

"I don't see why we couldn't still be lovers, do you?" he suggested slowly. "And as my *china,* darling, I would see that you wanted for nothing, of course," he suggested, for some reason hating himself for the offer, although why he should hesitate to make such a proposition to this little Gypsy who'd once been a *puta,* he had no idea. After all, it was surely a far better prospect than any those other men had offered her!

"Your *china?* I'm sorry, I don't know the word. What's a *china?*" she asked, almost holding her breath.

"My woman," he ground out with reluctance. "That's what we call a *gaucho's* woman here in Argentina."

"Ah, I see. Then a *china's* a *gaucho's* wife, you mean?"

The startling, transparent eagerness to her tone, the hope in it, cut his conscience like a knife. Was she genuinely naive—or was her ignorance a pretense, a malicious, annoying little game she played with him to make him feel guilty he wondered, feeling suddenly irritated?

"Not a wife exactly, no. They're not married, you see, except in common-law fashion," he explained baldly, knowing how brutal such a curt response must sound to her ears, but unable to think of a way to soften it and yet remain honest.

"But still, they live together? Sleep together? Make babies?" Her tone had altered now. It had an edge of understanding to it, and the dawning overtones of hurt.

Couple that with the stricken pride, bitter disillusionment, and no little rage he saw in her eyes, he now had all the ingredients necessary for a flaming quarrel on his hands, he thought, and saw his dreams of a long passionate night together slide forever beyond his reach.

"But of course," he snapped, guilt making his tone more brusque than he intended. "That is the custom," he ended with an indifferent shrug, staring at the ceiling.

"Well, to hell with your customs, *diablo!*" she spat like a cornered cat in a net, suddenly tearing free of his arms and jolting up-

201

right. Her golden eyes, so languid moments before, blazed now.

She brought back her clenched fist and smacked him full in the face, her blow connecting with his nose with a fleshy thwack! He yelped with the eye-watering pain and threw up his hands in self-defense, rolling away from her across the bed as the barrage of blows continued to rain down on him.

"*Perro! Canallo! Bastardo!* Krissoula Ballardo will never be your *china,* your kept whore!" she hissed, scrabbling after him. She clawed out and managed to lock her fingers in his hair, tearing at it and pummeling his head and shoulders like a wildcat. "You'd dare ask that of me?" She raised her chin and spat full in his face. "*Pah! Hijo de puta* yourself, San Martín! Whoremonger! *Bastardo,* I spit on your offer!"

"Enough!" he growled, catching both her wrists in a steely grip and shaking her. "Enough of this nonsense, woman! You'll never be *my* whore, you swear so proudly, eh?" he accused. "And yet just weeks ago you were willing to betray me, to sell yourself to a crazy, greedy old lecher for his stolen lands and wealth! To give yourself without love or thought of anything but gain to a man who's a murderer! Tell me, *minina,*" he mocked, "what's the damned difference whether you're Felipe's woman or mine? Only your price changes, no, little *puta?*"

She couldn't answer him. Couldn't speak a single word in her own defense, for he was right! The only difference between the two was that Felipe controlled the wealth of Tierra Rosa, while Esteban had only hopes of riches—and perhaps a very, very small claim on her heart, though she'd not swallow her pride to tell him so now, that bastard, not when he'd treated her so insultingly. Never, curse him!

"The *difference,*" she ground out through gritted teeth, "is that Felipe has offered me his name. He offered me marriage and position!"

"No, *querida,*" Esteban corrected her cruelly, standing and shrugging into his breeches. "He offered marriage to *Manuela,* not you—to the woman *I* chose for him because she happens to have Manuela's face! Felipe doesn't love you—he's in love with a ghost!"

Mortified, her cheeks flaming, she looked away, unable to face him as she grabbed her discarded wrapper from off the floor and slipped into it. Never had she been so humiliated, never, never, never! She knotted the sash with a savage tug, but when she turned back to face him, still furious, she saw that the anger was gone from his eyes. His lean, handsome face seemed sad now, as if already he regretted their harsh words, coming so hot on the heels of their

202

wonderful lovemaking.

"At least *my* offer was sincere, however insulting you may have found it, Krissoula," he gritted softly, hating the pain his words, however true, had caused her, and which he could read so clearly in her wounded eyes. "And it was made to you, and you alone, as a woman, with nothing to do with the deal we made in Barcelona. Can't you see, little fool? I'm in no position to offer you marriage, even if I wanted to!" he said frankly.

"Why don't you be honest?" she hissed, "and say what you really feel? That the fine *patrón* of Tierra Rosa you hope to be someday would never consider marriage to a little Gypsy slut! That's the truth of the matter, isn't it, my fine Don Esteban de San Martín?" she jeered bitterly with a toss of her ink curls. "I'm plenty good enough to warm your bed, to ease your *gorgio* lust, eh, but not good enough to be your wife, to bear your children!"

"Don't put words into my mouth, Krissoula," he snapped, his sapphire eyes intent. "Whatever you may think, I don't use women. I'm not that kind of man."

He reached out to touch her cheek, wanting to soothe her pain and her hurt pride with a caress, but she flung his hand away, still unable to look him in the face.

"Aren't you?" she challenged.

"No," he said quietly.

"Then just what kind of man are you?" she sneered, her lips twisted and ugly in her bitterness.

"An honest one, I hope! Come, little one, be reasonable! Surely you wouldn't rather I'd lied to you, make you wonderful, false promises of a rosy future for the two of us, in order to bed you?" he demanded softly. "I promised you pleasure, darling—nothing more, but nothing less, either. If you thought otherwise, I'm sorry."

His sapphire eyes searching her golden ones, he reached out to take her hand, but she flinched away as if he'd made to strike her instead.

"No! Don't touch me. Not now. Not ever again!"

Hands dropping to his sides, he watched as she fastened and refastened the silk sash of her robe about her waist, and saw how unsteady she was, how her usually graceful, tapering fingers fluttered clumsily, like a bird's crippled wings as it tried to fly. Ignoring her protests, he covered her chill little hands tightly with his own, and tilted her heart-shaped face up to his as he drew her to him.

Her eyes came up to meet his at last, and to his shock he saw that there was the sheen of tears in their depths. He stared, stricken, for he'd never seen the proud, feisty Krissoula even come close to weeping before. She saw the pity that filled his eyes, and couldn't bear that he should look at her in such a way.

"Get out, San Martín!" she whispered hoarsely. "Get out of here and don't come back—ever!"

She would have whirled away and fled across the room from him had he not grasped her elbow to hold her back.

"Don't, *querida!* I can't leave you like this, damn it!"

"Why not?" she said coldly. "I mean nothing to you, after all. Like you told me once before, *hombre,* you paid my price, you bought your pleasure. What else would you do with your *puta* after bedding her, but toss her a coin and leave?"

He could feel the tense yearning in her body to break free, to be gone from him, to be anywhere else but there, beside him, and he was overwhelmed with self-disgust. She was so very lovely, so very, very proud—so surprisingly naive, with her pretty dreams of marriage and happiness-ever-after. How could he have overestimated her worldliness, her ease with men, her vulnerability, so badly? He'd taken her self-assurance at face value, figuring she, of all women, must know the score where men were concerned, and been encouraged that she'd wanted him as badly as he wanted her. But right now, he couldn't have felt more guilty if he'd discovered he'd raped an innocent virgin, so huge and betrayed were her golden eyes!

He smoothed her wild mane of hair down about her shoulders, neatening it idly with restless fingers, playing for time and hoping in the interim to find some words to mend things between them a little. But no glib words or soothing catch phrases came to mind. What was done was done, and there was no turning back. He sighed and gently grasped her chin between his thumb and forefinger, tilting her face and forcing her to look up at him.

"At least let me kiss you good-bye before I go, Krissoula *mía,"* he whispered. "We owe each other that much, surely . . . ?"

So saying, he lowered his curly dark head and pressed his lips to her unresponsive, wooden ones. She flinched and moved sharply backward before he could deepen the kiss as he'd intended, and jerked her head away.

"No, San Martín," she said hoarsely, her upper lip curled with contempt, her nostrils flared. "Your time is up, *hombre,* and a whore's time is as precious as Gypsy gold, no? Just get out—go!"

He left.

Chapter Sixteen

Tomás dangled his arms over the corral fence and watched as Esteban gingerly put foot to stirrup and eased himself into the saddle of the new black-stockinged bay mustang he'd bought at the last horse fair in Córdoba. Something remote in his friend's brooding expression drove the smile from his lips and left him frowning.

In his opinion, something was badly wrong with his friend today, and Tomás had an uneasy hunch that that something concerned the golden-eyed señorita.

Esteban had never been the most even-tempered of men for as long as Tomás had known him—almost eleven years now. He was cursed with a hot temper when wronged, and would redeem himself with a murderous, single intensity of purpose that was frightening to behold. Yet for all that, Tomás knew he was also fairer than most men, and that Esteban's anger, however explosive, was blessedly short-lived and rarely undeserved. In other words, he was not the type of man given to brooding and hugging a grievance to his heart.

Still, unless his observations were way off the mark this time, Esteban was brooding about something today, as he had been for the past month. Surely he couldn't be in love, Tomás considered idly? In love with the tempestuous, beautiful Doña Krissoula, who was as far above him as the moon above a clod of earth? Had he tried to follow through with his attempts to seduce her that day he'd interrupted them in the stables, Tomás mused—their guilty expressions had given much more away than they'd realized!—and been haughtily rebuffed? Ah, *sí*, perhaps that explained his black mood, for Esteban—with his dark good looks, his flashing sapphire eyes, his roguish charm—was not accustomed to women refusing him! Rather, they dropped into his hand like plump, ripe grapes from the vine, ready and eager to be sampled . . .

Tomás sighed. Whatever the cause of his friend's preoccupation, one thing was certain: Esteban had no business trying to break a spirited wild mustang with such a mood on him, when a split second's distraction could cost him his life! As the head *domador,* the horse-handler of the *estancia,* it was his duty to ensure that no unnecessary risks were taken. What had he been thinking of, to go along with Esteban's decision to break the bay to the saddle today, he wondered gloomily? But . . . it was too late to stop him now. He was already mounted. And Esteban, like a stallion with the bit firmly between its teeth, was impossible to halt once set on his course . . .

Countless hooves had worn away the grass from the space enclosed by the split railings of the corral. Only churned dirt and dust remained underhoof now. From the center of the dirt enclosure rose a tall shaved pole, and attached to it by a rope halter stood the wild bay bronco, deceptively calm now. Its wild, rolling eyes had been blindfolded by a length of cloth in the South American way.

Esteban made himself comfortable in the saddle, wound the reins securely about his fists, and checked to make sure his feet were tucked deep into the stirrups. Certain he was ready, he jammed his felt *chambergo* down on his head and nodded curtly to the groom, Ignacio, who waited close by. Deftly Ignacio loosened the rope halter, freeing the mustang from the restraint of the pole. In almost the same move, he slipped the blindfold from its eyes and the bay's former calm evaporated like fog burned off by the morning sun!

Like a rocket, the bronco suddenly leaped into the air, all four hooves leaving the ground simultaneously in a startling way that wrenched shocked gasps from the onlookers! She skewed her rump around as she landed in a vicious, corkscrewing jolt that flung Esteban several inches up and to the side of his saddle, and left him momentarily flying in mid-air by the seat of his pants. Yet, he hung on and even regained his seat briefly before the bay bucked again. The watching *gauchos* straddling the rail whooped their approval of his riding skills with admiring cries of "Olé, San Martín!" and "Bravo, *mayordomo!*"

"That's a wild one there, eh?" old Roberto observed, nodding at the bronco and rider circling the corral in a series of explosive, firecracker springs and furious bucks that threw up clods of dirt.

"The horse or the man, *viejo?*" Tomás asked with a doleful grimace.

Roberto chuckled gummily. "I meant the horse, young Tomás— but then again, our beloved *mayordomo* appears out of sorts himself today, eh—not up to breaking a bronco, unless in the old *gaucho* way!"

The "old" way of breaking a wild horse was considered cruel now by many, and was a method rarely used, for it damaged a mount's spirit irreparably. The method involved having the *gaucho* mount a saddled wild bronco, which he immediately spurred and whipped mercilessly to bring it to full gallop, before it could so much as buck or recover its wits. Then he rode the animal without mercy, covering many miles until it was exhausted, its sides heaving, its heart close to bursting. After such cruel treatment, the mustang knew who was master. Invariably, a bronco broken in this fashion would be too beaten in spirit to protest the weight of either saddle or rider ever again.

A former *gaucho* of some reputation himself, Roberto was a shrewd one where reading horses or men were concerned, and to his eyes, Esteban's mind was elsewhere this morning.

"My gold says the horse will win, and Señor Esteban will bite the dust! Is it a bet, sonny?" he cackled, black eyes bright with anticipation.

Tomás pursed his lips. "The mare means business, true, *viejo*, but his rider's more stubborn than any mule! He won't let the bay best him—*especially* not in the foul mood he's in today! *Sí*, it's a bet, you old rogue!"

They both turned curiously to watch as a woman approached them, for a woman was a rare sight here at the corrals, which were considered male territory. Tomás' eyes widened when he saw that the woman was none other than the doña, looking trim and competent in a divided riding skirt and a short tailored jacket of a buckskin shade, topped by a flat-brimmed sombrero with a vicuña skin band around the crown. Her inky hair flowed loose beneath it to her mid-back, and her slender hips swung gracefully as she drew closer. *Caray!* Little wonder Esteban was preoccupied, he thought fleetingly. She was breathtaking!

"Buenas tardes, señorita," Tomás welcomed her, whipping off his own felt hat and feeling heat blaze up his throat to sting his olive cheeks as he clasped it to his chest. "It is not often these humble corrals are graced by such loveliness as yours," he observed gallantly, Spanish fashion, making a half bow from the waist. "Therefore, you must surely be looking for someone, *sí, doña?*"

"Not anymore," she confided with a frown. "I just came to watch the horse-breaking for a few minutes before heading home. I rode out here to visit Lupe Buenaventura, but her husband José told me she'd gone to help out at Tierra Rosa for the day, so we crossed paths, I suppose," she explained with a disappointed sigh.

"Then perhaps—if she has nothing better to do, of course!—the doña would care to amuse herself by placing a small wager?" Roberto suggested slyly, though his wrinkled mahogany face was as innocent as a babe's. "Last time you were here, I remember the señorita was very lucky at rolling the 'bones,' *sí?*"

Krissoula's smile widened. Her topaz eyes sparkled. Her cheeks warmed with fresh color. "Ah, so I was!" she agreed, remembering that day only too well because of the unforgettable night with Esteban that had followed it. "What is it you're wagering on, *viejo?*"

"The endurance of the bronco, against that of her rider, señorita. My money says the horse will win. Señor Tomás here says the rider. What do you think?"

Krissoula glanced appraisingly at the animal. "Let me study the 'field' for a moment or two before I make my choice, eh, *viejo?* It's only fair, after all!"

Accordingly, she turned and leaned over the railing as Tomás was doing, her golden eyes trained critically for several minutes on the twisting, plunging mare. A wild one, indeed, with a strong, deep chest, powerful hocks, and a fiery spirit! Her tío Ricardo would have sold his soul for such a horse! But when her gaze traveled upward to assess the mettle of the *gaucho* astride its back, her smile abruptly vanished as she realized, for the first time, that the rider they were discussing was none other than Esteban. She hadn't recognized him with his bandanna pulled over his lower face to keep the dust from his nose and mouth. The shock of seeing him so unexpectedly left her face pale and darkened her eyes with remembered hurt and wounded pride, yet she managed to keep her expression carefully bland as she set her jaw and turned back to Roberto.

"The horse," she gritted, feeling a fresh tide of anger rising through her to stain her cheeks with apricot color. "I'd put my money on the bronco any day—if I had any money, that is!"

Roberto chuckled gummily, gave Tomás a triumphant "I told you so" look, and the three of them turned back to watch the bronco-breaking.

The bay still seemed fresh, despite her violent maneuvers to unseat her rider and the strings of foam that flecked her chest and shoulders. Nothing seemed to matter to the maddened animal now except flinging its hated burden, the man, from its back, and running free across the Pampa to rejoin her wild herd in the Chaco, or the windswept lands of Patagonia to the northeast.

Dark-stockinged legs working like pistons, the mare suddenly plunged and kicked up her rear heels, almost launching Esteban forward over her head. He hung on tenaciously, one arm stretched up and out as a counterbalance to the horse's wild gyrations. Just as suddenly, the mustang catsprung sideways to the left the minute it had all four feet on the ground, and followed it up with a bone-jarring veer to the right that made the onlookers sigh in sympathy for the rider shaken to and fro like a rag doll in the jaws of some violent monster. And then, equally unexpectedly, the mare halted. She stood quite still, a shudder running through her that rippled and bunched the muscles beneath her lathered coat. Eyes rolling, mouth sagging open, she lowered her head dejectedly and nickered, and the *gauchos* let out a rousing cheer, believing the beast broken.

Yet even before the sound had fully died away, the mustang suddenly bucked again, sunfishing the unsuspecting Esteban—who'd relaxed his guard, also believing the horse bested—clear into the air! The reins were ripped from his hands. His booted feet were torn free of the stirrups. His lean, tall body described an arc in the air that seemed—to Krissoula's horrified eyes—to last forever, and then he handed with a sickening thud in the dirt, and lay still.

At once, the bay mare reared up, its black-stockinged forelegs hammering the air. A wild, primitive scream of triumph tore from its mouth as it lunged viciously at and over the fallen man with teeth bared.

At once the watching *gauchos* sprang to life! Hurriedly, they scrabbled under the rails to aid the fallen man, Tomás reaching him seconds ahead of the rest. Two of them acted to draw the mare's enraged attention from Esteban, waving their hats and arms in the air, while a third attempted to throw a lariat over her head and lead her back to the tethering post. Meanwhile, Tomás knelt at Esteban's side and ran his hand over his friend's arms and legs, torso and head. Incredibly, he discovered no broken bones; other than for being winded, the ranch manager seemed to have gotten off lightly, with only a badly split lip and a small yet deep graze that was bleeding freely on his forehead. Blood trickled down to sting his eyes. The smarting pain obviously roused him, for he groaned and opened them.

"*Jesús y Maria!* What the hell hit me—!" he growled, his sapphire eyes furious.

"The ground, *amigo,*" Tomás supplied casually with a grin of relief. "Only the ground! Tell me, *hombre,* do you hurt anywhere?"

209

"Other than for feeling like I've been run over by a steam engine, you mean?" Esteban muttered wryly and added an obscenity loaded with self-disgust. *"Perdición!* I'd have to say no."

"Get up then," Tomás ordered mercilessly, stepping back. "And get out of here! I've work to do, if you're finished taking your damned siesta in the middle of my corral! And Esteban—"

"What?" his friend snapped, sitting up and gingerly fingering his scrapes with a furious scowl.

"Don't think of getting back on the mare today. You can break her some other time, *amigo,* when your mind's on the job at hand. Agreed?"

"The devil I will!" he exploded.

"Sorry, but that's my decision. You're through here, for today," Tomás said firmly. "I'm the *domador,* after all, *amigo,* not you. You can manage the ranch any way you choose, but the horses are my business, understand? And watching you break your damned neck isn't part of my job! Go home, Esteban. Clean yourself up and get some rest. I'd bet you'll be feeling like *two* locomotives ran over you when you're stiffened up tomorrow morning!"

Old Roberto joined them, and gave a wheezy chuckle. *"Sí,* so would I! And talking of bets, hand over my winnings, young Tomás! Didn't I tell you the bay would win?"

"You bet against me, you old scoundrel?" Esteban demanded in an aggrieved tone as he hauled himself to standing and staggered across the corral to retrieve his lost hat.

"He did," Tomás confirmed with a grimace, fishing in the pocket of his money belt for the wager. "And that's the very last time *I* put my hard-earned money on you, my friend."

"Let me up on her back again, then, Tom," Esteban suggested. "You could go double or nothing with this old thief here, eh?"

"The devil I will!" Tomás snorted. "Besides, if the sky's anything to go by, we're in for some heavy rain before long. And when it comes, this corral'll be six inches under mud in minutes, unfit for anything but a hog wallow! Be sensible for once in your life, *amigo.* Go on home."

As if on cue, they all heard the low, ominous rumble of thunder far off in the hills, and the pale sky seemed to darken accordingly. Esteban saw the broiling dark mass of the thunderheads rolling over the Sierra de Córdoba in the distance and he nodded, knowing Tomás was right.

"All right, damn it. I'll see you tomorrow." He moved stiffly away to where his horse, Barbaro, waited, and mounted up, giving

210

them a wave of farewell as he rode away.

It was only then that Tomás remembered the señorita. He glanced about, curious to see any exchange between the pair, but she was gone, and so was her little palomino mare. He had a momentary twinge of misgiving as he looked up at the rapidly darkening sky, for the scent of rain tanged the air, and there was that heavy, oppressive feeling to the atmosphere that presaged a storm brewing now. Ah, not to worry, he reassured himself. The señorita was no fool, and she was an expert horsewoman. She'd sense the coming storm, too, and head Girasol straight for the *hacienda* to outrun it, he was certain.

The last thing on Krissoula's mind was returning to the *hacienda!*

For the past month, Sofía had fretted about the restless, preoccupied, brooding mood she'd fallen into, and had driven her to distraction with inquiries about its possible cause, curse the woman.

Numerous times, she'd come perilously close to screaming, "Leave me alone, for the love of God, Sofía! Can't you see I'm not ill? Can't you see it's the pain in my heart that has made me this way? I'm hurt, Sofía, hurt and angry—and *sí,* maybe even a little crazy, in love with a man who feels nothing for me, who'll never believe I'm not the *putana* he took me for! That's why I'm so quiet, Sofía, don't you see? I'm afraid if I open my mouth, all the hurt will come pouring out, and with it the truth—that it's him I want. That no matter how he's used me, blackmailed me for his own ends, I haven't been able to *think* of anyone but him since the night we made love! That the thought of betraying him, of marriage to Don Felipe, makes me die a little inside with each passing day, because all I can think about is Esteban de San Martín, curse his soul!"

But of course, she could tell Sofía no such thing, and so she'd bottled it all up inside her until today, when she'd seen Esteban again and that strange duality of love and blistering hatred had filled her anew. Was it possible to loathe someone so intensely, and yet at the same time be unable to think of anyone but them? To love them with a passion that was all pain, and precious little joy? Ah, *sí,* crazy as it sounded, it was possible all right! She was living, hurting proof that it was. She'd felt as if she'd tear apart with grief, with wounded pride and helpless, misdirected love when she saw Esteban in the corral a little while ago. Unable to give vent to her pain in tears, she'd had only two outlets left her—her dancing or her riding. Since dancing was out of the question, she'd ride, she determined, ride till she'd driven him from her heart! Consequently, she'd run from the corral to her horse once she'd seen he was unhurt . . .

Now, her cheeks flushed and her hat bouncing on its cord against her back where it had fallen off, she realized her foolishness. Girasol was exhausted—badly in need of rest and rubbing down—but the swift gallop Krissoula had kicked her into earlier had put them many miles distant from the hacienda. A storm too imminent to outrace was darkening the sky with bruised iron-gray and purplish clouds that were swollen and threatening with rain. Thunder boomed a staccato *zapateado* over the mountain ridges, and an occasional flicker of lightning snapped bony, white-bright fingers in the brooding sky. The tang of ozone hung like a pall in the air. Unless she found shelter, and soon, she was in for a drenching, at the very least. At worst, she ran the risk of her and her horse being struck by the lightning, exposed on the open Pampa as they were.

As if the weather had read her thoughts, a massive forked arm of light streaked down, and a distant *quebracho* tree exploded in a torch of fire with a crack as loud as a pistol shot. A pampas fox who'd made its den deep beneath the tree's roots streaked past them, its gray fur singed, and Girasol reared up in terror. When her forelegs touched earth, she was off, exploding like a bolt of lightning herself in a stampede of blurred gold.

Fortunately, Krissoula was no novice where horses were concerned. She quickly recovered her seat and hung on for dear life, devoting every ounce of her strength to steering the mare away from obstacles that might cause them to fall, rather than wasting her energy on trying to halt her mount's wild flight. Eventually, when her panic lessened, the mare would slacken speed of her own accord. Meanwhile, it was her rider's job to make sure they didn't come to grief . . .

Rain began lashing down like stinging whips as Girasol galloped wildly across the vivid green Pampa, soaking through Krissoula's cord jacket to the blouse she wore beneath in a matter of moments, and chilling her to the bone. Her hair was a sodden cape that fell heavily over her shoulders in streaming rattails long before Girasol finally slowed to a canter, and then a walk.

Krissoula blinked against the heavy curtain of rain, catching droplets on the tip of her tongue. She was panting heavily, her breath all but snatched away by the storm's fury as she looked about her. Surely there was shelter of some kind hereabouts, she thought as she kneed Girasol on through the blinding downpour—

at the very least another little *puesto* or line-camp used by the *gauchos* here on the far western reaches of the *estancia*? Common sense dictated there must be, if only she could find it!

At last, after what seemed an eternity of aimless riding through the miserable downpour, she spied through the sheeting rain a small cabin nestled snugly in a hollow up ahead. Built of whitewashed adobe, it boasted a stone chimney from which smoke curled up to be shredded and whipped away by the rain and wind. A corral with a sturdy *ramada* attached to it led off to one side, she saw. Beneath its shelter huddled a string of matched bay horses, maybe six in all, their heads crossed over each other's backs for comfort.

In such foul weather, surely the cabin's owner wouldn't turn even a stray dog away, let alone a woman, she thought, confident of a welcome, and kneed Girasol forward.

By the corral fence, she slipped from the mare's back and was about to lead her beneath the cover of the *ramada* before approaching the cabin's front door when a huge, shaggy dog came rushing out at her from somewhere. It was barking furiously and dancing around her on massive paws, as if ready to lunge for her throat and tear it out at any moment! Its barking was deep, baying, and aggressive even above the dull roaring of the rain, and the expression in its amber eyes was a threatening one.

Krissoula tossed her wet hair over her shoulders and turned to face the animal with her fists on her hips.

"Enough of your loud voice, Señor Perro!" she snapped sharply and confidently, advancing on the animal a step or two through the mud puddles. "Is this how you greet a guest? How you offer your master's hospitality? *Bribón!* Shame on you!"

The dog's furious barking was abruptly silenced by her firm scolding and her utter lack of fear. He stood there with his head cocked curiously to one side now, his ears pricked up, heeding her authoritative tone. Apart from the shagginess of his soaking coat, he could have been a wild wolf from the deep forests of the Rhine, Krissoula thought uneasily—and then she heard him whine an apology.

Ah! So, he might look like a fierce wolf, but he was tame for all that! She smiled and held out her hand for him to sniff. Dogs, like some people, often acted aggressively when afraid, she knew. By showing him she was to be respected but not feared, she'd defused his vicious behavior.

"There! That's much better, boy," she praised softly as the dog edged forward to smell her hand. He swiped her palm with his long pink tongue and his tail began to wag in greeting. "However, the longer we stánd here, exchanging greetings, the wetter I'm getting! Where's your mistress, eh, *perro?*"

As if the great red brute understood her words, he flung his massive head around and bounded across a muddy stretch of dirt to the cabin, barking joyfully now. His tail whisked back and forth as he scratched and whined at the wood plank door. To her relief, it opened.

"About time you came home, you old rascal! Where've you been carousing, eh—?" began a deep, masculine voice—which abruptly trailed away to startled silence.

Krissoula raised wide eyes to Esteban's shocked, battered face, and felt the blood leave her own. *His* cabin? *His* dog? Inwardly, she groaned. *Dios mío,* was she cursed by God, she wondered as their eyes met? Was there to be no escape for her, no place she could run to be rid of him? But even as she thought it, she knew in her heart that there was none. Even should they be parted by a dozen oceans and countless mountains, he was firmly lodged in her heart to stay . . . damn him!

Her glance flickered quickly away, and then she flung about and started running back the way she'd come to find her horse, leaping puddles and squelching through mud, caring nothing for the drenching rain now. *Madre,* she had to get away! It was far, far more important to put distance between them than seek shelter, despite the very real threat of being struck by lightning—!

Esteban caught up with her in a half-dozen strides and she heard him utter a curse as he grasped her elbow and flung her about to face him.

Their eyes met again, dark sapphire crashing into gold for moments that were an eternity . . . And then, without a word passing between them, he suddenly hauled her hard against him by the upper arms and crushed his lips down over hers, kissing her with a brutal, savage hunger that rivaled the storm raging above them.

The hurt he'd caused her, her wounded pride—*Dios, nothing* mattered in that moment carved from time except that she was in his arms, that he was holding her fiercely, as if he intended never to let her go again! Uttering a helpless cry, she twined her arms about his neck, cradled his head between her palms and leaned into his hard body. She kissed him back with an openmouthed hunger that equaled his own.

The rain streamed down over their faces as they clung together, clinging in droplets to their lashes and hair, collecting in tiny rivulets and pools in the crevices of their tightly meshed bodies. Neither of them noticed or cared. The world could have come to an end, in that moment, and the lovers would have known nothing, so caught up were they in their own cataclysmic explosion.

When at last Esteban abruptly released her, they were both breathing heavily. Her breasts heaved beneath her sodden clothing. His bare shoulders rose and fell as if he'd run a mile flat out.

"What the hell are you doing here, *bruja?* Why did you come? Why must you torment me this way? Damn you, witch! Damn you . . . !" he rasped harshly, his face a mask of fury—and confusion.

"Hijo de puta!" she hissed above the roar of the rain, ashamed and angry at her easy surrender to his punishing arms, his savage kisses, which had so quickly fired her blood. "Let me go! Take your filthy paws off me! You flatter yourself, *hombre,* to think I came here looking for you! I was looking for shelter, nothing more—!"

"The devil you were, witch," he rasped, his deep-blue eyes blazing. "Tell me you didn't know this was where I live? Ha! You'd be a liar! Everyone knows this cottage is mine!" He grinned cruelly and gripped her wrist, yanking her back against his rigid body so that her small, firm breasts were crushed hard against his abdomen. "No, my darling little liar, we both know why you really came here—what it is you're really looking for! Well, you've found it, *querida!* By God, you've found it!"

Lightning flashed then, and as the bright-white flare lit his darkly tanned face, it was like looking up into the dangerously handsome, tortured face of El Diablo himself.

Chapter Seventeen

In the wake of the lightning flash a sudden bolt of thunder boomed ominously overhead, distracting her attention from him fleetingly. In that instant, his arms snaked about her waist. With little effort, he dragged her clear off her feet and into his sinewy arms, gripping her so tightly she could hardly breathe.

"You animal! Put me down!" she hissed, furious as she tried to squirm free. "*Bastardo!* Dirty *canalla!* Let me go, I tell you! You're wrong—you're a madman—you're *loco!* I don't want any part of you, you filthy *campesino.* By the Virgin, I swear it!"

"After that kiss?" His lip curled cruelly, and he shook his head in reproof. "Be careful on what you swear, little *bruja,* for God punishes liars—!"

With that, he turned on his heels and strode swiftly back to the little cottage through the drenching rain, with Krissoula held fast in his arms. He kicked in the door to clear his path, and kicked it violently again to close it in his wake. Like a man gone deaf, he ignored completely the furious curses she screamed at him, seemed numb to the hefty barrage of blows she rained down over his head and shoulders from clenched fists.

She glimpsed his bed, heaped with downy sheepskins, along one wall in the far room of the cabin, and her belly squeezed with a treacherous mixture of anticipation and fear in the moment before he dropped her unceremoniously onto it.

"There! I've put you down, darling. Satisfied?" An evil grin thinned his lips, and his sapphire eyes glittered wolfishly.

"A curse on your bastard head, *hombre!*" she seethed.

"Curse or no curse, you'll take off those wet clothes," he snapped, adding caustically, "After all, it was to find 'shelter from the rain' that you came here, right? We must see our beloved doña made warm and dry, then, eh?" He laughed his scorn.

"Go to hell, San Martín!" she spat. "It'll be a cold day in hell

216

before I take off my clothes for you again!" Her eyes were like golden shards of topaz glass in the ruddy shadows as she crouched there on his rawhide cot, like a small wild animal with its claws unsheathed, glowering fiercely up at him as she prepared to lash out.

"I said strip off, Krissoula," he ordered, knotted fists planted on his hips as he towered over her, "and quickly, or I'll have to do it for you."

"Pah! You think so, eh?" came her jeering retort. She tossed her wet hair. "Well, I think you're not man enough to make me do *anything* I don't want to do—!"

Immediately the words were out, she could have bitten her tongue, cursing herself for challenging him so rashly.

"No?" A thin smile split his chiseled lips as he suddenly reached out and twisted her long, wet black hair around his fist, jerking her roughly to her feet. "Are you quite sure, *querida,*" he challenged in a silky tone that left her speechless, "that I'm 'not man enough' to do *anything* I set my mind to?"

His wicked sapphire eyes holding her transfixed, his free hand found the front of her jacket and deftly slipped the leather buttons free of the buttonholes. Grasping the lapels, he wrenched the sodden jacket from her arms and tossed it aside, while she wriggled and tried to escape his tight, painful grip in her hair, but could not. After, he uncinched her belt buckle and yanked her up, onto her feet, using the running loop like a noose to tug her roughly to him.

"Still sure, *gatita?*" he taunted full in her face, his hot breath singeing her cheek, a mocking smile curving his lips.

"Bastard!" she spat, shoving him forcefully away with her palms thrust against his chest.

"Bitch!" he countered crisply, jerking her roughly to him again. "What's the matter, little tease? Got cold feet and wish you hadn't come sniffing around here like a bitch in heat after all—is that your problem?"

"How dare you—!" she exploded, but deaf to her protests he continued in a rasping rush:

"—But then, that's how it's always been with you, eh, *querida?* Your eyes say 'yes,' you want me! Your body comes alive, sings under my touch. When I hold you, you're as hot and eager for me as I am for you, but—afterward? Ah, darling, afterward, when passion cools, you tell me 'no'! You swear that from the first, you never wanted me as a man! Well, I'm done playing your little games, Krissoula!" he threatened. "I'm tired of you growing hot

217

and cold, and tormenting me this way. It's time you made up your mind about us, once and for all. Time to decide whether you want to be my woman, or waste your time trying to make your marriage to my uncle a reality, rather than the sham it is. But don't worry, little one, I won't disappoint you if your decision's what I think it will be—!"

"Pah! You overestimate yourself, you arrogant—strutting—rooster—! I don't want you—I've never wanted you! You forced me, *sí,* you forced me—!"

"Then you won't be surprised if I 'force' you again, eh, *bruja?"* he breathed.

His fingers encountered the hooks that held the fronts of her blouse together and easily freed them. He drew a quick, involuntary gasp at the sight revealed as he yanked the garment down over her shoulders to her elbows, effectively pinioning her arms to her sides.

Beneath the blouse, her thin, lace-edged camisole was soaked, plastered to her body like a second skin, and all but transparent. Her pointed breasts showed through the sodden covering as blurred golden mounds. At their summits, her taut nipples ruched the filmy cloth, making tiny, darker hillocks there that invited his touch, his mouth, and he smiled triumphantly. Oh, she wanted him all right!

"Fickle and unreasonable you might be, but you're a lovely little bitch, Krissoula," he observed softly, the timbre of his voice low and purring now, like a jaguar's low growl. His sapphire eyes turned darker with passion as his long brown fingers strayed to trace the outline of those soft curves, circling each jutting little peak in turn. *"Dios, minina,* I want to bite you, like a vampire! I want to nibble at your little ears, your fingers, your throat . . . to kiss your breasts. To touch you here, to taste your sweetness on my lips and feel the fire begin . . ." He pressed his palm against the very pit of her belly, and something treacherous and eager deep within her stirred in response to the warmth and arousal of his touch, quivering, surging . . .

His erotic threats excited her, he knew, for she belatedly flinched away as if his touch had burned her, and telltale color rose up her throat before his eyes. Heat flamed through her, centering, no doubt, where his fingers rested lightly upon her chilly body, scant inches from the hidden core of her womanhood.

"Did I give you leave to touch me?" she ground out, anguished by her body's treacherous response.

"I told you, I don't plan on asking permission anymore, *minina,"* he came back with more than a hint of sensual menace in his tone.

"Only on taking what I want."

Her heart skipped a beat. She drew a short, ragged breath and forced a contemptuous laugh that sounded brittle and frightened to her ears. "That's what you think, *canalla!*"

He shook his head, fire glinting in his ebony hair, and advanced the step that she had taken backward to close the gap between them. "No, *bruja,* that's what I *know* . . . !"

She slapped him hard then, the sound of her palm striking his cheek brutally loud on the firewood hush. The blow, loaded with her fury and indignation, was hard enough to have rocked him on his heels, but he only threw back his dark head and laughed in contempt.

"For that, I think you'll forfeit the remainder of your clothes, darling Gypsy! A fair exchange, no? The loss of my dignity for the loss of your—modesty?"

His eyes! Caray, how they smoldered—how they consumed her, as if already he'd stripped her naked! Warmth and weakness flooded through her at even the thought of him doing just that. She trembled inwardly, yearning to surrender, wanting to melt, to let him do with her as he would, but she'd gone too far to back down, now that she'd hit him. To let him win, let him treat her as casually as he would treat his *china,* his kept woman, would convince him she'd agreed to accept that role in his life, that she was willing to accept his passion—when what she wanted was his heart, his love, his trust. Pah! She may as well howl for the moon as yearn for the love of this lusting *diablo,* she thought bitterly. And she wouldn't—couldn't—accept anything less than his love, ever again.

Accordingly, she kicked out, aiming a vicious toe at his shin. But he wore knee-length boots of fine cordovan leather, as did she, and the kick pained her toes far more than it pained him!

He laughed again in that mocking, profoundly disturbing way he had, and stepped closer. "Careful, *minina.* You know as well as I that there's only one way to break a wild filly! Don't make me tame you by force—not when we both know the truth: that you want me just as badly as I want you! That our fights fire your woman's passions, make the blood run hot and wild in your veins—and make the loving that comes after even sweeter! That's really why you came here, after all, no? To fight, and then make love with me? Denying it any longer would be a waste of what precious little time we have, eh?"

"You filthy animal—!" she screamed, looking frantically about her for a weapon, but in the Spartan cabin, there was nothing close at hand that she could use. "I told you the last time, I want nothing more to do with you, and I mean it, I don't, I don't—!"

He took a step towards her, and she shrank up against the bed, feeling the hard ridge of the frame pressing against the back of her knees. Again, he advanced, leaning up against her, and her legs buckled.

She sprawled backward across the rough cot and he followed her down, pinning her to the sheepskins with the weight of his body. He grinned in triumph, trapping both flailing wrists above her head in his grip, and then he dipped his dark head to cover her throat with kisses, to nibble at the delicate lobes of her ears as he'd threatened to do, until she was breathless. His warm, damp breath, his scandalous, filthy, *wonderful* promises in her ear, filled her with shivery anticipation.

"You're going to admit it, Krissoula," he swore, and then his tongue lightly traced a path over her throat to the tiny hollow at its base, tickling like a feather. "You're going to tell me that you want me to take you, and admit that's why you came here, and put an end to these childish games you play, mmm, *querida?*"

"I don't want you," she lied, insistent. "No. You're wrong, so wrong!"

"What is it you want then?"

"From you—nothing!" she denied.

Yet her fingers slackened their desperate grip on his shoulders and moved caressingly upward to tousle the dark commas of hair at the nape of his neck.

His hand slipped downward, releasing her wrist to stroke the sleek line of her flanks and thighs pinned beneath him, finding the sensitive, silky flesh they concealed. She gasped as he thrust aside her remaining garments and slid his hand against bare, shivering flesh to the hidden, heated heart of her.

"Ah, little one, how warm and soft you are here," he murmured as he caressed her intimately, moving his fingers deeply inside her in maddening, rhythmic strokes. "Do you feel how your body welcomes my touch? How warm and wet you grow when I caress you, *querida mía?* Ah, *sí,* you want me, darling—want me badly, as a woman wants a man! How can you deny it, when your body tells a different story? Admit it, little one . . ."

"Please—!" she implored, the words ground out in an anguished gasp.

"Please what, *minina?* Please stop? Or please, please, Esteban, go on?"

"Don't," she begged, "don't humiliate me like this!"

"Then admit it, little one. Tell me you want me—that you came here to find me, to make love with me again on any terms! That you'll be my woman, no matter how we parted the last time!"

His lips seared her flesh as he pressed his hungry mouth to her brow, her eyelids, her cheeks, the corners of her mouth. "Admit that for whatever reason, you've missed me this month as much as I've missed you. That you came here to find me, because you wanted me as much as I've lain awake nights, hungering for you—"

His fingertips grazed the sensitive bud of her womanhood, teased it, and she moaned low in her throat and tightened her grip in his wet hair. He gently stroked her there again and again, and felt the impact of full arousal suddenly leap through her like a jolt of lightning as she arched her body upward to pursue his touch. "Well, *minina?*" he asked softly, his voice a low, husky whisper.

"Damn you, yes!" she hissed, "Yes, I want you—but because . . . because *I love you,* damn your soul! Can't you see that? Couldn't you tell? I love you, damn you, you blackmailing brute—and I want more than this—more than being your mistress, your whore—I want your love!"

Her wailed confession, wrung from her like blood from a stone, stunned him speechless. He drew back, incredulity stamped on his darkly handsome face, for never had he imagined for a minute that his golden-eyed virago might be in love with him! Such a possibility had never crossed his mind, not after the way they'd met, and the way he'd coerced her into helping him with threats of imprisonment. He'd thought only hatred and resentment could flourish between them after such a beginning. Such fierce emotions could engender equally fierce passion between a man and a woman, he knew—but love? No, never love!

His gut was tied up in knots, his emotions in turmoil as he drew away, rocking back onto his heels to stare at her. Her face was pale, so very pale, and she couldn't meet his eyes, he noted. Worse, she was shivering violently now, but whether from the effects of her soaking, her reluctant confession, or a combination of both he didn't know.

Oh, God, it all made a crazy sort of sense now, her violent reaction to his suggestion that she become his mistress that last time, her bitter comment that she was good enough to be his *puta* but never his wife, her headlong flight each time they'd made love that he'd written off as the result of guilt, or maybe simple perverseness on her part. No. It was none of those things. She'd been running from herself—from the emotions she feared to let him see, or even suspect she harbored! Her fierce Gypsy pride would have locked her tongue more surely than any key. Given the way she was, she'd probably been completely unable to voice her words of love for him, fearing he would spurn them—or worse, laugh and belittle her, and throw them back in her face. And—given the complexity of his own feelings for her—he might well have done so. *Sí,* he just might have, rather than swallow his own arrogance and admit that he—

"You're shivering," he observed suddenly instead, a lame comment since he could hear her teeth chattering, and she was slowly turning blue!

Not a word was spoken by either of them as he quickly and methodically stripped her remaining few sodden garments from her. He hung them over a chair by the crackling fire to dry before turning to her—curled naked and trembling upon his bed—as if he were some beautiful dark-skinned savage, kneeling to worship at a pagan shrine.

His striking hawk's face was dark and unreadable in the shifting ruddy light as he took up a rough cloth and dried her, turning the mundane task into an exquisitely pleasurable interlude for them both. Moving the cloth about her throat, rubbing thoroughly around each taut breast, sweeping languorously across her belly and buttocks and down the lovely, graceful arch of her back, he toweled every inch of her until the blood moved through her veins like mulled wine and her flesh glowed rosily both with inner warmth and from his touch.

At last, he tossed the cloth aside and stretched out beside her, gazing silently down at her. The mood between them had changed; they both sensed it. Her confession had altered things, shifted them to another level, another depth, another gentler tempo. Was he angry? she wondered. What was he thinking now? At least he hadn't laughed at her, thank God! She could bear anything but that . . .

Locks of wet black hair were plastered to his brow and temples like inky commas, sleek and seal-like. She yearned to brush them away, to touch him, caress him somehow, but could not bring herself to move. A lethargy filled her, as if telling him, admitting her feelings to herself aloud, at long last, had taken the substance out of her. She still wanted him so badly that to touch him spelled disaster, and yet—he hadn't said he loved her, too. Aiiee, *Madre,* he thought her a Gypsy thief, a *putana* who drugged and duped her marks! She'd been stupid to dream he could ever care for someone like her . . .

His body was bared to the waist, must have already been so when he'd opened the door to Rojo's scratchings. In the firelight, his lean torso, so golden-brown, so wonderfully braided with muscle and cords, gleamed from its sprinkling of raindrops as if oiled. Across the flesh of his rib cage rode the old, silvery outline of a strange scar that looked—at least to her dazed eyes—as if someone had tried long ago to carve their initials deep into his chest, beginning with the letter "A."

Feeling his eyes devouring her nudity in the flickering firelight and shadow, she moaned low in her throat, biting her lower lip to silence the pleas that welled treacherously on her tongue. Let him make the first move now, she decided. It's not up to me anymore. If he still wants me, let him be the one . . .

With hungry eyes, Esteban took in the delicate beauty of her little face, the fluid lines of her throat and shoulders. His gaze lingered on the pale gold of her high, pointed breasts, tipped with honey-colored steeples, the ebony fluff at the pit of her belly framed by the slender, almost boyish, jut of her hips, and he knew he was lost. *Dios,* he wanted her more than ever! Wanted her more than Tierra Rosa, more than his father's name, or justice against the man who'd murdered him. Wanted her more than anything this side of heaven!

It's more than that, you fool! She's had the courage to admit it, so why can't you? You love her, fool! came a nagging, insistent voice in his ear that he didn't want to hear. *That's why she has this effect on you. That's why she makes you so angry. Despite her past, despite everything, you love her!*

He wetted his lips, hesitating. If he surrendered to the fierce emotions within him now, there'd be no turning back, not for either of them, he sensed intuitively. But with little inner struggle, he surrendered and let emotion rule . . .

Dipping his sable head, he began to savor each jutting, honey-colored rosette with his mouth, the tip of his tongue flicking teasingly across the pert crests, one by one. His lips were hot and hard, greedy for the taste of her that had plagued his days, and left his nights sleepless. With a growl, he drew each swollen nubbin deep into his mouth, drinking and drawing on the sweetness of her flesh as if it were some pale, exotic fruit whose texture must be thoroughly savored. She tasted of warm, womanly flesh, of her own elusive female musk, of fresh rain, and the subtle wild orchid soap with which she'd bathed that morning. The hardness at his groin bucked, demanding release from his straining breeches.

". . . *Dios,* I'd never dreamed a month could be so damned long, my love!" she thought she heard him mutter, but his breath was hot against her ear, doing strange things to her breathing, and she couldn't be certain of anything anymore, except that she wanted him beyond all reason, even if he'd decided to ignore her confession of love.

He kissed her shoulders, tonguing circles of honeyed fire over her smooth curves until heat flamed through her, centering in her mouth and loins. Her lips felt swollen and bruised from his ardent kisses. Her breasts were full and taut from his caresses. Deep in her belly, deep in her womanhood, she felt white-hot and pulsing with desire. Ah, *sí,* clear down to the tips of her curling toes, he set her afire and glowing with the pleasure he aroused in her!

Cupping a breast in one hand, he fondled the firm little mound while his mouth flickered over her rib cage, like lightning dancing over the hills outside the cabin, and heard her moan softly. When he came to her belly, she shrank from his nuzzling lips, but he pressed her down to the bed. With the very tip of his tongue, he circled the tiny rim of her navel as he leaned over her, and then darted hotly within it, like a hummingbird sipping nectar from the throat of a pale-gold flower. She gasped and arched her hips off the sheepskins with shock at the ticklish torment his caresses aroused, reaching out, seeking the hard ridge of him with impatient hands to draw him to her.

But, laughing low in his throat, he held her down with a tanned hand planted firmly on either side of her hips, and continued his delicious assault. He trailed lips and tongue everywhere over her flat belly, nuzzling the satiny ridges and fragrant hollows made by her hip bones beneath her smooth skin until she was crying his name like a prayer, over and over, pleading with him to end her torment.

And then she felt him shift his body to kneel between her thighs and grew still with expectancy. Holding her breath, she waited for him to shuck off his breeches and take her, to fill her with himself. But he did neither of those things.

"Ah, *querida,*" he whispered huskily, his warm breath fanning the triangle of ebony curls he was caressing at the pit of her belly and making her tremble uncontrollably. "I'm going to taste every inch of you, my golden witch—!"

She gasped in shock as he parted her thighs and slid his palms beneath her bottom to raise her hips.

A moment more, and she felt his damp curls brush against her inner thighs as he nestled his head between them. The branding heat of his mouth seared her nether lips with kisses, kisses more intimate than she'd dreamed possible, for Miguel had never loved her this way, although they'd been man and wife.

The pulsing that throbbed in her ears, her heart, her loins, coalesced, mounting rapidly to a deluge of wild, throbbing pleasure that threatened to engulf her as his lips and tongue worshiped the hot, wet core of her woman's body, his hands anchoring her firmly in place so she could not evade his mouth no matter how wildly she squirmed.

She tastes like the sea, he thought, moving his mouth against her honeyed well, the restless sea! Calm and quiescent one minute, as the waves lap lazily at sandy shores, and in another fierce and raging, whipped into stormy, salty furor by the wind!

She cried out and arched her head back, her fingers kneading desperately through Esteban's inky curls as skillfully he brought her to rapture with his mouth alone. A moment more, and she was flung over the crest, whirled headlong into the velvet arms of an ecstasy that was blinding, shattering in intensity.

While she still uttered birdlike cries of fulfillment, he unfastened his breeches and slid his hard body up and over the satin length of hers. He took her lips again and again in long, lingering kisses, twining her dark hair about his throat as he did so.

Her mouth parted eagerly to the pressure of his, and he plunged his tongue deep inside it, taking possession of the hidden sweetness there and stroking her tongue with his own. In another moment, he'd entered her with a single fluid thrust that stole her breath away!

Knowing he'd already given her the release she craved, Esteban raised her hips to take him fully, and rode her as he needed to reach his own release, to burn the fever from his body. He thrust deep into the tight sheath of her womanhood with an almost savage urgency filling her time and time again. She'd recovered a little by now, and her arms came up to embrace him, to caress his broad back, murmuring silly little love words against his ear that drove him to distraction. How big he is, she thought dazedly, how hard and ready, how wonderfully male, like a healthy young bull. And she loved him . . . loved him . . . loved him so!

Caray, she's so damned lovely, he thought! All-giving, all-passionate, all female—all that was woman and mystery! Her eyes were dark-lashed pools of dreamy gold now, gazing up into his, reflecting the amber flicker of the fire in the stone hearth as he possessed her, as she gave herself to him. He fancied he could dive into their shimmering, adoring depths, and never want to surface! Her lips were slightly parted, revealing the sparkling line of her pearly teeth. He couldn't resist another kiss. The hardened tips of her breasts rubbed erotically against his own dark-furred chest as he thrust deeply into her, as he drank from the wine her mouth so deliciously offered. The friction of her satiny flesh sliding back and forth against his harder, rougher body drove him to madness.

Time and again he thrust, wanting to possess every inch of her, driving deep and full into the sweet, tight warmth of her womanhood. It was as if she were a raging fever in his blood that could be sweated out, a she-demon that could be exorcised by the rites of passion! But . . . he knew now that she couldn't. Like the Indians of the rain forest and the jungles, he was addicted to her, as addicted as strongly as they were to the leaves of the coca plant. *Dios!* A month of nights he'd lain awake, thinking of her and wishing she were in his arms, here in his bed, silky and soft beneath him. A month of brooding, restless days with every minute, each second, spent in thoughts of her, wishing he could relive the last night he'd made love to her all over again, and instead have it end with Krissoula smiling and content, pledged to be his woman. Instead, they'd parted in anger and hurt, her eyes spitting hatred like golden embers and a curse like acid dripping from her lips. Since then, his life hadn't been worth living. If she'd bewitched him like this after thirty short—agonizing!—days, how much worse would he feel in a year, a lifetime, without her . . . ?

"Now, *querido,* now!" she cried throatily, her grip tightening as she rocked with him as one.

A muffled roar broke on the ruddy shadows as a shattering climax exploded through his body. He drove deep into her for the last time and she cried out and tensed in pleasure as he grew rigid above her. Another second, and she felt the hot leap of his seed spring into the very depths of her, heard her name torn once off his lips, and end in a gasp.

After a little while, he rolled to her side and gathered her snugly in his arms so that his chest cradled her weary head. Together, they slept, their limbs loosely entwined in the afterglow of their loving.

The fire had died down to a heap of white ashes with glowing red embers at its heart when Krissoula awoke over an hour later.

She could hear the rain still drumming heavily on the roof and the angry mutterings of the distant thunder, which sounded muffled within the snug confines of the cabin, but was proof that the storm hadn't yet ended.

Propped on one elbow, she gazed down at Esteban's face, so relaxed in sleep. A wave of such tenderness filled her, she thought she might really be able to cry for once. Ah, *sí,* she loved him, without a doubt, and although he hadn't said he loved her in return, she was strangely glad it was out in the open, for it seemed as if an enormous weight had been lifted from her shoulders. She still couldn't cry as yet, but the feeling of wanting to remained, stinging like sand behind her eyes.

226

How handsome he was, her beloved, his features strong and even, commanding as any matador's. His cheeks and jaw were faintly bluish with beard-shadow, and felt rough to her touch. The purplish graze at his brow, the puffy swelling where his split lip had opened again from their passionate kisses, only heightened his masculinity, she thought. Unable to resist this unguarded, approachable Esteban, she leaned over him and lightly pressed her lips to his. In response, his arm tightened to draw her closer and he murmured, "Ah, *querida mía,* we were something, eh . . . ?" but did not waken.

"*Sí,* we were something, all right, darling," she murmured sadly to herself, yet she smiled as she idly caressed his powerful chest with her fingertip, tracing the line of dark hair that furred it down to the hairline ridge of scar tissue that puckered the flesh across his rib cage. Her first impression earlier had been correct, she saw. The letter "A" had been carved upon his body with a knife, a long time ago. She leaned over and tenderly traced the scar, kissed it, wondering what such a marking had done to his fierce pride? Or—could he possibly have done it himself as a boy, perhaps as a dare or some youthful badge of honor, she wondered? "A" for his father's name, Aguilar, perhaps, so long denied him? She gave a mental shrug. It was possible.

Her belly growled then, reminding her that she was hungry and that the luncheon hour had come and gone long ago. *Caramba,* she wasn't merely hungry, she was starving—hungry enough to eat a horse!

Untangling Esteban's weighty arm from about her waist, she slipped from the sheepskin-strewn bed to the fireplace, shivering as she added a fresh log from the wood-box to feed the ruddy embers. She checked her discarded clothes, which he'd draped over two chairs set before the fire to dry, smoothing the wrinkles from them as best she could. They were ruined, and the state they were in would inevitably result in a barrage of questions from Sofía. But—somehow, she didn't care anymore. Not about Sofía's scolding, nor about Felipe, nor even her future. All that mattered now was the man sprawled asleep in the bed across the cottage from her—and her growling belly, of course! The future and fate must take care of the rest . . .

Still naked, she explored the two neat but tiny rooms, finding coffee beans in a sack upon a shelf in the first, a small grinder, and a coffeepot. Moments later, she had a black kettle heating over the fire with coffee brewing, and was rummaging about for something to eat. Madonna, she was starving!

She found a half-loaf of dry bread, a length of sausage, a wedge of cheese, and a bowl of speckled brown eggs in a grilled meat-safe. A string of onions and peppers hung from a peg set in the wall. Humming a lively *fandango* that matched her surprisingly buoyant mood, she set about fixing them both a meal, breaking the eggs into the basin and beating them with a spoon, chopping spicy *chorizo* into meaty coins, dicing onions and peppers, and tossing everything into a black skillet to cook over the fire when the coffee was done. The simple little domestic task made her feel warm and content inside. Was this the way it would be if they were man and wife—or even man and mistress, she his *china,* she mused? The thought of being Esteban's mistress didn't hurt so much now, somehow. Had her feelings on the matter altered so much in a month, or had those empty, pain-filled days merely served to show her how life without him would be, and convinced her that being with him on any terms was better than nothing, better than living without him—?

"Well, well! You look as if you know your way about a kitchen, Doña Krissoula!" observed a teasing, idle voice, and, startled, she flung about to see Esteban, awake and already half dressed, sitting on the side of his bed, watching her. He was grinning as he ran his hand through his disheveled hair. "I must admit, this is the first time I've ever had a naked woman cook for me, though! I wonder if it's my appetite for food or for something else that will be piqued, *minina!"* He rolled his eyes wickedly.

To his delight, she blushed charmingly, covered her breasts with her hands, and retorted, "I had no choice, *bribón!* My clothes are still wet!"

"Here, then, I suppose you could put this on, if you must," he offered with a sigh of regret, and tossed her a clean chambray shirt from a neatly folded pile set atop a chair. "If it were left to me, I'd keep you just the way you are, but alas, *minina mía,* you might catch cold—and I have no curiosity to make love to a sneezing woman!"

She tossed a damp rag at his head, but he ducked, it missed, and they both laughed easily, like old friends, old lovers.

Moments later, she was beckoning him to the little table, looking adorable in his shirttails, her hair a wanton tangle of curls about her shoulders now that it was dried, a little girl's tangled mop.

"I could find only the one plate. You go ahead and eat first, then I will."

"We shared the same bed, *bombón,* why not the same plate, mmm?" Esteban suggested, and speared a bite of her impromptu omelette on his fork. He offered her the first bite, and took a second for himself. Tasting it and rolling his eyes in pleasure, he exclaimed in surprise, *"Caray!* It's good! Here, have some more."

She pouted and rudely stuck her tongue out at him. *"Hombre!* Did you think it wouldn't be good, then? Did you think a *gitana* wouldn't know how to cook, but could only dance and play the tambourine and *dukker* your fortune?"

He grinned wickedly. "I did wonder. A woman who's as good in the kitchen as she is in bed is a rare find!" His smile faded, and he set his fork down and regarded her seriously. "But then, there're so many things about you that I don't know—that I never bothered to ask. We have all the time in the world to talk, since the storm won't blow over until morning, I doubt. Tell me about your life before we met, *minina.* Tell me who you are—all about yourself."

Who was she, indeed? Ha! That was a good one! Was she the fiery Krissoula Ballardo, "La Reina," former Queen of Flamenco and the intended of Don Felipe of Tierra Rosa—or Krissoula, the barefoot Gypsy dancer whose poor heart ached with love for a man she could never have for a husband?

Before, she hadn't wanted to think too much about what she was getting herself into. She'd simply gone along with Esteban's plans as much for her own benefit as his. After all, despite his blackmail threats, if she was completely honest with herself she knew she could have escaped him at any time over that year she'd spent in Barcelona, tediously learning the ways of a lady, simply by slipping away from her tutors, or later, Sofía, and disappearing into the farthest reaches of Spain or Portugal or France like a lost chord. And, despite his threats, he'd never have been able to find her unless she wanted to be found, she knew! Be honest for once, Krissoula, she told herself! You stayed on, went along with his schemes because you were greedy, and saw a chance for something better. Ah, *sí,* the lure of gold had proven too strong for the Gypsy inside her, who prized and coveted its glitter as no other.

After the grief and disillusionment that marriage to Miguel had brought her had passed into bitter memory, her ambitions had seemed enough, the only reason she needed to keep going. She'd show the world and everyone in it that she could spit in their eye, that she needed no one but herself! Only what Krissoula wanted, needed, coveted, had mattered, she'd hardened her heart and told herself, but now—all that had changed. The promise of a life of comfort, of wealth, ease, and security was no longer enough; not nearly enough! She wanted a strong man to love and to be loved by. She yearned for a heart's companion to confide in, so she'd never be alone anymore. She wanted badly to share her life with someone, taking whatever the future brought them, good or bad, laughter or tears, and to treasure all the wonderful, *ordinary* times strung between them like precious links in an old gold chain. That was the true wealth in life, love and caring, and having someone to share it with, she thought. That was the "gold" this little Gypsy now coveted above all other wealth.

And perhaps—if God was good and forgiving of her many sins—she wanted another child someday, perhaps many babies, to fill the arms left empty and desolate by her Nicki's loss. A large and loving family on whom to shower the love she'd bottled up inside her. If the truth were known, she wanted Esteban de San Martín to be that someone to share her life, to shower her love upon, to father those babes.

But—what if she told him the truth, the whole truth of her past, and he didn't believe her? Or worse, if she told him everything, and it made no difference? Bastard born or no, he was the son of Alejandro de Aguilar, son of a family counted amongst the esteemed Two Hundred in Argentinian society. Blue blood flowed in his veins, while in hers there was only the blood of the Rom, the Gypsies, a people looked down upon, despised for centuries as dirty, thieving vagabonds, without principles or honor. She daren't hope for more than she had right now, for to do so, to be greedy, could breed only disappointment and bitterness. She must be content to share his bed, if not his heart, and grateful for having that much of him, at least . . .

"Are you afraid to tell me?" he pressed, turning her face up to his. "Don't be, little one! My own past was not so different from yours, I'd bet. You've nothing to fear from telling me."

"Me, afraid, *gorgio?* Of course not!" she insisted with a trace of her former defiance that he recognized now as armor, erected to shield her from hurt. "It's just that—well, there's really very little to tell you that you don't already know," she lied flatly, her golden eyes flickering quickly away from his.

"Try me!" he insisted.

"No! Eat, *hombre,* before the food gets cold. I'll pour us some coffee."

"Damn the coffee and tell me, Krissoula," he insisted, and the stubborn glint in his eyes told her he wouldn't be satisfied by less.

"Oh, very well," she agreed grudgingly at some length. "I'll tell you—but don't blame me if my story makes you yawn!"

"I doubt that, somehow!" he observed, and settled back to listen.

Chapter Eighteen

"I was born nineteen years ago last February, in Sacro Monte on the outskirts of the city of Granada, which is in Andalusia, Spain, and quite the most beautiful place in all the world," Krissoula began.

"My birth was considered a shameful one amongst my people, for my father was Greek, a *gorgio*—one not of our Romany blood. Worse, I was a bastard child, for my mother, Katarina, had not married her handsome Greek fisherman, neither in our Gypsy way, nor any other. I suppose—I suppose I should be thankful that Nikolas, the man who fathered me, was handsome and pleased her more than most had, for she stayed with him longer than with any of her other lovers—long enough for her to tell him she was with child before he sailed away. If not, I suppose I should never have known who had fathered me!"

She darted him an uncertain smile, which quickly vanished, before continuing. "Anyway, after I was born, my mother sent word to Niki that he had a baby daughter, and to everyone's surprise Niki came to the caves where my people lived in winter months to see me. He even stayed long enough to give me a name, too. 'Krissoula!' he told my mother as I nursed at her breast. 'Call my little daughter "Krissoula," Katarina. Back home in Greece, such a name means golden one, and it suits her!' And so, I became Krissoula.

"When I was only a few months old, my mama grew restless and made the mistake of choosing her newest lover from amongst the young men of our band—a man who'd already chosen a woman. There was a terrible knife fight between the two rivals, and blood was spilled, tempers roused. The council met to decide what was to be done about Katarina's shameful behavior, and their decision was that she be cast out of my uncle's band as a troublemaker.

"Katarina laughed in their faces, my aunt, Tía Isabella, told me

231

when I was old enough to understand, and told them 'good riddance!' She tossed her head and told the Old Ones she intended to wring some fun out of life if she had to choke it by the neck to do so! With that farewell, she gave my aunt the care of me, packed up her few belongings, and was gone one dark night. None of the Ballardo band has seen her since, and until this day, she is considered dead by my people, her name never spoken aloud, as is our custom. I was raised by my mother's brother, Ricardo, and his wife, Isabella, but kept my mother's family name, Ballardo, as my own."

She took a sip of her coffee to wet her throat, and stole a glance at Esteban, relieved to see he was listening quietly to her story with an expression more compassionate than either shocked or judgmental in his eyes. Encouraged, she went on, gazing dreamily into the flames that danced on the stone hearth.

"My childhood years were happy ones, for the most part. My aunt and uncle doted on me, for none of the babes my aunt carried had lived longer than a few months after their births. I became the daughter that life had denied them, their hope and joy. Tío Ricardo was a horsetrader by profession, and there was little he did not know about horseflesh. It was from him I learned to love horses, for he taught me to ride almost as soon as I learned to walk—and to do the trick-riding that you saw the time I rode Girasol bareback across the Pampa—!"

Amazingly, she actually blushed on recalling that day, and Esteban thought he'd never seen a more lovely sight than that telltale apricot color blooming in her cheeks.

"And how you rode, *minina!*" he remembered, flashing her a teasing grin as he added with raised brows, "Much better than you kissed, as I recall!"

"Bribón!" she scolded. "Let me get on with my story . . . !"

"Tío Ricardo and the others of our band took pity on me, a motherless, fatherless child, and I'm afraid they all spoiled me shamefully. I loved the winters we spent in our snug cave, which was as clean and cosy as any *gorgio* house. I looked forward to the long, lazy summers, too, when we turned our painted *vardos* into homes on wheels, and took to the open roads of Europe for the horse fairs. We traveled through vineyards heavy with grapes, dreaming in the Andalusian sunshine. We wound our way through the almond and lemon orchards of Málaga, with the scent of citrus tangy as wine in the air. We saw the raisin crops drying in the sun, and the olive groves with their twisted, stunted trees covering the windswept hillsides that reached down to the seashores. And beyond lay the Mediterranean, the most brilliant turquoise you can imagine, under dazzling Andalusian skies . . .

"I didn't go to school, but then, I had no need to—! I was given an education few are lucky enough to receive, in the school of life! The whole wide world was my schoolhouse, and my uncle and experience the only teachers I needed!

"Tío Ricardo would drive our *vardo,* pointing the way to this great city and that town, and tell me the marvels and the history of each wonderful land we traveled through. My own thirsty senses supplied the rest, for I was a curious little one, even then! I've seen all the great cities of the world with my very own eyes, Esteban. Wonderful, magical cities like Paris and London, Venice and Rome—oh, all of them! And I learned the languages spoken in each land I visited over the years, almost as well as my own Romany tongue—French, Italian, and English, as well as my own Spanish. I learned to appreciate the God-given talents of Europe's greatest artists, musicians, singers, and dancers with my own eyes and ears—not through another's, described in the dry, colorless pages of a book. Oh, life was one marvelous adventure in those days, unraveling day after day, week after week, like an endless shining ribbon leading into the future!" she declared, golden eyes shining, too, but then she bit her lip and her smile dimmed. "But then, when I was sixteen and already long past a marriageable age by our Romany standards, everything changed. I met a man—a boy, really —whose name was Miguel. He was a fisherman, and I . . ."

Esteban, watching her intently as she talked, heard Krissoula describe her first encounter with the handsome young fisherman when her band camped on the common land outside his Mediterranean village with twinges of jealousy that Miguel, not he, had been the one to meet her first. How beautiful she must have been at sixteen, he thought, an innocent beauty with the radiant aura a young girl wears in the flush of first love surrounding her like a halo! Could she possibly have been any lovelier than she was now . . . ?

Fascinated, he watched the proud way she held her head, with that great mass of glossy hair spilling in wild ringlets down over her shoulders like ebony ribbons. He saw how her magnificent eyes reflected her emotions like mirrors of amber glass as she spoke, dancing and alive with happiness one moment, or huge and tragic with remembered sorrow, or dark with tempestuous anger, in another. He gazed at her creamy beige-satin skin, remembering its

233

texture under his hands earlier and the way the merest blush of apricot color could seep into her cheeks with a bold glance from him, and make them bloom like wild roses. Ah, *sí,* she had beauty in abundance, yet there was character stamped on her face now, too, that youth and innocence could not have suggested. And beneath the beauty, giving it substance and fire, lay a core of strength, he sensed, the strength that comes when steel is forged in fire. He guessed that her story would be one of struggle, of soaring joys and profound sorrows, and that life had tried her bitterly in its forge of experience; that much he could read in her eyes. But, she'd risen from the testing fires like the legendary Phoenix, stronger than before, where another might have been bowed and broken, consumed to ashes by the testing. She'd survived, he reflected, by her sharp wits, by drawing on her inner strength, just as his mother had once survived, raising him to manhood in the slums of Buenos Aires to become, against all odds, a man he was not ashamed to be. A man of honor, of principles and pride, and, he hoped, of compassion and humility, too.

"You're not eating?" she observed, interrupting her tale. "Perhaps I should stop . . . ?"

"No, no, don't worry about me, *minina,* I'm listening, that's all. Go on," he urged, aware that her voice had trailed away into a hush broken only by the snap and crackle of the fire as it consumed the fresh logs with which she'd fed it before he awoke. Her expression was distant with memory as she twined a restless finger through a stray inky curl. "What about this man, this Miguel of yours? Tell me everything about him. I want to know!"

"Well, as I said, Miguel was young and very handsome, but quite different to the men of our band in that he was quieter than they. He had less arrogance, less flash and daring about him, than the *gitanos* I'd known. In my innocence, I mistook that quietness for a thoughtful, caring turn of mind. 'My Miguel is a thinker!' I told my uncle proudly, but Tío Ricardo was as good a judge of men as he was of horses. 'Beware, *sobrina,'* he warned me, 'that you do not judge a man's silence as proof that he is capable of deep emotion. Too often, a silent man is simply one who has nothing to say, like a stream that appears deep because of the rocks and weeds that overhang it, giving it darkness and a semblance of depth when there is nothing but dangerous shallows.'

"He was a wise man, my uncle Ricardo, and I should have listened to him, but alas, I did not! I was young, and fancied myself in love—!" She shrugged expressively, and pouted in the way

234

Esteban was fast coming to recognize as one of the endearing little things he liked about her. "What else can I say, except that I thought back then I knew everything, as the young always believe! I disobeyed my uncle, and ran away from my people. And, by so doing, became an outcast from our Romany band, like my mother before me.

"Miguel and I were married quietly in a Catholic church, with only a handful of his friends to witness our wedding. Miguel's family and the people of his fishing village shunned the ceremony. They were against us marrying, too, you see. As Tío Ricardo had considered my Miguel a shallow, spineless *gorgio,* his family had no liking for Gypsies, either—and especially no affection for the bold *gitana* wench who'd dared to marry their precious only son! They muttered about the slyness and thievery of my people, and said in my hearing that our women were slovenly, dirty animals without morals or honor. Creatures who made poor mothers for the litters of children they bred like rabbits! Aiee, the hurt their insults caused me! But I told myself it didn't matter what they said or thought, because I had Miguel, and Miguel loved me. That, I was so certain, would be enough!

"But little by little, in the months following our wedding, I noticed Miguel begin to change. Where before he'd teased me about the things I was ignorant of, now it seemed he criticized me at every turn and had little patience for my mistakes. He praised the housewives' skills the girls of his village had learned when they were little more than babes in arms, and which I'd never had any need to learn. At first, he treated me this way only when we were alone, and I was thankful I could hide my shame. But over the months, that changed. Miguel took to belittling me and poking fun at me openly before his family, his friends, and they—seeing my own husband treat me in this fashion—took their cue from him and added to my misery. Oh, the cruel insults they threw at me, the names they called me! But Miguel, curse his black heart, uttered not a single word in my defense! Rather, he laughed with them and egged them on, until in my misery I grew even clumsier!"

She grimaced bitterly as she remembered those unhappy times, and her usually graceful fingers twisted about themselves, drawing Esteban's compassionate gaze with their agonized, fretful movements. She, clumsy, whose every move possessed a dancer's grace? *Dios,* how he'd love to choke that callow Miguel by the throat . . . ! Instead, he reached across the table and stilled her hands in the warm clasp of his own, urging, *"Calma, querida.* Their cruelty is

235

all in the past now. Finished. Done with! They can't hurt you anymore, Krissoula . . . so go on, tell me the rest."

"Well, just when it seemed things couldn't get any worse than they already were, I discovered I was with child. Oh, Miguel might have mocked me before others, but he'd never denied himself his husband's rights to my body!" she said bitterly. "His lovemaking was a rough and hasty, selfish act. I know that now, but back then, I knew little of how things were meant to be in a marriage bed. I'd come to our wedding a sixteen-year-old virgin, you understand, and had known no other man but him!"

She bowed her head and blushed. "U-until you, Esteban, I had no other lover with whom to compare my husband, you see? Oh, I'd felt my blood run swift and hot with desire for Miguel, of course! But in my innocence, I'd never dreamed that a woman could find as much joy and pleasure in making love as a man. I have you to thank for teaching me how it should be . . .

"Well, anyway," she continued her story, obviously flustered by her intimate confession, "I—I hoped that having a babe might improve things between Miguel and me, but, if anything, it only served to drive us further apart!

"When my belly began to swell, Miguel would scowl and ask me if I was sure the child was his—if it were not perhaps some other man's brat, a *gitano*'s bastard conceived when he was out at sea, fishing. He'd ask this of me, his own wife, the woman he'd sworn before God to love, honor, and cherish!" she recalled bitterly. "His lack of trust pained me more cruelly than any blow from his fist could have, for a Gypsy's word is his—or her—honor, and in a church and before God, I had sworn to honor and love no man but him, to give myself to no one but him. Miguel made me doubt myself in those months, Esteban, to question my own worth. He took away my pride, my independence, my confidence, until at last I came to wonder if perhaps the things he accused me of might be true? Perhaps I was a wicked woman, deserving of his contempt? Why else would he and his family, his friends, despise me, when I tried so very hard to be a good wife to him . . . ?

"Then one afternoon, while Miguel was out at sea, my labor pains started. While I was still able to walk, I went to my mother-in-law's house and told her that the babe was coming. I went to the midwife's in the village, and warned her that my time was near. Then I went home and waited, trusting that they would come to me in my hour of need, certain that no woman—however unfeeling, however cold and pitiless—could let a young girl deliver her first child all alone, with no mother of her own to help her. It was full dark before I realized that I'd have to deliver my baby alone. Those hateful bitches never came!"

She sighed heavily, and in the firelight her eyes were enormous, shiny with unshed tears, the long, dark lashes spiked and wet. Emotion filled Esteban as he imagined her, so young, so terribly frightened, as that long night wore on, and her birthing pains increased in force, and with them, her pain and desperation. His grip tightened, her small hands completely enclosed by his own now in an effort to comfort her so that he could feel her trembling violently as she relived that dark and endless night. He wanted badly to hold her, comfort her and make the hurt and terror she was reliving go away, and so on impulse, he drew her from her seat and onto his lap, holding her close while she poured out the rest of her sad little tale with her head cradled heavily against his shoulder, his hand caressing and soothing her hair.

"Nicki was born just before dawn, after a night of hell, for it was no easy birth. *Dios,* how I envy women who can drop their babes with the ease of a bitch whelping her pups! It was not so for me, alas. I was smaller then, my hips narrow, and my son—my beautiful, beautiful son!—was big and healthy, a vigorous child. I struggled and screamed. I wept—*Dios,* how I wept!—as the night crept slowly away, inch by inch. Just before dawn, the pains began coming in waves that towered higher and higher before crashing down over me, tearing me apart. I moved in and out of consciousness as if it were a sea that ebbed and flowed without ending. When the moment came, I pushed and pushed, but it seemed an eternity before the child tore himself free of my womb. I lifted him from between my legs and held him in my arms at last, trembling with exhaustion and joy. I had a knife put by, and I managed somehow to find the strength to cut and tie the cord myself. I bathed the blood from his little face and head, then wrapped him in the clean shawl I'd made ready. I was too tired and weak, too sore, to do anything more. I fell asleep, exhausted, with my infant son cradled in my arms."

"Pobrecita!" Esteban murmured huskily, moved by her story which, told so simply, was more touching than great eloquence.

"I awakened to find my mother-in-law standing over me, reaching for my babe like a she-devil sent from the depths of hell. 'Give me Miguel's son!' she shrieked at me. 'It is not fitting my grandson should lie in his own filth, as his Gypsy slut of a mother enjoys doing!'

237

"Something cold and angry filled me that she—the spiteful bitch who'd not stirred herself to help me even in my hour of greatest need, nor come to offer a word of encouragement—could find fault with me yet again. My anger gave me strength. I told her no! I told her, 'Go away and leave us alone! The baby is mine, you hear me, *mine!* You watched me carry him alone these past nine months, knowing I had no mother or friends or family near to advise me, without a word of compassion or concern from you, or your coven of sisters. No, *suegra mía,* you left me to labor all alone, to give birth to my firstborn in terror and ignorance! Well, I don't need you anymore, you old witch! I'll raise my son as I gave him birth—alone, without help from you!'

"She argued, but I think she sensed that I wouldn't be persuaded. In the end she went away and left me alone. I'd regained a little of my strength by then—partly on account of my anger, I think!—and so I got up and washed myself, changed the soiled bed linen. I made myself drink a little goat's milk, and went back to bed to nurse my baby, my little angel, Nicki, for the first time."

Her eyes were dreamy now, her expression poignantly tender in a way Esteban had seen only once before, as she had held Lupe's little son Paulo in the kitchens of Tierra Rosa.

"I called my baby 'Nicki' after my father, you understand, for my aunt had told me once that my father's hair was brown with threadings of gold, as was my babe's. Besides, I wanted no name that was any part of Miguel and his family, not for *my* child!" she added fiercely, her golden eyes glittering in the firelight like the eyes of a protective she-hawk defending her young. "At last, I told myself, I had someone to love and to love me—someone to make the hatefulness of my life easier to bear. What did it matter if my people had cast me out? If Miguel didn't love me? If his family and the villagers despised me for my Gypsy blood? Nicki shared that blood with me, and he was *mine.* I swore I'd never give him up! As long as we had each other, it was enough . . .

"Things were a little better for a while, after Miguel came home that night. He told me he was sorry that he'd doubted he was Nicki's father, for any fool with eyes to see could tell who'd sired him. His father's name was written in his face!

"Nicki grew to look more like him every day, and Miguel, to his credit, seemed to love his son. As our babe grew, I stupidly began to hope that things would get better, and that Nicki would bring us closer together. I was so wrong, so blind, so foolishly trusting! Miguel's love was all for the babe. He had none left for—for me. So

238

it went on, until one day in September, when Nicki was four months old . . ."

It had been dawn, she remembered with agony in her heart, and the sky had been glorious, flushed pink and gold beyond the cottage window. The cocks had been crowing loudly to welcome the new day. Waking to find her breasts full and tender with milk, she'd been a little surprised that, unlike other mornings, Nicki's cries to nurse had not roused her. Dropping a kiss on Miguel's cheek, she'd slipped from the bed and gone to take Nicki from his wooden cradle, intending to carry him back to the warmth of the bed and nurse him there.

". . . but as I looked down at him, I saw that he still lay fast asleep in his cradle, instead of kicking free of his blankets and gurgling for my breast as he did each morning. I picked him up and held him close to my face to kiss him. It was then that I felt his cheek. He was so chilled to my lips. His little body seemed rigid within the blankets . . ."

She'd bared her breast in readiness for his hungry mouth, and cuddled the sleeping babe to her body, hoping her warmth would warm him. She'd crooned the loving, silly little nonsense words that mothers do as she pressed her lips to his brow this time—and found it still cold. Not merely chilled, but icy, waxy cold. She'd begun to tremble uncontrollably, for only then had she admitted to herself that his little body was also cold and stiff in her arms beneath the blankets. Too still, far too stiff . . .

God in heaven, noooo!

A dark shadow of foreboding had moved through her, freezing the scream of denial on her lips, strangling the sobs in her throat as she'd unwrapped the blankets and seen—oh, God!—seen that her precious babe was . . . was . . . !

She'd heard screams then; terrible, heart-rending screams, but in her madness and grief, she'd not known them for her own.

"I unwrapped my Nicki's blankets, telling myself it wasn't so, it couldn't be so—I wouldn't *let* it be so. He was sick, just sick, I promised myself that he'd get better, I'd see that he did. Yet there was no sign of sickness, no mark upon him, nor a movement—be it ever so slight—from his perfect little body. I shook him. I pleaded with him to open his eyes. I breathed air into his mouth in the Gypsy way. 'Nicki, my heart, my life, for the love of God, wake up for your *mamacita!*' I cried. I fell on my knees and begged God to forgive me my sins—I swore I'd do anything, *anything,* if He'd just let my baby breathe again, please God, let him be alive and well, not dead . . . not dead . . . anything but dead! But Nicki . . . my Nicki lay like a doll in my arms, as cool and stiff as wax . . .

"My screams woke Miguel, and he tore Nicki from my arms and struck me hard across the face, knocking me to the floor. 'What's wrong with him?' he screamed at me. 'What have you done to my son?' Aiee, *Dios,* he accused me of killing our baby—the only joy of my life! I knew in my heart then that he'd never love me again, no matter how I tried to make him care. That he'd always believe deep down inside that I killed our babe out of jealousy, because just days before, in anger and hurt, I'd accused him of loving our son more than he loved me. I knew then that my love for Miguel had died, too. In that moment, how I hated him!

"At the funeral, everyone came to share Miguel's sorrow, while I sat alone and uncomforted, my heart swollen to bursting with a grief I could share with no one . . ."

Sí, she recalled, her apparent composure in the wake of such tragedy had earned her the villagers' open contempt, but then in all honesty, their contempt had always been hers, the only "gift" they'd ever freely given her, curse them all!

"A heart of stone, has that one!" they'd whispered loudly enough for her to hear. *"Look at her! Not a tear does she shed for her poor dead child!*

"But what else could you expect from a Gypsy slut like her, eh? Everyone knows how the Gypsies are—dirty, cold-hearted devils all, dabbling in fortunes and witchcraft!"

"Strange, wasn't it, her being the one to find their babe dead that morning? Not a mark on his little body—nor a whisper of sickness in the days before—to give reason for his death, either, poor little mite!

"The work of witchcraft, like as not—or else she ignored the child, that lazy good-for-nothing, too fond of her sleep to hear her child cry out . . . !"

"When their hateful whispers became too much, when the agony threatened to tear me apart and fling me headfirst into madness, I got to my feet and danced!" she continued defiantly, tossing her head and challenging him with her eyes to condemn her. "Barefoot, in my one white dress—for it is not black, but white, we *gitanos* wear for mourning—I drew my shawl over my face like a veil and danced and danced and danced because—because I *had* to! You understand why, don't you?" she whispered beseechingly, and she saw Esteban nod solemnly, saw the tears glistening on his cheeks in the firelight as he wept silently, although her own cheeks remained strangely dry.

Ah, *si*, he understood all too well! Her words had recalled a day in his own past, a day not long after his mother's death, when the young cutthroats of Barrio San Timéo had tried to part him from his stolen loaf of bread. The crimson rage that had filled him then had been his grief and rage over his mother's death exploding in violence, though he hadn't understood that until much later in his life, when he was grown. Everyone expressed their grief in their own way, and in their own time, and he understood only too well what Krissoula's dancing had signified to her. He knew what it was to weep on the inside, where the pain was hidden but no less wrenching . . .

"Miguel didn't understand, of course," she continued sadly. "He didn't have it in him to understand! Nor did his village understand, either, how a mother could dance at the funeral of her infant son! They called me murderer, whore, Gypsy slut, but I laughed in their face and kept on dancing—and pitied them their shallowness, their ignorance, their prejudice, and the hardness of their hearts.

"After that night, I think I was a little mad, for a time. I tried once or twice to talk to Miguel, hoping perhaps that in our shared grief we could rekindle a spark of love amongst the ashes of what we'd lost. But it was no use. Miguel turned away from me with only hatred and accusation in his eyes and on his lips, though I ached for the comfort of his arms about me or the solace of a gentle, understanding word. The love between us—if it had ever truly existed—was gone. The desire, too. After that, Miguel rarely came to our cottage when he came home from fishing. He'd be gone till the wee hours, and then put out to sea again at first light.

"One morning, about six months after Nicki's death, they carried my husband home to me on a door, as still as my babe had been. There were bloody wounds in his chest and belly—stab wounds, I knew. My evil ways had driven him to another's arms, the villagers said, to a woman whose man had tired of her loose ways, and who'd surprised her making love with my husband. Spanish tempers flare hot and swiftly into violence, as well you know, eh, *querido*? A quarrel had started. Knives had been drawn, and Miguel was the loser. They buried him alongside our child."

She sighed heavily. She'd wept a lifetime of tears in the days that had followed her son's death, had believed ever since she had no tears left to shed. Dry-eyed, she'd learned of Miguel's death not a year later. Dry-eyed, she'd followed his youthful body consigned to a grave beside their infant son's, without a single outward sign of

241

grief. It was as if her heart were encased in ice, and nothing could melt it, set it free to love again. She was numb to pain, to joy, to passion, to all the gamut of human emotions, her senses dulled. It had been easier to go through the motions of living that way, and so she'd chosen to remain numb, blocking off feeling until doing so had become second nature to her.

"Scarcely had the grave been filled when the villagers turned on me like a pack of wolves," she continued in a wooden tone. "'There's nothing more for you here, *gitana!*' they jeered. 'Be gone with you, back to your own dirty kind!'

"They had stones to drive me on my way, and no reluctance to use them. Cut and bleeding, I ran for my life. I don't think I stopped until I reached Barcelona! And when I did, when I finally stopped running and had time to think and take stock of all that had happened, I found the innocent, loving girl I'd once been no longer existed! I'd grown hard and cynical, wary of men, determined to use them as they'd sought to use me. I swore that henceforth, I would live for myself, for Krissoula Ballardo—and El Diablo take anyone who tried to stop me! Happiness had been denied me, I told myself, and so I would have a life of riches and comfort instead."

"You never thought that maybe your flamenco could turn a profit?"

"No, not then! At that time, I didn't dream I might be able to turn my one small talent to any gain. I owe that opportunity to you, Esteban!" She smiled bitterly before adding, "No, *querido,* the back streets of Barcelona soon taught me another lesson. That there was only one thing a woman possessed that commanded a price. Her body."

Her harsh words dropped like heavy stones into the yawning silence, and Esteban felt his heart constrict. He'd been expecting it, and yet even so, it was a shock to hear her confirm his fears aloud. Involuntarily, he released her hands as if they were scalding hot. So, it was exactly as it had seemed, after all. She'd sold herself, he thought jealously, and to his shame—for all that he understood very well why she'd done so—he couldn't squelch the anger that filled him, to think of her loveliness squandered on countless, lusting men for the price of a coin. That that coin had meant the difference between starvation and survival to her didn't seem to carry the weight it should have, and his feelings showed in his face.

Krissoula saw the change in his expression and gave a bitter, sad little laugh as she drew herself from his arms.

"So you judge me, too, my love, and find me guilty? But of

242

course, you would! After all, you're a *man,* and there's always something a man can do to make his way in life, no? How could I have expected you to understand what it's like to be a woman in these hard times, when a young girl without husband or father or brother to protect her is easy prey? But despite what you're thinking, you can rest easy, Esteban. It wasn't that way. I suppose I was lucky, for I never became any man's *puta*—though perhaps selling myself might have been the more honest road to take, rather than what I did. *Sí,* I used my body, but not, I swear, in the way you're thinking. I used it to steal."

He was ashamed at the weight that lifted from his shoulders when she denied selling herself, yet he was relieved beyond words. He was who he was, the sum of all that had happened to him in his life, and he was too settled in his ways to change them now. Memories of the fresh young girls he'd seen used and abused by men in the *barrios,* who had gradually grown old and raddled with disease, the bloom of their youth squandered before its time, were too repugnant to reconcile with his new feelings for Krissoula. Such women soon became numb to emotion, their feelings cauterized, their hatred of men the only thing that kept them going. No! He hadn't wanted to learn that his suspicions had been right all along, that Krissoula had been hard on the road to becoming one of them when he met her . . .

"How did you survive, then?" he asked, curious, although still half afraid of what her answer might be.

"I met a man called Hector Corrales—a sly, drunken sot who lived for his bottle and little else. We met in a tavern one night when I tried to pick his pocket, and he made me an offer to join him. It seemed his 'partner'—a woman, of course!—had died in childbirth. He was looking for someone to replace her. They'd worked as a team, he told me, the woman enticing the men to enjoy her favors in some sorry room above a convenient inn. She'd produce a bottle of cheap wine, and suggest they share a drink together first, and when he wasn't looking, she'd slip a sleeping draft into the pigeon's glass. While the 'marks' slept, Hector and the woman would empty their pockets, and their victims would wake up to find themselves without a woman and robbed of coin. It was a crude trick—one as old as time itself—but the beauty of it was, it worked, time and time again! Dazzled by a pretty face and the promise of a lusty tumble, the stupid old goats followed me like lambs to the slaughter, and lost what few coins they possessed! That, Esteban, was how I survived, on the bones of Saint Sara, I swear it! And then one day, that greedy Hector made the mistake of selecting a well-dressed, handsome foreigner as my mark, and—! Well, the rest you know, eh?"

She forced a smile, yet her eyes were haunting as they locked with his, imploring him to believe her.

And I, like your Miguel, like your Hector, set out to use you! Esteban brooded, his expression dark and unreadable. *I left the* barrios *because I refused to be used for Rolón Severino's dark purposes, and ended up using a young, desperate girl who'd already suffered far too much for my own!* He shook his head, filled with self-disgust. *You son of a bitch, San Martín! Your thirst for revenge has warped you, twisted you into a man I hardly recognize—or want to admit to becoming . . .*

"You—you don't believe me!" she cried, misreading his expression for disbelief and springing to her feet. "Pah! I knew I was wasting my breath!"

She'd made it to the door and flung it open before he caught up with her.

"No, Krissoula, that's not it! I believe you! I swear on my honor as a man that I do, every single word!" he reassured her, planting his arms on her shoulders and pulling her back against him. He rested his chin on the top of her head and sighed heavily. *"Sí,* darling, I believe you. And if I seemed angry a moment ago, it's because I wish with all my heart that I'd never involved you in my schemes, Krissoula. *Todos los santos,* you've had more than enough pain in your short life, little one. Far too much!"

"It's still raining," she observed several moments later without commenting on his words of self-reproach.

Standing in the open doorway, Krissoula leaned back against Esteban's broad chest and they watched the rain teeming down in silvery sheets together. She saw how the raindrops dimpled the muddy black earth, or stirred ripples in the inky puddles, and felt warm inside—warmer, lighter of heart, than she'd felt in years. He believed her. He trusted her. He'd said so! Being there with him, watching the rain, was a moment she'd never forget, for never had she felt more safe, more protected, than she did right now, leaning against his strong body, his arms curled about her.

"So it is," he agreed softly in answer to her comment. "You'll have to stay here until it eases up."

"Sí, I suppose I must," she agreed without any regret.

For a few moments more, there was a comfortable silence between them. She could feel his heartbeat against her back, the

244

warmth of his body surrounding her, his breath in her hair, and somehow it was a more intimate moment than any they'd shared before. Far more intimate than making love.

Then Esteban slipped his hands down her arms and curled them about her waist, drawing her still tighter to him.

"Do you know what the rain says, *minina?*" he asked her in a voice she'd never heard him use before, one that sounded charged with tenderness, with hesitancy and some other emotion she couldn't define.

"No," she murmured with a slow smile curving her mouth. "Tell me!"

"It says, 'I love you, Krissoula.' Can't you hear it?"

Her heart skipped a beat, and a fierce, wild joy blazed through her. She turned quickly in his arms to face him, and gazed searchingly up into his sapphire eyes, her face grown suddenly radiant.

"I—I think I can, yes!" she whispered, aware of the sudden acceleration of her heart. "And do you know what else the rain says, *mi amor?*" she asked in turn, her voice tremulous with feeling.

"No, *querida mía.* I can't even guess," Esteban answered her with a slow, tender smile of his own.

"It says, 'Krissoula loves you, too, San Martín!'" she murmured, her golden eyes shining amidst their fringing of thick lashes. She buried her face against his chest and added shyly, "The rain says that I love you, *querido mío,* and—and that Krissoula never betrays the ones she loves, nor lets them down. I'll find the papers you need, I swear I will, somehow! You will have Tierra Rosa, and the justice you seek against Felipe, or my name is not—"

"Hush . . . To hell with the papers," he whispered, a knot clenching in his throat. "They're not important now. You are! I love you, *minina.* I know now that I need you. And *Dios,* woman, how I want you! Come to bed, Krissoula. Come back to bed."

"I will—soon, my love!" she promised. "But first, there's something I have to do . . ."

She turned back inside the cabin, and took up the sharp knife she'd cut the vegetables with. Before he guessed what she was about, she'd turned the point against her palm and nicked the flesh there. A ruby droplet welled on the pale gold of her skin, glistening in the firelight, and she held her palm outward, towards him, as if in offering.

"I want to swear a blood oath to you, Esteban, after the customs of my Romany people. An oath that only death can sever, if you accept it?"

"What oath?" he demanded almost curtly, angry that she should wound herself on his account. He came quickly back to her, and took her hand in his, his expression concerned, for the droplet had become a crimson trickle now.

"An oath of love and loyalty!" she murmured earnestly. "On this day, and by the lifeblood that runs from my body to mingle with your own, I swear never to betray you, Esteban de San Martín. To be loyal to you, to love you, to belong to you as your woman, for as long as there is breath in my body, and blood in my veins. For as long as you still want me in return . . ."

"Be careful what you swear upon, beloved," he warned her for the second time that day, his voice choked, "for I'm a greedy man!"

Taking up the knife, he slashed a small, deep cut in his own palm. His eyes met hers, and sapphire locked tenderly with gold. "You see, *gitana*, I wouldn't settle for less than a lifetime!"

So saying, he took her hand in his, and pressed their palms together so that their blood commingled, Gypsy to *gorgio*.

"My love, my heart, they're yours," he whispered huskily. "As am I . . ."

Fingers clasped tightly, he drew her into his arms, and to the bed.

Chapter Nineteen

For a second time that night, Krissoula wakened from deep sleep with a horrible start, her heart pounding, not knowing at first where she was, or with whom, nor what had aroused her so abruptly.

Lying there, afraid to move a muscle, she looked about her, yet saw nothing out of the ordinary. The fire sizzled as a trickle of rain ran down the chimney, but soon the amber flames had returned to their former lazy flickering over the whitewashed walls, spilling ruddy light across them that was contrasted with deep purple shadows. She could hear the heavy rain upon the roof, still falling with its pattering din, and could smell the fresh scent of it and the tang of rain-soaked earth in her nostrils, but everything seemed quite normal.

Her glance flicked from the pegs where Esteban hung his bridles and clothing, to the chimney breast, and thence to the wall built at a right angle to it in which had been set a small glazed window, now streaked with rain. The rivulets made weird patterns against the thick glass, creating the illusion of a horrible, flattened face pressed against the small panes!

With a shudder, she forced herself to look on, examining the next wall, but then for some reason, some sixth sense or heightened instinct sent her gaze veering back to that same window again. The impression of a face, staring in at them, was still strong. Far too strong! Indignation and concern swept over her. Dear God, there *was* someone out there, she was certain of it now—someone who was peeping in at them, spying on them while they slept—and who knew what else they'd witnessed earlier!

Remembering belatedly that the sheepskins had slipped from her naked body, baring a breast, she surreptitiously pulled them up to cover her, almost in the same move taking Esteban by the arm and shaking him awake.

"What's wrong, *querida?*" he mumbled drowsily, stifling a huge yawn.

247

In a guarded undertone, making no sudden moves that might alarm the voyeur, she murmured, "I think there's someone out there, watching us through the window!"

And as if in agreement, Rojo—dreaming by the fire—suddenly came awake and hauled himself bolt upright, a growl rumbling deep in his throat, his hackles raised so that in the firelight he looked like a fierce wolf with a heavy ruff about his neck.

"You're imagining things, *minina,*" he told her, cocking a sleepy eye at the small, square window opposite his narrow cot. The aperture was divided into four by wooden crosspieces, and he could see nothing unusual about it. "It's only the rain, distorting the windowpanes. Go back to sleep, darling. It'll be morning soon enough . . ."

But even as Esteban sat up, the massive dog, Rojo, lumbered to its feet and began scratching and whining frantically at the door, and as Esteban's words died away, the animal began barking furiously to be let out.

"Maybe you're right," he hurriedly acknowledged, and had tossed the sheepskins aside and stepped into his breeches in almost the same move. Taking up his pistol, he moved quickly to the door, unbolted it, and flung it open.

At once, Rojo sprang forward, bounding out into the wet night with loud, baying whoofs that grew more and more frantic and excited with every second. He quickly disappeared, swallowed up by darkness.

Krissoula slipped on the blue cambric shirt Esteban had loaned her, and came to stand behind him, hurriedly buttoning it.

"Was there someone there?" she asked, peering beyond him into the darkness beyond the cottage.

"Sounds like it, if Rojo's any judge. Stay here, while I go and take a look around . . ."

He strode outside, obviously expecting her to obey him, yet Krissoula had no intention of staying alone in the cottage while he disappeared into the night—not after all the lurid tales of Indian attacks she'd heard about! Padding on bare feet through the mud a pace or two behind him, clad in only his shirttails, which barely covered her bottom, she followed him outside.

At first, their eyes had to adjust to the darkness and the steadily falling rain, but then Rojo's barking, a little way off in the distance, drew their attention to the slight rise which lay beyond the cottage. For a brief moment, a running figure was silhouetted against the lighter sky beyond, followed closely by the bounding dog in full-throated cry.

"You were right," Esteban acknowledged, his eyes narrowed. "But whoever they were, Rojo's seen them off for the night. And it doesn't look as if they had time to steal anything. The horses seem calm enough."

"Who do you think it was?" she asked, curious despite his calm reassurances.

"A squatter, probably. There're a handful of them trying their hand at farming along the boundaries of Tierra Rosa's lands. Trouble is, they waste their time in gambling and drinking at the *pulperías* in Rosario, instead of working their land, so when they've nothing to eat, they decide to pay me a visit and steal what they can carry off! It's not the first time it's happened—and it probably won't be the last."

"Well, I'm glad I wasn't imagining things!" Krissoula said with feeling. "But you know, it's strange—I had the strongest feeling I'd seen that face before somewhere, although its nose was squashed up against the glass." She frowned thoughtfully, oblivious to the steady downpouring all about them, and of the sky growing steadily lighter to the east, heralding the imminent dawn.

"Maybe in a nightmare," Esteban teased with a grin, chucking her beneath the chin. "But now, if it's all the same to you, mi'lady, I've had enough of a soaking for one night. I'm headed back to that warm, dry bed we left! Last one back to the cottage pays a forfeit!" he challenged.

"What forfeit?" she demanded, tossing her wet hair over her shoulders.

"Oh, I'll think of something, don't worr—hey! That's cheating, you little minx!" he roared as she suddenly took off at a run to get a head start on him, sprinting like a nymph around the rails of the corral and leaping the puddles like a fleeing deer as she raced back towards the cottage.

Over her shoulder she taunted him merrily, "All's fair in love and—waaarrrhhh!"

The word ended in a startled yelp as she lost her footing in the slippery ground and slithered through thick black mud, landing on her bottom with slime all over her legs.

"Oh, no! I'm covered in it!" she wailed, grimacing as Esteban slithered to a halt alongside her, chuckling wickedly and without an ounce of pity in him.

"Serves you right, *minina!*" he told her, fists on his hips. "Cheaters never win! Didn't you know that?"

249

"You horrible cockroach!" she accused, pouting. "If you were a true gentleman, *bribón,* you'd help me up, instead of standing there laughing!"

"You don't deserve it—but I will, anyway," he agreed, extending his hand to her.

She clasped it, a devilish gleam in her golden eyes and a mischievous grin tugging at her lips—a grin he could hardly discern in the gloom and rain! Her hand securely clamped to his, she suddenly tugged backward and, taken by surprise, Esteban was jerked forward, lost his footing, and sprawled into the mud alongside her.

"You little witch—!" he roared. "I'll make you eat this damned mud for that little trick!" Growling threateningly, he grasped her neck and tried to force her head down, Krissoula helpless with laughter and trying furiously to wriggle from his tight grip. She squirmed free of his hands at last and tried to crawl away on her hands and knees, but before she could struggle to standing, he gripped her by the ankles and yanked her back down onto her belly.

Over and over they rolled, until they were both covered from head to foot in the slimy mud, both of them choking with muffled laughter. His hand vainly tried to entrap her waist, yet with her body wet and muddy, it was like trying to hold fast to a slippery eel—impossible! And, somehow, it was deliciously erotic, too, their bodies slipping and slithering against each other, and wrestling in the cool, wet mud. Somehow, Krissoula's shirt ended up lost in the mud, and their childlike tussling took on a far different overtone, becoming one loaded with sensuality as Esteban's hands slipped everywhere over her sleek, naked little body, relishing the feel of her slippery female curves and the firm, mud-slicked mounds of her breasts beneath his caresses, while Krissoula thrilled to the sensation of his muscular torso under its oily coating of clay. Their laughter became teasing endearments and thickened breathing as they kissed and strained against each other, oblivious to the pattering rain and the occasional rumble of thunder and flicker of lightning on the distant hills.

"Mmm," Esteban murmured huskily, coming up for air after a kiss that had fired his passion for her all over again. "Let's go inside, before we give the owls an eyeful they won't forget!"

"Again?" she squeaked, incredulity in her tone, and her lithe body shook with laughter against the hard lines of his where they sprawled wantonly in the mud, legs entangled.

"Afraid so," he confirmed without regret and with no little

fervor, his sapphire eyes—the lashes spiked and wet with rain—gleaming roguishly in the meager light. "There must be something about this mud—it could rejuvenate a dead man!" he teased her, tugging on her lower lip with gentle teeth. "Maybe I'll patent it, and grow rich as Midas!" he whispered hotly in her ear, and goosebumps sprang out on her arms. "Now, for the love of God, *minina,* are you coming inside?"

"Why should we?" she asked archly, shaking her sodden curls like a little wet hound shaking itself dry. "What's wrong with right here, mmm?" she asked coyly, her slanted golden eyes wicked as she side-eyed him from beneath her sooty lashes. "Unless, of course, you have no—adventure—in your soul, eh, *gato?"*

A broad grin curved his lips and danced in his eyes.

"All right, you wanton little minx, you asked for it! Here, it'll be!"

Esteban, riding Barbaro, escorted a yawning and bleary-eyed Krissoula back to the *casa grande* soon after dawn the following day, to find the *hacienda* in uproar over her disappearance.

Tomás had rounded up some of the other grooms and several of the *gauchos* and they'd formed a search party, which had ridden out through the swirling rain and across the darkened, storm-washed Pampa to look for Doña Krissoula when she'd failed to put in an appearance by teatime the afternoon before. Also on Tomás's orders, they'd returned shortly before dawn to swallow a hasty breakfast and swig hot coffee at the bunkhouse before resuming their search in the drizzling rain that was still falling in fine but heavy sheets.

Sofía, who came running out to meet the pair as they rode up to the front of the hacienda with no regard for the weather, appeared gray and gaunt with worry as Esteban dismounted and went to assist Krissoula in doing the same.

"Until the next time, remember that I love you, *querida,"* he mouthed, his back turned to the duenna as Sofía hurried towards them. His hands, spanning Krissoula's slender waist as he lifted her down from her horse, tightened a little in the second before he released her. His dark sapphire eyes tenderly consumed her, betraying his reluctance to let her go after the glorious night they'd shared. They'd made love several, wonderful times, at last falling into exhausted sleep in each other's arms. Waking up to find Krissoula curled trustingly, lovingly, in his arms had been an experience he would never forget. He added softly, "Ah, *perdición,*

251

the 'next time' already seems an eternity away! Let's finish this today, and tell Felipe he can go hang—that you're mine, eh?"

"No! I love you, *querido!"* she whispered back, her golden eyes warm and radiant with love as she gazed up into his. "And I want you to have all that is rightfully yours! I'll keep on looking until Felipe returns to the *casa.* And don't worry, I won't take any risks—I have too much to lose now, mmm? I'll come to you just as soon as I can, I promise, and we'll be together, like last night . . ."

"No more fighting?" he murmured, smiling, formally taking her hand and going through the motions of kissing it in polite farewell.

"No more fighting, *gato.* Only loving, from here on!" she agreed tenderly, and reluctantly drew both her eyes and her hand from his with a polite inclining of her head.

In a louder voice for Sofía's benefit, she said, "I cannot thank you enough for finding me and bringing me home, *señor mayordomo!* That terrible storm—it was so very frightening!" and she gave a delicate shudder, every inch the *hidalga.*

Smothering a grin at her outrageous lie and the practiced ease with which she told it, the little minx, Esteban made a gallant bow and also said in a loud voice, "Think nothing of it! It was my pleasure to be of assistance to you, Doña Krissoula. I'm only grateful you were not harmed by your frightening experience. But now, with your permission—?"

So saying, he turned away, gathered the horses' reins in his fists, and led his bay stallion and Girasol towards the stable.

Krissoula turned to Sofía in the same moment that Sofía, uncharacteristically demonstrative today, flung her arms about Krissoula's neck, and sobbed, "Oh, *niña, niña,* you're home, safe and sound! Where were you all this time, child? And just look at you—your hair, your clothes! Whatever happened last night? Aiee, *niña,* I was so very, very frightened for you!"

"There, there, Sofía, stop blubbering, do!" Krissoula urged, embarrassed by the woman's unexpected show of affection. She patted her duenna's back. "I'm home safe and sound, as you said, and that's an end to it, eh? Dry your eyes, now, there's a dear."

"But—you were gone all night, *niña!* All night, in that terrible storm, and the lightning and thunder—! Señor Tomás and his men could find no sign of you, nor your horse. Aiee, I was so afraid you'd been struck by lightning, that you were dead out there, somewhere, or carried off by bandits or those savage Indians! How could you do this to me, Krissoula? How could you ride off without telling me where you were going? How could you make me worry

252

so, you thoughtless girl!" Two bright spots of color rode high in Sofía's pale cheeks now as her relief at seeing her charge safe and sound was rapidly replaced by anger.

"You were taking your siesta when I decided to leave, Sofía, and I am not a child, to have to ask your permission for every little thing I want to do! I decided to visit Lupe and her son again, but they weren't home, and so—" she shrugged, "I decided to go riding across the Pampa instead." Her eyes dared Sofía to scold her, but Sofía, having spent a sleepless night imagining every horrible little thing that could have befallen her charge, had gone beyond caring about Krissoula's explosive temper.

"What? And after Don Felipe expressly forbade you to go riding! Madonna, what a wicked girl you are! Well, we shall see if you're quite so defiant after I have told him of your escapades in his absence, *niña!*" Sofía blustered, looking for all the world as mad as the proverbial wet hen. "*Sí,* we shall see! I, for one, am done with your disobedience!"

"Pah! To hell with Don Felipe!" Krissoula flared, stamping her foot and tossing her hair, and Sofía gasped and crossed herself as if before her eyes her charge had suddenly sprouted horns and tail, and smoke were pouring from her nostrils. "Felipe's a miserable, spiteful old man who wants no one to be happy or enjoy anything in life, and I'm done with following his silly, petty little orders, or— for that matter—yours!"

"Krissoula!" Sofía cried, aghast at her charge's behavior. Her hand flew up to cover her mouth, to soothe her pounding heart, as if she didn't know quite *what* to do with them.

"And don't 'Krissoula' me, either, Sofía! What's done is done, and what happened yesterday can't be changed, so you might as well be relieved that I'm home, safe and well, and forget about it. Carrying tales to Don Felipe will only cause more unnecessary trouble for all of us. And besides, there's always the possibility that if you tell him about yesterday, he'll ask questions and find out about our *first* visit to Lupe—which was also in disobedience to his orders—remember, Sofía? The visit on which *you* accompanied me? Still, if you're prepared to deal with Don Felipe's anger, that is your business, no?" she finished casually but with a sharp eye on her duenna, who was sputtering in confusion and looked as if Krissoula had struck her.

"But—but you promised to say nothing of that, Krissoula, on condition that I gave in to your wishes?" she whispered.

"And I won't," Krissoula promised, a little more gently, "unless it comes out—as it surely must *if* you tell Don Felipe about last night . . . ?"

She slipped her arm around Sofía and smiled winningly. "Come, come, there's no harm done, really there isn't, Sofía darling! A few wrinkled clothes, a sleepless night—nothing more. Let's just forget all of this, go inside and have breakfast, and pretend nothing's happened, agreed?"

"Do I have a choice, *niña?*" Sofía asked, tight-lipped.

Krissoula felt an uncomfortable pang of guilt for a moment or two, although she tightened her jaw and answered, "We always have choices, Sofía, and I've made mine. It's now up to you to make yours, to decide whether you answer to Don Felipe or me, or only to yourself. For my part, as of today I'm done with trying to behave like that dead woman, the saintly Manuela. Finished with pretending to be the meek, spiritless creature Don Felipe wants me to be! From now on, I shall be myself, and if *el patrón* finds Krissoula Ballardo, with her taste for dancing, bright colors, having fun, and all her other faults unacceptable as his future wife, then we'll just have to live with that decision, and adjust our future plans accordingly, no?"

So saying, she swept into the house with a bearing as haughty as any Spanish infanta of the blood royal, despite the wrinkled, deplorable state of her riding outfit and the tangled condition of her hair, leaving poor Sofía no choice but to trail inside after her, close to shedding fresh tears over Krissoula's unkindness, but bravely fighting them.

Chapter Twenty

Esteban stabled Barbaro and Girasol, and made his way to the bunkhouse where the hands were enjoying a hearty hot breakfast, sheltered from the drizzling rain by an overhanging thatched roof under which a long trestle table had been set up, with several rough wooden benches pulled up to it. Over a dozen men were seated at the table, swigging steaming *maté* or hot, black coffee laden with sugar, and enthusiastically forking up platters heaped with a breakfast of eggs and *chorizos*, thick pan-fried steaks, beans, and folded tortillas dipped in *salsa*, which Angelina and her daughters had prepared for the wet, hungry search party's return.

He took off his hat and set it carefully beneath the bench out of the way of careless feet, sliding his long, lean body into the empty seat beside Tomás.

"There you are, San Martín!" Tomás greeted him with an unusual lack of warmth. "I hear you found the señorita safe and sound?"

Esteban met Tomás's eyes and he winked. "Indeed I did, Tomás," he acknowledged. "She was forced to seek shelter for the night and wait out the storm, but she's quite unharmed, other than for being a little damp." He had no intention of lying to his obviously angry friend, and his statement covered the truthful facts of the matter without, he felt, any need for elaboration. "You did a fine job, *muchachos,*" he praised the *gauchos* and ranch hands seated about him. "I'm sure the señorita would want me to convey her thanks to you for your efforts last night."

"And what of you, *Señor Mayordomo?*" came a sneering voice laced with innuendo. "Did the lovely doña also convey her thanks to you for *your* efforts last night?"

A bray of loud, bawdy laughter erupted from some men, but was abruptly cut off. A crackling silence, broken only by the soft patter of the rain, followed, lasting for seconds that seemed endless.

"If you mean for escorting the señorita back to the *casa grande,* yes, she was very grateful," Esteban said softly at length, refusing to rise to the man's crude taunt. "That *is* what you meant, isn't it, Luis?"

The slim, sharp-featured *gaucho* with oily black hair and a straggly moustache smiled from his seat clear at the other end of the table, showing tobacco-yellowed teeth. "But of course, *Señor Mayordomo!*" he purred. "What else could I possibly have meant?" He slyly side-eyed his companions and grinned. "Forgive me for asking, señor, but—where did you say you found her?"

Esteban's jaw tightened, and a dangerous spark kindled in his sapphire eyes. "I didn't say, Luis," he said in a tightly controlled voice, his hands knotting into fists on the scarred tabletop. "But what difference does it make where I found her?"

"Oh, none at all, señor, none at all!" Luis disclaimed, inspecting his dirty, broken fingernails. "It's just that Señor Cabral sent Pepé and me in a westerly direction last night, searching for Doña Krissoula, and we saw a horse very like the palomino mare she was riding in the *ramada* by your cottage. Pepé wanted to ride up to the house, and ask you if you'd seen the doña, señor. But I said to Pepé that we must, of course, be mistaken. That the mare could not have belonged to the señorita, for surely if it'd done so, our *mayordomo* would have escorted her safely back to the *casa* long before nightfall, no?"

A titter ran through the assembled men, and the muscle in Esteban's jaw worked violently.

"If you have something to say, Luis, then go ahead and say it—unless, that is, you're too much of a coward to do more than make insinuations?" he urged silkily, aching to wrap his hands around Luis's scrawny throat.

"No one calls Luis a coward and gets away with it!" Luis flared, jumping to his feet. His bloodshot eyes were ugly, narrowed slits now. "If you want me to speak plainly, señor, then I'll do so!"

He turned to the twin rows of expectant faces uplifted towards his, bracing his palms on the tabletop. "*Compadres,* while we were risking our necks last night, out riding in the lightning and rain across pot-holed land where a horse can break a leg or a man his neck, our dear *mayordomo* here was snug and dry, with the woman we were searching for safely in his cabin! It was a long, foul night, eh, *amigos*—or, at least, it was for us! I wonder how the lovely Señorita Krissoula and Señor Esteban kept themselves busy all that time?" He wetted his lips and smirked. "I'd wager a month's pay it was not by betting on the fall of the 'bones' or by playing cards, eh, *amigos—?*"

His leer faded abruptly as an enraged Esteban leaped clear across the table in his direction with a roar of fury, knocking dishes every which way and hurling Luis backward to the dirt. Like quicksilver, Luis drew his wicked *facón,* his long-bladed dagger, from his boot cuff and sliced through the air scant inches from Esteban, narrowly missing his exposed face.

"What's the matter, San Martín?" Luis jeered. "Forced to defend your pretty little *china's* good name, are you, eh? Well, it's a little late for that, no, *hombre!* She doesn't have one to defend, not after last night!"

"You'd best shut your filthy mouth, *hombre,* while you still have one to shut!" Esteban seethed, tightening his grip and effectively silencing Luis, whose face was turning a mottled purple.

Luis forced the dagger in his fist downward, bringing it perilously close to Esteban's back, forcing him to release his own throat. Instead, Esteban swiveled sideways and gripped Luis's wrist, squeezing hard in an effort to force him to release the weapon. With a cry from Luis, it fell to the mud, and Esteban, gritting out an obscenity, kicked it viciously away from them both. Their flailing bodies sent scratching chickens flapping away, clucking with fright, and set the dogs to barking furiously with excitement.

The *gauchos* and hands had left their seats by now, food forgotten, and were circled around the pair, urging them on or placing bets on the outcome as if it were one of the bloody cockfights they so enjoyed, while from the kitchen doorway, a tense Mama Angelina and her startled daughters looked on, the pale-faced cook wringing her hands in her apron.

"Enough!" Tomás snapped, hurrying forward, his usually gentle face tight with anger. "Break it up, both of you!"

"Stay out of this!" Esteban ground out, breathing heavily. Luis put his second's distraction to good use and clipped him craftily under the jaw, sending him flying backwards.

"Why, you son of a bitch—!" Esteban lunged forward. His own knotty fist smacked full into Luis's mouth, splitting the hand's lip and loosening teeth. Blood poured down his chin, as it did from Esteban's wounds of the day before, now reopened. With a roar, he leaped at Luis again.

"The devil I'll stay out of it!" Tomás growled. "You, Ignacio! Take Luis! I'll handle this hotheaded fool!"

Tomás leaned over the scrapping pair and gripped Esteban's collar, hauling him off Luis, who was wildly trying to get in another punch as Ignacio did likewise to him. A second pair of men volunteered their services and, although not without a struggle that threatened to degenerate into a full-scale riot, they at last managed to pull the two furious men apart. Chests heaving, expressions murderous, they faced each other, held in check by Tomás and Ignacio.

"Luis, damn it, you're fired!" Tomás said grimly. "This isn't the first time you've stirred things up with that loose lip of yours, is it? Well, I've had it with you! Pick up your things and go!"

"Pah! And what about him?" he jeered, nodding his jaw at Esteban. "You would fire a man for telling only the truth, Señor Cabral, and let the man who plays with *el patrón*'s intended go unpunished? Where is the justice in that, eh? Pah! I spit on you, Cabral! Spit on you, and on Tierra Rosa!" he vowed, and did exactly that, a phlegmy missile landing scant inches from the toe of Tomás's boot. "You'll pay for this, San Martín!" Luis warned, jabbing a stubby brown finger in Esteban's direction. "By all the saints, I swear it. Someday, you and your woman will pay!"

With that, he slung off Ignacio's hand and stalked away.

Tomás released Esteban's arm and ordered the other men to return to their meal.

"Well?" the *domador* asked his friend, his expression still furious. "Are you satisfied now, blockhead?"

Esteban smiled thinly. "I'd have been more satisfied if you'd let me finish what I started, *amigo,*" he gritted, spitting out a piece of gravel and wiping his mouth on his sleeve.

"You expect me to stand by and let you kill a man for speaking the truth, however crudely?" Tomás shook his head, his gentle face tense. "No, Esteban, I couldn't let you do that, friends or no! After all, we both know that Luis was right, don't we? I rode out to your cottage myself in the wee hours, intending to ask you to join the search party. I saw the mare, instead. That's when I signaled the others to return to the *casa grande,* my friend. You see, I didn't see the point in having good men spending the night riding around in circles on a wild-goose chase, looking for a woman who wasn't really lost! Damn! What the devil's come over you lately? You must be mad, *hombre,* to think this won't get back to Don Felipe's ears! What happens to your position here when it does? And what happens to the girl, tell me that, eh, my friend—or don't you give a damn?"

"Oh, I give more than a damn, my friend! And don't worry, Tomás, I'll take care of everything," Esteban growled uncomfortably, knowing in his heart that, as usual, Tomás was right. He hesitated, then added with difficulty, the words wrenched out of him, "I'm in love with her, Tomás—and Krissoula loves me. Just as soon as I can get things figured out, she's leaving Don Felipe and Tierra Rosa. She's coming away with me."

"What's this? Then you're abandoning your efforts to reclaim the *estancia?*" Tomás whistled through his teeth in surprise. "Aiee, *Dios!* I never thought to hear that!"

"Nor I," Esteban agreed with a grim smile, then winced and fingered the purplish swelling at his jaw. For all his slim build, Luis's fists had packed a hefty wallop! "And you don't know the half of the hell I've been through to come to that decision! Krissoula and I were—well, I'll tell you all about it someday, the whole story. But meanwhile, I've finally realized that I've been wasting the past two years of my life, trying to pin my father's murder on my uncle, and in trying to recover Tierra Rosa. I've finally admitted to myself that, if there was ever any written proof of my birth, Felipe's probably destroyed it. If not, it would have surfaced by now. And, unless that son of a bitch confesses, I'll never be able to prove he killed my father that night. So. I've finally seen the light! I've decided it's time I gave up chasing shadows, and got on with the rest of my life. With Krissoula."

Tomás nodded in understanding and approval, and clapped his friend warmly across the back. "I'm glad to hear it, my friend! Perhaps there's a slim hope for you yet, now that you've given up your crazy idea of revenging Don Alejandro's death. After all, is there not an old saying that goes, 'Revenge is an empty cup, acceptance a full one'? I wish you both good fortune and happiness, my friend, with the beautiful woman you have chosen. And if I'm not mistaken, I believe time will prove the two of you well matched . . . !" He chuckled and shook his head as he clapped Esteban across the shoulders.

"That sounded more like a threat than a wish for my future happiness, Tomás!" Esteban protested.

"Take it any way you want to, friend—I have better things to do!" He whipped his *chambergo* from his head and clasped it to his chest, his brown eyes shining as he looked over Esteban's shoulder.

"Why, *buenos días,* Señorita Estrella! I should have known that the rain ceased to fall, only because an angel had appeared!" he complimented her in true Argentinian fashion, nodding at the brightening sky, where a weak sun was trying to shine through. "And how are you this morning, señorita?"

"Thank you, I am very well, Señor Cabral," Esteban heard Estrella respond shyly as she came towards them. "I—I just wanted to tell you, señor, how very much I admired the way you stepped in and put an end to the—the trouble. It was so brave of you!" Her gentle brown eyes shone with admiration, and Tomás puffed up like a rooster.

"Ah, but it was nothing—all in a day's work, señorita . . ." he heard Tomás disclaim with an effort at nonchalance which didn't deceive Esteban for a minute! "Perhaps you would do me the honor of taking a little walk with me through the gardens? The rain has stopped, no, and look, I believe the sun is coming out . . ."

Hiding a smile, Esteban retrieved his hat and headed for the stables. Tomás and Estrella were well matched, both shy, gentle people; decent people. They were as different from him and his fiery, tempestuous *minina* as day is to night—and he wouldn't have wanted it any other way!

But, curiously, he found himself looking forward to a time—one hopefully not too far in the future—when he could take Krissoula walking through a flower-filled garden somewhere with his arm about her waist, and not give a tinker's damn who saw them . . .

It was two full weeks before Krissoula and Esteban were able to find a way to be alone together again, and each day they spent apart plodded by as if on feet of lead.

Felipe returned from wherever it was he'd been, seeming smug and filled with self-importance and a simmering excitement, barely repressed, but divulging nothing of his mysterious business or his mysterious associates, except for an odd comment to Krissoula over supper one night, when he asked her, "So, my dear, tell me— how would you like to preside over a supper table of two hundred guests someday, eh?"

Krissoula had raised her brows in surprise at his question, but she finished chewing her meat before answering, "Two hundred? I hardly think we'd have room for two hundred guests here at Tierra Rosa, Felipe! The dining room is far too small to handle more than sixty, at most, for a sit-down dinner, no? We might manage a wonderful buffet, though?"

"Here, *sí!*" Felipe scoffed. "But—I was not talking about here, dear heart! I was wondering how you would enjoy being the hostess for sumptuous dinners and balls in Buenos Aires, with distinguished guests from the capitals of the world at your table, eh?" he'd asked, smiling and cocking dark brows in her direction.

"Don't be silly, Felipe!" she'd chided prettily, softening the caution with a smile. "Why, it's not as if you're one of President Mitre's Cabinet and in the least likely to have to host State visits and so on, is it, my dear?"

"So long as Bartolomé Mitre is in control, regrettably no," he admitted, and shot her a sly look. "But—perhaps poor Presidente Mitre's days are numbered? Perhaps the rich and influential of Argentina have wearied of a man who concerns himself overmuch with the welfare of the poor and the disadvantaged, and who find his plans to educate the masses a stupid waste of revenues, far better spent elsewhere? Perhaps they're ready for someone new? Someone who'll see that the wealthy landowners, the rich bankers and businessmen of our country, are given the positions and rewards they so justly deserve, for making Argentina the prosperous land it is," he declared pompously. "And, Krissoula, when that day comes, the new *presidente* will perhaps remember his friends and backers with gratitude, and see that positions of power and respect go to those who truly deserve them."

"To those who got rich carried on the backs of the peasants, you mean? To those who grew fat and sleek on the lifeblood of the poor and oppressed?" she asked innocently, her eyes round and guileless.

His features had tensed with annoyance. "*Caray!* I should have known a mere woman couldn't hope to comprehend the intricate workings of government and politics! Enjoy your supper, Krissoula *mía,* and put this complex matter out of your pretty little head . . ."

Hiding a smile, Krissoula had taken his advice and devoured the remainder of her delicious meal, making a mental note to tell Esteban about the incident. Could their peculiar conversation have something to do with whatever it was Jaime Ramirez and Felipe were up to, she'd wondered?

As she and Esteban had agreed, she'd not told Felipe that she was breaking their betrothal as yet, although she itched to do so! But she knew she'd been acting much cooler and far less meekly towards him since he'd returned home from Córdoba. She couldn't seem to help it, somehow.

Ever since the night of the storm, when Esteban had awakened her to his wild, sweet passion and crowned that glorious night by telling her that he loved her, she'd found it harder and harder with each passing day to keep up the front of "dutiful *novia*" for that old goat Felipe's benefit. She wanted to tell the whole wide world about the man she loved, and who loved her and wanted to make her his bride!

Perversely, however, her very coolness—instead of making Felipe grow distant himself, or become angry, as might have been expected—had an unforeseen reaction. To her dismay, he became increasingly *more* attentive! At every turn, he appeared to be laying in wait for her to appear, and spoke more and more often and more and more eagerly of their impending marriage in the month of October, which was now only a few weeks away.

On rising from her siesta in the afternoon, she'd find Felipe waiting downstairs, eager to take tea with her. He never failed to put in an appearance at supper, and had even insisted she accompany him on several little outings, one to the lake a few miles northeast of Tierra Rosa for a picnic which—to her secret delight—had been rained upon, and another time to the little church in a nearby village to hear their wedding banns formally read aloud by the priest for the first of the required three times—a circumstance that had made her belly churn with dread!

Her only escape from Felipe's company was the privacy of her own room. But too much time spent alone there inevitably resulted in her thinking too much about Esteban, and wishing—wishing with all her heart!—that she were in his arms, that they could be together, and done with all this silly pretense once and for all.

To occupy her time, she turned once again to Manuela's diary for entertainment, eager despite herself to read the account following Manuela's marriage to her beloved Alejandro of the "melting brown eyes," for head over heels in love as Krissoula was, she thrilled to anything as romantic as a wedding—even one that had taken place decades ago, before she was born. *Perhaps,* she dreamed wistfully, *someday soon I will be married to* mi querido, *and we will live happily ever after, like in the very best of fairy tales . . . ?*

But that night's reading proved a bitter disappointment. Manuela's last entry had ended with:

". . . and so tonight, Dear Diary, I fall asleep knowing I will awaken to a lifelong dream, and be married at last to my Alejandro! Fly quickly past, Night, for Morning will see me his bride!"

Heady stuff, no, Krissoula had thought with an impish grin, and it was with a sense of keen anticipation that she'd turned to the next page, ready to be thrilled by accountings of weather and wedding gown, flowers and ladies-in-waiting—only to find the harsh, ugly black scrawl that covered the next page nigh indecipherable, and dated some *four months* after the wedding!

262

Disgruntled, she was tempted to consign Manuela's disappointing outpourings to her chamber pot, where, in her opinion, it properly belonged, but in the end thought better of it, and sulkily returned the journal to her drawer.

Dios! If only there were something for her to do—something to drain off her restless energy and impatience, and turn her thoughts away from Esteban, all alone by the fire in his little cottage. He'd be smoking a *cigarillo* with his shaggy Rojo leaning cosily against him as they gazed into the fire, and thought of—her? Oh, *sí*, she hoped so! She smiled dreamily, resting her chin on her fist as she imagined Esteban's handsome face lit by the ruddy glow of the fire, his sapphire eyes glittering as they reflected its light. Aaaah! She hugged herself about the arms. If she closed her eyes, she could almost feel his warmth surrounding her, smell the unique, male scent that was his in her nostrils, and which was as dear and familiar to her as her own hand. What would the future bring them, she wondered? Happiness? A family? Ah, *sí*, she could well imagine Esteban as a fond papa, bouncing their little ones on his knee, if her poor little Nicki's arduous birth had not ruined her body for the bearing of other children.

Far from her dreamy fantasies deadening the ache in her breast for her beloved, they only served to sharpen it. Soon she was again pacing the flowered carpet in her room like a restless wildcat, confined by the bars of a cage. *Caramba!* If only she could see him? She had to see him! Aiee, *Madre,* if only there was a way—!

Ah, but she *could* see him—and more—she thought suddenly, pulling up short, if she really wanted to. After all, his cottage wasn't far away, not on horseback? Excitement filled her. She could climb down over the balcony as easy as breathing! After all, she'd done it before!—and from there slip out to the stables. She'd need no saddle to ride Girasol, just a rope halter. In a matter of minutes, she could be riding through the night to Esteban's arms, and return before dawn pinked the sky—and neither fussy Sofía or that old goat Felipe need be any the wiser, asleep in their little beds!

The idea of hoodwinking the pair was a delicious one, and made her giggle. Why not? She asked herself. She'd do it, and laugh at the shocked and delighted expression on Esteban's face when he opened his door to find her there!

Krissoula was not one to linger overlong once her mind was made up. Acting swiftly, she pulled on a dark skirt and blouse, tossed a dark cloak over them, and made her way out onto the balcony.

In less than fifteen minutes, she'd reached the stables, had bridled Girasol, and led the mare quietly to the wrought-iron gates of Tierra Rosa, which boasted a pineapple design, the symbol of hospitality. Another minute, and she'd swung astride her mare's bare back and was off, racing over the darkened Pampa under the light of the full moon; winging her way to the arms of her lover—unaware of the jealous eyes that marked her departure, or of the bare brown feet that doggedly followed her path . . .

"Minina, you minx! How did you get here?" Esteban exclaimed in delight, gathering her into his arms and covering her throat with hungry kisses on answering her knock at his door.

"On Girasol, of course! How else, *tonto?"* she retorted cheekily, squirming under his ticklish kisses and pleased by his obvious happiness at seeing her. "Come, come, *querido!* At least let me get inside before you attack me, *bribón!"*

"Ah, but I can't wait!" he growled huskily, grinning broadly. "Even another minute without you is a minute too long!"

Nonetheless, he closed the door behind her, tucked her hand through his elbow, and led her across to the fireplace. Sheepskins had been strewn on the floor before it to make a cozy bed by the hearth.

"I was lying there, gazing into the flames, thinking of you," he confessed as her eyebrows rose quizzically, "wishing you were here with me, *querida."*

She leaned up on tiptoe and kissed him lightly on the lips. Her kiss confirmed her suspicions. His lips tasted of rum. "Ah. You've been drinking a little, no?"

He grinned down at her again and dropped a kiss on the tip of her little nose. "No, *minina.* Actually, it was a *lot*tle! *Caray,* I've missed you so these past weeks! I thought a shot or two of *caño* at the village *pulpería* might numb my heartache."

"And—?" she asked archly, cocking her head to one side as she looked up at him. "Did it work?"

"Not a chance, worse luck! Two shots—and I was still thinking of you. Four shots—and I was singing your praises to the poor proprietor and a handful of drunken *gauchos.* Five—and they'd politely asked me to be on my way—said I was depressing their customers with my *Tristes!* So you see, nothing worked, darling—until now!"

"I'm glad to hear it!" she teased, her golden eyes sparkling, her

264

lips a glistening invitation. "I'd hate to think you'd found an easy substitute for Krissoula in a bottle, *gato*. Now quickly, won't you undress me, *mi amor?*" She pouted prettily. "I want to be beautiful for you. I want to be naked for you. I want to lie in your arms and have you kiss me and hold me tight in these wonderful, strong arms, and make love to me all night long!" she whispered ardently, caressing those arms.

"You ask so much of me, woman, but—" he grinned roguishly, "a poor man can only do his best, no? Turn around, *querida* . . ."

Nimble fingers unfastened the hooks at the back of her blouse— most of them left unfastened to start with, or fastened wrongly, since she'd dressed without help! The same nimble fingers unbuttoned and drew down her skirt. Except for a thin camisole, she was quite naked beneath her outer clothes, and she laughed huskily at the bemused expression on his face as he saw her curves revealed through the brief, filmy garment.

"Are you shocked that I came here so—ready—to be loved?" she asked, flirting her sooty lashes at him as she ran her hands down over her body in a way calculated to drive any normal man to distraction.

"Come here, little tease, and find out . . . !"

He reached for her, but she backed away, out of his reach, laughing in a delightful, smoky way that made the hardness at his groin tauten unbearably.

But soon, he had her backed into a corner of the cottage with no escape, and was sliding the ribbon straps of her camisole down over her shoulders, then her arms, baring her lovely, pointed breasts and upper body inch by glorious inch. Eyes darkening with passion in the firelight that played over her, he slid the flimsy camisole down over her lower body. His hands brushed her bare skin in a sweeping caress as he did so. As the undergarment slithered down to her ankles, she gracefully stepped from it and stood before him with a pounding heart.

"You're lovely!" he whispered, cupping her little heart-shaped face between his hands as his dark eyes searched hers. "So damned lovely! You wear the beauty God gave you like a queen wears a crown, Krissoula *mía* . . ."

He ducked his head, and she closed her eyes and offered her lips to his hungry mouth, gasping as he kissed her long and hard and so thoroughly she was breathless with longing when he broke away. He kissed her throat, then moved his head lower to the valley between her breasts. Kissing the very tips of each one, his lips were like the brush of feathers on her bare skin.

She moaned and laced her fingers through his crisp hair, feeling the fire ignite in her body, fanned by his ardent caresses. Almost on his knees at her feet now, he kissed her waist and the curves of her hips. He teased the indentation of her navel, and nuzzled the ebony fluff of curling hair that crowned the joining of her thighs. She was quivering now, he noticed, trembling with desire and scarce able to stand unaided. Straightening up again, he took her hand and led her to the sheepskins, lying down and gently tugging her across him.

"The fire's warm. Our bed is soft. And you—aah, you're here, in my arms, sweetheart!" He brushed a tendril of inky hair from her flushed cheek, and smiled up at her. "I must have been *loco* to think there was anything else I wanted in life."

Smiling, she leaned up on her elbow where she lay across his chest, and traced the angle of his cheek and jaw with her fingertip. She liked the way his lashes looked, so thick and dark against his tanned complexion. Liked the way his cheekbones jutted just a little, giving his face a savagely handsome, hawklike cast, the rough feeling of his stubbled cheeks and jaw.

"You sound like a poet when you speak to me that way, 'Steban!" she murmured, and kissed his lips very softly. "Your words make me so excited—almost as excited as your touch."

She stuck out her tongue, and delicately ran it along the margin of his lips, trailed it down over his chin, then along his obstinate jawline to his ear. Once there, she circled the tiny pink tip around the sensitive whorl of flesh, and nibbled at the lobe. He gave a great shudder and drew away, unable to bear her teasing torture in his arousal. She laughed huskily, delighted by his response. "So, my fine *gato*," she demanded seductively. "Do you like the 'poet's words' Krissoula whispers, too?"

"I do!" he agreed roguishly. "But—there's something I like better!"

He raised her above him, so that one of her breasts was angled above his parted lips and greedily suckled at the swollen crest for a moment or two before drawing it deep into his mouth, swirling his tongue around and around the sensitive bud until she squirmed and ground her hips down hard against his flanks.

"Aiee, *diablo!* Don't torture Krissoula so!" she cried softly, but he only laughed and turned his full attention to her other breast, arousing it as he had the first.

Little gasps were breaking from her parted lips, and her eyes were half closed, heavy-lidded, when his hand skimmed down her sleek little body to cup her bottom, then plunder the warmth between her thighs.

"Yes, oh, *sí!*" she whimpered as his fingers deftly pressed apart the soft folds, seeking entry, teasing the hidden bud of her passion.

She was ready, more than ready for him, he could tell, and it had been too damned long since they'd made love the last time—! Gripping her hips, he lifted her astride him, watching her expression change in the flickering, ruddy firelight from one of languor, to one naked with desire as she slowly lowered herself onto his thighs and took him deep inside her.

Leaning back, she undulated her hips, fitting herself perfectly to him in a sensual way that made him groan and clench his teeth with the sweet agony of pleasure that shot through him. Black ringlets tumbling down over rounded bare shoulders, her firm breasts jiggling just a little with her sensual gyrations, she rode him passionately, mercilessly; rode him until he could bear the denial no longer and had to take her. With a growl, he hauled her down across his chest and rolled her beneath him, parting her thighs and thrusting deeply into her again and again, until she cried out her pleasure in the self-same moment that he, with a roar that shook the rafters, found his.

For a while, they slept in the fire-warmed cottage, light and shadow playing across the whitewashed walls and Rojo snuffling contentedly in his sleep by the hearth. She was awakened to more kisses, to more caresses, by a laughing Esteban, who gathered her up into his arms and declared he was insatiable, that he couldn't get enough of her. Lazily this second time, they explored each other's bodies, kissing and fondling each other gently, learning what gave the other greatest pleasure, building their passion slowly, exquisite moment by moment, and finally slaking their hunger in an unhurried coupling that ebbed and flowed, rose and fell, like a lazy, wonderful warm tide, before finally granting them the sweetest release of all.

Sleek and content as a kitten after a full bowl of the most delectable cream, Krissoula sighed and cuddled up against Esteban, nestled in the crook of his arm with her palm resting possessively on his hairy chest.

"Ahh, *querido*, you were so wonderful!" she murmured drowsily, happily.

"Mmm huh," he mumbled sleepily. "I know."

"*Bribón!*" She smiled, tousling his chest hair. "You know, I laughed when I first read Doña Manuela's diary," she observed

267

idly. "Her singing Alejandro's praises over and over sounded so childish and foolish. But—I know better now. I know *exactly* how she felt when she wrote those words! Love does that to you, no, *querido?* It makes you giddy—"

"What diary?" he asked suddenly, no longer sounding sleepy. "What did you say, *querida?*"

A momentary pang of guilt filled her as, belatedly, she remembered she'd said nothing of finding Manuela's diary to Esteban, planning at the time to keep any secrets it might reveal to herself, or perhaps destroy it if the information its pages held had proven a threat to her plan of double-crossing him and marrying Felipe!

"Doña Manuela's diary. She—she wrote about how much in love with Alejandro she was, and it sounded silly to me at first, and so I—"

"Manuela's diary? Where did you find it?"

"In her room, of course, tucked in a drawer. But it isn't important, believe me—"

He sat bolt upright, running his hands through his disheveled hair. "In her rooms! And when was this?"

He looked straight at her, straight into her eyes with his own penetrating sapphire ones, and something within her quailed.

"A—a few days ago," she whispered, looking quickly away, looking anywhere but at him.

"No. You're lying to me—I can see it in your face!" he accused softly, and gripping her chin, he turned her face up to his. "When, *querida?*" he repeated.

"Oh, all right!" she snapped crossly, furious that unlike everyone else, she couldn't seem to lie to him. "I found it a—a few weeks ago."

"What! And you said nothing about it to me?"

"I told you, it didn't seem important!" she defended herself, sitting up and gathering one of the sheepskins around her. "And it's not—it's just a lot of silly nonsense about falling in love and—"

"You should have told me anyway, Krissoula—and let me be the judge of its importance!" he snapped, infuriated. Then a thought occurred to him. "Exactly why *didn't* you say anything about it before, Krissoula? Because you didn't think it was important—or because you had some other reason? Because—just maybe—you were still planning to double-cross me and marry my uncle, perhaps?"

"No! That's not so!" she protested, yet still found she couldn't

268

meet his blazing eyes.

"Isn't it? Pah! Look at you!" he accused, his voice a razor's edge now, cutting her to the quick. "You can't even look me in the face and swear it, can you? Can you, damn it—?" he repeated more angrily, gripping her elbow and shaking her. "You little cheat! You still intended to double-cross me, didn't you, even after I warned you that night what would happen if you tried it! You still planned to go through with it!"

"All right, damn you, yes!" she hissed, tossing her head, her own golden eyes blazing into his now. "I planned to double-cross you and marry Felipe, despite your warning that night, I admit it! Are you satisfied now? But then—then we spent the night together, and I knew I loved you, Esteban, that I'd loved you for a long, long time and that I couldn't betray you," she whispered imploringly, "and everything changed."

"Not everything, *minina,*" he said coldly. "You had ample time the night of the storm to tell me about the diary. Why didn't you, if by then 'everything had changed'?"

"Oh, I don't know!" she flung back at him. "I suppose—I suppose being here with you, I forgot! Besides, there's nothing in the diary that can help you prove your claim, I swear it! It's just a young girl's thoughts and feelings, that's all it is. I'll bring it to you—you can read it for yourself! Please, Esteban, you must believe me, I wasn't planning to double-cross you, not now, not this time, I swear to you!"

"How can I believe you, Krissoula? How can I trust you, when you've lied to me so many times already?" he demanded.

"Because I ask you to!" she pleaded. "Because I swore a blood-oath to you that I'd never betray the one I love!"

"Love? Ha! Are you sure you love me?" he asked bitterly, his mouth an ugly, twisted shape in his disillusionment. "Are you sure you didn't discover something that could support my claim in Manuela's diary, and decide to switch alliances and marry a rich *young* fool, instead of an old one?"

She dealt him a ringing slap across the cheek, so loaded with fury he rocked back on his heels, his head sharply averted.

"Devil take you, whoreson dog!" she spat, outraged by his accusations. "How dare you accuse me of any such thing! *Caray,* I must have been crazy to come here tonight—crazy to risk everything—crazy to think I loved you—and even crazier to think for one minute that you loved me—! It's Tierra Rosa you really want, and all that goes with it, isn't it? You never loved me, San

Martín! You only said you did to make sure that I—your stupid little Gypsy accomplice—would come trotting after you, dutifully bringing you any information I found, like a faithful hound retrieving a stick you'd thrown for it. *Loco,* that's what I am! I really didn't see it, till now! Like a fool, I b-believed you when you said you loved me—"

She hurriedly tugged on her clothes and started for the door, trembling with hurt and fury, to find Esteban blocking her exit.

"Move!" she hissed. "Out of my way! I'll not stay here a moment longer!"

"Angry or no, I love you, Krissoula."

"The devil you love me! Move, I said! Step aside!"

"No. I won't let you go like this."

"I'm not giving you a choice, *hombre.* I have my pride, too, you know—and I don't stay where I'm not wanted nor trusted. Out of the way—and quickly, *gato!* I have to run back to the *casa grande* and tell my dear Felipe every little thing you've said, so that we can make plans to rid ourselves of you, once and for all!" she jeered, her golden eyes blazing, her lips thin with fury.

"Krissoula, for God's sake, stop it—!"

But in answer, she brought up her knee and slammed it hard into his groin, taking advantage of him being doubled over by pain to push past him and fling herself through the door, running out into the night like a wild thing.

Before he'd fully recovered, she was gone, a slim black silhouette with her long, inky hair streaming behind her like a banner in the wind, riding swiftly away.

Chapter Twenty-One

Somehow, she made it back to Tierra Rosa, although she did so more as a result of Girasol's unerring instinct for finding her stable than from any credit due her rider, whose eyes smarted with tears that refused to fall, unable to find the path.

Long before the walls of the *hacienda* came into view, her anger had gone, leaving her with a cold, empty misery in her heart instead. How joyful she'd been when she slipped from her room that night, imagining only a few blissful, stolen hours in the arms of her lover awaited her, and a future filled with happiness at his side stretching before her. But now, in the space of a few angry words, a few rash threats born of pride, she was alone again. A lump filled her breast and her throat constricted painfully. *Sí,* more alone than she'd ever been before, somehow. Her street urchin's courage failed her now, in the hour when she needed it most. She couldn't find it in her to tell herself it didn't matter, she could go on without him, and spit in the world's eye at the unkind blow fate had dealt her yet again. She wanted to crawl away and cower somewhere dark and small, curled in a ball like an injured wild animal, and blot out the hurt. To wail and sob and shriek until the ache in her heart, the longing for those precious few days of happiness with Esteban, dissolved and became a more bearable, dull throb.

Coupled with the misery was a feeling of anger at herself, anger at the stiff pride that had deafened her ears and hardened her heart to his words. *"Angry or not, I love you, Krissoula,"* he'd said, and his eyes had beseeched her to stay, even as her pride had urged her to run and go on running, rather than risk still greater hurt. What was the point in staying, in hearing him out, when nothing could come of it? He hadn't trusted her! Even after the blood-oath she'd sworn, he hadn't trusted her, or believed in her loyalty. As Miguel had dared to doubt he was her child's father, Esteban had doubted she was telling the truth about Manuela's diary. And what kind of love could exist without trust? No. She was glad she'd run, glad she'd hurt him! She ignored utterly the nagging little voice of her conscience that reminded her she'd given Esteban precious little reason to trust her to date. The voice that insisted trust must be earned, and was never given gratis. If he'd really loved her, she told herself stubbornly and quite irrationally, he'd have known instinctively that she was telling the truth . . .

The remainder of the night seemed endless to Krissoula in her upset. She couldn't sleep, and when morning came a pounding headache behind her eyes and an upset stomach had added to her discomfort; she, who'd never known a day's sickness in her life! Wanly telling a concerned Sofia that she was feeling unwell and had decided to spend the day abed, she lay there on her back, staring up at the ceiling, wishing with all her heart that she'd not gone to Esteban's cottage the night before . . . that she'd kept quiet about the diary . . . that she'd stayed there and tried harder to convince him of her loyalty and her love . . . that she hadn't planned to double-cross him, ever . . . oh, she had a million regrets for the words she'd said in anger, or left unsaid on account of wounded pride!

She really did feel ill by the time she dragged herself out of bed and dressed for tea that afternoon, weak and shaky and exhausted. Yet, nevertheless, she surrendered to the faint but persistent pangs of hunger stirring in her belly, certain she'd feel much better if she ate a little something—after all, she always had in the past!

Yet the sight of those heaped platters of golden-brown *empanadas,* plump with their fillings of meat and spices, and the fishy smell of Angelina's dainty salmon-and-cucumber sandwiches —which she usually loved!—made her stomach heave. Paling, she hurriedly excused herself and fled the *sala,* finding her way instead to the kitchen, where her wan complexion and obvious listlessness easily produced the tangy apples she really craved from Angelina's store of fresh fruits, along with the kindly cook's admonishment to rest until she was feeling much better.

To her surprise, on returning to her room she found she was able to sleep, and dropped off thinking about Esteban, and wondering how she could possibly think of sleeping for even a minute, when her poor heart ached so for him . . .

When she awoke, it was already full dark outside her window. The pale moon had risen and the stars were twinkling far above. She felt a little better, she discovered, stretching, although the ache was still there, in her breast. Perhaps it would always be there from

272

here on? she thought miserably. Perhaps it would never go away, and she'd carry the hurt she felt in this moment to her grave, like a battle scar, though a hidden one received on the battlegrounds of love, rather than war. Pah! What a goose she was, allowing her thoughts to dwell so on a man like San Martín, she told herself! *Put him out of your head,* tonta! *Find a way to show him he means nothing to you, and spit in his eyes!* she told herself sternly.

She forced herself to get up, with enormous effort, and poured water from an ewer into the porcelain washbasin, stripped off and bathed herself, then briskly toweled dry. The water had refreshed her considerably. Sitting before her dressing table, she took up a brush and mercilessly brushed her hair until it shone like a rippling blue-black waterfall about her shoulders. Her toilette completed, she pulled open a drawer to find fresh underclothes—and her eyes fell once again on Manuela's cursed diary.

What if Esteban's suspicions had been right? she wondered reluctantly. What if there *was* something written between those fusty pages she'd missed that would prove Alejandro de Aguilar had fathered him, after all? Some bitter, jealous comment that Manuela had made when she discovered her faithful duenna, Maria de San Martín, had become her husband's mistress and borne him a child, perhaps? It was possible, she had to admit . . .

Oh, to hell with it—and with him—! To hell with all of it! She'd had enough of San Martín, enough of Felipe and Tierra Rosa, of all of it! She was done with chasing shadows and searching for imaginary papers. The whole idea was ridiculous, a waste of her time . . .

She started to turn away from the dresser, but the idea that the very information she'd been searching for all these weeks might be there, in the next few pages, just waiting for her to read it, was a tantalizing one, and not easily ignored.

With a muttered curse, she scowled and snatched up the diary, resigned to spending an hour or two in reading. Besides, reading the diary *had* become something of a compulsion almost, of late, and since she knew she'd never be able to sleep, why try? The bitter quarrel between Esteban and her was still too fresh in her mind; the hateful things they'd said to each other still too raw and smarting to allow her to fall asleep easily. She'd read until her eyes ached and she could no longer stay awake, she determined, drawing the apples she'd begged from Angelina's pantry earlier to munch on while she did so.

Settling herself comfortably across the bed on her elbow, she opened the diary to the last page she'd read, then turned to the one following. The date scribbled at the top of the page read June, 1836, as she remembered noticing the night before—a date four months after the last entry, which had been shortly after Manuela and Alejandro's marriage in March of the same year. The handwriting was so erratic, it seemed almost to want to jump from the pages, and was disturbing somehow.

"*. . . unlike other little children who feared the dark, I was never afraid of the night before this,*" she read. "*I loved to sit in the gardens of Córdoba after the sun was gone down, enfolded in darkness as if it were a velvet cloak. The shadows were not to be feared. They were my friends in solitude! The quietness and serenity of mind I found there drew me closer to God.*

But all that has changed now, since that night made for joy became one of shame and terror. The gardens no longer hold comfort and peace of mind for me, but have become conspirators who offer concealment to my enemy. And I fear so to be alone! I dare not sleep without a lamp left burning to chase away the frightening shadows, or my dearest Alejandro or Maria close beside me for comfort. I trust no one and nothing to be as it appears anymore, for I have learned to my grief that the most familiar of faces can conceal the features of the beast. The beast that even now grows within me . . ."

Krissoula crossed herself with a shiver at the last, and then bit deep into the tart green apple, wondering as she crunched on it what it was Manuela had learned to fear—or if, quite simply, she had somehow gone mad? She shrugged, unable to unravel the heart of the matter from Manuela's cryptic scribblings. They were too different in personality for Krissoula to be able to put herself totally in Manuela's skin and decipher her hidden meanings.

There were several other entries in succeeding months, all in the same troubled vein, Krissoula discovered. She skimmed quickly through them, until another entry, written in October of the same year, caught her attention.

"*My prayers that I would be delivered from this torment have gone unanswered. The physician has told Alejandro that all is well, and he expects no difficulties when the time comes. How, I ask, can God permit such evil seed to flourish? Why was it not cast out, in answer to my prayers?*

Maria remains my strength, my comfort, yet although she tries so hard to sympathize, I sense she envies me a little, in her barren widow's state. Alejandro remains constant, the pure, golden light

*that keeps me going, when all else is darkness and despair. In truth,
I do not deserve his understanding, nor his forgiveness, I know. He
deserves so much more! I am tainted, soiled, unworthy to be his
wife, and yet he swears he loves me, and that nothing can ever
change that love. He tells me again and again that the fault lies not
within me, but in the heart of that other one. If only I could
convince myself of that! Blessed Madonna, I pray each night that
he speaks truly, and that when the time comes, as it someday must,
his feelings will not have changed . . ."*

Krissoula set the diary aside and stared long and hard at the
puddle of light spilled from the lamp, considering what she'd read
for several moments before flicking back through the pages to the
earlier entry. *Sí,* there it was, the part that had stuck in her mind:
"*. . . that night meant for joy became one of shame and terror,"*
Manuela had written.

Now, she pondered, What night would Manuela — being the kind
of woman she'd been—have considered meant for "joy"? She
frowned. Taking into account Manuela's blissful expectations of
her marriage to Alejandro of the "melting brown eyes," she could
only be referring to her wedding night, could she not? *Sí,* she must
be. And something terrible had happened on that night, to change it
from one of joy, to one of "shame and terror" . . . ?

Shame. Could the loss of her virginity at Alejandro's hands have
turned her mind, Manuela having been delicately, religiously
raised, Krissoula wondered? No. She thought not, else why would
Manuela write so fondly of her husband in the months afterward?
Surely her writings would be bitter, hate-filled, in all references to
him, if that were so? Therefore, it could not have been Alejandro
who had caused her shame and terror on her wedding night, but
some other man—the "beast" hidden by the "familiar" face, in the
"gardens that offered concealment" to her enemy! There! That was
it. It had to be!

Chills ran down her spine. Someone Manuela knew and trusted
had lain in wait for her in the gardens and taken her innocence on
her wedding night—and that man had not been her bridegroom,
Alejandro de Aguilar!

Alejandro had obviously been told of what had happened, or had
learned of it somehow, but he'd reassured his distraught bride that
the sin was not hers, but "lay in the heart of that other one." *Caray!*
What rare kind of man had he been, this saint, this Alejandro de
Aguilar! Krissoula thought with a wry grimace and a rolling of her
eyes. A *gitano* bridegroom, cheated of his bride's dowry of

275

innocence, would have torn out the guilty man's heart, and eaten it alive while it yet pumped! Such compassion was almost beyond her understanding—almost, until she remembered that Alejandro had loved Manuela to distraction, and would have wanted above all things to protect her, even at cost to his honor.

"The beast that even now grows within me," Manuela had continued on that later date. Beast? Had the woman somehow believed herself contaminated by the evil lust that had cruelly taken her innocence from her? She frowned, her thoughts exploring one possibility, then another. What would logically grow inside one after such an experience? Revulsion for all men, perhaps? Self-loathing? A feeling of being unclean and unworthy of the husband she loved? *Sí.* All possible. That would explain the rumors abounding about the Aguilars' marriage, and the gossip that Manuela had never shared her husband's bed. Was that the "beast" she spoke of?

Or—Krissoula amended, excitement suddenly filling her—could Manuela have been speaking *literally?* She flipped hurriedly back through the earlier pages, and there was her proof. A thrill of excitement ran through her, for the meaning was obvious when the writings were read in a certain light; Manuela had been left *encinta,* with child, by her attacker! And not unnaturally, she'd loathed the babe she carried, the "evil seed" that God had let "flourish" in her womb; loathed the knowledge that the man she thought of only as an animal, a shadowy "beast" springing from the darkness of the gardens, had impregnated her.

Dios, she had to read on now, couldn't stop there! She had to discover if Manuela had safely birthed her unwanted babe, and if so, what had become of it? Had Alejandro persuaded her to give the infant up to an orphanage? Or had it—mercifully, for Manuela's sanity, at least—been stillborn, as so many children were in these hard times, when childbed fever and hemorrhage claimed so many women in the lying-in period, and their infants with them?

There were no further entries for over a year, Krissoula noted, glancing at the dates that headed each page, but when the jottings continued, the handwriting was much improved, less wildly erratic than before and more like the earlier scribblings.

"It is soon to be over, thanks be to God. We leave here tomorrow. Perhaps, when we are far from Mar de la Plata, and settled in at Tierra Rosa, my life will take on a semblance of happiness and normalcy once again, and I can forget these terrible months?

Maria, my rock, has once again stepped into the breach, and has

276

undertaken the infant's care. What would we do without her, Dear Diary? And yet, in all honesty, she seems to find the prospect no hardship, but a welcome solution. She dotes on it at every turn—as she has since the day it was born. I've tried, at Alejandro's urgings, to accept it, and yet find I cannot! Something in me revolts when it is near; the memory of its beginnings grow too sharp and painful to bear. How could any creature so innocent, so small, so impossibly like my Alejandro, have grown from such wickedness and sin? In truth, it is a mystery that only God, in His wisdom, knows the answer to!

Today, I asked Alejandro if he will seek to revenge himself against the one who dishonored me by demanding a duel. But he smiled strangely and patted my hand, and told me not to worry. He said that there were other, better ways to accomplish vengeance than by bloodshed, and that the child itself would be his revenge. Alas, I did not understand what he meant, for I am of less subtle a nature than he.

Alejandro has found a little house for Maria and the infant, and has purchased it for their use. It is in my own beloved town of Córdoba, close by the university. He has grown to love the child these past months, I know, and am not surprised that he should do so. Before we were married, Dear Diary, he told me that a glandular illness amongst the estancia's children when he was twelve had left him unable to father children himself. I know that secretly, he hopes in time my feelings for the babe will change, and that I'll grow to accept it and let it be raised as our flesh and blood at the estancia, for as do all men, Alejandro feels the need for an heir, a son to follow in his footsteps. But in my heart, I fear that day will never come. Even my love for my husband, my desire to be an obedient wife to him and my wish to please him in all things, can never override the loathing I feel for the boy, and for the vile act that created him . . ."

Trembling with the excitement of her discovery—and its shocking import!—Krissoula hurriedly scanned page after yellowed page like one possessed. But the succeeding pages of the five-year diary were taken up with Manuela's thoughts and feelings, the little triumphs and disappointments of her everyday married life, which, despite the pall cast over it by its black beginnings, despite the rumors Mama Angelina and her daughter Luisa had once hinted at, had seemed a happy one, after a fashion.

And then, Krissoula's eyes fell on another entry, and her heart skipped a beat. There! It was as she'd guessed, she realized, a shiver running through her. Now, all but one piece of the puzzle—the identity of the child's father—was solved, the mystery answered!

"*A secret, Dear Diary, I have a wonderful secret to share with you!*" Manuela's words bubbled in obvious high spirits. "*Alejandro and I are truly man and wife at last! His gentleness and patience with me have finally been rewarded. I no longer shrink from his touch and my duties as a wife, but welcome him to me with open arms and a fierce, sweet joy.*

"*I have been wondering these past few months how I could ever hope to repay my husband for his kindness, or show him the depth of my love, and now I think I have the answer. It came to me this morning, while at prayer in the little chapel here at Tierra Rosa. As I gazed up at the statue of the Blessed Madonna with the Christ Child in her arms, I thought of Maria and the boy, banished to Córdoba by my bitterness, and, wonder of wonders, the hatred inside me was gone, utterly gone! There was even a spark of yearning inside me to look upon the boy's face, a curiosity to see how he has grown in the two years since I last set eyes upon him. I know what I can do, Dear Diary, to make Alejandro a truly happy man! I will travel to Córdoba tomorrow, and see Maria and him. And, after Maria has seen that I'm fully recovered from my decline, I'll tell her the wonderful news, that she and the boy are to come home to Tierra Rosa, where they truly belong. When Alejandro returns from the city next week, he will find the family—the true wife and son—he has wanted for so very long awaiting him. Dear Diary, I'm so happy, and so very frightened all at once. Can I be a good mother to my son? Can I make the past two years of my neglect up to him? Or have I left it too late to even try?*"

The love, the excitement, the new serenity and peace of mind the woman had found with her resolve shone out from the pages like a warm, glowing light. Her subsequent writings recounted her journey to the university town of Córdoba, and her merriment at seeing the shock on poor Maria's face when she'd opened the door to find her former charge and mistress standing there, tearfully begging her and the three-year-old toddler to come "home," and imploring their forgiveness.

And then, but a few short days later, Manuela's newfound joy—so fragile, so fleeting—had fled once again as she recounted how her happy plans had fallen in ruins about her:

"*Where did I go wrong? Blessed Mary, what did I say to Maria to make her take the child and flee? She seemed so eager, so happy for me, so relieved that I'd finally recovered, I never once suspected she was not sincere—! Blessed Mary, I can scarce believe she could have done this to us, not my Maria, not my dearest companion of so many, many years! And yet, in all honesty, is it really so hard to understand? I have no one but myself to blame! Maria cared for the boy from the moment of his birth when I, his natural mother, offered him only hatred and rejection! Where are they, God? Where has Maria taken my son? Show me where to find them, Madonna Mary, before my poor Alejandro is destroyed by grief!"*

But neither Alejandro nor his heartsick Manuela had ever been able to find the boy, the child who had been Esteban. And nor did Maria de San Martín ever return to Córdoba. Unwilling to relinquish the son she'd loved as her own from the day of his birth to the mother who'd spurned him, Maria de San Martín had taken the boy and vanished as if she'd never been!

And Manuela, who'd intended only to bring her husband joy, was left overwhelmed with guilt that she'd been the one who'd precipitated the woman's abduction of the boy; a guilt and sadness from which, Krissoula fancied, Manuela had never fully recovered. Her sorrow was written between the lines in the diary, etched in the sadness of the deep-blue eyes that looked out from her portrait . . .

Krissoula set the diary aside with a tightening of her jaw and a smarting behind her own eyes, more moved by the sad little tale than she cared to admit. Poor, poor Manuela, condemned to a lifetime of self-reproach and remorse for her well-intentioned act. Her life had been wasted from that day on—could have seemed little more than a marking of time on the road between sorrow and an early grave, unless—?

No! Manuela's life needn't have been wasted. Her good intentions need not have been for nothing, Krissoula amended with a suddenly racing heart and a surge of determination, not if she could help it! For, by her diligent scribblings, Manuela had unwittingly supplied her son, Esteban, with the proof he needed to regain Tierra Rosa, to at last come home, where he belonged, to stay.

A thrill ran through Krissoula. This couldn't wait till morning. She had to tell Esteban what she'd discovered tonight—now, right away! Their quarrel seemed negligible now, no more than a silly, impassioned lovers' spat. It would pale to the insignificance it deserved alongside her revelations, she was certain. *Caramba*, how happy he'd be when she told him, when he saw his dreams at last fulfilled!

Not pausing to dress, she tore garments from her drawers and armoire, and bundled them up in a shawl, tucking Manuela's diary snugly within their depths. She could dress in the stables. Clad only in her robe, she blew out the lamp and quickly slipped through the French windows and out onto her balcony for the second night running.

A few minutes more saw her sprinting across the courtyard and out to the stables beyond, as she had the first night.

It was dark within them, the shadows warm and pungent with the smell of horseflesh, droppings, and straw. She made her way between the two rows of stalls, coming at last to that of Girasol. The mare nickered in greeting, and nuzzled at her pockets in search of treats in the patches of gray moonlight that fell through the opened half-doors of the stall.

"Later, my pet," Krissoula whispered, taking a bridle from a peg and slipping it over Girasol's velvety nose. She'd need no saddle, accustomed as she was to riding bareback, she thought thankfully. "First, we have a job to do, *comprende,* my golden one? Then you shall have your reward."

Suddenly, Girasol's ears pricked back. She gave a shrill whicker and shied nervously, coming close to knocking Krissoula off her feet with her blond hindquarters. Further down the row of stalls, she heard Dorado give a nervous whinny, and kick out violently at his wooden partition. Krissoula tensed, wondering what it was that had so unsettled the animals. Had a pampas fox, grown bold in search of an unwary chicken for his supper, prowled too close to the *hacienda* . . . ?

And then, a lantern's light flared into view, temporarily blinding her with its brilliance, and she realized she was no longer alone in the stables. She gave a cry of protest, and reached up to shield her dazzled eyes. When she drew them away, she could see again, and her heart sank. Fear fluttered dark wings in her belly. A grinning Alfredo Flores was standing there, blocking her escape, and at his side stood a livid Felipe, his hawk's face a dark mask of fury. So. Now she knew. Little wonder Dorado had been unsettled by his hated master's presence . . .

Surreptitiously, she kicked at the bundle which lay at her feet, consigning both her clothing and Manuela's diary to the straw of Girasol's stall.

"What is the meaning of this, Krissoula?" Felipe demanded angrily. "What are you doing here at such an hour?"

"I was restless," she began hesitantly. "I couldn't sleep. There didn't seem any harm in coming here to be with the horses, señor."

"She lies!" 'Fredo jeered, grinning malevolently as Krissoula's face paled in the lantern's light. "She always lies! It's all as I told you, Don Felipe. Remember, I showed you the shawl she left behind when they'd lain here in the straw together weeks ago? While the rest of the household sleeps, this wicked one slips away, and rides through the night to meet with her lover! I've followed them and seen them sinning together, she and *el mayordomo,* San Martín. I've looked through the windows, and seen them naked." His cold black eyes gleamed like wet stones.

"You're mad!" Krissoula denied bravely. "It was as I told you, Felipe. Don't listen to this malicious *peón*'s lies! I wasn't sleepy, and so—"

"Lies, doña!" 'Fredo persisted, cutting her off. "If what you've told *el patrón* were truly the case, then why is this nag bridled, eh? Explain that if you can, doña!" he challenged slyly, jerking hard on the bridle she'd slipped over the mare's head, so that Girasol nickered in pain as the bit tore her gentle mouth.

Wetting suddenly dry lips on her tongue, Krissoula looked from 'Fredo's cunning black eyes to Felipe's furious, disbelieving deep-blue ones.

"Well?" he demanded.

To her dismay, she could not find the words to answer him.

Flinging about, she ran from the stable, blundering clumsily up against partitions and tack in the distorting moonlight and gloom, her heart pounding frantically.

"After her!" she heard Felipe shout, and then crashes and thuds followed as Flores lunged in pursuit.

She sped like a wild thing across the stableyard, heading for the towering wrought-iron gates, never letting up her pace for an instant. Yet the gates were locked, and though she shook them frantically till the metal clanged mournfully on the dewy hush of night, she could not open them.

Like a cornered, hunted animal at bay, she whirled about to face her pursuers, her back pressed painfully up against the ornate iron scrolls, her golden eyes wild with fear as Felipe and Alfredo came closer and closer.

"It's no use running, my dear," he said softly. "No use at all!" Turning to a grinning Alfredo, he ordered, "Saddle Dorado and the mare for Señorita Ballardo and myself, then round up a few of your friends and pay a little visit on our dear *mayordomo*. Tell him I'd like very much to speak with him immediately, Alfredo—and don't take no for answer! The lovely doña and I will join you at the corral, *comprende?* I'm sure she wouldn't want to miss this for the world!"

The pair exchanged malevolent grins.

"*Sí, señor,* I understand very well!" Alfredo smirked, darting a glance across at Krissoula. She didn't look near as cocky now as she'd looked the day she'd screamed at him for beating that golden devil of a stallion, he thought smugly.

"What are you going to do to him?" Krissoula cried.

"Do? Well, my plans are very close to being fulfilled, my dear! Soon the *estancia* will be sold, and I'll have no further use for Esteban de San Martín, nor his managerial skills. He's expendable, since he's outlived his usefulness, and I think it's high time he learned who's the master here, once and for all, don't you? And lest we forget, dear heart, there is, of course, also the little matter of the two of you! No man of honor could ignore that. I wonder what your lover will say when I describe how you betrayed him to me, dear heart? How you confessed to your little affair, and threw yourself on my mercy, begging my forgiveness?"

The color drained from her face, and her eyes grew stark with horror. "No!" she breathed. "I beg you, Felipe, don't! Beat me, if you will—send me away—do anything—*anything*—but that—!"

But in answer, Felipe only smiled.

Chapter Twenty-Two

Moonlight silvered bridles and bits and glinted off the dark eyes of the six men who silently sat their horses less than twelve feet from his door.

Throwing off the sleep that fogged them, Esteban's eyes narrowed, for two of the men he knew, without needing to see them either up close, or in a good light. One was none other than 'Fredo Flores, the lazy good-for-nothing *mestizo* ranch hand he'd fired for cruelty to the horses. The other, slighter one mounted alongside him was Luis, the same sly, foul-mouthed *bastardo* who'd insulted Krissoula and drawn a knife on him. The rest didn't look familiar, but appeared the low, rough *hombres* that could be found lounging up against the bar in any country grocery store-cum-saloon or *pulpería*, swilling raw *caño*, gambling, and getting into drunken knife fights to the death within their quick tempers, their small store of patience, and their pea-sized brains.

"Well, well! *Buenas noches,* Señor de San Martín," Alfredo sneered, tipping his greasy *chambergo* in a mockery of respect. "It is my hope we did not wake you from a good night's rest, *señor?"*

His *compañeros* sniggered or grinned broadly.

"All right. What is it you want?" Esteban growled, running his hand through his sleep-rumpled hair with a quick, impatient gesture. "State your business, and get the hell out of here, Flores!"

"Such impatience to be rid of your guests? Tch! Tch! How inhospitable of you, señor!" Flores complained in a wounded voice, clicking his teeth. "But, very well, if that is what you wish, I will tell you at once why we are here. We came to bring you an invitation from Don Felipe, *mayordomo*—a most important invitation to join him at Tierra Rosa, right away."

Esteban snorted in grim amusement. "Is that so, 'Fredo? Well, you can tell my uncle that any 'invitation' you boys have from him can wait until morning, *hombre*—or till hell freezes over, for all I care!" he said with marked contempt, turning back into the house.

At his feet, Rojo whined uneasily, then growled deep in his throat. The massive dog could smell the menace the men gave off as powerfully as his master could sense it in his gut—like a foul miasma leaking into the air. Esteban reached down and placed his palm firmly on the dog's massive head to restrain him. Beneath his fingers, he could feel the dog's energy quivering, bursting to be freed, and the rumbling anger in the animal, directed at the intruders.

"Just get going, 'Fredo, and take your *compinches* with you. I don't like you—my dog here doesn't even like you!—so crawl on back to whatever snakes' nest you slithered out of, and let me sleep—before I do something I won't regret . . ."

"Perhaps I used the wrong word, señor?" 'Fredo amended softly, his teeth yellow-ivory against his dusky *mestizo* complexion in the moonlight as he grinned. "Perhaps I should have said I bring you a *summons* from *el patrón,* rather than an invitation? You see, he wishes to speak with you right away about a matter of the utmost importance to both of you. The so-lovely señorita."

Esteban froze in the act of going back inside, one foot planted on the threshold, one hand resting on the doorjamb. His back was to the riders. "Summons, you said?" he repeated levelly, without turning around.

"Why, *sí, señor!*" 'Fredo confirmed. "You see tonight, the so-lovely Doña Krissoula told her betrothed that she cannot marry him! In tears, she confessed to him what everyone at Tierra Rosa has known for quite some time . . ."

"And what might that be?" Esteban snapped, his jaw tightening in an effort to control his temper.

"Why, señor, surely *you*—of all men—should know the answer to that! Don Felipe surprised the señorita in the stables tonight, preparing to ride here, to her lover's bed. When *el patrón* confronted her, she threw herself on her knees at his feet, and confessed to Don Felipe that she'd foolishly given herself to another man. And of course, she had no choice but to name the man who'd dishonored her. Esteban de San Martín. You, señor! Ah, it was so very touching! How the señorita wept, and begged Don Felipe to be merciful, to avenge her lost honor, and—well, you know how it is, eh? Our *patrón* is a tender-hearted one, no? A man easily moved by the tears of a pretty woman! You understand now why *el señor* wishes to speak with you right away?" 'Fredo shook his head in a mockery of sympathy for his master. "It is enough to drive any man to madness—even to murder, perhaps—to learn his woman has been used by another, no?"

His lips peeled back in a foul, yellowed grin. In the moonlight, his eyes were small and ratlike, shiny black beads of cunning.

Fighting the rage boiling up inside him, Esteban swung slowly about to face 'Fredo, his expression a chiseled mask of cold fury. His eyes were deadly, glittering blue dagger slits that caught the moon's silvery rays like the surface of a darkened lake, or sharpened blades of steel.

"You've delivered your 'summons,' 'Fredo. I'll take it from here. Meanwhile, get the hell off my land! Ride on out, before I make you wish to God you'd never come here tonight!"

He met 'Fredo's eyes unflinchingly, his expression dark and implacable, although inwardly he cursed himself for a fool for not pausing to buckle on his gunbelt before answering the door at such an hour. But then, he'd imagined his late-night visitor was Krissoula, her temper flown, come to mend their furious quarrel and spend a few stolen hours in his arms, making up. He certainly hadn't been expecting this . . . !

A muscle danced in his jaw. Was 'Fredo lying, he wondered—or had Krissoula really thrown their affair in Felipe's face? Could she have been so outraged and furious following their quarrel that she'd gone back on her promise and betrayed his scheme after all? Thrown everything away for the sake of marriage to a wealthy *hacendero?* Had she—or was 'Fredo lying through his teeth, as his gut instincts suggested? He gritted his jaw to force such futile questions from his mind. Time enough to ask her later, when he was well rid of 'Fredo and his cronies . . .

"Ah, but I regret that we cannot leave, señor," 'Fredo was saying in response to his gritty dismissal. "Not until we have seen *el patrón's* wishes carried out. You will come with us, *mayordomo."*

The fawning edge to his voice was gone now, and with it the thin veneer of civility he'd adopted. He sounded coldly gleeful, anticipatory, Esteban thought, the hackles at the back of his neck starting to prickle in warning.

At his feet, Rojo growled deep in his throat again, trembling with rage. Like his master, the dog sensed the menace these dark riders exuded, smelled the threat they posed to his beloved Esteban, and itched to react.

"The hell I will, *peón!"*

Suddenly, Rojo's master took a fluid back step through the threshold of the door, intending to slam it shut behind him and arm himself before any of the dark riders realized his intentions!

But in the same moment, a seventh man Esteban had not been aware of—this one on foot and alongside him, hidden by the deeper shadows cast by the cottage until now—leaped after him, his pistol raised and brandished in Esteban's face. In the second before it would have slammed home, the man's well-placed knee blocked the door from closing.

"No, San Martín, not so fast!" the seventh man gritted. "We won't make it that easy for you, you bastard—!"

"Get 'em, Rojo!" Esteban roared.

There was a threatening snarl, and in another heartbeat Rojo answered his master's command!

Like a maddened wolf, he hurled himself at the man, blocking the door from closing, leaping for the attacker's throat with a snarl of blind fury.

The man flung about, his arms raised to shield his face from long, yellowed fangs. Esteban was forgotten as the full weight of the huge, shaggy animal slammed up against his chest, toppling him backward to the ground. A brief yet violent struggle ensued, the man screaming and trying desperately to escape both the weight and the powerful squeezing jaws of the animal as Rojo's sharp teeth sank deep into the soft web of flesh between his throat and shoulder. He roared an obscenity and convulsively fired the pistol still clutched in his fist at point-blank range. A muffled explosion rocked the night. The silence that followed in its wake was deafening. Then, with a low whine, Rojo rolled heavily off the man to the dirt and lay still, a ragged hole in his shaggy chest.

"Damn you, *hijo de puta!*" Esteban roared, leaping across the inner room for his pistol. But in the same moment, the other men—who'd dismounted by now—had rushed the house. Like rats streaming from a sinking log, they shoved and elbowed their way through the door.

Esteban had no time to find his weapon in the ruddy shadows; no time to do anything more than put up a brave defense of himself with his bare knuckles, landing several hefty punches to left and right that sent his attackers reeling and staggering with yelps of pain.

Yet, in the close confines of the cottage, a true defense was impossible! He was outnumbered seven to one, and each time he successfully landed a punishing hook or a cracking, meaty punch, another man sprang to take the place of the one he'd sent flying.

In a matter of moments, two of Felipe's burliest henchmen had him pinned by the shoulders to the sawdust floor. They kept him immobilized with their weight. Although he put up a fierce fight to break free, he knew it was as good as over when 'Fredo raised his pistol and squatted alongside him. The flat-featured *mestizo* lodged the metal barrel hard against a point just above and forward of Esteban's ear, breathing heavily.

"It would give me very great pleasure to blow out your stinking brains, señor!" he rasped, and for an endless moment, Esteban believed he might do exactly that. With the hard ring of the barrel cutting deep into his temple, cold and deadly, he waited for the click that would be the last sound he ever heard . . .

But then, he felt the pressure withdrawn, and looked up to see 'Fredo turning the weapon about, holding it now by the barrel. The *mestizo* cracked him hard across the side of the skull with the pistol butt. A blood-red sea filled his vision, before everything went black. With a low curse, his head slumped sideways, and he lay still.

"You should have killed the damned bastard, *amigo!*" growled Luis, as Esteban folded. "I, for one, would have enjoyed seeing his brains splattered across the floor!" He was nursing a closed black eye and spitting blood and pink-stained spittle. A loosened tooth slipped from his mouth and he spat it away.

"Ah, me, too, *hombre,* me, too! But a bullet would be too quick and easy for the likes of him!" 'Fredo rasped back, his bright, feral little eyes gleaming cruelly as he hefted a hard kick into Esteban's ribs. "But Don Felipe has a more entertaining end planned for our beloved *mayordomo,* as you'll see shortly, my friend . . .

"You, 'Salo, get this whoreson onto a horse—but tie him good, hand and foot, in case he comes to. Me and him have an old score to settle. I don't want any slipups now! The rest of you—fire the house and drive that fine *tropilla* of bays over to my cottage. They'll bring a fortune at the next Córdoba horse fair!" He snickered malevolently. "After all, it's most unlikely that our fine Señor de San Martín will ever be needing either his house or his horses again, eh, *amigos . . . ?"*

Esteban came to with a groan and a mumbled string of obscenities, to find knives of pain slicing through his arms and back, his shoulders. Holy Mother, what could have caused such agony? But then—he remembered the night riders—remembered Rojo springing like a wolf—remembered the shot—all of it!—and his sapphire eyes snapped open amidst a welter of bruised and swollen flesh.

He could barely see, but dimly realized he'd been taken to the horse-breaking corral of Tierra Rosa and that he'd been lashed to the tethering pole there. The corral was lit almost as bright as day under a full, milky moon, and across the corral, beyond the railing, he could see his hated uncle standing there with Krissoula, pale-faced but pressed close beside him. Cozily close.

So. That was the way of it. 'Fredo had been telling the truth, after all, he realized, his gut tightening with a peculiar mixture of bitter anger, hurt, and grief. The greedy little bitch had betrayed him after all, he realized heavily. She'd sold him out, that Judas-witch, in return for her place as Felipe's bride, and a comfortable future as *la patrona* of Tierra Rosa. Betrayed him, despite her touching promises of love and loyalty, and her Gypsy blood-oaths! By God and all the saints, he'd kill her if he survived this, woman or no, he swore, squeezing his eyes shut to drive out the agonizing image of her beautiful, treacherous face . . .

His wrists had been shackled together way above him, lashed securely by lengths of wet rawhide to the tall, shaved post used to tie wild broncos for breaking. His feet dangled a few inches above the ground, forcing his shoulders and arms to bear the weight of his entire body. A narrow length of rawhide had been run around his head and forced between his lips, lashed tight and effectively preventing him from making anything but garbled, grunting sounds. Like a goddamned animal. A pathetic animal, trussed for the slaughter. A blinding rage roiled up inside him. He wasn't afraid of dying, hell no, dying was easy! But—he'd be damned if he met death this way, helpless and bound, denied the dignity of defending himself to the last! He tried to move his fingers, to embrace the pole above him in an effort to relieve the tension on his shoulders. It was useless. His fingers were numb, and, besides, the pole was too smooth and broad to grant any purchase, even had they not been . . .

He flexed his hands in a futile effort to loosen his bonds and restore sensation, perhaps even squirm free if they slackened a little, but whoever had tied him had been thorough. The bastards had bound him so tightly, the wet rawhide had bit into his flesh. Warm blood was already trickling down his knotted arms and slipping over his throat and bare chest, for, at some point, they'd stripped him to the waist, too, he realized. The remains of his shirt hung in tatters from his belt.

"So, you've come back to us at last, San Martín!" jeered his uncle's voice, carrying across the moon-washed corral. "I'm glad to see it! Now we can get on with your little lesson as to who's the master here at Tierra Rosa, and who's the servant, *sí?* And by the way, this will be your very *last* lesson of any kind, my young *mayordomo!* Krissoula has told me how you soiled her, used her. How you forced her to lie with you, and robbed me of her innocence," Felipe gritted, trembling with fury. "As her former betrothed, my honor demands that this insult be avenged, with your life, San Martín! Alfredo!"

"*Sí, señor?*"

"Are you ready—?"

"No! You're lying!" Krissoula screamed in denial, trying desperately to twist free of Felipe's cruel grip on her wrist. "You lie, you old goat! I told you nothing of the kind, nothing—!"

"You know, I'd been expecting something like this from you, sooner or later, San Martín," Felipe continued as if she hadn't cried out, forcing her arm up and behind her so that she was pressed tight against his body. The pain of her twisted arm, of bone and socket grinding against each other, made the blood drain from her face. "You're too like your damned father, aren't you? Bastard born or no, you've always wanted things your way. Always wanted to be first in everything, and to hell with anyone else! The pair of you always grabbed the best for yourselves, whether it was land or riches—or women. First, Alejandro married my Manuela, the woman *I* loved, and now this—! You've soiled my Krissoula, cheated me of the woman I chose to replace my lovely Manuela. What was your plan, mmm, San Martín? To see Felipe saddled with your discarded whore? To laugh behind my back as I made your soiled dove my honored bride? Eh, San Martín, was that it? Was that what you wanted? Well, you've failed, do you hear me? It is I who will have the last laugh now, *nephew*—both on you, and on this little slut!"

His expression contorted with fury, he nodded to 'Fredo.

The *mestizo* grinned as he drew on a pair of tight black gauntlets and took up an evil-looking bullwhip, flicking the long, tapering lash expertly. It spiraled like a slim black snake flexing its coils over the powdery dust of the corral. He tested his grip on the braided leather handle, and, satisfied, nodded to his master in return.

"I am ready, *Señor Patrón,*" he said softly, excitement glittering in his eager eyes as he coiled the whip's long tongue in readiness. A streak of spittle glistened on his lip. "Just say the word."

"Then begin," Felipe ordered harshly.

He strode back to the corral fence, forcibly dragging Krissoula after him by the wrist. She was still wearing only her yellow silk wrapper, the clothes she'd planned to change into hidden in the straw of Girasol's stall, along with Manuela's diary. Her inky black hair was a disheveled torrent of ebony curls in the moonlight against its gleaming pallor, but her normally vivid coloring was ashen, her golden eyes enormous with horror as Alfredo brought back the whip and raised it high above his head.

"God in heaven, *noooo!*" she screamed.

Alfredo's arm came down.

He laid the cruel lash across Esteban's bared back, and there was a violent, cracking sound as leather bit deep into fragile flesh. The blow sounded like a pistol shot on the hush, and Krissoula flinched and moaned as if she'd been struck herself, feeling sick to her stomach. They'd kill him, she knew it. Oh, dear God, they meant to kill him . . . !

Esteban jerked against his bonds as a white-lightning pain seared through his back, a stripe of agony laying his flesh open and raw as bloody meat. Yet not so much as an agonized grunt escaped the rawhide gag. Eyes squeezed shut by the supreme effort it cost him, he clamped his jaws and remained rigidly silent.

"You're mad!" Krissoula whispered, terribly, terribly afraid for her beloved's life, her anger at him dissolved in the face of this awful threat. "Please, señor, please—I beg you, don't do this! You must order Alfredo to stop, you must!"

"Oh, but I can do anything I want—I am doing it, Manuela! I'm *el patrón* here, after all, and I can do anything I want *to* anyone I want! Your precious Alejandro will be screaming for mercy before I'm done with him. I wonder if he'll still think you were worth such agony then, eh, my beauty . . . ?"

It was useless to reason with him, to remind him that she was not his beloved Manuela, she realized, but she had to do *something.* Had to stop him before he had Esteban killed . . .

"You're quite right, *mi amor,*" she said softly, no longer fighting Felipe's cruel grip. "Alejandro, he is nothing compared to you. Nothing! But—he is still your brother, no? And a mortal sin would be on your conscience if you killed him, Felipe. Send him away, *querido mio,* if you want to be rid of him. Banish him from Tierra Rosa for the rest of his days! But I beg you, think of your immortal soul, and put an end to this whipping! I'll—I'll do anything you want me to, Felipe, anything at all, if only you'll let him go—for our sakes, not his. Please, Felipe, you must! Think of your immortal soul! I'll do anything, my love—!"

She was babbling in her desperation, her slim fingers clawing at his arm in supplication. But he flung them off as if she were a pariah, and instead gripped her chin between his cruel fingers, so brutally she feared her jaw would snap in two.

"Anything, little *puta?*" Felipe ground out hoarsely, his hawk's dark face thrust into hers. "*Caray,* how prettily you plead for your lover's life when he's about to lose it—! How cleverly you lie when it suits you to lie! Oh, I know who you are, girl—I know you're not my Manuela. You could *never* be my Manuela, not in a million years. She was good, my Manuela. She was innocent. A saint! And she was pure, Krissoula, pure as the driven snow. She would never have given herself to a man like San Martín, while you—! Who knows how many others had you before him, eh, a dancer like you? Well, it's my turn now, dear heart! You'll dance to my tune tonight, learn how to please Felipe as you pleased San Martín, on your pretty back!"

She swallowed her revulsion and nodded. "*Sí,* Felipe, *sí,* I'll do anything, anything you ask—if you'll only let him go? I still look like your Manuela, remember?" Krissoula reminded him, desperate now to save Esteban. "I still have your Manuela's face. You can pretend I'm her, I'll *be* her for you! You can call me by her name. You can dress me in the clothes she wore—just name it, and I'll do it, I don't care! Only—only for pity's sake, make Alfredo stop!" The blood was running dark down Esteban's back, glistening like spilled wine in the moonlight, and her heart felt torn in two.

"No!" Felipe spat, his eyes like igneous sapphire coals. "You must be punished, as Manuela was punished! Like her, you chose another to love and rejected me. Any man can possess your body, no, Krissoula? But San Martín has it all, else you would never defend him so fiercely. He has your love, your heart—even as his father, Alejandro, stole my *querida's* heart! But Alejandro paid—and so will his cursed son!" He smiled cruelly, and nodded yet again to the waiting Alfredo.

"Flay him!" he rasped. "Flay the son of a bitch to within an inch of his worthless life. Flay him until the blood runs. Until he calls me 'master,' and begs my forgiveness and mercy!"

Alfredo eagerly plied the whip again, swinging his arm up high and wide to load the lash with all his wiry strength, and make each blow a telling one.

Once, twice, three times in agonizing, drawn-out succession, the whip came down across Esteban's broad bare back, patterning it with bloody, crisscrossed stripes that showed dark even in the

291

moonlight. Other lashes followed, until Esteban lost count of how many the *mestizo* had dealt him. Yet he did not so much as groan even now, even when the pain flamed through him in crimson heat waves, and blackness shot with golden daggers of agony crowded his vision. The *barrios* of his youth had taught him well how to withstand pain; a lesson learned at cost. He'd not give his uncle the satisfaction of crying out—! *Never!* It would be better to die than weaken and beg for mercy like a cringing dog . . .

"Remove the gag, Alfredo," Felipe snapped. "Let's hear what he has to say for himself now!"

Alfredo stepped towards the dangling man, drawing his long-bladed *facón* from his boot. The wet rawhide gag bit too deep into San Martín's flesh to permit the knot to be untied, and so he slid the slim blade between rawhide and flesh, and slit it with an easy flick of his wrist.

"Answer *el patrón,* you bastard," 'Fredo urged, grinning, for San Martín's face was a river of blood and sweat, his sapphire eyes agonized, his arrogance a thing of the past.

"Well?" Felipe sneered. "Do you acknowledge me as *el patrón* now? Do you beg my forgiveness for what you've done to the girl? Let me hear you say it, San Martín!"

"Your—your forgiveness? Acknowledge the—the bastard who killed my father as my master?" Esteban gritted in a hoarse, painful croak that carried on the stillness nonetheless. "*Never,* Uncle! It'll—it'll be a cold day in hell before I call you anything but murderer! *Murderer!*"

He clamped his jaws tight, concentrating all his remaining strength on removing his mind from the dazzle of pain that tore at him again and again as Alfredo, urged on by the livid commands that his uncle—furious the whipping had not cowed him—delivered now. Alfredo wielded the bull whip over and over. And with each cutting stripe, Esteban bit back a scream of agony and swore that his uncle would pay. That Krissoula would pay. That somehow, someday, *sí,* that greedy bitch would pay . . . !

Others had left their homes now, roused by the brutal sounds rupturing the night's silence and disturbing their sleep. Over Felipe's shoulder, Krissoula saw old Roberto wearing a flapping white nightshirt come hobbling down the dirt street between the *jacales* belonging to the ranch workers. The *viejo* came to an abrupt halt, gaping in horror at the scene in the moonlit corral before him. To her relief, he spun about and quickly hurried away, unnoticed by Felipe or his men, who were intent on the bloody spectacle before them. Surely he's taken his mule and gone to Tomás Cabral for help, she thought, hope rising through her. If only she could buy them a little time . . .

Manuela's diary.

The way to do just that popped into her mind, and was so very obvious, she cursed herself for a fool for not thinking of it sooner! Surely if she told Felipe what she'd learned tonight—the information she'd been planning on carrying to Esteban—he'd have to stop this madness—? Madonna, he must . . . he had to! Her beloved's life depended upon it!

"Listen to me, señor," she begged urgently, "and listen well. Esteban de San Martín is not your brother's son—but he *is* Manuela's! Your hatred of him all these years has been for nothing, don't you see?"

"Lying won't help your lover now, Krissoula," Felipe said with a pitying smile. "It's too late for anything to help him now, but the mercy of God. Manuela's son? Manuela had no sons, nor daughters! You must try again, think of a better lie, dear hearts!"

"Please, señor, you must listen to me, you must! I'm telling the truth. I found Doña Manuela's diary in her rooms while you were away, and I read it, all of it. It's all written down there, for anyone to read.

"Maria de San Martín was never Alejandro's mistress, no matter what the gossips said," she explained quickly, the words tumbling from her in a torrent in her eagerness to end Esteban's torture, "nor were the two of them the parents of the child she raised. Alejandro couldn't have been his father—he could sire no children of his own! An illness amongst the *peóns'* children when he was twelve had left him unable to father children."

Felipe had grown very still now, listening to what she was saying despite himself, and, encouraged, she continued in a rush:

"No, Felipe, Alejandro wasn't Esteban's father, and nor was Maria his real mother. Maria de San Martín was only the woman who raised him, the nurse who cared for him from birth and grew to love him as her own. It was really *your Manuela* who was his mother! She gave birth to a son in Mar de la Plata, where she and Alejandro stayed for over a year following their wedding, do you remember? But she rejected the child from the moment of its birth, and gave it over to Maria to raise. Someone Manuela hated— someone she feared—attacked her in the gardens on the night she and Alejandro were wed! This man got her with child, not Alejandro. He's *not* your brother's son, Felipe—but he is

293

Manuela's. If you ever truly loved her, as you claim, spare her son, spare him for her sake, I beg you!"

"The day my brother and Manuela were wed was a hot, sultry one at the end of summer—the month of March, as I recall," Felipe murmured in a low, thick voice. When she looked up into his face, she saw that his dark sapphire eyes were distant and dreaming. They'd taken on a glazed look.

"That evening, while the *mariachis* were playing and everyone else was dancing, I surprised Manuela taking the night air on the patio that overlooks the lake. I took her arm and persuaded her to come for a walk in the gardens with me, while Alejandro was busy playing the perfect host with their wedding guests." His upper lip curled in a sneer of contempt at mention of his brother's name.

"When we were alone, I begged Manuela to listen to reason. I tried to make her see the truth—that it was me she really loved, not my cursed brother! I kissed her then, but she cried and rubbed the taste of my lips from her mouth as if it were poison.

"I was angry, so very angry, for she struggled to escape me—I, Felipe, who loved her, and would have given my very life for hers! I took her wrists and dragged her deeper into the garden, where no one could hear her cries. There, I begged her to run away with me, to leave her new husband. But she laughed in my face. She told me that she'd never leave Alejandro, never. That he'd been her love, her life, since she was fifteen years old, and that she felt nothing for me.

"I knew then that there was only one way to convince her of my love—to stop her from becoming Alejandro's, body and soul. And so, in the mud and wet leaves alongside the iris pond, I claimed her, Krissoula, dressed gloriously in her bridal white, like an angel. I claimed her, and made her mine."

"God in heaven, *you?*" Krissoula exclaimed, her hand flying to her throat in horror.

"*Sí!*" he hissed. "It was me! I claimed her as if she were my own sweet bride on our bridal bed . . . She was innocent, of course, and my darling screamed and tried to fight me off, but—I knew it had to be done. It was the will of God. *You understood, didn't you, Manuela, that I had to be cruel, for kindness' sake?* I thought that afterward, she'd come to her senses and run away with me. That she'd have no choice. But—I misjudged her. Manuela ran back to my brother. She stayed with him as his wife for the rest of her life. I gained nothing from what I'd done except the undying hatred of my lovely Manuela, who never spoke nor looked at me ever again."

To Krissoula's disgust, she saw that there were tears in his eyes as he finished in a strangled tone, "For her, it was as if I ceased to exist the night she wed my brother . . . as if I was beneath her contempt!" He buried his face in his hands and wept, releasing Krissoula's wrist to do so.

"And you never once suspected, did you, you evil old *diablo!*" Krissoula whispered softly as the last part of the puzzle finally dropped into place. Her heart thudded crazily. "Are you still so blinded by your jealousy of Alejandro—a dead man!—that you can't see the truth, even when it spits in your eye?"

"What truth?" Felipe snapped, his sapphire eyes suspicious now as his silver head snapped up. "What are you babbling about now, girl?"

"The truth about Esteban, of course! What else? About the man your 'Fredo is whipping to death even now! Don't you understand? Doesn't what you did that night and what I just told you add up to anything, in your mind? Manuela became *encinta* by the man who violated her on her wedding night! And you were that man, Felipe—you! Esteban's, not Alejandro's son, you old fool—he's *yours!*" she flung at him triumphantly.

Felipe's face paled under olive skin. His sapphire eyes blazed with outrage. "Liar!" he snarled. "I would have known, somehow, if Manuela had carried my child. But you're wrong—she didn't! She didn't even tell my brother what I'd done, she couldn't have! He'd have called me out, shot me dead, if she'd breathed a word of it!"

"No, Felipe," Krissoula denied softly. "That's where you're wrong. Manuela told her husband *everything!* But—your brother was a clever, resourceful man. He decided on a different punishment for the terrible thing you'd done to Manuela—a far greater punishment than simply killing you. Alejandro let you *live* with your guilt, Felipe, knowing you loved Manuela but could never have her. Knowing you coveted Tierra Rosa, but that it belonged to him. Knowing you'd sired a son, but would never win his love for yourself! Alejandro knew he could never father children of his own, and he quickly grew to love the little boy himself, Felipe. He loved the fine son you'd unwittingly granted him—the one thing left that he wanted, and which money could not buy him! And out of your lust, your jealousy, your hatred, you granted him that last wish, Felipe—you!"

"Shut up!" he ranted. *"Silencio, bruja!"*

And she did look like a witch in that moment, with her black hair stirred by the nightwind around her shoulders, and her golden eyes blazing into his . . .

"Exposing you would have caused Manuela further shame and hurt, yet could have changed nothing," Krissoula continued, "—and Alejandro loved her so, Felipe, truly loved her with all his heart! Doña Manuela de Córdoba y Aguilar gave birth to her babe, Esteban, the November after they were wed, according to her diary. Your son, Felipe. Your blood. Your seed. But—in the eyes of the law—his mother was lawfully married to Alejandro at the time of his birth. That makes Esteban de San Martín Alejandro's legitimate heir, no? *He's the rightful master of Tierra Rosa!* Ironic, is it not, that it's your own flesh and blood who will oust you from this *estancia!* That the child born of your wickedness and lust will take from you all you hoped to gain! Alejandro won! He had the last laugh, after all, you crazy old fool—!"

She threw back her head and laughed in scorn, her golden eyes withering him, shriveling him with her contempt.

"No, no, you lie!" he seethed, his face contorted as he shook his head back and forth. "I don't believe you! I was waiting for Alejandro that last night when he went to stable his horse. I begged him to lend me the money I needed to save my exporting business in Brazil from ruin—but he refused. He told me I should have learned to manage my finances better, and turned his back on me.

"I tried to reason with him, but he wouldn't listen. He made me angry—so very angry! He had so much, while I had so little, and he intended to will it all to his bastard son by that common peasant bitch, Maria! And so, I took up a crowbar and hit him across the skull. He fell to the straw, blood pouring from his nose and ears, his mouth, and I knew he was dying. Yet even as he lay there, his lifeblood draining from him, he said nothing! Not that he knew what I'd done to Manuela—nor that she'd borne my child—*nothing,* you hear me, witch? 'Did you really hate me so much, Brother?' he whispered—but that is *all* he said before he breathed his last. Then I whipped his precious palomino stallion until it reared up, trampling his body, hiding what I'd done. Only Jaime Ramirez knew the truth. He followed me out, and he saw what I'd done, that cursed leech. No, witch, you lie! San Martín's my brother's son, not mine!"

"But can you be sure of that, Felipe? You'll find Manuela's diary in the secretary in her rooms," she lied breathlessly, knowing the journal was still safely hidden in the straw of the stables, for Esteban, and for his future—if he lived. "Go, Don Felipe! Go read the bitter truth for yourself, and when you have, weep, old man!"

she jeered. "But meanwhile, señor—order Alfredo to release *your son!*"

To her endless relief, the look of doubt and shock still filling his grayed olive face, Felipe wetted his lips and raced off to do as she'd suggested, flinging himself astride a nervous Dorado like a madman. He had to find the diary, had to see if everything the girl had said was true—and if it was, destroy it! Tierra Rosa was his! He'd earned the right to the *estancia, por Dios!* Son or no, Esteban would never take it from him . . .

When he'd gone, Krissoula whirled back towards the corral, agony in her expression, dread in her heart.

"You heard your master, *hijo de puta!* Throw down your whip and be gone with you—now!" she hissed to Alfredo, her golden eyes blazing, her little fists planted aggressively on her hips as she stalked towards him, her skirts swishing. "The rest of you whoreson dogs, *ride*—before I take this whip to your backs!"

She picked up the whip Alfredo had flung down and flicked it with a smart, ear-splitting crack across the hard-packed dirt. By the terrible anger in her raging golden eyes, the contemptuous twist of her lips, the men had no doubt that she'd do exactly as she'd threatened. She took another step towards him, and 'Fredo started running for his life.

The *mestizo* and his companions hurriedly took to their horses without any need for a second telling, and whipped and spurred them away from the corral at a gallop. No one turned to watch them go.

"Tomás, Roberto—all of you, quickly, come!" she cried, turning to the openmouthed men huddling by the corral. "For the love of God, cut Esteban down, cut him down, but—gently, *hombres,* gently, *por favor!*"

Tomás and three other *gauchos* carefully supported his weight, while another cut Esteban down. They lifted him and placed him facedown on a door that two others had brought in readiness to carry him. He was barely conscious and his back—his poor, striped back—was bleeding freely. Krissoula's heart turned over in dread. A knot clenched her throat. He couldn't die—not now, when he had everything to live for—he just couldn't—!

She hurried to accompany the makeshift stretcher as the men carried Esteban from the corral, headed for Lupe's cottage. Tears sparkling in her eyes, she took his limp hand and lifted it to her lips to kiss, pressed it to her cheek. The light pressure of her lips roused him, and he turned his head to look up into her face.

"You judas witch!" he rasped hoarsely, and she recoiled in shock at the hatred in his agonized eyes. "One day, you'll pay for your betrayal, Krissoula! B-before God, I swear it! *Dios*, what a fool I've been! I should have known better, eh? Should have expected this! In a *gitana's* eyes, not even love can dull the glitter of Gypsy gold—! Not even love can lessen greed!"

She abruptly released his hand, stunned by his bitter, hate-filled words, and her mouth dropped open in a silent cry of despair, of denial, as she stood there and let the *gauchos* carry him away. She'd remember the betrayed look in his eyes till her dying day . . .

Tomás caught up with her. Seeing her wounded expression, he shook his head.

"Don't let the stupid things he's saying bother you," the *domador* advised gently, "or try to explain. Save it for later! Right now, señorita, with the pain he's in, that hothead doesn't know what he's saying—and besides, he wouldn't hear you, anyway. You'd just be wasting your breath! We all heard what you told Don Felipe—and I'll see that he's told, too, when the damned, hotheaded fool's able to understand and appreciate it all, have no fear. He loves you, doña! He wanted to forget Tierra Rosa and avenging his father's murder and take you away with him. He told me that much. Everything will be right between the two of you when he's well again, Doña Krissoula. Believe me, everything will work out!" the head groom reassured her with an uncertain smile, for he had never seen her so strangely still, so petite and vulnerable as she was now.

"Will it work out?" she asked Tomás softly, her golden eyes wounded and resigned, like a small animal shot through the heart in the second it realizes it is dead. "No, *amigo* Tomás, I don't think so. Esteban believed Felipe's lies, did he not? He believed so easily that I'd betrayed him! Under the circumstances, how can anything be right between us ever again? How can there be true love in a man's heart, if there is not also trust—?"

Leaving him with that sadly voiced little question, and the disturbing memory of her lovely golden eyes shining with unshed tears, she turned and walked slowly away to her waiting mare.

Chapter Twenty-Three

"I think there's a village or a camp of some sort up ahead, beyond the cane fields. See the smoke rising above the trees? We'll be able to rest there, Sofía—and maybe find a meal for ourselves into the bargain!"

Sofía nodded, her lips tightly pursed. In truth, she was afraid to part them, not knowing what would spill out if she did, for her mind was whirling in confusion. So much had happened—so much had changed since that morning—that she was still half numb with shock!

As a new dawn streaked the charcoal sky with pink and gold, she'd awakened to hear Krissoula's furious poundings at her door. Fearing the *estancia* was under Indian attack—or on fire, at the very least—she'd tossed aside the bedcovers and run to answer it. At once Krissoula—pale of face and obviously distraught—had thrust past her and into the room.

"Close the door, Sofía," she'd commanded curtly. "I've much to tell you, and little time to do it, so come, sit down and listen!"

Sofía, astonished by her charge's startling brusqueness but silenced from asking questions by her obvious upset, had done so. And the story Krissoula had proceeded to pour out with little preamble and no pauses whatsoever had left her speechless in its wake.

In moments, she'd learned that the girl she'd so carefully attended was far from the convent-raised señorita she'd pretended to be; no *hidalgo*'s orphaned daughter at all, but a Gypsy thief! She'd also learned of the elaborate plan the *mayordomo*—that handsome devil, San Martín!—had contrived, tricking Don Felipe into making an offer of marriage to the girl to give his accomplice, Krissoula, the opportunity to search the *casa grande* from floor to ceiling for proof of his birth, and thereby his claim to Tierra Rosa.

She'd also heard, openmouthed and round-eyed in disbelief, how

Krissoula's discovery of Manuela's diary had led to the astonishing revelation that the doña had been Esteban's natural mother, and also what amounted to a confession of guilt on Don Felipe's part for the murder of his brother, the late Alejandro de Aguilar.

Little by little, it had all come out, like some fantastic tale of murder and mayhem penned for the scandal sheets! She'd learned of Krissoula and Esteban's initial animosity towards each other as blackmailer and reluctant spy, which had become instead a passionate affair and, Krissoula had believed at the last, true love. She'd heard all about Krissoula's rash threat—made in hurt and anger—to betray San Martín, in return for Don Felipe's name and a wealthy life, and of Alfredo Flores's hatred of the pair, which had caused him to spy on them and report what he'd learned to his master, and make it seem as if Krissoula's threat had been carried out—oh, all of it! So much it had made Sofía's head spin!

"But now, it's all over. I must leave here, Sofía," Krissoula had concluded at length, pacing up and down across Sofía's carpet in a way that had made the older woman's head—already buzzing—dizzy beyond belief. "I've done what San Martín wanted me to do, and it's finished. I have no place here, not now—and nor do I want one!" she'd insisted proudly, tossing her long black mane over her shoulders with a defiant gesture and no little trace of bitterness in her tone. Remembering the diamond-studded, vulgar betrothal ring Felipe had given her, she wrenched it from her finger and flung it across the room. "I'll leave here, taking nothing that belongs to him or Felipe—not a horse nor a single coin!—and the devil take San Martín, and his promises of payment for a job well done!"

"But why are you telling *me* all of this?" Sofía wondered aloud, thoroughly confused.

"Why? Oh, because you've always been kind to me, Sofía—though God knows, I've given you little reason to be! Because I felt you deserved an explanation, at least, before I left. And because I wanted to—to tell you that I—I'm deeply sorry that San Martín and I used you for our own ends."

"Ah. I see," Sofía echoed faintly, and her lower lip quivered in a way that tore at Krissoula's heart.

"Aiee, *Dios,* what will become of you after last night, Sofía—?" the girl cried, flinging herself on her knees at Sofía's feet and wrapping her arms about her duenna's trembling legs. "Tierra Rosa belongs to Esteban now, if he survives Felipe's whipping. And for all his arrogance, San Martín has a soft heart beneath that *diablo*'s temper. Perhaps—perhaps he'll let you stay here, until you have

300

other plans . . . ?"

"But what of Don Felipe, child? Surely he'll not meekly accept this unwelcome news, and leave the *estancia* to Esteban without a fight?"

"I think you're probably right," Krissoula agreed. "But I don't know what will happen! The last I saw of Don Felipe, he was headed here in search of Manuela's diary. He's a sly old fox, and must have realized that if he wants to keep the *estancia,* he must find the journal and destroy it, before anyone that matters reads its contents." She grinned ruefully. "I wonder if he's also realized by now that without what he confessed to me, Manuela's scribblings mean very little? Sooner or later, surely he must! But long before that time comes, I mean to be far away from here, from him—and from that cursed San Martín! God knows what Felipe's up to now! I met Mama Angelina on my way back to the house—Tomás had sent for her to tend Don Esteban's wounds? She said Don Felipe had passed her and her daughters, riding Dorado at a gallop across the Pampa towards Esteban's cottage. He must have come here, discovered I'd lied about the diary being hidden in Manuela's secretary, and assumed I'd left it in Esteban's safekeeping. Whether he'll be back here, and how he might treat you in the future should he decide to do so, I cannot say . . ."

Her voice trailed away in misery. She rocked back on her heels and looked up at Sofía like an apprehensive child expecting punishment.

Sofía stood, her shoulders braced, her back ramrod straight.

"Your concern on my behalf is commendable, but quite unnecessary, *niña.* I am Sofía de Alicante y Moreno, and, to date, the Morenos have never been beggars," she said quietly, but with enormous pride. "Nor have we stayed where we were not wanted. Under the circumstances, I shall leave a letter of resignation for Don Felipe, pack my bags, and leave Tierra Rosa at once. It is the only proper thing to do. And, as soon as it is possible to do so, I shall return to Spain. So you see, my dear, your concern for me is quite groundless."

"You have money?" the girl had asked bluntly.

Sofía had blinked rapidly. "Money?"

"Sí! For your passage on a ship to Spain?"

"I—well, no, not really! My room and board as your duenna were taken care of, naturally, but—I was paid no money to speak of."

"But without money, you're stranded here in South America,

Sofía—as am I! What ship would take you, without money for a cabin and your passage? No, Sofía. You must think again!"

Sofía had racked her brains for a way out of her predicament, but they had all come down to the same thing; without money, leaving South America was impossible. In fact, without money, any future at all was impossible to comprehend! How would she exist, Sofía had wondered then, dread creeping through her, without a roof over her head? Without food and clothing and all the other, necessary things she'd taken for granted throughout her forty-two years of peaceful existence?

Shortly after her papa had died from the long and unpleasant illness through which she'd nursed him selflessly, her oldest brother Raymundo had taken over the Morenos' family home where Sofía had lived all her life, as befitted the new master. With him had come his family: a wife, her harpy sister-in-law, Bianca, who'd always disliked and resented her, and their litter of four uncouth, noisy sons.

Sofía had known from the first that she was neither wanted nor needed there, and that they'd be happy to be rid of her. She'd served out her purpose. She'd run the household for Papa after her dear mother's death, and sacrificed her own chances for marriage and a family in the process. And, when he'd become ill, she'd nursed their father for the last five years of his life, performing the many duties—sometimes far from pleasant ones, too!—of a nurse for the helpless yet complaining, spiteful old man he'd become, without thanks or thought of any reward, nor any help from her brothers Raymundo and Frederico, or her selfish older sisters, Carlotta and Elena. *Dios,* no, they'd had their own families to keep them busy, thank you, they'd told her! They'd no time for Papa. Besides, as the youngest daughter of the family, it was Sofía's *duty* to care for the old man, they'd insisted, and mouse that she was, she hadn't argued.

It was Papa's former physician, astutely guessing her difficult situation, who'd told her about the man looking for a chaperone for his nineteen-year-old niece, Krissoula. Señorita Ballardo, he'd added, was a dancer of flamenco, and soon to begin her first professional tour of South America—a tour on which her uncle was unable to accompany her—and Sofía had jumped at the chance, she recalled. Anything had seemed better than the thought of having to stay on with Raymundo and his wife and sons, where she was neither needed nor wanted! Worse still was the thought of being forced to humble herself and admit to them in the process that she had nowhere to go. Her pride—as compelling as

302

Krissoula's in its own, far less flamboyant way!—had recoiled from that! Besides, the prospect of traveling to a new country, and what promised to be an exciting life as the lovely, volatile dancer's chaperone, had stirred a long-dormant spark of adventurous spirit in her spinster's breast. *Why not?* she'd decided. *Why not, indeed!* She had nothing to keep her in Spain, so what had she to lose? At least in leaving, her dignity and pride would remain intact!

And now, it had come to this. No position. No funds. No future . . .

She'd been very close to tears as her eyes met Krissoula's, and she'd seen in them a mirror of her own despair, coupled with something more: a depth of hurt so deep it would forever scar her soul! *Pobrecita.* Poor little one. Despite her wickedness, the girl had suffered from her Esteban's rejection last night. *Sí,* she could tell! She'd been with her too long, come to know her moods too well, for Krissoula to be able to hide her hurt from her duenna. And, Sofía realized with a start of surprise, over the months she'd grown quite fond of the girl who, for all her willfulness and her hoydenish ways, possessed an affectionate, open and generous nature that shrank from hurting others. *Dios!* Her heart quite ached with compassion and the urge to take the poor child in her arms and console her, like the daughter she'd never had; to tell her she knew only too well what it was to love a man, and lose him. Hadn't she loved Juliano with all her heart? And hadn't he sworn he loved her, too, and promised to be patient and wait until she was free to marry him, when her papa had fully recovered? Faithless Juliano! He'd heartlessly married another woman, an heiress, but a few weeks before the old man had passed away, and she'd never forgotten the pain, never truly forgiven him . . .

"Well?" Krissoula had demanded after her long silence. "Have you thought of a way?"

"I have," Sofía had declared, far more firmly than she felt. "Since you've brought me to this pass, I think it only fair that *you* should get me out of it, no, young lady? If you're planning on leaving Tierra Rosa, well, then, so am I. We'll leave here together! After all, two heads are better than one, no?"

"You're a crazy old woman!" the girl had exclaimed scathingly. "I don't know where I'm going, nor what the future might hold for me. It will be dangerous for one woman. Two might prove disastrous—perhaps even deadly! I'll be living on my wits and little more, Sofía. You're mad to even think of coming with me. No. I travel alone!"

"I have wits, too," Sofía reminded her pertly, "and though perhaps they are less razor-edged than yours, my dear, surely they can be sharpened?"

Krissoula's expression had softened a fraction. "But—there may well be times when I'm forced to go against the law, Sofía! To steal or cheat in order to survive? Will you be with me or against me, then? A help or a hindrance?"

"With you!" she'd replied without a pause. "And a help! After all, *niña*, I may be deplorably old—by your reckoning, anyway—but I'm no fool, for all that. I have a few good years left in me yet, I do believe," she'd insisted with a sardonic little smile. "And I want to survive, too. Very badly."

"You're sure you want to? There'd be no regrets later if I agreed?"

"If it's a choice between casting my lot with yours, and facing the anger of either Don Felipe or Don Esteban, I'll take my chances," Sofía confirmed with a shudder. Angry men reminded her too much of her loud and domineering papa, whose explosive temper had terrified her.

"Very well! You can come. You have ten minutes to make ready. Bring only what you must, and no more than you can tie in your shawl and carry easily. Oh, and Sofía, wear some stout walking shoes, if you own a pair. I'll meet you downstairs." She'd started for the door, then paused before going through it. "And by the way—?"

"Sí, niña?"

"—Gracias!" Krissoula had murmured, almost shyly, blushing as she bowed her head. "I think I'm glad you're coming with me. I suppose I've grown used to having you around!" It was the closest she'd ever come to admitting her fondness for Sofía aloud, and Sofía had smiled.

"Oh, don't thank me yet, *niña*. After all, I need you far more than you need me, I shouldn't wonder!" she'd said with twinkling eyes. "And besides, I'll probably prove a millstone about your neck before day's end—one you'll be only too happy to unload in the nearest pond!"

"Never!" Krissoula had whispered fervently. "I have few enough friends to throw such a dear one away so rashly." In a sharper voice she'd urged, "Hurry, now!"

And in a blink, she'd gone.

Sofía had hurried to do as bidden, and here they were, far from Tierra Rosa, surrounded by the rolling flatlands of the vast Pampa on one side and the whispering forest of the canefield on the other

304

with dusk fast approaching as they neared what appeared to be a little village, the first they'd come to on what promised to be a long, hard walk to the city of Buenos Aires, over a hundred and fifty miles away.

The village was no true village, they saw as they skirted the thorny chapparal and clumps of twisted *quebracho* trees that had hidden it from view, but for a handful of grass-thatched, crumbling adobe huts little better than lean-tos. These sorry dwellings were clustered haphazardly about a disreputable-looking *pulpería,* as the South Americans called the little country mercantiles that doubled as taverns, before which a number of horses had been hitched to a drunken rail. A ruined adobe church, its bell tower empty and silent, lay off to another side.

Many men were scattered about the area in various attitudes of boredom, some smoking, one idly tossing a knife into the center of a circle scratched in the black soil, another braiding a *reata* from long strips of rawhide. A third gold-toothed lout was tossing the *taba* knucklebones, while his companions laid noisy wagers. Meanwhile, other more industrious fellows were busily straining together to heft three large wooden boxes onto the beds of three little *carretas,* the two-wheeled country carts which were usually drawn by mules or oxen. *Boxes?* Krissoula thought, and swallowed uncomfortably. No. They were not merely wooden boxes, she amended silently. What the men were loading onto the carts were, more accurately, rough-hewn—coffins! She resisted the urge to cross herself, and clasped her hands primly together before her instead.

All of the men working looked up, startled, at sight of the two disheveled women approaching, and exchanged sharp glances with their fellows. As they walked across the tiny plaza, one entranced young fellow staring at Krissoula with admiring eyes lost his grip on his end of the casket. It slid back off the cart between his hands and thumped back down to the ground with a noisy thud and a peculiar clatter, landing upright and shuddering.

To Krissoula's horror, the lid came partially unnailed by the impact. When it jolted loose, she was granted an unwelcome glimpse of the coffin's contents! Her complexion paled. She darted a sidelong glance at Sofía, who was looking about her in obvious distaste. Clearly, her companion had seen nothing awry, except for the sorry state of the little cluster of buildings. With any luck, she meant to keep it that way and beat a hasty retreat, hungry or not . . .

In the same moment that Krissoula's eyes widened, one of the men—obviously a leader of sorts, for he was directing the lading—stepped away from the carts and strode quickly to greet the women, effectively blocking Krissoula's view while his men righted the fallen coffin. Standing over six feet in his horsehide boots, he was tall for an Argentine and proportionately broad of shoulder. Across his chest were crisscrossed twin cartridge belts, and in his sash was stuffed a brace of well-polished pistols. A *bandolero,* she wondered—or something else?

Eyes narrowing, Krissoula watched him draw nearer, noting the bright intelligence in the dark eyes that came alive, gleamed with male appreciation and undisguised suspicion, as they flickered over her. He boasted a drooping yet tidily trimmed, fierce black moustache that curved around his upper lip, but other than that, he was clean-shaven. Dressed in a *gaucho*'s black jacket with full breeches tucked into the cuffs of his boots, he appeared much like any one of hundreds of men belonging to these parts. And yet—there was an arrogance to his stride that set him apart from the other men. He had an almost military bearing that, to Krissoula's shrewd eye, struck a discordant note in such a placid rural setting . . .

"*Buen día, señoritas,*" the man greeted them, sweeping off his *chambergo* and offering them a polite bow. "As you can see, our village has a sad duty to attend to today—the transportation of the remains of our poor *compañeros* to the town of Rosario for burial. Three of my men fell afoul of a party of Auracanians this morning. They paid with their lives for their bravery in defending our horses . . . Ah, but enough of our problems! Forgive my poor manners and tell me, what are you doing here, señoritas? Why have you come to our little *pueblo?* Have you, perhaps, lost your way? The hour is very late for two young ladies to be abroad unescorted no?"

Before Sofía could answer, Krissoula did so with a breathless, "Oh, indeed it is quite late, señor! And you were perfectly right—we have lost our way! What a clever one you are to guess!"

Sofía's jaw dropped, for Krissoula's patronizing manner made her sound like a fawning little half-wit! But before she could wonder aloud what madness had come over the girl, Krissoula continued in an equally breathless rush. "My cousin and I are from the city, you know. We were lucky, I suppose, to find work as maids for Don Felipe at the great *estancia* of Tierra Rosa—you know of it, perhaps?"

"Roughly."

306

Thank God, Krissoula thought. "Well, we were supposed to be there by dusk tonight, but my uncle Ricardo's cart broke down soon after noonday, and so he told us we must walk the rest of the way! And so—well, here we are, señor, two very tired and very hungry girls, and aiiee, how our poor feet hurt, too!" She grinned inanely, and fluttered her lashes at him, and the man's guarded watchfulness visibly relaxed. "Could you tell me, señor, if Tierra Rosa is very far from here?"

"Quite far, I believe, señorita. I've never been there myself, but I understand it's a good day's walking distance from here. You certainly couldn't hope to reach it by nightfall."

"Oh!" Krissoula gasped. "Do you hear that, Sofía? We shan't reach it by nightfall."

"And the road is very dangerous in these parts—there are many bandits hereabouts, and wild Indians, too," the tall, moustached fellow added solemnly.

"Do you hear, Sofía—bandits, no less—and wild Indians!"

"Not to mention potholes, in which one might break a slim, pretty ankle."

"Break an ankle!" Krissoula echoed, crossing herself. *"Madre!* What a predicament we're in! You see, I told you we should have stayed in Buenos Aires, *tonta!"* she scolded poor Sofía, who looked suitably confused. "But no, *you* wanted to leave the city, didn't you? *You* said it would be better for us to be in the country before the summer sickness returned this year. *You* always think you know everything! Aiee, what am I to do with you, eh, you silly goose!"

She bobbed the man a curtsey, muttered her thanks, and gripped Sofía's elbow, steering her away from the ramshackle cluster of dwellings and the hostile or frankly interested eyes of its inhabitants, back to the rough track hidden beyond the trees from which they'd come.

"Please, señoritas, can't I persuade you to stop and rest awhile? And perhaps share our supper?" the man called after them. "You're welcome to do so!"

"No, *gracias,* señor!" Krissoula called over her shoulder. "We're late enough as it is, thanks to this stupid one here! *Adíos!"*

Another man came to stand beside the first, and together they watched the pair of women scuttle quickly away.

"Did they see anything, Señor General?" the second man asked the first, whose hooded black eyes were still fixed on the rapidly retreating women.

"I can't be sure, Rico," his leader murmured thoughtfully.

"However, I believe we have no choice but to find out, under the circumstances. No?"

"What on earth is wrong with you?" Sofía hissed crossly as Krissoula hustled her along so quickly, her feet barely touched the ground. "I was hardly able to get in a word back there!"

"Walk now, ask questions later!" Krissoula ground out, forging ahead. "And walk quickly, Sofía—I want to be as far from that place as we can get before nightfall!"

"But, why?" Sofía demanded, running now to keep up with the girl. "I thought we'd find a meal there, and shelter for the night!" She tried to keep the plaintive note from her voice, but failed. She was hungry and tired, and it showed.

"In a camp filled with men, and not a single woman? *Dios,* what a hussy you've become, Sofía—and in such a short time, too, no?" Krissoula accused in a withering tone.

Sofía's face flamed, but Krissoula's accusation had the desired effect. The woman pursed her lips and asked no more questions, and except for the sounds of their noisy breathing, they continued on for perhaps two miles in silence before Krissoula halted. Fists on hips, she looked back the way they'd come. The rough track ran between the towering stalks of whispering green sugarcane, and were bordered on either side by deep irrigation ditches grown waist-high with weeds from the winter rains. The road behind them was empty. There was no sign that they'd been pursued, and Krissoula sighed with relief.

"This is far enough for now, I think," she muttered. "Head over there, Sofía, down across the ditch and up the other side. We'll rest awhile under the trees, and decide what to do next."

As the purple twilight faded to night they saw bats leaving their treetop roosts to hunt, heard the dry flap of their leathery wings. In the branches above them, birds twittered drowsily before settling down to sleep, and the melancholy hooting of an owl seemed to underscore their vulnerability. Soon after the last of the daylight had faded, the air grew noticeably more chill and damp. Dew silvered the blades of tall grass now in the twilight, and the wind lifted, making the cane stalks rustle like a thousand gossips murmuring under their breath.

Sofía was shivering despite the cloak she'd drawn from her bundle and thrown about her shoulders as she helped Krissoula forage about to gather dry kindling—small branches and twigs scattered about in the tall grasses, which the girl stacked for a fire. They badly needed a fire for warmth, for nights on the Pampa could be bitterly cold even in these late spring months. A fire would also serve to keep away any wild animals, like wolves or foxes or snakes, that might see them as easy prey. Darkness would hide the smoke, Krissoula reasoned, and she'd make a screen of branches to shield the flicker of the flames from passersby, so it should be safe to risk lighting a fire . . .

"How will you start it, *niña?*" Sofía asked eagerly, warming to the adventure now that they'd halted and the prospect of a night's rest loomed pleasantly ahead. "Will you rub two sticks together, as I was told *los indios* do?" she wondered aloud, convinced the capable Krissoula was possessed of survival skills that would have done credit to a woodsman, she had such a competent look about her. And besides, Gypsies were used to living off the land, were they not?

In the deepening twilight, Krissoula regarded Sofía with scathing disgust. "Why on earth would I do such a stupid thing, Sofía? Rub some silly twigs together, when we have *fósforos?* Aiee, *caramba,* where is your common sense!"

To Sofía's chagrin, she drew a bundle of long kitchen matches from her shawl, and struck one against a stone. At once, it flared with yellow light, which Krissoula touched to the stack of kindling and dried grasses she'd gathered. In moments, the puny flame was catching the grass, smoldering, then glowing cheerfully as the twigs caught and fed. Krissoula fanned them with her hands.

Embarrassed by the withering expression on Krissoula's face, Sofía hesitated for some time before venturing to ask, "Well, now that we're settled, might I ask why you acted the way you did back at that village?"

Krissoula sat down with crossed legs and gazed into the fire with her chin resting on her fist. Her golden eyes reflected the flames in their depths as she muttered, "There was something wrong there. I knew it from the first! Call it Gypsy instinct or intuition if you will, but I could feel it in my bones, taste it on my tongue! That leader of theirs—he was dressed as a *gaucho,* and yet he strutted like a general, no? He also spoke Spanish more like a *porteño,* a city dweller, rather than any rough peasant. And not a woman did I spy, nor a little one, nor even a village dog nor a chicken scratching anywhere—did you?"

"Come to think of it, no!" Sofía acknowledged slowly, her admiration for Krissoula's astuteness glowing in her eyes.

"There, you see? I was right! Even a small village like that would have at least an old woman or two," Krissoula continued. "And then—I caught the eyes of one of those men—the ones loading the coffins? He let his end slip, and the lid sprang free for a second. Do you know what was inside it, Sofía—?" she asked in a low, breathless voice.

"Nothing so simple as a corpse, I take it?" Sofía said shakily.

"Dios, no!" Krissoula shuddered. "Worse! The coffin was stacked with weapons, Sofía—brand-new *rifles!* There must have been at least a dozen of them, wrapped in oilcloth!"

"Rifles!" her companion exclaimed. "But—why would those *peóns* have had so many rifles? Do you think they're planning a war?"

"Probably not a war, *amiga mía,* but a revolution—? *Sí!* And that would mean that those men were—were *revolucionarios,* would it not?"

"How very astute of you to guess, my 'featherbrained' *muchacha!"* drawled a low, mocking male voice. "And what a pity you did!"

The two women looked up in shock as General Hernando Zamora stepped soundlessly from the shadowed cane at their backs, and into the glow of their little fire.

The snout of the long black rifle he carried was aimed at Krissoula's heart.

Chapter Twenty=Four

"You almost convinced me that you were as foolish as you wanted us to believe, señorita," Zamora purred, running a long, elegant olive finger down Krissoula's cheek.

At gunpoint, she and Sofia had been marched back down the rough track to the little village they'd left less than an hour before. The three little carts had vanished, Krissoula noted—no doubt driven off to a new, secret location—and the dirt square in the midst of the abandoned village was deserted save for Zamora's motley little army and their mounts, and a crackling fire about which the band had congregated to cook and consume their evening meal. Now, standing before the moustached man his men openly addressed as "señor general," Krissoula's mind raced with a way to get them out of this predicament . . .

She contemptuously jerked her head away from Zamora's hand, making no attempt to conceal the distaste she felt for him. "Really, General?" she replied with marked sarcasm, and added curiously, playing for time, "What was it that gave me away?"

"The eyes, lovely one, the eyes!" Zamora confided with a wicked chuckle. "Your ways were those of a featherbrained little *bombón*, yet those golden eyes were too bright, too alive and intelligent by far to match your silly words! Perhaps I could persuade you to join our cause, señorita? We can always find a use for such a clever, beautiful spy."

"We?" Krissoula countered. "Surely you speak only of yourself, Señor General!"

"*Sí*, especially myself," Hernando Zamora agreed amicably, his black eyes devouring her lovely face in the torchlight. "The burdens of leadership rest heavily on a man's shoulders. From time to time, it is necessary to lighten those burdens with the little pleasures of life—and what better way to do so than in the arms of a lovely woman?"

He gripped her upper arms and pulled her hard against him so that her breasts were painfully crushed against his cartridge belts. With a low, triumphant chuckle at her expression, he ducked his head to hers to steal a savage kiss, then recoiled with a startled curse as her vicious teeth sank deep into his lip. He wiped a trickle of blood away on his knuckles and glowered at her.

"Stick to what you do best, Zamora—overthrowing governments and presidents—and leave me alone!" she hissed. "You'll have better luck deposing a good man like Presidente Mitre than you will at bedding me!"

Her scoffing tone drew a furious scowl from Zamora—and a ripple of uneasy laughter from his watching men that was quickly subdued by a murderous glare from their leader. In his outrage, the general thrust her away from him so roughly she lost her balance and sprawled backward to the dirt.

"Take this little *ramera* and the other skinny *puta* to the church!" he barked, his black eyes igneous with anger at this loss of face, the insult she'd paid to his male pride. "Perhaps come morning, you'll be ready to sing a different tune, eh, *muchacha*? A short tune necessarily, since you'll both be killed before we move out at dawn—unless you try to make yourself a little more—agreeable, shall we say?

"If not—well, perhaps we'll see how you like being bound and spreadeagled over a wagon wheel, *muchacha*, and how defiant you can manage to be after my men have used you, one after the other? There are seventy-five of them in all, girl, and no woman could survive such an ordeal. Think about it, eh, golden eyes?"

He cast Krissoula a chilling smile that made her pale despite her air of bravado. Yet in answer, as two of his men roughly hustled Sofia and her away, she spat at him over her shoulder, "Better dead than *your* whore, General!"

Zamora's men flung them inside the ruined church, slammed the door in their wake, and left them in total darkness.

"*Dios mío,* what is to become of us?" whispered Sofía, sinking to her knees. Her legs refused to hold her any longer, a result of an exhausting day's march, no food, and sheer terror combined. "Do—do you think it was wise to make that awful man so very angry, *niña?*" she asked with the mildest hint of reproof in her tone.

"What other choice did I have, tell me that?" Krissoula snapped irritably, prowling about and exploring the inky confines of their makeshift prison with her bare fingertips. Her body ached with fatigue, screamed for the sleep denied it for two nights in succession now, and yet she dare not relax, not yet.

"If I'd been willing, Zamora would have taken me to his bed,"she continued, "—then seen us shot without blinking an eye while he buttoned his breeches! This way, the shoe's on the other foot for a while."

"I don't understand?"

"Well, I made a fool of Zamora by laughing in his face, no? And proud men like him can't stand being made to look weak or small—especially not by a woman, and especially not in front of their men! I'd bet right now that cockroach is planning ways to make me beg for my life come morning!" She laughed harshly. "He hopes by forcing us to spend the night here in darkness, with only our fears for company, that he'll break me, make me grovel and promise him anything he wants, if only he'll spare us. That way, he'll regain his men's respect. But he still means to shoot us, even if I let him bed me, Sofía, make no mistake on that count!"

"But why! We've done nothing to him!"

"That's where you're wrong, my friend. He can't risk letting us go now. We've seen the rifles, guessed their purpose. If we escape, we could carry word of Zamora's plans to overthrow General Mitre to *el presidente* himself!

"But—with the grace of God—by defying him the way I did, I've bought us a little time, don't you see, Sofía? And we need all the time we can get to think of a way out of here!"

Ages passed, and not another word was dropped into the yawning black silence by either of the women. Sofía was too overwrought for conversation, Krissoula too preoccupied in getting her bearings.

Her hands told her they were in a large, blank-walled room within the ruined church. Three of the walls were sturdy, but the fourth had crumbled in places, leaving a gap large enough to crawl through, a result of the adobe succumbing to the elements over the years. Rain had leaked through a hole way above in the vaulting roof, from which several tiles were missing. By craning her neck, Krissoula could make out a patch of dark cloud far above, lightened from behind by a skulking moon and the distant glimmer of a single star. Escape that way—up and over the rooftop—was a possibility, except for one important missing element. Lacking a fly's singular talent for scaling smooth, bare walls, she had no way to get up there! Besides, prim, staid Sofía could never follow such a lead, even could she find a means to climb up there herself. There had to be another way . . .

"Stay right where you are, Sofía," she whispered, breaking the long silence. "I'll be right back. There's another room beyond this one—I can feel a hole in the wall. I'll see what's beyond it and come right back to you, I promise. Maybe there's an opening those *revolucionarios* overlooked, and we can escape. Wouldn't that be wonderful, *amiga?*"

Sofía murmured shaky assent, warning Krissoula, "Be careful, *niña!*"

Krissoula picked her way through the rubble in the darkness, and squeezed through the hole. Like a blind woman, she groped her way about this second room as she had the first. Immediately, she realized she must be in the nave of the church, for this area was far larger than the first. Sounds echoed. Moreover, puny moonlight spattered down in weird, patchy formations through the remains of the shattered stained-glass window beyond the altar, giving her a little light to see by.

She stopped in her tracks, able to discern several hulking shadows in the gloom, to feel the warmth and smell the sweat of something animal and alive. Mules! Why, there were the three carts she'd seen earlier! General Zamora hadn't detailed some of his men to drive the caches of rifles to a safer hiding place, as she would have expected. He'd cleverly hidden them here, practically under her very nose! However, he obviously intended to move the weapons out in the not too distant future, for the mules were still harnessed into the traces, and her outstretched hand and the reappearing moon's benevolent light also revealed the presence of the coffins, still loaded onto the wagon-beds.

Come on, Krissoula, think, think! she urged herself, racking her poor, tired brain to the very limits. *The* carretas *and the mules are plenty to work with, are they not,* gitana? *Surely you can come up with a plan using both carts and mules that would see you set free?* Sí. There must be a way! Was she dead from the neck up, that she could think of none—?

She looked at the carts again, saw the sturdy wheels and the patterns the moonlight made on the stone floor as it silhouetted the spokes, and like a wheel her mind spun, picking up one idea, discarding it for another. What if she and Sofía hid aboard the carts until the doors were opened, and then whipped the mules into a gallop and careened through them and into the night, leaving Zamora and his men gaping after them?

. . . dead from the neck up! nagged a little voice in her ear.

Fool! That wouldn't work! Zamora's rebels had enough rifles

and more than enough horses to overtake them in minutes, and riddle them with as many bullet holes as a sieve in the process!

... *dead from the neck up!* came the voice again, insisting she had missed something, and this time, she listened to that voice. Dead. Mmm, all right. But 'dead' what? What was that inner voice trying to tell her? Dead men? Of course. And what did dead men need? Nothing but their—coffins!

She stepped towards one of the mules and petted its nose, letting it smell her and grow accustomed to her scent so it would not bray in alarm and alert Zamora and his band outside. When it seemed the animal accepted her presence, she clambered up into the *carreta* and crouched alongside the simple casket of rough-hewn white wood, tugging at the lid.

Blessed Saint Sara, what luck! She'd hit the mark first time! It was the casket which had fallen off the cart earlier, and the lid was still loose. She heaved with all her strength, and it slithered aside, torn free of its remaining pair of nails. As she'd expected, the coffin was lined with rifles, each barrel wrapped in oiled cloth, each stock of fine, polished wood protruding. Unfortunately, that was not all there was inside—*Dios,* no, she realized with a gulp. There was a corpse in there, too! A very dead, very stiff corpse . . .

Forcing herself to look down into the casket in the sickly moonlight, she saw a pair of wide-open eyes staring sightlessly back at her, framed by a face that was young and not unpleasing—save for the neat little hole between those startled dark brows. The young man's body was still dressed in the smart blue uniform of Presidente Mitre's personal guard—the same uniform she'd seen worn by the soldiers stationed outside the presidential palace, the Casa Rosada, in Buenos Aires. The fringed epaulets and gold braid and buttons gleamed slyly in the light . . .

Krissoula turned away, feeling sick. This was by no means the first dead man she'd ever seen, but his youth and his startled expression reminded her so much of Miguel that morning two years ago when they'd brought him home to her that her belly heaved. There was no need to wonder who'd slain the young officer, no need at all! No doubt *el Presidente* Mitre's spies had gotten wind of the imminent attempt to overthrow him and his government and stage a revolution. Accordingly, the young officer and his company had been sent out into the countryside to find and crush the revolutionaries long before they reached the city, but had run afoul of Zamora's little army instead. The other two coffins, she knew, would contain still other bodies. And, heart thudding, belly

315

churning, that knowledge supplied the very idea she'd been seeking . . .

It took, she estimated, close to an hour to do what she had to do, and she was trembling with exertion when she was finally done with the first part of her plan.

Using a stout piece of metal she'd found in a corner—it appeared to be a large metal hinge that had fallen off a door—she'd managed to lever off the lid of a second casket to reveal, as she'd expected, a second corpse, this one far uglier and more frightening in death than the first, its face an openmouthed mask of blood and horror. Then, huffing and puffing and straining, she'd managed to drag the unwieldy corpses from the caskets inch by inch, until their own weight had toppled them over into the carts. From there, it had been an easy matter to roll them out of the carts and onto the stone floor, an onerous task that their very stiffness mercifully aided, for it was like rolling logs. After that, it had seemed relatively easy to drag them by the ankles back to the hole she'd crawled through. Neither of them had been large men, and for a woman she was strong, although petite.

"Sofía!" she'd hissed through the opening.

"Sí?"

"Follow the sound of my voice and come here. I need your help."

"All right." In moments, she heard scufflings, and then seconds later Sofía's outstretched hand encountered Krissoula's warm one and clasped it like a lifeline.

"Did you find a way out?" she asked hoarsely, and Krissoula knew that in her absence, the older woman had been weeping.

"In a manner of speaking, sí, I think I have," Krissoula said grimly. "Here. I want you to hold onto this and pull with all your strength when I give the word, comprende?" She paused and licked her dry lips, wondering how best to continue. "And Sofía—you are not to scream, or faint, or do anything that might annoy me, like crying, you understand? Promise me, Sofía?"

"I promise," Sofía rashly agreed, remembering the bold vow she'd given Krissoula before they left that she would help, not hinder.

"Good! I knew I could rely on you!"

And yet—aiee, Blessed Mother, it took all of Sofía's willpower not to scream and faint when—on placing her hand where Krissoula instructed—she encountered a waxy cold, very stiff foot, fringed with rigid, icy toes, and then another foot, equally gruesome.

"*Madre de Dios, niña!* What in God's name have you done!" she whimpered.

"Just pull for all you're worth, *tonta,* and I'll tell your later—unless you'd rather join this one, eh? No? Ah, I thought not, somehow! Now, pull, *amiga,* pull!"

Somehow, with a strength born of desperation, together they managed to pull the two bodies through the small opening and into one corner of the first room. That being accomplished to a critical Krissoula's satisfaction, they bundled the uniformed corpses in their own cloaks, Sofía moaning softly all the while. Hopefully, to a cursory glance under a raised lantern, it would appear that the two women were fast asleep, should anyone come to check on them . . .

"Now, do you have my shawl and the things inside it?" Krissoula asked, breathing heavily with exertion.

"*Sí,* it's here, next to mine."

"Good. Pick them both up, and take my hand."

Krissoula led Sofía through the hole in the wall and into the other part of the church. In the sickly moonlight, the caskets with their lids removed had a macabre appearance, and Sofía crossed herself and muttered a prayer under her breath. "Those men, were they—?"

"*Sí,*" Krissoula confirmed, tight-lipped. "Three of Presidente Mitre's most trusted guards, tucked in for their eternal rest with a lining of the *revolutionarios'* rifles! Our General Zamora has a twisted sense of humor, no?"

"But what now? Why did you want the—the bodies moved back there?"

"I'll tell you now, Sofía darling," Krissoula purred in a voice so soft and gentle Sofía had to blink to reassure herself she wasn't dreaming, "but you must trust me to know what's best for us, and promise to do everything I tell you to do—no matter how frightened it makes you or how unpleasant it may be—agreed? Remember, Sofía, our lives and our honor are at stake here!"

"I'll—I'll try."

"Very well. Here's how it goes. You will climb into that cart, and into that coffin right there—the taller one of the two—and I will replace the lid. No, no, curse it, Sofía, stop it, stop it! You swore you wouldn't do that!" Krissoula hissed sharply, reaching out and shaking her shivering companion, whose teeth were chattering uncontrollably.

"Get into a c-c-coffin—! Aiee, no, no! I can't do it, *niña,* I just can't! I won't—! Ask me anything but that—anything, anything!"

"Nonsense! If I can do it, so can you. Besides, I checked my plan, and the coffins are poorly made—there's more than enough air coming in through the boards for us to breathe. Once you're safely in place, I'm coming back here to set fire to the church. It'll take a few minutes, but once it catches well the smoke and flames should set up a fine panic amongst Zamora's men." Her golden eyes gleamed as she relished the thought.

"But we'll be trapped—burned alive!"

"The devil we will, *tonta!* Think about it, Sofía. Which is more important to Zamora—us, or his precious rifles? The *rifles,* of course—and we'll be right in the midst of them! When the alarm goes up, Zamora will give the order to open the doors and drive the *carretas* to safety long before he remembers us, and sends anyone to check on our well-being, *if* he bothers to think of us at all! By that time, those poor dead fellows next door will in all probability be unrecognizable, and there's a better than even chance that Zamora will believe that *we* perished, if he finds their charred remains. In either event, I'm certain he won't think to look inside the coffins in all the confusion. Probably he'll send men on horses out searching for us, believing we escaped some other way. We simply wait until the coast is clear, jump out and go on our way. What do you say?" It was a good plan, a viable plan, and she felt deserving of a small crumb or two of appreciation—which was not offered by Sofía.

"You're mad! You're quite mad, *niña!*" Sofía babbled, her brown eyes almost starting from her head in the moonlight.

"Pah! Think what you will! I'd rather be mad and alive than sane and dead! Now, are you going to get into that coffin like a good girl, Sofía—or must I help you?" she asked sternly. She was fully prepared to knock Sofía senseless for her own good if the woman refused, but hoped it wouldn't come to that.

"How long must we stay inside?" Sofía asked in a very small voice.

"For as long as we have to," Krissoula told her firmly, making no promises she couldn't keep. "For my part, I intend to catch up on my sleep while I'm in there, I don't know about you!" she joked. "Now, up with you—and be brave!"

She felt how Sofía trembled as she helped her to clamber up into the *carreta,* and stretched her length gingerly between the neatly arrayed rifles, and felt pity weaken her—an emotion she steadfastly drove out of her mind. Time enough for comforting and pity

318

later, when they were free—

"I can't stop thinking that a dead man was in here a few moments ago!" Sofía squeaked like a frightened little mouse, her lower lip trembling uncontrollably.

"Believe me, it's not the dead men you have to watch out for, *amiga*—it's those rogues that are still breathing!" she teased wickedly. *"Vaya con Dios!"*

She reached over and gave poor, clammy Sofía a peck on her icy cheek, thinking fleetingly that she made a pretty fair replacement for a corpse before hefting the weighty lid over the woman and settling it in place. "Can you breathe, Sofía?" she asked. "Knock once if you can?" A reassuring if timid knock sounded in reply, and Krissoula let out the breath she'd been holding and clambered down from the cart.

The nave of the church had obviously been used by those blasphemous Zamora dogs as a stable before tonight, Krissoula realized, but she was grateful it had, for she needed straw for her purpose. Carrying a bundle of it, she crawled back to the first room, and heaped the straw up against the door. Taking one of the precious *fósforos* from her bundle, she lit it and touched the yellow flame to the dry straw. At once, a pungent singed-grass odor filled the darkness, and then a small, crumbling, traveling column of light stretched out along the edge of the door, growing wider and more orange by the moment as it licked at the crumbling, termite-eaten wood. She crouched there until she was certain the fire wouldn't go out, then beat a hurried exit back to the other room.

In less than a minute, she was settled in "her" coffin, the lid dragged over and replaced.

Muttering every prayer she could recall to every saint she knew, she closed her eyes and listened to the pounding of her terrified heart as she began the long wait.

Chapter Twenty-Five

It seemed forever but could only have been minutes later when Krissoula heard crashes and cracklings outside, muffled by her wooden tomb. The stuffy air in the coffin now also held the acrid scent of smoke which, mingled with the odors of the oily gun-casings and the faint sweet-sour odor of death, made her gag.

Sweat rolled in rivers down her throat and breasts, and her palms were as slick as if she'd greased them with butter. Aiee, *Dios,* this was torture indeed! What if she'd judged Zamora wrongly? What if the fire traveled too swiftly for his men to save the rifles, and with them, Sofia and her? Blessed *Madre,* they'd be burned alive!

But she need not have worried. As she'd shrewdly figured, Zamora would allow nothing to come in the way of his revolution!

After seeing the two women imprisoned, he'd sat by the fire swigging wine from a leather *bota* while poring over maps and diagrams, planning how best to overrun and attack the Casa Rosada's complex deployment of loyal presidential guards. He'd hoped, by concentrating on such vital matters, to subdue the niggling anger in his breast that the golden-eyed *puta* had caused by belittling him in front of his men—and to forget the lust for that same woman which made his breeches strain uncomfortably across his swollen groin.

Beside him, offering unwanted suggestions from time to time, sat Ramirez, a wealthy *hacendero* from the north who'd ridden into the abandoned village an hour or two ago. Zamora personally disliked the man, but he was no fool for all that; far too clever to look a gift horse in the mouth. Ramirez had played a major part in his plans from the very first, two years ago now, by finding wealthy rebel sympathizers willing to finance his revolution, which were always costly projects at best, requiring vast sums of money for arms, supplies, and the inevitable bribes. Ramirez expected, in return for his assistance, that he and his friends would be given plum government posts when Zamora was sworn in as the new president in Mitre's stead. They'd been discussing this very prospect when one of the general's soldiers yelled the alarm.

"*Fire!* Fire in the church, General!"

Leaping to his feet, Zamora had run across the square towards the crumbling adobe mission, and seen for himself the smoke pouring out from beneath the plank door. That cursed woman! That conniving little *ramera* had done this, he thought, trembling with rage. Well, they could both be roasted alive for her pains, he swore, murder crawling in his black eyes like hungry maggots . . .

"The guns, you fools!" he'd barked, hurling orders interspersed with curses to left and right. "Martinez, García, unbolt the doors! You others, drive the *carretas* out before they go up in smoke! Run, damn your stupid hides!"

The village well was dry—had been for years. The nearest streambed was half a mile distant, the river closer to three long miles away. Extinguishing the blaze was out of the question! Standing with his fists planted on his hips, his head thrown back, Zamora saw the rear roof and walls of the church—where they'd thrown the female prisoners earlier—collapse inward with a boom and a hungry roar, and smiled with grim satisfaction. He saw orange flames and showers of amber sparks blaze like fireworks against the indigo night sky, whirled like fire demons by the wind, and for one dreadful moment, his smile faded, and he believed his plans had fallen in ashes along with the church: that the wind must surely carry the fire onward to the nave where his arms were stored, before his men would drive them out to safety . . .

The heat inside the coffins had grown intense, unbearable over the past few minutes. The sounds beyond the claustrophobic wooden walls were loud and frightening. Through the chinks in the lid of the coffin, Krissoula could see glimpses of red and orange light. Flames, she realized, panic foul and furry on her tongue. The fire was spreading so quickly—*too* quickly, surely?

She bit down hard on her lip to quell a sob of panic. Soon! Oh, dear God, someone had to come for the carts soon! Surely Zamora didn't mean to sit back and watch while his precious rifles melted down to worthless scrap? He couldn't—she'd been counting on the rifles being of the utmost value to him!

Oh, Blessed Mother, don't let me have misjudged him! Don't let me be proven wrong, because if I am I'll have murdered Sofía—!

she begged silently, wondering with a deep, pervading sense of dread if Sofía was all right, or if in her terror her heart had given out, and she were dead inside her wooden cage . . . ?

The mules were braying with fear now, moving around so violently the *carretas* were skewed to and fro, the two women inside the coffins jolted mercilessly about, which added to their terror.

A shot rang out, then another, and then, wonder of wonders, Krissoula saw through the chinks that the darkness had lightened measurably beyond her narrow cage! Her spirits soared with relief. At last, they were coming! Simultaneously, she heard the scream of rusty hinges as the wide church doors were flung open, and felt the flames roar louder and leap up with a *whoooosh* to twice their former size, as fresh air rushed into the church to feed them. Harsh voices raised in panic sounded close by, and moments later she felt the cart lurch as a driver leaped up to take the reins.

"Yeeaaah! Get up there! *Andalé! Andalé!*" the soldiers yelled, slashing the reins across the terrified mules' rumps.

The carts bolted forward and out into the night, wooden wheels rolling and clattering for several minutes across uneven ground until they finally shuddered to a halt.

"You cut it too blasted close there, García!" Krissoula heard Zamora bark. "I'd have had you shot if you'd failed!"

"I could not help it, *Señor General!*" the soldier protested. "The bolts on the doors were too hot to slide free with our bare hands—we had to shoot them off to get at them! Look at my hands, señor—they are blistered!"

"So I see," Zamora acknowledged pitilessly. "But what're a few petty blisters when weighed against our glorious cause, eh? You'll be well rewarded for your loyalty when I'm in control of this country, never fear, García. The important thing is the weapons are safe. I think it best we move out, immediately. There's no telling who's seen the fire on a clear night like this, eh, Ramirez, nor who might come to investigate the cause?

"Rico, pass the word! Have the men saddle up and prepare to move out on the double. As for you three, drive the carts on to the next rendezvous! Follow the Paraná's course until you reach the ferry at San Nicolas, about fifty miles southwest of here. Make camp, and wait there till we join you. I'll send an escort with you—just in case there are more of our beloved presidente's men out looking for us. Jump to it, men!"

"At once, General!"

"Lucky for you your men were successful in saving the rifles,

322

Zamora," Ramirez observed softly, gazing up at the inferno the church had so swiftly become. "That's why I came here tonight—to tell you that the 'goose' who supplied our golden eggs is, regrettably, no more!"

"Aguilar's dead?" Zamora rasped, darting the weasely Ramirez a swift, searching glance.

"*Sí,* Zamora, our dear *compañero,* Felipe, is dead. The fool was never much of a horseman—he was overly fond of the whip and the spur, you know the type? God knows why he took it upon himself to try making the ride to my *estancia* by night, but try it he did—! The stupid bastard paid for his foolishness with his neck. His horse stumbled in a pothole, they say, and threw him, and now his bastard nephew stands to inherit everything. A nephew who is not, I might add, a fellow who'd be in the least sympathetic to our cause!"

"And why not?" Zamora demanded, reluctant to let any possible source of backing for his revolution be so summarily dismissed. "Will my new government not benefit the wealthy *hacenderos* such as this nephew you speak of, and put the illiterate peasants back where they belong—where they were before Presidente Mitre came to power with his government of bleeding hearts—crushed under our bootheels?"

"Ah, *sí,* that would normally be the case, I agree. But this one's had a taste of poverty for himself, apparently, General Zamora—and those are the hardest to convince that right is on our side! This San Martín fellow was raised in the *barrios,* you see. Rumor has it he goes back to La Ciudad de los Niños several times a year to distribute staples to those filthy little bastards who live on the mudbanks—a sort of Lord Bountiful, one might say, eh?" Ramirez disclosed with a sneering smile. "No, Zamora, with Felipe de Aguilar dead and gone, you can kiss the Aguilar fortune goodbye. There'll be no more help from that direction! I trust, however, that you'll remember my past efforts on your behalf, and act accordingly when you are sworn in as *el presidente* of our beloved Argentina?"

With that pointed comment, Ramirez strolled away to his horse, leaving Zamora scowling after him.

Krissoula—who'd overheard every exciting tidbit of this exchange through the coffin, of course—was now quivering with excitement. She'd heard Ramirez's voice, and had recognized it at once as belonging to Felipe's weasely friend, Jaime Ramirez, the one she'd put in his place the night of the *asado.*

323

So! Her gut instincts about the man had not been wrong, after all! He was every bit as sly as she'd believed, and—from the sound of it—had either persuaded or duped Felipe into supporting Zamora's revolution, believing he'd be given a government post in return for his financial help! Little wonder Felipe had been steadily draining Tierra Rosa's finances. But now, if Ramirez were to be believed—and there was no reason to think he might be lying to Zamora—Felipe de Aguilar, their "golden goose," was dead! Ah, but that was welcome news. She felt no grief or pity for his parting whatsoever . . .

The carts moved out soon after, bumping along the rutted track that stretched across the Pampa, headed—if Zamora's orders were being followed to the letter, southwest, some fifty miles downriver, fifty miles closer to their original destination of the city of Buenos Aires. How kind of General Zamora to see them transported by cart! Krissoula thought with a wicked grin, stifling a chuckle of laughter. She much preferred riding to walking, however unusual her conveyance might be!

Her fear—whether it was premature or not for it to do so—had completely evaporated now. Instead, a giddy sense of euphoria had taken its place. What would the driver of the cart do, she wondered impishly, should she throw off the coffin lid and sit bolt upright like one returned from the dead? Without a doubt he'd piddle himself in sheer terror, she considered, and had to press her hand over her mouth to stifle a giggle.

Still smiling, she at last succumbed to the monotonous rhythm of the cart's wheels. It rocked her like a cradle until she fell fast asleep.

When she next opened her eyes, she glimpsed bright blue sky through the cracks of the coffin's lid, and, much closer, tree branches heavy with green leaves crisscrossed this way and that. They'd stopped while she slept, she realized, and the soldiers had probably attempted to conceal the *carretas* from curious eyes under heaps of brush.

She lay very still, and craned her ears for some sound. Flowing water, and the distant murmur of voices. Dare she hope the *revolutionarios* had made their camp some distance from the place where they'd concealed the carts? She waited several more agonizing, long moments to make sure no one was nearby, then tentatively raised the coffin lid. Sunlight dazzled her eyes, but they quickly adjusted. She peered over the casket's rim and looked around. Perfect. Oh, thank you, Madonna!

They were deep in a thicket of bushes on the crest of a steep slope that led down to banks of the Piraná River. The mules had been unharnessed, and were cropping the grass nearby along with the horses, while the drivers and their escort—six, maybe seven men as well as the other three—were sprawled about a fire on the riverbanks, cooking a meal. The smell of woodsmoke, spicy coffee, and frying fish carried on the morning air, reminding her that she'd not eaten in almost forty-eight hours. Her mouth watered, and her belly growled loudly in agreement. Still, there'd be no food coming their way, not yet. First, she had to let Sofía out, and then they still had to get away from here . . .

Her heart dropped like a stone when she raised the other loosened coffin lid. In the brilliant sunshine, Sofía's complexion was so pale and bloodless it appeared translucent. Her narrow features were pinched, the high cheekbones prominent under ashen skin. Her eyes were closed, not so much as a lash flickering to indicate she was still alive.

Biting her lip, Krissoula picked up Sofía's limp hand and began slapping gently at her wrist in an effort to revive her friend without alerting the soldiers. Oh, she couldn't be dead, she just couldn't be, she thought desperately, chafing Sofía's other hand now. And then, so suddenly Krissoula wasn't expecting it, Sofía sat bolt upright, her brown eyes wide and staring.

"Are we dead?" she demanded, the words bursting from her. "Are we dead yet, *niña?*" She looked dazedly around, as if surprised that heaven should appear so disappointingly worldly, with trees and sky and soil as she remembered.

"Not by a long chalk!" Krissoula whispered, grinning so broadly in her relief that her face came close to splitting clear in two. "You just fainted, I think. *Caramba!* My plan worked, Sofía! Better than that, we're less than a day's walk from the city! But come on, out with you. We're not free and clear just yet—look down there!"

Sofía looked, saw the soldiers guffawing around their campfire, and clambered out of both coffin and cart with a nimbleness and alacrity that quite astonished Krissoula. Hiding a grin, she replaced both lids on the coffins and gestured Sofía to help her clear the brush which had concealed them away from each cart's wheels. This task done to her satisfaction, she hefted her shoulder up against the cartbed, and began pushing.

"What now?" Sofía demanded indignantly.

"You don't think I've gone through all this just to see Zamora's revolution succeed, do you?" she hissed back. "Besides, this slope is surely a gift from God, a sign that El Señor Himself favors our good

325

Presidente Mitre," she added slyly. "So push, Sofía—and let's send Zamora's guns to a watery grave in the Piraná!"

They pushed the *carretas* and, as she'd anticipated, together they were able to edge the wheels over the rim of the slope. The weight of the cart and the incline did the rest. One after another, the little two-wheeled carts rumbled silently down the hill and tipped into the muddy river.

The first tumbled in with a splash, and that loud splash was the first warning the soldiers had. By the time they'd realized what had happened, the second *carreta* was fast approaching the riverbank, the third halfway down the hill and rolling faster with each passing second as it picked up momentum!

The soldiers ran about this way and that like chickens with their heads axed, screaming futile suggestions at each other. Others raced for the last cart with a bravado that was suicidal, while, meanwhile, Krissoula hefted Sofía up onto the back of one of their horses and leaped astride another for herself.

"Hang on for all you are worth, *amiga mía!*" she sang out. "Your first riding lesson is about to begin!"

With a wild whoop of triumph, she leaned down and slapped Sofía's horse across the rump, before digging heels into her own.

While the soldiers tore off boots and shirts and dived into the deep waters of the Paraná to try and retrieve at least some of the lost weapons, the two horses took off at a gallop, unnoticed, the women riding astride them. The other freed mounts of the *revolutionarios' remuda* milled about for a few minutes, and then both horses and mules followed suit, leaving their distracted riders afoot.

Ah, *sí,* Krissoula believed in being thorough—she'd left nothing to chance! It would be many months—perhaps years—before Zamora was able to replace his lost weapons and stage his little revolution.

"Viva el Presidente Mitre!"

Chapter Twenty-Six

Three afternoons later, a horse-drawn tram set them down at the end of the trolley tracks, far from any place that Krissoula recognized as even vaguely familiar from her last visit to the city of Buenos Aires.

She offered Sofía her arm to help her alight from the trolley, and as it trundled away Krissoula happened to glance across at her friend's tired face and saw the dismay that widened her eyes.

Looking about her, she immediately understood Sofía's horrified reaction, for the retiring, refined woman was as out of place here in the hurly-burly of the *barrios* of Buenos Aires as she'd once been herself in the drawing rooms of Barcelona!

There were no tree-lined boulevards down here by the wharves of Barrio la Boca, as there had been in the rich *porteño* areas of the city, only rickety piers of wood or stone thrown together in haphazard fashion to carry pedestrians over the unsavory mudflats of the Plata.

Neither were there any sidewalk cafés or fashionable tea rooms, where the elegant sound of clinking china carried above the well-modulated murmur of polite conversation. There were instead a number of rowdy taverns jostling for space on the wharves, and whorehouses that catered to sailors, ringing with boozy songs, snarled obscenities, and lewd propositions!

No romantically gas-lit plazas with wrought-iron lampposts and bubbling fountains were to be found here, with fashionable ladies taking the afternoon air beneath frilly parasols; no frivolous shoppers for furs and jewels and perfumes, as in the plush establishments of Calle Florida that catered only to the wealthy. Here there were only the noisy open-air markets, reeking of fish and fowl, fruit and vegetables, and, come nightfall, the only lighting you'd find were hissing resin torches set in sconces along the walls, torches lit by *el sereno,* the nightwatchman who called the hours.

And the only "strollers" hereabouts after dark would be the whores and their masters, or mulatto and Negro washerwomen walking wearily home with their huge laundry bundles balanced atop their tignoned heads, or burly tattooed stevedores headed for dimly lit bars and smoky cafés, and the cribs of the women.

The back streets that led away from the wharves of Buenos Aires's Rio de la Plata and which housed the city's poor boasted no fancy sidewalks of cobblestones, or granite brought from the island of Martín García, or even humble planking for pavements. They were a confusing maze of narrow, twisting streets of compacted dirt, Krissoula saw, little better than quagmires today after the rainstorm of the afternoon and night before. They promised to be no grander than rutted alleys even when the sun baked them hard as adobe at the height of summer, she thought as she took Sofía's elbow and they trudged onward, headed for God-only-knew-where.

Rotted fruit, vegetable peelings, and even the bloated, fly-blown bodies of dead animals littered the winking brown puddles, drawing swarms of shiny blue flies in the steamy afternoon heat. Oozing black mud soon splattered the hems of Krissoula's and Sofía's gowns, and splotched their stockings. Rivers of sweat glued their clothing to their spines and drenched their hair, the humidity making Sofía's as limp and forlorn as wilted lettuce, and Krissoula's even more tightly curled than usually.

Leche! It was too much! Ignoring the appreciative, or scornful, or more often openly curious stares of passersby, Krissoula dropped her shawl bundle of belongings and hoisted up her skirts, tucking the folds into the belt at her waist so that both her petticoats and dress cleared the dirty streets. Let them gawp at her, if they wished! If they hadn't seen a pair of trim ankles or a couple of slim bare calves before in their miserable lives, then more was the pity and here was their chance! This was neither the time nor the place to allow any qualms of false modesty to influence one, she decided firmly, attempting to set an example for Sofía to follow. Practicality was what counted here.

"Niña!" Sofía exclaimed, shocked. "Everyone can see your ankles!"

"Sofía, please don't start!" Krissoula snapped, her own exhaustion and fears for their future making short work of her small, threadbare store of patience. "Don't you understand? Don't you see? That part of our lives—that time when allowing anyone even a glimpse of our ankles was a sin—is *over,* done with! In the *barrios,* no one will give a damn what we say or do, or if we're modest women or brazen hussies! It's the strong who survive here, Sofía, and our strength will be the only calling card that matters, here on. If we show any weakness or fear, we'll go under! And—since this is one of my two remaining decent gowns—I intend to make it last for as long as possible. Remember, there won't be any others when these are past repair. If making them last means showing my ankles so that the hems stay clean, then so be it! And Sofía—unless you want that gown of yours to look like a dirty rag, do the same. Hitch up your skirts, and to hell with modesty!"

To Krissoula's horror, Sofía's eyes filled with tears that spilled over and trickled down her cheeks. Her entire body quivered. At once Krissoula was filled with remorse for the sharpness of her tongue. *Dios,* she'd expected too much too soon of the woman, that much was obvious! The escape from Zamora and his men, those gruelling hours trapped in the coffins, must have taxed Sofía's reserves of strength to breaking point. She'd have to take things slower, a little at a time, if she wanted the older woman to adjust and adapt to her new life. If not, there was a good chance that Sofía would simply give up, overwhelmed by their changed circumstances. And giving up here would mean a slow, miserable death . . .

"Oh, Sofía, don't cry, please don't? I can't bear to see you this way!" Krissoula implored, taking the older woman's elbow and steering her into the relative privacy offered by the gloomy mouth of a littered alleyway. "What is it? Tell me," she urged, slipping her arm around Sofía's narrow shoulders, which were heaving with her sobs. "You came through our last adventures so bravely—can this really be so terrible after all that?"

"I'm afraid, *niña,* so very afraid!" Sofía managed to blurt out between noisy sobs. "Look at these streets—all these rough, shifty-eyed people—ayee, *Dios,* they frighten me so, *niña!* It's as if—it's as if they're from another world, a frightening, threatening world which I know nothing of. How shall we survive, Krissoula? How will we eat? How will we live?"

Krissoula's jaw tightened. She squeezed Sofía's shoulder. "Dry your eyes, Sofía, and stop worrying. We'll be fine, I promise. I'll take care of you, you know I will. Haven't I looked out for you this far? Soon you'll see that although people are poor in these parts, they're still human beings with good and bad among them, just like you and I. Poor as they are, they're more like you than you'd ever have thought possible, you'll see."

"Really?"

"Really. It's just that here, it's keeping your family fed and decently clothed and warm that's important, rather than scrabbling to keep abreast with the latest fashions and who's who in society circles. Being poor has a way of stripping off all the shams and pretenses in our lives. Airs and graces and appearances don't count here. Food, water, shelter—survival, Sofía, that's what it's all about, *survival's* what matters here! Anything more is a gift from God." *Or stolen,* she added wryly to herself.

"And can we survive?"

"Can we? You dear, silly goose, of course we can! The great Krissoula and her wonderful companion Sofía can survive anything! No difficulty too large or too small to overcome!" she boasted flamboyantly. "Is that all that's frightening you? Why, you silly thing, we'll not only survive—we'll wring some happiness out of doing it, too! A month or so, and you'll wonder what on earth you were so worried about, I promise you," she lied brightly, hoping against hope she was right as she forced a brilliant, optimistic smile.

"Here, let me help you to hitch up your skirts like mine, and we'll be on our way. I want to find us a good, snug place to sleep before nightfall." *Because the* barrios *will really come to humming life after dark, and in ways you're better off not seeing just yet, my innocent Sofía!* she added silently, keeping her expression bland as she helped a trembling Sofía to tuck her skirts into the sash at her waist.

"I'm sorry, *niña*. I don't know what came over me—! Please, forgive my foolishness?" Sofía begged, gamely sniffing back her tears, and Krissoula leaned forward and on impulse kissed her cheek and hugged her warmly.

The affectionate gesture strengthened them both, bound them closer and dispelled the terrible desolation of their predicament. At least they had each other for comfort, and as long as they did, they were not alone. "Consider it forgiven and forgotten," Krissoula declared, "and come on!"

They walked and walked down endless streets that all had a shabby sameness about them, until Krissoula's feet were blistered and weeping and she itched to tear off her ridiculous high-heeled slippers and go barefoot for comfort. What on earth had possessed her to suggest to Sofía that they change into their best garments while still on the outskirts of the city that morning? She must have been crazy!

Sofía, hobbling along beside her, seemed even less comfortable than she, though to her credit she uttered not a murmur of complaint. That was one of the things Krissoula had discovered she

330

liked best about Sofía, and would perhaps prove the single quality to see her through this chapter of their lives: her ability to come to terms with a situation eventually, accept the inevitable, and then do her very best to make the most of it despite her fear.

For all that it was late afternoon, the sticky October heat rose in humid waves all about them, ripely pungent with the smell of decaying rubbish and offal, and, oftimes, something worse. The odor was so fetid in places that Sofía clapped her hand over her mouth to stifle a gag.

They'd left the wharves, the brothels, the rowdy saloons and bars that lined Corrientes Street and others like it far behind them by now, and Krissoula was relieved. Sofía's frequent, shocked gasps at the brazenness of the gaudy, barebreasted prostitutes strutting up and down there, or hanging half out of upstairs windows, and the flashy men who touted the women's tired favors on every street corner, had begun to grate on her nerves.

The area they'd entered was called La Boca, the *barrio,* or district, where the grand homes of the original Spanish colonists who'd first settled Buenos Aires still stood, though sadly run down and neglected now. Buildings rose directly from either side of the narrow streets, some of them boasting balconies of black wrought iron that almost met in the air above their heads and obscured the dazzling blue of the sky.

Formerly the spacious homes of the well-to-do, each house now housed many families. Women lounged in doorways and gossiped or argued while their children swarmed around them, clung whining to their dark skirts, or else played in the gutters. Through the opened doorways, Krissoula glimpsed empty courtyards beyond the high, blank walls that enclosed them, where several lines of wash hung out to dry. In one, a number of chattering women bent over washtubs and scrub-boards. In another, groups of men squatted on the flagstones and played cards or dice. In yet another, a bleary-eyed, rowdy group of drinkers eagerly watched the outcome of a lively, bloody cockfight.

A few narrow grilled windows, not unlike dark, suspicious eyes gouged out from the stained adobe walls, overlooked the streets. In places, efforts had been made to brighten the surroundings a little. Pots of tired-looking geraniums wilted in the heat within peeling wooden window boxes and fluttered faded red petals to the muddy streets below where they settled like drops of old blood.

On another street, garrulous old women dressed in black came out with their pitchers and basins to purchase water from the water-wagon that trundled up and down the rutted streets, a commerce

331

that Krissoula noted and which filled her with dismay. Watching the water-seller fill their vessels by means of a tap set in the enormous wooden barrel anchored atop his cart, she thought, Dios, *is even vital, life-giving water not to be had without a price here?* Obviously not, and that being the case her little store of money—garnered from the sale of the stolen horses that very morning!—would last less time than she'd optimistically planned! The sooner she found work of any kind, the better, she determined grimly.

They crossed another street and entered the area known as Barrio Irlandes where the rich brogue of the Irish poor, driven from their native Ireland by the potato famines, was thick enough on the sultry air to slice with a knife.

The famines had brought desperate Irish immigrants to Argentina in droves and some estimated their numbers at as high as thirty-five thousand Irish in Buenos Aires's province alone, she recalled someone telling her! The more industrious or most fortunate among them had found the better life they sought in South America, profitably turning their old talents to becoming successful sheep ranchers or shepherds, and building a secure future for their large families from the flocks that grazed the rich grasslands of the Pampa. Others had found themselves little better off than they'd been in Ireland, and had ended up here, in the back streets of the city, with a *barrio* named for their people.

The next *barrio* they passed into was smaller, less densely populated than the last, its limits perhaps only two blocks in all. From the open doorway of one dark *taberna* they skirted, Krissoula caught the wink of copper pots adorning the walls, smelled the distinctive aniseed aroma of *aguardiente,* and heard the chords of a softly played guitar. Snatches of the heated yet good-natured arguments of old men within the tavern carried outside to the street, and were in a language she recognized as oh, so very familiar, and which tore at her heartstrings.

Romani! They must be passing through the Barrio de los Gitanos, the Gypsy quarter, she realized, yet she made no move to slow their path. Rather, she hurried Sofía along, chivvying her to keep up a spanking pace that chafed her own blisters unbearably. The thought of lingering here, of begging lodgings for the night amongst the Gypsies, never crossed her mind, for she was certain she'd find no ready welcome there, for all that the inhabitants were of her own blood. In Spain, she'd been considered an outcast, "unclean" since her marriage to a *gorgio*—a non-Gypsy—and in *gitano* eyes, she was no longer of the Rom. Like one who'd died, she

332

knew the Ballardo band had never spoken her name aloud since that day. It was the Gypsy way of things.

Furthermore, it was also customary that respectable Gypsy women never traveled anywhere without either their father or another close male kinsman to escort them, and defend their lives and honor. Her solitary state would tell these Gypsies of the *barrios* all they needed to know of her shameful past, and there was no sense in trying to lie or pretend it was otherwise. As a woman alone, she was branded with her sins as surely as if someone had carved them into her brow!

Naked children, all brown as berries with flashing, sloe-dark eyes and raggedly cropped hair, played with a scrawny puppy in one crumbling courtyard they passed, while their mothers laughed and chatted noisily about a fire, over which bubbled a black kettle filled with savory lamb stew that smelled mouthwatering. In their swirling flowered skirts, prettily embroidered blouses, and fringed shawls, they could have been transported straight from her beloved Andalusia, she thought, and Krissoula's heart grew even heavier. Perhaps they didn't belong here. Perhaps there was no country, no people, to whom she could truly belong, ever again. Who was she now, anyway? Krissoula Ballardo, "La Reina," the Gypsy dancer who'd taken the *aficionados* of flamenco by storm on two continents? The widow of the *gorgio,* Miguel? Or Esteban de San Martín's cast-off *china,* the woman he believed had betrayed him and almost cost him his life? *Dios,* she didn't know anymore, she realized with a mounting sense of panic that greased her palms with sweat! She didn't know who she was—!

One of the women in the courtyard spotted the pair then. With a knowing wink to her companions she left the cooking fire and sidled up to Sofía, stepping in front of her to block her path.

"Your fortune, lady? Let me look at your hand, dearie, and see if your lines are as lucky as your pretty face?" she cajoled.

"Go away!" Sofía blurted, wrenching her hands from the woman's nut-brown fingers.

"Come, come, now, just a little silver piece, pretty lady!" the young Gypsy woman wheedled, her green eyes bright with mischief as she plucked at Sofía's untidy bundle of belongings. "A silver coin, and I'll tell you your heart's desire, that I will! Please, fine lady, my little ones are hungry, and I've another coming soon . . ."

There was a whining, insistent edge to her voice now, and Sofía shuddered and seemed ready to bolt as she hissed, "Don't touch me, you dirty thieving Gypsy! Get away from me!"

"Saint Sara's blessing on your children and yourself, Cousin, but *caray!*—we are even poorer than you!" Krissoula hastily cut in in her Romany tongue which, though a little different from the woman's, she knew would be understood well enough.

The woman's eyes widened in amazement. "Why! You're Romany, no?" she demanded eagerly, her scowl at Sofía's insult miraculously diminished as she turned now to Krissoula.

"Sí! Gitana española—Spanish gypsy. My uncle was—is—Ricardo Ballardo. Perhaps you've heard of him in the old country?"

"Heard of him? But of course! The Ballardo name used to be a legend at the horse fairs in España when I was a little girl! Who among us hasn't heard of the great Ricardo? Come, Cousin, won't you honor us by joining the Reyes band for supper? Believe me, there is always plenty to share with those of the true blood—and a bed under the stars in the courtyard, too, if you're weary and need a safe place to lay your head?" She nudged Krissoula and winked.

Krissoula bit her lip, before plunging on, *"Gracias,* but you should know who I am before you ask me to share your supper, don't you think? And perhaps once you do, you'll take back your invitation, for I won't lie to you, not when you offer your hospitality." She bit her lower lip. "I—I was cast out of my uncle's band back in Spain."

"Cast out? But, whatever for?" the woman asked, her lips twitching at the young woman's serious expression. "You don't look very wicked to me! Did you kill a man, then? Steal from one of your own band? Sleep with your sister's husband?"

Krissoula smiled wryly, for the woman's teasing manner was infectious. "Nothing so easily forgiven, alas! I made the mistake of falling for a *gorgio,* and taking him as my husband. That's why I was cast out."

"Ah, then you're guilty of a very serious crime indeed—that of poor taste in men, eh, Cousin?" The woman rolled her eyes. "Imagine, choosing a cold, pale-skinned *gorgio* over a hot-blooded, passionate *gitano!"* the gypsy woman retorted with another merry wink. "But poor taste or no, come with me anyway, why don't you? Perhaps my husband or brothers will have something to say about you joining us, but I'll put in a good word for you with my father, never fear. You look in need of a square meal and a good night's rest to me. I'll see that you get both."

"Wait!" Krissoula cried as the woman turned back towards the courtyard. "My friend here—what of her?" Of course, she couldn't accept the woman's invitation unless it included Sofía.

"Why, bring the whey-faced *gorgio* with you, *gitana*—if she'll agree to sharing a meal with a band of 'dirty, thieving gypsies,' which I doubt!" The woman grinned wickedly but not unkindly at Sofía, who looked like a terrified rabbit about to faint from fright.

With a relieved nod, Krissoula turned to Sofía and explained the woman's offer in rapid Spanish, ending, "It's getting late, Sofía, and I want us somewhere safe before dark. The woman is kind, however she may seem to you. She's asked us to share their supper and says we can sleep in their courtyard for the night, if we wish. What do you say? Shall I accept for us?"

Sofía fearfully eyed the darkening sky and the way the shadows were beginning to stretch out and fill the narrow alleys like spreading black ink, and crossed herself nervously. Surely anywhere was better than spending the night out in the streets and alleys filled with who-knew-what vermin, human or otherwise, after dark?

Suddenly shamefaced, she swallowed and stammered, "*Sí*, go ahead, *niña*. And—and please, tell the woman that I'm very sorry for my rudeness earlier, but that I—I was afraid of her, and didn't know what else to say. Tell her that I'm—I'm grateful for her offer, and that I accept with pleasure."

Krissoula did so, giving Sofía an approving grin. The other Gypsy woman's surprisingly easy acceptance of her, and Sofía's surprisingly rapid agreement, had suddenly boosted her flagging spirits! The future seemed a little brighter now, no longer completely without promise. A dim but steady light now shone at the end of the future's long, dark tunnel, for if they had friends, they had wealth beyond imagining . . .

"*Bueno!* Then come along with me," the woman declared. "And by the way, my name is Carla Valde. And yours—?"

"Krissoula. And my *gorgio* friend is Sofía."

"*Con mucho gusto, Krissoula y Sofía.*"

Linking her arm through Krissoula's, Carla led them to the group of other curious Gypsy women in the courtyard.

One by one that evening, the menfolk of Carla's father's band, the Reyes, returned to the courtyard, loud with laughter and good humor. There were several arrogant, attractive younger men amongst them, and soon Krissoula could not help but become aware that they were watching her admiringly—though Gypsy manners prevented them from rudely whispering to Carla to ask who she was. Carla eased the uncomfortable, tense moment with her easy smile and open manner, and quickly introduced them.

"Come, Papa, and meet our guests for supper—and perhaps for

335

the night, too. They are from the old country, isn't that wonderful? This here is Señorita Krissoula, and her *gorgio* friend, Doña Sofía. Krissoula, Sofía, my papa, Armando Reyes," Carla declared proudly.

"An honor, Señor Reyes," Krissoula murmured politely, bobbing a curtsey to the man, for as her uncle Ricardo had done, Armando Reyes wore the golden earring of a leader in one earlobe and was deserving of her respect.

Among gypsies, few men were accorded this honor on a lasting basis. The *gorgios* might speak romantically of Gypsy kings and princes, queens or counts yet in reality the old titles, if they'd ever truly existed as legend suggested they had, had long since passed into memory. A Gypsy attained leadership nowadays only by proving his wisdom and his ability to lead his people in times of trouble. And when that danger ceased to exist, so, in many cases, did a chieftain's authority. Matters of Gypsy law and discipline were customarily decided in a democratic manner, by the vote of a council, not a single man. The council convened as need dictated. Armando Reyes, like her uncle, "Count" Ricardo, had obviously proven himself worthy of permanent leadership of his band.

"Your daughter's hospitality does credit to your name, Señor Reyes," Krissoula complimented the man.

"As your beauty graces our humble company, Señorita Krissoula," Armando replied gallantly and with true Gypsy formality.

A man of middle height, he was stockily built with large, attractive features that implied a generous heart. His tanned cheeks were ruddy with color, and his eyes a sparkling green flecked with amber, like Carla's. His hairy arms bulged with muscle where his shirt-sleeves had been rolled up to the elbows, and his broad belly strained the corduroy cloth of his breeches and spread the fronts of his brown leather vest just a little. A smith by trade, she guessed by his burly build and ruddy complexion, or a farrier; perhaps even both.

"So, tell me, Señorita Krissoula, where are your menfolk?" Armando asked congenially, looking about him. "I'd enjoy reminiscing about the old country over a little wine!"

It was the question she'd been dreading answering, and her mouth suddenly went dry. Yet Carla again stepped into the breech, murmuring, *"Con su permiso, amiga?"* and receiving Krissoula's grateful nod, she quickly explained her new friend's exile from the Ballardo band.

"Caray! So that's how it was, *pobrecita,"* Armando murmured

sympathetically at length, and added a heavy sigh. "But are we *gitanos* not all exiles here in this strange new land of South America, cast adrift by the rest of the world we knew? And like our wandering cousins, the Jews, did we not have to leave the lands that gave us birth to travel the byways of all lands, and make them our own? Knowing this, could we turn away this daughter of the true blood who has no kinsmen to defend her, nor to put food in her pot, simply because she once loved a man who was not one of us? I, Armando Reyes, say no! I say let her stay. I say let her become one of us and start a new life here in Barrio Gitanos, if that is what the señorita wishes." He paused before adding, "But—Armando's voice is just one of many. What say you, my sons, my cousins, my brothers?" he asked, turning to his fellows.

The majority of Armando's companions echoed his sentiments wholeheartedly—especially three of his handsome sons, Carla's younger brothers, Franco, Joaquin, and Leonardo, who eyed Krissoula as covetously as if she were made of Gypsy gold! Yet there were enough who remained silent, who eyed her with open suspicion and mistrust and dislike, that Krissoula accepted Armando's welcome with mixed feelings. Armando and Carla would see that no harm came to her or Sofia for the time being, but when Armando was gone, his ability to control his people went with him. Then, she'd be on her own, and her trusty instincts warned her she must be on her guard . . .

God only knew what the other dwellers of the various *barrios* put in their cooking pots that night, but there was no shortage of tasty food in the cooking pots of the Reyes band! Lamb stew, seasoned lavishly with garlic, onions, parsley, and other spices, and thickened with tiny, fluffy dumplings, eaten along with chunks of crusty bread, lined empty bellies. Conversation and laughter about the blazing fire in the center of the courtyard and tongues oiled and loosened by free-flowing wine poured from leather *botas,* replenished weary spirits.

Krissoula, wearing a lazy smile, leaned back from the fire's ruddy glow and patted her belly in appreciation. *"Caramba,* what a feast!" She smiled slyly and arched her brows. "Such tender mutton could only have been stolen, *amiga!"* she told Carla.

"But of course!" Carla acknowledged with an airy wave of her hand. "Is it not said by our people that the flesh of a stolen animal always tastes sweeter than any other?" She giggled, then nodded towards Sofia. "Look, *niña,* your friend is fast asleep and snoring! Let me find a quilt to cover her with. It grows cold here at night, for all that the days are hotter than Hades."

337

When she'd seen Sofía snugly bundled up in a brilliantly embroidered orange and yellow quilt in a cozy corner of the courtyard, safely nestled alongside Carla's two children, Krissoula returned to Carla and the fire. While some of the men smoked their pipes and talked of the past, and green and golden summers spent in other countries, others brought out their guitars and softly began to play while one of their number mournfully sang:

> When I play my guitar,
> I'm home again,
> Back in the fields about Sevilla.
> I smell the roses' perfume
> And my thoughts return to you—
> To how you kissed me through the lattices
> And stole my poor heart.
> You put it in a cage, *gitana,*
> Then you threw away the key.
> Now, like a captive bird I sing
> Only sad songs.

> *Caray,* your dark eyes
> Are stars, *gitana,*
> Shining in the night!
> And your lips are red, *gitana,*
> Red as wine.
> Do you think of me a little
> When the nights are long and lonely?
> Or did you find another's lips
> To kiss you through the lattices . . . ?
> Did you find another's heart to imprison,
> Without caring?

"Memories of our beloved Spain, and lost sweethearts! Death and sorrow. Jealousy and betrayal. The place may change, but the songs—never!" Carla observed as her brother Franco's voice floated out over the courtyard. Carla saw that as he sang, his eyes were riveted on Krissoula's face, breathtakingly lovely in the play of light and shadow from the dancing flames of their fire. "Do you miss the old country? How long have you been here in South America, Krissoula?"

"Since last fall."

"And before that?"

"Why, Spain, of course, where else? My family and our band, the

338

Ballardos, lived much of the year round in the caves of Sacro Monte—you know, in the hills of Granada?"

"Why, *sí*, I've been there many times!" Carla agreed excitedly.

"My uncle Ricardo's home was the biggest and most beautiful of all the Gypsy caves to be found there, with arched ceilings and doorways like a little Moorish palace. My uncle, his father, and brothers carved our home from the rock themselves, when Ricardo was still a young man," she added with a touch of family pride. "The walls were always whitewashed and hung with pretty copper pieces, polished and gleaming just like yours are, Carla. The floors were flat and even, and my aunt Isabella kept them neatly swept, with dried herbs sprinkled about to sweeten the air, and a braided rag rug or two for warmth underfoot. We even had a chimney, like a tiny bell tower above the caves' surface, so that the smoke could escape! I remember in the summer we traveled all over Europe with the caravans, moving from horse fair to horse fair, but we'd spend the winters there in the caves, snug and dry, and I loved those nights by the fire."

"Ahh, you still miss your family, *sí*? I can tell. *Caray*, it must have broken your heart when your band cast you out?" Carla observed with a sympathetic sigh.

"*Sí*, it hurt me more than I dreamed anything could! After—after my husband was stabbed during a quarrel, I had nowhere to go, no one to turn to. Aiee, Carla, the bitterness that grew in my heart frightened me, changed me from the woman I'd once been! I used to think often of those long winter evenings we spent in the caves then, when I was alone."

Her golden eyes grew dreamy as she gazed into the amber flames of the fire before continuing. "I used to remember how, when the nights were dark and chill, Uncle Ricardo would sit by the fire like this and sip his *aguardiente*. With his throat well wetted, he'd start singing one of his favorite *cantes*. One by one, his brothers would begin to accompany him on their guitars, strumming a lively *zambra* or a sad *seguiriyas*, depending on his mood—just as your brothers are doing tonight."

Carla nodded in understanding.

"Some evenings the atmosphere would be light and gay, the wine spilling freely along with the laughter, just like this one. On other nights, the *cantes* my uncle sang would be *cantes jondos*, desolate with despair. His voice would sound rough and harsh with sorrow, even crack a little with the emotion pent up inside him. Then my aunt would remember the three little children she'd borne him, and how each one had died before reaching the anniversary of its birth, hardly tasting the joy of life before breathing its last. Before long, his grief would call to her own and fill her heart and soul to bursting. Suddenly, she'd get to her feet and leave the fireside, a look in her eyes to make a stone weep tears of blood! Aiee, *caramba,* it was little wonder they called her 'La Grande,' for with the sadness upon her she would dance the flamenco, and *Dios mío,* how she could dance! The graceful *filigrano* of her arms and her hands alone could convey all her sorrow and heartache, and lay it bare to the world, or send her laughter and her joy of life soaring to the topmost peaks of the mountains! Oh, Carla, the *duende* of their dancing and singing would seep into the listeners' hearts, their minds, their very bones!" Her golden eyes glowed with an inner radiance as she remembered. "I know very well, for so it did with mine."

"And did you learn to dance, too?"

"Learn to dance? I would have to say no! Flamenco is something one feels, the way I understand it. It cannot be learned, for it is woven of the heart, the soul, the feelings, and expressing one's emotions cannot be taught or learned like ciphering or numbers, eh? No. To my mind, the flamenco can only be felt—in here," she explained simply, touching her breast, "and so that is how I came to dance for the first time. One night, Tío Ricardo sang, and I was a little girl again. I remembered weeping for my mother Katarina, who'd run away and left me when I was only a few months old, and yearning for the father whose smile I'd never known. I don't really remember standing up, but I must have, for the next thing I knew, I was dancing—pouring my soul into the dance, creating my very own *duende.* When I was finished, the old men were weeping, the women, too, and there were tears in my uncle's eyes. 'Truly, *mi sobrina,* never have I felt such soul, such emotion, such *duende* in one so young and so untried as yet by life! One day, mark my words, you'll be the greatest *bailaora* in all of Spain!' he said." Krissoula realized that she'd gone on at some length, and blushed. "Oh, forgive me! I didn't mean to bore you—!"

"*Caray,* I have it now! You're the one they call 'La Reina,' aren't you?" Carla exclaimed, slapping her palm against her brow. "I knew your name sounded familiar to me, somehow. You're Krissoula Ballardo, La Reina, the one they call the Queen of flamencos, *sí?* The one who danced at the Ópera Florida last fall, yes?"

"*Sí,* I'm called that by some people," Krissoula admitted reluctantly, her dismay at Carla's discovery evident. "But please, don't tell anyone else who I am, nor where to find me should anyone

340

ask—promise me, Carla? Betray my trust, and I could pay with my life."

She shivered, despite the warmth of the evening and the crackling fire that cast a ruddy glow upon her flushed face, before adding, "You see, there's a man—an Argentine named San Martín—who might come looking for me. He'll stop at nothing—not even murder, I believe—to avenge the wrong he thinks I did him!"

Carla looked deep into her haunted golden eyes, and her own green ones suddenly brightened. To her mind, her new *gitana* friend was overly solemn, overly fearful. She was safe here, protected by her own kind, so what had she to fear? After all, life was too short to spend so much of it in melancholy thought! Like good red wine, life had to be freely poured, then relished to the last sparkling drop with gusto and flair, not doled out in miserable little glassfuls, always fearful that there'd be none left for *mañana*. That was the way the miserly *gorgios* doled out the joy in their life—and their wine! It was not the way of the carefree Rom.

"Pah, don't worry so much," she reassured the girl airily, "no self-respecting Argentine *gorgio* would dream of looking for you here in Barrio Gitanos!" She winked and grimaced horribly. "You know how we Gypsies are, all 'flea-ridden, light-fingered devils, wallowing in our own filth, performing strange magic and witchcraft rituals on innocent *gorgio* children, and casting spells to left and right before we eat them—!'" She nudged Krissoula heartily in the ribs and laughed merrily.

Her infectious good humor succeeded in making Krissoula smile.

"Nevertheless, I swear—on my honor as one of the true blood—that I won't give your secret away, if that's what you wish, although there is a small price for my silence and your supper," she teased. "Please, won't you dance for us, Krissoula?"

Krissoula nodded, her tension easing. "Of course, it would be my pleasure. But not just this minute, Carla, *por favor?* Maybe a little later tonight instead, eh? Right now, my mood is wrong for a lively dance," she apologized, hoping she wouldn't seem bad-tempered or ungrateful. "Talking about Sacro Monte and my family—aiee, it stirred too many memories, I think! You do understand?"

Carla nodded and squeezed her hand. "Of course. I'll look forward to watching you dance later."

With a wistful nod, Krissoula wandered away, wanting only to be alone. But as always since leaving Tierra Rosa five days ago, she found her thoughts turned not to the family she'd left behind her, but to Esteban . . .

341

Chapter Twenty-Seven

"*Caramba*, my friends, surely this must be heaven, for here comes an angel!"

"Angel? Manolito! Have you no eyes, *hombre?* That's no angel, but a graceful goddess who walks on air!"

The extravagant, loudly voiced *piropos,* or compliments, of the young men lounging on the street corner brought an amused smile to Krissoula's lips, but she modestly lowered her eyes and continued on without giving any sign that she'd heard them, as was expected. Young men paying such flowery compliments to an attractive woman who caught their eye were as much the tradition here in Buenos Aires as they'd been in the cities of Old Spain. A decent woman enjoyed the men's extravagant flattery, but never acknowledged it in any way!

Two more corners to cross, and she'd be in the Barrio San Timéo, only a stone's throw from the *taberna* where she'd found work as a dancer three nights ago, thanks to Carla's many contacts amongst the Gypsy communities of the city, she thought as she hurried past the baker's house.

The baker, an old man with a pot belly, snowy hair, and moustaches named Señor Mendez, had been kind enough to give her directions to the Taberna Cádiz that first night, when she'd become hopelessly lost in the maze of darkening streets. Tonight, as always, he was standing on his stoop when she approached with a fat orange cat cradled in his arms, and enjoying a slim cigar. He nodded a cordial greeting to her, and offered her the advice he'd offered her every night so far.

"You should find yourself an escort, señorita! It is dangerous for a pretty young woman like you to walk alone in the *barrios* after dark!"

She smiled back and thanked him for his concern, saying, "God will protect me, Señor Mendez. He must, since I have no one else to do so. *Buenas noches!"*

She waited for a mule-drawn cart piled high with firewood to pass, and then crossed the street to the opposite side. Her heart fluttered nervously as the next corner came into view, and she bit her lip as knots of tension began to tighten in her belly. On the past two nights, a man named Antonio had taken to waiting there for her to pass by, and she was a little—no, more than a little!—afraid of him.

Antonio Malvado, she'd discovered from the serving girls at the Cádiz, was a *compadrito,* or "little godfather." It was he who ran Barrio San Timéo, he who owned the loyalties, body and soul, of most of the young men who lived there, whom he commanded like a military general commanding his troops. By virtue of intimidation, he controlled most of the *barrio's* other inhabitants, too. It was Antonio who decided the laws by which everyone in "his" *barrio* would live and who saw that his men carried these laws out, meting out either favors or harsh punishments as his own sense of honor, whim, or volatile mood dictated. It was Antonio who controlled the pickpockets and cutpurses and the houses of ill repute in the *barrio,* and took his "cut" of the profits from each; Antonio who was behind many of the burglaries in the rich *porteño* heart of Buenos Aires, and who enjoyed a life of comfort and ease behind the high walls of his crumbling mansion on Calle Pajaro, while the people of his *barrio* went hungry or sick. And unluckily, she'd caught this hateful creature's roving eye and—apparently—his fancy, when all she'd wanted to do was to live quietly and inconspicuously, and have nothing whatsoever to do with men. What bad luck dogged her heels, she thought with a troubled little frown, and her graceful, lightfooted passage faltered a little.

Sure enough, Antonio Malvado was lying in wait there on the corner again tonight, flashily dressed in tight black breeches and a tailored black frock coat, the snowy folds of the stock at his throat in sharp contrast to the somberness of his flashy sateen attire. A cape lined in scarlet swung elegantly from his slim shoulders, and he wore the full brim of his black felt hat pulled down low over his eyes at a rakish angle that gave him a decidedly sinister air. Ever the strutting dandy, he always sported a flower in his lapel, and for the past two nights that flower had been a rosebud—a yellow one in honor, he'd told her just last night, of her golden eyes and the rose-trimmed topaz gown she always wore to dance at the tavern.

The rose affectation was just a showy part of his attempts to court her, she knew that in her heart, but remembering how the audiences at the Ópera Florida had once tossed yellow rosebuds onto the stage after her performances, the gesture made her uneasy. What if someday, someone who'd seen her dance at the theater put two and two together, as Carla had done, and Antonio discovered who she really was, and that she was hiding in the *barrios* of Buenos Aires in fear of her life? That would give him a hold over her, would it not? Give him the leverage he needed to force her to do his bidding and become his woman. Ah, *sí*, she knew he wanted her that way, for the lust in his eyes was unmistakable! She shuddered. Handsome enough he might be, in a slim, catlike way, with countless other women always at his beck and call, but he held no appeal for her, none whatsoever! The thought of sharing his bed, of his hands upon her body, filled her with crawling disgust. *Sí*. For some reason—perhaps the knowledge that he traded in fear and force, and maintained his own comfortable lifestyle amidst the poverty of others solely by means of the vices he exploited?—he filled her only with the utmost distaste and contempt. There could be no future for the woman unfortunate enough to belong to such a man, she knew, for she'd seen his kind before, in Barcelona. He'd use the poor woman up, debauch and exploit her, and then discard her for another, fresher young face and body when her novelty palled and she ceased to amuse him. She only prayed he'd tire of his unsuccessful attempts to flirt with her without incident, and find someone else to pester . . .

Her knees shook as she drew level with the man and she pulled her fringed shawl tighter about her shoulders, keeping her eyes down. *Leche!* Her legs felt boneless and more insubstantial with every step she took! Her poor heart was pounding with fright as Antonio swept off his hat and stepped from the shadows, and her faint hope that he'd already given up on her crumbled. He made her a courtly bow, yet the eyes he raised to hers as she faltered in her brisk passage past him were speculative and insolent, rather than gallant. Hooded, hot black eyes that consumed her like live coals.

"Your loveliness outshines the stars, señorita. The moon hides behind a cloud, embarrassed to compete with your beauty and suffer the shame of losing!"

His *piropo*, delivered in a smooth, oily tone, was probably the result of hours of practice before a mirror, judging by the knowing grins and nudges his two henchmen exchanged behind his back, Krissoula thought with contempt, yet she was too intimidated to let him suspect her true feelings, much less voice them.

"You are too kind, señor," she murmured expressionlessly, her eyes riveted to the dirty street beneath her feet. "I have done nothing to deserve such flattery, I'm sure." And with that dismissal, she attempted to step past him and carry on her way.

But Antonio Malvado quickly stepped before her, blocking her retreat. She was brought up short, unable to evade him without making her distaste obvious. His scent—of spicy cologne—filled her nostrils, and she found it subtly repulsive. Esteban had always smelled so wonderful, so clean and masculine, she thought with a sudden pang of helpless longing . . .

"Barrio San Timéo is no place for a woman without a man to escort her, señorita," Antonio said silkily, his eyes caressing her pale, lovely face. She was illumined by the puny glow of a tallow streetlamp behind them, since gas lights were only to be found in the wealthier parts of the city, yet even in so poor a light, her vivid beauty glowed like flame. "Aren't you afraid to be out alone after dark, little one?"

She managed to give a nonchalant shrug and a wry smile, and pretended she hadn't heard the endearment that dripped so easily from his lips. "Day or night, we must all learn to live with our fears and overcome them, must we not, señor? And a poor widow such as myself must eat. The money I earn from my dancing puts bread on the table. It's as simple as that. Hunger, señor, can always conquer fear."

To her surprise, he nodded and smiled in approval and even, she fancied, with agreement.

"Sí, that's how it is. I was not always the compadrito here in Barrio San Timéo, you know, señorita," he revealed with a pompous little smirk. "I, too, have known what it is to go hungry, and to be alone and afraid. But I'm in a position now to help those less—fortunate—than I, those too weak and defenseless to fend for themselves, such as your lovely self," he bragged, swaggering a little with pride. "Allow me to offer you the services of my boys here, Juan and José. They would be most happy to escort you from your home to the Cádiz each evening, and to see that you reach there safely afterwards. What do you say, pequeña?"

"A very generous offer, señor. I thank you, but I cannot accept. I do not know you, after all, and to do so would not be proper. Good night, señor."

Before he could protest or press his point, she inclined her head, quickly sidestepped him, and scuttled down the block. The bright lights spilling from the familiar taberna up ahead acted as a welcome beacon in the gloomy street, along which darker alleys

345

opened up, awaiting the unsuspecting like hungry, cavernous mouths.

Antonio's expression darkened as he watched her flee him, growing ugly with thwarted purpose. He rammed one fist into the open palm of his other hand. Damn the girl! He'd expected her to accept his offer of protection with eagerness, and was unaccustomed to women brushing him off so casually. Nevertheless, the dancing girl had done so—and under the guise of propriety, too, the cold little bitch! Who the hell did she think she was, anyway, eh, to give the *compadrito* of Barrio San Timéo the cold shoulder?

Yet—and now he grinned—it was her very resistance, her coolness and act of indifference towards him, quite as much as her vivid loveliness, that fired his lust so strongly! It had been a long, long time since he'd viewed winning a woman's favor as a challenge. Years since he'd enjoyed the thrill of playing the "hunter" and pursuing a reluctant female quarry, with all the exciting little uncertainties and nuances of the chase that came before the "kill." However coolly she treated him, he had no intention of giving up on the beautiful Krissoula Ballardo. He wanted her, curse her soul, and Antonio Malvado always got what he wanted, one way or the other! Sooner or later, she'd have to give in, and her surrender would be all the sweeter for the wait, he thought, a thin smile splitting his lips as he imagined her petite, curvaceous body naked beneath his save for her cloak of midnight hair, writhing in pleasure as she begged him with golden eyes and lush lips to take her, swore she'd do anything he asked of her, anything at all . . . The notion that she might not find him attractive as a man, might never welcome his advances, never share his bed, never once entered his swollen head. A woman refuse the *compadrito*? Ha! Never! Not if she valued her life, anyway . . .

"You, Juan, and you, José, I want the woman followed when she leaves the Cádiz at dawn, understand? Find out where she lives, and with whom—everything about her! I'll be at the tavern, meanwhile. Don't bother me unless something important comes up, *comprende?*"

And with that, he left the ugly pair and followed the path the young woman had taken to the Cádiz Tavern. There—as *compadrito* of Barrio San Timéo—the best seat in the smoky tavern was always reserved for him.

The Cádiz Tavern was crowded to bursting that night. The

346

number of patrons had grown steadily over the past two evenings, and the proprietor, a Spanish-Italian named Luigi, was pleased to see his serving girls running about like chickens with their heads lopped off, trying to keep up with the barrage of orders for beer or wine.

"Wonderful, 'Soula! Wonderful! Business has never been better! It's your dancing they come for, you know, *niña*, not the cheap red wine and poor beer I serve them. Keep it up, and I'll soon be a rich man!"

Luigi rubbed his pudgy little hands together greedily, and watching him through slitted golden eyes, Krissoula's temper was thoroughly nettled. Thanks to her, eh? And yet that piggy-eyed, sweaty-pawed little fat man paid her so poorly for her talents, she doubted she'd be able to see Sofía and herself decently fed each day on her earnings, let alone provide them with any of the other necessities of life! She'd only accepted the job on condition that if the customers increased, so would her pay, yet Luigi had made no mention of that! Better she set the greedy old goat straight this very night, and show him she wouldn't be taken advantage of, not at any price! If Luigi's customers liked her dancing so much, then the customers of other taverns would, too, she reasoned confidently. She didn't have to stay at the Cádiz.

"Oh, I'll keep it up—but only if you make it worth my while, *gorgio!*" she told him. Her golden eyes were still narrowed, her nostrils flared with contempt, her little fists planted on her hips in an aggressive stance. She tossed her inky mane of hair over her shoulder and sashayed across the taproom towards him, her topaz skirts swishing as her hips swayed to and fro. *"Caramba!* You couldn't find an organ-grinder's monkey to dance for what you pay me! I want double from now on, starting tonight. And if my price is too rich for you, I'll leave and find myself another tavern—make someone else a 'rich man'!" she spat out in a scornful tone, her lip curled in derision.

Luigi scowled. Damned, thieving Gypsies, they were all the same, all lazy, sly, untrustworthy scum, male or female alike. You felt sorry for them, hired them out of the goodness of your heart, and this was how they repaid you—by demanding more and more money! Ungrateful, slothful bastards!

In that moment, he'd forgotten completely the night his former *bailaora,* Florinda, a temperamental *mestizo* woman, had walked out on him in a fit of rage and left him with a saloon filled with disgruntled customers threatening to go elsewhere. Forgotten completely how the Gypsy girl, nudged forward by the woman, Carla, had stepped from the shadows and begun to dance. Conveniently forgotten that Krissoula had held himself and his handful of bleary-eyed old patrons spellbound with her sensual, utterly feminine grace and the depth and passion of feeling she managed to convey with her dancing. Ah, yes, all that was forgotten, thrust out of mind by her outrageous demands! He'd call her bluff, he decided, put the little bitch in her place once and for all, and teach her that Luigi da Costa couldn't be pressured into doing anything by the likes of her . . .

"Only three days you work here," he roared, his meaty, gnarled old fists clenched, the twisted veins and liver spots standing out on them like snakes, "and yet already you threaten to leave me, you *demand* an increase in pay? *Basta!* Enough of your demands! Shut up, I say, bitch! Another word from you, and I'll throw you out on your backside, and to the devil with your precious dancing! Perhaps you'll be able to make a living spreading your legs, but by God, I'll make certain you never make a living *dancing* on them again if you leave the Cádiz!"

"*Sí,* you'd love to do that, wouldn't you, you evil old devil! You'd enjoy throwing me out and having someone break my legs—but you won't, will you, Luigi? You're too greedy for that—and you know these legs can make you money!"

"Just shut up and get out there and dance!" Luigi snarled. "And don't tell me what I will or won't do. Dance, Gypsy slut! That's what you're paid for, after all!"

"All right, I'll dance," Krissoula gritted, much to Luigi's surprise, though he noticed her eyes were still hard as nails with purpose. "But when I'm finished tonight, I'm leaving the Cádiz, and I won't be coming back, threats or no threats. Not, that is, unless you agree to pay me what I'm worth—!"

"Never!" Luigi sputtered, almost convinced she was bluffing but too furious to consider his rash threat if she were not.

She shrugged, stirring inky curls about her finely boned, exquisite little face. "Very well, if that's your last word—*Adios!*"

With that, she slipped out into the smoky public saloon, leaving Luigi seething in her wake.

He started to follow her out, intending to continue their quarrel, but then caught sight of Antonio Malvado seated at a nearby scarred table. He paled as the *compadrito* beckoned him over with a lazily crooked finger.

Luigi wove his way between the press of customers to Antonio's table. Even with his cape and hat removed, the *compadrito* still had a sinister appearance, a combination of his lean, cruel features and the jagged silvery ravel of an old scar that ran from beneath his left ear to his chin, as if someone had once tried to slit his throat, and bungled the job.

"Why, Señor Malvado! What an honor to see you here ag—"

"Button your fat lip, da Costa!" Antonio drawled. "We both know you're about as glad to see me as the devil himself!" A faint smile quirked his mean mouth. "I overheard you quarreling with the dancer, *sí*? I want to know what about." He lounged back on the rough wooden bench and gripped the bottoms of his vest fronts, waiting.

"The Gypsy dancer?" Luigi licked his dry lips before answering, choosing his words carefully. The *compadrito* had never visited his tavern socially before the Gypsy girl started dancing there three evenings ago, except to collect the monthly "protection" money he squeezed from all the tavern keepers of his *barrio*, and to enjoy an occasional bottle "on the house." Luigi was no fool. That Malvado had been here every night since the girl started working as a dancer could mean only one thing; he was interested in the woman. Therefore, he must be very careful how he answered. He plastered on a smile, and kept it there by the dint of sheer terror, teeth bared like a grinning tiger's.

"No, no, Señor Malvado, quarreling is surely too strong a word, señor!" he protested, his palms slick with sweat as visions of a watery, precipitous grave in the Rio de la Plata suddenly filled his mind. Others who'd crossed Malvado had ended up there, he knew, a thin blade skewered in their hearts or stick-pinning their guts. He was getting old, *sí*, but he had no wish to die before his time! Accordingly, he continued in his fawning manner. "You know how these dancers are, señor—they're artists, and notoriously temperamental. And besides, our lovely Krissoula's a Gypsy, too, which doesn't help, for everyone knows how unpredictable *gitanos* are, even at the best of times! No, señor, we had a little disagreement—about the young lady's payment for her dancing, that is all. Nothing you need to concern yourself with," he finished hopefully. "As you will see, the problem has already been solved. She'll be dancing in a few minutes."

"She asked for more money, didn't she, Luigi, my friend? And, of course, a shrewd businessman like yourself would have agreed to give it to her?" Antonio suggested silkily, his eyelids drooping down to curtain his eyes in a way that reminded Luigi of a snake, if snakes

349

had eyelids.

A shiver ran down Luigi's spine as Antonio's jaw hardened and he pressed, "You *did* agree, didn't you, my old friend? You see, I have a certain interest in the young lady's well-being and happiness. I would be most—upset—should I hear she is less than satisfied in her work for you here . . . ?"

"Well, I—I agreed to think about it," Luigi blustered, lying to his toenails. "I would have given her a little more in due course, anyway, since she's working out quite well—but she wanted double, Señor Malvado! Double!"

"Double, eh? But that sounds quite reasonable to me, under the circumstances. Just look around you, Luigi! Have you ever seen so many thirsty customers in here at one time before? I'd say business is good—five hundred percent better since the young lady began entertaining your patrons. Certainly good enough to make me question why your payment for last month's protection is long overdue, eh . . . ? Perhaps—with your business so obviously booming—I should consider raising *my* fees and hiring the lovely señorita to dance for my own personal enjoyment? What do you say to that, *amigo*? Or—*sí*, perhaps you'd prefer a little swimming lesson instead. Do you know how to swim, *pibe*?"

Luigi turned gray, and wondered if he'd shame himself by losing control of his bladder, so great was the fear Malvado's words struck in his heart. "Please, señor, no! There's—there's no need for that! I—I understand completely what you're saying, and I know I deserve your anger, but I swear, I'll make it up—it's as good as done!"

"When?" Malvado drummed his fingers on the table.

"You'll have my payment first thing in the morning, I swear on the Blessed Virgin!"

"And the señorita?"

"I'll double—no, I'll triple!—the dancer's pay, I swear I will!"

Luigi had leaned forward over the table in his pathetic eagerness to convince Antonio he meant what he said. In his panic, his flailing arm knocked against the green glass bottle of wine set before the *compadrito* and sent it flying. Uttering an obscenity, Antonio quickly jerked back on the bench before the red river could stain his expensive breeches. The ruby wine dripped from the table to the sawdust dirt floor, pooling there, to Luigi's horrified eyes, like a congealing river of blood. His blood, he thought, gulping . . .

"Please, forgive my clumsiness!" Luigi cried. "Gina! Fetch another bottle for Señor Malvado at once. Cojo, the mop—and quickly, you ugly good-for-nothing!"

"Don't forget our little talk," Antonio snapped, waggling his finger threateningly at Luigi as a buxom serving girl set another full bottle and a clean glass before him with a frozen-on smile. "Whatever the girl wants, she gets, understand?"

"I understand, señor. It's as good as done," Luigi whined, his upper lip oily with sweat. His collar felt like a garrot, slowly strangling him, and the pressure in his bladder was agony. "And now, if you'll excuse me, of course, I have much work to do—? Enjoy your evening, señor. The wine is, of course, on the house."

With that, Luigi flung about and fled on rubber limbs for sanctuary, which in his case was the rear of his saloon, where he had his living quarters and storerooms.

Cojo, the Cádiz's young handyman, was loitering by the opening between the taproom and the saloon, leaning on his broom with a rapt expression in his soulful brown eyes as he watched Krissoula move gracefully to take the floor. In the same moment, the flamencos' guitars began to play. The noisy saloon customers fell silent as the Gypsy girl started to dance, and Cojo's eyes misted over as her graceful arms wove sinuous patterns in the smoky, torchlit air. Light flashed off her earrings and glittered in her eyes, and her yellow skirts flew up to reveal the slender, pale gold of her bare legs, moving in intricate patterns or furiously stamping so that her scarlet slippers became a hypnotic blur of color that tore a sigh of admiration from Cojo's lips.

Luigi followed his handyman's rapt gaze, and his features twisted in fury. Like the man who trips over his own feet and kicks his faithful, innocent dog, terrified Luigi needed a scapegoat on whom to vent his terror and fury at Malvado. He found it in poor Cojo. With a curse, he drew back his fist and fetched the crippled lad a hefty clout across the side of his head with a force that flung him off balance, to the ground.

"You lazy slug! Is this what I pay you for—to ogle the pretty girls? Get out there! Clean up the mess by Señor Malvado's table before he has us both enjoying the waters of La Plata!"

The short, slight young man hauled himself upright, clumsily dragging his left leg. His twisted features were a mask of pain as he limped awkwardly away to do Luigi's bidding.

Chapter Twenty-Eight

Krissoula's mind was blank with exhaustion when dawn broke the next morning. Her body ached with fatigue. But the pealing of the church bells from all over the city reminded her—no work tonight. Thank God, it was Sunday today, the day of rest, and the Cádiz would be closed. What a relief!

Gathering up her belongings and bidding a yawning, bleary-eyed farewell to her guitarists, Andres and Jesús, and the singer, Francisco, she gave the crippled handyman, Cojo, a farewell smile.

"See you tomorrow night, *muchacho!*" she told him, and watched his poor distorted face light up with joy as she stepped from the tavern and out into the street.

Time and time again the evening before, and well into the wee hours of Sunday morning, the appreciative patrons of the Cádiz had applauded wildly and called for encores of her dancing. She'd done her best to please them, though the emotional drain the *duende* of the flamenco exacted of her left her emptied for hours afterward, like a shell or a husk with no core.

How long could she keep up this pace, she wondered wearily, trudging back along the narrow streets towards the Barrio Gitanos? Until there was nothing left in her to give? Until there was no past sadness or joy left to draw upon to fire her movements, but only a terrible numbness that made her dancing equally empty and unfeeling, like a wooden puppet's dance? If that day ever came, she'd be finished, broken spiritually and physically, she knew, but what other alternative did a woman have, here in the *barrios?* If she wanted to eat, she could either dance until she dropped, or she could sell herself, as Luigi had implied, it was as simple as that! She'd dance, she decided with a shudder as she imagined her alternative, dance until she dropped, if need be—or even find herself a partner to fleece the unwary as she and Hector had once done in Barcelona. Anything—even the life of a thief or a pickpocket was better than a life spent on her back . . .

There were few people about on the streets at that early hour; one or two red-eyed carousers returning to their homes after a night's drinking, a few old women dressed in somber black with shawls over their heads, hurrying to early Mass. The latter eyed her with sour disapproval and crossed themselves as she passed, no doubt believing her vivid yellow satin dress the trappings of a whore returning to her crib after a night's work. A scrawny dog or two barked furiously as she went by, cats slunk into the shadows like shifting shadows themselves, but other than that the streets were strangely hushed at this hour of the morning, miraculously empty as the sun came up drenched in a golden haze that quickly flooded the city. Glorious light seeped down into the grimy, forgotten cracks of Buenos Aires that were the *barrios'* streets, like melted honey pouring over a waffle, bringing with its misty gold the promise of yet another stifling-hot, steamy day.

With the sun's rising, the *barrios* also stirred. Cocks crowed. Cows lowed to be milked. Babies cried, and with a pang of memory, she heard their mothers crooning as they hurried to nurse them, and thought, *Ah, Nicki, my little Nicki!* and wondered if she'd ever be able to remember the good times without also feeling the pain. Children tumbled from their straw pallets and began to play, their laughter and squeals muted behind the forbidding walls of the crumbling courtyard houses that were their homes. The yeasty smell of bread baking and *beignets* frying rose from Señor Mendez's bakery, along with the dark fragrance of Brazilian coffee floating, spicy and rich, on the morning air. Her belly growled with hunger, reminding her that she'd not eaten since noon of the day before. Would Sofía have breakfast ready and waiting for her this morning? *Sí,* surely she would! She'd learned well enough herself by now how to cook them a simple meal, and shouldn't need Carla's help.

Her appetite whetted by the thought of warm tortillas smeared with honey, and spicy *chorizo,* she quickened her step. Turning a corner, she saw the water-vendor, Giovanni, leading his blinkered horse down the street towards her. The poor nag was drawing a weighty barrel-cart, and women were coming out of their homes with assorted vessels to buy its master's ware; the unpalatable yellowish water of the Plata. The vendor gave her a roguish, gap-toothed grin as he caught sight of her, recognizing her from past mornings when they'd exchanged greetings.

"*Hola,* pretty early bird! I see you have an admirer this morn-

353

ing!" he called cheekily, slopping water into a woman's earthenware pitcher.

"Admirer?" she echoed in surprise. "What do you mean, *hombre?*"

"Unless I'm mistaken, someone's following you, *signorina!*" the water-seller said in a teasing voice, throwing her a wink and nodding over her shoulder. "He ducked back in that last alley when he saw me watching him."

"You're sure?" Krissoula asked, stifling the overwhelming urge to turn around and look.

The man shrugged. "I could be wrong, but I don't think so. Be careful, eh, *bellissima?*"

"I will, *gracias,*" she promised gratefully.

She carried on, yet didn't take the route back to Carla's courtyard she normally used. Instead, she intentionally chose a circuitous one that twisted and turned back and forth.

Sure enough, she discovered after only a block or two that the water-vendor had been right. Someone was definitely following her! Twice she'd suddenly turned and looked back, only to see the shadowy form of a short, slight fellow hurriedly duck into some alcove or other, obviously reluctant to be spotted. One of Malvado's men, she wondered apprehensively? Had Antonio set his thugs to following her? He must have, curse him! After all, who else would go to such trouble on her account?

She reached the Reyeses' courtyard far later than usual, but was satisfied she'd thrown off whoever'd been following her by her twisting route. She decided she'd mention that she'd been followed to Carla, and see what her practical friend suggested she do about it, but the minute she stepped into the courtyard she could smell trouble, and she completely forgot all about being followed.

Sofía was standing close by the fire, her long mousy-brown hair still in braids from the night before instead of neatly swept up, as was usual for her. Her narrow face was pale and she was trembling—Krissoula could see that even from a distance. She looked as if she was trying to shrink into herself. Another woman— Carla's surly sister-in-law, Delora—was facing her, her fists planted on her hips. Delora's sharp, swarthy features were even more belligerent than usual.

". . . Well, I say she stole them, right from under my nose, Carla!" Delora accused shrilly. "Surely you won't take this *gorgio* bitch's word against mine, eh?"

"What's going on here?" Krissoula asked quietly, stepping between the circle of women to stand at Sofía's side before Carla

354

could answer.

"Ask her, why don't you!" Delora spat, jerking her chin at Sofía. "Ask your friend, the tortilla thief, here! She's so useless, she can't even make her own tortillas!" she jeered. "She has to steal from other women!"

"Sofía?" Krissoula asked gently, receiving a shrug from Carla.

"No, it's not true, Krissoula, I swear it!" Sofía whispered brokenly, wringing her hands. "You know Carla's been teaching me how to make tortillas?" Krissoula and Carla both nodded. "Last night after you left, I made a stack for your breakfast this morning. I wanted—aiee, Krissoula, I wanted to surprise you and make you proud of me by having everything perfect and ready when you came back this morning! So, I got up at daybreak and fried the tortillas, and had them keeping warm while I went to ask Carla for a little honey—you know how you love honey on your tortillas? But when I came back, that—that hateful woman and her husband and their children w-were e-eating th-them!"

"There! You see how it is? Just because we're Gypsies, this outsider thinks she can call us thieves and cover up her own light-fingered ways!" Delora screamed. "Well, she's not getting away with it, not this time!" With a whirl of grubby skirts, Delora flung about and snatched up a cooking knife, springing at Sofía, who screamed in terror and hurriedly backed away.

Carla at once sprang between the two women. She swirled about and wrenched Delora's wrist down to her side, squeezing hard to force her to drop the knife.

"That's enough!" she snapped, her green eyes angry and crackling. "I saw Sofía making the tortillas last night myself, Delora, just as she said. *Gorgio* or no, she's not lying. It's you who are in the wrong here, for taking her tortillas without asking first, and trying to cover up your rudeness. Tell her you're sorry, and let's have an end to the matter, eh, sister?"

Delora's lips curled in derision. "Me—tell that dried-up old hen I'm sorry? Pah! Never! And whatever you might say to defend her, to side with a *gorgio* against your own blood, Carla, I know the truth. If she made any, she burned her own tortillas, likely as not, and stole mine to replace them. She's a thief, and a *gorgio,* and one's as bad as the other, to my thinking! We don't want her here—none of us do. She's a parasite upon all who live here, taking the food from hungry mouths when there's precious little to go around as it is. Tell her to go! Get rid of her!"

"If Sofía goes, then I leave, too," Krissoula said firmly. "I've known Sofía for over a year. She's my friend and I believe her when she says she's innocent. Why, she'd no sooner lie or steal than would the Blessed Pope himself!"

"You go with her, then!" Delora hissed. "Go live somewhere else with your precious *gorgio* friends! Some of us here have no liking for you, either, come to that. You put on airs, Krissoula Ballardo—if that's who you really are! Don't think we haven't noticed the way you talk to us sometimes, as if you were some grand *hidalga* bitch and us, your lowly *peóns*. Go, damn you—!"

"They stay," Carla cut in sharply and in a tone that brooked no refusal. "My father and the other men of the council make the rules here, and they voted in their favor. Everyone here knows you're too lazy to make food for your children or your man, although *you* know how, so don't condemn poor Sofía for something she cannot help. She tries very hard, and she's learning a little more every day. She does all the darning now, and helps with the little ones without being asked and without complaining. In fact, she does far more for her keep than you do, lazy one, and earns what little food she puts in her mouth! What's more, very soon Krissoula's dancing will more than pay for their share of everything here, so stop complaining and get back to your children, where you belong. Look at them, poor little mites! Their faces are grubby and their hair needs combing, and their clothes are little better than dirty rags. You should be ashamed of yourself! Look to your little ones, sister—and don't let me hear of you picking on Sofía again, or else!"

"Or else what?" Delora sneered, fists on hips.

"Or else I'll tell my brother to beat you, as he should have done years ago!" Carla threatened with obvious relish.

Delora seemed ready to continue the argument, but then thought better of it. Her black eyes gleamed nastily. She looked straight at Sofía and smiled in a gloating, malicious way that drained what little color was left from Sofía's sallow cheeks.

"A Gypsy curse on you, *gorgio* bitch!" she murmured darkly, brandishing her clenched fist in Sofía's direction, and then she flung about with a swirl of grubby, tattered petticoats and stormed away.

"Perhaps we should leave, as she said," Krissoula said worriedly. "I knew some of your band didn't like the idea of taking us in, but I'd hoped—"

"Oh, *leche!*" Carla snorted crudely. "Those that objected do so because of how they are. They'd protest that sun up there, just to keep it from shining, if it pleased their contrary little minds. Forget about them. Sofía, it took courage to stand up to that witch my

356

brother married the way you did—well done! We'll make a *gitana* of you yet! Now, I have plenty of tortillas, freshly made this morning and keeping warm, and I'd be happy if you'd accept some in place of those Delora's children ate. What do you say, mmm, Sofía? Will you forgive us?" When Sofía made no answer, Carla looked at Krissoula and shrugged.

"What is it, Sofía *mía?*" Krissoula asked, slipping her arm about the trembling woman's. "The quarrel's over and done with now, don't you see? You can relax and forget it. You won, and nobody believes for a minute that you're a thief, really they don't! Please, speak to me, Sofía," she ordered, more sharply, shaking the still woman. "Say something!"

"She cursed me!" Sofía said with a low, despairing moan, her hand flying up to cover her mouth. "She cursed me, and now I'll die! Everyone knows that's what happens when a Gypsy curses you! You die, Krissoula!"

"Ayee, *caray,* don't be a fool, Sofía! If Delora's curses are as good as her palm-reading, you'll live to be a hundred and ninety, at the very least! Believe me, I know!" Carla reassured her. "Isn't that so, Krissoula?"

"*Sí,* of course it is! I've met only a handful of our people who had the gift where *dukkering,* seeing the future, is concerned, but Delora certainly doesn't strike me as one of them!" Krissoula confirmed. "Come on, you silly old dear, borrow some of Carla's delicious tortillas and show me how well you're learning to cook. Those drunken sots at the Cádiz made me dance all night. *Caramba!* I swear my legs are two inches shorter than when I left here yesterday." She grinned. "What's more, I'm st-a-a-a-rving. Find me some food before I faint away, Sofía *mía!*"

Her teasing served to get Sofía moving, as she'd hoped, but did nothing to rid her eyes of their haunted look as she trailed away after Carla. Krissoula sighed. Perhaps only time could help superstitious Sofía forget Delora's silly threats, she decided—day after day after day of simply waking up and finding one was still alive, and by so doing disprove the curse.

It was Monday evening before she remembered being followed. Would her mysterious "shadow" try to secretly dog her path once again tonight, she wondered as she readied herself to leave Barrio Gitanos? There was only one way to find out! Asking Carla to keep an eye on Sofía and warning Sofía to steer clear of Delora, she set off for Barrio San Timéo and the Cádiz Tavern.

Chapter Twenty-Nine

Unknown to Krissoula, she was not the only one being stalked that sultry Monday evening as she made her way to dance in Barrio San Timéo. Another, sinister shadow was even at that moment stalking thousands of innocent inhabitants of Buenos Aires, yet unlike whoever it was following Krissoula, this enemy was invisible to the naked eye—not even human.

This other stalker played no favorites. It preyed on wealthy *porteños* and lowly *barrio*-dwellers alike, paying heed to neither station nor sex, age nor youth. Numbered among its earliest victims were an Army lieutenant and his beautiful *mestizo* mistress; *el presidente*'s own secretary and his quadroon whore; a handful of mulatto washerwomen and a dozen high-born *criolla* ladies. Drooling octogenarians, plump, pretty chambermaids in the flower of their youth, and toddling babes who'd barely tasted life all fell indiscriminately to this silent, deadly assassin. Priests and nuns were not spared its dreaded embraces behind the hallowed walls of their churches and convents, nor were the lowliest sinners in the depths of the wharf-front stews. The assassin's name was well known, its visit each summer was dreaded, but nevertheless it was impossible to avoid, although many families who could afford to do so fled the city for their remote country *estancias,* and prayed it would not join them there. Long before this most unwelcome guest deigned to leave the city of Buenos Aires that stifling summer, cholera would have claimed the lives of thousands.

Unseen and uncontrolled, it bred indiscriminately in wells dug too close to stinking outhouses—both the outhouses of the *barrios* and those perfumed cupboards in the courtyards of the rich. It proliferated on unwashed fruits and teemed unseen in the milk and on the hands of unsuspecting carriers.

Giovanni, the water vendor, delivered it to one's door—quite unknown to him, poor fellow, of course!—pouring it straight into your pitcher in the mornings to enjoy along with your coffee. Those who sought a little relief from the sweltering heat of summer in the city by immersing their sweating bodies in the yellow waters of the Plata—as was the custom on sultry summer evenings for the rich and poor of Buenos Aires alike—found it lying in wait for them there, too. Within hours of the first case of cholera being diagnosed, people were falling sick all over the city. Within the week, they'd either recovered, or were dead. Carts rumbled up and down the city streets, piled high with corpses wrapped in sheets to be taken for mass burial outside the city limits, and the stops the cart made on its macabre rounds were tragically frequent. Few streets were spared the sight of a weeping family huddled together in a doorway as they watched a beloved mother or father, a cherished son or an adored daughter's body being added to the gruesome load.

Fortunately, under such distressing circumstances, the inhabitants of Barrio Gitanos were, like the Jewish Quarter, a people apart from the rest of the *barrio* dwellers. Alienated and insulated by differing customs, religions or centuries' old superstitions and suspicions, their quarters remained free of the cholera epidemic for far longer than those of their neighbors. Fear and mistrust had made the Gypsies outcasts among other peoples, and now that very separateness served them well—for a time, at least. Consequently, life in Barrio Gitanos went on as normal, with Krissoula leaving Carla's courtyard for the Cádiz Tavern each evening shortly before dusk, and returning in the early hours of the next morning, exhausted.

She was still being followed in the days succeeding the quarrel, she'd discovered, but didn't have the opportunity to mention it to Carla until three evenings after the incident with Sofía and the "stolen" tortillas. Carla, in her turn, at once told her father, Armando, all about it, and despite Krissoula's protests that she wasn't in the least afraid, and that she was certain it was someone Antonio Malvado had set to keeping an eye on her for reasons of his own, Armando Reyes had insisted on taking action.

"You are one of our blood, Krissoula, and for as long as you remain here with my band, it is my duty to protect you," the burly leader had informed her gravely. "My son, Franco, will keep an eye on you for a while, *sí*, Franco?"

"But of course, Papa! I would be honored to protect and serve the señorita!" arrogant Franco had replied with a blushing eagerness and pride that drew laughter from everyone gathered nearby, for by now it was all too obvious to the Reyes band that handsome young Franco had eyes only for lovely golden-eyed Krissoula, and would have followed her to hell and back without being asked, if she'd only given him a smile or two of encouragement!

To be honest, it amused Krissoula to think that, as she made her way through the shadowy streets, Franco was diligently following whoever it was following her, though over a week passed before he was able to apprehend the man. And when he did, the results were surprising . . .

That morning, she'd gone home earlier than usual, leaving the Cádiz in the wee hours while it was yet pitch dark, despite Luigi's initially heated protests that she must stay. In the end, though, he'd relented and agreed that she could leave early—as he'd given in to her wishes more and more often since the night of their argument over her pay, much to Krissoula's surprise. He'd acted in an almost fatherly manner as he told her to be careful going home through the pitch-black streets. He'd even gone so far as to offer her a lantern to light her way, which she'd accepted, although she knew she had nothing to fear, not with her fierce, handsome watchdog, Franco Reyes, lurking somewhere in the shadows to defend her, armed with fourteen inches of the finest Toledo steel!

She was eager to get home, for three days of festivities would begin today, starting at dawn that morning with the wedding of Gina, a fourteen-year-old Gypsy bride from the next courtyard, to her betrothed, Alonso, a young *gitano* who belonged to another Romany band, the Zambras. Their wedding would be celebrated in the old Gypsy traditions, in place of a formal religious ceremony or Catholic exchange of vows.

The young man had, as was the custom, cleverly abducted the "reluctant" bride from her people's courtyard several days before. Subsequently, he and his friends had carried her off to his own home. The bride's parents had been duly informed of their daughter's "abduction" and asked to give their consent to the couple's marriage. They had, naturally, agreed, and the date for the wedding had been decided by both sets of parents as today. This morning, the old rite of ascertaining the young girl's innocence in the traditional way would take place at the home of the groom, and then would follow three or more days of loud and lively celebrations, with music, singing, dancing, drinking, and feasting. Krissoula's Ballardo band had long since relinquished the old Gypsy wedding rituals for the more modern, formal Catholic exchange of vows between young couples in the sanctity of a church, and she was both curious and eager to see the goings on.

She was only two plazas from home when she heard a cry and the thuds and grunts of a scuffle in progress behind her. She quickly spun about to see a huge, furry black rat go scampering away in a patch of fading moonlight, before making out the bulky shapes of two men grappling wildly in the gutters at her back, rolling over and over in the dirt and refuse with arms and legs flailing wildly.

"I've got you now, *canalla!*" she heard Franco hiss angrily. "I'll teach you to follow innocent women and scare them half to death!" Straddling the man's chest, his knees pinioning his captive's arms to the dirt, she saw Franco draw back his fist, obviously intending to do his teaching in the most rudimentary method possible—with his bare knuckles.

A garbled, nasal protest choked out of the fallen man, yet the tone was unmistakably that of someone pleading desperately with Franco not to hurt him. And—to Krissoula's dismay—she suddenly realized she recognized the man's incoherent whimpers! Hitching up her skirts, she raced back down the darkened street towards the pair, her lantern swinging wildly and splashing crazy arcs of golden light hither and thither as she ran.

"Wait!" she cried breathlessly, abruptly skidding to a halt. "Don't hit him, Franco, please! For the love of God, wait!"

"What?" Franco exclaimed, his fine head jerking back in indignation. His sulky lower lip jutted belligerently. "And why not, eh? This dirty *canalla* deserves the beating I mean to give him, following you like a panting dog each day!"

"Please, just do as I ask, Franco?" she pleaded. "I know him, I think, and I'm certain—if he's who I think he is—he'd never mean to hurt me, even if he was following me!"

"Hold the lantern high over here, then," Franco grumbled. "Let's have a look at the dirty little bastard before I let him up. If he's not who you think, he'll be sorry, I promise you!"

Krissoula held the lantern aloft, and Franco grasped the man's hair and jerked his head around so that his face was bathed in the lantern light. He recoiled at what he saw, revulsion filling his handsome features.

"Dios mio!" he gasped as he saw the man's face, deformed by a harelip, and he quickly dragged himself off the man, wiping his palms on his thighs as if they were soiled before hurriedly crossing himself.

"Cojo?" Krissoula asked gently, and held out her hand to help the crippled young man to his feet. The lad hesitated, then accepted,

361

lurching upright to stand beside her. "What are you doing here, *muchacho?* Why have you been following me?"

"Ah! So, you do know him, then?" Franco demanded rudely, cutting in before the youth could reply.

"Of course I do," Krissoula retorted, irritated by Franco's insufferable behavior. "I said I recognized him, didn't I, *tonto?* He's a—a friend of mine from the tavern—aren't you, Cojo? He does odd jobs here and there for Señor da Costa, right?"

Cojo nodded eagerly, then his enormous brown eyes slid uneasily in Franco's direction, as if he feared the young man might leap at his throat again.

"So tell me, why on earth have you been following me?" Krissoula repeated gently. "Did Luigi ask you to?"

Cojo hung his head and shook it slowly to and fro. "No, señorita."

"Why'd you do it, then?"

"Mahlvahdo," Cojo whispered in his nasal, jawing voice that chewed up words and spat them out almost beyond recognition, unless you were accustomed to listening to him speak, as Krissoula had become. "He's a bahd one, he is, but he loikes you, señhorita. I wanted to—to—" He seemed to be searching for the right word, but was unable to pronounce it for several seconds before managing to grind out, "prohteck you, *si?"*

He looked up at her hopefully then, and Krissoula knew by the adoring expression in his beautiful, long-lashed brown eyes that in his own way, the crippled handyman of the Taberna Cádiz was every bit as besotted by her as was Franco! *Madre,* she'd never even noticed! A lump formed in her throat and her eyes prickled. Was that why Cojo had always chosen to do his sweeping just before she began her dancing, and then leaned on his broom and watched, transfixed, while she did so? Was that why he'd followed her? Because he was concerned for her safety, too? She remembered then his poor crippled foot, clubbed and twisted from the birth that had also left his lip deformed, and the difficulty with which he took even a single step, and her heart went out to him. Cojo, poor, dear Cojo, scarce able to put one foot before the other without pain, and yet he'd followed her back and forth through countless streets, day in and day out, without a word to her, merely to protect her from Antonio Malvado and his men! *Dios mío,* she wanted to weep at the sacrifice the lad had made, at the pain and exhaustion he must have borne, and all for her sake!

"What'd he say?" Franco asked impatiently. "I can't understand a cursed word he's babbling!"

"That's all right, Franco. I understand him perfectly well! Cojo told me that *compadrito* Antonio Malvado's a bad man, and that he was afraid he'd do something to hurt me. He was following me to try and protect me, if that was the case, that's all—just like you were doing, Franco. Right, Cojo?"

"*Sí!*" Cojo agreed, nodding eagerly. "*Sí!*"

"And I suppose he jumped me thinking I was one of Malvado's men!" Franco jeered sourly.

"*He* jumped *you?*" Krissoula exclaimed, wanting badly to laugh at the incongruity of the bony youth with his twisted foot grappling the strapping, healthy young bull, Franco. "I thought *you'd* surprised him!"

"You needn't laugh, Cousin," Franco said stiffly, his annoyance obvious. "If I'd been the one to attack him, he'd be dead now, with my dagger skewering his guts."

He said the latter with such dire relish, Krissoula was hard put to stifle a giggle, for both young men were like fighting cocks haggling over a favored hen, with their feathers ruffled and their spurs extended!

But instead of laughing, she respected their dignity and told them both gravely, "Then I'm grateful I was able to stop you *both* in time! If not, I would have lost one—perhaps two!—wonderful, loyal friends, as well as the best bodyguards in the world, no? Thank you both, from the bottom of my heart . . ."

"All right, all right, that's thanks enough. We've wasted enough time here already," Franco said gruffly, embarrassed by the warm smile she gave him, which made him feel as if his joints were turning to butter. "Alonso and Gina's wedding's this morning, remember? If we don't get a move on, it'll be dawn before we get home, and the drinking half over with."

"Do you think the others would mind if Cojo joined us?" Krissoula asked impulsively.

Franco scowled and shrugged. "I doubt it. There'll be so many people, I'd be surprised if they even noticed one more, though with his looks, *Dios,* they just might! Let the little runt come, if it'll make you happy. I'll settle it with my father. But keep his ugly face out of my sight, eh?"

"I understand," Krissoula said solemnly, and added with disarming innocence, "And thank you for being so—so wonderfully gracious about your invitation, Franco."

Franco's brows crashed together in a dark scowl and his jaw

tightened, for something in her tone suggested she was teasing—or worse, chiding—him. But before he could ask her if that was the case, she'd turned from him and was talking to Cojo who, Franco had the most uncomfortable feeling, she liked quite as much as she liked him. *Caray!* Surely the monstrous youth couldn't be his rival for Krissoula's favors, not with that leering face like something out of a nightmare, or better yet, the gargoyles that decorated the eaves of the cathedral! The idea was preposterous, and yet . . .

"There's to be a wedding in Barrio Gitanos today," Krissoula was telling Cojo meanwhile. "There'll be music and dancing, and dozens of good things to eat! Oh, it'll be fun, *amigo,* I promise you, for we Gypsies know how to enjoy ourselves better than anyone. Won't you come—that is, if you've nothing better planned?" Krissoula urged the young man, yet offering him a reason to refuse, if he so wished.

"Will you dahnce at the wedding, Krihhoula?" Cojo asked, his eyes brightening like newly minted copper coins.

"I suppose I might—if I'm asked," she flirted, lowering lashes modestly.

"Then Oi'll come, if you're thure no one will mind," Cojo agreed gravely. "Oi'll ahhsk you!"

"It's agreed then. Wonderful! Let's go!"

With one of them on either side of her, Krissoula was well protected as she hurried home that morning!

But even as the oddly matched trio moved on down the street, two other men stepped from the shadows.

"Well, well! Whaddya make of that, eh, José?" one asked the other in *lunfardo,* the *barrio* dialect that was part Spanish, part Italian, and more often a weird combination of both.

"What I make of it isn't worth thinking about!" Juan growled. "It's what *el compadrito* makes of it that counts! Guess we'd better go tell him, eh?"

"Do we have a choice?" José countered, picking his teeth with a small gold toothpick.

"I suppose not. But the boss won't be happy, hearing his dancing girl's been traipsing about with her men friends—especially not after the way she's been brushing him off as if he stunk like yesterday's sour milk . . . !"

"You think I don't know that? *Merda!* Let's get it over with, and the sooner the better, to my mind . . ."

Chapter Thirty

Despite the early hour, the Reyeses' courtyard was a scene of frenzied activity when, shortly before dawn, Krissoula tripped through the wide-flung gates, her arms linked through Franco's on the one side, and Cojo's on the other.

Seated by the fire, Armando Reyes was smoking his long-stemmed clay pipe, interspersing puffs with issuing suggestions here and there and gesturing with the smoking piece for emphasis. His daughter, Carla, wearing a bright scarf over her dark head to keep the sweat from running into her eyes, was busy presiding over the cooking, the other women, and the fire, and seeing to the final preparations of the food they would take with them to share at the wedding feast—chicken and roasted racks of lamp, beef stew and huge platters of fresh salad vegetables from the market—but somehow, Carla still found a spare moment for a smile to welcome Krissoula home.

"Why, there you are at last, Cousin!" she cried, her green eyes sparkling as she brandished a ladle in Krissoula's direction. "So that old *bribón*, Luigi, let you go early after all, eh?"

"*Sí*, he did—but not without an argument, of course!" Krissoula laughed, her tiredness lifted by Carla's effervescent spirits. "He wouldn't be Luigi unless he grumbled, eh?"

"*Sí*, maybe not!" Carla allowed with a grimace. "So, who's your new friend there?" She nodded towards Cojo.

"Señora Carla Valdez, allow me to introduce Señor Cojo, of the Taberna Cádiz! It was Señor Cojo who's been kind enough to follow me home these past days, Carla—just to ensure my safety, you *comprende?* And so to show my gratitude, I've invited him to the wedding celebrations. It is all right, isn't it?" She frantically signaled a plea over Cojo's shoulder with her eyes, and Carla's smile widened.

"Ah, I see!" she exclaimed. "But of course it's all right, you silly goose—one more won't make a bit of difference! The Zambras' courtyard will be filled to overflowing as it is, and what's an extra mouth or two amongst so many?" She wiped her hands on her apron and bobbed a curtsey. "It's an honor to meet you, Señor Cojo. True gentlemen willing to offer their protection to a lady are so hard to find these days—especially so in this part of town!" She laughed smokily, her laughter generous and genuine and infecting all about her with smiles, Cojo among them. Why, Krissoula thought, he looked as if he'd died and gone straight to heaven, so merry were his brown eyes and his wide, if painfully misshapen, grin! "Won't you make yourself comfortable until everything's ready?" Carla continued, as always a warm and perfect hostess, no matter their humble surroundings. "Sofía, pour a mug of coffee for Señor Cojo while he waits. And fetch another for my poor brother, too, eh, with lots of sugar—he appears to need some sweetening this morning, the sourpuss! What's wrong, little brother? You look as if you've been eating lemons . . ."

"Enough, Carla . . ." Franco growled, and scowled threateningly. He glowered at his sister, nodded curtly to Krissoula, turned on his heel, and strode away.

Carla giggled. "Aiie, *Madre mía,* that insufferable, arrogant peacock! What on earth did you do to him this morning, Cousin? He acts like a jealous little boy who's been told he can't have something he wants—and we all know what he wants is you! He's been lovesick over dozens of women before, but he's never fallen as hard as he has this time, I think. Tell me straight, *gitana*—has Franco a chance to win you, or are thoughts of that Argentine, Esteban, still keeping you awake nights?"

Krissoula's lips pursed. Her golden eyes darkened. "I told you, didn't I? I want nothing to do with men, Carla! Not Franco nor Esteban—nor any other, come to that! They've brought me trouble enough in my life, *gracias!* Now, what can I do to help?" she inquired, deftly steering the conversation away from the painful matter she was still ill at ease discussing.

"Pah! I won't hear of you helping! After all, you've been working all night, *loca,* dancing for those drunken animals at the tavern! What you *can* do for me is have some coffee to refresh yourself, and sit down and relax for a few moments. When you're revived, then you can busy yourself—by prettying up for the wedding!" Carla insisted in her big-hearted fashion. "Sofía more than made up for your absence last night—she did the work of three women, I swear, didn't you, Sofía, chopping and dicing and peeling onions till she cried, *pobrecita!*" The thinner, older woman blushed with pleasure, despite her red-rimmed eyes that amply bore out Carla's claims, and Carla hugged her boisterously. "You know, I like this skinny little friend of yours, *amiga*. You were right—she's a *gorgio*, no doubt about that, but she *tries,* she really tries to fit in and pull her weight. Why, even my father remarked on it, and he's not one who's easily impressed. Now, if only our lazy Delora was more like her, we'd be ready to lea—! Why, scat, you naughty little monkeys! Geraldo, Francesca, shame on you!"

She broke off to shoo her two giggling children away from the platter of food she was arranging, threatening them with the ladle, yet the laughing, green-eyed boy Geraldo managed to grab a drumstick and made off with it, shrieking with triumph, while his little sister followed him empty-handed, wailing with disappointment and sucking her thumb. "Aiee, *Dios,* be off with you, too, Cousin, and let me get on, or I'll never be done here!" Carla cried in mock despair, and, giving her a warm hug, Krissoula gratefully did as bidden.

The sky was tinged with dawn's rosy pinks and silvery golds when the Reyes band set off down the street for the Zambras' courtyard. A little canvas-covered wagon drawn along behind them carried kettles and platters of steaming food, while the women and girls— all colorfully dressed in their finest ruffled skirts and fringed shawls, their hair elaborately dressed with dramatic Gypsy spit curls and the ears dangling with heavy gold hoops, carried baskets of flowers and walked alongside or behind.

The traditional Gypsy wedding flower was the almond blossom. But, failing to find any almond trees in the depths of the South American city and surrounding areas, the men had ridden out into the countryside and had gathered whatever they could find—or, Krissoula suspected, had "borrowed" several of the more exotic varieties of flowers—from the gardens of the palatial villas to be found to the north of the city! There were red and pink roses, white carnations, and waxy-white gardenias. There were exotic hibiscus bugles of yellow and scarlet, miniature pale-yellow jasmine bells, and the tissue-fine magenta, crimson, or purple petals of bougainvillea, all wafting a sea of perfume about their noses. Even the donkey hauling the little cart had its bridle decked with flowers for the festive occasion! Daisies had been woven in its short, shaggy mane and a battered straw hat with holes for his long ears garlanded with still more wildflowers—the work of the little children who, scrubbed and combed and finely dressed, scampered in and out of the cavalcade, playing tag and teasing each other in shrill, excited voices.

Not to be outdone by their womenfolk or children, the men sported ruffled white shirts this morning, crisply starched and pressed by their women. The elegant full sleeves had deep cuffs at the wrist, and over them they wore black felt vests embroidered with twining patterns of flowers and vines in bright reds and golds and blues. Elaborate leather belts or the traditional satin sashes cinched their waists and held up full-legged breeches tucked into leather boots at the knees. Some of the men played their guitars as they strolled along, and the narrow streets of Barrio Gitanos rang with the lively foot-tapping chords and merry laughter, ribald wedding jokes and good-natured teasing and singing.

The Zambras family greeted their guests with warm hugs and obvious pleasure, admiring new babies, clasping hands, exchanging back-slapping welcomes, gossipy tidbits, and how-have-you-beens? Krissoula was introduced around the gathering, received a wholehearted welcome, and afterwards found herself, Sofía, and Cojo a comfortable corner of the courtyard from which to watch the goings-on, spreading an old blanket over the flagstones to cushion their hardness and to keep clean the full skirts that billowed about them when they sat.

Krissoula watched with keen interest as the bridegroom's parents officially welcomed the nervous fourteen-year-old bride's mother and father. Then she saw a wrinkled, officious-mannered old woman hobble forward from somewhere, wearing a black lace shawl draped over her balding head. Señor Zambra received her with the respectful air of one receiving a bishop.

"Ahh. Here we go! The old witch is ready and waiting to do her duty! Aiee, *Dios,* that poor *niña!*" Carla—who had joined them—muttered in Krissoula's ear. "The girl looks ready to faint, eh—and little wonder! If you ask me, it's a barbaric old custom, long past its time! It should be done away with, no?"

As they watched, the old woman took the girl's trembling hand in her gnarled mahogany one and, followed by the bride's mother and the bridegroom's parents, led her away to the privacy of one of the many rooms leading off the open courtyard.

"What's going to happen in there?" Krissoula asked curiously, nodding in their direction. "How will they exchange vows without the groom?"

"You mean you don't know what goes on in there?" Carla exclaimed, her green eyes wide and incredulous at her friend's ignorance. *"Caramba!* And you call yourself a Gypsy of the true blood?" she teased scornfully.

Krissoula shook her head. "Not a clue, I'm afraid. You'll have to forgive my ignorance, but the Ballardos were Catholics, you see— we celebrated our band's weddings with a priest, in a church!"

"Lucky for you, *niña!* In the traditional way of things, that old woman's task is to verify that the bride's a virgin, before the marriage can be considered consecrated. Only once she's done so are they considered man and wife. You saw the white silk handkerchief the old *bruja* carried?"

"*Sí?*" Krissoula acknowledged, frowning.

"Well, with his parents and her mother as witnesses, the old woman will verify Gina's purity by pushing the handkerchief up between poor little Gina's thighs. If she is pure, the act will break her maidenhead, and the kerchief will be removed stained with her virgin blood. Then she and her man—Alonso over there—are considered married, and we shower Gina with flowers and songs in praise of her purity."

Krissoula gulped, remembering the loss of her own virginity years ago on her wedding night. While no less uncomfortable and admittedly an act clumsily executed on an overimpatient Miguel's part, at least the emotional moment had been a private one between her and her new husband! Poor little Gina would have no such privacy. "I think I agree with you," she murmured fervently, crossing herself. "The old ways are barbaric!" She paused for a moment, deep in thought. "But—what will happen if she doesn't bleed? What if she's not a virgin, or if her maidenhead had been accidentally broken in some other way?"

Carla grimaced. "You have to ask, knowing our people and the short fuse of our tempers, the importance of honor and pride and the purity of one's bride for a *gitano* man? In a word, Cousin, what would happen is—murder! That's what happens! The groom's family would be furious at the bride's father for trying to wed his wicked daughter to their beloved son. They and the bride's family would probably get into a terrible fight to the death. Knives would be drawn, tempers would be all too ready to flare, old enmities and grudges would be remembered and dragged up yet again—! Aiee, *caray!* You know how it is! We're a hot-blooded people, no?"

Krissoula grimaced. "I can imagine only too well, *sí,*" she agreed vehemently. "Oh, look! They're coming back out already!"

The bride's father came forward to meet the returning bride and her witnesses, and his wife beamed and nodded to him. Proudly, the smiling father took his daughter's trembling little hand and bussed her pale cheeks soundly as the toothy, grinning old crone held aloft the pure white silk kerchief, opened like a banner for all the gathering to see. It was stained with drops of bright red blood, and the guests roared their approval and praises.

"Ah, the precious 'scarlet roses'!" Carla exclaimed, then added with a relieved giggle, "Gracias a *Dios,* the poor girl's passed the test! Now the parents will show her their admiration and good wishes, and then the newlyweds will be put to bed. *Dios!* I do hope the happy pair aren't shy, and won't waste any unnecessary time in consummating their wedding! I'm starving, and we won't get to eat till that's all over and done with!"

"Carla!" Krissoula exclaimed, shocked by Carla's insensitivity. "Shame on you!" But Carla only grinned wickedly and gave a shrug as a man's deep voice began to sing:

> On the white kerchief
> Scarlet roses bloomed.
> Flowers of innocence,
> Blossoms of purity.
> A virgin maid,
> This lovely *gitana*—
> She brings honor to her father's name.
> Smile upon her, happy bridegroom,
> For she is beautiful,
> And will bring you joy . . .

The Gypsy guitarists began to play the lovely wedding songs, the *arboreas,* while the two sets of parents knelt on the ground about the smiling bride's feet. The proud young groom looked on, his dark eyes riveted to his shy bride's face, his arms crossed over his chest, while the two mothers and fathers performed a lovely dance Krissoula had never seen before, one danced in Gina's honor. Still kneeling and using only their upper bodies and graceful arm movements, they accompanied the lively music in a dance of adoration.

When they were finished, the bride's father and mother led the girl towards the groom, while his parents led him across the courtyard to meet her halfway. The pair shyly clasped hands, exchanged quick, nervous smiles and as quickly looked away, obviously embarrassed. With their parents to escort them, the newlyweds were taken at last to the flower-strewn wedding chamber, where they were left alone at long last to consummate their union.

"Dios mío! It's a wonder any bridegroom can perform his

husband's duties after such a ritual, eh, Cousin?" Carla observed with a sly grin and a hefty nudge that landed in Krissoula's ribs. "But then, you know our *gitano* men—lusty *hombres* to the last breath, eh, Coz?" She winked.

"I wouldn't doubt it," Krissoula agreed with an exasperated smile.

An hour later, after countless *arboreas* had been sung, the shy bride and groom emerged arm in arm from their bridal bower, blinking at the bright light in the courtyard after the shadowed chamber they'd shared. They had the dreamy-eyed look of lovers, Krissoula observed, and tears pricked her eyes, which she hastily scrubbed away with her knuckles.

It was mid-morning by now, and the golden summer sun was high in the sky, the air growing warmer and more sultry and humid with every passing moment.

The music changed with the reappearance of the couple. The guests gathered around, making a huge circle all about the crimson-cheeked young bride. Fourteen-year-old Gina was beautiful in her scarlet wedding finery and golden jewelry as she began to dance, quite alone. Women ran forward to shower her with flowers as she danced in the midst of the circle of Gypsies, until everywhere she stepped the flagstones were carpeted with blossoms, and several petals had been prettily caught in her snowy lace *mantilla* or in her cascade of luxuriant black hair. Carla and Krissoula gathered up handfuls of blossoms, and urged Sofía to do the same. Joining the other women, the three of them showered their blossoms over the bride and wished her good health, happiness, and the blessing of children in her new life.

The formal parts of the traditional Gypsy wedding ritual having been completed, the guests in the courtyard were finally allowed to succumb to their high spirits and celebrate in grand style! The kettles and platters of food that weighed down trestle tables rapidly vanished into hungry mouths. Bottles and leather *botas* filled with wine were soon being passed freely amongst the men, loosening tongues and oiling voices. Loud and lively music set restless fingers snapping and feet tapping, and several of the gathering sprang into the open courtyard and danced, whirling in wild abandon as the gay mood of the day moved them. Backs arched, their long fingers and graceful arms snapping or describing lovely patterns in the air, the women danced, looking like exotic, bright flowers themselves as they moved about the drab courtyard. Their ruffled skirts swirled or flew up as they furiously stamped their heels, revealing snowy petticoats and slim brown legs. The men stamped and clapped as they circled the women with a great air of arrogance and haughty disdain, their dance a proud, virile counterpoint to their women-folk's utterly feminine, graceful movements. Sofía, seated on her right, was entranced, Krissoula saw, and Cojo, sitting cross-legged beside her on her left, seemed little less so.

"You were right all along, *niña,*" Sofía said softly, her eyes still on the dancing. "You said there would be good times as well as bad in our new life here, and there is. This is one of the good times I'll remember for the rest of my days!"

Krissoula smiled, for it seemed Sofía had at last forgotten her fear of Delora's spiteful curse. "I'm happy you're enjoying yourself, Sofía. You see, you needn't worry about the future anymore. The bad times are over, behind us. We'll be all right now, I just know we will! This life might be harder than your old one—a far cry from what you've been used to in the past—but it's not so bad if there are times like this, is it?"

Sofía reached across and squeezed her hand. "No," she agreed softly, tears shining in her eyes, "It's not bad at all, *amiga.* Thank you for standing by me, when you could have left me behind to face Don Felipe's wrath alone."

But quite unknown to Sofía, Krissoula was wrong. It would have profited her to ask old Granny Zambra, who had the Romany gift of "seeing," to look into her palm and *dukker* her future from the lines etched there. If she had, they would have learned that the bad times weren't behind them. They had yet to begin . . .

Night had fallen and tiny stars sequinned the indigo sky yawning above the *barrios* before Krissoula finally succumbed to Cojo's urging and agreed to dance for the merrymakers.

"Pleath, Krithoula?" Cojo implored her nasally, his magnificent brown eyes soulful. He looked down at his feet, at the crippled, clubbed one in its odd, crudely fashioned boot of black leather that had given him his name, and she saw his lashes grow spiked and dark with tears. "You, who are so graceful, do not know how it ith to be cursed, to be a cripple like me, for El Señor blessed you with two lovely, healthy feet. Always—even ath a little boy in the convent of San Timéo, where I was raised by the good sisters—I have yearned to walk straight and sure, like others, and to be able to danth and sing. I feel the music here, in my heart. I hear it in my mind. But my clumsy legs and my lips and tongue will not obey me. My harelip cannot form words for others to understand, you see, and when I sing, it's like the gargling of a frog. My singing and danthing is the danthing of a freak, a clown—something to poke fun at, to be pitied. But when you danth—aiee, Señorita Krithoula, my heart dances with you! I forget that I'm only stupid, clumsy Cojo, the crippled boy!" he finished, smiling. "Please, danth for me?"

Krissoula nodded her heart going out to him in love after his impassioned speech. She tried to imagine how it must be, to want so badly to dance, and be unable to do so, but could not. She had always taken her strong, healthy limbs and her talents for granted, she realized, suddenly ashamed of herself. "For you, then, Cojo—only for you!" she promised, and she stood up, draping her flowered shawl over her tall haircombs as she made her way to where the musicians were seated.

She whispered in the guitarist's ear, and a moment later the chords of a well-known *flamenco zambra* carried over the noisy laughter and chatter of the assembled guests, many of whom had grown a little drunk on wine and good humor by now. Heads lifted and curious, appreciative eyes turned in her direction as the singer began to sing, and Krissoula began to dance to the words:

> You think I didn't see you
> As you followed me
> Through the streets of Sevilla.
> But I saw your dark eyes, *gitano*—
> They gave you away!
> Why follow me in secret,
> Like a bandit,
> When no other has spoken for me?
> Ask my father, shy *gitano*,
> If he will give you my hand!

The words of the song were teasing yet gentle ones, and Krissoula's lips curved in a playful smile as she danced before Cojo, the fringes of her shawl spraying about her, her bare golden arms weaving lovely, graceful patterns against the darkened star-strewn sky. Her high-heeled crimson slippers—a little scuffed and battered now, true, nevertheless nimbly stamped and whirled in rhythm to the full-throated song of the guitars.

> Your eyes fill my dreams,
> Handsome gypsy boy!

373

A thousand silver pieces,
Would buy just one of your smiles!
Don't be shy, my dark-eyed one,
For I won't refuse you . . .
Your smiles will be many
When I hold you in
In the garland of my arms,
And drown in the pools of your handsome eyes . . .

The crowd had grown hushed as they watched Krissoula dance, for the aura she created, the *duende* with which she danced, captivated them all. Playful, flirtatious, teasing—perhaps a hint naughty and sensual—it was a romantic song perfectly suited to a wedding feast, and her dancing expressed its sentiments as few flamencas could convey it. Her golden eyes sparkled in the torchlight, and her red lips glistened, parted to reveal a fleeting glimpse of the pretty, pearly sheen of her teeth as she smiled only at the ugly, short young fellow with the twisted foot, they noted with surprise and—on Franco's part—more than a little jealousy.

She was halfway through the final verse when a sudden commotion from the direction of the street brought the throbbing chords of the guitars abruptly to silence. The singer's voice broke off with a startled, "What—!" as several men elbowed and shoved their way into the courtyard, rudely thrusting aside the guests and knocking the guitars from the musicians' hands to the flagstones.

One slim man, his fists on his hips, strutted into the open, hushed circle, and looked about him with a scornful smile.

"So! It's a wedding feast we're having, then, is it, my gypsy friends? It seems you must have misplaced my invitation, eh? Nobody celebrates in Barrio San Timéo without the blessing of the *compadrito!* Nobody—!"

Krissoula's throat went dry as she flung about to see Antonio Malvado's cold, black eyes staring fiercely at her across the courtyard, no longer flirtatious and benevolent, but angry and threatening.

The *compadrito's* men flanked him on every side, pistols in their belts, or long-bladed knives already in their fists. From the ugly expressions on their faces, she knew they meant trouble, and that, at heart, she was the cause. She, and Malvado's lust to possess her.

Chapter Thirty-One

"Go back to your own part of the *barrios,* Malvado!" Papa Zambra growled, his fingers tightening over the hilt of the dagger he wore at his belt. "We *gitanos* have never allowed you to rule our lives, and nor will we ever do so. Go! You're not wanted here—not tonight, nor any night!"

"Wanted or no, I'm here, Zambra, and I intend to stay. It will take more than the likes of you to get rid of me—" Antonio's eyes flickered over Zambra's shoulder and back towards Krissoula in a way that made her skin crawl with revulsion, "—unless, that is, I get what I came for." His expression left no one in any doubt as to what that "something" was.

Armando Reyes stepped forward, placing his bulk between Krissoula and Malvado and physically announcing his band's support of the Zambras' leader, and his protection of the girl.

"If you mean the woman over there, *hombre,* forget it!" Armando said softly. "The señorita belongs to my band now, and is under my protection. She has no wish to go anywhere with you—is that not so, señorita?" he asked Krissoula over his shoulder, without taking his eyes from the godfather.

Krissoula's heart was beating so swiftly, it made her chest ache. *Por Dios!* Malvado must have finally grown impatient of the flowery compliments and subtle hints he'd tossed her way without response, and had decided to press his suit in more forceful terms! The last thing she wanted was to go anywhere with him—but if she refused, a bloody confrontation between Malvado's men and her Gypsy friends was inevitable.

"Please, señor, I don't want any trouble!" she pleaded, trying to sound calmer than she felt. "Perhaps we could talk about this in private, yes—outside, in the street?" Perhaps once outside, she could talk Malvado out of this foolishness, make him a few false promises to get rid of him and prevent any blood being shed by her friends?

"You'll go nowhere with this *canalla*, señorita," said a deep, calm voice, and Krissoula watched in surprise as a man she hadn't seen before stepped from the crowd to join Zambra and Armando Reyes.

"Why, Papa Severino!" Antonio exclaimed, his dark brows rising in surprise. He seemed, Krissoula thought, markedly taken aback. "I didn't know you'd be here. It's been a long time, no?"

"Not long enough," the man said coldly. "I'd hoped the rumors I'd heard about you were wrong, Antonio. I'd hoped you'd grown up a little since the old days, and become worthy of the title of *compadrito* of San Timéo. A pity, isn't it, that you haven't? You're still the bad little boy I remember from the old days, eh, 'Tonio—taking what you want by force when you can't have things your own way? Be off with you, *pibe*, before I lose my temper, and these good people here and I have no choice but to get rid of you by force!"

"Ha! Do you think I'm scared of your threats?" Malvado jeered, wetting his lips. "Surely you forget, Papa Rolón—I'm a *compadrito* in my own right now! I don't have to take my orders from you, nor from anyone else."

"In Barrio Timéo you're *compadrito*, Malvado. But here, in Barrio Gitanos, no! Here, you're nothing—less than nothing!" Rolón Severino declared in his mild yet somehow threatening tone. With the merest movement of his head, two Argentine men sprang forward, took Malvado by the elbows before he could react, and wrenched his arms painfully back and up behind him. A knife flashed as it was drawn from the boot of one man, and glittered in the torchlight as Severino's bodyguard pressed it across Malvado's windpipe.

"You see what I mean, *pibe?*" Severino asked amiably. "Here you are nothing! Now, tell your little trained monkeys to back off, understand, or I'll have my nephew here slit your throat from ear to ear, *comprende?*" Severino smiled thinly. "Our mutual friend might have hesitated to do murder to you once, and left you with only a pretty scar, but I have no such reluctance."

For a fraction of a moment, it seemed that Antonio Malvado might be foolhardy enough to resist. The tension in the horrified onlookers—Krissoula among them—mounted to crackling fever pitch in the time span before the *compadrito*'s shoulders slumped in defeat. Accordingly, no one noticed when Delora slipped away from her husband's side, using the others' riveted attention as a cover for her absence. Moving quickly from shadow to shadow, she left the courtyard for the darkened street beyond, unobserved.

"Very well," Antonio rasped at length, hatred glittering in his black eyes. "You win, Severino—this time. José! Juan! Put up your blades and get going, damn you! You, Stefano, and you, Roberto, that's enough, you hear me? We're leaving, boys."

At a nod from their boss, Severino's bodyguards released Malvado, and he dusted himself off as if their touch had contaminated him. He turned as if to leave the courtyard, but then, to everyone's surprise, he hesitated, plucking the yellow rosebud from his lapel as he swung about to face Krissoula.

"I'm leaving, *querida,*" he said softly, his tone laced with menace, his thin lips curled, "and for now, you may think your friends have won. But you haven't seen the last of Antonio Malvado, I promise you! I want you, woman—and Antonio always gets what he wants, one way or the other. Some fine day, you'll come crawling to me for help, pretty one! And when that day comes, you and your friends will wish to God you'd left with me tonight—!"

He fixed a long, intent look upon first Franco, and then Cojo, Sofía, and Carla in turn, before tossing the rosebud contemptuously at her feet and striding quickly away after his men.

Krissoula looked down at the wilted blossom, then muttered a blistering curse and ground it to shreds under her high heels; a defiant, scornful gesture that drew roars of approval from the formerly hushed crowd.

"Music!" Señor Zambra ordered in a loud voice, clapping his hands. "Eat! Drink up, everyone! Are we cowards, *amigos,* to have our Gina's wedding ruined by that scum? Never, I say!"

At his urging, the musicians resumed their playing, and the hum of conversation and laughter resumed little by little, even louder and more boisterous than before as a result of the unpleasant interruption. Smoldering-eyed Gypsy men, egged on by their volatile women, bragged of what they would have done should Malvado's men have started a fight. Outrageous boasts flew thick and fast about the courtyard as one man or another demonstrated his skills with a blade on an innocent loaf of bread, or an unsuspecting chicken breast.

Krissoula, her legs still trembling, took advantage of the distractions to go to Armando and thank him.

"But I didn't want to cause any trouble for anyone," she murmured afterward. "I—I hope Malvado won't take his anger out on anyone else because of me?"

Armando patted her shoulder in an awkward yet affectionate gesture of comfort. "Enough, *niña!*" he scolded. "You have no man to protect you, and since you are one of us now, what else would we do but defend you? Besides, we are not children, to fear such a bully as Malvado! If he plans a reprisal for tonight, he'll find he's bitten off more than he can chew, eh, friends?"

"*Sí!*" echoed the men around him heartily, their dark eyes fierce.

"There, you see? Come, little one, forget about Malvado, and enjoy yourself! You've seen the last of that rogue, I'd wager, thanks to our friend Rolón here!" He chucked her under the chin, as he so often did Carla, with the gruff affection of a fond uncle.

"I must thank you, too, señor," Krissoula murmured, reaching out to clasp the one-eyed man's hand in thanks. He nodded as he gazed at her, the black leather patch he wore over his left eyes lending him the air of a sinister pirate.

"You are more than welcome, señorita," Rolón Severino replied, "but unlike my friend here, I wouldn't take Malvado's threats so lightly. I've known him since he was a young puppy, running wild in the streets with his followers like a pack of scavenging dogs. That one's as hard and as sly as they come, with no notions of honor. It's a rare woman who has the courage to refuse Antonio, and it's when he's thwarted that he's at his most dangerous! Be careful, señorita, and take my advice. Don't put yourself in a position of owing our 'friend' any favors, unless you're prepared to pay his price, *comprende,* little one?"

Wetting her lips, Krissoula nodded and whispered, "*Yo comprende bien, gracias, señor.*"

The remainder of the guests appeared to have regained their former good spirits, but not so Krissoula or Sofia, who were subdued now, and unsmiling. Cojo fetched them both a glass of red wine, anxious to restore the color to their cheeks, but for the two women, Malvado's threats had ruined the wedding festivities, and even his bright thanks for the dance she had performed for him could not bring a smile back to Krissoula's face, Cojo saw sadly and with a surge of renewed hatred for Malvado filling his breast.

It was a relief when, an hour or two later, Carla came to them and suggested they return home. The wedding party would continue for two or more days, but it would have to continue without them.

As the Reyeses' womenfolk prepared to bundle up their sleepy children for the return to their own courtyard, no one saw Delora slip back to her husband's side wearing a smug smile—no one, that is, except for Cojo, whose soulful brown eyes missed nothing where Krissoula was concerned. He noticed the burning, malicious glance the sharp-featured Delora cast the girl across the courtyard, and he frowned. What, he wondered, had caused that gloating look, her expression of triumphant hatred . . . ? What mischief had she been up to?

Chapter Thirty-Two

Esteban stood in the gloom, looking up and down the darkened streets as memories crowded in on him, both painful and pleasant. How many years had it been since he'd last stood in this very place, he considered, poised to knock at this very door? Ten years? Eleven?

Eleven, he decided, though it didn't really matter. He'd been twenty years old that last time, and he'd seen his thirty-first birthday just last November. Those eleven years had flown past, and he'd changed more than he realized. He felt it strongly—just as he sensed that here, everything had stayed much the same.

The streets were as he remembered—oh, perhaps a little shabbier, perhaps more densely populated, but intrinsically the same streets, although they seemed smaller, narrower than his memories had painted them. The smells were the same as those he remembered, too; the aromas of hundreds of cooking pots abubble with the pungent reek of the evening's meal: of tomatoes, garlic and spices, of onions and peppers and tripe, of *ravioli* and *pulchero* or sickly sweet, overripened tropical fruits—pineapple and banana, orange and limes, underlaid by the stink of the river, the Plata, mingling with but never quite masking the smells of poverty and dirt, decay and despair. And disease . . .

Ah, sí, I can smell the stink of death and sickness here again, he thought sadly, remembering that other summer—many years ago now—when cholera had stalked the city of Buenos Aires as it did this year, and would each and every sweltering summer to come, if no cure were found.

That time, the dreaded wasting disease had torn from him the mother he had loved, gentle Maria de San Martín, and in the aftermath of her death, it had ultimately brought him here, to this very house, and to the notice of Papa Rolón Severino, who'd taken him off the streets, healed his hurts, fed him, protected him, raised

379

him to manhood, and loved him like a son.

Was he still alive, Esteban wondered uneasily? And if he were, had he forgiven him for leaving, for turning his back on the opportunity to be *compadrito* in Rolón's wake? He shrugged. Forgive him or no, he'd known he had to leave. Papa Rolón's kindness had become a noose around his neck, stifling him, albeit the noose was woven with cords of love. He'd had to go to become his own man, to seek his own identity and his own destiny far removed from the benevolent yet destructive shadow of Rolón Severino. He'd found that destiny at Tierra Rosa, whose vast rolling grasslands and sweet, fresh air had seemed like heaven on earth after the narrow, confining streets of the dingy *barrios,* with their rigid code of honor, their fierce, often misplaced loyalties, and the deadly bloodfeuds waged between enemy *compadritos* and their gangs of cutthroats and thieves. Life had been held cheaply in the *barrios,* but Esteban had learned at too early an age how very precious and fleeting life truly was; far too precious to be squandered for an imagined insult, another man's pride, or some woman's faithless heart.

Krissoula, he understood now, had seen the same futility in such a life, and had—in her own female fashion and, in all truth, in probably the only way she knew how—tried to escape it by taking any opportunity that came her way to get out. Was she here somewhere, he wondered, alone and afraid in these darkened streets, scrabbling out a living for herself and Sofía—or had he already lost her for all time to cholera or some other untimely death? The thought of her perhaps being dead made sweat spring out on his brow and palms, and filled his gut with the sick, awful weightiness of dread. She couldn't be dead! She couldn't, for he loved her—! He had to find her, tell her so. He flicked his head to rid it of such an unbearable thought, and beat heavily upon the door before him with a clenched fist, before he could change his mind and do the easy thing and leave.

"Who is it?" came a muffled female voice long moments later.

"Have you forgotten your little brother's knock already, then, *bombón?*" he answered, his heart pounding.

He heard a muted gasp, the sound of a bolt being hurriedly slid back, and then the door swung open and the years rolled away like the skin peeled from an onion, layer by layer: the past rushed up to meet him and became one with the present. As he'd expected on hearing the voice, Rolón Severino's only daughter, Theresa, stood in the doorway, her tiny mother—dressed all in black—hovering

380

anxiously at her elbow and peering nearsightedly over her daughter's shoulder. A sensation of déjà vû filled him, for he'd played this scene a thousand times before.

"Theresa," he said quietly, smiling down at the openmouthed girl briefly before turning to her mother, who had a veined brown hand clapped to her birdlike bosom in shock. "Mama Rosa! It's been a long time, no? *Dios,* how I've missed you both!"

"Esteban, mi hijo? Can it truly be you?" Rosa Severino exclaimed, tears of happiness filling her eyes as she saw, after so many years, the man she'd raised like a son, standing there. She held her arms wide to embrace the tall, broad-shouldered man who moved into them and lifted her clear off her feet, hugging her tightly as he whirled her around and around. "Still slim and light as a reed, mmm, Mamacita!" he declared, swallowing the clenching in his throat.

"And still a flattering rogue—as ever!" Rosa declared fondly through her tears. "Come, come inside with you, mi Esteban! Theresa *mia,* come inside also, and close the door, *niña.* Whatever will our neighbors think to see you dawdling on the doorstep at such an hour with a strange man!" With a tremulous smile, Rosa brushed away her tears, gripped Esteban's arm, and chivvied and scolded him down a dark hallway smelling of cabbage to the family *sala,* talking all the while. Theresa trailed in their wake with far less enthusiasm than her mother exhibited.

In the *sala,* Esteban saw the same heavy, carved furniture, the same fussy lace doilies gracing the highly polished wooden furniture; smelled the same old scents of lemon-oil polish, wax, and lamp oil, and the faint odor of mothballs that underscored them all, that he remembered from the past.

The table was set for two, everything proper and in its place—an expression, he'd always suspected, of Mama Rosa's secret need to bring order to the ordinary, everyday facets of her life as the wife of *compadrito* Rolón Severino; a peculiarly dual existence which had aspects that were far, far from the ordinary.

True, Rolón Severino was a good man; a fine husband, a peerless father, a devout Catholic, in many ways. Hadn't he taken an unknown urchin off the streets, seen him nursed back to health, counseled him through his difficult teenage years, taught him the art of survival in the *barrios?* Hadn't he always shown a gruff affection to his shy daughter, attending her first communion, her confirmation, throwing a lavish celebration for her fifteenth birthday, like any good Spanish papa? And hadn't he always

381

protected his little wife, Rosa, whom he adored, and seen that everyone showed her the respect she deserved, without ever once forgetting an anniversary or a special time? *Sí,* he had!

But there was also another, darker side to Papa Rolón. Esteban knew all about it, and Mama Rosa certainly did—though she might deny it even to herself. In all probability, so did Theresa know of this other Rolón, the man who led a secret, separate life as *compadrito,* and whose word was second only to that of God— maybe.

Rolón could be ruthless when crossed, merciless in visiting vengeance upon his enemies. He'd not become *compadrito* by virtue of his compassion nor his kindness, *Dios,* no, that much was certain, nor had kindness kept him in that position! Nevertheless, the dwellers of Barrio la Boca respected him, perhaps even loved him in their own way, much as cowed children will love a stern and unforgiving father, with a desperate, twisted love. After all, they were *his* people! He protected them from outsiders, and repelled those jockeying to take his place; other would-be *compadritos* who might, they feared, have proved far harsher than he. True, he favored those who did things his way, but he also upheld the rights of the weak or poor against those stronger than themselves, though God help those who defied him! *Sí.* The immaculate order of Rosa Severino's house was in direct proportion to the disorder of her husband's secret life . . .

"Come, *hijo,* sit yourself down, and I'll fetch you a plate. Aiee, how handsome you've grown, *niño,* but *caray,* how lean you are, too, *mi pobrecito!"* Rosa fussed, clicking her teeth in fond disapproval. "A bowl of my *pulchero* will fatten you up. You'll eat with us, no? Of course you will! My Theresa will keep you company while I'm off to the kitchen, *sí,* Theresa *mía?"*

"*Sí,* Mama," Theresa agreed flatly, still with marked lack of enthusiasm, and Rosa Severino beamed and scuttled off, oblivious to anything but her joy at seeing Esteban again.

"She doesn't change, does she?" Esteban observed with a wry smile.

"Mama? No, I suppose not. She's too old to change now. Maybe we all are."

"So. How have you been, Theresa?" Esteban inquired, taking a seat at the table uninvited. He felt uncomfortable at being left alone with the young woman, for her displeasure at seeing him again was marked. She sat stiffly in a straight-backed chair set close to the door, her slim, pale hands clasped in her lap, her dark head meekly—

or sullenly—bowed. Her doelike prettiness had faded over the years, he observed, watching her in the usually flattering glow of the oil lamps, like a perfect white blossom will bruise and fade when hidden too long from the sun. The last time he'd seen her, she'd been beautiful, an oval-faced Spanish Madonna with beige satin skin like magnolias, and long, straight black hair streaming like a waterfall about her shoulders.

Had he caused that wilting, he wondered fleetingly, feeling a momentary twinge of guilt? But then, the moment passed as swiftly as it had come. After all, he had nothing to berate himself for. Nothing! He had made the girl no false promises back then, given her no reason to expect more of him than the teasing brotherly interest and affection he'd always felt for her. Her expectations of more between them had been a result of her father's wishful thinking—and perhaps, her own.

Papa Rolón had planned that Esteban de San Martín should marry Theresa Severino, his only daughter, with never a thought given to ask if he wished to do so or nay! No, it had simply been decided. The great *compadrito* of La Boca had spoken, and Rolón had assumed that that would be that!

It had been then that Esteban—already restless to prove himself as a man, eager to leave the *barrios'* rigid confines and find his own place in the world beyond the shadow of the forceful man who'd raised him—had felt the noose of Rolón's love tighten about his throat. He'd known he had to get away before it was too late, and had dared to tell Papa Rolón so. As he'd expected, Rolón had been stunned when Esteban had defied him and quietly refused to marry Theresa, becoming incredulous and then furiously angry by turns.

"So! My beloved Theresa is not good enough for our fine Señor Esteban de San Martín—is that it?" he'd rasped.

"Perhaps it's that she's too good for me, Papa," he'd countered. "I love her like a sister. I'd protect her honor with my life, you know that. But love her as a woman, a wife—?" He'd shrugged. "No. I cannot marry Terecita."

"Ingrata!" Rolón had growled, and slapped Esteban hard across the cheek, snapping his head back. "Ungrateful wretch! Is this how you thank me for dragging you off the streets? For giving you a home, and a family who loves you?"

"As I love you all, Papa," he'd replied quietly, his face livid with the marks of the blow. "You know I can never repay you for all you've done for me! But my marrying Theresa would be wrong. We don't love each other, Papa—not in the way we should. And she deserves a man who loves her, not one who would marry her out of gratitude to her father, or out of guilt. I could only bring her unhappiness, I know it."

"And you think that leaving San Timéo and finding this true father of yours will make *you* happy?"

"Who knows? I know only that the life here is not for me. I must find another."

"Even if your leaving breaks my Rosa's heart?"

So, he would manipulate him, eh, mercilessly pull at his heartstrings?

"*Sí*, Papa," he'd acknowledged softly, "even then. Letting go of our children, letting them live their own lives in their own way, is all a part of life, too, just as much a part as bearing them and raising them. In her heart, Mama knows this, and so, Papa, do you. In time, you'll come to accept it."

"Go, then!" Rolón had ranted, his square olive face mottled with white in his anger. "Get out of my house—get out of my sight, you ungrateful wretch! And if this life of yours doesn't work out, don't think you can come crawling back here! Our doors will be closed to you from this day, Esteban. You are no longer welcome here."

"Must it be this way?" he'd asked, anguished. "Can't we part without this harshness between us? With a door left open—one that swings in as well as out?"

"No. It must be this way! You've made it so—you leave me no choice!" Rolón had said stonily, his eyes coldly furious, and he'd turned his back on the tall young man.

"Wrong! There's always a choice, Papa," he'd said softly, "as long as we don't leave it too long to make it." There was no answer from the older man. "Very well. Then I'll be going. *Adíos, compadrito,*" he'd said with acidic emphasis on the latter word, and without further ado, he'd left the *barrios* behind him . . .

"It brings back memories for you, coming here, doesn't it?" Theresa asked shrewdly, watching his face, and Esteban realized with a start that she hadn't answered his question—or if she had, that he hadn't heard her do so, so lost in thought had he been.

"*Sí,*" he agreed heavily. "Perhaps too many memories!"

"Good ones—or bad?"

"Good, most of them. I owe your parents so much, Theresa. Far more than I could ever hope to repay. And I love them. My only regret is that I left with harsh words and bad feelings between us, remember?"

"Oh, I remember," Theresa said coldly. "And I remember why

384

you left, too." She bit her lower lip and looked away, hiding her expression in shadow. He knew if he turned her face to the light, he'd see tears sparkling in her sad brown eyes.

"Do you?" he asked, and frowned. "Do you really?"

"Because you didn't want to marry me," she blurted out, and covered her mouth with her fist to staunch a sob. "That's why you left! Do you think a young girl would ever forget that, Señor de San Martín? That she could ever bring herself to forget your rejection of her? I loved you, Esteban! I thought you loved me, too, but I was wrong."

"No, Theresa, that's not so—and you know it, too, in your heart! You always thought what your papa wanted you to think, *hermana,*" Esteban corrected her gently. "You convinced yourself you wanted what *he* wanted you to want, in order to please him— never considering what you truly wanted from your life. Think back, Theresa. It was soon after he lost the sight in his eye that Rolón decided I should follow in his steps as *compadrito* of La Boca, and that we should be married. No doubt he'd realized he was mortal after all, and that there was a better than even chance that he wouldn't live forever. That he just might grow old, as other men do, and someday lose his grip on the reins of La Boca. He could not—would not!—allow that to happen, and so he came up with a solution. What better way for him to remain in control of things than through a younger man, one who possessed the youth and the vigor he was destined to lose? Through one whom he could control? He planned to do so through me, with Esteban de San Martín as his son-in-law, the husband of his beloved Theresa! How we felt about each other or what we wanted never entered into it!"

"That's a lie!" she cried hotly, springing to her feet, all apathy gone.

"No, I don't think so. Nor do I think you loved me, not in your heart, not in the way a woman loves a man. You convinced yourself you did because it was what your papa wished. Be honest, Terecita! Can you truly say that you once thought of me with passion and desire, as your husband, your lover, in all the years we were growing up together like brother and sister?"

"You make my father sound like some kind of monster!" she protested, avoiding answering him.

"Rolón?" Esteban laughed. "No, Theresa, not a monster! But he is—as well you know—a very strong-willed man. One determined to have his own way in all things, and one who knows how to go about getting it, how to inspire loyalty and love in others, how to manipulate them in the name of love. Those are the very qualities that make him capable of controlling La Boca, that make him a strong leader, as well as a ruthless enemy. Tell me—is he still angry at me, after all these years?"

For the first time, Theresa smiled, her small, oval face lighting up. "Oh, come, Esteban, you know Papa better than that, surely! I doubt you were halfway across the city before he regretted the dreadful things he'd said to you, and wished he could get you back here to stay, on any terms! Truly, he's missed you, *hermano*. Missed you more than he'd ever admit to Mama and me."

Esteban nodded soberly. He'd missed Rolón Severino, too.

"And Malvado?" he asked, knowing he couldn't put off the question any longer. Involuntarily, his brown hand strayed to his abdomen, and he lightly touched the scar concealed by his clothing; the letter "A" which Antonio Malvado had carved into his chest when he was only ten years old.

Theresa nodded, and distaste filled her expression. "Ah, *sí,* he's still alive, more's the pity! It is as if, like a cat, he has nine lives! He recovered from your reprisal for Papa's injury, and he's grown steadily more vicious and cunning ever since! He's *compadrito* of Barrio San Timéo now, did you know?"

Esteban's mouth twisted in a grimace. "I didn't, but it doesn't surprise me. He gave up on the idea of taking over the running of La Boca, then?"

The woman nodded. "*Sí.* He had no choice! After you left, and my father had recovered his strength and resumed his position as *compadrito* here, he used paid informants from among Malvado's cronies to find out the names of all those responsible for his ambush and the loss of his eye."

"And?"

"One by one, Malvado's men were found floating in the Plata."

Theresa shuddered, her distaste at confessing this evidence of her father's dark side plain on her face. "Antonio decided he'd had enough, that he'd never be able to take over here as long as my father still lived. He moved in on Barrio San Timéo instead, and, little by little, he took it over. That's where Papa's gone tonight—to a wedding in the Gypsy quarter there. The Gypsies bow to no one, you see, recognize no *compadrito* as their lord, and I think they fascinate Papa for that very reason, for he has many good friends in Barrio Gitanos. But he should be home very soon. He'll be happy to see you again, I know, *hermano.*" And she was pretty again as she smiled for only the second time since his arrival.

"And I him," Esteban said with feeling. "Besides, I need his help, Theresa. He may well be the only one in Buenos Aires—or all of Argentina, for that matter—who can help me."

"Help you to do what?"

His eyes flickered away from hers as he muttered, "To find someone."

Theresa nodded. "Ahh, I see. This—someone—it's a woman, yes?" she asked, but it was more statement than question. Why else would he have been unable to meet her eyes?

"*Sí,* a woman," Esteban agreed reluctantly.

To his surprise, Theresa rose and came across the room, slipping her arms about him in an affectionate, forgiving hug. "Don't worry, little brother. Wherever she is, Papa will know how to find her!"

Mama Rosa returned then with the platters of food.

Chapter Thirty-Three

"Carla, did you borrow my golden hoops?"

"Without asking you? Silly! You know me better than that!" Carla retorted. "Look again, Bianca. You must have misplaced them."

"I know I didn't," the young woman protested with a worried frown. "And I've already looked everywhere twice! They were here just yesterday morning, though. I remember, because I couldn't decide whether to wear them for the wedding or not. In the end, I wore my silver ones instead, and left the gold behind."

"What's going on? Someone's missing something?"

"*Si!* Bianca's lost her golden earrings, Elena, nothing to get excited about. I'm sure they'll show up sooner or later," Carla explained casually as a third woman hurried over to them. She had a basin of water at her feet, a cloth, and a scrap of soap, and was kneeling down and bathing her little daughter—a pretty moppet with huge black eyes—in the warm rays of sunshine that flooded the courtyard.

"I'm glad you're sure!" Bianca snapped waspishly. "Meanwhile, what am I to tell Eduardo if he asks what I've done with them? They were his wedding gift to me, Carla, and you know how sentimental—and quick-tempered—he can be!"

"Perhaps there's a magpie in our courtyard then, for I'm missing something, too!" Elena revealed with a grimace. "My silver combs—the ones my grandmother left me?—they're gone!"

Although she managed to pacify Elena and Bianca for the time being, they were not the only women to have valuables missing, Carla discovered as the morning wore on. Another woman had lost the small store of tiny golden sovereigns from England and the silver guinea pieces from Spain with which she'd planned to dower her daughter; still another an expensive shawl of Brussels lace, irreplaceable here in South America. Angered and upset by their losses, the women quickly fell to squabbling about other matters and Carla, still feeling drained from the wedding festivities the day before, found her patience quickly worn thin before the day was half over.

"Enough!" she snapped, covering her ears. "I can stand no more of this—your bickering has given me a headache! Return to your belongings and search them once more. If the items you've lost haven't been found by suppertime, then we'll tell my papa when he comes home. He'll decide what's to be done about it."

"Meanwhile, where are your dear friends, Krissoula and Sofía?" Elena asked pointedly, her brows arched. "I don't see them anywhere!"

Her friends murmured in agreement, "*Sí*, where are the pair this morning? They should be up and about already, since they left the Zambras' courtyard long before everyone else, mmm . . . ?" Their implication was obvious.

"As did I, remember, Cousins?" Carla gritted, furious. "And they were with me until we turned in for the night."

"Ah, *sí*, of course! But after that—what then, Carla? What about after you fell asleep, eh?"

The women exchanged smug, knowing glances that infuriated Carla. She threw down the cloth with which she'd been polishing her copper pots, sprang to her feet, and planted her fists on her hips. "*Caray!* I've had more than enough of your insinuations!" she snapped. "Krissoula and Sofía have gone down to the riverbank to wash their clothes, satisfied? And as for those sly eyes you make at each other, I tell you my friends have stolen *nothing* that belongs to any of you! They'd never do such a thing!"

"No, Carla? But what about that time Delora accused the *gorgio* of stealing her *tortillas?*" Elena reminded her. "It's said there's no smoke without fire, eh?"

"Delora was lying through her teeth that time, *muchacha!*" Carla hissed. "*Dios mío!* I'd have expected such behavior from my sister-in-law, but never from you two. What's wrong with you all today? You should be ashamed of yourselves!" She looked about her, suddenly suspicious. "By the way, where *is* Delora this afternoon?" She grimaced. "Somehow, I can't imagine that one missing out on all of this—!"

"She fed her children breakfast, and then took them with her to the marketplace," Elena disclosed.

"She did, did she?" Carla echoed, rolling her eyes. "Well, well! That doesn't sound like our lazy Delora to me! Perhaps the summer's heat's affected her mind, no? Or—perhaps her wonderful gift of the 'sight' forewarned her that there'd be trouble this morning, and she decided it would be better if she were far away when the storm broke, no?" Her sarcastic smile quickly faded. Her green eyes flashed. "Now, the rest of you, get out of my sight, before I lose my temper! We'll sort this matter out tonight, when Krissoula and Sofia are here to defend themselves."

The women obediently scattered, for no one wanted to be anywhere near Carla should her legendary Reyes temper be lost, and Carla returned to polishing her copper pots—the few valuable pieces she'd been able to bring with her from Spain, of which she was enormously proud. Something was definitely wrong, she thought, and the knowledge that there might well be a thief amongst their numbers troubled her. Could Delora know something about this . . . ? It wasn't like her to leave the courtyard to run errands unasked, and that in itself seemed suspicious, evidence of *something,* only of what, she was uncertain. She gave a shrug. It was no use dwelling on the problem. When everyone was gathered about the evening fire for supper would be the time to bring the matter up for her papa's consideration. She'd worry about it then.

Krissoula and Sofia knelt on the muddy riverbank under the fierce summer sun and brilliant azure skies. Their skirts were hiked up and fastened securely at the waistband in a way that bared their legs to mid-thighs. After all, the squelching mud was everywhere and while legs were were easily washable, skirts were but poorly so!

Their laundry was spread over the rocks. After they'd energetically scrubbed it clean, they rinsed the soap from the clothes in the yellowish river water before draping the garments over still other rocks to bleach and dry in the hot sunshine. They were not alone at their tasks—far from it! Despite the cholera epidemic that had driven many *porteños* to become hermits in their own homes out of fear of contagion, life had to go on, and so did the wash have to be done! On every side of Krissoula and Sofia, mulatto and Negro washerwomen were likewise busy at their laundry, as well as other working-class Argentines or Spanish women. Baskets of soiled or newly washed clothing were everywhere and although the hour was still early, the river already bore a foamy scum of soap and froth.

It was just one of many times Krissoula and Sofia had come to the Rio de la Plata's banks to do their laundering, but it was a task they'd come to welcome and look forward to as a brief respite from the stifling climate of Barrio Gitanos, and the Reyeses's courtyard.

The strain of several people living in a confined area in one another's pockets had begun to tell.

She and Sofía, lacking families and being newcomers, had not been given one of the many little rooms opening off the Reyeses' courtyard, but slept outside, under stars in the open air each night. In all honesty, sleeping in the open was no hardship, not in the sweltering heat of a South American summer! Krissoula knew she'd have gone *loca* penned in a single, stifling room. No, it was the lack of privacy for dressing and bathing that bothered her, and she knew it mortified poor, painfully modest Sofía.

Carla had been kind enough to offer her her and her husband's room from time to time, but Krissoula had only taken her up on her offer when she and Sofía wished to bathe and needed the privacy of walls and a door. Carla had a family, and they needed their own place. Besides, Carla had already done more than enough for them, to Krissoula's thinking, without this added demand on their goodwill.

Consequently, laundry excursions to the riverbanks had become breathing spaces where she and Sofía could talk together openly and air their grievances or opinions without fear of offending their hosts in any way. Besides, the coffee-skinned washerwomen they met there were kind to them, and it was great fun listening to them teasing each other outrageously in their lilting voices, or else shamelessly propositioning the red-faced young men who made the mistake of wandering along the rickety wooden piers erected over the sloping mudflats!

Seeing those piers, Krissoula couldn't help remembering her arrival in Buenos Aires. Once their ocean-going vessel, the *Rosamundo*, had dropped anchor in the roadstead of the Plata— over five miles from the city itself—launches had arrived alongside the *Rosamundo* in small flotillas to carry the passengers to shallow water, which was still more than a mile from dry land. From the shallows, the passengers and their baggage had been transferred to ox-drawn carts with enormous wheels and, more than a little damp and uncomfortable, they had at last been carried in these cumbersome vehicles to the piers. The whole clumsy procedure of disembarking had lasted over two hours in all! Krissoula had found the various stages in the process wildly amusing, but not so poor Sofía, who'd suffered terribly from *mal de mer* when they sailed from Spain, and who'd never discovered her sea legs. The news that they could only reach firm, dry land once again by a series of uncomfortable stages that left them soaked had been the final straw, the last indignity! Krissoula had had to have a sleeping draught prepared for the distraught and weeping Sofía once they reached their hotel, just to calm her down!

Krissoula glanced across at Sofía, watching her for a few moments unobserved. Sweat rolling off her brow, her mouse-brown hair curling in the humidity, the older woman pounded, rinsed, and wrung out her linens as if to the manner born. She hid a smile. She doubted Sofía's reactions would be the same now, she'd changed so much! She'd probably dismiss such minor inconveniences and excitements as negligible, bless her, she thought fondly!

"*Hola,* Krissoula-girl! Sofía, chile, a good mornin' to you!" a mulatto washerwoman, newly arrived, sang out, dropping her load of wash from her head and settling her plump body comfortably not far from them. "Say what, girl, I heard there was big trouble in Barrio Gitanos las' night an' I thought straightway 'bout you, girl! Heard tell there was a fight 'tween Severino and Malvado, eh?" She winked. "Two bulls in one pen, no?"

"It came close to it," Krissoula admitted, wondering bemusedly how news could travel so fast and over such distances in the *barrios.* "But, *gracias a Dios,* their quarrel was ended before any blood was spilled."

"Heard that fight was 'bout a certain wo-mon, too?" Consuela continued archly. "Anyone 'Suela might know, girlie?"

Krissoula grimaced. "I'd say you know very well already, Consuela!" she retorted, unable to repress a smile. "Yes, the fight was about me! That cursed Antonio Malvado has the eye for me. Aiee, all the women in Buenos Aires he can pick and choose from, and that rogue wants me, curse his black heart!"

Consuela clucked in dismay, her broad smile gone. "Then you'd best keep a sharp eye out, darlin', and a slick tongue in your head if you ain't got any likin' for the mon, 'cos he's jest about as bad as they come in these parts—and believe me, honey, we've got plenty bad mons here already! Careful what you say 'round that mon, real careful. Make him angry, and you're as likely to end up in here, honey—" she motioned, nodding at the dirty river water, "as you is in his bed!"

"Don't I know it!" the Gypsy girl agreed gloomily.

Consuela gave a deep, throaty chuckle which set her golden earrings swinging. "Now, now, girlie, on second thought, it ain't so bad as all that! Things get too hot for you in Barrio Gitanos, you jest come see 'Suela. Ain't nobody gonna bother you at the Bamboo Cage, no, sir—not with Mama Zita keepin' her eagle eyes on the girls, bless her!"

Krissoula grinned. Consuela had told her the first time they'd met that she worked as a washerwoman and serving girl at the Bamboo Cage on Corrientes Street, a waterfront tavern that fronted for the well-known—and very popular—bordello, of which Mama Zita—or more properly, Señora Margarita Alvarado—was the madam! A huge woman of mixed black, Indian, and Spanish blood, Mama Zita had something of a reputation for being able to keep perfect order in her domain. Not even the *compadritos* dared to tangle with the mountainous female, whose memory for slights and double-crosses was as huge as her body and, it was rumored—if she liked you—her generous heart.

"Sorry, 'Suela, but I'm not about to escape Malvado's bed just to fill one in the upstairs rooms at the Bamboo Cage!"

Consuela looked wounded. "Did I say you should, girlie?" she demanded, and gave a prim little sniff. "No, I weren't thinkin' 'bout you doin' that—I was thinkin' 'bout you dancin' there, girl! You're dancin' at the Cádiz, so why not at the Bamboo in Barrio la Boca? At least it'll get you out of Malvado's way, eh?"

"Dance? Mmm. That's an idea! But—I wouldn't have expected the Bamboo's patrons to be *aficionados* of flamenco, somehow?" she said doubtfully.

Consuela roared with laughter, her small breasts jiggling beneath her thin, colorful blouse. "Lord, girl, where in heaven have you been? It ain't the flamenco them mens flock t'Zita's place t'see!" Consuela giggled. "It's that wicked *molonga* and the *tango* that fires up their blood and perks up their skinny lil' roots!" She rolled her eyes and grinned broadly, her plump, pretty face shining with sweat beneath her colorful *tignon*. "An' I reckon you could do them dances real well, girlie, yes I do! I seen how you swing them hips and flash them sassy golden eyes, girl!"

Krissoula giggled, for Sofía—overhearing the latter part of their conversation—was now openmouthed with astonishment, or more accurately, shock.

"But—the tango's banned in Argentina!" Sofía exclaimed. "And by el presidente himself!"

"Oh, not over at the Bamboo it ain't, Sofía, honey," Consuela said wickedly, and Krissoula laughed. "Ain't *nothin'* banned over there! An' the only president what counts is Mama Zita! Her word's the only law there is!"

"I've always wanted to try my hand at dancing the tango, ever since I first heard about it," Krissoula confessed.

"Then what's stopping you, eh, girl? Come on back to the Bamboo with me, and you can meet Mama Zita this afternoon?"

"Oh, no, really, I couldn't, Consuela. Armando Reyes promised he'll take care of Malvado for me, and if not him, Rolón Severino. We'll be all right with the *compadrito* looking out for us, really we will. Besides, I'm not ready to leave the Cádiz just yet. It took me ages to get that slug, Luigi da Costa, to pay me what I'm worth, and I'll be damned if I'll give up just when things are looking up!"

"All right! Have it your way, then. Jest remember, you ever in trouble, you come find Consuela at the Bamboo. She'll see you set right."

"Gracias, amiga," Krissoula thanked her. "All finished, Sofía?" she asked, turning to her companion.

"Except for these. I've folded everything else, but these are still a little damp. We can take them home wet and hang them to dry there, I suppose?"

"Of course we can. Look! Here's Cojo coming to meet us already! We're finished just in time. Hurry up, Sofía. I want to stop off at the market on the way home. I've had this craving all day to stuff myself on boiled shrimp, of all things! Ready?"

She took up half the bundle, smiling a welcome as Cojo limped shyly towards them, his arms already outstretched to help her. He insisted on carrying their bundles, as always, and without protest Krissoula thanked him and accepted, gesturing Sofía to do the same. She was rewarded by a dazzling glow that kindled in Cojo's brown eyes and warmed her heart. Those eyes told her better than words could how much her casual acceptance of him as a person meant to him. Her refusal of his help, out of pity for his crippled foot, would have destroyed him!

"Adíos, 'Suela! See you next week!"

"Surely, 'Soula-Girl, surely! An' don't you forget what I said, you hear, honey?"

"I won't! *Hasta luego!"*

The fish stall at the open market in the plaza off Calle Corrientes was far from crowded, for the people of Argentina seemed to care little for the bounty of the sea, much preferring beef to sea foods. The stall holder was delighted to have such an eager, attractive customer, and enjoyed the haggling he entered into with Krissoula, finally agreeing on a price with her and scooping dozens of fine fresh brown shrimp into a cone of white paper.

"Enjoy, pretty one!" he teased her roguishly, and winked as he generously added an extra pint, free of charge.

"I shall indeed," she promised flirtatiously. "And I will think of no one but you, my fine *pescador,* as I pop each delicious one into my mouth." She blew him a naughty kiss from puckered lips, and he clutched at his heart as if struck by Cupid's dart.

"Do so, beautiful one, and for every little shrimp I catch, I'll think of no one but you!"

"Promise?" She grinned, her golden eyes sparkling, her ebony curls flying about her in the dazzling light as she whirled away to find Sofía and Cojo, waving goodbye. "*Adiós, pescador*—and good fishing! See you next week—perhaps!"

The lad, Cojo, and her friend were at a stall farther down, haggling with the vendor over the price of some sewing thread and papers of needles, Sofía's small store having grown depleted since she'd taken over much of the darning and fine sewing for the Reyes band.

"I want to look around a little," Krissoula told Sofía. "I won't be long, so take your time. I'll meet you back here in a little while, yes?"

Sofía nodded agreement, but Cojo, ever protective of his beloved Krissoula, followed her as she strolled among the various stalls, jostling and elbowing her way between the knots of people crowded about some to inspect the wares offered, or passing by those that held no interest for her without a second glance.

Huge golden pineapples with their spiky crowns—the South American symbol of hospitality—were much in evidence on the fruit-sellers' stalls, as were huge bunches of yellow bananas that reminded Krissoula of candelabras. Oranges lemons, and limes were piled in baskets alongside hairy coconuts and bushels of Brazil nuts, lengths of sweet sugar cane for the little ones to suck on, or sacks of rice and grains.

Dark-skinned Indians had stalls which offered silver trinkets and carved wooden idols and masks, animal skins, and woven ponchos and blankets in bright, natural colors, as well as gaudy red parrots in bamboo cages. The parrots made Krissoula stop and look in wonder, for she'd never seen such large, colorful birds, and couldn't believe it when Cojo explained to her that they could be taught to talk, and sounded amazingly human when they did so.

"You're teasing me, no?" she accused.

"Honest, Krithoula, I'm not!" he protested earnestly. "Askth the Indio—he'll tell you."

"It is true, señorita," the Indian man confirmed in broken, heavily accented Spanish, giving her a gap-toothed grin. "This one here, he swears worse than any *gaucho!*"

"From where do you come?" she wondered aloud, gazing at the brilliant red feathering and huge, powerfully curved beak of the macaw in question.

It interrupted its preening with one foot raised to stare back at her, its head cocked suspiciously to one side, and a bright, beady black eye fixed unblinkingly on her for a moment before it solemnly muttered, "Awwk! Go to hell, *hombre!* Tch! Tch! Tch! *Hijo de puta!* Awwk! You've no *cojones,* sailor, none at all! Awk!"

Krissoula's eyes widened. She dared a glance at Cojo and they both burst out laughing. What, she wondered, would prim Sofia have said about this!

"My people catch these birds in the jungles of the Amazon, señorita," the Indian explained eagerly, sensing a sale as he saw the delight and amazement in her face. "You like this wicked one, no? Perhaps you buy, yes? I let you have him very cheap!"

"I'd love to, but—!" she grimaced and shook her head ruefully. "I'm sorry, señor. I've already spent more than I could afford on these shrimp! Some other time, maybe? Come, Cojo."

They moved on across the plaza, and it was only then that Krissoula caught sight of a dark, open doorway fronting the plaza, above which hung a swinging sign painted with a cage—a bamboo cage, in which a faded red parrot much like the one she'd just seen had also been painted. She halted, and her eyes lit up. So! This was the infamous tavern where the wicked *malonga* and the sensual *tango* were danced! The bordello cum tavern was sandwiched between an ill-lit café and a rowdy pool hall, from which blue cigar smoke escaped as if from the pit of hell, and the crack of cues against balls sounded sharp as pistol shots on the sultry air. Many other saloons, dance halls, and bordellos also fronted the square, and even at this early hour seemed to be doing brisk trade, judging by the noises escaping the establishments and the gaudily dressed and painted whores lounging in the doorways or draped over upstairs balconies. There were bursts of bawdy male laughter and shrieks of female merriment, drunken singing and guitar and tinny piano music, along with the wheezing of concertinas or accordions. Gazing at the inviting doorway of the Bamboo Cage—"inviting" simply because it was not closed!—Krissoula had an irresistible urge to go inside this den of iniquity. Just a quick look couldn't hurt, surely, and would satisfy her curiosity once and for all . . .

Turning to Cojo, she instructed, "Here! Hold my shrimp for a moment, would you? I'll be right back!" and headed towards the tavern doorway before Cojo, lost under a mountaintop of laundry and her paper cone of wet shrimp, could protest.

She heard him call after her, "Wait, señorita! No! Come back here! It ith a wicked place!" as she did so, but she ignored him . . .

Chapter Thirty-Four

At first, it was so gloomy within the Bamboo's smoky taproom that Krissoula stood stock-still yet again, suddenly blind in the dark after the brilliant light in the sun-drenched marketplace outside. But gradually, she was able to distinguish forms and the lighter spaces between them, and wove her way between benches, tables and customers, heading towards the puddle of light spilled by a solitary oil lamp set high on the wall.

She was halfway towards the space she'd chosen to watch the goings-on when suddenly several sconces lit simultaneously sputtered into light, so bright they made her blink like an owl! A stirring blast of music sounded, violins, guitars, and trumpets blaring. Sensing all eyes turned expectantly to her, she looked frantically about, then dived quickly for the dark perimeters of the taproom and concealment.

As she did so, a male and a female dancer ran from behind a curtain and took up their stances in the torchlight. Fascinated, her alarm forgotten, Krissoula shrank back into the shadows to watch, leaning up against a wall adorned with lengths of bamboo lashed together, from which hung small green parrots in cages, and even— she saw with surprise—chattering little monkeys that reached between them to tug her hair.

The *bailaora* was a reed-slim woman dressed in a tight emerald gown, with bell sleeves and heavily ruffled skirts. She wore her hair pulled back from her handsome, angular face and twisted into a heavy knot at her nape. The knot was adorned with a single frilly white orchid. Two enormous emerald teardrops, which must have been worth a small fortune, Krissoula judged, dangled from her earlobes.

Her partner was a lean man, his features concealed in the shadows cast by his broad-brimmed sombrero, which was held in place by a cord beneath the chin. He wore a full-sleeved white shirt, the front ruffled but tieless at the collar, and above it a short black bolero vest. A cummerbund of emerald satin spanned his narrow waist, and below it his slim hips and long, lean legs were encased by tight-fitting black breeches that ended in stilt-heeled boots. Those lean flanks and long, powerful legs reminded her forcefully of Esteban's, she realized with a wistful sigh . . .

She bit her lip, forcing her wandering thoughts back to the dance the pair were about to perform, as the music swelled into a passionate rhythm that drew the rowdy patrons' attention like moths to flame. Silence fell, and a crackling expectancy filled the taproom.

Krissoula could hardly believe her eyes as the pair began to dance, performing what could only be the wicked *tango,* the outlawed dance she'd heard so much about on her arrival in Buenos Aires, and longed to see and dance for herself! It was a dance of sharp, exciting contrasts, she realized very quickly, and therein lay its magic and appeal. The dancers seemed either haughty and remote, or atremble with unbearable passion in turn! The music was alternately slow and winding, filled with the heartbreak of the violins' silvery weeping, or loud and stirring with the triumphant blasts of the trumpets. The music was sometimes peculiarly erotic, but then again, quick and compelling, seeming almost martial in its measured underbeat. The very uncertainty of it all was guaranteed to hold the audience's rapt attention, for it was not unlike a coveted love affair whose outcome is uncertain! Will he, won't he? Will she, won't she? Torrid affair—or rejection and heartbreak—that was the way Krissoula would have described it!

From the first, the dancers' eyes were locked on each other's faces with a jealous intensity, as if no one else existed in the world for them, and they were quite alone in the crowded taproom.

The woman's half-closed, sloe-black eyes were inviting. Her pouting scarlet lips were curved in a smile that could only be described as seductive as she gazed up at the man. As the music drifted lazily on the smoke haze—the trumpets winding about a dreamy melody that sounded almost Eastern in origin—the man took his partner by the hand and pulled her smoothly into his arms, holding her so close her breasts and hips were pressed against his lean chest and flanks.

Then he clasped her hand, slipped his free arm about her waist, and strode her across the sawdust floor, one, two, three, four steps. There, on a dramatic note from the guitars and trumpets, he flicked his head and arched the woman fiercely against him, gazed still

398

deeper into her eyes and dipped her backward across his thigh, arching her so low to the floor that her hair brushed the sawdust, and her breasts and hips were thrust high and proud in offering. The man leaned over her, their mouths a hairsbreadth apart, their breaths commingling, their bodies almost touching their entire lengths, as if they were naked and making wild, passionate love before everyone. Then in another second he'd raised her, flung her away from him, then whirled her back into his arms as if to say, "You see? I can do with you as I will! I am your master, woman! As I command, so shall you dance! As I command, so shall you give yourself to me!"—or at least, that was how it seemed to the fascinated Krissoula, who watched with bated breath!

The male dancer turned the *bailaora* this way and that as he willed, and like a brilliant emerald flower, she moved wherever he commanded, a graceful cape in the hands of a bullfighter, a fan in the hands of a skilled coquette; flirting, challenging, flowing about him, moving with him, almost—but never quite!—touching him, as if she were not a separate being, but a supple, fluid extension of his body. Slow and sinuous, their dancing conveyed a sensual magic and excitement that was wildly arousing to the onlookers, Krissoula among them. Her face flamed as the man's hand glided through the air, as if he were not dancing, but intimately caressing his partner's lissome body, and somehow it was as if it were *her* he was caressing, and not his partner, and goosebumps sprang out on her arms!

Alternately, the woman would mold herself to the man's slim thighs, her eyes closed, her red lips breathlessly parted as he rocked her gently to and fro, else she'd stalk haughtily around him with her slender back arched, brazenly grazing his shoulder with her breasts, or brushing her hips against his flanks. And then, arms extended, their cheeks touching, they'd begin that haughty, catlike stalking all over again, or he'd spin her across the floor like a whip driving a spinning top in time to the hypnotic music, he virile and masterful, she completely feminine and yielding—but both of them passionate, oh, so damnably passionate!

Krissoula's face burned in the shadows as she watched. Her heartbeat quickened, for the stirring tempo and the erotic quality of the tango's rhythm and the pair's dancing had fired her blood, reawakened her female body, brought back vividly memories of passionate moments spent in Esteban's strong arms, his bed, the scented straw of the stables. She could remember all too clearly his kisses, the way he'd caressed her—times she'd hoped forever forgotten, buried. *Caray!* It was as if she could feel the lazy glide of his palm over her breasts even now, sense the tingling sensation of his fingertips tracing circles on her ankles, the pressure of his hand molding her calves as it traveled slowly, inching up under her skirts, fumbling and worming a sweaty, damp path between her knees . . .

"Diablo!" she spat suddenly, indignant and furious. "Dirty *bastardo!* Take your filthy hands off me, you randy toad!" and whirled to strike out at the rogue who'd boldly slipped his hot little hand beneath her petticoats to fondle her bare legs and buttocks as she watched the dancing, entranced and oblivious to his groping. Her open palm landed smartly against a balding head with a loud smack, and its owner yelped.

"Hey, *bombón,* not so rough, eh? I can pay!"

"Maybe you can, *hombre*—but this *muchacha*'s not for sale!" she hissed, her golden eyes brilliant in the light.

"All my girls have a price, honey," said a smoky, deep voice. "If your favors aren't for sale, you've no business in the Bamboo!"

Krissoula swung about to see the biggest woman she'd ever seen standing before her, smoking a slim black Cuban cigar in a long ebony holder banded with gold. She was dressed in a tentlike gown of wild yellows and reds that reminded Krissoula of the parrots she'd seen outside, in the marketplace! Her features might once have had some small claim to prettiness, but if they had, that prettiness was now buried under necklaces of fat that rendered her throatless. A button of a nose and a small red mouth, heavily rouged, were her only discernible features. Her enormous breasts were like pillows, billowing just inches from beneath her triple chins. Far below them swung a huge belly, massive under its cloth draperies. In sharp contrast, however, there was nothing slack or flaccid about the woman's eyes! They were so dark as to appear black, and snapping with shrewd intelligence under lids layered with blue paint.

"Consuela—a friend of mine—works here," Krissoula managed to stammer once she'd recovered from her initial shock, craning her head up to look into the towering woman's face. "She told me about this place. You—you must be Mama Zita?" The Spanish name, meaning "little rose," brought a nervous giggle to Krissoula's lips now that she was confronted by its ponderous owner who, if she was a rose at all, could only be an overblown one.

"None other!" Mama Zita confirmed, and her eyes sparkled wickedly as she added in a wry tone, "Now, I wonder how you knew?" Her gaze flickered appraisingly over the girl, and she seemed to approve of what she saw, for although taken aback, she'd recovered quickly and seemed not in the least afraid of her—as many people, male or female, often were. Mama Zita grinned. She liked a girl with spirit, and so did her patrons.

"Get lost, Enrico!" she snapped at the gaping man who'd fondled Krissoula's legs, and a mammoth arm encircled Krissoula's shoulders in a fond bear hug that came close to snapping her ribs and shoulder bone. "Try that again, and you'll lose those itchy fingers, *comprende?*" she added casually over her shoulder.

The man needed no second urging. With a mumbled apology, he pushed through the spectators nearby and vanished into the crowds.

"There! That's better!" Zita declared with a throaty chuckle. "Now, honey, what're you doing here—you lookin' for a job? Truth is, you're kind of skinny for a whore, eh? Our South American men—well, those *hombres* like a woman they can grab a hold of, child. A plump armful of woman who's plenty soft and rounded— more like me, you could say!" Her belly quivered as she chuckled in that deep, smoky way she had, which reminded Krissoula of the muffled rumble of a volcano, about to erupt.

For all her worldliness, Krissoula colored crimson. "I'm no whore!" she bridled, indignant. "'Suela told me that sometimes you need dancers here, and I—I was curious to see this 'tango' everyone on the streets is talking about."

"You're a dancer?" Zita said speculatively, turning the girl about and eyeing her up and down as if she were a little puppet or a doll.

Krissoula shrugged modestly. "*Sí,* I've done a little dancing in my time—but the flamenco's really my dance. I've never tried anything like this," she explained, nodding towards the entertainers.

"But you could learn, no? *Sí,* I think so. You look like a sharp one, to me! So, what did you think of it?" Zita asked curiously, nodding towards the dancers, whose number had ended now. They were taking their bows and the crowd was going wild and growing raucously loud with its stamps and whistles of applause and pleas for encores.

Her golden eyes flickered away from Zita's piercing black ones. "I think I could do it, yes. But—it's very different from the flamenco—much slower and—and very—arousing, no?"

"Ah, but that's exactly the way I want it, *niña*—what Mama Zita counts on! Why, my 'business' upstairs booms each time the *tango's* performed, and when the men get hot around the collar—why they drink twice as much! My little gals hardly have time to catch their breath or a wink of sleep anymore—and that's good for the Bamboo, no?" She smiled and arched her brows, taking in Krissoula's petite but curvaceous body with a shrewd, knowing eye. She was a tiny little thing, but there was an earthiness, a sensuality to the girl that went beyond mere looks. Her customers would go wild to see this golden-eyed kitten dance the wicked tango . . . "Well? You think you could do it, little one? Just say the word, and you're good as hired!"

"Me, dance the *tango*? Well, I don't have a partner, but—*sí*, I'm sure I could!" She sighed. "I could—but I can't! If you'll forgive me, señora, I really should be going. I—I have friends waiting for me in the plaza, and they'll be worried about me if I'm gone too long."

Mama Zita frowned and shrugged. "Have it your way, then, honey, but remember, any friend of 'Suela's is a friend of mine. We go back a long way together, Consuela and me. You need a job, you just come back and see Mama Zita, *sí*? I'll find you a partner, don't worry about that, if you want to work for me. You know, I think I could get to like you, little one! After the way you belted that Henrico—!" She chuckled. "*Sí*, you'd do just fine here, honey!"

"Thank you for the offer, but I really must go—!" Krissoula gasped out, and made her escape, weaving her way through the drunken customers to the bright sunlight and fresh air of the plaza, where Sofía and Cojo were anxiously awaiting her.

Mama Zita smiled as she slowly circled around her saloon, her very size and her fearsome reputation effectively keeping would-be troublemakers in their place. She needed no "bouncers" to keep the peace. At six feet five inches tall, she dwarfed all of the men in her establishment in height, and easily tripled the largest among them in girth.

"*Buenas tardes*, Don Miguel! Are you and your companions enjoying yourselves, señores?" she inquired politely of one well-dressed young man.

"You know better than to ask, Zita!" the man replied, and his friends chuckled agreement as Zita moved on.

"Why, by all the saints, it can't be—!" she exclaimed moments later. "San Martín, you handsome devil, is that you? *Hombre, Gallito*, where've you been all these years!"

"Buried in the countryside, Zita, *mi corazón!* How've you been? You're looking magnificent, as ever!" Esteban flirted, standing and giving the mountainous woman a smacking kiss on her rouged cheek.

"Pah, be off with you, flatterer!" she scolded, giving him a playful shove in the ribs that all but hurled him backwards to the sawdust floor. "I've gained a little weight, and you know it, *bribón!*"

"Just a little perhaps—but that only means there's more of you to love, Zita, *querida mía! Sí,* all the more to love!" he teased, his sapphire eyes twinkling, his fondness for the woman unmistakable. "Can I buy a lovely lady a drink?"

"No, handsome! The 'lovely lady' will buy you one! We'll go upstairs to my private rooms. Maybe Consuela would like to join us, an' see how her *gallito,* her 'Little Rooster' has grown, after all these years!" She nudged him again, but forewarned this time Esteban had nimbly backed out of her reach. "Come on, honey, it's quieter upstairs. We'll split a bottle, an' you can tell me what you've been up to since I saw you last, yes?"

With an engaging nod and a grin, he gallantly took the madam's elbow and steered the magnificent Zita to the staircase at the rear of her saloon, never suspecting that he'd missed the woman he sought—and whom he'd come to the Bamboo to enlist Zita's help in locating—by a matter of minutes . . .

Chapter Thirty-Five

"The council of Gypsies has voted, Krissoula Ballardo. It has been decided that you and Doña Sofía must leave our *barrio*, tonight, and without delay."

Leave tonight! Pale and trembling, Krissoula heard Armando Reyes's sad voice and ominous verdict as if it came down a long tunnel. From somewhere inside herself, she managed to respond with a nod, wondering how a day that had progressed so happily could have ended like—like this.

She and Sofía had returned to Barrio Gitanos from the marketplace to find themselves accused of theft. Armando had listened gravely to the charges made against them by Elena and Bianca, and asked them if they had anything to say in their defense.

"We have stolen nothing, Señor Reyes," Krissoula had insisted with quiet dignity.

"Nothing!" Sofía had echoed, wringing her hands.

"Then you have no objection to having your belongings searched?"

"None whatsoever, señor. We have nothing to hide. Go ahead and make your search."

But Krissoula hadn't really been very surprised when their shawl bundles had been emptied out onto the flagstones before everyone in the council, and the missing belongings found so conveniently— no, miraculously, she amended bitterly—among them. A pair of heavy golden earrings had been found knotted in the long fringes of Sofía's shawl. A hoard of English sovereigns and silver guinea pieces had spilled out of the toe of one of Krissoula's scarlet dancing slippers. Another shawl, of Brussels lace, had been found carefully folded inside one of her chemises.

Of course, they'd indignantly denied any knowledge of how the stolen items came to be there. It was as plain as noses on their faces to her and Sofía, Carla, and even Armando Reyes himself, that they'd been made scapegoats by someone, "set up" to be blamed for the thefts, but the council of elders had not been so easily convinced of their innocence. They'd voted and the majority had ruled. The council's decision had been to banish them from the Gypsy quarter that very night. And, as much as he might dislike the council's decision, Armando had no choice but to act upon it.

"I cannot tell you how very much it pains me to ask you to leave, Señorita Moreno," Armando told a shaken Sofía with tears glistening in his green eyes. He reached out to take her hand in his, seemed to catch himself doing so, and instead patted her shoulder awkwardly. "Perhaps I could speak to a few friends . . . do something . . . ?"

"That won't be necessary, Don Armando," Sofía had insisted with a little sniff. "The Morenos have never been beggars. I would rather leave than stay here where everyone believes we are c-common thieves!" But her voice broke at the latter, becoming a sob, and her proud stance crumbled. Oh, it was all very well to be proud, but the prospect of spending the night—maybe many nights—unsheltered and unprotected in the alleys and streets of the *barrios* terrified her.

"Enough, Sofía!" Krissoula said sharply, her head held proudly, high, her stubborn little chin thrust determinedly skyward. "We will go. But, before we leave, I have two things I'd like to say, with your permission, Señor Reyes?" The burly Gypsy nodded, giving his assent. "First," Krissoula said loudly and clearly, "I want to swear to you all one last time, and with God as my witness, that despite all evidence to the contrary, Sofía and I have stolen nothing from any one of you who've been our friends since we came here two months ago! Secondly, we'd like to thank the Reyes band for its many kindnesses in taking us in when we were desperately in need of help. *Muchas gracias, gitanos,* and—and farewell."

She turned to look at the circle of faces surrounding her, meeting each pair of dark eyes for the barest instant before moving on. Some of the Gypsies had the grace to uncomfortably look away, unable to meet her searching golden gaze, while others stared boldly back with contempt and open condemnation.

"Guard your belongings well, my friends," Krissoula added softly, "for when we go, the thief remains yet in your midst! Come, Sofía!"

With that, she swung her tied bundle of belongings over her shoulder and strode resolutely towards the gate in the courtyard wall that led to the street. Sofía and Cojo, who returned to the courtyard with them, hurried after her.

Carla looked around the circle of Gypsies much as Krissoula had done, her green eyes filled with disgust.

"Tonight, you have made me ashamed that I am of the Rom—that we share one blood!" she hissed, and then she turned and ran after Krissoula, reaching her before she disappeared into the already darkened alleys of Barrio San Timéo.

"Krissoula, don't go! Please, come back to the fire. I'll stand good for you tonight, and tomorrow we'll find a place for you somewhere else. You're both innocent, I know that. Somehow, I'll prove it! Stay here tonight."

Krissoula hugged her. "I know you want to help, Carla, but I think it best we go. Whoever it is that hates us enough to set us up this way may not stop at making us look bad, given a second chance. Next time, there could be blood spilled, innocent people hurt. I don't want that on our consciences! Thank you for everything you've done, *amiga*. You and your papa have been so good to us—we'll never forget you. Tell Señor Reyes and Franco that we appreciate everything they've done, and that we're sorry for any trouble we've caused them, would you?"

Carla's eyes brimmed with tears. "Of course I will. That goes without saying. But—what will happen to you now? I'm afraid for you both! What about Malvado—?" She gripped Sofía's hand and squeezed hard.

"Oh, don't even think about him, Carla! Your father and Rolón Severino scared him off. He won't dare bother me again! We'll be all right, I know it. I'm used to taking care of myself, and I can take care of Sofía, too—right, Sofía *mía?*"

"Right," Sofía agreed bravely, though her lips quivered and her color was poor. She kissed Carla's cheek and returned the warm grip of the Gypsy woman's hand with marked affection, obviously reluctant to release her. "Each time I make a tortilla, I'll think of you and your lessons, Carla, both with gratitude and—and affection. I—I wasn't very nice to you at first, I know that, but I—I'll really miss you, Carla, my dear. Kiss those darling children of yours goodbye for me, and—and God be with you all . . ." Her voice broke, and she turned away, blinded by tears and unable to continue.

"And with you both. *Adiós,* my dear friends! Take care of them for me, Cojo!" Carla cried, her own tears flowing freely now.

Cojo gave a curt nod and blinked rapidly.

With that, they set off down the street, Cojo—holding himself as erect as his crippled foot would allow—walking protectively alongside the two women, taking Sofía by the elbow.

Carla watched them until they'd turned the corner and were lost from view, and then furiously scrubbed the tears from her eyes with her knuckles and hardened her expression.

Green eyes narrowed, she swung about and stormed back to the courtyard, determined to give the council and the members of her Gypsy band a good piece of her mind for the second time that night—and this time, by God, she vowed, they'd listen, or her name was not Carla Francesca de Reyes y Valde! And when—and if—that sneaking Delora ever returned, she intended to wring the truth out of the woman somehow, even if she had to tear out her hair, or throttle her to make her talk—! Delora was at the bottom of all this, she was certain, could feel it in her bones, and Carla intended to see her guilt proven if it was the last thing she ever did!

To Krissoula's enormous relief, Cojo found them a safe place to sleep with relative ease that first night, in the little church of San Timéo. Saint Timothy's doors were always left open to offer sanctuary to fugitives or the troubled of heart, he told them confidently, and added with a twinkle in his eyes that, unlike the ears of the *gitanos,* the ear of God was a compassionate one, and His understanding infinite.

Krissoula—exhausted and still upset by their return to Barrio Gitanos from the market that afternoon, to find the Gypsies in uproar and demanding justice of Armando Reyes for the theft of their valuables, was only too glad to follow his suggestion, though she couldn't quite manage to summon a smile despite his attempt at cheering them up, not just yet. She simply let him lead them to the little church without protest. At least within San Timéo's sturdy stone walls, they'd be safe for the night, she hoped.

By the flickering, comforting light of the tall white candles lit upon the little altar, looked benevolently down upon by the many statues of the saints in every corner, Krissoula and Sofía spread out their cloaks. Stretching themselves out upon the cold flagstone floor with their bundles tucked beneath their heads for pillows, they tried very hard to sleep.

Meanwhile, Cojo propped himself up against a stone pillar, prepared to stand watch the night through over the two women he'd determined to protect at all costs.

They'd both been kind and understanding to him, he thought as the long night inched slowly away towards morning. From the very first, Krissoula had treated him like another human being, rather than a monstrous freak, in a world that was rarely so gentle to those with his obvious shortcomings. Sofía, too, had been gentle and protective, like he imagined a mother would be.

His own mother had abandoned him on the steps of San Timéo only hours after his birth, no doubt horrified by the disfiguring cleft in his upper lip. He had no idea who she'd been; rich or poor, good or bad. The nuns of the convent of San Timéo had been his mother and father both, yet the abandoned children they'd cared for had been many and their caretaking of him had left little room for affection. They'd seen that he was fed and kept clean, and shabbily yet adequately dressed in well-laundered castoffs, and that was that. Then, when he was twelve—and old enough by their reckoning to earn a living for himself—they'd found him work doing odd jobs for Luigi da Costa at the Cádiz Tavern.

All his life, Cojo felt as if he'd been pining for something; maybe for affection and closeness with another human being? Or simply to be treated as an equal, instead of a carnival freak. He'd yearned, too, for a little beauty and grace in his harsh, empty existence, where a kick or a shove or a brutal curse were his only lot, rather than kindness and laughter, kisses and hugs. As he'd matured into manhood and begun to notice girls and young women with more than a casual interest, he'd seen how they flirted and coquetted with other lads and he'd ached to be one of them—had seen how their lovely faces had altered, their smiles fading when they caught sight of ugly Cojo. Sadly, he'd been forced to face up to the terrible truth; no girl could possibly love a gargoyle like him! And little by little, his hope that someone would look beyond his disfigured outer shell to the beauty of soul, the boundless love, the capacity for endless loyalty that existed within him, had died. And then, he'd met Krissoula, lively, lovely Krissoula, whose dancing was magical and whose smile without pity or mockery, and who teased him and scolded him as if—as if he were no different from anyone else. She'd accepted him without reservation, without pity, from the very first, and for that, he loved her as he'd never loved anyone before. Consequently, he'd let no harm come to her or her friend, Sofía, not if he could help it. He'd guard their lives with his own.

When morning broke over the city in a hazy golden flood of light, the women awoke to find that Cojo had been busy while they slept.

"Askth no questions as to where our meal came from, and I'll tell you no lieth, señhoritas!" he declared proudly in his nasal voice that both women understood with little effort now. Why, they'd grown so accustomed to him that they noticed neither his difficulty in talking nor the deformity that split his lip! He was simply Cojo, the slight orphaned lad who, in the space of a few short days, had become a true friend, standing beside them in their troubles.

From somewhere, Cojo had found a loaf of fresh bread, a little hard cheese, and a length of *chorizo*. With a proud smile he set the food before them, sliced it into portions with his knife, and bade them eat with the air of a king providing for his court. Krissoula, reluctant to hurt the lad's feelings although she had lost her appetite the night before, managed to swallow a few bites of the dry victuals, but Sofía turned greenish, jumped to her feet, and fled outside the church with her hand clamped over her mouth. Moments later, they could hear her retching violently.

"She doesn't like what I brought!" Cojo exclaimed, obviously hurt that his efforts had been so violently rejected on Sofía's part.

"It's not that, silly," Krissoula reassured him, squeezing his hand. "I think Sofía's still too upset by what happened last night to eat. She's afraid for our future, too. Fear has a way of killing your appetite, no?"

"I suppose tho," Cojo agreed. "Should I see to her, or will you?"

"Neither of us," Krissoula said after considering for a moment or two. "We'll wait here and when she comes back, we'll pretend we haven't even noticed she left. You know Sofía, Cojo! The last thing she'd want is for us to see her at her worst—it would embarrass her terribly."

Cojo grunted agreement. Whatever Krissoula said must be right, he reasoned, gazing at her adoringly. She was right about so many things! And even if she had slept the night on the cold, hard floor, and if her long black hair was tumbled this way and that, he still thought her the most beautiful woman he'd ever seen, let alone known. She looked especially lovely this morning, with the dawn sunshine streaming through the stained-glass windows from behind the altar. The multicolored light played about her head like a rainbow-colored halo. Why, she could have been a goddess—or even a saint.

"Saint Krithoula!" he spoke aloud, almost reverently. "The saint of danthing, grace, and beauty!"

Krissoula blinked, then giggled. "Oh, Cojo, you *niño loco!* I might be many things, but a saint—! *Caray!* Never! Being so good all the time would be far too dull and boring!" She punched him in the ribs and his solemn expression vanished as he laughed along with her. Both of them rolled about like children, rough and tumbling on the hard stone floor of the church, their laughter echoing in its empty, vaulted confines.

"A good morning to you, my children!" greeted a merry-faced little gnome of a priest as he shuffled in through the doors to robe himself for the early-morning Mass he'd soon be celebrating. "The gift of laughter is a precious thing to bring to the House of God, and one He's seen too little of in these hard times of sickness and death, I'm sure. May He bless you both!" The priest made the sign of the Cross in the air over them, but then frowned. "However, there's a señora outside who feels far too ill to laugh at anything, I'm afraid. She is, perhaps, a friend of yours?"

Guiltily, Krissoula nodded, sitting up and smoothing herself down in an effort to regain some semblance of neatness. "Sí, Padre. I'm sorry. I'll go and see to her at once! When she's recovered a little, we'll be on our way. Thank you for the use of your church for the night. We—we were desperate."

"Oh, don't thank me, Daughter," the priest declared with a dismissing wave. "I'm only the 'caretaker' here, for this is God's house, not mine. If you would thank your landlord, you must thank Him!"

Smiling, she and Cojo gathered up their belongings and hurried outside, to find Sofía sitting on the steps looking wan and trembly.

"Better?" Krissoula asked anxiously. It was far worse than she thought. Sofía looked terrible.

"Much," Sofía lied, forcing a thin smile.

"Then let's be on our way," Krissoula decided. "We need to find somewhere other than the streets to sleep before nightfall."

Long before noon that day, three things had become painfully obvious to both Cojo and Krissoula.

The first was that lodgings would be hard to come by, despite the little money Krissoula had in her possession, for everywhere they asked to rent rooms, doors were abruptly slammed in their faces, or they were sent packing in no uncertain terms by curses and vicious dogs set to worry their heels. The reason for this hostile treatment was also the second truth that was forcefully brought home to them: that whereas in the insulated *barrios* in which Krissoula and Sofía had lived and worked, the summer cholera epidemic ravaging the city had made few inroads, elsewhere an atmosphere of terror stalked the citizens of Buenos Aires as the disease spread like wildfire. Any stranger or newcomer was a possible carrier of the dreaded disease, and was therefore to be shunned and chased away.

Down every street they walked, they saw further evidence of the dreadful holocaust that left Krissoula silent and stunned. Usually crowded market squares were empty and forlorn-looking, only a few squashed and rotted fruits to show there had ever been a market at all. The taverns and shops hereabouts had closed their doors and had a similar air of neglect and abandonment. Not once did they spot a water-vendor with his barrel-wagon and horse, nor a night-watchman hurrying home to his bed, nor a streetgirl with a tray of some tasty wares or other, loudly singing their praises. No children played in the dusty streets, nor pestered their mothers as they gossiped on the stoops of the houses, for women were nowhere in evidence, any more than men. There were only dogs wandering the streets, the sorry animals so thin their ribs showed beneath their mangy fur.

Alternatively, rough wooden wagons piled high with corpses sewn into shrouds fashioned from sheets soon became an all too commonplace sight, as did the weeping relatives who huddled in doorways and watched their loved ones carried off to the communal graves outside the city limits. Large crosses painted on far too many doors betrayed that the inhabitants behind them were under strict quarantine, with one or more family members stricken. So shocking were these signs of the devastation the cholera had wrought, that both Cojo and Krissoula—who'd set off so optimistically that morning—soon fell silent as they trudged aimlessly down deserted street after street, holding Sofía up between them, for the third truth was that Sofía—despite her protests to the contrary—was far from recovered from her bout of sickness. Time and time again that day, they'd had to help her over to a ditch or gutter, where she'd retched and lost her stomach. She'd grown more ill and weaker by the hour and Krissoula could not quite rid herself of the dreadful, growing suspicion in her heart that her friend had somehow also fallen victim to the dreadful cholera.

By nightfall—which found them still without a roof over their heads, or any place to lay them, her suspicions had become convictions. Sofía had joined the numbers of the stricken. In a week, she'd be either recovered—or dead.

"Well, Gypsy?" Antonio Malvado asked contemptuously, lounging back in his chair at the Cádiz Tavern and drawing on his

411

cigar. "What have you to report?"

"Just that my plan worked like a charm, Don Antonio—as I promised you it would the night of the wedding!" Delora Reyes crowed, her sharp features split in a triumphant, malicious grin. "The two of them were thrown out of Barrio Gitanos last night by our council!"

"And where are they now, woman?" Malvado demanded. "If you've lost track of the girl, you can forget—"

"No, no, Don Antonio, I know just where they are! In an alley off Caballo Street—you know, close by the slaughterhouses?" Delora cut in hurriedly. "I followed them, and they're not going anywhere, believe me!"

"How can you be so sure of that?" the *compadrito* snapped, irritated by the cocksure woman's manner.

"Because they've been refused lodgings at every turn, on account of the wasting sickness—and because the old *gorgio* bitch is sick herself, and slowing them down!" Delora explained with obvious relish.

"Them? Ah. You mean Krissoula and the other one."

"And that Cojo. The lad with the monster's face is still with them!"

"Ah." Malvado nodded. "Is he now? He could be trouble."

"*Sí.* But trouble easily dealt with, Don Antonio, no?" a lisping, almost childlike voice, observed.

The voice came from the shadows of an alcove at Delora's back, and at first she thought it was witchcraft, for although she turned about, she could see no one there. But then, the shadows shifted and a dark, squat bulk separated itself from the gloom and waddled forward into the stream of sunshine, whirling with dust motes, alongside Don Antonio's chair, and she gasped, for the speaker was a dwarf.

He stood perhaps three and a half feet tall, yet his torso was that of a giant. He was bull-necked and bullet-headed as he squatted there, picking his dirty, broken nails with the point of a wicked little knife. His soft, lisping voice was so at odds with his horrific appearance, it was all Delora could do to keep her twitching fingers from making the sign to ward off the evil eye, for she recognized him now and her belly churned with foreboding.

The dwarf was known to everyone in the *barrios* simply as "Bobo." He was loathed and feared throughout the back streets of Buenos Aires and even beyond, for it was common knowledge that he was Antonio Malvado's shadow, his personal bodyguard, and

412

his eager executioner. If someone proved troublesome to Compadrito Don Antonio Malvado, Bobo's piggy, cold black eyes were the last ones they ever gazed into as his beefy arms squeezed the life from their bodies in a massive bearhug that snapped bones and burst blood vessels as easily as kindling. His small stature was no handicap, not in his profession. Tall men or short men, he dispatched them all with the same smiling relish. Ah, Bobo loved his work, and he did it well.

"True, Bobo, very true," Malvado agreed mildly, favoring Bobo with a faint smile. "Da Costa!" he roared, pounding his fist down on the tabletop so hard and so suddenly that Delora actually jumped in fright.

"*Sí,* Don Antonio?" Luigi babbled, coming at a run to Malvado's table wiping his sweaty hands on his dirty white apron.

"I've decided you'll have to close down the Cádiz for the time being. If our mutual friend, the dancer, decides to come to work tonight as usual, you're to tell her you've closed down—that you're not reopening until the winter, after the sickness has burned itself out. Understand?"

"Close down? But, sir, I'll be ruined!" Luigi da Costa protested, sweat breaking out on his fleshy brow and palms.

"I'm not asking, *pibe,*" Antonio said silkily. "I'm ordering!" He smiled. "Or perhaps you'd rather have my little friend Bobo convince you of the wisdom of obeying my orders without protest?" He arched his brows.

On cue, Luigi cast a desperate, terrified look at Bobo, who grinned, showing broken yellow teeth, clasped his massive paws together, and cracked his knuckles so loudly, both Delora and Luigi flinched and paled under their olive complexions.

"But—if I may be so bold as to ask, señor—what are you waiting for?" Delora suggested, obviously nervous. "I've told you where the girl can be found, no? Why not simply have Sen-Señor Bobo here bring her to you?"

"Why? Because that would be too easy, *gitana!* No, no, that wouldn't suit at all. I want that haughty bitch to come crawling to me for help!" Antonio said with a gloating smirk. "I want that proud little Gypsy *slut* to taste desperation, and to finally realize that only I, Don Antonio Malvado, *compadrito* of Barrio San Timéo, can help her. She'll beg to be my woman on her pretty little knees before I'm done with her! And when I am . . ." he paused, ". . . she's all yours, Bobo, my friend. A little reward for your loyalty and good work in the past, shall we say?"

413

Delora gave a malicious smile, and Bob simpered and giggled happily at the thought.

"It's no use," Krissoula whispered, exhausted by the combined effects of the sweltering January heat the following morning, and by disappointment after yet another lodging house—the eighth or ninth they'd been to—had turned them away. "We may as well accept it. It's the streets, or nothing for us!"

They'd passed the previous night in a fetid pitch-black alley, where the sultry silence and stifling heat of the night had been punctuated by the squeaks and scurries of huge, furry rats, the yowls of mating cats, and by Sofía's low moans of discomfort. Her vomiting had increased in frequency overnight, and the terrible loosening of her bowels had begun—both symptoms typical of the dreaded cholera. Krissoula was certain by now that her initial fears were correct, and she was desperate to find someplace where she could attempt to nurse her poor Sofía, somewhere she could see the sick woman bathed and her clothing changed, able to lay down her head in cleanliness and a bit of comfort.

"You mustn't give up," Cojo urged in an attempt to encourage her, for he'd never seen Krissoula so dejected and beaten. "Tell you what, you stay with Sofía this time. I'll go and see what I can find, thall I?"

He made the offer cheerfully, but Krissoula guessed what he must be thinking; that if she could find nothing for them, with her unmarked face and her strong, whole body, how much more success would he have, looking as he did? "No, no, I'll go. You've already done more than enough," she told him gently. "Do you think I don't know how hard it's been for you with your poor foot, what with all the walking we've had to do—and it's not out of pity I'm mentioning it, either, just plain fact! You stay here and rest up a little, while I try again." She forced a bright smile she was far from feeling and added, "You know, somehow, I feel a little luckier now! Perhaps I'll be back with good news this time, *sí?*"

"I hope so," Cojo acknowledged fervently. "And bring some water, too, if you can get some." He nodded towards Sofía, who lay on some old sackcloth they'd spread upon the ground. "I've seen the wasting sickness before, and she needs to drink a lot of water, if she's to pull through."

"All right. I'll do what I can," Krissoula promised. "You know, I think I'll try the Cádiz this time, and ask that old goat Luigi if he'll put us up. After all, he's expecting me there to dance tonight, as usual. Maybe I could threaten not to dance, and wring something out of him that way!" she suggested with a trace of her old spirit. "Da Costa'll do anything to keep the money rolling in, that avaricious old slug!"

Cojo scowled. "No, don't go back there! I don't like the idea of going to him for anything, Krithoula. He's Malvado's puppet—terrified of him, he is—and he could tell him—"

"Oh, I can take care of Luigi, Cojo, I promise!" she declared confidently. "He's all talk and no substance. Now, *adiós!* I'll be back just as soon as I can."

But to her horror, she found the doors of the Cádiz had been bolted shut. She hammered upon them, and at length heard Luigi's muffled voice from behind them, telling her to go away.

"No, I won't go away—not until you open up, you hateful little man!" she insisted. "Come on, Luigi, at least open the door and let me talk to you!"

But despite her pleas for him to open up and talk to her, he answered with a string of obscenities and a gruff order for her to go away, keeping the door obstinately closed.

"But please, Luigi, I beg you, we—I need a place to stay for a while!" she pleaded, swallowing her pride with a humility born of despair. "I'll dance for you, in return for food and board—how about that?"

"If you need lodgings, try the courtyard on the corner of Calle Rios," he yelled back. "I hear they have a room for rent there. But in any case, don't come back here, *gitana!* I'm not reopening the Cádiz again until after the summer plague's ended, understand? Now go away!"

"Well, thanks for nothing, you miserable, greedy old goat!" she yelled back, hands on hips, her golden eyes blazing. "And see if I ever dance for you again come winter!" and she made a crude gesture at the closed doorway before flinging about and trudging off in the direction he'd suggested, towards Calle Rios. It was worth a try, even if that slug Da Costa *had* been the one to suggest it. They were desperate, and beggars couldn't be choosers.

The house Luigi had suggested was in one of the poorest parts of the *barrios,* a crumbling old villa with weeds grown up about its foundations, and signs of damp blotching the dirty adobe walls with slimy green maps. Her spirits sank, for although the place was a dismal one, appearances notwithstanding it was obviously still inhabited. A mangy donkey was tethered in the courtyard, whisking flies away with its long ears and tail. A scrawny milk cow with dried up udders regarded her solemnly from melancholy brown eyes. Chickens scratched halfheartedly in the dirt. She rapped on the main door, and to her surprise it was answered by a gnarled little old man who eyed her suspiciously.

"*Sí?*" he growled.

"I—I need a room," she stammered.

"For how many?"

"There's three of us—but one room would be more than enough," she amended hurriedly. "You see, we—we have nowhere to sleep!"

His dark eyes flickered over her rumpled clothing, and a gleam flickered in their rheumy depths. "Sleep, eh, that's a good one! No whoring, *muchacha!* I run a decent place here." He cackled with laughter, as if the idea of him running a decent place was an amusing one.

"I'm not a whore!" she protested, her face flaming. "My—mother—and my brother and I have just arrived in the city from the Pampa. We need lodgings, just a place to cook our meals and sleep while we look for work."

He gave another gummy cackle. "Work? *Caray!* You'll be lucky, girl! But if you have no money, and no work to earn any, how'll you pay for your lodgings, eh?" he asked slyly.

"Well, we do have a little set by—enough for a few days' lodging—I swear it!"

"Then I'll want two days money, in advance."

"Agreed," she promised, hope welling up inside her.

"No signs of sickness in your family?"

"Of course not!" she protested, crossing her fingers so the lie wouldn't count. "We're all strong and healthy!"

He nodded finally. "All right. You can stay. But any trouble, and you're out on your pretty little rump, understand, girl?"

She nodded eagerly and took her leave, stumbling out into the sun-drenched street as if she'd been told she'd inherited a castle, complete with fortune. Unable to believe her good luck, she ran all the way back to Calle Caballo, and down the alley that ran alongside the slaughterhouse where she'd left Sofía and Cojo.

It wouldn't be easy, slipping Sofía past the old man's watchful eyes in her condition, but they'd manage somehow, she told herself. The important thing was that they had somewhere safe to stay, thank God!

*   *   *

416

"Well?" José asked, coming out from another room to join the old man after the girl had gone. "Did she take the bait?"

"Like a hungry piranha in the waters of the Amazon, Señor José!" The old man cackled, and held out his gnarled brown hand expectantly.

José flung a handful of coins in his general direction and strode out of the crumbling building into the blinding sunlight that beat down on the dirt streets, leaving the old man to scrabble in the dust for his payoff.

"So? Did it work?" Juan, lounging against the outside wall, asked him eagerly.

"Without a hitch," José replied, his ugly face with the crooked nose screwing up in what passed for a grin.

"Good! The boss'll be pleased, for once, I hope, curse him!"

"Oh, I hope so, too, Juan. I surely hope so. That Bobo—I don't like the way he's been eyeing me lately. *Madre,* I don't like it at all!"

"*Dios!* Just look at this place! Cockroaches and cobwebs in every corner—and there're rat droppings everywhere, Cojo! Why, only a pig would live in such a filthy place, no?"

"Wrong, Krithoula!"

"Wrong?" she demanded indignantly.

"Uhhuh. No self-rethpecting pig would ever live here!" Cojo corrected her solemnly.

They exchanged happy, foolish grins, for as awful as the room leading off the courtyard was, it was far, far better than sleeping in a stinking alley without a roof over their heads!

"Let's get Sofía settled, then I'll see if I can't borrow a broom from our generous landlord to clean this place up a little," Krissoula decided, looking about her with a critical eye.

"While you do that, I'll go down to the river for water. Will you be all right alone until I get back?"

"Of course I will! Here, take this and buy us something wonderful to cook for supper—and get some soup bones to make broth for Sofía, if you can. The market on Corrientes Street hasn't closed down yet, I don't think."

With a nod, Cojo was gone with half of her precious store of coins.

Alone now, Krissoula knelt beside Sofía, biting her lip to keep the tears from falling as she saw how sunken her friend's cheeks had become over the past few hours, and how very pale she was.

"We have a home now, Sofía," she whispered, holding the

woman's bony hand in hers and rubbing it. "Can you hear me? Don't worry, dear Sofía! You're going to be all right, you'll see! In a few days, we'll have you up and about again. Things'll be better now, I promise. I'll get you through this, I swear it!"

A terrible guilt welled up in her breast and lodged like a heavy stone in her throat. It was all her fault that Sofía was here now, lying at death's door—all her fault for wanting to lead an easy life of wealth and luxury in her bitterness following Miguel's betrayal and little Nicki's death, and of not caring who she hurt or used in the process. If Sofía died, her death would be on her conscience for the rest of her life!

She'd promised the woman she'd get her through this, but could she? And did she really have the right to make any such promise? No, she realized miserably, only God could make such a promise with any certainty of keeping it. And He seemed to have deserted them . . .

Chapter Thirty-Six

"Four days they've been holed up in those miserable lodgings, yet there's still no sign of the girl growing desperate?"

"Far from it, señor," Juan reluctantly informed the godfather, his shifty-eyes rolling every which way but at Malvado. "She looks tired, *sí*—but—but far from desperate. That ugly cripple fetches the water from the river each morning and evening. She washes the sick woman's clothing in a tub and spreads it out to dry in the sun before going back inside their room—I've seen her for myself. Then she sweeps and cleans and cooks, like any woman. But," he added eagerly, "their money must be close to running out, Don Antonio! You see, the crippled lad's taken to stealing what he can from the market for them to eat!" Juan declared with an air of triumph, certain this little tidbit of information would appease the godfather. It didn't.

"Pah! 'The crippled boy fetches water.' 'The cripple steals what he can from the market,' that's all I hear from you two! And as long as he continues to do so, you stupid fools, the golden-eyed bitch will *never* come crawling to me!" Malvado exploded, his expression ugly, and Juan leaped backward, out of range of those flashing dark eyes that promised hell to pay.

Malvado uttered a curse and sat back, fingertips braced together in an arch, deep in sullen thought for a minute or two, before drumming his well-manicured fingers on the tabletop before him while his cohorts watched his every mood anxiously and waited with bated breath for his next word. They had good reason to be afraid. The *compadrito* was in one of his unpredictable moods, and his men had learned to their cost that at such times he was even more vicious than usual; might as easily order you "snuffed" out like a candle for some imagined slight, as to grant you some unasked-for favor or other, in his present frame of mind . . .

"Under the circumstances, I think it's time we cut off young

Master Cojo's services, don't you, friend Bobo?" Malvado murmured softly at long last. His black eyes gleamed. "Our little Gypsy dancer must fend for herself and the sick woman alone from now on, poor *niña,*" he murmured sarcastically, and flashed the squat, toadlike creature who waited in a shadowed corner a broad, foxy grin.

Bobo grinned, his bulbous, fleshy lips peeling back to show a mouthful of yellow teeth so crooked, his mouth resembled a churchyard filled with leaning tombstones made green with lichen. A self-taught assassin, Bobo made up for his lack of intelligence and height in width. His head was almost square, and as smooth and bald as an egg, his scalp always slick with sweat. His massive, hairless chest bulged under a black leather vest, which he wore without a shirt. Armbands of leather studded with brass nailheads encircled his bulging upper arms, which ended in small, peculiarly childlike, pudgy hands. A similar belt cinched his thick waist and emphasized his slight paunch. With the immense size and power of his upper body surmounting them, his legs were stubby and short, unlike other dwarves who were well proportioned even if smaller than average, but he was no less powerful for all that. Clad in breeches that reached only to his knees, his calves bulged like some massive ape's, a comparison his simian forehead and overly long arms did nothing to dispel. His lower legs and feet were bare and crusted with filth.

"*Sí,* Don Antonio! Bobo will take care of the problem for you at once," he lisped, his piggy eyes bright with animal cunning. He flexed his brawny arms and lumbered to his short legs, obviously eager to be about the task his master had indicated. He was a man who enjoyed his work, was Bobo, and in seconds, he had gone.

Malvado grinned in satisfaction after the brute had left. He waved a dismissal to Juan and José, and found himself alone again at last, surrounded by the tangible proof of his wealth and power—costly furnishings, rare artworks, silver candlesticks, rich Turkey carpets, and the like. And enclosing it all was the lavishly renovated Italian-style villa he maintained on Calle Pajaro, secluded from prying or jealous eyes by a high wall of crumbling, weed-grown adobe. Not bad for little Tonio, the street urchin, whose mother had been a waterfront whore and his father her "pimp," eh, he thought smugly? He'd come a long way in his thirty-six years, *por Dios,* and with no thanks due anyone but himself! The shabby walls effectively concealed his wealth from those he preyed upon, and kept him removed from the dirty streets and poverty of the *barrios* upon which he fed like a parasite upon its weakened host.

He poured himself a glass of red wine and leaned back comfortably to sip it from a French crystal goblet, his imagination fancifully toying with visions of the gypsy beauty on her knees at his feet, naked and pleading with him to help her. Soon, she'd have no other choice but to come begging to him, or starve, he reflected smugly. He'd have broken the fierce pride and stubborn will her people were filled with once and for all! And, once the irritating matter of the cripple had been taken care of, he'd have covered every angle, right down to the smallest detail. Thanks to the woman, Delora, the dancer's own people, the Gypsies, had disowned her, as—for that matter—had everyone else! He'd seen to it that his men passed the word amongst the people of the *barrios* that the consequences of either aiding or hiring the *gitana,* Krissoula Ballardo to dance could prove dangerous—even deadly —and he knew that without work, without friends, without money, she'd have nowhere left to turn!

And when, broken and humbled, she came to him and threw herself on his mercy—as he knew, ultimately, she must!—he'd exact his payment from that graceful, lissome body of hers; use her again and again until he'd wearied of her golden Gypsy charms. By then—he smiled evilly—he would have taught that proud bitch once and for all time that no one, man or woman, refused the *compadrito,* Don Antonio Malvado. *No one.*

And then, afterward—? He shrugged, dismissing the matter of the girl's disposal as negligible. He'd promised Bobo he could have her, but if not the dwarf, there were any number of the foulest kind of brothels in his *barrio;* brothels that catered to men of the lowest, most perverted and cruel tastes, and they were always short of women. Any one of them would be pleased to take a beautiful gypsy wench slightly used . . .

"Cojo!"

"*Sí?*" He turned and looked back towards the doorway he'd just left, where Krissoula leaned against the doorjamb. Her black hair was still tousled from sleep, her cheeks were flushed, her golden eyes heavy-lidded and dreamy-looking. With a pang and a peculiar feeling of foreboding, he thought she'd never looked more beautiful than she did this morning, and the love swelled in his youthful heart.

"Won't you have some *maté* before you leave? It's already

brewed. I don't like you going out on an empty belly."

"The sooner I leave, the sooner I'll be back with something to fill *all* our empty bellies," he retorted with a grin. "Don't mother me, Krithoula. I'll be fine!"

"You're sure?"

He nodded. "I'm thure."

"Very well." He turned to leave. "Cojo—be careful, eh, little *amigo?* Don't take any risks. Sofía and I, we need *you* far more than we need the food, you know?"

Her words filled him with an unaccustomed feeling of pride. They needed him! "Don't worry, Krithoula. I'll be fine. I'll be back in time for *siesta,* never fear. *Adiós!"*

She waved him a smiling goodbye, and with a wink Cojo set off, limping down the sun-baked streets.

Although it was still early yet, the sun was already hot and hazy over the city with the promise of yet another sweltering day. As he trudged along, he thought of the evening before, and a cozy little glow rekindled in his belly.

Seeing Sofía made comfortable for the night, he and Krissoula had left their one-room quarters and gone out to sit about the fire in the courtyard. They'd talked and talked like old, old friends will do, even when they're together frequently. She'd told him about her family, of Uncle Ricardo and Tía Isabella and Spain, and how she'd lost a husband and a child, and alone and afraid and embittered by her past, had turned to thievery for her living. She'd even told him of that man, Don Esteban, whom she'd loved, ending:

"Don't be like me, my friend, and think that wealth and an easy life can solve everything, heal all wounds, for it can't. Without someone you love to share it, even a life of riches can be as hollow and empty as a drum . . ."

Cojo had known by the expression of longing in her eyes that she still loved the Argentine, Esteban de San Martín, even now, whatever she said otherwise to hide it, and he'd felt jealous beyond words. She'd seen the yearning in his face and had reached out, gently stroking his cheek.

"Don't be jealous, young Cojo. I'm way too old for you, my lad!"

"Too old!" he'd protested sourly. "Pah! What's three years—what's your nineteen to my sixteen?"

"But I'm only nineteen by the calendar. In here, where it counts, and in here," she'd added, touching her head then her breast, "I'm far, far older than you in terms of experience! Please, don't lose your heart to me, my friend, for my heart's used up—taken—and

I've none to give you in return. Besides, you'll find someone of your own someday, with a brand-new heart all shiny and empty and ready to love. You'll forget poor Krissoula Ballardo then," she'd suggested with a twinkle in her eye.

"Never!" he'd denied fiercely. "Besides, who'd want to love a gargoyle? It would be the old tale of Beauty and the Beast all over again!" he'd said with no little bitterness.

"Eh, and in the fairy tale, didn't the princess grow to love the beast for the goodness and beauty inside him? You know she did! The way we look on the *outside* doesn't matter so much, Cojo, don't you see? It's just a shell, and, besides, if looks mattered as much as everyone thinks they do, half the world would remain unloved and unwanted, for I've seen few enough pretty faces in my time! No, it's what's inside you that counts. Remember, Cojo, I'm a Gypsy, and I can read the future, so believe me when I say that one day, some day, there'll be someone special for you. And she'll be *very* special, I know, because she'll be clever enough to look beyond your poor lip and your foot to your beautiful brown eyes, and see through them clear down to your heart. And when she does, she'll be dazzled by what she sees, helpless to resist you. In her eyes, you'll be a prince, Cojo—Prince Charming!"

"Oh, you're just teasing me!" he'd countered, but he'd been pleased nonetheless by her teasing prediction—and yes, just a little hopeful, too. More hopeful than he'd ever been before. Her reassurances had gone a long way to making him feel better about himself, to give him confidence. He only wished he could do the same for her; could rid her eyes of the sorrow he'd glimpsed from time to time in their long-lashed golden depths. They'd talked some more after that, and she'd told him she'd put the Argentine behind her, that her love for him was now a thing of the past, but that wasn't true. She murmured his name constantly in her sleep, and tossed and turned all night, making little whimpering noises that brought tears to his eyes . . .

An hour later found Cojo hovering, itchy-fingered, alongside a stall in the half-deserted marketplace of Plaza Corrientes, eyeing the vendor's wares—baskets of long, crusty bread loaves—and the vendor himself, in turn. He was waiting for the moment when the baker's watchful eyes strayed from his goods to strike!

Stealing was new to sixteen-year-old Cojo, for the good sisters at the convent foundling home of San Timéo—where he'd been raised from the moment he'd been abandoned on their doorstep, just a few hours after his birth—had taught him that stealing was a mortal sin.

Consequently, he'd always tried to be honest and good, to labor long and hard to put food in his belly rather than break the Commandments by taking what belonged to others. Though his life had been far from easy, he'd succeeded in eking out a living despite his deformities, and despite the contempt in which he'd been held.

But now, with the cholera epidemic choking the people of the city in a fist of terror, nobody dared to hire him, and he knew why. The Argentine poor were a superstitious folk at the best of times, relying heavily on their *curanderos,* their witch doctors, for guidance, rather than trusting in themselves and in God. Having little of material value and still less self-confidence, they were eager to blame their misfortunes on influences they felt beyond their control; another's "evil eye" could make one ill; bad luck was the result of evil forces or a jealous influence in the house, an enemy's ill will, or a neighbor's envious eye. Cojo knew they feared his twisted lip and misshapen body, which were, to their thinking, a sure sign that his mother and his birth had been cursed. That being the case, they thought the bad luck which had dogged him from birth would somehow rub off on them, and leave them stricken. And what better way for *el diablo* to work his will than through the wasting sickness? No. He could look to no one for assistance. If he intended to find food for Krissoula, Sofía, and himself, stealing was the only way left to him, and God forgive him for his sins . . .

He frowned, knowing he'd never get the act of thievery down to the slippery, graceful art the urchins of the Ciudad de los Niños had elevated it to. He was too clumsy for that, too easily recognizable. Besides, with his cursed clubbed foot slowing him down, a swift getaway was impossible! He had to rely on stealth rather than speed, and pray he could stuff a loaf of bread beneath his shirt and draw his vest over it to conceal the telltale bulge, before the vendor spotted him . . .

The seconds seemed endless as he waited his chance, and then—miracle of miracles!—a garrulous old woman dressed all in black stopped to exchange a few words with the baker, and his opportunity came. Quick as a flash, Cojo took it!

His brown hand darted out, clamped over the bread, and snatched it up. In the same fluid move, he'd stuffed the long loaf up under his shirt and turned slowly away from the baker, drawing the fronts of his shabby leather vest together over his stolen prize as he began to limp casually away. He moved unhurriedly, snail-like, as if he had all the time in the world, thank you very much—while his poor heart thundered like a cannon in his bony breast, and sweat dampened his palms with fear. Only on account of the love he bore Krissoula would he ever endure the panic he was feeling now, he vowed with fervor: only for her.

He'd taken only three shuffling steps when he sensed eyes upon him. Feeling the blood drain from his face, he looked up guiltily, expecting to meet the eyes of the baker, hot and angry with accusation, or at the very least the pitying and disgusted glance of someone who'd remarked his handicaps. But instead, his eyes met the cold, piggy, black eyes of Bobo—and that, aiee, *Dios*—that was far worse, for the squat toad of a dwarf was *smiling* at him—!

Bobo's legendary smiles were terrible to behold, for it was common knowledge in the *barrios* that to see the murderous simpleton smiling could mean only one thing; he had a job to do for his beloved master, Malvado. And there was only one "job" the godfather would entrust to that animal . . .

A sensation of weakness and the cold sweat of foreboding swept over Cojo as Bobo took a rolling step towards him. Where could he hide? How could he hope to outrun Malvado's executioner! Executioner? Ah, *sí,* he knew by the look in Bobo's eyes that he'd been sent to kill him, and he also knew why . . .

He looked wildly about for help, and inspiration struck. With a hefty shove, he pushed the loaded stall before him, knocking it aside. The flimsy wooden structure toppled easily, baskets of bread rolling everywhere, the ruins of the stall itself blocking Bobo's path.

"What the devil did you do that for, you troublesome cur—!" the baker yelled, angrily brandishing his fist.

"It was him!" Cojo panted, pointing accusingly in Bobo's direction. "He did it, señor, not me—!"

"Why, you clumsy ape—!" the baker growled. He rolled up his sleeves and started towards Bobo.

In a matter of moments, the foolish baker would realize exactly who he'd tangled with—the crowds of onlookers jostling forward to watch the fight would see to that—but meanwhile, he might be able to escape—!

Without looking back, Cojo started limping across the square, ducking into the first alley he came to. He was breathing heavily already, and more frightened than he cared to admit, but he still had the bread and he still had a chance—and that was more than he'd dared to hope for a few moments ago.

Thinking quickly as he hitched along, summoning what speed he could from his one good leg and dragging his clubbed and useless one like a weight behind him, he wondered where he could run to?

What bolt-hole could he use to escape Bobo, and lie low for a few days? The room on Calle Rios where Krissoula and Sofía awaited his return was out of the question. He'd not lead Malvado's henchman back there, and endanger his friends! Nor could he go to the Cádiz Tavern. Luigi was too deep in the *compadrito's* pocket to be of any use, and, besides, the Italian had little fondness for him. The church of San Timéo would offer no sanctuary against that blasphemous slime, Bobo, either, for the idiot toad had no respect for God, nor His House. So. What other alternative did he have? Cojo thought and thought as he scuttled along, and at last came to a decision. There was only one other place where he might be safe, where he could guarantee he'd be taken in and hidden, despite his deformities. He'd go to the Ciudad de los Niños! he decided. "*Sí!* The City of Children!" he repeated under his breath. "My friends there will hide me till it's safe to leave!"

The Ciudad de los Niños was a shantytown of pitiful shacks, many of them constructed from broken wooden boxes, sackcloth, branches, and loosened boards—anything that had been discarded by others which could be pressed into service to build a crude shelter. There were hundreds of such lean-tos on the mudflats of the Plata in summer months, and hundreds of orphaned or unwanted children living in them; children the orphanages of the city of Buenos Aires had no room—or wish—to house. The children—ranging in age from little babes abandoned by their mothers to youths or girls of ten or twelve who cared for the little ones as best they could—lived on the charity of those precious few who seemed to care about their plight, and who brought them what little food and money they could spare. They earned whatever else they needed by selling the old clothes and bones they found by rummaging through littered alleys, and also from the proceeds of their pickpocketing and outright stealing. That's where he'd go—to the Niños!

His flight had purpose now, his pace had new direction, although it seemed circuitous, for he followed a route that wound through countless alleys and zigzagged between narrow, densely shadowed streets that took him closer and ever closer to the river.

Past seedy cafés and smoky pool rooms, Cojo hobbled on, his bad leg screaming with pain, his other, stronger one exhausted, darting a glance over his shoulder from time to time to see if he was being followed. Thank God, there was no sign of Bobo! His relief was so great, scalding tears smarted in his eyes; tears both of gratitude and of loss, for even should he escape the dwarf, it was doubtful he'd ever be able to go back to Krissoula—whom he loved with all the fierce, sweet innocence of a lad's first love—or to kind, motherly Sofia. It would be too risky to try it, when doing so could only place the women he cared for in greater danger. Better he should just disappear, at least for the time being. Perhaps his old friend Sancho or one of the other Niños would carry a message to them for him, so they'd know he hadn't deserted them by choice in their hour of need? The idea encouraged him, and he forced a little more speed from his poor legs, his breathing escaping from between his teeth and twisted lips like a panting animal's, run to ground.

He lurched out of a narrow alley into blazing afternoon sunlight. There were fewer buildings about now, but what there were cast sharp black shadows on the ground. Standing on tiptoe, he could just make out, above the rooftops of the warehouses hereabouts, the crisscrossed dark masts of the ships that waited to unload their cargoes in the roadstead of the Plata. A mile more, and he'd be there, and home free! *Gracias a Dios,* a little farther, and he could rest!

The shanties of the Ciudad de los Niños came into view, baking under the summer sun and the brilliant azure of the sky, while beyond, the Plata winked a yellow-brown eye. He let out a cry of joy and triumph—and as abruptly silenced it.

No.

No!

Not now—

Not when he was so close—

He could hear someone squelching purposefully across the mudflats behind him.

Dread in his heart, he forced himself to stop, to turn and look back, and his bowels squeezed with dread. Fear and exhaustion froze him in place. *Blessed Virgin, protect me!* he prayed silently, reaching for the wooden rosary about his throat and drawing the little silver crucifix to his lips, before he reached for his little knife.

Bobo the dwarf was less than three yards behind him—far too close to outrun a second time. Even worse, Cojo saw that he was still smiling.

Krissoula lit the single candle they possessed, and set it on the windowsill in a puddle of melted wax. Eyeing the swiftly darkening sky outside, she bit her lower lip, feeling sick to her stomach with worry. Where the devil was Cojo? What could have happened to make him so late? Had *los botónes* picked him up for stealing? Was he even now sprawled in a filthy cell somewhere, frightened and alone? *Caray,* he'd never been gone for so long before! He'd always returned way before nightfall with something for them to eat brandished triumphantly in his hand, and a shy smile of pride that he'd found them food wreathing his poor, dear face. Something was awry. She could feel it in her bones—but *what?*

Sofía stirred across the single room, her restless thrashing diverting Krissoula's thoughts from the boy. She hurried across to the woman, and knelt by her side.

Sofía's skin looked yellowish and wrinkled, even in the candle's flattering light. A gentle pinch, and the folds stayed put, instead of springing back, as was normal. Her gentle brown eyes seemed to have sunk deep into their sockets, and were ringed with dark shadows. Poor, dear Sofía! Over the past few days, she seemed to have dwindled almost to nothing. Never a large woman at the best of times, there was little more to her now than skin encasing angular bones. And yet—thank God!—she was alive, and that was the most important thing. She'd passed the crisis point in the disease, if Cojo's knowledge of the cholera could be relied upon, and now would have to start the long convalescence to restore her to her former health and vigor. She'd need good food, and lots of it, along with rest. How, Krissoula fretted, was she to provide the things Sofía needed, with only a few pesos left to her name, and no work by which to earn more?

"Krissoula?" came Sofía's dry whisper.

"I'm here, *cara mía,* don't worry," she softly reassured the sick woman as Sofía's eyelids fluttered open. "How are you feeling?"

"A little better, I think. Thank God, those awful cramps have gone! Could I—could I trouble you for a sip of water?"

"It's no trouble at all, Sofía. Better than that—I have a little beef broth warming—just for you, mind—rather than plain old water. The broth will make you strong and beautiful again, Sofía. It'll put meat on your bones, so that when next you see that handsome Armando Reyes, he will have eyes for no one but you!" she promised with a teasing smile, for Carla's widowed father had seemed to admire gentle Sofía very much while they lived in Barrio Gitanos, and Sofía had not seemed displeased that he should do so. As she'd hoped, a tired and wan but genuine smile curved Sofía's mouth.

"My dear, wicked girl . . . the things you say . . ." the woman murmured fondly.

Krissoula went outside into the courtyard where a cooking fire still smoldered, and fetched Sofía the last of the broth in a little bowl. She'd made the broth from some fine meaty soupbones that Cojo had begged from the slaughterhouse yards two days before, cooking it with a handful of stolen rice and a little salt begged from her crotchety old "landlord." Fearing the broth—which was rich in nourishing marrow—would spoil in the summer heat if allowed to cool, she'd kept the small pot Carla had given her simmering all day and all night. And at last, the vast quantities of water and broth she'd managed to spoon into Sofía to replace the liquid that had passed from her body in such alarming amounts seemed to have done the trick, as Cojo—himself a recovered victim of the summer plague some years before—had told her it would.

Having helped the convent sisters nursing the stricken in other years, Krissoula had realized that Cojo had probably learned as much about the mysterious wasting disease as anyone else. She'd opted to follow his practical suggestions to replace the fluids lost from Sofía's body as quickly as possible, rather than resorting to the amulets and charms the *curanderos* were urging superstitious, frightened folk to garland themselves with—at robbers' prices, of course! In between hours spent painstakingly spoon-feeding the sick woman, and in scrubbing Sofía's pitifully few garments again and again so that they would be fresh and clean for rewearing, she and Cojo had dulled their own hunger with some overripe bananas he'd found—or stolen—from somewhere. Not a feast, by any means, but enough.

She remembered how she'd gorged on Mama Angelina's *empanadas* and juicy steaks, savory *pulchero* and spicy chicken, and although her mouth watered, she felt ashamed of the greedy, thoughtless child she'd been then, stuffing herself at every meal as if it were her last. Oh, Saint Sara, what she'd give for such wonderful treats right now; to see Sofía and Cojo with full bellies and sleek smiles! She'd never again take food for granted, or see it wasted, she vowed, if only God would help them this time . . .

"I think Delora's curse has failed, no?" Sofía murmured after she'd obediently swallowed the last of the broth. A wry smile played about her thin, pinched lips. "I believe I might live, after all, thanks to you, my dear *niña.*"

"Mmm? Oh, of course you'll live, *tonta.* Only the good die young, eh, so you must have been very bad in the past!" Krissoula reassured her, patting her hand almost absently. It was obvious even to the recovering woman that her thoughts were elsewhere.

429

"But you still look so drawn and frightened, child? Why? Have I—have I been such a burden on you?"

"No! Don't be such a goose!" Krissoula scolded, sharply bringing her thoughts back to the present. "Wouldn't you have done the same for me, were I in your place? *Sí,* of course you would! We're friends, Sofía, and I don't know about you, but we women of the Rom don't take a friendship lightly! We stick together through thick and thin . . . Now, finish your broth and get some sleep. Look! It's dark outside already."

It was dark. The narrow, single window framed a midnight-blue sky, sequined with stars. The air was sultry and still, only a single vagabond current fluttering the sackcloth that curtained the opening. The draft raised a shiver down Krissoula's spine.

She went to the window and stared out once again into the dusty street beyond. It was dark and empty, except for a mangy dog scavenging the alleys for food. *Where is he?* she wondered, a knot of apprehension tightening in her belly. *Where can he be?*

Krissoula knew it had to be a dream, but she didn't want to wake up!

She was dancing—dancing with Esteban—dancing the deliciously immoral tango, and *Dios,* how wonderfully they danced!

They were in the taproom of the Bamboo Cage, crowded with noisy patrons. She wore a ruffled gown of scarlet, and had heavy gold hoops dangling from her ears. Her feet and legs were bare, and the sawdust strewn over the flagstones was warm and soft to her toes. He wore a ruffled white shirt and breeches that molded to his thighs, and a low-brimmed sombrero that hid his eyes, yet she knew—oh, yes, she knew, somehow—that they were dark with desire for her.

Like a matador swirling his magenta cape, he draped her about him, their bodies touching, the steady throb of his heart palpable against her ear. Then he took her hand and flung her violently away, only to spin her back into his arms with a mocking smile.

"You will make love with me, *querida!*" he commanded, his voice low and sensual, arousing her.

"Here?" she whispered, her heart fluttering like a bird's beating wings. "But—there are people watching us!"

"What of it?" he growled roughly. "I've paid your price. Make love with me!"

The music was compelling, a jungle heartbeat woven around

with melodies that were slow and dreamy and sensual. The tempo touched some pulse that lay dormant deep within her belly, bringing it to throbbing life. He took her by the hand and guided her across the room. His gaze locked to hers, he halted and swung her across his thigh, arching her so low to the ground that her hair swept the sawdust beneath them. As he leaned over her, their bodies scandalously touching, she saw that his eyes were as she'd imagined—sapphire pools made lambent with passion.

"Surrender!" he whispered in her dream. "Surrender, my golden witch!"

And heedless of the eyes upon them, he pressed his lips to the hollow that lay at the base of her throat, then lower, to the start of the valley between her breasts. Somehow, as in the manner of dreams, her gown dissolved, whirled away like wisps of smoke and she was arched naked across his powerful thigh. His lips were playing at her breast, tasting her satin flesh, teasing each dark-gold nipple to aching, swollen life, and it was wonderful, so wonderful to feel his mouth upon her . . .

But then she heard a snicker of laughter from the watching crowd, and she tensed, remembering they were not alone.

"Please, *querido,* stop! Everyone's watching us!" she whispered, wanting to cover herself, to hide from the lust-filled eyes that feasted hotly on her body and spied upon their lovemaking.

"Let them!" Esteban rasped, raising her up and twirling her naked across the floor, moving her fluidly back and forth in time to the music as he willed, as if he were the whip that drove her, and she the spinning top that must twirl and spin and obey his commands. He ground her body against him, welding their hips together, lustfully stroking the curves of her bottom as he pressed her to him. She could feel the fiery ridge of his manhood riding hard against her belly, and then his hungry lips found hers, parting the softness of her mouth with the fire of his own, kissing her thirstily, greedily as he lifted her astride his flanks, filled her with his swollen shaft, began to ride between her thighs in an urgent, masterful way that drove her to distraction. She moved to meet him, matching the thrust of her hips to his, no longer caring that there were eyes upon them, nor hearing the hoarse, thickened voices of the crowd urging him on as he plunged and thrust and took his pleasure of her body.

"I love you! I love you still!" she cried.

"The little puta *loves him! Oh, how she loves him!"* the voice of the crowd jeered.

"Why didn't you trust me?" she implored, searching his dark, enigmatic face for an answer as he rode her on and on. "I made a blood-oath, remember? I swore to be loyal only to you!"

"I wanted to trust you—God knows, I wanted to! But you lied to me, darling. You hid the truth, left things unsaid that should have been shared! You swore you'd betray me, remember—? What else was I to think? Trust is earned, *querida.* Earned—not given!"

"Give! Give! Give!" the crowd roared. "Caramba, *see how she gives!"*

"But I didn't mean it!" she sobbed. "I was angry, but I would never have betrayed you, *querido,* never—not when I love you so! You are my heart, my soul, my breath! Please, Esteban, you must believe me. It was Alfredo who told Felipe about us, not I. Please, oh, please, I can't go on without you. My life is empty. It means nothing anymore. It's not wealth I crave, it's you, *querido,* you! Aiee, Madonna, I need you so!"

"Too late," he whispered softly. "Too late . . ."

Desperately, she reached out to hold him, to tell him it was never too late, never! That she'd spend the rest of her life making up to him, earning his trust, if only he forgave her. If only he loved her still—! But her arms closed on air. His beloved face and form dissolved, melting away until she hugged only herself about the arms. Cold, naked, she tossed and turned on the cold dirt floor, hearing his last words echoing over and over through her mind, while the crowd whispered and roared with laughter at her shame, chanting the words again and again to the beat of a drum:

"Too late! Too late! Too la—"

She sat up with a heart-rending jolt, cold sweat beading her brow despite the stifling heat of the night and the closeness of the small, square room. She'd fallen asleep while waiting up for Cojo, she realized, and now someone was pounding on the door. A voice was calling her name. Still shaken by the nightmare, she stumbled to her feet, going to the door and pressing her cheek to the wood.

"Who is it?" she asked hesitantly.

"You don't know me, señorita, but I come from San Timéo's. Cojo—your friend, the crippled boy—he sent me to fetch you! Hurry, señorita, there isn't much time!"

Hastily, she unbolted the door and flung it wide open. A boy stood on the threshold, ragged and dirty and breathing heavily as if he'd run some distance.

"To fetch me? But why? Where is he? Why couldn't he come himself?"

"He is at the church, señorita, and he has been hurt—very badly hurt. He—he asks that you come at once, señorita!"

"Lead the way," she whispered, her heart in her mouth. "Oh, my God, *niño*, lead the way—!"

Cojo lay on a cloak which someone had spread over the stone floor of the church. His pallor in the light of the many candles the priest had lit was ghastly. A trickle of frothy blood had escaped the corner of his mouth, and his beautiful brown eyes were already dimming as death stole through him, inch by terrible inch. Icy with dread, she met the priest's eyes as he concluded the last rites, and saw him shake his head sadly.

Kneeling beside Cojo, she took his cold hand in her own, lifting it to her lips and kissing it.

"Krithoula?" Cojo whispered uncertainly. He coughed, and another bubble of bright red blood escaped his twisted lips.

"*Sí*, I'm here, darling," she choked out. "Krissoula's here."

"I—I tried to get a-away. But—but this—this cursed leg—made me too slow. I lost the bread, Krithoula! Now you and Sofía will—will—go—hungry!"

"Hush, hush, never mind the bread, darling," she murmured, lifting his head to cradle it in her lap. She caressed his dark hair, which was damp with sweat and soiled with dried mud. "Please don't worry about anything, not any more. You see, I found work today, isn't that wonderful? A good job, dancing at a decent tavern. From now on, there'll be chicken and rice in our cooking pot every night, Cojo, and more of your favorite herb dumplings than you can possibly eat!" Her voice broke with the lie, and the priest reached out and gripped her shoulder to steady her. She looked down, and saw through a mist of tears that Cojo was smiling.

"Really?"

"Really! You and me—why, we'll make pigs of ourselves, eh, little brother, eat—eating those d-dumplings!" she promised, blinking rapidly. "And then poor So—fía—Sofía will scold us for our a-awful table manners."

Wearily, he nodded once and his brown eyes closed. The breath caught in her throat and she thought he was gone before he opened them once more—though with obvious effort—a second or two later.

"I'm so tired. Will you dansth for me until I fall asleep, Krithoula?" he whispered. "You know how much I love you—love to watch you dansth?" And he gave a great sigh, as if a weight he

433

carried had suddenly grown too heavy to bear. Fresh blood bubbled from the corner of his mouth, and Krissoula stifled a sob of anguish.

"For you, darling, Krissoula is always ready to dance," she whispered brokenly, and, leaning forward, she kissed his cheek and his poor misshapen mouth with a tenderness that brought tears to the eyes of the priest and the watching boy. "Are you ready?" she asked, and with a barely perceptible nod, Cojo acknowledged that he was.

Straightening up, she stood and draped her shawl over her head. She locked her gaze to his and softly, huskily, in a voice that broke now and then with unshed tears, she sang the song she'd danced just for Cojo at Alonso and Gina's wedding. Her full skirts swirled like flowers about her as she danced barefoot in the light of the candles which bathed her in their light.

> You think I didn't see you
> As you followed me
> Through the streets of Sevilla,
> But I saw your dark eyes, *gitano*—
> They gave you away!
> Why follow me in secret,
> Like a bandit,
> When no other has spoken for me?
> Ask my father, shy *gitano,*
> If he will give you my hand?

"Señorita. You can stop now. It is over, alas," came the priest's voice, laden with pity.

But the Gypsy girl seemed deaf to his words, numb to their meaning. On and on she danced, singing her song, a half-smile playing about her lips, her graceful body moving in time to the rhythm. Tears were flowing unchecked down her cheeks and shining in the candlelight as she sang hoarsely:

> Your eyes fill my dreams,
> Handsome Gypsy boy!
> A thousand silver pieces
> Would buy just one of your smiles!
> Don't be shy, my dark-eyed one,
> For I won't refuse you.
> Your smiles will be many

When I hold you in
The garland of my arms,
And drown in the pools of your handsome eyes.

She grew still as the last trembling note of her song faded into silence, and the priest sought for words to ease the deep sorrow in her eyes, her tragic face.

"Come, now, little *gitana*. Take comfort that his pain in this world is ended, Daughter," he advised her gently. "Now your Cojo sleeps in the arms of the Blessed Mother, in Heaven Above."

She glanced up at him sharply, and to the priest's surprise, she gave a disclaiming, brittle little laugh that rang through the hushed church.

"Sleeping, Father? *Dios,* I hope not! I surely hope not! If there *is* indeed a heaven, and there is indeed a God who is good and kind and just, as the church would have us believe, then Cojo isn't sleeping—he's dancing, Father! Not sleeping but—but *dancing,* and *running* and *walking*—and on two strong, whole legs . . . !"

Before his eyes, she crumpled to her knees, buried her face in her hands, and wept.

Chapter Thirty-Seven

The next few days passed in a painful blur for Krissoula. She spent the days crying, the nights crying, the hours, minutes, even the seconds, in crying, as if, after two years without tears, now that they'd started, she couldn't staunch them.

She cried with wrenching grief and aching loss, knowing she and Cojo would never again affectionately tease or rough-house together, as they'd done while he lived; that the lad would never find the girl of his dreams. She sobbed with outrage at the unfairness of his passing; at the youth and innocence, the simple honesty and goodness his untimely death had robbed the world of, and asked the four walls again and again, *Why him, Madonna? Cojo never hurt anyone! Why him?* But if God, in His wisdom, had a reason, He never answered her.

She wept bitter tears of anger, too, that an animal like Malvado could order a decent human life extinguished at his whim, with no more thought given the deed than blowing out a candle, or treading a cockroach underfoot. And even when she'd cried herself out and could weep no more, her questions remained unanswered, her heart aching with sorrow.

She'd learned from the priest and the ragged urchin boy, Sancho, who'd come to find her, exactly how Cojo had died, and also why. The meaty hands of some toadlike madman, a dwarf named "Bobo"—who, they told her in frightened whispers, worked for the *compadrito,* Don Antonio Malvado—had picked Cojo up and crushed him, had held him fast in a terrible bearhug. His massive arms had broken every single bone in the frail crippled lad's body. A splintered rib had pierced Cojo's lungs, and death had been inevitable; just a matter of time.

Sancho, self-appointed "king" of the City of Children—wherever and whatever that might be—had heard Cojo weakly calling for help shortly after nightfall, and had searched the mudflats to find him. He and some of the other children had managed to lift their crippled friend onto a dog-cart and carried him to the church, as he'd asked them to do. There, Cojo had begged Sancho to find Krissoula and bring her to him, knowing he was dying, and wanting to warn her that the *compadrito* would stop at nothing to have her, not even if it meant murdering her friends.

At last, Krissoula had understood Esteban's outrage over his father's senseless and untimely death, his relentless resolve to see his murderer pay for what he'd done. The same fury, the same raging thirst for revenge, now choked her own breast. Someday—she swore, trembling all over with uncontrollable emotion—*sí,* some fine day, this despicable "Bobo" creature would be called to account for what he'd done, as would his hated master. Poor Cojo's blood cried out for vengeance!

She remembered how she'd given the little priest, Father Pedro, all of the money left her, imploring him to say a Mass for Cojo's soul, and to see the boy decently buried.

"No common, unmarked grave for him, please, Padre?" she'd whispered, fearing Cojo's pauper's death would see his poor, broken body consigned to one of the anonymous mass graves dug for the cholera victims.

The priest had looked down at the pitiful handful of pesos she'd forced on him, and she'd known in her heart that there was not enough for what she asked, not nearly enough. Yet the priest had nodded, and she'd seen in his eyes that it would be done as she'd asked, nonetheless. She'd thanked him and left, and somehow found her way back to Sofía and the room they shared. Now, she had to go on living, to pull herself together—for Sofía's sake, if not her own. She owed it to Cojo. He'd given his life for her sake, and she must survive, or his sacrifice would have been in vain . . .

"Señor! Señor! *Hola,* señor, *hola, hola!*"

A chorus of cheeping young voices greeted Esteban as he strode across the squelching mudflats through the City of Children, dwarfing the ramshackle little shanties as he wove between them on mud-splattered boots.

From every lean-to, children poured out to follow him, until a score of them danced at his heels. Like the Pied Piper of Hamelin, he led the children on in a giggling, yelling tide, until they came to the shack of boards and stolen sailcloth from which the "King" of the City, named simply "Sancho," ruled his domain, along with his younger sister, Lourdes, who was their "Queen." In his arms, Esteban carried two heavy sacks of cornmeal flour, and slung over his shoulder, their necks tied together, a half-dozen dead chickens.

"There'll be tortillas tonight! Yippee!" cried one little girl, her ragged dark hair flying behind her as she raced on bare feet to tell her friends the wonderful news.

"And chicken!" screamed another in delight, jumping up and down like a bouncing ball. "Chicken! Chicken! Chicken! *Gracias, señor! Gracias!*"

Sancho emerged from his dwelling with the dignity of his position, arms crossed over his thin chest. His huge dark eyes met Esteban's gravely, and he nodded once before his gaze flickered to the largesse in his arms and slung over his shoulder. He extended his hand in greeting, and Esteban shook it, man to man.

"Welcome to the Ciudad de los Niños once again, Señor San Martín!" Sancho greeted Esteban. "We did not expect you back again so soon!" he observed, gesturing the adult to take a seat upon a rickety stool set before his hut.

Against his better judgment, Esteban put aside the sacks and chickens and sat, his long legs almost folded up under his chin on the low stool. Dozens of children, some naked, others dressed in assorted rags, squatted in the dirt all about them, or crowded at their backs. They peeped shyly between their fingers at him, or giggled behind their palms when he glanced their way. He winked at one or two of them, tickled others in the ribs, before turning his attention to the matter at hand.

"I've come to ask you a favor, Sancho," Esteban said solemnly. "A big one! I need your help, you see."

"*You* need *our* help, señor?" Sancho echoed, hiding his surprise as swiftly as it flitted across his narrow, sun-browned face with an attempt at a serious, grown-up expression. "But of course, if it is in our power, you'll have it, señor! What is it you want us to do?"

"I'm looking for a woman."

Sancho blinked, then grinned wickedly. "A good-looking *hombre* like you, señor, must ask Sancho's help for that—?" He chuckled, looking ten years old for once, instead of ten-going-on-a-hundred. "Have you not tried the Plaza Corrientes, señor?" he asked innocently. "I have heard they have many pretty women there at the Bamboo Cage?"

"You little rogue—you know damned well I didn't mean that!" Esteban grinned, reaching out and ruffling the boy's ragged black hair. "No. The woman I'm looking for has a name—unless she's

438

using another one. It's Krissoula Ballardo. Golden eyes. Long black hair. A small, slender woman, and very pretty, too. She might be a dancer. Have you heard of her, by any chance?"

"Krissoula Ballardo?" Sancho repeated slowly, playing for time while he considered how to answer the man's surprising question.

Moments before his death, his friend Cojo had asked him to swear something; to swear never to reveal the whereabouts of his friend, the woman Krissoula, to anyone. And now, not even a week after he'd made that promise, here was Señor Esteban, of all people, asking him to break it! This matter, Sancho decided, would need careful thought. A hasty answer in the negative might cost them the generous gifts of food and clothing which Señor Esteban had brought them at regular intervals for as long as Sancho could remember. They all depended upon him, and he couldn't let the *niños* suffer because he'd answered rashly, and without thinking it through from every angle. On the other hand, if he gave Señor Esteban the information he wanted, he'd be breaking his word to Cojo! And a promise given to a friend on his deathbed could not lightly be broken, if a man was honorable . . .

"Why are you looking for this woman, señor?" Sancho asked curiously, gazing with a steady intensity into the Argentine's deep-blue eyes. Esteban did not look away but met his searching look unflinchingly, he saw.

"Because I love her," he answered the boy simply. "And because I want her back, with me, where she'll be safe. There were misunderstandings between us, you see. We—quarreled—and she ran away, believing I hated her. I went to Rolón Severino for help—."

"*Compadrito* Severino?" the boy asked in awe.

"*Sí,* that's him. Severino said he'd met her, and that she was well and living with her people, the Gypsies, in Barrio Gitanos. I went there, but she'd gone—vanished! Consuela—the mulatto woman who works for Mama Zita at the Bamboo Cage?—told me much the same story. She said she knew Krissoula, and that she and her friend, Sofía, used to come down to the riverbanks to wash their clothes, but that she hasn't seen her in over a week. I love her, Sancho, and I'm afraid for her life! 'Tonio Malvado wants her for his woman, you see?"

He knew, Sancho having been raised on the streets, that there was no need to say anything more, nor to explain the baser facts of human nature to the boy. There was little this man-child hadn't seen in his ten short years. Boys and girls grew up quickly in the

439

barrios, as well he knew, having been raised here himself. They had no choice.

"Ah," Sancho said softly, nodding in understanding. He hated Malvado with a passion. "Then I'll see what I can do. I'll keep my eyes peeled and my ears pinned back, and tell all of the *niños* to do the same, all right, señor? If I hear anything, where can I find you?"

"I'm staying with the Severinos. You can send word to me there."

Sancho nodded. He'd go and see the woman, Krissoula Ballardo, and tell her that Señor Esteban was looking for her. If she wanted San Martín to find her, then surely he could break his promise to Cojo with a clear conscience . . . ?

Esteban felt a tugging at his sleeve, and looked down to see a little girl of about four or five years old gazing hopefully up at him. Her tiny hands were clasped primly in front of her over a pot belly—swollen with hunger, rather than puppy-fat. Her angelic little face was grubby beyond belief, yet her shoulder-length, curly black hair was glossy, despite its dirt and tangles. He smiled, his blue eyes twinkling. They'd met before!

"Ah. Señorita Bonita, is it not?" he said gravely, bowing in a formal way that made the little girl giggle shyly.

"Sí, señor," she murmured, bobbing her head in a sketchy curtsey.

"And what is it you want of me, señorita?" he asked, knowing very well what it was she wanted, but playing her delightful little game.

"Did you bring us *bombóns,* señor?" she asked, her dark eyes shining.

"Bonita, I told you you're not to ask for things!" Lourdes, Sancho's nine-year-old sister and self-appointed mother of the little ones, scolded sharply. "We are not beggars, after all! Tell Señor San Martín you're sorry for your rudeness!"

Bonita's lower lip trembled. A suspicion of a tear sparkled in her eyes. "I am very sorry, señor," she whispered.

Esteban's heart squeezed. He reached out and took a wispy tendril of her hair in his fingers, tugging it gently. "Don't apologize, Bonita. You see, I do believe you've done me a service, because I did bring candy—it's right here, in my pockets—but I'd forgotten it was there, until you reminded me. Perhaps Lourdes would let you help me find it?"

He looked inquringly up at Lourdes for permission, as did Bonita, both with a transparently eager expression.

"May I, Lourdes? Please?" she begged.

440

The older girl, scarcely more than a baby herself, had an infant of perhaps three or four months straddling her skinny hip, like a far older woman. Her fiercely proud expression softened, and for a moment, he was painfully reminded of Krissoula, and her indomitable pride. Anger filled him, that these children—the future of Argentina—should have had their own precious childhood taken away. Sancho and Lourdes should be playing with tops and lead soldiers and dolls, or climbing trees and tumbling with kittens and puppies, doing all the things that children love to do—not scratching out a living here in this filth, playing mother and father to little ones not much younger than themselves! Still, he had the chance to change things a little now, as he'd dreamed of doing for so long. With his uncle dead and his origins confirmed by Manuela's diary, Tierra Rosa would soon be his, her wealth at his disposal. Maybe he couldn't change the entire world, nor right the unfairness of life that left innocent children starving while men like Malvado grew fat and sleek on the spoils of evil, or men like Hernando Zamora plotted the overthrow of decent rulers who wanted to change the lot of the poor for something better, but he could make a beginning here, in the Ciudad de los Niños, and hopefully watch it grow from an acorn to a tree . . .

"Well, Lourdes?" he asked again, his own expression beseeching, and Lourdes smiled and gave a nod of assent, flattered that el señor had asked her permission.

With a squeal of delight, Bonita plunged a grimy little fist deep into the pockets he held open, drawing out peppermint sticks and lollipops, striped humbugs, cinnamon twists and gob-stoppers, licorice whips and bitter-lemon drops galore. Generous hearted, she handed out the spoils to the children, who suddenly crowded around, voices strident and fingers waggling for a share of the rare treats he'd brought them.

The others content, Bonita chose a bright red lollipop for herself, and Esteban lifted her up onto his lap to eat it. Cuddled in his arms, she sat there contentedly, quiet as a mouse. Her little pink tongue turned bright raspberry as the lollipop grew steadily smaller and smaller.

"Your eyes—they are so blue, señor!" she observed, looking up into them with a curious expression, and patting his face with her sticky little hand.

"And your tongue, it is so red, señorita!" he teased back, planting a smacking kiss on her cheek. She giggled and squirmed and hid her face in his chest.

441

"Will you stay for supper, Señor Esteban?" Lourdes offered shyly. The señor's visits were reason enough for a celebration in the *ciudad*. He nodded, and the children clapped their hands and screamed with delight.

"He's staying! El señor's staying!" they shrieked.

"I'd like that very much, Lourdes. No one makes chicken just the way you do. Thank you!"

Lourdes turned bright pink with pleasure, and was obviously flustered by his compliment.

"Oh, look, Bonita's fallen asleep in your lap, señor—and with her fingers all sticky, too! Let me take her from you before she makes your fine shirt dirty, *sí . . . ?*"

Esteban waved her away. "No, Lourdes, there's no need. She's not hurting a thing. Let her sleep, while you get your work done. You have your arms full with that *niño,* already!"

"Matteo? Oh, he's no trouble, no trouble at all! Sancho, have the boys build a big fire for me. Paco, fill my kettle with water. I have chickens to cook tonight!"

Flashing him a grateful, happy smile, Lourdes hurried away.

Corrientes Plaza was brightly lit by sconces that cast their flaring light over the flagstones in long puddles, Krissoula saw as she turned the corner.

There were people about even at this late hour, some drunk and reeling unsteadily, others heading for the taverns with a purposeful air and a thirsty look about them. It was as if, in this small pocket of Buenos Aires, the cholera held no power; as if the residents—all whores, pimps, saloon-keepers, madams, gamblers, or their patrons—had in ostrich-fashion decided to pretend the epidemic didn't exist, and therefore it had left them untouched!

The Bamboo Cage seemed to be doing brisk trade across the square, people coming and going, loud music drifting out on the sultry night air, along with occasional shrieks of laughter and bursts of bawdy song.

Krissoula drew a deep breath. Well, here she was. It had come down to this at long last, despite all her promises to herself. After two days of going hungry, of listening to Sofía moaning in her sleep, but remaining stoically cheerful and uncomplaining in her waking hours, bless her, desperation had forced her to choose, and Krissoula had made her decision at last.

No one would hire her, and if she had to work, she had no way left her by which to earn money but by stealing or selling herself. And, since selling herself—however distasteful—seemed by far the safer course, after what had happened to poor Cojo, she'd decided to do just that. She drew a deep sigh. It was now or never, and for Sofía's sake, it had better be now . . .

Setting her jaw, she stepped from the shadows and began walking along beneath the torchlight which spilled from the sconces fixed to the walls.

She tried to stroll in a way that would attract a mark's roving eyes, as she had long ago in Barcelona, with her head held jauntily and her hips swinging with a seductive jiggle that promised a man some lively bedsport, rather than betray the defeated, cornered way she was feeling. Oh, Lord, inside she trembled so, she feared she'd be sick all over her scuffed red slippers! She couldn't be doing this, she told herself, she couldn't possibly have sunk so low—but she was. She had. There was no turning back, not now. She had to be strong, and go through with it, for Sofía's sake, and for her own . . .

A man was coming in the opposite direction. She saw his eyes light up when he'd looked her over. She gulped. *Caray!* She could smell him even from here! The reek of garlic and onions, sweat and unwashed flesh commingled and rose in a stench from him, making her want to gag! *Not him, oh, God, not him,* she told herself, and steadfastly looked in the other direction, intending to walk on past him. But as she'd half-expected, seeing his eyes kindle, a meaty hand locked over her elbow, swinging her about.

"*Hola,* pretty one!" the man drawled with a drunken slur, leering down into her startled face. He was even uglier close up than from a distance, and smelled foul . . .

"Take your filthy hands off me!" she hissed, her golden eyes stark with revulsion.

"Hey, no need to be so unfriendly, is there? Give me a little kiss, *pequeña!*"

"Over my dead body!" she spat, and shoved hard against his chest with both palms.

In his drunken state, the man was in no condition to press his intentions on her. He lumbered backward and lay in the filthy gutters, grumbling loudly about women in general and Krissoula in particular, while she bolted.

It took her a good ten minutes to get herself under control again, and by the time she had, she'd decided on a different tack to take. Instead of letting a man choose her, she decided she would choose the man! Ducking into the shadows, she stood quite still and watched the men coming and going from the taverns, looking for one who did not repulse her to the point of nausea.

One she discarded as too fat. Another looked mean-tempered and liable to get rough with a woman. Still another appeared too old, another too dirty and unkempt, another too down-at-the-heels to pay her price, another too—another too—aiee, *Dios!* Who was she fooling? She just couldn't bring herself to do it, not like this! She clenched her fists within the folds of her skirts. She didn't *want* to do it! And that being the case, she'd never be able to pick a man in any way to her liking.

Oh, Esteban! She swallowed, fighting the prickling tears that burned behind her eyes. *Dios,* how her heart cried out for him. How her body clamored for the nearness and comfort of his in her misery and fear, while knowing it could never be again . . . But—perhaps if she chose someone who resembled him in some small way, and tried very hard to convince herself it was him, she could go through with it, she thought hopefully.

An hour later, she'd found the courage from somewhere to try again. A young man had exited the Bamboo Cage and was striding across the plaza in her direction. She knew at a glance that he wasn't really Esteban, but there was a self-assured arrogance to the way he walked that reminded her a little of him, and he was dark-haired and neatly dressed in a sailor's flat cap and navy-blue reefer jacket. Perhaps that fleeting resemblance would be enough? She bit down hard on her lip, worrying it, drawing blood.

Before she could change her mind, she stepped out of the shadows and began walking towards the fellow, her hips swaying jauntily, her head cocked invitingly to one side with a little half-smile playing about her lips. The sailor smiled back as she neared him, showing her a glimpse of white teeth, and slowed his rolling gait. She fluttered her lashes, and her heart skipped a beat. He was interested, all right. He'd stopped . . .

"A good evening to you, *caballero,*" she purred throatily, fighting down the urge to run like the wind and never look back. Fists planted on her hips, she swung her hips gently to and fro.

"Ah, and a good evening to you, too, *muchacha!*" he responded, his smile broadening. "Enjoying the evening air?" He winked broadly.

"But of course," she agreed prettily. "It's a beautiful night, no?" She wetted her lips with the very tip of her tongue, so that they glistened with moisture in the torchlight. "And you, señor? Are you also enjoying the air?"

He chuckled, his brown eyes hungry. "I can think of something better to enjoy than the air, *chiquita*—you! Tell me, pretty one, are your favors for sale?"

"To such a handsome *caballero,* but of course!" she said brightly, wanting instead to cry as the heat of shame filled her cheeks. "Do you have a room somewhere, perhaps, where we could be comfortable—?"

"A room? That's rich! Who needs a room, *chiquita?* I only want to tumble you, not marry you—!" he scoffed crudely, and her illusions that he was Esteban vanished like pricked bubbles. He curled his arm so tightly about her waist, she couldn't squirm free, and plastered her up against him. "This alley's good enough for what we want, no, sweetie?"

"I—I suppose so," she whispered, her thoughts chaotic.

Moments later, they were in the depths of a stinking ink-black alley. The stranger stood before her, one hand planted on either side of the wall at her back so that she couldn't escape. She was close to fainting from sheer panic—!

"Well?" he rasped thickly. "Surely you're not shy, a girl like you! What are you waiting for? Lift your skirts, and let's have at you, wench!"

In the darkness, she sensed him busily unfastening his breeches to free his member.

She fought down a sob of terror and managed to speak, saying flatly, "The money first, señor." Perhaps she could snatch it from him and run?

"You take Rodriguez for a fool?" he jeered as if he'd read her mind. "No, *chiquita!* I'll have you first, and if you're lively and please me, why, then I'll pay you . . ."

She tried to protest, to demand that he pay her first, but his fingers locked around her chin, holding her fast. His mouth ground wetly down over hers, brutally stifling her cries. His other large hand swooped down the front of her *camisa,* tearing the strings that laced the bodice before he encountered her breast. He fondled her roughly, tugging on her flesh and tweaking cruelly at her nipple in a way that filled her eyes with tears of pain.

"Ah, that's what I like, wench! Nice, firm little *tetas,"* he growled thickly as he tore his mouth from hers and smothered her throat with wet kisses and painful bites that made her wince with pain. "Are you as nice all over I wonder, mmm? You smell clean enough, at least."

In the darkness, his hands moving over her body felt like something out of a nightmare, as if some awful monster, unseen, unknown, pawed and ravished her at will. His knee jammed up against her thighs and roughly pried her clamped knees apart. Pressed back against the hard wall, the man's lower body grinding against her hips with his lust, her spine throbbed with pain and she could hardly keep her balance! With mounting horror, she felt him grab at her hems and roughly shove her skirts up clear to her waist. He fumbled beneath them, fighting her fingers as she tried desperately to tug down her skirts. He won, and with a groan of triumph he pulled aside her undergarments. His rough fingers plundered the warm, bare flesh between her thighs.

Oh, God, how could she have been so wrong about him? He wasn't like Esteban. He was nothing at all like him! He was crude and hateful, and no matter how much she tried, she couldn't convince herself that this—this crude, rutting animal was the man she loved and desired! No matter what it cost her, or Sofia, she couldn't sell her body to him, not at any price! She had to get away—had to—!

"Please, señor, no! I've changed my mind!" she panted, struggling to extricate herself from his grip.

"The devil you have, *china!*" he rasped, his breathing thick with lust. "Once ole Rodriguez is good and hard inside you, poking away, you'll sing a different song, I promise you, sweetie! Now, lean back now, there's a good girl, and spread those thighs a little wider for me, eh—? Damn but it's cursed awkward, standing like this, but—well, there's the fun, eh?"

She felt the hard, hot ridge of his manhood prodding against her belly, seeking entry. Felt his rough fingers poking and probing to bring her soft female core against that hardness, and the last shred of her resolve snapped clean in two.

"I said no, damn you!" she spat, and brought up her knee as hard as she could, slamming it into his engorged groin. In the same instant, she shoved him hard, and with his breeches unfastened and dropped about his knees, he lost his balance and went flying backward with a groan of pure agony.

"I'm—I'm poxed!" she lied. "I—I can't!"

With that, she whirled around and stumbled her way out of the pitch-dark alley, blubbering like a babe in arms until she'd found her way through the terrifying, absolute blackness, and back to the brightly lit plaza, where she retched violently in the gutter before racing away, as fast as her legs would carry her.

Once again in the familiar territory of Barrio San Timéo, she fled as if the hounds of hell snapped at her heels, not halting until she saw the squat silhouette of the church of San Timéo on the corner just ahead of her. With a sob of relief, she flung herself up the steps, opened the door, and almost tumbled inside, a fugitive desperately seeking sanctuary.

After a few moments, she'd cried herself out and her composure had improved a little. Yet, still trembling, she made her way between the hushed pews to the altar, where tall white candles burned as comfortingly as they had on the night she and Cojo and Sofía had taken refuge within these same walls; as brightly as the night when she'd danced for the dying boy . . .

Kneeling at the altar rail, she clasped her hands together and prayed. She implored God and the Blessed Virgin, and Saint Sara—the saint unrecognized by the Catholic Church, but nonetheless best loved by the Gypsies (for she was reputed to have been a Gypsy herself)—to give guidance and help to her and Sofía.

"*Sí,* there was sin in my heart tonight, Heavenly Father, but I couldn't help it. I was desperate!" she explained a little defiantly, her voice low and husky with unshed tears, echoing a little on the hush with the vaulted ceiling. "I didn't know where to turn for help, or what else I could do to get some money, and so—*sí,* I tried to sell myself. It was wicked of me, I know, but I need money for food, Madonna, or we'll starve! Please God, help me, show me what to do? Give me some sign that will show Your Will in this, I beg you! And if—and if it is Your Will that we should starve, then give me the grace and humility and strength to accept it?"

Still kneeling, she waited, hoping against hope for some tangible response, some outward sign that her prayer had been heard, a sudden lightning bolt streaking down out of the clear night sky, perhaps, or a rainbow arching in the dark of night. But there was no such miracle. There was only the gloomy comfort of the ancient church, the pungent scents of hot wax and musty old pews and wilted flowers, nothing more. Her faith—tenuous at the best of times—wavered, and came perilously close to being snuffed out and replaced with anger. Sofía was good and kind, a decent woman! How could God stand by and let her die, even if she was too wicked herself to bother about saving? But then—hadn't He allowed Cojo to die without lifting a finger to save him?

She got stiffly to her feet and started back down the aisle the way she'd come in, heading towards the same door through which she'd entered. She was mindful as she did so that she dare not leave poor

Sofía alone for too much longer. Although the worst of her illness was behind her, she was still weak, and far from well. Certainly not strong enough to defend herself, should the need arise.

As she reached for the wrought-iron ring of the door and opened it, a shaft of silvery-gray moonlight fell at her feet, illuminating a scattering of yellow rose petals on the weathered stone floor.

A coincidence, she thought, her heartbeat quickening as she crouched down to pick them up? The residue of some joyful wedding celebrated earlier that day—or the sign she'd asked God to give her? If so, His indications seemed clear. El Señor obviously intended that she should enlist Don Antonio Malvado's help. And if, in the process, it should happen that Cojo's death was somehow avenged, his murderer brought to account, then that must also be the will of God, must it not—?

She shrugged fatalistically and hardened her jaw. The meaning of the rose petals was clear. The outcome, whether it was success or failure, was in El Señor's hands, now . . .

Chapter Thirty-Eight

Sancho, his head down, his hands thrust deep into his pockets, started eagerly down the street towards the rooming house on the corner of Calle Rios, where he knew he'd find the señorita and her friend, as he had the night Cojo had been attacked and killed.

He'd be glad when he had told Krissoula that the señor was looking for her, and got it over with, he thought. After the many kindnesses Don Esteban had shown him and the *niños,* lying to him—or rather, lying by omission—didn't sit well on Sancho's conscience! And besides, Sancho had a hunch that Don Esteban de San Martín—although a wonderful friend—would make an *equally* deadly enemy. There was something lethal in his deep-blue eyes that threatened hell to pay if he were crossed, or caught someone he trusted—someone he'd hitherto considered a friend— lying to him. Sancho shuddered. The sooner he got this over with, the better off he'd be, and the better he'd feel!

He ducked into a doorway as he neared the crumbling old adobe house, for there were a number of people outside it, as well as a horse-drawn cart and an elegant, covered carriage drawn up to the front entrance.

Eyes narrowed against the brilliant sunlight, Sancho risked a hasty glance around the doorway, and his dark eyes widened in shock; his heart skipped a beat. The people were none other than Malvado and his goons! They'd gotten here before him! Even from a distance, he could make out Malvado's beefy "lieutenants," the ones known on the streets as José "Toothpick" Comadreja, and Juan "The Nose" La Rata—and they were carrying someone, lifting someone into the cart! Sancho gulped. A body? *Aiee, Dios mío,* no! Not the lovely señorita—?

But then, he saw the young woman, Krissoula, come flying out of the house and scream at the ham-fisted men, and he sighed with relief.

"Careful with Doña Sofía, you stupid, muscle-bound fools! She's a sick woman—not a sack of cornmeal to be hefted about, *comprende?* Lift her gently, *hombres,* gently! If you harm so much as a single hair on her head, the deal between your *jefe* and me is off—understand, Don Antonio?" she hissed.

"Perfectly, *mi corazón,*" Malvado purred stroking her arm possessively, and although the señorita flinched and her golden eyes flashed—Sancho could see that even from his hiding place—she made no attempt to dash his hand away. "Careful with the old hen, boys," the godfather ordered amicably. "I don't want my pretty little *bombón* upset, not on any account, you hear me, *muchachos?*"

With a chuckle, Antonio slipped his arm about Krissoula's waist and walked her to the carriage, handing her up inside it. Krissoula gave one last, anguished look up and down the street, and then ducked into the vehicle, settling herself on the shiny black leather seat with such vehemence, the carriage rocked violently. Malvado followed her inside. Moments later, both vehicles drew away, and the dusty street was deserted once more.

Sancho let out the breath he'd been holding and stepped out of the doorway, into the sunlight. He picked up a pebble, and flung it irritably at the wall. It pinged away and landed once again in the dirt. A fierce scowl screwed up his features. He'd come too late, so what should he do now? He was furious with himself for not coming here last night, instead of waiting till morning!

On his deathbed, Cojo had asked him to warn Señorita Ballardo that Malvado meant to make her his woman at any cost, but now she appeared to have gone with the *compadrito* willingly! Had she really—or had that last look of panic she'd cast up and down the street been a final, desperate plea for help?

He chewed on his lower lip for a few seconds, before coming to the conclusion that his gut instincts were sound. Although Malvado hadn't employed any force—or at least, none that Sancho had witnessed—the lovely señorita hadn't truly wanted to go with him, judging by her expression. He'd follow the carriage, find out where Malvado had taken the woman, and then find Don Esteban and tell him everything he'd seen. He'd let him decide what should be done!

Sancho took off down the street at a run.

Malvado's carriage swept through the open gates of his villa on

Calle Pajaro, and two of his men jumped down from the vehicle to close the heavy doors in its wake.

It's like a cursed jail! Krissoula thought gloomily, sitting tense and silent beside the godfather, her hands clasped tightly together in her lap.

Despite the defiant air she'd worn earlier, inside her belly churned with foreboding as the heavy gates closed behind the carriage, like a trap closing in. Aiee, *Dios,* was she crazy, or merely stupid, eh? She'd willingly placed herself at the disposal of a man who could coolly order an innocent, crippled boy killed, just to be rid of him! And as for poor Sofía—well, her poor friend would soon be in the hands of strangers at the Bamboo Cage, where Krissoula had asked Malvado to take her.

The *compadrito*—afraid of catching the contagious wasting sickness to which Sofía had fallen victim—had staunchly refused to allow the recovering woman to accompany Krissoula to his villa.

"Time enough to have your serving woman join you when she has fully recovered her health, *mi amor,"* he'd said. "I will, however, see her taken anywhere else your little heart desires to be cared for, and have my men leave her caretakers with enough money to see that she lacks for nothing. Do you have someplace in mind?"

Consuela! The mulatto washerwoman's kindness and friendliness towards them had come to mind then—as had her offers of work. So had Mama Zita's fearful reputation for independence, and her refusal to knuckle under to any of the *compadritos* popped into her thoughts.

Accordingly, Krissoula had casually asked Malvado to see Sofía taken to the Bamboo Cage and given into the care of Consuela there. At least she could be reasonably sure Sofía would be safe there, under Mama Zita's watchful eyes, so that even if—God forbid!—she was thwarted in her plan to revenge Cojo's murder, and ended up floating facedown in the waters of the Plata herself, Malvado would not find it too easy to take out his fury on her friend; not if she was in the formidable madam's care!

Biting back a curse, she blinked away angry tears and steadfastly stared out of the carriage window as the vehicle lurched to a halt before several shallow stairs.

Despite the shabby, run-down walls that enclosed it from prying eyes, Malvado's villa was something to see! Built of whitewashed adobe, the upper windows were shaded with gay red-and-white-striped awnings. Below them, built directly into the walls, were ornate stucco window boxes jutting out from the walls like portly

451

bellies. From them trailed brilliant red geraniums. An arched *corredor,* tiled with dark-red tiles, encircled the villa's lower story, with many enormous polished wooden doors opening off it. Every few feet along the *corredor,* an earthenware pot had been placed, from which a vine or a plant splashed attractive greenery, or a trellis rose, heavy with scented, waxy-white bugles, alternating with mossy little statues of naked cherubs in various lewd poses. The lower windows, heavily shaded by the *corredor,* were arched and grilled with black bars of twisted wrought iron, probably as a protection against forced entry. Seeing this, Krissoula grimaced. Did that master of thieves, Malvado, so fear his own kind, then? she thought wryly.

Malvado caught her expression and mistook it for one of surprise.

"Ah, you see, you never dreamed that Antonio would have such a palace for his queen, eh?" he crowed.

She shot him a contemptuous look. "On the contrary, Don Antonio, I anticipated no less of you," she said silkily, adding, "A gaudy palace for a gaudy popinjay, no? It is only fitting!"

Antonio paled with anger under his olive complexion, and his long, narrow features hardened. He took her by the wrist and gripped it so cruelly, she winced.

"You would do well to remember your manners, my little flower," he ground out, thrusting his face into hers so that his hot breath, reeking of garlic and Parma violets, fanned her cheek. "As long as you are my guest here, and the other woman dependent upon my good will, it would be wise to keep a civil tongue in your head, understand?" He smiled. "After all, my little yellow rosebud, *you* came begging to *me* for help, remember?"

"*Sí,* I remember," Krissoula acknowledged grudgingly but in a softer tone, and to her relief, Antonio released her throbbing wrist.

"That's better," the *compadrito* murmured, pleased that he'd been able to bring her to heel with so little effort. Her earlier defiant expression had tarnished his satisfaction that she'd finally sent for him that very morning, and meekly asked that he take her in on whatever terms he chose.

"So long as you behave, you will want for nothing. Fine food, clothes—even expensive trinkets, perhaps—will all be yours, as my woman. But cross me, defy me, and—well, I don't need to tell you how very dangerous that could be, do I, darling?" He smiled. "Nor how very angry it would make me! You're a clever girl. You can figure it out, no?"

So saying, he sprang easily down from the carriage and reached inside to lift her after him. His hands spanning her slender waist, he set her on the ground before him. He didn't release her at once but held her there, clasped to his body. His eyes were hungry as they took in her startled, lovely face.

"Ah, how I've burned for you, Krissoula," he whispered hoarsely. Giving in to the urge that had ridden him from the moment he'd first set eyes on her, he twisted a hand through her glorious black hair, jerked her head around to meet his, and ground his mouth down over her lovely, lush mouth in a wet and brutal kiss.

He was breathless when he released her, 'and his black eyes simmered with lust; his groin ached. But apart from an angry, swollen look to her mouth, Krissoula seemed totally unmoved by his passionate advances; cold and haughty, with her chin held high. He chuckled. What a woman she was, so defiant, so spirited! He could scarcely wait to try her; to see if her nature was as passionate and fiery in his bed, as it was out of it.

"No kiss for me in return, my icy Krissoula? No fire for the man who's saved you from starvation? Ah, but that will come, little flower, given time! I will teach you how to please me, and very soon you'll burn for me just as I've burned for you."

He chucked her beneath the chin like an indulgent uncle, that suave pig, that oily swine, and with only the greatest effort, Krissoula managed to stand there mutely and let him. She swallowed the furious torrent of curses and insults she longed to hurl in his sly, narrow face. She curled the fingers which ached to rake his cheeks like talons into harmless fists within her skirts. *Easy, Krissoula,* she warned herself. *Don't get carried away, not yet! Don't let him force your hand, or suspect why you really came here. There's plenty of time to get mad, and to get even . . .*

"Toothpick!" Malvado bellowed.

"*Sí,* Don Antonio?" José responded at once. He came running at the sound of his master's voice like an obedient dog, panting and breathless.

"Show Doña Krissoula to her room, and see that she's made comfortable!"

"At once, *jefe!* At once!"

"I think you'll be quite cosy in the accommodations I've chosen for you," Antonio assured her. "Your rooms adjoin my own, you see—discreet but convenient, no? I expect you'll want to rest for the remainder of the day—perhaps the rest of the week, too, since I've

453

pressing business to attend to—so I'll look forward to you joining me for dinner the first time on Saturday evening, yes? I have a small celebration planned for that night, you see, in honor of a new—business venture of mine, shall we say? I can think of nothing that would impress my future partner more than the sight of a beautiful woman like you on my arm, and believe me, dear one, this friend of mine is a man with a future in Argentina—one it would be well to impress. I should like very much for you to do whatever he wishes to please him—you understand what I'm saying, Krissoula?"

"In these rags, I doubt I could impress a beggar, señor," Krissoula murmured distastefully, pretending ignorance although she understood only too well what he was implying! It would please Malvado if she should agree to play the whore for his new partner, should the need arise! Gritting her teeth, she added, "And the yellow gown I wore to dance is ruined beyond hope."

"Ah, such little matters have already been taken into consideration, and will be taken care of in good time, rest assured, Krissoula! The mistress of Antonio Malvado will lack for nothing. Gowns, jewels, furs, perfumes, you'll have them all, *if* you please me. You'll be the envy of every woman in Buenos Aires! I'll have gowns brought for your selection from Maximilio's salon first thing in the morning! Perhaps I'll even allow you to dance that evening for my important guests, eh, *mi corazón?* A little flamenco from the old country to stir the passions, fine wines and good food, will go far towards oiling the wheels of commerce between us, no?"

"Whatever you say, señor," she said dully.

"I'm glad to find you so amenable, my dear. "But—just in case you should later decide my hospitality is not completely to your liking—I've appointed one of my most loyal men to—shall we say?—act as your bodyguard. Señorita Ballardo, I'd like you to meet my old friend, Bobo. He's a little short, as you can see, but what he lacks in height, he more than makes up for in terms of loyalty to me. Bobo, go along with José and your new mistress, and see that she comes to no harm, eh?"

Krissoula's head came up sharply at Malvado's mention of the hated name she recognized so very well.

A monstrous, dwarfed figure lumbered out from the shadow of the *corredor.* It was almost as wide as it was tall, with arms as long as an ape's, and a bald, square head that was greasy with sweat. Bobo's fleshy lips peeled back from his yellowed teeth in a smile as they faced each other.

"Buenos días, señorita!" Bobo lisped. "Welcome to Villa Malvado!"

454

Golden eyes blazing with hatred, Krissoula looked into the cold, emotionless eyes of Cojo's murderer, and bile scalded her throat.

"*Buenos días,* Señor Bobo," she said softly, smiling down at him, and suddenly, she was the old Krissoula once again; the crafty Gypsy girl and thief, Krissoula the *gitana,* who'd been fearless and cunning, and unafraid of the consequences as she boldly chose her "marks" on the streets of Barcelona, and sidled up to them with a lazy, tempting smile. "I can tell that you and I are going to be great friends, no, little Bobo?" she purred silkily, extending her slender hand to the dwarf. He took it almost reverently in his own small, pudgy paw.

She almost laughed aloud at the bewildered delight on Bobo's ugly face as he stood on tiptoe to kiss her hand. Dwarf or no, the hateful little toad was still a man, and one smitten by Cupid's dart, if ever she'd seen one! She could see it in his adoring, piggy little eyes, which came alive as he ogled her. Well, she'd use that infatuation to good purpose, fan it and encourage it for all it was worth in the coming days, she thought bitterly, curse his murdering soul. And, hopefully, one day use it against him!

He'll pay, Cojo, my friend! she vowed silently. *Never fear, he and Malvado will* both *pay for what they did to you! Krissoula will see that they do!* she swore.

In an upstairs room at the Bamboo Cage, Esteban stood looking down at a wan-faced Sofía with a stern expression.

"I swear to you, Doña Sofía, that I mean Krissoula no harm, whatever she's told you!" he repeated. "The threats I made that night were the empty threats of a man driven crazy by pain. By one who believed himself double-crossed by the woman he loved. I *must* find her, Sofía, before she comes to some harm. Damn it, woman, tell me where she is!"

"I believe you, Don Esteban," Sofía protested weakly, frightened by his angry expression, "and I swear I would tell you—*if* I knew! But Malvado's men took me one way in a cart, and the señorita and he left by carriage in another! I don't know where she is, I tell you, my *pobrecito!*"

"Ah, but I know, señor!" piped a young voice from the doorway, and both Consuela and Mama Zita and Esteban turned in the direction of the voice.

"Sancho! What the devil are you doing here?" Esteban exclaimed.

"That pretty little piece, Dolores, was downstairs. She has a soft spot for me—well, you know how it is with women, eh, señor?" The boy rolled his eyes expressively. "I told the little *bombón* I was looking for you, and she let me in, just like that!" Sancho boasted, snapping his fingers and swaggering a little.

Esteban grinned and nodded. *"Sí,* I know all about your wiles with the ladies! But—about Señorita Krissoula? Do you really know where Malvado's taken her?"

Sancho nodded gravely. *"Sí, señor,* I do! She's at his villa on Calle Pajaro. She's been there for the past three days, ever since they brought the other woman here," he added, nodding towards Sofía, who was almost buried amongst the snowy sheets Consuela had tucked about her. "I've had some of my boys watching the place while I tried to track you down, señor, and they tell me there's something going on there—all kinds of comings and goings!—but that the señorita hasn't set foot outside the walls since the moment she arrived." He grimaced. "It's taken me three days to find you, Don Esteban! *Por Dios,* you're not an easy man to pin down, señor!"

"Ah, but being elusive's only good common sense, knowing how Malvado feels about me, eh, *chico?"* Esteban said with a wink. "The *compadrito* and I are old enemies, remember? It was I that left him with that pretty necklace of scars about his throat, in repayment for the attack he ordered on Rolón Severino all those years ago, which cost Papa Rolón an eye. Malvado's never forgiven me for that! If he knew I was back in the *barrios,* he'd do whatever he had to do to see me floating in the Plata some fine morning, with a knife in my back! A moving target is far harder to hit than a still one, no? So, I keep moving!"

"Ah, I see what you mean, señor!" Sancho agreed admiringly, and grinned.

"That something that's been going on over at Malvado's place—I think I know what it is, sweetie," Mama Zita, who'd been silent until now, divulged to Esteban. "That slime is planning a celebration of some sort—and on a large scale, too! He sent one of his boys over here on Tuesday to tell me he needed the best of my girls and some dancers to entertain his guests at an *asado* Saturday night. Money was no object, he said, so I agreed, naturally."

Mama Zita chuckled, and her huge breasts and belly jiggled alarmingly under the voluminous folds of her purple and green gown.

"Ah, did he now?" Esteban echoed thoughtfully, and there was a hint of excitement glittering in his sapphire eyes now. "Tell me all about Master Malvado's plans, would you, Zita, my plump little dove?"

Zita giggled girlishly. "Are you thinkin' what I'm thinkin', *gallito?*" she asked in her smoky voice.

Esteban nodded slowly. "Oh, I wouldn't be a bit surprised, Zita. No, not a bit!"

Surprisingly, Malvado was true to his word, and didn't bother Krissoula in the days following her arrival at his villa. After two stifling days pacing four walls, she almost wished he *would* bother her, for, like a prisoner, she rarely left the fancy room he'd chosen for her, except to use the outhouse in the courtyard, or for a rare meal taken downstairs in the dining room alone, with José and Bobo hovering attendance.

A selection of designer gowns arrived from Maximilio's salon exactly as he'd promised the morning after her arrival, along with a terrified little woman who proved to be the designer's fitter: as did several jewelry cases lined with black velvet from a prestigious jeweler's on the Calle Florida, a well-known and expensive shopping district in the wealthy heart of beautiful Buenos Aires.

Under normal circumstances, Krissoula would have relished the opportunity to pick and choose from amongst such expensive baubles, as would any woman. But, knowing the price Malvado expected her to pay for such trinkets, she could find little pleasure in selecting them. However, she forced herself to choose several gowns, and then stood impatiently on a low stool while the fitter pinned and tucked the garments preparatory to making the necessary alterations. Then she chose necklaces and earrings, bracelets and jeweled hair clasps to accompany her selection, before, with a bored yawn and ill-concealed impatience to be done, she waved the jeweler away. The emeralds would look well enough with the apple-green taffeta. The topazes would complement the gold and bronze of the silk. She chose the cold fire of diamonds for the white gown—she had a special reason for selecting *that* one! she thought with a hard, secretive little smile—and rubies for the wine-red.

Her choices made, she allowed the woman to select a few blouses and skirts and a day dress or two, along with the underthings, stockings, and slippers to accompany all of her selections, and then dismissed both the jeweler and the fitter with a muttered curse, flinging herself across the bed to think the moment she was alone again.

The way she saw it, she had only until Saturday to do what she'd

457

come here to do: to revenge Cojo's murder on both Malvado and Bobo. After Saturday and his guests' departure, Antonio would waste little time in making her his mistress, and she'd sooner plunge a knife into her own breast than give herself to that murdering slime! What she needed now was a plan—and a good one, at that . . .

"Kiss you?" she jeered, contempt curling her lip. "You're a bigger fool than I thought, Bobo—a powerful ape, all right, but a fool nonetheless, if you think I'd give you the time of day, let alone kiss you!"

Fists on hips, she flung her mane of black tresses over her shoulders and laughed at the dwarf.

It wasn't Bobo's size that revolted her, not at all. She'd met and considered her friends many little people like him—both men and women—who'd worked in the carnivals, fairs, and circuses her uncle had traveled with while journeying all over Europe with the Rom. She'd always found them to be delightful people, good natured and generous and perfectly normal except for their short stature. Bobo, however, was a law unto himself! His short stature had embittered him, she felt, and made him hate and resent with a passion anyone of normal height; that bitterness, coupled with an intelligence falling somewhere between simpleton and complete idiot, had created a monster with little intellect who delighted only in using his strength to kill, and who took a malevolent joy in generating fear.

"Say what you want, witch!" the dwarf continued. "But you'll be mine when Don Antonio's bored with you, like it or not, you'll see. He pwomised me!" Bobo lisped, giving Krissoula a sly, gleeful, excited look that made her flesh crawl as if it were his pudgy paws traveling over her body, rather than his piggy black eyes. "You won't talk so mean to me then, because you'll be mine, and I won't let you. You'll kiss me, too—any time I want you to!" he boasted.

"You won't have that chance, you ugly, stupid little toad!" Krissoula spat, golden eyes flashing dangerously. "I'd kill myself before I kissed you, or let you kiss me! Besides, your precious Malvado's all talk. He only says he'll give me to you. Behind your back, he laughs at you—makes fun of you and calls you small and stupid! He says he'll never let a monkey like you have me! Can't you see, Bobo? The things he promises you—they're just his way of making you do what he wants, *estúpido!*"

"You're lying!" Bobo, his expression crestfallen, flared up, his massive fists balled at his sides.

"No I'm not. I heard him! Are you such a simpleton you can't see that he uses you, just as he uses everyone about him? When you've served your purpose, he'll have one of his men kill you. Maybe it'll come as a knife in your back, or a pistol ball between the eyes, who knows? But some fine morning we'll all hear that poor Señor Bobo has been found floating in the Plata and you'll be history, slug!"

The dwarf wetted his fleshy lips on his tongue, his simple mind obviously disturbed by the prospect she'd suggested. "We'll see about that!" Bobo, obviously nettled, cried truculently. "Oh, we'll see about that, you stupid Gypsy!"

So saying, he started to lumber away, and Krissoula panicked. It was too soon!

"Go ahead," she urged softly after his retreating back, "tell the don what I've told you! Force his hand! Spill your guts, Bobo! Of course, Malvado will deny everything. He'll swear it isn't so, insist that you're his number-one man and that nothing can change that. But maybe—just maybe—everything I've said is true? If it is, he just might decide to get rid of you right away if you start stirring things up, and find someone else to keep an eye on me . . ."

Bobo halted, a stupefied, perplexed expression on his face as he swung about to face her. Obviously, she'd confused him thoroughly now, as she'd been hoping to do. She'd been working on him for the past three days now, alternately flirting with him and then scorning and belittling him until Bobo didn't know what to do, or who to believe, or which way to turn. She'd planted the seed of doubt about Malvado in his simple, bestial mind, and in such empty soil, watered by a deeply ingrained insecurity, the suggestion had straightway taken root. Bobo didn't know whether to consider the *compadrito* his friend or his enemy anymore: didn't know whether Krissoula liked him and wanted to be his friend, or loathed him with a passion—which was exactly what she'd hoped to bring about!

"My poor, poor little Bobo," she purred softly, and walking across to him she steeled herself and lightly pinched his fleshy jowl. "You just can't trust anyone anymore, can you, you poor little man? Ah, well, that's life! You do what you want, eh? As for me, I'm going back to my room now, to get ready for the fiesta. Maybe I'll even let you watch me get dressed, if you're a good little toad . . . How would you like that, mmm? Coming?"

With a low, seductive laugh, she sidled away, her hips swinging under her full skirts, her bare shoulders gleaming like satin in the sunlight that also struck blue highlights in her shining mane of curls.

With a confused grunt, besotted Bobo lumbered heavily after her, simian arms swinging, short legs churning—and a foolishly eager smile on his face.

Upstairs once again, Krissoula drew the gown she'd selected for the *asado* from the massive armoire. The gown she'd chosen to wear for that Saturday evening was the one of white satin. An appropriate choice, she'd decided, for, unknown to Malvado, white was the Gypsy color of mourning, and *Dios*, she felt far more like mourning than celebrating! Wearing it would be her own, secret show of defiance!

She ordered Bobo to summon serving girls with kettles of hot water, and after they'd done so, promptly dismissed him, slamming the door so forcefully in his disappointed face that she almost broke his nose!

There was no key or bolt with which to lock the door against him, and so she propped heavy chairs beneath the outer door by which he waited, and also under the doorknob to Malvado's suite. Certain she would not be interrupted, she proceeded to take a long and leisurely bath in the enameled tub, soaking up the steaming, perfumed water. After all, why should she hurry herself? She was in no haste to play the hostess for Malvado and his cronies! She'd enjoy a long, lengthy soak in warm, scented water for the first time since she'd run away from Tierra Rosa. And Malvado, curse him, could go hang!

As she lathered the sponge and washed herself, she considered all the activity that had been going on since daybreak. Trestle tables had been set up in the courtyard—several of them, indicating Malvado was expecting far more than a handful of guests to join him tonight. Not one, but two carcasses of beef had been speared on the *asadors* and were even now roasting over the charcoal pit, along with several brace of lambs. The succulent aroma was everywhere! Many cases of wine and kegs of beer were stacked in one corner of the courtyard in readiness, and other delicious odors had been wafting from the kitchens all day, aromas so delicious, her belly had growled in anticipation, and her mouth had watered continually.

Then, an hour or so ago, shortly after *siesta,* a carriage had pulled up before the front doors of the villa. By drawing aside the lace draperies that curtained her window, Krissoula had seen at least eight giggling, squealing women tumble from it, all gaudily dressed with plumes and sequins in their hair, their bright, revealing gowns ablaze with paste jewels and glass beads. *Whores!* She'd recognized their type instinctively, and her brows had risen in surprise. Well,

well! That slimy Malvado had obviously spared no cost or thought for his guests' entertainment, if he meant to provide them with women for their pleasure, as well as food and wines! She also glimpsed the couple who'd danced the wicked tango that time she'd gone to the Bamboo Cage, the woman in the emerald gown accompanied by the tall, lean man who'd partnered her.

What the devil could Malvado be up to, she wondered idly? Was he planning a grand hoist on El Banco de Buenos Aires, and hoping to woo his unnamed guests into partnering him? On burglarizing the Casa Rosada itself, and stealing *el presidente*'s silver plate? She grinned. Whatever dirty mischief he had up his sleeve, it promised to be on a grand scale, what with all the trouble he'd gone to—and that would make his ultimate come-down at her hands all the sweeter!

She sighed as she leaned back in the warm water, and squeezing the sponge over her shoulders, she closed her eyes. Unbidden, Esteban's handsome face filled her mind, yet, to her dismay, she couldn't picture him nearly as clearly or as sharply as she once had, and her heart ached with misery.

Time, that great healer, was attempting to soothe her hurt by making her memories of him less easily recalled—but her stupidity was not so easily forgotten nor forgiven. How different her life might have been, if only she'd controlled her hot temper that last time they'd argued, and stayed and heard him out instead of running off so childishly! After all, Esteban had been right, she could admit that to herself now, for all the good it did her. She'd done precious little to prove herself trustworthy to him, so could she really blame him for questioning her motives, when her actions had suggested she still meant to double-cross him? No, not really!

But, instead of calming down and listening to what he had to say like a mature, grown woman should have, or instead of explaining all over again about Manuela's diary and how she'd honestly believed it of little importance, her wicked tongue had run away with her; her stupid pride had overruled all common sense. With heavy sarcasm, she'd threatened to betray him to Don Felipe, so that when Felipe had ordered Esteban brutally whipped, it had seemed as if she'd done what she'd threatened to do!

What normal man wouldn't have believed her guilty, under the circumstances? No, she had no one to blame but herself for the situation she was in now, and no one but her stupid, prideful, hot-tempered self to blame for its outcome. Nor anyone but herself to blame, ultimately, for Cojo's senseless death! If she hadn't fled

Tierra Rosa, she'd never have been forced to dance for her living at the Cádiz Tavern; Malvado would never have seen her and wanted to make her his woman; Cojo would never have fallen for her, and tried to protect her—he'd still be here, alive and well. No, nothing in life happened by chance. Everything had a cause and an effect, and she'd been the cause of Cojo's death—just as she would be the cause of Malvado's and Bobo's!

Stepping from the enamel slipper-shaped tub, she padded—barefoot and dripping water—to a dresser, and pulled out a drawer. From beneath the little pile of shabby garments she'd brought with her to Malvado's villa, she withdrew a small, sharp knife. It was Cojo's knife, and had been found by Sancho the night of his death, buried in the mud beneath her friend's poor, broken body. It was only fitting that Cojo's own knife should be the instrument of her revenge—!

White had never been her best color before, but that night, when she'd finished dressing and turned to consider her reflection in the cheval looking glass, she was well satisified with the effect she'd created.

Her skin—still fair since those months spent in Barcelona out of the sun at Esteban's orders—was the color of creamy beige satin, with the faintest tinge of rouge at the lips and cheekbones to give her a little color. Against the gleaming white of the gown, the subtle contrasts of color—inky hair, rosy cheeks, pale beige complexion—was lovely. Her eyes, slanted and fringed with sooty lashes, needed no help from her paintbox; her excitement gave them all the sparkle she could wish for! She'd brushed her hair until it crackled, and had then swept it up into a tight knot at the crown and fastened it with a diamond hair clasp, from which wanton ringlets tumbled flamboyantly down over her shoulders, and wispy tendrils framed her face. Diamonds winked at her throat and earlobes, too, and drew the eyes to the deeply plunging neckline of the gown, and the thrust of her hard young breasts. Her shoulders were bare, the sleeves of the gown full, filmy puffs that hid her upper arms almost to the elbows, and the skirts were very full, emphasizing her slender waist. She'd do, she decided with a last critical glance. *Sí*, she'd do very well!

"Enjoy, Malvado!" she hissed under her breath, "for if all goes well tonight, the last thing you'll see on this earth is little Krissoula Ballardo in her mourning gown!"

And with that grim promise, she raised the hem of her skirts and tucked Cojo's little knife into the lacy garter at her knee.

Chapter Thirty-Nine

Night had fallen over the *barrios* like a purple cloak long before the first of Malvado's mysterious guests arrived. They came slipping through the gates in groups of two, or three, or four, like shadows, handing their horses into the care of the *compadrito*'s henchmen, who led them away.

The moon rose way above like a golden grapefruit hanging in some lofty bough, surrounded by starry pinpoints of light that looked like fireflies. Far below, in Villa Malvado, torches had been lit on every side of the courtyard, and their flames hissed and writhed in a sultry little breeze, scented heavily with flowers and spices, that did little to cool the steamy night air.

Fanning herself with a spray of fluffy ostrich plumes, Krissoula watched the furtive arrival of Malvado's guests with mounting curiosity leaning idly against a trellis by the foot of the stairs.

At least thirty men had slipped through the double-doored gateway over the last hour, which she guessed had opened in response to some password or other—she knew, because she'd counted them! More were arriving with every passing minute, either singly or in small groups. Who could they be, she wondered, for none of the men seemed in any way special—certainly not important or influential enough to have warranted such painstaking preparations for their enjoyment as those undertaken by Malvado! What the devil was he up to?

The men, for their part, wasted little time in getting into the festive mood! Squeals of delight greeted their arrival as the whores from the Bamboo Cage launched themselves into their arms. The rough-and-ready fellows, long denied the company of women, judging by appearances, were soon actively enjoying the charms of the squealing girls Malvado had ordered brought over from the Bamboo Cage. Some of the women were draped across the men's laps, and the lusty rogues had their hands plunged down the girls' bodices to squeeze a plump breast, or else their busy fingers were lost beneath the women's skirts. Still others had lost patience, and had decided to slake their lust in the shadows of the courtyard, judging by the female giggles and strangled male grunts and rustling she could hear. Other men headed straightway for the liquor tables, while still others heartily took up platters and heaped them with food, devouring Malvado's feast like hungry dogs, as if they'd been denied a decent meal for many weeks.

She turned at the sound of her name, to see Antonio leading a newcomer to meet her. The man was tall and moustached, and had a military bearing to him, but his features were hidden by the shadow of his black felt *chambergo*. She saw his lips split in a wide grin as Antonio introduced him, but only dimly heard Malvado's introduction as the man swept off his hat and stepped forward to take her hand.

"Zamora!" she exclaimed in shock, paling beneath her rouge. Her hand flew to her mouth in horror.

"Well, well, I'll be damned! So you're *Compadrito* Malvado's new mistress, eh? I can't tell you what a great pleasure it is to meet you once again, my 'feather-brained' *muchacha!*" General Hernando Zamora said with a smirk. His eyes gleamed under heavy black brows, and his teeth were white and wolfish beneath the dark curve of his moustache as he took her hand in his and held it fast in his grip.

"You know my woman?" Antonio asked suspiciously, obviously nettled by Hernando Zamora's familiar manner with the beauty he planned to make his mistress.

"Know her? Why, this lovely little bitch and I are old friends—or should I say, old *enemies*—eh, señorita? It was this very woman I told you of, remember, Malvado—the one who caused the loss of one hundred and fifty of our new rifles, sent at great cost from North America? One hundred and fifty fine weapons lost, lying useless in the mud at the bottom of the Paraná!" he hissed, spittle flying with his vehement tone. "Your actions forced us to postpone our plans for many months, señorita—a circumstance that I find extremely difficult to forget, let alone forgive. But then—" and he smiled, catlike, "I have never been a forgiving man, alas!"

"Neither am I a forgetful or forgiving woman, General Zamora," Krissoula countered boldly, yanking her hand from his grasp. "Nor one to meekly accept the fate life hands me! You intended to kill Sofía and me when you realized we'd seen your little cache of arms, didn't you? What was I supposed to do! Meekly accept death at

464

your hands—or fight for our lives? No. I did what I had to do, señor—without regret. I would do the same again, given half the chance! Presidente Bartolomé Mitre is far from perfect, but he *is* a *porteño* himself, a man who was raised in this very city. From what I've heard since I came here, he's concerned about the future of Argentina, and is striving to build a better life for all the people of this country, rich and poor alike. To provide honest labor for every man willing to work by expanding the *estancias* and the farms. Try to overthrow him, General Zamora, and every able-bodied citizen of Buenos Aires will rise up against your *revolucionarios* to make certain you fail!" she told him with relish, and with her fists planted firmly on her hips as they were now, she appeared quite capable of rising up herself, and defeating Zamora's little army single-handedly!

"You've grown rash since we met last, my dear," Zamora observed through tight lips. "Openly challenging me the way you are—! Why, it's foolhardy to say the least, don't you think? For myself, I hardly think you're in any position to threaten anyone!" He turned to Antonio. "For my own peace of mind, Malvado, I want this little hellcat safely locked away, until after the coup has been accomplished."

"Very well, General," Antonio agreed slowly and with obvious reluctance. "I'll see it done as soon as I've—"

"On the contary, *compadrito,* the pleasure of seeing this little bitch securely locked away will be all mine!" Zamora cut in with a smirk. "You offered me my pick of the women here tonight, do you recall—and I choose this woman! I have an old score to settle with your lovely little whore, as well as an old threat to make good on! If you'd be so good as to show me to your room, wench?" he said with a sneer, and he gripped Krissoula's wrist, jerking her towards the *corredor.*

"Antonio, no! Don't let him do this!" she implored Malvado over her shoulder, but she could see from his expression he'd not lift a finger to help her escape Zamora. No! He was too much in awe of the general who aspired to be president . . . !

With a shrug, Malvado's eyes slid away from the pair, and he turned back to watching Zamora's men, who'd grown rowdier still now on account of the enormous quantities of liquor they'd swilled down. His black eyes gleamed as minutes passed, and as he watched the goings-on his breathing grew steadily more rapid and thick, for the scene all about him resembled nothing so much as a Roman orgy, with the men and their whores coupling on every side, some lined up to take their turns at one or other of the wenches. Damn that Zamora! Future president or no, why should *he*—the *compadrito* of Barrio Timéo—be forced to act the voyeur, while the woman he wanted obediently spread her legs for the general, before he'd even once sampled her charms himself? He'd been a fool to tell her to please Zamora, or to offer the man his pick of the women. What man, after seeing Krissoula, would have chosen another . . . ?

Springing to his feet, he stalked across the courtyard to the stairs, headed for Krissoula's room. He brushed off the anxious offers of assistance from his men who came running to ask what it was he needed, and started up them alone.

Krissoula stumbled as Zamora shoved her forcefully inside her room, losing her footing and falling heavily. He slammed the door behind him and at once sprang after her, flinging her over onto her back before she could scramble to her feet.

Smiling in his catlike fashion, he gripped the neckline of her gown and tore it from her body, exposing her breasts in one vicious move. With a smile, he hauled her to standing and tossed her onto the bed like a rag doll, where she lay stunned for the moment by the suddenness of his attack, trying to draw the torn edges of her clothing up to cover her.

"There'll be no escaping me this time, *ramera,*" he promised her, unfastening his belt and drawing down his breeches. "You'll do as I say without question this time, or feel the sting of my belt across those charming little breasts—and perhaps across your bottom, too? *Sí,* I like that idea! There's nothing better for firing a woman's passions than a sound thrashing to make her obedient and hot for a man!"

Black eyes glittering, he raised his shirt over his head and hauled it off, then strode to the bed naked, laughing as he saw her eyes stray to the hairy hugeness at his flanks, and widen in horror.

"Ah, *sí!* He's all yours, my little slut—if you can take him all, that is, eh? But first, you must be punished for your defiance the last time we met—!"

He dropped heavily to the bed and flung her hands away from her breasts, covering them with his own and kneading cruelly, tweaking her sensitive nipples until she cried out in pain. She tried to squirm free of him, but with a curse he slapped her hard across the face and ordered her to be still.

Her head ringing from the blow, she did so, cringing as he

466

methodically proceeded to rip the remainder of the white gown from her, tearing off her petticoats, her camisole, her drawers, leaving her naked except for her stockings and garters. *The knife!* Oh, dear God, he'd find the knife any second, hidden along the outer side of her right thigh—the one farthest from him! But to her relief, he seemed satisfied when she was stripped, and in a thick, rasping tone, he ordered her to turn over, onto her belly, and kneel before him on the bed.

"No!" she protested in a choked voice, terrified by his order. Dear Lord, what did he intend to do to her?

As if he'd read her mind, he grasped her upper arms and forced her over onto her belly, slamming her down with a hard hand pressed against the small of her back so that the breath was forced from her in a sickening whoosh as she hit the mattress.

"I said up on your knees, bitch!" he commanded. "I want your little bottom in the air, ready to receive my punishment. Up, I say!"

Choking back a sob, she raised herself to kneeling as he'd commanded, and with dread in her heart sensed him moving about behind her. He stroked the quivering cheeks of her buttocks in a lascivious, gloating way that made her face burn with mortification, then took his broad belt, running the leather thong through his fingers almost lovingly.

"Four or five strokes should be sufficient, I believe, to both punish you and make you hot and ready for me," he said thickly. "What do you think, golden eyes?"

"Go to hell!" she flung back at him.

"Still not tamed? Then let's say a round half-dozen, to drive the impudence from you, shall we? And don't forget to say 'thank you' for my lenience, girl, so I'll go easier on you!"

He waited, but when, after several moments, she still said nothing, he clicked his teeth angrily. "Come along now, *say* it! Say 'Thank you for being so forgiving, General Hernando! I know I'm deserving of your punishment.'"

But she wouldn't, couldn't say it! Wouldn't play along with his sick, sadistic little game. Before she had time to spit back a retort at him, his belt whistled through the air and cut down across her exposed buttocks, leaving a bright pink welt across her tender flesh that made her yelp in pain and drop down onto her belly with a sob.

"You're a bad, bad little girl, Krissoula!" he growled. "Come along now, girl, get back up, on your knees, with that bottom in the air, before Papa Hernando loses patience with you, and doubles your spanking!"

"Come and make me, you *hijo de puta!*" Krissoula ground out, fumbling her hand along her side to slip the little knife free of the garter.

"You dare to defy me still!" Enraged, Zamora leaped at her, flinging her violently over onto her back.

In the same instant, her hand rose and she slashed downward with the knife, stabbing him deep in the side of his throat where it met his left shoulder. She sprang away from him, off the bed, as blood spurted from the wound, spattering the sheets with crimson gouts. He moaned and slumped onto his belly, the pool of blood spreading slowly beneath his head. From the looks of him, he'd be masterminding no more coups against Presidente Mitre—not in this life, anyway . . .

Gulping, her mind racing, Krissoula drew a coverlet over him with trembling hands, arranging it so that Zamora seemed to be sleeping, the bloodstains hidden. That accomplished, she wiped the blade clean and returned the knife to her garter, then hurriedly dressed herself again, this time donning the wine-red gown.

Smoothing down the skirts, she slipped from the room, taking deep breaths to calm herself. She was shaking uncontrollably and felt sickened to her stomach, close to heaving up the contents of her belly. Aiee, *Dios,* she'd never killed a man before! And, despite having stabbed Zamora in self-defense, she felt no triumph, no joy, no satisfaction at having killed him, as she'd expected. Rather, she felt peculiarly emptied of emotion, save for a feeling of self-disgust. Life was a precious thing—a gift from God—and it was not for mortal hands to take the life of another, however deserving of death that someone might be. How on earth could she bring herself to kill Malvado and Bobo, feeling such revulsion for killing? *How—?*

"Oh! Don Antonio!" she exclaimed, pulling up short at the head of the stairs to see Malvado climbing up them towards her.

He frowned. "Where's Zamora—?" he asked suspiciously, looking over her shoulder to the deserted *corredor* beyond.

"Zamora? Why, where else would he be, señor, but—but sleeping in my bed! That puffed-up braggart, he talked grandly of his talents as a lover—but it was all over for him in a matter of moments!" she jeered scornfully. "I thought—I hoped!—that perhaps you might enjoy watching me dance," she wheedled, "just for you, instead of wanting me locked away for the night, and so I changed into something more appropriate. You like it, 'Tonio?"

She twirled about for his inspection, and her new, coquettish manner towards him seemed to please him, for he murmured,

"Very much, my little flower! And by the way, Krissoula, you did well tonight—with Zamora, I mean. I'm pleased! From now on, I'll share you with no one, understand? You're my woman, and after tonight, there'll be just the two of us, favorites of the new president of Argentina!" He grinned wolfishly. "And darling—I'm no empty braggart like Zamora, believe me!"

"Oh, I do, I do!" she simpered, taking his hand in hers. "Come, Tonio, let's go back downstairs," she coaxed. "I have a little dance number planned that will set you afire—a wicked tango, no less! And then later—" she giggled and flirted her lashes at him, "well, who knows what I have planned for you, mmm, *mi compadrito?*"

Smiling, he let her lead him back down the stairs to the crowded courtyard.

The slow, serpentine melody of the tango drifted out over the courtyard, drawing the attention of the revelers and halting them in their busy pursuit of pleasure. All heads turned to the lovely young woman who stood in the center of the courtyard like a slender flower, poised to dance.

Krissoula, the burgundy satin of her gown gleaming like spilled wine in the torchlight, began to move, both improvising her movements and drawing on those she remembered seeing at the Bamboo Cage as she stalked and twirled, tossed her head haughtily, or pirouetted her hips, moving sensuously in time to the fascinating music.

And then, all at once, she was no longer alone. A tall, lean man was partnering her, taking her hand and leading her masterfully across the flagstones, spinning her from him, then reeling her in to arch her back across his thigh, dipping her lower and lower until her hair brushed the ground and their bodies all but touched their entire lengths, just like in her dream the night Cojo had been killed. Glancing curiously up into his bearded hawk's face, a squeak of surprise escaped her lips, for she found herself gazing—not into the face of the male dancer from the Bamboo Cage, as she'd expected—but into the blazing sapphire eyes of—*Esteban!*

"Don't say anything," he warned softly as he leaned over her, his mouth almost touching hers, "just keep dancing, *querida*—and for once in your life, listen!"

Chapter Forty

She listened, and she did, for once, obey his commands. Together, they danced the wicked tango, growing closer and ever closer to the double gates that enclosed the courtyard, working their way step by torturous step towards escape!

It was agony to maintain the pretense of dancing: to smile and twirl and dip and spin as if nothing untoward was happening, but somehow she managed, and was rewarded by Esteban's wink and his approving murmur of, "Good girl! That's the way!" as she swayed in his arms in time to the soaring music.

Twelve feet from the gateway, and he dipped her once again, arching her deeply across his thigh as he gazed into her eyes. "We're almost home free, *querida!* Keep it up," he murmured, and he brushed his cheek against her own.

"*Caramba!* Get rid of the beard, *hombre!* You feel like a prickly hedgehog," she retorted cheekily, though her shaky tone belied her attempt at bravado, and Esteban grinned as he raised her to standing and whirled her at arm's length. She was fire and spirit, courage and beauty, all rolled into one incredible woman—and *Dios,* how he'd missed her! How he'd dreamed of holding her in his arms again—though never, to be honest, exactly like this!

Six feet from the gateway, and they were almost home free!

Krissoula's heart was pounding in nervous anticipation as she whispered, "What now?" as they extended arms, clasped hand, and stalked haughtily across the flagstones.

"When I give the word, break away!" he gritted under his breath. "Up the beer barrels and over the wall! Can you do it, *minina?*"

"Can a flea bite?" she demanded scornfully, nervousness lending her voice an extra bite. "Of course I can do it, *loco!*"

He nodded amused approval, and swung her around so that his body was between hers and Malvado's line of vision, giving her a little cover. "Now!" he rasped. "Go for it!"

She was off and running for the stacked barrels the minute he gave the word, yet she'd taken only a couple of steps when Malvado sprang from his seat to his feet.

"You, by the gate, stop her! Head her off!" he roared, and at once his men sprang forward, blocking her escape.

With a foul curse of defeat, she spun about and ran back to Esteban, clinging to his arm as Malvado stalked across the courtyard towards them.

"The game's up, San Martín. I've seen through your foolish little masquerade. You can't have the girl, so why don't you let her go and we'll finish this once and for all between us, you and I? And don't bother to try anything reckless, my friend. You can't hope to win! You see, I have the upper hand here, not you."

The music died away, its last, startled chord like the squall of a strangled cat as the musicians abandoned their playing one by one. As all heads turned to watch the confrontation between Malvado and San Martín, an uneasy hush grew and spread throughout the courtyard, broken only by the hiss and roar of the resin torches as they writhed in the night wind, and a single nervous giggle from one of the whores that was abruptly silenced.

"Like the last time?" Esteban asked softly, mockingly, an undercurrent of menace to his tone as he pushed Krissoula behind him. His fingers slowly curled, became knotted fists bunched at his thighs, she saw, her mouth dry with apprehension. "You thought you had the upper hand then, as I recall—but you were wrong, eh, *compadrito?*"

"Ah, but this isn't like the last time, San Martín! No, not by a long chalk. You see, this time, you didn't take me by surprise! This time, I was *expecting* you to show up here, sooner or later. I have been ever since my boys told me they'd heard on the streets that you'd come back to the *barrios,* looking for her." He jerked his head in Krissoula's direction. "You see, San Martín, there's nothing that goes on in the *barrios* now that I don't know about first! Nothing that can be kept a secret from me, the *compadrito* of San Timéo!" he boasted, tugging at his lapels and swaggering a little.

Malvado smiled, his sloe-black, glittering eyes heavy-lidded and sly. "My lovely flower, Krissoula! She was the perfect bait to draw you into my trap, no? What a fool you were all those years ago, Esteban, *mi amigo!* What a stupid, principled fool! You really should have finished me off when you had the chance, *pibe*—what was it, ten, eleven years ago? But—luckily for me, eh?" he chuckled, "you lacked the guts! Those pretty principles of yours stayed your hand—wasn't that the story you gave that poor Severino, after he'd raised you to become *compadrito* of La Boca in his footsteps? After he'd loved you like a father? Planned to marry you to his only daughter? How you repaid him for his generosity, eh, San Martín bleating that you couldn't take another man's life in cold blood!" the godfather jeered. "That human life was 'too precious' to squander!" Malvado chuckled scornfully and inspected his polished nails. "Why should now be any different, eh? You were a coward then—and my money says you're still a coward, yellow through and through! You're still a gutless excuse for a man, San Martín—without the balls to do the things a real man must!"

"Haven't you learned yet? It doesn't take courage to kill someone, Malvado!" Esteban gritted in a voice like iced steel, each word dripping into the crackling silence like a sizzling drop of acid. "Nor does it take balls, as you put it," he added in a withering tone, "to order a harmless boy brutally butchered because he didn't fit in with your plans! No, my friend, it's the coward's way out you've taken, having others do your dirty work for you, while you hide behind these tall, safe walls with your clean hands and your manicured nails, and enjoy the good life! If that's your measure of courage, then I pity you, Malvado! I despise you. I *spit* on you, *compadrito,*" Esteban scoffed, "for despite your fancy clothes, you're still nothing, whatever you may tell yourself!"

Esteban knew his words had struck home when Malvado paled with anger under his olive complexion. He saw how a nerve danced along his jaw, and how the ugly necklace of scar tissue about his throat grew livid and angry as a purplish tide of fury rose up his neck. He'd put that scar there himself eleven years ago, he recalled, in bloody retaliation for Malvado's gang's attempt on the life of Rolón Severino, which had cost the *compadrito* of La Boca an eye but it gave him no satisfaction to see the damage he'd inflicted. Rather, he wished fervently that in this one instance he could have swallowed his reservations about taking another's life, finished the job, and killed Malvado . . .

He continued. "No, Malvado, I'm not afraid of you! And whether you like it or not, Señorita Ballardo is leaving here with me. If you have something different to say, then go ahead, say it. Try to stop me, *hombre*—if you're man enough to try it alone, without calling your muscle-bound goons to bail you out! But personally, I doubt you've the *cojones* to go one-on-one with me in

472

a fair fight. Even as a boy, Tonio, you were only brave when you ran in a pack like a wolf, preying on those who were weak and unarmed or alone. Well, my money says you *still* need that pack, you scum!"

"Ah, but you've missed the whole point, San Martín!" Malvado said silkily, controlling his mounting anger with enormous willpower on his part. "You see, the beauty of being *compadrito* is exactly that—being powerful enough and important enough to have countless *others* do your bidding. I don't *need* to dirty my own hands on you in order to keep the woman here. I can simply summon a dozen others to do it for me, and know it will be done, while you—" he sneered, "—have no one to back you, San Martín!"

"No?" Esteban said softly, a pitying smile curling his upper lip with contempt. "Ah, but that's where you're wrong, *compadrito!* Not everyone in Barrio San Timéo fears you! There are others—like me—who know what a coward you really are—"

Fists planted on his hips, he glanced up at the high mildewed walls that surrounded the courtyard and bellowed: "Sancho!"

"*Sí*, Don Esteban!" came a loud young voice in immediate response, and Malvado's head snapped about in the direction of the speaker to see Sancho and a dozen or more of the older *niños* straddling one section of the high wall, scrawny bare legs dangling from ragged breeches. They were armed with sticks and knives and leather slingshots.

"Children?" Malvado snorted in contempt. "Be serious, San Martín!"

Esteban smiled. His lips quirked, but he made no comeback. "Franco! Armando!" he bellowed instead.

"Here, Don Esteban!" came the immediate response from the opposite wall. Malvado's head swiveled around as if jerked by a cord, to see the Gypsy menfolk of Barrio Gitanos there, armed to the teeth with *facóns*, the long knife-blades winking silvery fire in the starlight; at least twenty swarthy, muscular men poised to spring down into the courtyard below and do battle.

"Pah! What's a handful of cowardly, stinking *gitanos!*" Antonio dismissed them with disgust. "My men could finish them off like nothing—like beetles stomped underfoot!" he boasted, snapping his fingers.

"Severino!" Esteban continued, still wearing his lazy half-smile and watching Malvado with hooded, glittering eyes that, combined with his midnight hair and his lean, dark features, made him look like *El Diablo* incarnate.

At once Papa Rolón's face, roguishly eye-patched like a pirate's, appeared over the walls alongside that of Armando Reyes, as did the heads of several of his trusted lieutenants.

Esteban allowed his smile to deepen as he saw the first dawnings of fear fill Antonio Malvado's face, and his cocksure smirk waver just a little, for it was obvious that Malvado—who boasted he knew everything that went on in the *barrios*—had never discovered that the differences between him and Papa Rolón had been resolved and mended days ago, or that the hurtful words exchanged in bitter anger and in the heat and grief of their parting years hence had been forgiven and forgotten, thanks to the power of love.

"And last, but by no means least—!" Esteban murmured, swinging about to the watching crowd, and making a gallant half-bow and an expansive flourish with his hand. "Lovely ladies, if you'd be so kind—?"

To a woman, the gaudy whores Mama Zita had sent over from the Bamboo Cage untangled themselves from the arms of the *revolucionarios* and crossed the courtyard to stand at Esteban's back, fists on their hips, belligerent expressions on their painted faces. Some of them—the more audacious girls—took up empty wine bottles as they came, holding them by the neck and casually breaking them against the edges of the tables, leaving sharp, lethal weapons in their dainty fists that could carve a man to ribbons.

"There! I think that's everyone," Esteban observed casually. He cocked a raven-black brow in Malvado's direction. "Now. What was it you were saying, Don Antonio? Something about me having no one to back me up . . . ?"

"Bobo!" Malvado roared, infuriated. "Get him!"

The squat dwarf erupted from the shadows, his huge arms raised, his short legs pumping like a runaway locomotive as he barreled towards Esteban.

"Forget it, toad—!" Krissoula ground out, and scant feet before the midget assassin reached Esteban, her dainty slippered foot shot deftly out, into his path.

The squat dwarf blundered and tripped heavily over her foot, crashing to the ground with a piglike squeal of pain. Before he could recover, Krissoula sprang after him, stomping down on his wrists and scrabbling fingers with her high-heeled slippers in a lively *zapateado* as he tried in vain to push himself up, off the ground!

"Take that for my Cojo, you squealing piglet!" she stormed. "And this! And this, too, you sniveling, butchering toad!" she raged, and Bobo whimpered and cringed and begged for mercy, trying to roll away, but could not evade her barrage of blows. Krissoula leaped on his back, her knees lodged against his spine to hold him down. She yanked on Bobo's ears until he shrieked in pain. She pummeled at every inch of his body with her clenched fists, battering his bald head, his shoulders, his back, hammering at his torso like a woman gone mad.

"Toothpick! *La Rata!* Help him, you stupid fools!" screamed Malvado, looking about him frantically for assistance, and his loyal lieutenants came running.

Seeing their beefy rush to aid the dwarf who was bent on subduing his woman, Esteban saw red. Springing forward with a roaring curse of fury, with a matador's lithe grace he ran to intercept their mad rush.

José met the oaken thunderbolt of Esteban's knotted fist as it slammed up and under his jaw in a cracking uppercut. Juan doubled over with a piledriver solid to the belly, tasting bitter bile on his tongue as he cradled his aching guts. Esteban flung around to encounter yet another of Malvado's lieutenants, and caught the shimmer of a blade singing its way towards him. He ducked to avoid it, then leaped after the goon who'd thrown the knife, wrestling him to the ground.

And as if the move on his part were a call to arms for his companions, all hell broke loose in the courtyard as over a score of men scrabbled over the villa walls and dropped into the patio, eager and ready to join him in the fight!

Sancho and the *niños* loaded up their slingshots, and peppered the godfather's men and the drunken revolutionaries both with a hail-shower of hefty rocks, launched from the safety of the high walls of the villa where they were unreachable themselves! The *compadrito*'s lieutenants tried helplessly to dodge the barrage of sharp stones that stung their bodies and gouged their cheeks, while the *niños* kept up a stream of insults, jeers, and victorious "Gotchas!" that were equaled only by the unending stream of missiles they launched with such devastating—and deadly!—accuracy, one after the other.

Simultaneously, the painted whores from the Bamboo Cage turned on the revolutionary soldiers they'd serviced so amorously just hours before like squalling, spitting alley cats, punching and pinching, scratching and biting, kicking and pulling hair, much to the astonishment and dismay of their earlier paramours! The whores battled the soldiers like rouged, befeathered, and sequined

Furies, slamming trays or stools down over their heads. They also hefted well-placed knees into defenseless groins, and whooped with glee as they left their victims unconscious, huddled in piles on the flagstones, or draped untidily across trestles and benches, nursing their hurts.

Meanwhile, the fierce *gitanos*—led, of course, by Armando and Franco Reyes, and Papa Zambra of the Zambra family—sprang down from the high walls and into the courtyard proper, where they demonstrated their Gypsy knife-fighting skills and their notorious hot-blooded, violent tempers to good purpose, much to the dismay of General Hernando Zamora's men, and the godfather's startled goons, who were no match for the fierce and angry Gypsies without their rifles. They saw the lusty thirst to spill blood in the *gitanos'* sparkling black eyes, saw the razor-edged steel of their *facóns,* noted their gleaming, white-toothed smiles—and tried to run!

Pandemonium reigned supreme in the courtyard!

Prized fighting cocks, freed and spilled from their broken wicker coops by lurching bodies, started miniature battles of their own, blood and crimson-and-orange feathers flying as they flew at each other with hackles raised and spurs brandished, screaming their barnyard challenges. The dogs bristled and snarled and barked furiously, flying into snarling tangles of fur and yellow fangs. Men punched and cursed. Fists swung and connected. Boots stomped and kicked. Knuckles bled. Nails raked. Teeth and pink-stained spittle trickled down split lips and dripped off battered chins, and blackened eyes purpled and puffed up, their owners groggily reeling about like drunkards as they dazedly sought out other opponents.

Esteban threw off the last of Malvado's men—a lout named Stefano—at long last, and cast apprehensively about him for Krissoula. His gut lurched in foreboding when he glimpsed her beyond a mass of grappling bodies nearby, for that foul little slug Bobo had managed to throw off her slender weight and had staggered to his feet. The ugly dwarf was leering gleefully as he lumbered closer and closer to the frightened girl, for he had her backed into a corner from which there was no escape!

Krissoula was desperately lashing out with her hands and feet, trying to hold Bobo back, to prevent him from coming close enough to curl his arms around her slender body in the deadly embrace that was his trademark. Once he'd done so, the dwarf would take her slender form in a massive bearhug, one that would snap every bone in her body like dried twigs, and rupture her blood vessels, burst her fragile lungs, as he'd once done to poor Cojo, she knew.

476

"Get away from me, you slimy slug!" she threatened. "Look to your precious master, why don't you, before San Martín chews him up and spits him out—like yesterday's spoiled mutton!"

Out of the corner of her eye, she saw Esteban in the instant he spotted her own dilemma. Grim-faced, he started heading quickly towards her, but the faint hope that he'd rescue her from Bobo flared up and just as quickly died. She'd suddenly noticed Hernando Zamora, swaying unsteadily on the stairs at Esteban's back, a drawn pistol held slackly in his fist, his black eyes glittering feverishly. *Aiee, Dios mío, el general was still alive! She hadn't killed him, as she thought!*

In the same moment that she spotted him, the ashen-faced general raised his rust-soaked arm to shoulder height, and made ready to fire the pistol, curling his finger about the trigger and squeezing—

"Behind you!"

She screamed the warning, and Esteban threw himself aside in the nick of time as Zamora fired. The ball whistled past his cheek and carved a trough in the wall beyond as he leaped for the general's legs, throwing his arms about Zamora's knees as he tackled him and brought him crashing to the ground.

Esteban's one thought was to finish Zamora and get to Krissoula before Bobo harmed her! And yet, despite his wounding, Zamora was still incredibly strong. Over and over they rolled, Zamora's wound reopening and blood splattering them as they both struggled to gain the upper hand.

Relieved, Krissoula saw that Esteban had leaped to safety, but had no chance to watch the outcome of the ensuing fight with Zamora, for Bobo, simpleton that he was, nevertheless proved cunning enough to put her momentary lapse of attention to good use. He lunged for her, his long simian arms going around her ribs like twin boa constrictors, tightening, crushing.

She felt the flood of her life-blood rush to her face, the pressure of it distending the veins at her throat, her temples, and forehead as Bobo squeezed, an unholy grin wreathing his grotesque face as he leered up at her.

"You made fun of me, didn't you?" he accused petulantly. "But you aren't making fun of me now, are you, my pretty?" he lisped, and gave a squeaky little chuckle. "Shall I give you a great big hug, *bombón,* like the one I gave that wretched cripple you liked so well? Or how about a kiss for your Bobo? Maybe a little kiss would make me let go of you, eh? Will you kiss me now, pretty Krissoula, in return for your life, hmm?"

Laughing, he pressed his fleshy wet lips to the exposed upper swells of her bosom, his arms still coiled agonizingly tight about her rib cage. Her pulse was thundering in her temples. Her breath was being choked off as his muscles bulged, and he increased the pressure of his grip about her ribs. Her struggles to free herself grew measurably weaker. *Dios mío*, she couldn't draw breath! She couldn't suck even a thread of air into her lungs! She was drowning, choking on her own saliva, her tongue, the used breath gurgling in her throat, sending fiery agony throughout her starving lungs, which felt close to exploding. Blackness began to crowd into her vision like inky wings; blackness pierced with daggers of blinding crimson and gold, though her eyes remained wide open and all but starting from her head. She was going to die . . . here . . . now . . . horribly . . . and there was nothing . . . nothing . . . she could do to prevent it . . .

"Kiss me, Krissoula!" Bobo lisped in a taunting, singsong voice that came at her from what seemed a great distance away. "Kiss me! Kiss me! Kiss meeee *aaaaaaaagh!*"

His taunt ended in a strangled scream. His arms loosened their grip and dropped from about her abdomen as he staggered backward, clutching his bleeding temple as he toppled to the flagstones.

Gasping for breath, Krissoula bent over, coughing and swallowing greedy gulps of air. She retched painfully until she'd regained her wind, her face blotched red and white, tears streaming down her cheeks.

When she was able to open her eyes again after several moments, hateful Bobo was sprawled at her feet, his fleshy lips parted in horror, an ugly gash at his right temple that was oozing blood in a puddle beneath his cheek. His piggy little eyes were now wide open and staring unblinkingly up at the sky way above, reflecting the flaring light of the hissing torches in their glassy depths. Off to one side of him lay a large rock.

Understanding slowly dawned through her foggy thoughts, and she glanced up at the wall beyond to see the lad Sancho perched there, staring fixedly down at the dwarf's body. A leather slingshot dangled limply from his brown hand, and there was a strange expression on the boy's face; one neither gleeful nor sad, nor regretful or smug.

"Thank you!" she mouthed gratefully in a hoarse voice. "You—you saved my life!"

Sancho turned his head to look down at her. "For Cojo," she heard him murmur woodenly. "I did it for Cojo! They both had their crosses to bear in this life, no? Cojo with his poor crippled leg and his twisted lip, and Bobo with his dwarf's shrunken body? But while that hateful ape chose a life of evil and murder, Cojo did nothing but good. He was my friend, and he loved you, Krissoula. It isn't fair! He didn't deserve to die!"

There were tears shimmering in the lad's eyes, she saw, and her own eyes filled and her heart swelled with pity that this child, this little boy, had had to learn at such a tender age what no grown man should ever have to learn; that life was rarely fair, and that when death came, it played no favorites, paid no mind to who deserved its coming and who did not. It simply was.

"No," Krissoula agreed softly. "Cojo didn't deserve to die. But now, thanks to you, Sancho, our friend will rest in peace. His blood will no longer cry out for vengeance. It is over, and we who are left must go on, and care for those who need us."

With a brief nod, his eyes met hers, and then Sancho disappeared over the wall.

Obviously, as far as the lad was concerned, there'd been enough fighting for one night. And more than enough of death to last a lifetime! For her part, she was inclined to agree with him . . .

She made to turn back to the fight, to find Esteban and help him if he needed her, but before she could do so, a wiry arm slipped about her throat from behind; the icy steel of a blade slanted across her windpipe.

"Don't make a sound, my flower!" Malvado rasped in her ear. "You're my passage out of here, *comprende?*"

Chapter Forty-One

"You'll never get away with this!" Krissoula whispered.

"No? Just shut up and get going!" Malvado hissed in an ugly tone.

Taking her wrist, he wrenched it up and behind her. With the point of the knife pricking in her back, he jerked her ahead, forcing her to circle around the chaotic battle scene in the courtyard to the gates that led out into the street.

Krissoula purposely made her pace a slow one, yet within moments the godfather saw through her little ruse and wrenched painfully on her arm, forcing bone against bone. "No tricks, my flower," he rasped in her ear. "We're going to do this my way, or not at all! If you don't want your precious San Martín to find you with a knife between your ribs, hurry it up!"

They reached the gates, and Krissoula looked frantically about her, spying Franco grappling with one of Zamora's mercenaries nearby, and Papa Zambra similarly involved with one of Malvado's men. She wanted to cry out, to call to them so that *someone* would know that Malvado was escaping, and that he'd taken her with him as his hostage, but she dared not distract the two fiercely struggling men. To do so could mean their deaths! Heartsick, she turned away as Malvado hefted open one of the gates and shoved her through it, knowing she was quite alone as he slipped through them in her wake.

"The next courtyard," he ordered harshly, his breathing raspy. "There are horses there. By the time your cursed friend realizes we're gone we'll be cozily aboard my ship, and bound for sunny Rio! I'll lie low there until the heat dies down a little, and who better than you, my little golden rosebud, to make my months of exile pleasurable ones?"

Krissoula wetted her lips but said nothing, instead concentrating her attention on trying to see her path through the gloom, looking for any avenue of escape she could take as they entered the second courtyard.

As Malvado had implied, the horses belonging to Zamora's revolutionaries had been stabled there, tethered to long hitching posts. There were dozens of them milling nervously about, nickering and fighting their reins as the *compadrito*'s fear and excitement communicated itself to them.

Malvado tore free the reins of two of the horses and grabbed Krissoula by the waist, tossing her up onto an unsaddled animal's back without preamble. He took her mount's reins in his fist while he clumsily mounted a second horse himself, needing several attempts and hissing a mouthful of blistering obscenities before he'd managed to clamber astride a chestnut's broad back and hook his feet through the stirrups.

Krissoula's golden eyes widened in excitement as she watched him mount up, for she'd immediately realized that the cocksure godfather was no hand with horses. Of course, he wouldn't be! City born and bred, Antonio Malvado had never needed to be a horseman! Settling herself securely on her mount's bare back, she wound her fingers through her horse's long, rough mane for purchase, and waited with bated breath to see what he'd do next.

He managed to mount, finally, and was heading his horse out of the courtyard into the street, leading hers behind it, when Esteban appeared through the gates of Villa Malvado with Zamora's pistol in hand. His eyes blazed when he saw the pair.

"No, you don't! Let the girl go, Malvado!" he roared.

"The hell I will, *hombre*! Yaah! Get up, there!"

In desperation, Malvado kicked his horse into a gallop, and the startled creature careened down the street, picking up speed as it towed Krissoula's mount in its wake.

Down gloomy narrow street after gloomy narrow street they galloped at suicidal speed, the walls of the houses on either side looming up and veering away in a wild rush that was dizzying. She heard a dog yelp and scatter to evade their onrushing hooves, glimpsed the glassy green eyes of a cat in the meager light as it sprang away, and then they were past and gone. Scant moments later, Krissoula heard the thundering hooves of another horse coming up fast behind them, and knew with a wild sense of elation and a quickening heart that Esteban was in pursuit! Blessed Saint Sara, she wasn't alone anymore!

On they rode through the darkened *barrios*, passing the little stone church of San Timéo with Malvado still leading her horse behind his own, the reins gripped in his fist, his whole attention devoted to keeping his precarious seat astride his mount's back. They careened past the Cádiz Tavern and streaked on towards Corrientes Street. Startled carousers flung themselves aside to avoid the wildly racing hooves as the two horses—trailed by a third coming up on them at speed—clattered into the torchlit plaza, passed through it and on. Krissoula saw Malvado vainly try to turn his horse's head down a chandlers' street that would have led them directly to the wharves and the vessel he'd mentioned, but his attempt failed. The frightened horse sensed his inexperience, and with the bit firmly between its teeth it refused to obey his command to turn, continuing on instead down a main thoroughfare crisscrossed by the narrow tracks set down for the horse-drawn trolleys that would lead them into the heart of the city.

The shabby *barrios* fell away behind them like a shabby worn cloak. Now, Krissoula saw, they were racing down one of the beautiful, broad, tree-lined *avenidas* of the city proper, the avenues or boulevards that made up the wealthy *porteño* district of Buenos Aires. Each deserted, elegant street here was well lit by gaslight and the ethereal silvery-gray wash of the full moon far above. Exclusive little shops offering perfumes and furs and jewels lined the colonial streets of Calle Florida which led off one of the avenues, each one boasting a colorful striped awning above its storefront to shade its goods from the fierce South American sun, and, instead of hard-packed dirt, there were pavements and streets of granite underfoot. The lead horse chose to turn onto this fabled street, and both mounts' hooves set up a noisy clatter as they sped over it that sounded deafening to Krissoula's ears, like the rattle of gunfire.

Hair flying behind her, she risked a glance over her shoulder, and saw that Esteban was now only a few dozen paces behind them.

"Shoot!" she muttered fervently under her breath. "For the love of Saint Sara, *mi querido,* shoot while you have the chance—!"

But Esteban didn't dare risk a shot at Malvado—not with Krissoula riding so close behind him! She realized that, and in the same moment, knew what she had to do!

Letting go of her mount's mane with one hand, she clumsily stuffed her skirts into the sash at her waist and kicked off her slippers, sending them bouncing across the street. Then, as she'd once done long ago as she rode pretty Girasol across the grassy Pampa, she squirmed her legs up beneath her, first one, then the other, until she was kneeling precariously on the wildly racing horse's back, while Malvado rode on ahead of her, oblivious to his hostage's exploits in his effort to retain his seat in the saddle!

Esteban's eyes narrowed as he saw what she was doing, and he knew she'd realized his predicament and chosen to take action accordingly. *Caray!* His gut squeezed with dread, and his heart thundered like a freight train out of control. *Jesús y María!* That *stupid*, wonderful little fool! She could easily break her neck if she fell, the speed her horse was going! Surely she'd never be so reckless as to try it—?

But nevertheless, he saw her rise slowly to standing, and balance there with her feet splayed wide apart on the horse's bare rump for balance, arms outstretched as a counterbalance like a circus bareback rider or equestrienne. A second or two more to get her bearings, and then she suddenly sprang from her mount's back. Arms reaching above her, she was flying in mid-air for heart-stopping, endless seconds before her fingers curled over and gripped the metal edging of a *confitería's* red-and-white-striped awning several feet above her.

She swung there by her arms like a little monkey, a broad grin of triumph curving her lips as Esteban thundered on beneath her. He had a clear target now, and surely he wouldn't be reluctant to take advantage of the chance she'd created for him? For a moment or two, she had cause to wonder, for Esteban made no attempt to shoot. "Do it!" she urged silently. "So what if you shoot him in the back? Malvado deserves no better! Shoot, *gato!"*

Malvado twisted around in the saddle, his olive face a pale moon in the silvery light, pallid with fear as he realized his hostage had flown, and that his lifelong enemy was angling his horse alongside him, obviously intending to tear him from the saddle. Clumsily, he drew the knife from his belt, and holding it by the blade sent it flying towards Esteban. In the same moment, Esteban raised Zamora's pistol to shoulder height and took careful aim.

The knife glanced harmlessly off his shoulder, yet his shot took Malvado exactly where he'd planned, solidly through the right shoulder blade. The force of the shot spun Malvado from his precarious perch in the saddle, and slammed him to the ground beneath his own mount's hooves. The horse lost its footing and twisted over onto its side, its weighty hindquarters pinning its fallen rider briefly before it hauled itself upright and shied away, eyes rolling, mouth agape. Esteban knew Malvado could never survive such a crushing injury, for he'd seen men pinned beneath their horses before, yet against all odds Malvado was still breathing as he reined in his own horse and swung quickly down from the saddle to crouch at his side.

The fancy gray frockcoat and snowy-white stock and silk brocade vest Malvado—ever the dandy—had donned for the *asado* were dirtied and ripped from the horse's hooves. The yellow rosebud he'd pinned in his lapel button was crushed, the petal bruised and stained with blood. More blood welled from his wounds to stain the pristine silk of his ruffled shirt. Turning his head at Esteban's approach, the mortally injured *compadrito* looked up into Esteban's face as his lifelong enemy knelt over him. Despite his grave wounds, he still managed a lopsided sneer.

"So, *pibe* . . ." he croaked hoarsely. "I was wrong! You had the . . . the guts to kill after all, eh? Who'd have thought it!" He coughed, a telltale trickle of bright red escaping the corner of his mouth.

"Like I said, 'Tonio, it doesn't take guts to kill a man," Esteban said heavily.

"Perhaps you're right, after all," Malvado whispered, an agonized expression filling his ashen face. "Truth was, I always envied you, San Martín . . . ever since we were *niños*. You had a mother to raise you, no? And when she was gone, you had Rolón Severino looking out for your skin, while I—? I had no one who cared. Maybe—maybe—I'd have turned out—better, given your chances, eh?"

Esteban's face remained implacable, stern and dark and unforgiving as he recalled what Sancho had told him of the crippled boy, Cojo, and Malvado's brutal decision to have him killed. He slowly shook his head.

"No, Malvado. Somehow, I don't think so. Other men grow up never knowing their parents or a mother's love, but not many of them choose the path you chose in life. It's the choices we make that make the difference, for better or worse, right or wrong, good or evil, despite the hand we're dealt coming into this life. You made your choices. Now you have to live with them."

"And die with them, too, eh, San Martín?"

Malvado coughed again after he'd spoken, and frothy bubbles escaped his lips, ghastly in the gaslight. When he looked up again, Esteban could see the light dwindling from Antonio's dark-brown eyes as death stole over his body inch by inch.

"*Chau, pibe,*" Esteban murmured in the *lunfardo* dialect of the *barrios.* "May God have mercy on your soul!"

Antonio sighed heavily. His head slumped to one side, and he breathed no more. There'd be a new *compadrito* of Barrio San

Timéo in a matter of weeks, Esteban knew, but it wouldn't be Don Antonio Malvado . . .

"He's dead?"

Esteban looked up at the sound of her cautious voice to see Krissoula standing a few feet away. The wine-colored gown she'd worn earlier was wrinkled and torn. Her hair was a wild torrent of inky curls flying about her grubby face. Her stockings were ripped, her feet bare—but never had she looked more beautiful to him than she did in that moment, standing beneath the gaslight with her slanted golden eyes looking inquiringly down at him as he knelt over Malvado's body!

"*Sí,*" he confirmed, rising to standing and striding towards her. "He's dead."

"What he said in the courtyard—about Severino raising you to *e compadrito* in his stead, was that true?"

"*Sí,* it was. I was—oh, about twenty years old then, I'd say. Malvado was young and greedy, and he wanted to take over Barrio a Boca for himself. He decided to have Severino killed, and move a on his district. He almost succeeded, too! Rolón lost an eye, and —I almost killed him in retaliation. I remember kneeling over him, *anting* to kill him, and I almost succeeded. I'd put the wound that eft those scars about his throat on him before I realized the futility f it all. If I'd killed Malvado, then his lieutenants would have come fter Rolón and his men in revenge, then we after them, and so on ithout end. Someone had to put an end to it, and I decided it aight as well be me. I'd seen more than enough of death by then."

Krissoula nodded in understanding. "So. How did you find me?" ie asked, curious.

"The lad, Sancho. He'd been following you and he told me where ou were," he explained. "But tonight was all Sofía's idea—the little aasquerade we pulled off with the dancing!"

"Sofía *mía? Dios!* Then I think there is hope for her yet, no? How she, the poor old thing?" Krissoula asked, unable to hide the ffection and concern in her tone despite her offhand manner.

"Much better. Good food has done wonders for her this past eek. And Mama Zita and Consuela enjoy spoiling her."

"I'm glad. She's been a good friend."

"You and I are blessed with a great many friends, Krissoula! arla Valde, Armando Reyes, and young Franco from Barrio itanos. The *niños,* of course. *Compadrito* Rolón Severino. The rls from the Bamboo—they all turned out when they heard I eded their help and that you were in trouble."

"I know! They were wonderful!" She shuddered. "I wanted to repay Malvado and that creature Bobo so badly for what they did to Cojo, but I couldn't bring myself to do it somehow. I'd be dead now, or on my way to some brothel in Rio, no doubt, if not for them—and you."

"Krissoula, I have something I must say to you."

"Oh?" she said casually, though her pulse suddenly raced and she was trembling all over. "What?"

He took a step towards her. "I wanted to say that I've finally figured you out, my fierce little kitten! Now I know that it's when you're most afraid, you curse like a trooper. You scream and rant and strike out at whoever or whatever happens to be closest to you at the time. Unfortunately, that someone's usually me! And then, when you're *really* afraid you might have to confront your true feelings, or face up to some unwelcome truth about yourself—then you run, Krissoula! Like a frightened little rabbit, you run! And do you know why, darling?" he asked in a softer, gentler voice. "You run because you're afraid! Because your damned Miguel convinced you that a Gypsy wasn't worthy of being loved by anyone. Somewhere along the line, you lost your pride and came to believe it yourself!"

"The *devil* I'm afraid, San Martín!" she exploded, lashing out at him with her hand and poking him hard in the chest with her index finger. "What have I to be afraid of, tell me that, eh? You, you think, maybe? Your terrible threats that night in the corral? Pah! Don't make me laugh, crazy one!" she jeered, her golden eyes wide with the dawnings of some new and naked, unexplained fear in their depths. She wetted her lips, her heart suddenly pounding so loudly she could hear its drumbeat in her ears, and her cheeks were afire. "I left Tierra Rosa because my job there was done. Because I needed no one—not you, not Miguel—no one! Not because I'm afraid of anything—!"

"That's where you're wrong, Krissoula. You were afraid—afraid that I'd never really loved you! And you were afraid to stay and find out, one way or the other. Rather than taking a gamble that you might be hurt again, you decided to take the coward's way out, and run," he said softly, his sapphire eyes turbulent under raven brows with the fervor of his emotions. He cocked his head to one side. "For love to work—for a man and a woman to live together happily—there must be give and take on both sides. Loving someone means trying to understand, and being able to forgive and forget and start afresh." He brushed the tendrils of inky hair away

486

rom her brow and gazed deep into her eyes. "I was wrong that night, *querida,* and I ask your forgiveness for the things I said then, the things I wrongly accused you of. I love you, Krissoula. Never doubt it! Marry me Krissoula! Come back to Tierra Rosa with me as my bride!"

"How can I help but doubt you?" she asked in a small, strangled voice. "How can there be love without trust, eh? Tell me that, *gato!*"

Gravely, he reached inside his jacket and without hesitation drew from an inner pocket there a thick, calf-bound volume which she recognized.

"Manuela's diary, Krissoula, as well you know," he observed, holding it up between them. "The writings within these pages hold my future. Without this journal to prove my claims to Tierra Rosa, the *estancia* can never be mine. My dreams will never be anything more than ashes, the residue of burned-out hopes. You asked about trust? Well, I give this into *your* keeping, Krissoula, to prove my trust in you," he murmured. So saying, he placed the journal in her palms, folding her slender fingers around the worn binding. "Do with it as you wish. The choice is yours, just as it's your choice and yours alone whether you want to be my bride, and to spend the rest of your life with me. I can't force you to marry me nor to love me, *querida.* But if, by some wonderful chance, you should want to find me, I'll be staying at Rolón Severino's for a day or two."

So saying, he tenderly brushed a knuckle against her flaming cheek. "Whatever you decide, take care of yourself, *minina. Adiós!*" he murmured, then he spun on his heel and strode back towards the horse he'd ridden. The animal was skittish after the wild ride and the shot, and he spent several moments in talking quietly to it, calming it preparatory to riding away.

Stunned for a second, Krissoula stared openmouthed after him, Manuela's journal hugged to her breast. Despite his declaration of love, he was leaving her, she realized. Leaving his future, his dreams, in her hands, to do with as she wished! She swallowed. He was trusting her to decide a matter that could make or break him, and he'd said—he'd said he loved her—had begged her forgiveness—and asked her to be his bride—! She looked down at the stained calfskin volume in her hands, and her eyes blurred with tears. *What son you birthed, Manuela,* she thought. *Despite his natural father, what a man he is!*

When she looked back at Esteban, he'd gathered the horse's dangling reins in his fist and had hooked his toe into the stirrup. He'd meant what he said. He was leaving!

The wrenching loss of the past two months without him returned full force. Memories of desolation and emptiness washed over her. How many nights she'd longed for him! She couldn't bear to stand there and meekly watch him ride away! After all, it didn't have to be that way again, it didn't! All she had to do was swallow her stupid pride and call him back; to take a chance and walk that step in his direction, to meet him halfway instead of running—as she'd told herself a thousand times she should have done long ago. She gnawed at her lower lip. Saint Sara's bones, could she bring herself to do it, to forgive him as everything within her cried out to do, and take that chance on love . . . ?

She stood there in an agony of doubt, a welter of indecision, a small, slender little figure beneath the hissing gaslight wearing a forlorn expression on her lovely little face, and with nervous fingers that clenched and unclenched about the journal.

Esteban swung his lean body up and over the horse's back. He settled himself and gathered the reins in his fists, before turning the stallion's head about, touching his heels to its flanks, and starting the horse forward. He saluted her as he made to ride away, and the finality of his farewell galvanized Krissoula into action at last.

"Wait!" she blurted out in a strangled voice.

He reined in the stallion, and turned in the saddle to look back at her inquiringly. *"Sí?"*

"You—you can't go like this! I won't let you!"

"No?" The bastard wanted to smile. She could tell!

She swallowed a scathing retort and said instead, "No! Someone has to ride to the Casa Rosada, and warn Presidente Mitre about Zamora and his revolution, no? So is—is there room on that—that nag of yours for one more?" she asked hesitantly, her voice shaky with emotion and an edge of fear.

"Is that your only reason for wanting to come with me?" he asked sternly.

"Yes!" she said too quickly, and then as quickly amended with a red face, "No! Of course not, *loco!"* She paused. "I—I love you San Martín! And—and I want to be with you, always. Oh, damn you, *querido,* must I beg? Take me with you!" she implored, her defenses crumbling.

"In that case, if there's no room on the horse, I'll *make* room," he promised, laughter in his voice, and he held out his hand to her. "Come on, you stubborn little minx, up with you!"

With a wild, unladylike whoop, she crammed the diary down her cleavage, hoisted her skirts to mid-thigh, and flew across Call

Florida, showing a delicious amount of bare golden legs to the crowd of onlookers that had gathered in the process. Clutching his outstretched hand, she nimbly vaulted up behind him, settling herself comfortably across the horse's broad rump. Another second, and she'd slipped her arms tightly about his waist and clasped them together over his belt buckle, while she pressed her cheek flat against his broad back.

"I was wrong, too, *querido,*" she grudgingly confessed in a muffled voice from behind him. "I suppose from the first, I gave you no reason to trust me, eh? After all, the first time we met I tried to cheat you, to drug you and rob you blind! And then, later, I even plotted to double-cross you and marry your uncle for his money and his lands." She sighed heavily and added in a small voice, "I—I suppose I'm not much of a bargain, am I, *hombre?* Are you—are you quite certain that you want me?"

"Damned certain, kitten," he assured her, very firmly.

She knew by his tone that he was smiling as he said it, and she snuggled up against him with yet another sigh—this one of sheer happiness!

His body was strong and solid, warm and comforting against her burning cheek, and the scent of him—so dear, so familiar, so long denied her—was wonderful beyond belief. She planted a smacking wet kiss on his back and hugged him so tightly about the stomach that he grunted for breath.

"*Dios mío, gato,* how poor little Krissoula has missed your loving these past weeks!" she murmured with a pout. "You must get this thing with El Presidente Mitre finished very quickly, and then take me somewhere—anywhere!—we can be alone together. I think I'm not at all a patient woman, after so many lonely, empty nights without you—!"

Digging his heels into the horse's flanks, Esteban grinned as he urged the gelding in the direction of the Plaza de Mayo and the Casa Rosada, the Pink House, where the President made his residence. *Caramba!* Be damned if he wasn't feeling more than a little impatient himself—!

Chapter Forty-Two

It was that long chill hour that comes before dawn—when the stars are already paling and the moon has faded to only a foamy crescent in the charcoal sky—when Esteban's groomsmen came to "abduct" his all-too-eager bride and carry her off to the house of "his" family; the first step in the part-traditional, part-modern Gypsy wedding festivities that Esteban and Krissoula had decided upon to celebrate their union.

Acting gruff and arrogant and even a little threatening, a bossy Franco, Leonardo and Joaquin, Carla's younger brothers, along with young Sancho and Tomás Cabral (who'd been sent for from Tierra Rosa to act as Esteban's best man) arrived at the courtyard of Barrio Gitanos.

Before the gateway, the young men strutted noisily about and beat upon the bolted double doors, loudly demanding that the bride's parents—in this case, Doña Sofía Moreno and Armando Reyes, who'd been chosen to act as her family—hand the Gypsy maid, Krissoula, over into their care. To soften the "loss" of their daughter, they offered the pair gifts of the finest wine, platters, and spoons of silver and gold; bribes from the groom's family in exchange for the bride's virtue!

"Gold and silver—pah! Merely trinkets! For such a woman as this, no gift is great or costly enough!" Armando insisted pompously, hiding a grin. "She is a pearl, a treasure. Her beauty is beyond compare! Her grace, the stuff of which legends are made! Go home, you young rogues, and tell your master he has failed—that he must take another for his bride!"

"But he will have no woman but the lovely Krissoula, I tell you!" Tomás argued, warming to his role and playing it to the hilt. "Give up your daughter, Reyes, and you'll be a wealthy man! Refuse, and we will have no choice but to carry her off by force!"

"No, I tell you! Be gone! She is not for ransom to you rogues, nor

490

your master. Now, do as I say, and order your men to leave my house at once, Cabral—or else feel the weight of Armando Reyes's club across your empty skulls!"

It was all a wonderful, boisterous game! After the ritual attempts to prevent the groomsmen from "abducting" the bride by shaking sticks in their faces, and a great deal of loud, good-natured arguing, Armando Reyes pretended to weaken, and a lengthy session of haggling over the bride-price commenced. Finally, an amount was set and the bride's family "relented" and agreed to give up their "daughter."

With a fine, showy torrent of weeping on Sofía and Carla's part, they did so, Armando himself lifting Krissoula up into the flower-decked cart drawn by a donkey, which the groomsmen had brought with them for that purpose. The Gypsy chieftain managed a great show of fatherly grief over the loss of his precious "daughter," accompanied by much snorting and snuffling into an enormous red kerchief as Sofía lifted Krissoula's veil and kissed her, and Carla did likewise.

"Every happiness, *niña!*" Sofía murmured, hugging her fiercely. "Health and happiness and prosperity to you both!"

"*Buen suerte, amiga mía!* Good luck! And I must say, he's not so bad, your Esteban—quite passable to look at, even if he *is* a pale-skinned *gorgio!*" Carla whispered shamelessly, kissing her cheek and squeezing her so tightly Krissoula thought she'd faint.

With the crimson-dressed bride waving tearful farewells, interspersed with happy giggles at the antics of the groomsmen and her two friends, a heavily veiled Krissoula was carried away to the courtyard of the groom's family, and the home of Rolón Severino, where the wedding would take place.

The groomsmen played a wild accompaniment to the torchlit bridal procession as it wound its way through the darkened streets to Rolón Severino's house, the silver bells on the donkey's harness jingling merrily, the guitars strumming, the shaken tambourines chinking and rattling, the violins squealing, and many deep, rich male voices raised in noisy accompaniment. Gypsies ran alongside the cart and tucked golden coins into the bride's gown, veil, or hands, and wished her good fortune and happiness. Another carried a mirror before the cart, as was the tradition, to frighten away any evil influences that might mar the future prosperity of the happy couple. Others threw flowers before the little donkey's hooves, until the dirt streets were carpeted with fallen petals of red and white, pink and lavender.

Dawn had flushed the sky above the *barrios* a rosy pink, bordered with gold and cream streaks, when the cart finally creaked to a halt before the double gateway of the groom's house. These gates were likewise adorned with flowers, like an arched bower, and beneath them stood Esteban, awaiting his bride's coming.

He looked so tall—so tall, so dark and handsome!—she thought when she saw him. A vest of black embroidered with colorful flowers and vines emphasized the breadth of his shoulders, and a crimson cummerbund spanned his lean waist and set off his snowy, ruffled shirt. Black breeches hugged his narrow hips and flanks, and were tucked into highly polished black boots. His dark-sapphire eyes met hers behind the filmy folds of the veil, and Krissoula felt warmth bloom in her cheeks as his gaze caressed her. Her heartbeat quickened at the love and desire for her that glowed in their depths, and she looked quickly beyond him, to where Rolón Severino and his tiny wife, Mama Rosa, and their daughter Theresa waited.

Pride and eagerness in his bearing, Esteban came to the cart and handed Krissoula down, escorting her to the doorway, where Rolón smiled and solemnly welcomed her. He presented her with a loaf of bread, symbolizing his and his wife's approval of the wedding and their promise to support the happy couple. Krissoula nodded and smiled without uttering so much as a single word, for until the priest had pronounced them married, speech was forbidden her. Then, holding up a wineglass for all to see, Rolón set it down upon the ground, covered it with a kerchief and crushed it beneath his heel, shattering the vessel instantly.

"As this cup is broken, so are your ties with the past forever broken, my daughter! Welcome! Welcome!" he declared, his good eye twinkling with merriment, and the gates were flung wide open to permit the bride and her bridal party and family to enter.

A noisy, happy tide of guests and well-wishers, among them Sofía and Carla, streamed into the Severinos' courtyard in the couple's wake. Trestle tables had been erected on every side, and already whole carcasses of beef were slowly roasting on the *asadors*.

Esteban led the way between the tables, leading his bride to a flower-decked altar behind which waited the priest—the merry-faced little priest of San Timéo's church, Father Pedro.

Birds were singing a warbling *arborea* beneath the red-tiled eaves of Rolón Severino's house and the sun had risen over the city when the ceremony came to its happy conclusion. Esteban slipped a slim gold wedding band onto Krissoula's trembling finger, and the smiling priest, with tears in his eyes, pronounced them man and wife before God, and blessed their union.

Raising her up from her knees, Esteban lifted his bride's veil, took Krissoula tenderly in his arms, and kissed her deeply. She could feel the strong, measured throb of his heart beneath her fingertips as she joyfully lifted her face to his and offered her lips for his kiss.

"Now, and for always, *querida,*" he murmured ardently in the second before he released her, and his deep voice trembled with emotion. "You're mine, now and for always!"

"Yes! Oh, yes! For always, *mi amor!*" she whispered, tears of happiness prickling behind her eyes and lending them a dewy sheen.

Wild cries of *"Bravo!"* and *"Olé!"* and other roars of approval greeted them as the pair turned to face the gathering, and hats were torn off and flung high into the air. Krissoula's lovely face, unveiled now, wore a blushing radiance that would have dimmed the brightest candle. And Esteban—his dark eyes never leaving his bride's beautiful face—glowed little less so! Taking her hand, he led her away to the bridal chamber that had been prepared for them by Rosa Severino and her daughter, Theresa, where their marriage would be officially consummated prior to the commencement of the wedding feast.

As she turned to dutifully follow her bridegroom, Krissoula caught Carla's mischievous green eyes. Before she could quickly look away, she saw her friend wink, and then Carla wickedly and silently mouthed the plea, "Don't take all day about this consummation nonsense, eh, *amiga?* You'll have a lifetime together for all that, and I'm starving!"

Remembering Gina and Alonso Zambra's wedding, Krissoula turned bright pink and hid her face against Esteban's ruffled shirt in embarrassment, much to Carla's glee!

Alone with her new husband at last in the cool, shadowed chamber, Krissoula experienced a flutter of nerves, and an unexpected shyness. Suddenly, it was as if she'd never met Esteban before, not known his passionate loving; as if she were truly his virgin bride, and the marriage one arranged by their parents! Playing for time, she leaned down and buried her face in the flowers that decked the room, mass upon mass of them in bowls set upon tables and dressers, or strung in garlands from the four posts of the bed or about the narrow windows, inhaling their fragrance. Their scent was so pungent and heady, its sweetness almost made her reel with dizziness. She felt lightheaded and insubstantial with happiness, as if a gust of wind could whirl her away like thistledown. Across the room, her bridal bed awaited, the snowy linen sheets scented with lavender and edged with yards of lace. *Our marriage bed,* she thought, and her heart skipped a beat.

"Nervous, *querida?*" Esteban asked softly, coming to stand before her. His stern, handsome face was incredibly tender as he gazed down at her. He took her hand in his and kissed her fingertips, one after the other, until she trembled uncontrollably.

"A little," she confessed shakily, unable to look him in the eye. Her cheeks burned. "It's silly, I know, but I am!"

"Very silly," he agreed solemnly, his sapphire eyes twinkling as he smiled, "since you have nothing to fear from me, ever. I love you, Krissoula *mía,* more than anything this side of heaven, and maybe—*sí,* maybe even beyond it, you bewitching minx! I'll never hurt you, *querida,* I swear it. You're my life, my breath, my soul!"

She nodded, blinking rapidly, feeling doubly foolish now. "I know. Oh, I know that now! And I—I love you, too, my husband—so very, very much, I can't find the words to tell you how happy I am!" she whispered huskily.

She stepped towards him, rising up on tiptoe as he lowered his dark head to hers, cradling her face in his large, tanned hands.

They kissed, and his kisses were like the sweetest, most potent wines upon her lips, starting a fire inside her that promised to burn for a lifetime. Their bodies touched, the hard lines of his supporting her soft curves as she leaned against him. Her arms curled around his neck, drawing his ebony head down closer, closer, as she drank from his mouth. She clasped him fiercely, and the intensity of her graceful hands upon him, twining through his hair, stroking his shoulders, fanned the fires of his own passions. With a low, lusty growl, he slipped his arm beneath her knees and bore her to their bed.

The sweet scent of lavender filled her nose as he lay back upon the snowy sheets. Eyes dreamily closed, she sighed as she felt Esteban's hands deftly gliding over her, loosening the fastenings of her bridal gown, carefully removing it. He unpinned her lacy *mantilla,* uncovering her wild profusion of glossy black ringlets, undressing her inch by inch until she was cradled bare in his arms. His eyes adoring her beauty, he stripped off his own clothes and tossed them carelessly to the floor, made impatient with desire. Cords rippling across his back, his lean, brown body hard with muscle and sinew, he strode naked the two paces to the bed, and stretched himself out alongside her.

Taking a tendril of her inky hair between his fingers, he rubbed its softness, then with a groan of longing he buried his face in the sweet-scented mass of her hair, his hand finding and cupping a little pointed breast as he kissed her throat, her silken shoulders, the delicate knobs of her spine.

"I could spend a lifetime touching you, making love to you," he whispered ardently, "and never tire of the way you feel beneath my hands . . ."

"Ah, but Carla urged us to hurry," she murmured teasingly, her eyes half closed as she ran her hands over his broad torso and down over his hard flanks. *Dios,* how wonderful *he* felt! How she'd missed the way those powerful arms held her, the touch of his hands as he caressed her, the clean lines of his body as he loved her! He made her feel so safe, so protected and cherished, it was as if she were the only woman in the world! Mounting desire had robbed her of all shyness now. She wanted him so very badly, her need bordered on pain! "There'll be no feasting till we rejoin our guests, you know," she reminded him eyebrows arched as she drew circles on his hard belly with her fingernail. "The poor things will be famished!"

"To hell with our guests, and with Carla's urgings! Your friend is a crafty minx, and you know it," he growled in her ear, and his hot breath sent goosebumps rising in tingling waves down her arms. "And, my darling—if I have my way!—she'll be a *starving* minx, by the time we're finished here . . ."

"Poor Carla," Krissoula murmured drowsily, but with laughter in her voice, and gasped softly as Esteban's hot mouth worked its magic on her breasts, suckling gently and bringing them to taut, throbbing life. "Poor, poor Carla . . ." she repeated without a shred of pity to her tone, and held out her arms to embrace him with a fierce, sweet joy as he lifted himself onto her, gathered her into his arms, and claimed her as his bride.

After that, their guests were forgotten! There was only the wonderful magic of love and desire between them, the fire and the sweetness of their love that being parted had sharpened, rather than dulled. Together, they moved in passion's dance: a dance more fiery than the tempestuous flamenco, more sensual than the wicked tango, for it was truly the dance of love, and the expression of true love's desire . . .

As the sun rose over Buenos Aires, spilling light like honeyed golden syrup over the *barrios,* flooding the dark and winding streets with glorious light, Carla and her hungers were forgotten as the lovers sated their own.

*　　　*　　　*

Later, Krissoula lay half across Esteban's chest. One of his arms was curled possessively around her, the other hand toying with her hair.

"Are you sleeping, husband?" she asked him softly, savoring the sound of the wonderful new endearment on her tongue.

"Sleeping? *Dios,* no! I have better things to do than sleep, wife," he teased lazily, ruffling her hair and tweaking her little nose as she rose up on her elbows to consider him.

"Really, *gato?* What things?" she demanded coyly, her golden eyes bright with mischief.

"Oh, things like—thinking."

"Thinking! Now? When I am here in your arms, *bribón? Caramba,* you insult me! Surely you can think of something more romantic—more entertaining!—to do than thinking!" she chided, smiling broadly nonetheless as a lazy fingertip drew whorls around and around his flat brown nipples, laughter crinkling her eyes as they stirred and stood erect.

"Ah, but my thoughts were important ones," he assured her seriously, "for I was contemplating the possibility that nine months from today, by the grace of God—and only with much hard work on my part, of course!—you might hold our son in your arms, mmm, *minina?* I was jut wondering—having been raised by two very different 'fathers' myself—what kind of father I'll be—?"

To his dismay, his teasing words—instead of bringing happy laughter to her lips—made her dreamy smile abruptly vanish instead. It was replaced by a bitter twisting that had no place on her lovely little mouth, not on their wedding day. Frowning, he gripped her chin and tilted her face up to his, wanting to kick himself for whatever it was he'd said to sadden her.

"What is it, Krissoula?" he demanded sharply. *"Por Dios,* darling, what's wrong? Come now, enough of that long, sour face, my little bride! Your husband won't allow you to frown, darling, not today, of all days!" he scolded, trying to tease the smile back to her face.

But in answer, she remained unsmiling and slipped from his arms. She padded barefoot from the bed and across the room, going to gaze from the window which overlooked the street.

Doves were making a dustbath below; he could hear them cooing noisily. Yet even with her back turned to him, he could tell, by the way her slender shoulders heaved, Krissoula didn't see them through her tears.

"What is it?" he repeated, going to her and turning her by the shoulders to face him. "For God's sake, tell me, *minina!* We're husband and wife, and I will have no secrets between us now!"

"A son," she murmured, her voice choked with tears. "You long for a son—a baby I may never be able to give you! Remember, *querido*, the night of the storm, when I told you of my past, and of the birth of my son, Nicolas? It—it was a long and difficult birth, as I explained then, and I've often wondered since if my body suffered because of it. Now, I'm almost certain it did. Think, Esteban, just think! All the times we have loved together, I have never become *encinta!* Perhaps—perhaps my Nicki's birth left me barren? Perhaps I can never give you the children you want, the little ones I long so badly to hold?" Her voice, shaky at the start, broke then. With a great shudder, she turned, buried her face against his chest, and sobbed her heart out.

Esteban held her, stroking her hair soothingly until she'd calmed a little, before setting her at arm's length.

"Look at me, Krissoula!" he ordered sternly. Lower lip trembling, her lashes spiky and golden eyes swimming with tears, she did so.

"Good! Now listen to me, darling, and listen well, for I don't intend to repeat myself," he warned, tilting her chin so that he could look her full in the face. "You need have no concerns on that score, I promise you. Whether you're barren as a mule, or fertile as a rabbit, I'll always love you, Krissoula. Whether we have no children or a dozen, nothing will change between us. But—if you want children so desperately—why, then I could fill your arms to overflowing with babes! And not within a year or two, either, but before nightfall this very evening!"

Through her tears, she managed a tremulous smile at his ridiculous boast. "Before nightfall? Oh, you're *loco, gato,* as I've told you many times before! Before nightfall, indeed! Am I to have a litter, like a little mouse? Pah! Even a mouse could never manage that before nightfall!" He was teasing her, trying to make her feel better, she knew, and her heart swelled with love for the caring his efforts betrayed.

He scowled, his handsome face stern though his lips twitched with a suspicion of laughter. "'*Loco,*' is it, impudent wench! Well, maybe a mouse couldn't make good on such a boast, but your husband, Don Esteban de San Martín, is a man of honor, and of his word. We'll see who's crazy come dusk, *minina!* In fact, I will go so far as to make a little wager with you. If, by nightfall, you hold our babe in your arms, as I promised, then you must pay me a forfeit, agreed?"

"Forfeit? What forfeit?" she asked warily, knowing him for a tricky brute!

He grinned wolfishly. "Nothing too difficult, my dear. Just promise that if I win, you will spend a day and a night without leaving my bed, mine to command, mine to enjoy—a slave to my every lecherous whim."

She smiled. "Ah. I see. And if nightfall proves me right, and you wrong?"

"Then I, *minina,* will unfortunately have to spend a day and a night in *your* bed, your slave to command." He sighed heavily, as if the prospect alarmed him, but the lusty gleam in his eyes was much in evidence. One dark brow quirked, he added, "Agreed?"

She giggled at his foolishness and dashed away her tears, answering him, "It's a wager, you rogue!" They shook on it as she added archly with a flirt of her sooty lashes, "After all, your motto, 'Victory at any cost' is also mine, now that we are wed. And how could I possibly lose, eh?"

"How, indeed?" he agreed wickedly, and dealt her a smart slap across the bottom which made her yelp. "Now, we will return to our guests, and you shall do your bride's dance to keep everyone happy. And then later, when we've seen everyone busy guzzling Papa Rolón's wine and stuffing their faces with Mama Rosa's good cooking, you and I will slip away."

"Slip away? To where?"

"Ah, patience, *minina,* patience! You'll see, all in good time," he promised mysteriously, and try as she might, he'd say not another word on the matter.

It was over two hours before Esteban beckoned to her from across the courtyard, signaling that it was time for them to go on their mysterious mission. She'd danced her bridal dance, and been showered with blossoms and well-wishes from the female guests— among them naughty Carla, who chided her with flashing green eyes for taking so cursed long to consummate her marriage.

"Tonta!" she'd chided Krissoula teasingly. "You make us wait an eternity for such a feast as this, when you can have that pretty *gorgio* in your bed each night for the rest of your life—? *Dios mío,* I don't understand such a woman!"

"Liar!" Krissoula retorted heatedly. "You understand me very well, *amiga,* seeing as how you're easily as hot-blooded as I! And if you were me, you'd have done exactly the same and taken your time, fiesta or no fiesta!"

"Guilty," Carla had confessed with a giggle. "Aiee, but passion is both a blessing and a curse for us hot-blooded *gitanas,* no?" and with a flurry of her skirts, she'd danced away on her grinning husband Stefano Valde's arm, blowing Krissoula a flamboyant kiss.

Krissoula looked about her, a fond, satisfied smile curving her lips as she saw Sofía, flushed and animated, laughing at something Armando Reyes was saying. She appeared a little thin still, but was fast recovering her former vigor—and *sí,* she even looked rather pretty today in her borrowed Gypsy finery as the stocky widower, Armando, beaming happily, paid her some outrageous compliment or other.

On the opposite side of the long trestle table, a stern Rolón Severino was seated next to a pink-cheeked Theresa Severino, chaperoning his daughter and guarding her honor against the ardent attentions of arrogant, handsome Franco Reyes. He was shamelessly serenading her with both voice and guitar, his expression one Krissoula remembered only too well! There was no mistaking the look of infatuation for the *compadrito's* lovely daughter in Franco's burning dark eyes, nor the eagerness and interest in shy, modest Theresa's, who reminded Krissoula of a Spanish Madonna with her long straight hair, oval face, and huge, sorrowful eyes. Her smile deepened. Like it or not, Rolón Severino might well find himself Franco's father-in-law before too long, with a *gitano* grandchild or two to dandle on his knee, although he'd given up hope of his daughter ever marrying years ago.

Across the courtyard, the girls from the Bamboo Cage—all dressed in their finest—were putting on airs and graces and acting the grand ladies. They fluttered their lashes and cooed and fussed over Carla's handsome older brother, Ramón, the hateful Delora's former husband, like a flock of pretty parrots. Ramón, she noted, appeared not in the least reluctant to accept the girls' attention! Rather, he seemed to be thriving on it, and his children—scrubbed and neatly dressed and smiling as she'd never seen them smile before—with him, basking in the attentions of over a dozen surrogate "mamas." *Madre,* sad-eyed Ramón looked fully ten years younger! If he mourned the fact that the elders of Barrio Gitanos had elected to exile his deceitful wife from their band and thus end his marriage, he gave no sign that he cared.

The madam of the Bamboo, Mama Zita, was garbed in a voluminous, tentlike gown of brilliant orange for the wedding. She winked at Krissoula over her partner's—poor, red-faced Tomás Cabral's—shoulder as she steered him past her in the dance, ponderously but gracefully, very gracefully! Zita drew the long black cheroot in its slim gold holder from her rouged mouth long enough to complain, "Tell that husband of yours to talk Tomás here into staying in the city, would you, honey? God knows, I've tried to talk him into it, but he just goes on and on about some little *muchacha* waitin' for him in the Pampa! *Cojones!* I'd bet she ain't half the woman I am!" Zita finished with a despairing sigh.

Remembering Estrella's slender figure and modest demeanor, Krissoula couldn't muffle an unladylike snort of laughter. "Oh, she isn't, Zita!" she called after the couple. "She certainly isn't—I'll vouch for that! Keep working on him, *amiga*. Don't give up!" And she collapsed into giggles as she saw the horrified, anguished, *imploring* look poor Tomás gave her as the mountainous woman whirled him on, to the strains of the guitars and violins, his feet hardly touching the ground.

"Ready?" Esteban murmured suddenly in her ear, his arms going around her waist.

She gave him a quick, searching glance, but his expression gave away nothing of his plans.

"Ready!" she answered, and taking her hand, he led her away from the courtyard to the stable where Barbaro waited, already saddled and bridled.

With Krissoula perched sideways behind him, clinging to his waist with her full crimson skirts spread prettily over the horse's rump, they rode through the *barrios,* the bay picking its way easily over the sun-baked streets.

It was a little after noon. Sharp black shadows were everywhere, contrasted with patches of dazzling South American sunshine. From some courtyards came the soft strumming of guitars; from others, the laughter of children settling down for the afternoon *siesta.* Still other crumbling villas rang with the sounds of excited male voices placing wagers, and with the harsh screams of the fighting cocks as they flew at each other across the pit in a blur of feathers. Women in dowdy black gossiped and quarreled and laughed together on the whitewashed stoops, and on the street corners outside the cafés or saloons, the young men waited for the pretty girls to pass by, extravagant *piropos* burning on their lips.

This, ah, this was Argentina, Krissoula thought happily, the patchwork of good and bad, pretty and ugly that now spelled home, and *caray,* how much she loved it all, now that this man was finally hers!

She looked about her, puzzled when she saw that they were fast leaving the mazelike streets behind them, riding along one of the rickety wooden piers that rose three feet above the mudflats. Where on earth were they going? To a ship, perhaps, anchored far out in the roadstead of the Plata? Had he a honeymoon planned he'd said nothing of to her? Oh, she couldn't imagine what he could be up to, he rogue!

Reining the stallion in, Esteban dismounted and tied Barbaro's reins to a sturdy if weatherbeaten piling.

"*Hola, niño,* over here!" he beckoned a curious urchin who stared at them. "Keep an eye on my horse for me, eh?" And he tossed the boy a silver coin as he lifted Krissoula down to the mudflats beside him, grinning at her confused expression.

Beyond, over a mile distant from where they stood, the green-and-yellow River of Silver, the Plata, winked lazily in the hot sunshine, perhaps dreaming of the Spanish *conquistadores* whose sailing ships had once dropped anchor in her roadstead; treasure-seekers coming to the new land of South America with their own dreams of cities built of silver and gold, never thinking that the true wealth of South America was the fertile land itself. From here, Krissoula could make out the colorful tignons of the washerwomen, bobbing like brilliantly colored jungle flowers, and hear snatches of their lilting conversation borne on the breeze as they bantered back and forth. Eyes half closed against the light, she wondered idly if Consuela was among them . . .

"Come on with you, daydreamer!" Esteban urged, jolting her back to reality. Taking her elbow, he led her along. "We're almost here now. It's not much farther."

Fortunately, there had been no rain of late. In the fierce summer sunshine, the mudflats were baked even drier than usual, and walking across them not as squelching and messy as it might have been. Before long, Krissoula could make out strange shapes in the near distance; perhaps little buildings cluttered together? *Sí,* she was right, it *was* a village of some sort, she decided, frowning, shading her eyes and squinting against the light. A village with dwellings of a type she'd never seen before, neither adobe nor wood nor brick, and it was built so low to the ground the inhabitants must have been short indeed!

As they drew closer, she could make out rough shanties leaning in drunken, straggling rows, each low hut thrown together with an assortment of scavenged materials: planks and wooden boxes, sackcloth and sailcloth—even a few battered sea chests and trunks had been pressed into service for walls. Who on earth could be living here, she wondered, and Esteban, noting her quizzical expression, grinned but said nothing, curse him!

As they approached the tent city, small figures—silhouetted too darkly by the dazzling light to distinguish features—came out to watch the tall man and the slim, petite woman as they drew closer.

"Why, it's Señor Esteban!" exclaimed a shrill, excited voice.

"Señor Esteban's back again!" cried another child, and all at once a horde of similar little figures came pouring out of the village, racing from every direction to meet them.

"Children?" Krissoula exclaimed, astonished.

"*Sí,* children!" Esteban agreed, laughing as the tide of giggling youngsters clambered like puppies about their feet, begging him to carry them. She smiled as he stooped to lift a little girl with ragged black hair onto his shoulder, and kissed her cheek.

"You came back, señor, just like you pwomised me!" the little girl crowed, patting his blue-shadowed cheek in approval with a tiny, dirty hand.

"Ah, *sí,* of course I did, Bonita," he agreed, flashing Krissoula a teasing smile. He winked. "I always keep my promises to beautiful young ladies!"

Bonita beamed. She looked around from her lofty vantage point on his shoulder, biting her lip nervously before asking, "Did you— did you bring me another red lollipop, señor?"

Esteban shook his head ruefully. "No, I'm afraid not, *bombón!* But—I did bring you something else almost as sweet. Señorita Bonita, may I present my wife, Doña Krissoula de Ballardo y Aguilar?"

"*Con mucho gusto, doña,*" Bonita said, politely but very quickly, and again she captured Esteban's face between her little hands. "No candy, señor?" she asked in a loud, hoarse whisper, her angelic face with the enormous brown eyes crushed with disappointment.

"Sorry, *niña,* no candy today. Just a wife!" He grinned. "Perhaps tomorrow, you'll have lollipops, *sí—?* Now, be a good girl, and run and find Lourdes for me. I need to talk with her."

"Again? Oh, but you talked and talked with her just yesterday!" Bonita pouted.

"So I did," Esteban agreed. "But I have to talk with her again. Now, run!"

He set Bonita down, and, giggling, she flew away like the wind, racing over the mudflats with her hair and her ragged skirts flying behind her, yelling "Lourdes! Lourdes! Señor Esteban wants to talk with you! Again!" at the top of her lungs.

"She's adorable," Krissoula declared, smiling as she linked her arm through Esteban's. Looking down at the curly-haired little boy who'd slipped his thin hand into hers to skip alongside her, she added, "And so are you, *niño*. Oh, Esteban, they're all adorable! And you seem to be an old friend of theirs, no?" she accused.

"Mmm. You might say that," Esteban agreed, waving to an older boy who doffed him a cheeky salute and winked, patting bulging pockets. Esteban winked back at him, knowing full well what those pockets contained—and it wasn't pebbles!

"But—is this where their parents live? Here?" She looked around her in dismay. Poor as she'd been at various times in her life, she'd never known this abject poverty.

"Parents? The little ones here have none, *querida!* You see, this is the City of the Children, La Ciudad de los Niños. There are no grown-ups here, only orphans, or unwanted children who've been abandoned by their parents. Sancho and his sister Lourdes are their 'king' and 'queen.' It is they and they alone who care for the other *niños.*"

"But—Sancho can't be more than eleven or twelve himself!" Krissoula gasped.

"He's ten, *querida,* only ten—but he's learned more in his short ten years than other men learn in fifty!"

He stopped and took a step towards her, taking her in his arms. His expression was serious, all teasing done with.

"Right here is where my dreams begin, Krissoula, now that I have you," he told her earnestly. "From the day I left the *barrios* to find a better life for myself, I swore I'd never forget the Ciudad de los Niños, nor the poor little ones living here—children who were denied the chances that Rolón Severino granted me by taking me in after my—mother's—death.

"When Alejandro de Aguilar died, I expected to inherit his wealth. I told myself that my inheritance would make me a wealthy man, somebody who, with the help of God, would have the money and the position and the voice to use as he wished. I wanted to use my good fortune to make a difference in the lives of these little ones, who have no one but each other to care for them." His sapphire eyes shone with an inner fire and indomitable determination. "Now, thanks to you, that day has come."

Moved, she reached up and touched his cheek, her heart overflowing with love and pride for the fine, caring man she'd married. He could have regained his inheritance and conveniently forgotten his troubled past. He could have selfishly turned his skills and talents to amassing greater wealth for himself, and shared it with no one. Instead, he planned to use Tierra Rosa's prosperity to benefit others less fortunate than himself, the forgotten children of the mudflats. Truly, not one drop of Felipe's tainted blood ran in his veins! His compassion, his goodness, could only be the gift of his mother, the virtuous Manuela; his ambition and pride, a legacy of the fine blood of his Aguilar grandfather! Her eyes filled with tears for the second time that day. Oh, if only her uncle Ricardo were here now, he'd give his blessing for the man she'd chosen, she thought with enormous pride and a heart filled to bursting with love. He'd find a depth to this handsome *gorgio* she'd married that was far more to his liking than Miguel had proven!

"I love you," she murmured. "Oh, how I love you, you great, wonderful *gorgio!*" And she flung her arms around his neck and kissed him soundly.

"Ooo, look! They're kissing!" tittered one of the openmouthed little boys, who'd been watching their exchange with wide, curious eyes. *"Sí!"* another acknowledged in disgust, rolling his eyes, sticking out his tongue and clutching at his scrawny throat as if gagging. "Uhhhgg! Blaaggh!"

"Come here, and I'll kiss you, too, *niños!"* Krissoula threatened, and she puckered her lips and advanced a few steps as if intending to do just that.

The pair of rascals hurriedly scampered away, shrieking with laughter and clutching their hearts.

Krissoula laughed up into Esteban's face, then pretended to pout. "Well! How very insulting! Something tells me they did not welcome my offer!"

"Something tells me they might—if you make the same offer in a year or two. Ah, here's Lourdes at last!" he observed, nodding at someone over her shoulder.

Krissoula swung about to see a thin dark-haired girl of about nine coming towards them from one of the lean-tos. She had a naked baby boy slung comfortably over her bony hip, carried in a sling of tattered cloth.

"Hola, señores!" Lourdes greeted them. "I'm sorry, but my brother's not here. He said—at least, I thought he said—that he'd —he'd gone to *your* wedding, señor, and that he would bring us all something to eat when he returned?" She eyed Krissoula with open curiosity.

"And so he did, Lourdes," Esteban reassured her. "And, knowing my friend Sancho, he'll have picked the wedding guests' pockets to the last man before he can bring himself to come home! Krissoula, my love, I want you to meet Señorita Lourdes. She's the

504

'mother' to all the children you see here. Lourdes, my bride, Doña Krissoula."

"*Mucho gusto, Doña Krissoula,*" the girl murmured, bobbing Krissoula a curtsey. "Don Esteban is right, señora—about the children, I mean," she acknowledged, sounding a little embarrassed. "I do try to be a good mother to all of the little ones here in the City, but—it is not easy with the smallest of them—like little Matteo here. We lose more babies than we are able to save, señora. Fresh milk, it is so very hard to come by, no? We did find an old cow once—she had escaped from the slaughterhouse yards!—but her udders were dry, and we had to butcher her for meat!" She shrugged. "So, we manage as best we can."

"Can I hold the *niño?*" Krissoula asked, her heart going out to the girl and to the grubby moppet in her arms.

"But of course!"

Lourdes slipped the sling from about her shoulder, and carefully handed the baby boy to Krissoula. From amidst a filthy rag, a pair of thickly lashed button eyes the color of blackberries gazed curiously up at her from a complexion the color of beige satin—very dirty beige satin. A mop of inkly black curls crowned the baby's little head, and two tiny little fists found her finger and thrust it hungrily into a busy mouth.

"Aiee, Matteo, what an appetite you have, eh, darling?" Krissoula crooned, cradling the baby snugly against her bosom. *Dios,* he was thin! Far too thin for his age, she realized. No bracelets of baby fat plumped his wrists nor encircled his ankles. None dimpled his feet. His weight in her arms was like a bag of feathers. "I wonder where we can find a freshened cow for milk . . . ?" she asked herself thoughtfully, out loud.

"Why, Doña Krissoula's just like you promised me she'd be, señor," Lourdes observed happily, giving Esteban a shy smile. "What you told me yesterday was exactly right, no?"

"And what was it this rogue told you, mmm, Lourdes?" Krissoula demanded suspiciously, lifting Matteo over her shoulder to pat his little bottom.

"The señor told Lourdes that he knew a pwetty lady who loved babies—and even little girls, too," piped a young voice, and Krissoula looked behind her to see Bonita shyly watching her cuddling the baby with a wistful expression on her face.

"Oh, did he now?" Krissoula observed as she sat down on a low stool, lifted the baby to one side, and made room for the little girl on her other knee. She patted it invitingly to show she could sit there, if

505

she so wished. At once, Bonita eagerly clambered up and snuggled comfortably into the crook of Krissoula's free arm, fingering her glossy black curls almost reverently. "And what else did your wonderful Don Esteban say?" she asked the little girl teasingly, her golden eyes twinkling.

"He said—" Bonita racked her memory, wrinkling her little nose, "he said that the pretty lady would let me come and live with her, if Señor Esteban asked her very, *very* nicely, and said 'please may I'— and that she'd let me eat lollipops every single day!" she declared with a wicked, triumphant little grin.

"Bonita!" scolded Lourdes sharply. "Señor Esteban promised no such thing!"

"He did say the señora would take me to live with her, he did!" Bonita protested. "An' he said she liked babies so much, he reckoned she'd like armfuls an' armfuls of 'em—didn't you, señor?" she pleaded, looking to Esteban for confirmation.

"Hmm, I believe I did mention something along those lines, *sí,*" Esteban agreed uncomfortably.

"Perhaps it was more on the lines of 'filling my arms to overflowing' with babies?" Krissoula asked with a knowing grin, brows arched.

"Come to think of it, I believe it did go something very like that," he confessed.

"Were you so sure of me then, *bribón?*" she asked huskily, cuddling Matteo and Bonita closer, and feeling a deep, sweet contentment flow through her at the heavy warmth of their little bodies snuggled to hers. The aching for Nicki would always be there, she knew that now, but it could be eased, the sharpness softened, with other little ones to love. *Sí,* it could be . . . it would be.

"Very sure, *minina,*" Esteban confirmed, coming to stand behind her and the children. "Surer than I've been of anything in my life— except for my love for you."

"*Gracias, querido,*" she murmured, rubbing her cheek against his hand as he reached down to caress her.

"I discussed it with Sancho and Lourdes yesterday. They want us to take Matteo to raise, as well as Bonita, if you're agreeable? As Lourdes said, the infants are the hardest to care for here, with no fresh milk available. And as for Bonita and I—well, er, we're old friends, you see. Could you come to love her, too, do you think?"

"You have to ask, *hombre?* I already adore her! You know better than to think I wouldn't, you rogue! But—what about the others?

Oh, Esteban, can't we take them all?"

"I've been thinking about that for years, and I've come up with a solution, finally. The Aguilar house at Mar de la Plata where Manuela and Alejandro spent their honeymoon is a sprawling old place, very close to the beaches. It's far too big for one family to live in. The villa is mine, too, now. I've been planning for some time to make it into an orphanage, Krissoula, and to move some of these little ones into it before the next winter rains, if possible. I thought Sancho and Lourdes could run it, until I find someone older. What do you think?"

"It's a wonderful idea! But—Lourdes and Sancho will be much too busy learning how to be children again to run the place," Krissoula said softly, remembering Sancho's terrified face in the moment after he'd slain Bobo. "Did you consider asking Sofía? She's marvelous with children, you know, and I think she'd jump at the chance to stay here in Argentina. She has no ties in Spain to make her want to go back there."

"Sofía? There's an idea! I hadn't given her a thought as far as the orphanage was concerned—I'd assumed she'd want to come back to Tierra Rosa to live with us, but—I'll ask her, if you think she'd want to try it. You do think my idea could work, then?" he asked, his sapphire eyes so bright with hope, the contrast against his tanned brown face was startling. "You'll help me to make it all happen, Krissoula? God knows, I'll need your help!"

"How could I think of refusing, 'Papa' Esteban? We are a team, no? Two horses in the same shafts! Hills or valleys, joys or sorrows, we must pull together, no?"

He chuckled at her teasing words, but seemed pleased by them nonetheless. "Ah, Krissoula *mía,* I like what I'm hearing, but—promise me you'll never grow *too* biddable, eh? A red-blooded man likes a sprinkling of hot peppers in his food from time to time—and a little fire and spice in his life, too! A steady diet of syrup and cream is one that quickly grows dull . . . !" He paused and waggled a stern finger at her. "Which reminds me, *querida,* talking about spice in a man's life—what about our wager? The sun hasn't gone down yet, has it? I'd say I've won, wouldn't you? Your arms are certainly overflowing with little ones!"

"No, *querido,"* Krissoula answered him huskily, dropping a kiss to first Matteo's and then Bonita's little heads. *"I've* won—and far, far more than I ever dreamed of winning!"

Golden eyes shining with happiness in the blazing sunshine, she lifted her lovely face for his kiss.

Epilogue

"Aiee, *Dios,* I'm too fat to wear this for el presidente's banquet tonight!" Krissoula wailed, hurling aside yet another gown. "Please, Sofía, *dear* Sofía, fetch me a looser one—find *something, anything,* I can breathe in!"

Sofía sighed and looked long-suffering. For over two hours now, Krissoula had been trying on and discarding every one of her gowns—the trunk filled with gowns which Esteban had sent for from Tierra Rosa. They'd been left behind when they fled the *estancia,* and Tomás Cabral had brought them with him for Krissoula to wear when he traveled to the city for their wedding.

"If you refuse to curb your appetite and refuse to surrender to stays and corsets, then you must pay the price, *amiga.*"

Krissoula shot her friend a murderous look that would have withered leaves still green on the bough, and scowled horribly. "Pah! It's a little late for your scolding, no, Sofía? Already, I am grown fat! And in less than three hours, the banquet Presidente Mitre has arranged at the Casa Rosada will begin—! Aiee, *Madre,* what am I to do! Go naked? Wear a sack?"

She flounced across the suite in a fine fit of temper, golden eyes dangerously bright.

"You could plead a headache—?" suggested Sofía hesitantly. Much as she loved Krissoula, she had no eagerness to feel the bite of her tongue when she was in her present mood.

"A headache? Stay away, when my Esteban and I are to be the guests of honor? When the banquet was arranged by the President himself, in gratitude for stamping out Zamora's little revolution? No. No, no, no! Esteban would never forgive me! I would never forgive myself. And besides," she sighed, "I never have headaches. He'd know I was lying. He can always tell."

Sofía shrugged helplessly. "Then I don't know what you can do!"

Krissoula abruptly sat down on the edge of the bed, rested her chin on her fist, and stared sulkily at her reflection in the mirror across the suite. A scowling young woman with elegantly upswept hair and a cascade of ringlets spilling over one shoulder glowered back at her. It wasn't such a fat face, really, she considered, patting beneath her chin for signs that it was doubling. And besides, until her wedding two weeks before, she'd had precious little to eat after being cast out of Barrio Gitanos. How *could* she have grown fat on little or nothing? she thought crossly. And yet, somehow, she had! Her hips were a little fuller, her waist perceptibly thicker, her breasts bigger and as tender as they'd been when she'd—

Enough of that useless train of thought! She caught Sofía's speculative expression and grimaced. "Oh, no! I know what you're thinking, Sofía—you can't pretend, not with me—but you're wrong! It's too soon, and besides, I can't be—it's impossible!"

Sofía snorted. "Hardly impossible, *niña!* When was your last flow?"

Krissoula frowned, thinking hard. "October? *Sí,* I think in October. I'm sure that was it."

"And you haven't bled since?"

Krissoula shook her head. "Not once. But that's not really so unusual, *amiga.* My aunt, Tía Isabella, told me that often, when a woman has too little to eat and many worries on her mind, her monthlies cease. And besides, I've never been regular."

"But have you ever missed for three months before?" Sofía asked pointedly.

"Nooo," Krissoula admitted slowly, silently amending, *Only once before.* She was seriously beginning to wonder now if her suspicions were not, after all, a fact. Hmm. There *was* that—that suspicious craving she'd had for boiled shrimp with vinegar a few weeks ago, but surely that didn't mean anything? And, too—what about those times she'd felt queasy when faced by food—she, who had the appetite of a starving dray-horse, normally . . . ? Her heart started to beat very fast, and she splayed her hands over her belly and closed her eyes.

Could it be? Could the new hardness to her belly mean that a child of hers and Esteban's was growing there, beneath her fingertips? A wanted, beloved child who would someday be a little sister or brother to her angel, Bonita, and her handsome *hijo,* Matteo? Surely she would have known long before this, were that so! Unless—had she intentionally blocked such a possibility from her mind, fearing it was unlikely after Nicki's long and arduous birth, and reluctant to be disappointed? Or alternatively, had she secretly been *afraid* to face life with a child who could claim no father for its own, and so pretended even to herself that there was no child?

She stood there, her expression intent, more still than Sofía had ever seen her restless, active friend. And then, suddenly, Krissoula caught her lower lip between her teeth as a fragile, fluttering sensation quivered deep inside her, as if in answer to her unspoken questions. Her golden eyes widened with wonder.

"Aiee, Sofía!" she cried. "Oh, Blessed Madonna, Sofía—I think—I think you're right. I felt—something—move inside me, like a—like a new little butterfly trying its wings!"

Sofía sprang to her feet and ran to hug her. "Oh, Krissoula, really?"

"Really, really! Oh, Sofía, a baby!"

The door to Esteban's adjoining dressing room swung open, and her husband strode in, dark, handsome, and resplendent in a black cutaway coat and breeches, every inch the gentleman *hacendado*.

"Not dressed yet, I see, eh, *miniña?*" he observed fondly as he looked at his wife, immodestly standing there without a shred of shame in her semitransparent camisole, drawers, and stockings. He drew his eyes reluctantly from the delectable picture his wife presented, and looked with some curiosity at Sofía. *Dios,* what was wrong with the woman? She was grinning like an idiot, her smile so broad, he wondered amusedly if the rest of her face might not fall into it! A frown wrinkled his brow. On closer inspection, Krissoula appeared to be hiding a smile, too! Laughter tugged at the corners of her lush mouth. Excitement danced in her golden eyes.

"All right, ladies!" he said patiently, drawing a slim cheroot from his pocket and lighting it with a puff of gray smoke. "What have you been up to now, eh?"

"If you wouldn't mind, dear Sofía . . . ?" Krissoula asked Sofía, giving her a pointed wink, "I have something to tell my husband."

Sofía nodded and smiled knowingly. "Oh, but of course!"

With that, Sofía made a speedy exit, closing the door carefully behind her.

On the hotel landing outside the suite, Sofía waited for a few moments. Soon, just as she'd anticipated, she heard Don Esteban let out a delighted roar, which ended in a loud fit of coughing as he choked on his swallowed cheroot smoke. The coughing spasm was swiftly over, and then Sofía heard a merry peal of laughter from Krissoula, and her former charge's shrieked protests that she didn't "need to lie down at all, *hombre loco!*", but instead felt "like

510

dancing the night away!"

Straitlaced Sofía giggled happily. She'd sleep on the chaise in the children's room for the night, she decided, and see to their care herself. Somehow, she didn't think their new mama would protest just this once, under the circumstances. Unless she was far off the mark, it was unlikely the happy couple still planned to attend el presidente's banquet this evening, but intended to while away the sultry night in a far more amorous fashion; by making love.

"Oh, what wicked thoughts you have, Sofía Moreno!" the old maid scolded herself primly as she made her way down the hall to the children's suite, which adjoined their parents. "Enough wicked thoughts to earn you a dozen Hail Marys in penance!"

But even as she scolded herself, a little smile played about her lips, and her feet twitched with the unaccustomed urge to *skip* down the carpeted landing. Why, she fancied if she closed her eyes she could almost hear Krissoula's voice, scolding her in her irreverent, scandalous way:

"Shame, shame on you, Sofía *mía!* Such wicked thoughts for a gently reared señorita to be having!" before adding with a naughty wink and a smile, "Perhaps there is hope for you yet, eh, *amiga mía?*"

Sofía thought of Armando Reyes, and her smile deepened. *Sí,* there was hope for her yet. Considerable hope, in fact . . .

She gave way to her rare impulse, hoisted her skirts to show several inches of stockinged leg, and skipped like a goat down the hall!

Author's Note

Dear Friends,

To all the many, many readers who have written to tell me they enjoyed my last books, *Silver Rose* and *Desert Captive,* thank you all! The pleasure I get from your wonderful letters can't be measured. They brighten my days, and show me in no uncertain terms just how very warm and special you all are.

If you've written to me and not received a response by now, it could be that I never received your letter. I do answer all of my mail personally, although sometimes it takes a while, so please, write to me again in care of Zebra Books, 475 Park Avenue South, New York, New York, 10016 and they will forward your letters to me.

I hope you've enjoyed reading *Midnight Captive.* Until the next time, happy reading and much Aloha to each one of you!

P.N., Hawaii